A Cheney Sampler

Other Books by Glenn Alan Cheney

How a Nation Grieves:
Press Accounts of the Death of Lincoln,
the Hunt for Booth, and America in Mourning

Love and Death in the Kingdom of Swaziland

Poems Askance

Thanksgiving:
The Pilgrims' First Year in America

Neighborhood News

Law of the Jungle:
The Tenharim People and Environmental Anarchy in Amazonia

Frankenstein on the Cusp of Something

Journey on the Estrada Real:
Encounters in the Mountains of Brazil

Journey to Chernobyl:
Encounters in a Radioactive Zone

Acts of Ineffable Love

Life in Caves

Just a Bunch of Facts

The Merry Burial Compendium

The Cat Caboodle:
A Litter Box of Cat Facts and Curiosities

Bangs & Whimpers:
The Ends of the Earth and Other Catastrophes

Lurking Doubt:
Notes on Incarceration

Dr. Jamoke's Little Book of Hitherto Uncompiled Facts and Curiosities Regarding Bees

Notions from a Time of Peril

Passion in an Improper Place

His Hands on Earth:
Courage, Compassion, Charism, and the Missionary Sisters of the Sacred Heart of Jesus

Promised Land:
A Nun's Struggle against Landlessness, Lawlessness, Slavery, Poverty, Corruption, Injustice, and Environmental Devastation in Amazonia

Translations

The Best Chronicles of Rubem Alves

On Time and Eternity

Concerto for Body and Soul

Tender Returns

To the Ends of the Earth: Memoir of a Missionary Sister of the Sacred Heart of Jesus

Pensamentos

The Fancies of Littlenose

The Reform of Nature

The Size Switch

A Cheney Sampler: Excerpts from Works by Glenn Alan Cheney

by Glenn Alan Cheney

Cover art by Glenn Alan Cheney

Published by
New London Librarium
Hanover, CT 06350
NLLibrarium.com

ISBNs

Paperback:	978-1-947074-63-7
Hardcover:	978-1-947074-67-5
eBook:	978-0-9798039-8-7

A Cheney Sampler

Glenn Alan Cheney

New London Librarium

To Miss Montgomery

Contents

Nonfiction

Fiction

Translations

Nonfiction

From

Thanksgiving: The Pilgrims' First Year in America

Prologue

It's hard to track back through the events of history to figure out why, in 1620, 102 people packed themselves into a ship and sailed off to live on a distant continent. How far back should we go? At the very least we should step back a century and some to 1488, and we should go to Spain. King Ferdinand of Aragon and Queen Isabella of Castile y Leon had political reason to betroth their daughter Catalina to Prince Arthur, the eldest son of King Henry VII. Allied with England, Spain would be better able to attack France. King Henry, a Tudor, liked the idea of someone attacking France, but he also liked the dowry that would come with a princess. He also liked the idea of marrying royalty. As the first Tudor to rule England, he needed the recognition of a foreign monarchy to shore up his shaky claim to the throne.

The young couple weren't quite ready for marriage – she was three, His Royal Shortness only two – so it wasn't until 1501 that a fleet of Spanish ships delivered the sixteen-year-old Princesa Catalina and half her dowry to Plymouth, England. She and Arthur married in November. A few months later, they both took ill with infection. Arthur died. She didn't. The widow Catalina claimed that the marriage had never been consummated. The pope believed her. By special dispensation, he allowed her to betroth Arthur's little brother, Henry. Little Henry was twelve.

Despite the nod from God, young Henry protested, quite likely on the advice of his father, who was looking for some other way to keep the half of the dowry he'd already received. His son's marriageability might be more profitably applied elsewhere in the political squirmings of sixteenth century Europe. Things changed significantly when Isabella died. A complex balance of power shifted, and Ferdinand no longer needed to marry his daughter into English royalty. He was content to keep the half of the dowry they hadn't yet lost. Henry VII still hoped for the other half, so he held on to the girl until something could be worked out.

Before Catalina could return to Spain, the situation squirmed again. Big Henry died, and little Henry, the eighth, rose to the throne. Two months later, in 1509, with the blessing of the pope, he married Catalina. The people of England called her Catherine. The marriage worked for a while. Henry went off to war on the mainland, leaving his Catherine as Regent of England. While he tried to make France English, she tried to beat some sense into Scotland. Their shared interest in hegemony and war, however, wasn't enough to sustain their marriage. Catherine was bearing children at a reasonable pace, but they were dying at almost the same rate. Only one survived. To the dread of Britain, it wasn't a boy. It was a girl, and her mother gave her the most Catholic name she could think of – Mary. But Henry didn't need a Catholic daughter. He needed an English son lest the kingdom one day fall into the hands of a woman.

What he needed was a better wife. Divorce wasn't so easy in those days of devout Catholicism. One solution, he thought, might be to have the pope reconsider whether his marriage to his brother's widow had really been valid in the first place. If it wasn't, then perhaps a divorce or annulment could be granted. The pope didn't like the idea, perhaps because Catherine's nephew Carlos, the last so-called emperor of the Unholy Hardly-Roman Nonempire, had just sacked Rome and was closing in on the Vatican.

Meanwhile, in Germany, a young man named Martin Luther was asking the pope similarly difficult questions. It wasn't about divorce. He was a monk. Marriage wasn't his problem. His problem was the relationships between man, church, and God. As he saw it, a lot of religious responsibility ought to be shifted from popes and priests to individuals. Individuals, he said, should be responsible for their own repentance, their own actions and beliefs, their own souls, and their own relationships with God. In other words, they had to do a lot of thinking and praying for themselves, at least to the extent that God allowed. Repentance had to come from their hearts, not their wallets. This revolution in religious thought began when he nailed to a church door in Wittenberg his list of ninety-five "theses," or statements he wished to defend. That was in 1517. Luther's questions loosened a thread in the tightly woven tapestry of Catholicism. As it began to unravel, the pope's patent on religion in Europe began to break up.

As for the Henry's divorce issue, the pope could not bring himself to papally annul what had been papally approved, especially with Carlos's army at the Vatican gate. Henry's next best idea, then, was simply to start a new church that could recognize certain necessities. In 1534, with Henry's encouragement, Parliament created the Church of England (two centuries later known as the Anglican Church) with Henry himself as its Supreme Head. As such, he could, and did, grant himself a divorce. He dispatched his ex-wife/ex-queen to a suburb and within a fortnight married Anne Bolyn, leaving the people of England whispering about the nature of good and evil, right and wrong, marriage and divorce, and who truly had the right to impose God's will on Man. Some said the pope. Some said the king.

And some said neither.

Henry's subsequent execution of two wives, his devotion to war, his mistresses, divorces, drunkenness, and obesity did little to persuade the English that a king at the head of a church was any more moral than a pope in that position. Henry did manage to provide the Y-chromosome to a child, a sickly boy named Edward. When Henry died in 1547, he left England in the hands of a nine-year-old, the last of the legitimate Tudor males. Five years later, before really taking power, the boy died of tuberculosis and the measles.

By written will, Edward left his throne to a cousin, Lady Jane Grey, but she had little claim to the Tudor line. The real choice was between Catherine's Catholic daughter, Mary Tudor, and Anne Bolyn's daughter, Elizabeth, who was raised under the Church of England. Or, as those of the Catholic persuasion saw it, England could be led by Mary, daughter of the king's only legitimate marriage, or Elizabeth, illegitimate daughter of the king's paramour.

Technical legitimacy won out over the politics of religion. With more popular support than Queen Jane, Mary had the queen beheaded after just nine days on the throne. Mary then reigned for five years, from 1553 to 1558. During that brief period, she tried to return Catholicism to its former power and glory. All she succeeded in doing, however, was bankrupting the nation, losing its last territory on the mainland, and raising tensions between the Catholics and Protestants of England. Having three hundred Protestants burned at the stake for heresy did nothing to smooth relationships. All it did was earn her a memorable nickname: Bloody Mary.

Bloody died in 1558. By default, her half-sister, Elizabeth, rose to power. Elizabeth reigned for forty-five years, just long enough to clean up the political and economic mess that her vain and reckless father had left behind. She tried to quell the hatred between Catholics and the worshippers of the Church of England, but her defense of Protestantism elsewhere in Europe made it clear which faith she favored. She didn't do much to quell tensions among English Protestants, either. Worship outside the Church of England was prohibited but not prevented. Many ordained ministers trod a fine line between strict adherence to the Book of Common Prayer and sermons that suggested a different way of thinking.

Elizabeth never married. She lived until the end of 1602, when, for lack of successor, the reign of the Tudors came to an end. James Stuart, king of Scotland, succeeded her in 1603.

The early seventeenth century, then, found Catholics at odds with those of the Church of England, and those of the Church of England were at odds with Protestant dissenters, among them the Puritans and the Separatists. (Typical of religions everywhere, the definitions of these groups were by no means consistent, tending to vary from group to group, especially among dissenting groups who were striving to establish distinct beliefs.) The Puritans accepted the principle of the Church of England but wanted to purify it of its showy ceremonies, clerical vestments, and other remnants of papism. They sought these changes from within the established church.

The Separatists, a tiny group of loosely affiliated churches which never really identified themselves as "Separatist," were essentially Puritans who saw less hope of reforming the Church of England. Separatists weren't so sure that the Catholic church and Church of England weren't following parallel paths to the same fires of Hell. Whether they followed king or pope, their souls, they feared, would be doomed. They didn't want a Church of England any more than they wanted a Church of Rome. The very name implied that the church was subservient to or belonging to England. For them, 2 Corinthians was pretty clear about what they had to do: *Come out from among them and be ye separate, saith the Lord.*

What the Lord said, Separatists did, so they separated, devising their own church, a church where "church" meant neither an institution nor a building but a gathering of worshippers. They didn't meet in a church. They *were* a church. In their church, the clergy wore simple clothes and devoted more energy to sermons, less to ritual. Their church didn't have priests but a pastor. There was a difference. For one thing, the Bible said nothing about priests. For another, priests were appointed from outside the church. Then they came in and took over all interpretation of scripture, all communication with God. Separatist pastors, on the other hand, were more like shepherds, merely guiding their flocks in their interpretation and prayer. The pastors were ordained and thus might know a little more than their congregations, but they were as fallible as any other human.

Separatists didn't worship saints or celebrate saints' days. They didn't sing prescribed hymns, recite creeds, or chant prefabricated prayers. They didn't kneel to pray unless they felt like it. They thought it repugnant for a groom to give a bride a ring. They considered the celebration of Christmas and Easter idolatrous. Their holy days were the Sabbath, the Day of Humiliation and Fasting, and the Day of Thanksgiving and Praise. The Sabbath, Sunday, was, of course, a weekly day of rest and worship. The other two ad hoc holy days were declared as necessary. They declared a Day of Humiliation and Fasting when a downturn in circumstances indicated God's displeasure with unrepented sin – sin they were stuck with due to Man's inborn moral imperfection. When things went suspiciously well, they declared a Day of Thanksgiving to thank God for overlooking the inevitable sins of an undeserving people.

The Separatists believed that they could worship in a home as well as in a cathedral. The flexibility of worship space fit well with the threat of fines, arrest, torture, and death by hanging. With no identifiable church buildings, no central organization, no structured hierarchy, no sign out front, and no supreme leader besides God, they were hard to identify, hard to catch in the act, hard to eliminate as a threat to the Church of England. Each congregation took care of itself and reported to no higher authority. These isolated organizations worked well. Their cellular structure would eventually evolve into that of the Congregational Church in America, where each church is independent and the minister of a given church has risen as high as he can go. Hierarchically speaking, a Congregational pastor was, and still is, on a par with a pope.

But you wouldn't want to call a Separatist pastor a pope. The Separatists saw the Church of England's rejection of an omnipotent pope as a big step toward Heaven on Earth, but the appointment of a king to serve in the place of a pope just stepped back toward authoritarianism and its inevitable companion, corruption. The Separatists could not accept any authority standing between them and God. They didn't let a professional do their praying. They read the Geneva Bible and other books and applied their knowledge to religious decisions. They didn't think they were thinking for themselves. That would be impossible in a universe controlled by God. But they made every effort to figure out what God wanted them to think.

The Geneva Bible was known as such because it had been translated and published in that city. The Geneva Bible's primary translators were English Protestants who had fled their country under Mary's bloody reign. Their translation of the New Testament came out during Queen Mary's time. The Old Testament translation came out a few years later, during Elizabeth's reign. The margin notes of these editions made it clear that the satanic beast that was to emerge from the pit of Hell, the beast foreseen in Revelations, would be the pope himself. The pope had a rack for people who thought like that. Other side notes suggested the fallibility of kings. King James didn't like that part, and he had a gallows for people who did. He disparaged the Geneva Bible and ordered a new translation, a beautifully poetic version that came to bear his name.

The Separatists believed the Geneva Bible and accepted its notes. They recognized the possibility of error in translation, but generally they believed its every word, and if the word wasn't in the Geneva Bible, they didn't believe it. If their Bible didn't describe a ceremony, prescribe a prayer, mention a ministerial garment, or declare a holiday, they didn't accept it as part of their worship. The closest they came to recital of a prayer or the singing of a hymn was the recitation of a psalm, sometimes in melody, never in harmony, never with instrumental accompaniment. If they said the Lord's Prayer, they varied the words to fit the passion of the moment. They may have recited from Psalm 19: The statutes of the Lord are right and rejoice the heart: the commandment of the Lord is pure, and giveth light unto the eyes.

In the philosophy of John Calvin, the Separatists wanted to participate in the administration and theology of their church – an idea that ran contrary to papism, Roman or English. They wanted a voice in the election of their authorities– an idea that ran contrary to kings, queens, princes, dukes, marquesses, barons, counts, viscounts, viceroys, earls, assorted lords, and landed gentry in general, not to mention priests, bishops, archbishops, sufragen bishops, archdeacons, rectors, vicars, and curates.

It would not be accurate to say that the Separatists wanted to choose their authorities. At most they might use their individual voices to try to express the natural hierarchy that God had intended. Together they might approximate God's will. This wasn't egalitarian democracy, but looking back, we might see the seed of it. These were the kind of people kings didn't like, the progenitors of people who didn't like kings. They accepted the role of king as absolute ruler, but only in the earthly realm. Matters of God, Heaven, and religion were of a kingdom beyond the king's.

The Church of England itself was not uniform in all parishes. In some villages, the congregations leaned a little toward Puritanism. In others, they stuck with the prescribed rules of worship found in the Book of Common Prayer. The Puritans, too, ranged from radical to conservative, and the Separatists, off on the fringe of the radical side, were still trying to figure out what God wanted them to do. Psalm 107 said, Let them exalt him also in the congregation of the people, and praise him in the assembly of the elders. God was clear on that. But did he prefer a certain posture for prayer? Should the prayers include certain words? Did he want them to sing during worship? If so, what should they sing? And who should decide? And who did God want to be their pastors and deacons? And how should a person become a member of a church – by birthright or by choice? And what did God expect from members?

They weren't supposed to be asking these questions. The Church of England already had the answers. King James did not tolerate people who felt his church needed to be purified of false ceremonies, superstitious rituals, misleading interpretations, and other supposed remnants of papism. The congregational cell system did not succeed in protecting everyone from discovery. Preachers and writers – and not just Separatists – were hanged. Believers were imprisoned. Moses Fletcher was charged with attending the secret burial of a child, an attempt to avoid the ceremony of the Church of England. James Chilton's wife got in trouble for the same thing. Christopher Martin was cited for refusing to kneel at communion, then for refusing to follow Church of England ritual. Other Puritans and Separatists spent time in jail, in some cases the rest of their foreshortened lives. Prisoners often did not long survive the unsanitary filth of prisons and the rampant infections of overcrowding. Meals weren't part of the deal. Food had to be brought by outsiders and distributed by guards. A long prison sentence was often a death sentence.

Under these threatening circumstances, a minister in Babworth, Richard Clyfton, found himself evolving out of Church of England beliefs to the less ceremonious Puritan beliefs. From Puritanism he found himself wandering into the desperate realm of Separatism. His sermons were famous for contradicting the popish demands of the king's church. People in search of true worship – people serious about their relationship with God – came miles to hear him. Among his pious and curious congregation were William Brewster, of Scrooby, and a twelve-year old orphan named William Bradford. He had lost his father at the age of one and his mother at the age of seven, after which he was given to his grandfather, who died when the boy was twelve. An uncle then raised him and tried to turn him into a farmer, but he failed. The boy was weak and ill and far more inclined to read a book than shovel manure. His intense interest in the Bible and the meaning of the Scriptures led him as a young teen to Richard Clyfton's ministry. Hearing Clyfton, his thoughts turned radically liberal.

In 1604, King James tried to put a stop to the radical preachings of Puritans and Separatists. He demanded that all ministers conform to the Book of Common Prayer and the norms of the Church of England. Those who did not conform would be ousted from their churches. Clyfton and other "nonconformists" then had a decision to make: God or king.

Clyfton chose God. Ironically, doing so left him without a church, at least in the stone-and-mortar sense. But the Separatists offered another kind of church, one as separate from stone and mortar as it was from the earthly whims of a king. It existed where the faithful came together to worship in accordance with the word of God. One such place, just six or seven miles away, in the hamlet of Scrooby, was the home of William Brewster, his wife Mary, and their first two children. The Separatists of Scrooby needed a pastor. Clyfton needed a church and home. Brewster's place became both, and young Bradford became part of the congregation.

It was a bit run-down but otherwise a pretty nice place to live. It was owned by the Archibishopric and called the Manor House. It had known such visitors as King John in 1212, King Henry VII's daughter Margaret Tudor in 1503, Cardinal John Wolsey in 1530, and King Henry VIII in 1541. The people who assembled there to hear Richard Clyfton, however, were hardly of such royal stock. Rather, they were commoners with an uncommon need to make contact with God and to do God's will. Not the Pope's will. Not the king's will. God's.

Like Clyfton, Brewster had studied at Cambridge, a hothouse of Puritan thought. Cambridge students and professors were being arrested, imprisoned, tortured, and, in one case, strangled, and burned in a public execution. Brewster had good reason to toe the line of the Church of England, but his studies made him a thinking man. He worked under William Davison, a Puritan and British ambassador to Netherlands, which at the time was at war with Spain. During trips to Amsterdam and Leyden, Brewster witnessed the possibility of religious freedom.

In 1590, Brewster's father died. William inherited not only his property but his positions, including those of bailiff, innkeeper, and royal postmaster. He was short of aristocratic, but compared with the rest of Scrooby, he was someone to look up to. The Manor House was a six-acre compound with a moat on three sides and a river on the fourth. It had forty rooms and a chapel. It held the Brewsters. It held another Separatist family, that of Richard Jacksons. Now and then it may have held the Clyftons if they didn't feel like walking home to Babworth, which wasn't far away. When Clyfton lost his job there, he may have moved in with the Brewsters for a while. And once or twice a week the manor held a secret congregation of scores of underground worshippers.

Some of those worshippers were following their beloved Richard Clyfton, walking several dangerous miles to hear him. One of them was the orphan Bradford, whose teenage curiosity was being stuffed with Clyfton's Separatist thoughts. Another member was John Robinson, who had been a Fellow at Cambridge, then parish minister of St. Andrew's Church in Norwich, then a former minister with big ideas and no church.

In other words, King James' crackdown was backfiring. His attempt to force the faithful to conform was only forcing them underground. Rather than conform, they separated, and deposed ministers such as Clyfton and Robinson became the sparks of new Separatist fires.

Separatism was by no means a mass movement or an organized rebellion. The groups were small and far between. Each Separatist church – and there were only a few – operated not only secretly but independently. They didn't belong to a broader group or report to a remote hierarchy. They named their own leaders. They openly discussed their beliefs and confessed their confusions.

They did so at night, with lamps low, curtains drawn, shutters closed. No sign out front said "Separatist Church." They arrived and left quietly, surreptitiously, in small groups, aware that men were watching their houses and inquiring about their comings and goings. They knew they had committed capital crimes. They'd listened to a minister who had neglected to wear a proper gown. They'd failed to kneel to pray, and they'd prayed their own prayers. They'd read the wrong Bible. For this, they knew, they would someday have to pay.

Psalm 1 said Blessed [is] the man that walketh not in the counsel of the ungodly, nor standeth in the way of sinners, nor sitteth in the seat of the scornful, but still, things were getting worse. More people were getting arrested, their property seized, their lives threatened. When Mrs. Brewster gave birth to her second daughter, they named her Fear.

By 1607, it was clear that the Scrooby group had to leave England. They decided to move, en masse, to Holland, a country more liberal and socio-politically advanced than England. Though a small country, it produced half the books published in Europe. The University of Leyden, founded in 1575, was the first university in the area that is today's Netherlands. Holland's economy was already evolving beyond manufacturing in to the more sophisticated business of trading. The Dutch government tolerated any reasonably Christian religion. Holland looked like a good place for people who couldn't contain their thoughts.

King James, however, wanted errant thoughts contained. He allowed neither dissenters nor Catholics license to travel abroad. The Separatists had to bribe an English ship captain and pay an exorbitant fee to charter his ship to take them from Boston (a hundred miles north of London), east across the North Sea to Holland. Before the day of their escape, they quietly sold their houses, furniture, animals, and just about everything they couldn't carry. Under cover of darkness, a hundred and twenty-five desperate Christians sneaked down to the dock and rowed out to the ship with their worldly goods. But it wasn't just a ship. It was a trap. The captain had betrayed them. The ship's crew helped themselves to the Separatists' belongings until the sheriff's officers showed up. The officers hauled the Separatists back to the wharf, "rifled and ransacked them," William Bradford later wrote, "searched to their shirts for money, yea even the women, further than became modesty; and then carried them back into the town, and made them a spectacle and wonder to the multitude, which came flocking on all sides to behold them." They were stripped of their money, their books, everything of value. Clyfton, Robinson, Brewster and four others were thrown into two dark, filthy jail cells measuring just six feet by eight. The rest were ordered back to Scrooby. Following their trials, the jailed leaders were condemned to prison for a month.

Now refugees in their own town, the destitute Separatists had to beg for living space and food. They spent the winter there, living off the mercy of friends and family, no doubt to the angst and irritation of all.

With no jobs or homes to hold them, their benefactors surely eager to be free of them, their king hardly inclined to loosen his holy rule, the Separatists still had every reason to flee the country. Come the spring of 1608, they had to try again.

This time they hired a Dutch captain and devised a scheme to meet his ship at an isolated stretch of beach at the mouth of the Humber River, some forty miles north of Boston. For seventy-five or a hundred people to parade down the road to a remote beach would be too obvious. They had to split up. The men would walk in small groups. The women and children would load themselves and their bundles of goods onto a barge with Clyfton, Robinson, and Brewster. Under cover of darkness, the barge would sneak down estuaries and tributaries until it reached the rendezvous.

The ship arrived but the tide went out, stranding the barge in a mud bank somewhere in the dark. The men waited anxiously until the captain sent a longboat to get them. The tide wouldn't be in until well after daylight, so the men thought it best to move out to the ship. Some were on board, others still awaiting their ride, when the king's soldiers arrived, armed with guns and other weapons, some on horseback, others on foot. The men on the ship could only watch as the soldiers arrested their friends on the beach. The captain, himself in big trouble if he got caught, weighed anchor and headed for Holland. When the barge arrived, the women, children, and leaders were also arrested, though in the dark and confusion a few managed to escape.

It's hard to say who had worse luck – those on the ship or those left behind. The ship hit a storm that blew them nearly to the coast of Norway. For fourteen days waves pounded the boat until it nearly filled with water. It surely would have foundered had the application of intense prayer not succeeded where bailing had failed. They arrived in Holland but without their wives, children, friends, leaders, possessions, or any idea what had happened as they sailed away.

Back in England, the people under arrest suffered a similar storm, but one of courts rather than weather. Judges and magistrates passed them around – women weeping, children clinging to them, all of them destitute, homeless, hungry, and cold. Prison didn't seem fair because innocent children would be separated from their mothers, and the mothers had only been following their husbands. Fines wouldn't work because they had no money. After much misery, pleading and public wailing, the easiest solution was to just let them go, or at least disappear. Little by little, they made their way to Holland. Clyfton, Robinson, and Brewster were the last to go.

Once in Holland the Separatists took up residence in Amsterdam, then moved to Leyden a year later. In Holland they worshipped as they reckoned God wanted them to worship. Nobody stood between them and God; nobody told them what to believe, when to kneel, or how to worship. But Dutch liberalism turned out to have its drawbacks. Toleration, it turned out, provided protection not just for Separatists but for Jews, Turks, Arminians, Catholics, Anabaptists, and any other misguided group that felt like opening up a church founded on dubious interpretation of scripture. The Separatists knew enough to suspect and avoid such churches. The warning appeared clearly in Corinthians, that people would come preaching in the name of Jesus but would do so with lies.

Miscreant churches weren't the only problem. Separatist children were easing into the Dutch community, where "evill examples" tempted them into "extravagance." As the expiration of a Dutch-Spanish armistice approached, the army tempted young men to the arguably unchristian profession of soldiering. Protestants worried that a renewal of the Spanish Inquisition might reach Holland. It was not an unreasonable fear. Spain had controlled Spanish Netherlands – the areas now known as Belgium, Luxembourg, and a northern area of France – since 1579. Many of the English remembered Spain's Invincible Armada. Just twenty years earlier it had tried to invade England. Spain was not a distant threat.

Meanwhile, religion aside, the Dutch economy had stagnated, and the Separatists were low-skill laborers in a relatively high-tech country. Hard work earned wages barely sufficient for survival. They didn't see themselves getting ahead in life. After twelve years, they began to regret their move to Holland.

Then, in what was becoming a Separatist tradition, things went from bad to worse. William Brewster's press published a book titled Perth Assembly, about King James' questionable religious policies in Scotland. The books made their way to England and, inevitably to the king. Irritated yet again by separatist thought, he directed his ambassador in Holland to demand that the press be destroyed, its operator, William Brewster, arrested and extradited. The Dutch government, needing to keep England as an ally against Spain, cooperated. Authorities seized Brewster's press, but they couldn't find Brewster. He was in England. He now had warrants out for his arrest in two countries. Holland was no longer far enough from the Church of England – across the southern corner of the North Sea, yes, but apparently not far enough for survival. If the Separatists really wanted to separate, they needed more than a corner of a sea between them and the king; they needed an ocean.

Chapter Five

The People

History has come to know this whole group as the Pilgrims. The closest they came to seeing themselves as such was reflected in a line in Bradford's Of Plymouth Plantation: "So they left that goodly and pleasant city [Leyden] which had been their resting place near twelve years; but they knew they were pilgrims, and looked not much on those things, but lift up their eyes to the heavens, their dearest country, and quieted their spirits." This was apparently a reference to two lines in the Geneva Bible, Hebrews xi, 13-14: All these died in faith, and received not the promises, but saw them afar off, and believed them, and received them thankfully, and confessed that they were strangers and pilgrims on thc carth. For thcy that say such things, declare plainly, that they seek a country.

So if these people saw themselves as pilgrims, it wasn't as pilgrims on a pilgrimage from Europe to America. They were unsettled people on Earth, unattached to places or things, passing through on their way to Heaven. Or at least half of them were. Around fifty came from the Leiden congregation. Twenty-two were coming directly out of England. The rest were servents of the Leiden folks. So roughly half were just looking for something that London didn't offer. Bradford would refer to these people as "strangers." Twenty-five or thirty others – the number is unknown – were sailors who just wanted to make their wages and go home.

Forty-one of the hundred and two passengers were men twenty-one years of age or older. The average age of those whose ages we know was about thirty-four. Eighteen passengers were adult women, all married. We don't know the ages of everyone, but apparently of the thirty boys under twenty-one, almost half were not yet adolescents. Of the thirteen unmarried girls, four were adolescents. Several men left wives behind, and some of the couples left children, too. Three men came with teenage sons. Five young children came without their parents.

Richard Warren left his wife, Elizabeth, and five daughters. Francis Cooke left his wife, Hester, and four children, but he took his son John, who was thirteen or fourteen years old. Degory Priest left his wife, Sarah, and two daughters. Thomas Rogers took his oldest son, Joseph, but left a wife, Alice, two daughters, Margaret and Elizabeth, and a son, John. William and Dorothy Bradford left their three-year-old son John behind. The Brewsters took Love and Wrestling but left Fear, Jonathan and Patience behind.

Samuel and Katherine More didn't go, didn't even want to go. They had no religious issues to resolve, no need of a better life. They already had a pretty good life, at least in terms of stuff. Their problem was divorce, a particularly scandalous one. Some of their four children – maybe all of them – turned out to be hers but quite possibly not his. The biological daddy may have lived right next door. To relieve themselves of this problem and spare the children the embarrassment of bastardy, they gave all four to Separatists and paid the children's one-way passage to a place from which they weren't likely to return. Ellen, 8, went with the family of Edward Winslow. Jasper, 7, went with the Carvers. Richard, 6, and Mary, 4, were handed over to the Brewsters.

Little Humility Cooper also went without her parents. Her father had died, and her mother, for reasons today unknown, gave her to her uncle and aunt, Edward and Ann (Cooper) Tilley. Barely weaned from her mother's breast, she set off for North America. Though probably the youngest to board the Mayflower - little Samuel Eaton may have been a bit younger - neither he nor she would be the youngest to disembark in America.

Elizabeth Hopkins, Mary Allerton and Susanna White boarded the Mayflower pregnant.

Desire Minter, a teenager, went for much the same reason as Humility Cooper. She had buried her father in Leyden, and her mother had decided to remain there with him. She sent the girl off to support herself in a place where God would be more accessible. Under the wing or employ of John Carver's family, Desire would have constituted half an adult, entitling Carver to half a share in the venture's profit. In seven years she would be a free woman, albeit with little to show for her efforts.

Only two other girls were of marriageable age. One, Dorothy, was a servant to the Carver family. The other, Priscilla, daughter of William and Alice Mullins, was about sixteen. Desire, Dorothy and Priscilla boarded the ship with over fifty men who had no wives, at least none with them.

Not one passenger claimed the rights of noble birth or the authority of government title. None could claim a station above middle class. All but a handful were humble tradesmen. They were, for the most part, venture capitalists without capital and nothing to venture but their labor and lives.

William Brewster was one of the oldest of the passengers, probably about fifty-four. (John Carver was about fifty-five; James Chilton was around sixty-four; one or two others may have been about that old.) As a founder of the Separatist congregation in Scrooby and Elder of the church in Leyden, Brewster oversaw the behavior of his flock. He offered advice on issues of morality and admonishment for moral shortcomings. He was not, however, a pastor.

William Bradford had no title in the church, but he'd been among its most active members. He was twenty-three when he married a sixteen-year-old, Dorothy. They soon had a baby and named him John. Little John was three years old when his parents kissed him good-bye.

Myles Standish, in charge of security, held the kind of physical power that any military leader holds. He had his own weapons, including flintlock muskets and a sword long enough to skewer a bear. He knew how to use his weapons. Little is known of his life before he boarded the Mayflower. He was probably about thirty-six years old and had known combat in his defense of England in battles with the Spanish in Holland. He probably came from the Isle of Man. He was short and bearded, his face the color of a parboiled shrimp. He could quickly lose his temper over issues of stupidity or insolence. Years later, William Hubbard would write, in A General History of New England, "A little chimney is soon fired; so was the Plymouth captain, a man of very little stature, yet of a very hot and angry temper. The fire of his passion soon kindled, and blown up into a flame by hot words, might easily have consumed all, had it not been seasonably quenched." Once they got to know him, the settlers might well have worried about such a man being the most powerful among them.

Stephen Hopkins, who had worked as a merchant and clerk, was the only passenger with experience on the American continent. He'd sailed to Jamestown in 1609. Along the way, his ship wrecked on the Isle of Devils, in the Bermudas. There he, the crew, and several passengers spent ten months living off turtles, birds, mollusks, and wild pigs. When

Hopkins got caught trying to organize a mutiny against the governor – actually he just wanted to separate from the others and stay in Bermuda – the governor sentenced him to death. He wept and pleaded his way out of it, however, and the stranded survivors finally managed to build two boats that took them to Virginia. Hopkins eventually returned to England to find that his wife had died. In due time, he married a widow, Elizabeth Fisher, who soon bore a child, her first. He, Elizabeth, and their three children, Constance, fourteen, Giles, twelve, and Damaris, one, all signed up for the Mayflower and the adventure in America. Elizabeth was seven or eight months pregnant when she waddled up the gangplank for the last time, no doubt wondering whether this trip was a good idea.

John Carver and Christopher Martin had risen a bit above the working class. Carver and his wife, Katherine, had no children but took as servants John Howland, about twenty-one, William Latham, eleven, Roger Wilder, also a minor, and the young Desire Minter. It is unclear to what extent the Carvers considered these young people family, servants, or apprentices.

A few others took servants. Stephen Hopkins took Edward Doty and Edward Leister. William and Susanna White took William Holbeck. Christopher Martin took John Langmore. Samuel Fuller, deacon, took William Butten. William Mullins, a shoemaker and shoe salesman, took Robert Carter, two hundred and fifty shoes and thirteen pairs of boots.

Just about everyone else was a tradesman, farmer, merchant, or general roustabout. William Brewster had studied at Cambridge and worked for England's secretary of state. He later became a printer and publisher, specializing in religious issues, which is what had gotten him into trouble in Holland and left him a wanted man in England. William Bradford was a fustian weaver, Francis Cooke a wool comber,

James Chilton a tailor. Edward Winslow helped Brewster in the printing business. John Turner was a merchant. Francis Eaton was a house carpenter. John Alden, a barrel-maker, was hired to serve as ship's cooper. Isaac Allerton was a tailor. John Allerton, who may have been Isaac's brother, was a seaman. William Trevore was hired by the group to work as a laborer and seaman. Thomas Tinker sawed wood. Nothing is known of Thomas Rogers's profession, but according to tax records, the wife and children he left in Leyden were considered "poor." No one represented the government, a company, or any church save that of the essentially unstructured Separatist congregation. No one was paid to be a leader. They did not consider themselves equals, but they recognized that they were all in the same boat, none of them riding first class, all of them sharing a single debt, all of them bound for the same place and bound to suffer the same hardships. No one, apparently, intended to get rich quick on gold or the labor of slaves and then return to England.

So the Mayflower contained a cross-section of values that would become quintessentially American: the insistence on following the heart rather than the law; the inability to tolerate injustice; the audacity to demand authority over authorities; the courage to pursue happiness no matter how miserable it might make them, and to seek a better life no matter how much worse it might be; the wisdom of working together as a society for mutual benefit and personal profit. They believed in the power of the congregation. They would do their own thinking and make their own decisions. They would pray their own prayers. They would dig in their heels. The strong would bury the weak, perhaps suffer a moment of doubt, then remember the mercy of their God, and then get back to

Chapter Six

The Crossing

Someone in this group kept a journal of that first year. It would return to England aboard the Fortune in December 1621. Within a year it would be published in London in 1622 under the title Mourt's Relation. We do not know who "Mourt" was. No one of that name went to America on the Mayflower. A "G. Mourt." (with a period at the end of the name) signed a "To the Reader" introduction to the book, so it is widely supposed that the name was the abbreviated name of publisher George Morton. The publisher may have disguised his name because of the dubious legality of the Separatist settlement and the possible guilt by association of anyone who promoted their venture.

In all likelihood, the book has several authors. It includes a few letters signed with initials – two letters apparently by Robert Cushman, one by pastor John Robinson (who had remained in Leyden), and one by Edward Winslow. The main narrative of the book, however, has no names or initials to indicate an author. This narrative, a journal divided into five parts, reports events from the September 6, 1620 launch of the Mayflower until an expedition to the Massachusetts tribe in September, 1621. The most likely journalists are Edward Winslow and William Bradford. Governor John Carver may have contributed. The journalist or journalists tended to write in the first person plural – we – and the third person plural – they. Nowhere does a sentence use the pronoun I. In a few cases, he apparently refers to the writer himself and they includes the author. In many cases, a confusion of pronouns leaves us wondering who did what and exactly what happened.

The journalists may have written the narrative for various reasons. In the tradition of explorers, they may have been reporting on events and discoveries. They may have been reporting to investors. They may have been encouraging more people to come join the colony. As a real estate advertisement, however, it fails. It reports much suffering, alludes to much danger, and hints at the difficulties of starting from scratch under the duress of New England weather. Alas, it also falls short of an ideal history. It provides a bounty of information, but it leaves out such obviously significant details as the dates of deaths. It mentions only a few of the people who died and nothing about grief or burials. It reports little about the activities of daily life and the human conflicts that inevitably arise among people under great stress. Except for a quick allusion to a conflict just before they landed at Cape Cod, it mentions no arguments or disagreements. It expresses no regrets, misgivings, or second thoughts. It rarely mentions women and children. It says nothing of hunger. It admits to considerable suffering, but we have to look between the lines to imagine the conditions that killed so many people in so little time. If Mourt's Relation sold any real estate, it was only by neglecting to mention the absolute worst of the experience.

Mourt's Relation relates little about the voyage across the Atlantic. In sixty-seven words, it takes us from the launch on September 6 to the first sighting of land on November 9. That same sentence brushes off two months of terror and hardship with just five words: ...many difficulties in boisterous storms... One of those many difficulties would be the sheer stress of knowing that they had shoved off two months later than planned. They would arrive on the verge of winter with dwindling food supplies, no homes on shore, no friends outside their group, and no possibility of going back until, at best, spring. But the option of sailing toward difficulties seemed better than the pressures pushing them from behind: persecution by the king, financial demands from their backers, the sale of most of their possessions to pay for the trip, the lack of jobs or houses to go back to, the frustrations of delay, and the certainty that a cold and hungry winter in a strange land was safer than worship with a papal flavor.

While Mourt's Relation tells us little of the voyage, another source, William Bradford's Of Plymouth Plantation 1620 – 1647, gives us more details. He tells us that for the first few days, they sailed before a "prosperous wind" that did much encourage them. But prosperous winds didn't keep them from throwing up all over the place. Restricted to the windowless gun deck, unable to orient their balance to the horizon, the passengers suffered explosive bouts of seasickness. Without benefit of portholes or anything that would flush, they heaved their beer-soaked biscuits, their bits of cod, their oatmeal, pea porridge, and salted pork. Maybe Brewster offered a psalm to assuage them: He shows by the sea what care God has over man, for when he delivers them from the great danger of the sea, he delivers them as it were from a thousand deaths. They mount up to the heaven, they go down again to the depths: their soul is melted because of trouble.

An especially obnoxious sailor did what he could to make them feel worse.

...he would always be condemning the poor people in their sickness and cursing them daily with grievous execrations; and did not let to tell that he hoped to help cast half of them overboard before they came to their journey's end, and to make merry with what they had, and if he were by any gently reproved, he would curse and swear most bitterly. But it pleased God before they came half seas over, to smite this young man with a grievous disease, of which he died in a desperate manner, and so was himself the first that was thrown overboard. Thus his curses light on his own head, and it was astonishment to all his fellows for they noted it to be the just hand of God upon him.

For the next two months the passengers would live in a dim, wet world that smelled of seawater, vomit, chamber pots, animal dung, unwashed clothes, and every aroma the human body can produce, not to mention whiffs of the wine, tar, fish, and turpentine of cargoes past. They heard men snore, women weep, children whine, an oink-oink here, a cluck-cluck there, sailors thumping around the deck above. They heard each other pray. They heard the stutter of the tiller as it swung back and forth at the rear of the gundeck. They heard a continuous creaking of wood that spoke of the condition of the ship, the mood of the sea, the strength of the wind. Sometimes the creaking murmured that all was well; sometimes it screamed that man was not meant to sail across oceans. They read the tones of the shouts of the sailors to guess the ever-shifting degree of danger. When waves reared back and thundered across the upper deck, cold water dripped through the decking. During each four-hour shift, sailors manned two pumps to draw the water out of the bilge, up onto the top deck, where most of it ran to the sea but some of it dripped or trickled back down on the passengers. The passengers were moist at the best of times, soaked at the worst of times, and never truly dry, not for a moment, from late summer 1620 until mid-winter 1621.

During calm weather Master Jones may have let passengers come up onto the main deck for a bit of air, light, and exercise. At any sign of bad weather or any need to work with rigging, passengers had to descend immediately to their dim, dank quarters. If bad weather threatened, the crew fit the lids over the hatch, letting the passengers ride out the storm in the dusky gun deck.

The ship never stopped, never dropped anchor, never rested motionless. The passengers spent the entire voyage swinging between extremes of boredom and fear. Except for the occasional moment on deck, calm seas meant endless hours of sitting in one place, talking to the same people about a daily routine that never changed. But none would wish for more interesting weather. Winds brought waves that took the ship on a terrifying ride. The prosperous winds turned ferocious as the ship sailed into the middle of hurricane season. By sheer luck – or was it miracle? – the Mayflower would spend over two months in the North Atlantic without getting hit by weather of hurricane strength, but something mighty strong hit them, and more than once. Somewhere midatlantic, the Mayflower, so tall and solid at the dock, all but cowered under mountainous waves. At times the wind pushed her over so far that the mainyard, the fifty-foot horizontal yardarm from which the mainsail hung some forty feet above the deck, would lean over and grab the water. As the water pulled at it, it acted as a twenty-five-foot lever that tugged violently at the mast, making the whole ship shudder and groan as if trying not to tear in half. More than once Master Jones gave up trying to control the ship. When the wind grew too fierce, he gave the order to go "at hull." Working in a murderous wind, the crew pulled down all sails and every possible piece of rigging, reducing the ship to not much more than a hull with a barely waterproof lid. They lashed everything down tight, battened the hatches, barred the doors, tucked themselves into the forecastle, put out the fire, and prayed for God to do what Man couldn't. They feared a wave swamping the ship and dashing it to pieces. They feared broken masts and yards. They feared the wave that would lift the ship at one end but not the other, leaving one half of her supported by water, the other half sticking out into the air. She was a ship, not a bridge, built to be cradled, not suspended. The unsupported weight could well crack her in half. To avoid such structural stress, the helmsman would turn the ship to take the waves broadside.

But the broadside pounding put a lot of pressure against the beams that arched under the main deck and kept the hull from breaking inward. One beam, oak half a foot or more thick, warped and bowed as it took punch after punch from thousands of tons of water. The passengers didn't know much about ships, but they knew beams weren't supposed to warp. They also knew scared sailors when they saw them. With typical understatement, Bradford wrote, "there was great distraction and difference of opinion amongst the mariners themselves." The leaders of the passengers entered into consultation with Master Jones and his mates, suggested that maybe it might be wise to turn around and go back, that maybe King James was less dangerous than an angry sea. But Jones told them that they were already closer to the New World than the Old. He thought his Mayflower was actually in pretty good condition and taking the seas well. He'd seen her take a pounding like this for two weeks off the coast of Norway, but he'd eventually brought her into port. They might as well go west as east.

The Mayflower was probably at hull when a wave slugged her especially hard at just the right angle. The bent oak beam cracked like a cannon shot. As wave after wave washed over the topdeck, fear and cold water flooded down to the gun deck, inundating the terrified passengers, soaking everything as it sloshed back and forth across the deck. The ship's carpenter no doubt raced to the scene and was surely relieved to see water coming down instead of up. Still, it was a grave situation. With one beam broken, the others held less lateral pressure against the hull. Another good whack from the outside could snap another beam. In a matter of minutes, the Mayflower could crack in half, break up in the tumult of wind and waves, leaving a hundred-odd people foundering a thousand miles from land, clinging to each other and to pieces of wreckage, gradually weakening and watching each other disappear. But someone remembered the large house jack that had come on board. This was its moment in history. With wet and desperate shoulders and some fast turning of the jack, they forced the beam back into position, propped it with a post, and nailed it with a multitude of prayers, perhaps a psalm: They that go down to the sea in ships, that do business in great waters; He shows by the sea what care God has over man, for when he delivers them from the great danger of the sea, he delivers them as it were from a thousand deaths.

The beam held.

The Mayflower almost lost a passenger when John Howland went up on deck during heavy weather. As the ship rolled to one side, Howland slipped into the sea. Though he was powerless to resist the waves, the topsail halyard, which happened to be trailing in the water, happened to come into his hand, which he happened to close at the right moment. He held it as he sank what seemed to him several fathoms. The crew hauled him to the surface and used a boat hook or something to bring him up to the deck. Bradford described him as "something ill with it," as anyone might be after being snatched back from sure death. But he got over it. It may be a good thing he did. Within his cold, wet breeches he carried the genetic roots of the forty-first and forty-third presidents of the United States, George H.W. Bush and his son. Howland was also an ancestor of Edith Roosevelt, wife of Theodore.

Somewhere between England and America, Elizabeth Hopkins, wife of Stephen, mother of Damaris and stepmother of Constance and Giles, went into labor and delivered a baby boy. We do not know the date or the weather. The ship may have been smoothly tacking to the west, or it may have been in the throes of a storm. They named the boy Oceanus. His mother's breast may have tasted slightly of seawater.

The passenger population of the Mayflower returned to 102 with the death of William Butten, who expired on November 6. He was young, a servant to deacon Fuller. Nothing else is known of him. In all likelihood he was buried at sea. Passengers were probably allowed on deck to witness his shrouded body being lowered into the cold waves. Or maybe they watched from the gun deck as he was slid out a gun port. Separatists would not perform a religious ceremony – none was prescribed in their Bible – but passengers of the Church of England might have liked a traditional good-bye. As Master of the ship, Christopher Jones may have read from the Book of Common Prayer. William Brewster, in his capacity as Elder, may have later talked of life and death in a sermon, perhaps offering a piece of a psalm: For he is content with that life that God gives for by death the shortness of this life is recompensed with immortality.

Master Jones had to make this voyage with the simplest of navigation equipment. For direction, of course, he used a simple compass – a sliver of iron magnetized by the stroking of a lodestone. But the compass did not always point at the lodestar, the north star, Polaris. Magnetic north is neither below that star nor directly on the northernmost point of the planet. Rather, magnetic north wanders around the northern longitudes. Navigators had no idea why Plymouth (the one in New England, not old England) was at 18 degrees, 40 minutes in 1605 but at 13 degrees 40 minutes in 1620. A compass might bring a ship close to Plymouth, but the unpredictable variation in magnetic north could mean the difference between sailing in the ocean and sailing on a beach.

Knowing one's direction is of little use if one does not know how far one has gone in that direction. True, if a ship left Europe and sailed straight west (which, due to wind directions and water currents, it couldn't really do), it would eventually hit the landmass of the Americas. Hitting a landmass, however, is something seamen have traditionally tried to avoid. For obvious reasons, coming close is preferable. It is also preferable to arrive near the destination rather than taking a long and dangerous trip up or down the coast.

Measuring distance to the east or west was not easy. Neither the Mayflower nor any other ship of the time was able to calculate longitude at sea. To do so would require a genius as yet unborn and a clock as yet uninvented. Astronomers could measure the longitude of any place that had an accurate clock, but the constant tilting of a ship at sea made a mockery of pendulums. The only way to estimate longitude was to physically measure the distance sailed from a starting point at a known longitude, a process called dead reckoning. This measurement was made more complicated by a ship's inability to sail straight into the wind. It could sail west in an eastbound wind, but to do so it had to tack slightly northwest and southwest, back and forth, using the rudder and the angle of the sails to cut a course against the wind. The navigator would have to measure the distance sailed to the northwest and then to the southwest, then figure in the angle, then calculate how far due west the ship had actually gone.

The ship measured distance by dropping a triangular chip of weighted wood into the ocean and letting a nine-hundred-foot log-line feed out from a reel as the ship sailed away from it. The line had knots at certain intervals. They could be counted as they slipped through a man's fingers. But this measurement alone was hardly accurate. The ship was not on a stable platform. It was in water, and the water was moving. Navigators already knew more or less the direction that the ocean flowed at various points. In the North Atlantic, the Gulf Stream moved northeast off the coast of Virginia, then turned more to the east, then more to the north as if aiming to slip between the British Isles and Iceland. Water on the northern edge of that current peeled off to the north and west to flow up around the west coast of Greenland. There it passed a current coming down the east coast of northern Canada to curl around Newfoundland and down the coast of New England, just inside the northbound Gulf Stream. Closer to Europe, waters on the southeastern side of the Gulf Stream veered off to the south to sweep past Spain, Saharan Africa, and the Canary islands. There the current turned west toward the Caribbean. By knowing which current the ship was in, a navigator could assume that the ship was drifting in a certain direction at a certain immeasurable speed.

The navigator could measure speed two ways. One was by periodic calculation of changes in latitude, though that didn't really measure the ship's speed forward, not unless it was going due north or south. The other way was to count the knots in the log-line over a period of time. They used an hourglass to measure that time. By dividing the distance by the time, they calculated speed in "knots" per hour. If they knew the speed and it seemed to be constant, they wouldn't need to measure each and every nautical mile.

Determining latitude – one's distance from the equator – was a lot easier than calculating longitude. It wasn't necessary to measure physical distance traveled. Master Jones needed nothing more than a cross staff – a yard-long vertical staff with a horizontal crosspiece that slid up and down the staff. The vertical staff was marked in degrees. At noon – that is, the moment when the sun was highest in the sky, not necessarily at the moment the clock would have struck twelve if they'd had a clock – he would aim the crosspiece at the horizon, the vertical piece at the sun. The angle, noted in numerical charts and duly calculated, indicated the degrees north of the equator.

They measured depth with a 150-fathom line weighted with lead. This instrument was known informally as a dipsie. Nine hundred feet of water wouldn't be of immediate concern to a ship that needed just twelve feet to float, but any indication of ground beneath the sea was reason for people to start paying attention.

So Master Jones had to navigate across the North Atlantic using nothing but a few pieces of wood, a long string, a sliver of iron and a jar of sand. The ship would have to sail a constant zigzag as it tacked against the prevailing westerly wind, the general northeasterly flow of weather and water that followed the Gulf Stream, and the vast counter-clockwise cyclones that swirled up from the south. Storms blew the ship off course and made it difficult or impossible to keep track of distance. Clouds hid the heavens and horizon for days at a time, rendering the cross staff useless. The Gulf Stream constantly nudged the ship to the north and east.

Jones knew where he was going, but history does not know the course he took. He may have followed Columbus's route, riding the Canaries Current to the Canary Islands off the coast of Morocco at latitude 29 degrees, about as far north as Tampa, Florida. From there he would have sailed west around the bottom of the dead-calm, weed-choked Sargasso Sea, then turned northeast to take advantage of the Gulf Stream. Or as most ships bound for New England and Virginia did, he may have sailed southwest to the Azores, a thousand miles off the coast of Portugal at 38 degrees, then almost due west. Or he may have taken the shortest route, the great-circle around the north, where the globe narrows, to come down south on the Arctic current past Newfoundland – a tricky, risky route not recommended for a ship that could not calculate longitude. Whatever his course, Master Jones took sixty-five days to bring his ship and all his passengers, save young Butten, plus young Oceanus, minus the sailor who had died, to the coast of North America just one half of one degree north of his destination. He had aimed at the mouth of the Hudson but arrived a hundred miles north at Cape Cod. Had he sailed in an impossibly straight line from

Plymouth to Plymouth, he'd have sailed about 2,750 miles. If we assume that tacking added 250 miles and that storms didn't blow him too far off course, we bring the total to a hypothetical but conveniently round total of about 3,000. The Mayflower's average speed, then, would be a little under two miles an hour.

While they were on deck on November 6 to bid God-be to William Butten, the passengers may have noticed something changing. Master Jones most certainly noticed a change in cloud formation as the Westerlies off the continent hit the warm air over the Gulf Stream. As soundings found the bottom of the ocean, he'd have his crew alert for rocks and shoals. The crew would have noticed a change in the color of the water, and maybe even the passengers would smell the sweet air coming off the land. And on November 9, someone high in the rigging probably really did shout, "Land Ho!" Permitted or not, passengers could not have resisted coming up through the hatch to have a look at the New World. Quite likely they all rushed up and pressed to the railing, looking west. Their weight may well have tilted the ship to that side. At first it would have been hard to see, but as they crept closer at two excruciatingly slow miles per hour, they would soon glimpse the low, sandy hills of Cape Cod.

From
Love and Death in the Kingdom of Swaziland

Prologue

Once upon a time in the Kingdom of Swaziland, life was as good as it was going to get. The folk in the country lived in little round houses of mud, sticks, and reeds. They planted gardens and let their cattle wander around. The folk in the city found jobs, ate imported food, drove imported cars on paved highways. On Sundays, they went to church. They laughed a lot. They drank the tap water. In February, everybody got drunk on home-brewed amarula fruit hootch. In the rainy season, it rained. In August, everybody watched bare-breasted maidens perform the annual reed dance. The king would be there, perhaps to pick another wife. The Swazi culture, millennia old, kept everyone knitted together in a handful of vast families. Orphans were genealogically impossible.

They had their unspeakable side: black magic, witch doctors, social paranoia, chattel-women, abominable sacrifices. They used the same word for love, like, fornicate, and rape. But this culture, dark and bizarre by the standards of the white world, somehow worked to sustain them in a place of thorn bushes, pit vipers, and wars fought with spears and knobkierrie clubs. Seventy percent of the population was rural, and the level of ignorance wasn't advanced much beyond the dark ages. Illiteracy outside a couple of cities was general, beliefs almost prehistoric. Though Protestant and Catholic churches claimed over 80 percent of the population, age-old beliefs ran deep beneath the veneer of Christianity.

For many years Swaziland benefited from the racial nastiness of the neighbor that bordered the kingdom on three sides. When the world refused to do business with the South African apartheid regime, companies from that country set up camp in the little kingdom four hours east of Johannesburg. Though the country was landlocked and without a train line through South Africa or Mozambique to the coast, the economy boomed. King Sobhuza II reaped plenty of revenues and used them not only to take good care of himself, his 70 wives, and his 210 children, but to pass out food, sponsor clinics, support schools, fill potholes, and keep cities livable. He worked with the chiefs of chiefdoms to keep people happy. When he dispensed with the constitut`ion the British colonizers had imposed, no one cared. Everyone loved King Sobhuza.

Sobhuza died in 1982, but his successor, one of many sons, was only 14 years old. Two queen mothers ran the country in succession until the boy turned 18. He was in high school in England when they called him back to be groomed for the throne. In 1986, a week after his eighteenth birthday, he became King Mswati III.

Mswati didn't have much time to learn to be a king. In 1992, drought descended on Swaziland. In 1994, apartheid collapsed, the international boycotts stopped, and the South African companies went home. And then everybody started dying.

The Dust of the Place

Everybody was dying. That was what Sister Ana Maria de Oliveira said on the phone to her province superior, Sister Diane Dalle-Molle, when she heard that the Missionary Sisters of the Sacred Heart of Jesus, a.k.a. the Cabrini Sisters, were retracting her mission from Swaziland.

"We can't leave now," she pleaded. "Everybody's dying. Everybody." And she started crying. All the babies she and Sister Speranza D'Ambrosi had delivered, educated, raised to adulthood, and trained for a job were all dying. The work of three decades, a whole generation of people, a little impulse of hope for the struggling kingdom, was wasting away.

Sister Ana Maria said, "All we can do is go out to the homesteads and bring them some food and sit with them while they die. Children are everywhere. What are we going to do with all the children?"

Sister Diane had no idea what to do with the children. She was overseeing missions in several countries, from the United States to Australia to Taiwan. That was in 1997. Average life expectancy in Swaziland had already declined from 60-something to 56, and projections were tilting down at a Titanic angle. The sisters of the Sacred Heart had been in Swaziland for 30 years, maintaining a school and convent near Manzini, Swaziland's largest city, and a clinic in the harsh, dusty outback of the Lubombo district, a parish-based outpost called St. Philip's. Things had been going so well in the country that the sisters no longer felt needed. The world had more desperate places.

But then Sister Diane got a call from her General Superior in Rome. She'd heard of the decision to pull out. She said to Diane, "Don't do it."

And Diane asked, "Why not?"

And the Superior General said, "Just don't."

She had grabbed Diane's heart, but her managerial brain needed a reason.

"I can't give you a reason. We just need to stay if we are ever to do the work that God wants us to do. We have to stay in places that seem impossible."

Sister Diane went to see the situation. She flew into Johannesburg, then took a little plane into Swaziland, then took a car an hour down paved roads, then an hour down a bumpy dirt road. She found St. Philip's above the west bank of the Mhlatuze River, which, in the ongoing drought, often barely qualified as a creek. The mission consisted of a few low buildings that housed a little clinic, some staff, the parish priest, an elementary school, and a high school. The church was a dome supported by concrete arches, built, it would seem, to echo sweet Swazi hymns.

And there she found just about everyone dying. Ana Maria took her to some homesteads out among the thorn bushes. The average homestead was a small, circular, wattle-and-daub house with a reed roof. A fence of stick, stones, and thorny branches might surround the place. A few head of cattle and goats might be wandering around the scrub. A scarred and skinny dog might be sleeping in the dust. A few gristly chickens might be scratching around in search of infinitesimal bits of something edible. The houses had little or no furniture or even room for furniture. Rare was the house without at least one person slowly dying on a reed mat on the dirt floor. At one they found three girls lying on mats outside the house. They were 16, 17 and 18, all in the fourth and last stage of AIDS, all infected by the same man. One girl's uterus was distended from her body and covered with fungus. All three had fungal growths around their mouths and down their throats. Their mother was trying to care for them, but there was little she could do.

Cabrini's little clinic didn't have the technical capability to diagnose what the Ana Maria and Speranza knew to be the problem. Even if they could, they had no way to treat HIV/AIDS. Every day more leathery black skeletons staggered in on their spindly knobkierrie staffs. But treatment was superficial at best. The best the sisters could do was alleviate some of the symptoms. The people had to drag themselves back home to die.

And it was time for the sisters to go home, too. Ana Maria was 75, Speranza 85.

Diane wasn't one to walk away from dying people. She had to go back to New York to plead for Swaziland, but something tied her to St. Philip's. As she boarded the little plane to Johannesburg, she was still covered with grit. It was even in her teeth. When she pulled her shoes off to shake them clean, she realized that she loved even the dust of that place.

Back in New York she became more conscious of the oppressive enormity of her job as Provincial Superior. Though a nurse by training, she was overseeing 20 hospitals, clinics, and other institutions. Her congregation's hospital in New York – 1,100 beds, 500 employees – was struggling in the industry's maelstrom of regulations, law suits, restructuring, union demands, technology, AIDS, and soaring costs amid widening poverty. She was spending more in a month than the mission in Swaziland could spend in 20 years. She wanted out, and the outback of Swaziland was about as far out as a Cabrini Sister could get. She wanted to go there, she said, to save her everlasting soul. Her work in New York was God's work, she knew, but it felt like she was walking the other way.

Her board approved an extension of the mission. Ana Maria would go back to her native Brazil, Speranza to New York. Diane would replace them, downshifting, she thought, into a simpler life. She was 61. That was in 2004. Life expectancy in Swaziland had declined to 37 and was still dropping.

But Swaziland wasn't so simple. Instead of lawyers, bankers, union officials, consultants, administrators, and government regulators, she faced plague, drought, corruption, decimated families, legions of orphans, endemic rape, black magic, and ignorance rooted in an impenetrable culture. The government, medieval in its structure and its disregard for its people, obstructed change to any status quo and showed no concern for the well-being of citizens. Dr. Henk Bos had been at St. Philip's for a couple of years. He was the director of laboratories at the Cabrini hospital in Australia. As he handed the mission to Sister Diane, he offered no words of optimism, no illusions of a problem solved or solvable. He told her she would never be able do what she'd come to do, that the problem was impossible to solve. She didn't know what she was doing, didn't know what she'd gotten into. Then he got into the little plane to Johannesburg and flew away.

No Body on Earth But Yours

Diane had second thoughts. They pursued her into bed that night. Lying in the dark of that strange and scary land, she realized that Dr. Hank didn't understand who the Missionary Sisters of Cabrini were, that they had always done what they didn't know how to do, that they didn't surrender to impossibility, not when people were standing in front of them dying.

That disregard for impossibility had always been the history and mission of the MSC. The congregation was founded in 1880 by Frances Cabrini, an Italian woman who didn't let impossibility stand in her way. Dynamic and unstoppable, she founded and secured funding for schools, hospitals, and orphanages in the United States, Nicaragua, Argentina, Brazil, and Europe – all quite impossible for a woman at that period in history, yet she was able to accomplish it. She was canonized in 1946.

The congregation is of sisters rather than nuns, the former tending to go out into the world in with proactive charitable purpose, the latter tending to be cloistered and more focused on prayer. A nun is typically seen in a habit; a sister might well in bib overalls and rubber boots. The Cabrini sisters have a favorite prayer, a call to action by St. Teresa of Avila: "Christ has no body now on earth but yours, no hands, no feet but yours; yours are the eyes through which he looks with compassion on this world; yours are the feet with which he walks to do good; yours are the hands with which he is to bless men now."

Before they retired from St. Philip's, Ana Maria and Speranza put their hands and compassion together to pull off one more impossibility. They managed to get an orphanage built for 50 children. More precisely defined, it was a hostel, a place where children could stay most of the year. During school breaks they would go back to whoever had last been taking care of them. On the day the hostel opened, 98 children showed up. The sisters put them two to a bed. More showed up the next day. It was a lot of kids to feed, love, and clean up after. The local staff needed a lot of training in the art of raising children. For one thing, they had to learn that beating traumatized children is not the best way to discipline them.

Diane, too, had a lot to learn. She was the only white woman in an area raging with a worsening epidemic. She had one small health clinic staffed with a few Swazi nurses, and she had a hostel with well over a hundred children. She awoke every morning to find people dying on her porch. It was a lot for one woman to handle. She called her Provincial Superior in New York and asked if Sister Barbara Staley could be assigned to Swaziland. Barbara had a master's degree in social work and had done time in the jungles of Guatemala and the slums of Chicago. She knew how to work with children. She knew how to plan. She knew how to not just get things done but make them get done.

The province superior said no. Diane pleaded with all her heart. When that didn't work, she lied through her teeth. She said she needed Barbara for just three months. She knew perfectly well she was going to keep finding reasons why Barbara couldn't leave. Barbara arrived in late 2004.

Barbara knew how to devise a plan and then execute it, but there was little point in planning anything. As soon as she got off the little plane, she was dealing with immediate problems – the people dying on the porch, the venomous black mamba coiled up in a tree in the back yard, the dilapidated homestead headed by an unprotected prepubescent girl, the car stuck in the river. These problems didn't need plans. They needed immediate attention. Every day, starting well before dawn, Sister Barbara and Sister Diane had to confront the life-and-death urgency of right now.

And they didn't know what they were doing. They had never confronted an epidemic before and certainly had no idea how to treat HIV infection or AIDS. They had no one to advise them on anything. They had no idea how the medical system worked in Swaziland, no idea where to buy food for a hundred-odd children every day, how to train illiterate people, how to run a clinic staffed with nurses who believed black magic worked. They had no time to learn siSwati.

As they started to establish initial measures for dealing with the epidemic, they hit their first inexplicable wall. Everyone was deathly ill, and in most cases it was pretty obvious what the cause was. Step one toward treatment was to have blood tested, yet people were refusing. In fact, the people working with Diane and Barbara refused to even ask people to be tested. Not even nurses would do it. But it made no sense. Though the causes of HIV, from rape to polygamy, held no stigma, having the disease was embarrassing, and asking about it was insulting. The sisters hired Mr. Pius Mamba to provide the language and insight they needed to talk with people. He'd been raised in the rural culture, but he'd always been a Christian and had quite a bit of college education. He went out to the homesteads with the sisters to translate, but he, too, had difficulty asking about testing for HIV. He had to gradually, over the course of half an hour, lead into the question. "Forgive me for being so bold," he'd say. "It isn't me asking this, it's the Sister; she's white, you know...a little crazy; I'm just translating and I need this job, so I have to ask, if you could just try to understand that I don't mean anything by it..." And then all he could do was hope the question didn't lead to a curse that only a witch doctor could remove.

Oddly enough, once the question was asked, the answer was often a desperate yes. So in dark, smoke-filled huts, Diane drew blood. Because of the dim light, the tough muscle tissue of dirt farmers, the dark skin over collapsed veins, she had to use her bare fingers to find a vein and guide the needle in. Then she'd put the blood on ice to take to Good Shepherd Hospital for testing. Sometimes the blood spent the night in plastic bags in the refrigerator back home, in there with the food. It was the only refrigerator they had.

When the test for HIV came back positive, they would have to take the patient to the hospital. They'd be rumbling down unmapped dirt trails by 4:00 a.m. It was the only way to have enough time to pick up Mr. Mamba, find far-flung homesteads, talk people into allowing a blood draw, pick up patients, go to the hospital two hours to the northeast, take blood samples into Manzini for HIV testing, take other samples into the capital, Mbabane, for CD4 testing of white blood cell levels, and then go back to homesteads to inform those who had to go to the hospital the next morning. They packed as many people as they could into an old Toyota Venture, a mini-van modified to hold more passengers than it was built for. It had problems. It was a four-wheel drive vehicle, but only two wheels drove. The battery kept falling out. The lights kept going off. The tires kept going flat. A wheel kept coming off. Not built for off-road travel, the van tended to get stuck in rivers they were driving through, in soft sand, in puddles of dust. On the way to the hospital one night, just after repairs to the electrical system, the lights went out and flames licked out from under the hood. Diane couldn't stop for that. She held a flashlight out the window in case other cars couldn't see the flames coming down the road.

She was a nurse, not a mechanic, and she was at the wheel of a logistical nightmare. She wasn't even much of a driver, either. She didn't know how to drive a standard shift until she got to Swaziland. She didn't know what to do with a battery hanging under the engine, swaying by a cable. She didn't know how to change a flat until Mr. Mamba, who is blind, talked her through it one dark night. She learned to keep a flashlight in the car.

Good Shepherd wasn't much of a hospital. It certainly wasn't up to the challenge of an AIDS epidemic. HIV patients were laid out on the floor of a space not much bigger than a living room. A couple hundred more lay on the ground outside. The only doctor, an American from

California, was always angry and shouting, way over his head in patients, dealing with inadequate staff, dispensing inadequate medications, and working with inadequate equipment.

To simply leave patients at Good Shepherd wouldn't be much better than leaving them at home. They were as ignorant as could be, as humble as dirt, unable to understand instructions, afraid to speak up, mystified by the whole medical process. The sisters had to speak for, and think for, their patients. Mr. Mamba said to Sister Barbara, "You care more about these people's lives than they do."

The conditions at homesteads had declined from third-world to sub-human. The sisters came to homesteads so poor that people were walking around naked. They found young children trying to maintain a household while a tubercular parent in the fourth stage of AIDS lay fetid and suppurating on the floor in a cluster of jubilant flies. Water had to come from a river a mile or two or more away, and if the river was dry at that time of year, they'd have to dig. Due to the drought, no one had harvested a crop in a decade. Due to lack of people healthy enough to work, houses were falling apart, mud walls eroding, reed roofs disintegrating. As parents died, children got passed to aunts and uncles until they died, then to grandmothers until they died, then to neighbors, then to the grandmothers of neighbors. Children lost track of where they were born and who their parents were. Some lost track of their own names. As they distanced themselves from their families and homesteads, they lost their inheritance of family homesteads. Old women found themselves with herds of children from unknown places, everyone sleeping on the floors of their little houses, sharing smoky air with people coughing up blood. No one in the world offered any help except the two old white women in the old Toyota, and they were lucky if they made it to half a dozen homesteads in a day, half a dozen out of 2,500 around St. Philip's.

At one homestead, apparently abandoned after the roof fell in, they looked around, found nobody. They asked a neighbor who said there was a small baby being cared for at the house by a "troubled" young girl and an old man. The sisters went back to the house, poked around, found a rib-skinny dog crouched beside a pile of rags. In the pile of rags they found a rib-skinny little boy named Menze. They picked him up. He didn't stir. He wasn't quite dead, but almost. The dog could have told them that. It was just waiting. The sisters took him back to the mission and nursed him back into life.

These people weren't just patients. Barbara and Diane developed close relationships with many of them. When they died, they were friends dying – hundreds and hundreds of friends. The sisters didn't cry much, but once in a while it happened. It happened to Diane the first time she got out of Swaziland. It was in 2006, after two years in-country. She went to a retreat in upstate New York, a place for prayer and contemplation. On the second day she got to contemplating about all the friends she'd seen die. She started sobbing and couldn't stop. She just sobbed and sobbed and sobbed.

Barbara sobbed when a girl named Tanzele died. Both of her parents had died, and she had HIV and tuberculosis. Twice a week she had to walk 19 kilometers to a clinic for medication. She was 13 when the sisters took her into the hostel. In the magical way of Swazis, she became happy. Everyone loved her. She took her medications and went to school every day. She giggled with the other girls. She played a game that involved dodging a ball of wadded-up plastic bags while trying to fill a soda bottle with sand. She was so proud of her excellent report card. When she went home to stay with relatives during a school break, she contracted measles. Medical personnel and foreign aid workers didn't know what to do. They'd never seen anyone with HIV, TB, and measles. Barbara thought they didn't try hard enough to help her. When she died, Barbara wept – not just for the loss but for the fact of no one being able to save her. She wept for that and the reality that success had to be measured in such small increments. In Tanzele's case, it was a girl who was allowed to experience childhood for a few months.

There was hardly a day when either Diane or Barbara didn't decide to give up, to go home, to take on some other problem, one that could actually be solved. Every day was one day too much. But when they had time to stop and think about what they were doing, to relate their travails to Jesus, and to dispense with the notion of impossibility, they always managed to stay a little longer and go out to a few more homesteads to see what they could do. It's hard to walk away from people who are dying. In the dark of that strange and scary land, she realized that Dr. Hank didn't understand who the Missionary Sisters of Cabrini were and what they could accomplish when they felt it had to be done.

White Medicine in a Black World

People on the homesteads had no idea what was causing their maladies, which in a single individual were likely to include several sexually transmitted diseases. They might have tuberculosis that had spread from lungs to glands to bones. They often had Kaposi's sarcoma, a systemic viral infection that causes lesions on the skin, from soles to gums, down the gastrointestinal tract and into the lungs. They might have tumors under the arm, on the tongue, in the throat. They might have shingles as ugly and painful as a third-degree burn. They might have fungal growths down through the alimentary canal. They surely had chronic diarrhea. They had skin diseases Diane had never seen before. They had peripheral neuritis, an agonizing inflammation of the nerves of the lower leg. People in their twenties hobbled around like crippled elderly trying to keep their infected feet off the ground. Paranoid by the nature of their culture, they readily supposed they were the victims of a curse targeted at them as individuals. They didn't know how the disease spread, and when told, they didn't believe it. They believed what the "traditional healers" told them – that they had been cursed by a neighbor, that if the patient was a man, the prescribed cure might be sex with a virgin, or if the patient was a woman, the cure might be sex with the doctor himself. It might also involve little hash marks cut into the knuckles and other joints with a razor used on other people with the same medical complaint. Sometimes the healers, protective of their turf, told people to refuse the white medicine, that it would kill them.

The sisters recognized that they had to work within this culture. But they found it unfathomable. No one, not even the people they worked with, not even the ones with education and urban experience, was willing to offer more than a peek into its dark secrets. Ever since the English and Dutch colonization of the 19th century Swazis had learned to keep their African side veiled. The national motto, Siyinqaba, could be translated as "We are a fortress" but with the parallel meaning of "We are hidden; we are a mystery."

They spoke English with foreigners in a beautiful, off-kilter, almost poetic whisper, but they rarely said more than necessary. They answered open-ended questions with vague thoughts that seemed framed to tell the white people only what they wanted to hear. They answered yes-no questions honestly but with just one word. They were polite to the point of self-effacing humility. Women were reluctant to speak with men and afraid to speak with whites. When women came into the Cabrini clinic, they could not bring themselves to look at Diane. They stood half bowed, half turned away, speaking in a timid hush. The treatment and prevention of HIV had to begin with basic education: getting women to stand straight and speak up, and not just to talk with Diane.

They would have to stand straight and speak up to their doctors, their husbands, their chiefs, their sorceresses and witch doctors. But they were as comfortable doing this as American women would be singing operatic-style to all the men in their lives.

Behavior was inexplicable. People would get sick and frightened enough to come in for testing, but when they went home, they hit family problems. Their husbands wouldn't allow them to get treated. Or their sisters talked them out of it. Or their healers would offer a more traditional option. Or their preachers would tell them Jesus would heal them. One patient came in and said that her preacher had cured her. When he prayed over her, she could feel the moment she was healed. She didn't come back until she was almost dead. There was a staff member whose mother was a sorceress. He was a "default tracker" who excelled at going out into the outback to track down people who had stopped picking up medications. For three years he showed the symptoms of AIDS, but his mother refused to let him get tested. He died at the age of 35. They found him lying naked in a building, waiting for his spirit to return to his body. Then he couldn't be buried on his homestead because it was feared that the neighbors who had bewitched him with HIV would come dig up his bones to use for rituals.

As they grappled with the causes and prevention of HIV and orphanhood, they came to see how the culture itself was the crux of the problem. Women, especially those in rural areas, had no way to say no to sex. It didn't matter if the man was an uncle or someone else's husband or a stranger who happened to come along. It didn't matter if he was HIV-positive. Swazi culture instilled such submission in women that psychologically they could not bring themselves to resist sex. A girl might well be pushed into marriage as a young teen, especially if deflowered. Her father would be compensated for the loss by a payment of cattle. Depending on the girl's beauty, virtues, family connections, and extent of virginity, she could be worth ten or twenty cows, maybe more, maybe less. Her proposing groom would actually negotiate with her father, giving reasons why she wasn't worth as many cows as her father liked to think.

While women were submissive in sex, men were sexually unencumbered. Though a neighbor's wife was technically off limits, adultery was a matter of what one could get away with more than an issue of morality. An unmarried sister-in-law was fair game. Virginity was something to respect, but not out of concern for the girl. Rather, it was a matter of how many cows she was worth before and after. Once violated, she was obliged to marry. If the man already had a wife, well, now he had another, though it might cost him a few cows. The wives slept on the floor near their husband's bed. When he wanted to lie with one of them, he called her over. They had a special verb for that.

On the other hand, none of that is necessarily true. Swazi sexual mores are confusing, convoluted, and contradictory. Any non-Swazi claiming to understand it probably hasn't asked enough Swazis to explain it. Barbara and Diane certainly didn't understand it.

Alcohol aggravated the situation. Home-based bars, called shebeens, sold a cheap, sweet, creamy home-made hootch made from the amarula fruit. The fruit ripened in February. Everybody spent the next month or two drunk. Crime rose. Pregnancies increased. Disease spread. Dedicated alcoholics kept it up for the rest of the year. They hung around the shebeen all day, often leaving kids unattended at home. If the individual had TB, the close and palsy-walsy quarters of the shebeen facilitated its transmission. As the day's drinking built up, the benefits of condom usage got forgotten. Inebriation enhanced the beauty of the famished barflies, and desperation for another drink increased the acceptability of a man with money. If the individual was HIV-positive, which he or she probably was, the virus soon found its way into a nice, new bloodstream. And everybody took home some TB bacilli for the kids.

Pius Mamba, one of few willing to give the sisters a little insight into Swazi culture, defined sex as a matter of power exchanged for pleasure. Women lacked social and economic power and privilege–the privilege of sitting on a chair rather than on the ground, of learning a trade and earning their own bread, of owning land, of deciding whom they would marry and how many children they would have and whom their husbands would marry. Their power was pretty much limited to how easily they would provide the pleasure of sex. Mr. Mamba called it "transactional sex." Women gave sex to get something, be it food, a cell phone, a ride into town, or a withholding of violence. While psychologically they couldn't say no, they could set some conditions for yes. They could try to get what they could for what they had to do anyway. Though other Swazis weren't necessarily as cynical (or articulate) as Mr. Mamba, his explanation was credible. Sister Diane knew a woman who was having sex with a man she knew to be HIV-positive. Her justification: "I'd rather die later with a full stomach than die hungry now."

Culture was at the root of the problem, but Barbara and Diane hadn't come to Swaziland to cure culture. They weren't even there to push Catholicism. Not exactly, not that directly. Yes, they believed the world was better off where Catholicism and its values were a way of life; yes, they would like to see more of it in Swaziland; no, they were not pushing it on people. They did not engage in catechism. Their mission was health care and child care. Yes, they led their children in Catholic prayer and Catholic song. Yes, they took their children to mass every Sunday. But aside from religious guidance for the children in the hostel, the sisters were bringing the love of Jesus to the local people not by thumping a Bible but by providing example. As Diane put it, they were in circumstances where they were better off living the love of God than talking about it. They were teaching by doing, nurturing love by loving.

But the frustration of working with an incorrigible and uncooperative culture gave rise to anger. sisters aren't supposed to experience anger, and they certainly aren't supposed to show it, but it happened. Like all sisters and nuns who struggle with the world's intractable problems, Barbara and Diane have a certain fire in them. Without that fire, they wouldn't be able to do what they do. They probably wouldn't even try. It's a good fire, but like all fire, it can burn. There were times when they lost control and lashed out at somebody too stupid or sluggish to see what needed to be done. The negative impression left by these incidents would haunt them for years.

And they lashed out at each other, an inevitability when two people are exhausted and trying to solve problems which neither have seen before and which have no obvious solutions. But they were brief arguments free of ego or suspicion. They were both trying to accomplish the same thing, and they never had time for a drawn-out debate. They also understood the inevitability of failures along the way. Though a good deal of the time they didn't know what they were doing, at least they were doing something. Their failures were no worse than the default situation.

Toward the end of 2004, just months after the sisters arrived in Swaziland, the first free anti-retrovirals (ARVs) came into the country courtesy of the Global Fund to Fight AIDS, Tuberculosis and Malaria. At the same time, the President's Emergency Plan for AIDS Relief (PEPFAR), initiated by George W. Bush, started providing financial and technical assistance for promoting capacity, competence, and sustainability. The Global Fund was funded by donations from governments, the private sector, philanthropic organizations and individuals. The Bill and Melinda Gates Foundation was the largest non-governmental donor. The Global Fund provided (and carefully monitored) grants to governments to pay for medications and other materials.

In their first years dealing with the epidemic, the sisters could offer nothing more than access to health care – the blood tests, the rides to the hospital, the education. Columbia University's International Center for AIDS Care and Treatment Programs (ICAP) came to St. Philip's to help help raise the capacity of their local organization, Cabrini Ministries. Cabrini turned over its general clinic to the Severite Sisters, a diocesan order located at St. Philip's. On the next day, Cabrini opened a clinic dedicated to HIV/AIDS and TB. Big mistake. Because it was a new clinic, it had to go through all the government certification procedures again. But in time, as they increased their capacity, they would be able to test for HIV and TB and initiate treatments, avoiding the trips to Good Shepherd.

Anti-retrovirals, it turned out, worked better than sex with virgins and witch doctors. They didn't cure, but if combined with good nutrition, and if other illnesses were dealt with, ARVs could support immune systems enough for them to avoid the diseases associated with AIDS, prolonging life for more than a decade. They drastically reduced transmission of the virus through sex, and they could prevent contagion of newborns by their HIV-positive mothers.

In 2007, after knocking on innumerable doors and filing innumerable forms and beseeching innumerable government ministers and other officials, quite innocently neglecting to bribe everyone along the way, they got Cabrini Ministries registered as a not-for-profit. Around about that time, they gained a reputation for not only getting things done but implementing new programs quickly. They had no organizational bureaucracy holding them back, and they were far enough out in the sticks to be overlooked by the government. They became a model for how to most efficiently and effectively implement new projects.

Ironically, they were still flying by the seat of their calf-length skirts, figuring things out as they charged forward, finding solutions for impossible problems and moving on.

By this point, average life expectancy in Swaziland was edging down toward 32 years, probably lower in the Lubombo region. The national population was declining, something that had rarely happened anywhere on earth since the bubonic plague hit Europe in the 14th century.

Though working in a place dense with disease, the sisters themselves had no time to be sick. They had to be in a lot of places at the same time. Mbabane was in the northwest corner of the country. Good Shepherd hospital was in Siteki, in the northeast corner of the country. Manzini was in the center of the country. St. Philip's was in the southeast. They had to move patients, medications, and blood samples to most of these places almost every day. They had to buy food in Manzini for the homesteads because the medications certainly weren't going to work on people who were starving. They had to divvy the food up into packages for delivery. They had to keep track of who had to go back to the hospital, who had children not being taken care of, who was failing to take their medications.

In the middle of all this, they were raising over a hundred traumatized children who needed a consistent supply of food, clothes, showers, and school materials. They needed warm words of encouragement in a cold, discouraging world. They needed admonishments for the gaffes and misdemeanors of childhood. They needed someone to explain the facts of life to them, including the fact that sex was synonymous with death. Their hostel needed a poster depicting a young, happy, hip-looking black woman saying, "I can live without sex."

The sisters had to teach people, one by one, why they had to continue medication once they'd started. They had to deal with the people they found on their porch every morning. They had to drive a full car past desperate people waving their hands weakly in hopes of a ride. They had to keep the car from falling apart. They had to dig it out of the sand or push it out of the mud or find a tractor to haul it out of the river. They had to rush people to the clinic with snake bites. They had to triage children to decide who was most likely to die if they didn't get into the hostel. They stopped everything to pray with people as they withered from the earth.

To avoid operating an ad hoc HIV clinic on their front porch, they set up a slightly more formal clinic in an empty room that belonged to the parish. Medical equipment wasn't much more than a couple of plastic tables and a few chairs. The examination room and waiting room shared the same open space. They had no pharmacy, no medications to dispense. In hot weather they moved a plastic table out front.

They couldn't resist last requests. They bought meat for an old man who craved that little luxury before he died. They bought coffins for people. When a dying woman requested a Coca-cola, Diane drove almost 100 km down dirt roads to get her one. Barbara said that wasn't a cost-effective use of gasoline and time. Diane said suppose it was your mother. Barbara then remembered what they were doing in Swaziland. It wasn't just health care and child care. It was compassion. They were there to love – to love and to show love, to show that it's all right to love your neighbor, that love can make life better. The siSwati language didn't even have a word for this kind of love.

Death by death they came to learn that they were dealing with values beyond their understanding. The basic human values they had always assumed innate to all humans were just Judeo-Christian values not necessarily shared by all cultures. They noticed that there were no Down Syndrome children, no children with cleft palates, no congenital deformities whatsoever. But an unusual number of newborns accidentally died while their mothers were washing clothes at the river – drowned, eaten by a crocodile, bitten by a mamba, or meeting some other euphemistic demise. Mothers were capable of infanticide, something the sisters had simply presumed beyond the instinct of mothers. Even more inexplicably, many people seemed unconcerned with their own survival. The urge to live wasn't present in everyone, and neither was the urge to let-live.

The sisters couldn't conclude whether this disregard for the most fundamental values was part of the old culture or a new-born product of trauma and poverty. The two overlapped. There was a young woman in their area, for example, whose parents died of AIDS when she was 14. That meant she'd been caring for them and the rest of the family for four or five years prior. Her adulthood had begun at about age ten. Soon after her parents died, she was raped and impregnated. She had a baby and at some point contracted HIV. She became pregnant again and endowed her newborn son with the gift of a deadly germ. The sisters met her when she was 20. She was taking her ARVs and giving them to her child, heading her household reasonably well. In fact, she seemed exceptionally intelligent and capable, so the sisters hired her to work in the clinic. They taught her to drive. Soon she got a job in a nearby town. But within a few weeks, she started to change. She didn't do her work. She argued with co-workers. She started alienating neighbors who had been trying to help her. She stopped taking her ARVs, and then she stopped giving them to her little boy. And then the little boy fell into a bucket of water and drowned. He was 11 months old.

From

The Cat Caboodle: A Litter Box of Cat Facts and Curiosities

Your Tax Dollars at Work

The Central Intelligence Agency almost got its middle name revoked after the agency's innovative attempt to enlist a patriotic cat to the service of his country. This was back in the 1960s, when counter-Soviet espionage was most urgent. The CIA needed to know what its nuclear adversary was up to.

The top-secret plan: Surgically implant listening devices into a cat, code-named "Acoustic Kitty."

A former CIA officer described the gruesome process. "They slit the cat open, put batteries in him, wired him up," the officer said. "The tail was used as an antenna. They made a monstrosity."

Then they tried to train the cat–whose real name remains a government secret–to hang out on window sills, under park benches, and near embassy garbage cans, picking up and transmitting conversations.

To the surprise of the intelligence agency, training a cat proved difficult.

"They tested him and tested him," the CIA agent said. "They found he would walk off the job when he got hungry, so they put another wire in to override that."

Five years (a mighty long time for a cat) and $10 million (a mighty lot of money for a cat) later, they took the secret agent out for a trial run.

"They took [a specially equipped van] out to a park and put him out of the van," the CIA man said, "and a taxi comes and runs over him. There they were, sitting in the van with all those dials, and the cat was dead."68

A heavily redacted CIA report, released in 2001, said, "Our final examination of trained cats...for...use in the...convinced us that the program would not lend itself in a practical sense to our highly specialized needs....

Incendiary Cats

Cat bombs. Just what the world needs.

A few have reached the concept and even experimental level of development. Fortunately–for cats as well as other living things–cat bombs have never been deployed.

One of the earliest ideas, dreamed up around 1430, was an incendiary bomb that would be carried to the enemy on the back of a cat. It was called a "rocket pack," though it wasn't meant to make the cat fly. Instructions went something like this:

"Create a small sack like a fire-arrow...if you would like to get at a town or castle, get a cat from that place. Bind the sack to the back of the cat, ignite it, let it glow well, and then let the cat go so that it runs to the nearest castle or town, and out of fear it thinks to hide itself in the hay or straw of a barn, which will be ignited."

Some Idiot's Idea for a Cat Bomb

According to the Internet, the following is true.

Back during World War II, before the CIA got its name, the Office of Strategic Services got a brilliant idea to solve a complicated problem.

The problem: How to get a moving bomb dropped from a moving plane to hit a moving target, in this case, an enemy ship.

The solution: Strap the bomb to a cat.

Why a cat: Because a) cats know how to land on their feet, and b) cats hate water. Dropped from a plane several thousand feet in the air, the bomb-laden furball would attempt to get into a feet-first toward-the-ship position. That attempt would somehow guide the bomb toward the ship.

How the cat would actually guide the bomb was going to take a lot of experimentation, one cat per shot, each cat terminally precluded from learning how to do it right a second time. According to an animated illustration on youtube.com, the cat was inside a capsule with a window and a bomb. Strings attached to the cat's paws guided the bomb as the cat tried to land on its feet on the ship.

Under the urgency of war, the OSS skipped over technical concerns and went ahead and outfitted a courageous volunteer cat with a bomb and dropped it from a plane. The bomb missed the target. The OSS said that the cat had passed out at some point during its breathtaking–one can only imagine–descent and thus was unable to complete its mission. How the OSS detected the cat's lack of consciousness is another mystery in this story, which, though terrible, is just too interesting to ignore. Whatever the answer to these mysteries, there were no further attempts to use a cat to guide a bomb. One cat, and they were done.

Dogs and Cats in Space

Dog ventured into outer space long before cat.

Between 1951 and 1952, Soviet rockets carried nine dogs into space on several flights. Some were sent in pairs. The first pair survived. The second pair did not. Three of the canine astronauts made the trip twice. One dog, Bobnik, missed her dubious opportunity by escaping before her scheduled flight. Whether she made it to and over the Berlin Wall is not known.

The Russian street mutt Laika was launched on November 3, 1957 aboard the Sputnik 2. (Americans nicknamed her Muttnik.) The first living being to orbit the earth, she was supposed to live six days before her oxygen depleted. However, in 2002 it was revealed that she had died from overheating in the first few hours.

The French cat Félicette, a black-and-white female stray found on the streets of Paris, was launched on October 18, 1963. She and 13 other cats had been trained for the mission in high-G centrifuges and compression chambers. Her rocket was a Véronique. Unlike Laika's trip around the planet, her trip was suborbital, lasting only 15 minutes, reaching a height of just under 100 miles before her capsule parachuted safely to earth.

Four days later, another *astrochat* was launched, but due to technical difficulties, the courageous cat never again walked the earth.

Dog vs. Cat

Ever wonder why dogs defend their territory but cats don't? Both are hunters and can be very vicious. But cats are better built for fleeing. They can sprint faster and climb up a tree. Dogs, who long ago lived in packs, have found they're better off if they stand (with their friends) and defend their turf rather than run and try to climb a tree.

Ever wonder why cats are stealthier than dogs? It seems to be because cats are better sprinters. They can move fast but only for short distances. They have to get as close to their prey as possible. Dogs are better built for the long haul. They can hound their prey for a long time, so rather than sneak up on their prey, they wear them down.

When Cats Get High

What is it with catnip? That's a good question. Scientists have determined that the active ingredient in the Nepeta cataria plant is nepetalactone. A cat can detect as little as one part nepetalactone per billion parts of air.

Cats go ape when they smell catnip. When they find it growing, they roll around in it, get the oil on their fur, lick it off, then roll around some more. When they find a catnip-filled toy, they toss it around, claw it, clutch it, have a lot of fun with it.

Leopards? Cougars? Lynxes? Lions? They love the stuff, too. Tigers? Not so much. It depends on the tiger.74

An experiment with various plants found that nearly all domestic cats responded to some kind of olfactory stimulant. Almost 80 percent responded to silver vine, and about 50 percent to Tatarian honeysuckle. Catnip? One in three domestic cats couldn't care less.

How about people? Desperate marijuana smokers have been known to try smoking catnip, but all it does is make them feel not just desperate but stupid. However, an experiment conducted by two Marquette University researchers found that when people smoked tobacco that had been sprayed with catnip oil, they hallucinated as if on lysergic acid diethylamide (LSD). In that trans,cis nepetalactone is molecularly similar to LSD, it is possible that when cats are flipping out over catnip, chasing phantom butterflies, they may be tripping like hippies.

Odds and Ends

Cats do not think that they are little people. They think that people are big cats. This influences their behavior in many ways.

Most cats have no eyelashes. But they have 26 teeth.

Cats lack a true collarbone. Because of this lack, a cat can generally squeeze its body through any space it can get its head through. You may have seen a cat testing the size of an opening by careful measurement with the head. You may have noticed cats' tendency to get stuck in tight places. It's because they have no collarbone.

Unlike humans and dogs, cats do not suffer a lot from loneliness. It is a mistake to project our social feelings onto our cats. Cats are social to a degree, but they are far more concerned with territorial issues than we can even imagine.

Like birds, cats have a homing ability that uses its biological clock, the angle of the sun, and the Earth's magnetic field. A cat taken far from its home can return to it. But if a cat's owners move far from its home, the cat can't usually find them.

Besides smelling with their nose, cats can smell with an additional organ called the Jacobson's organ, located in the upper surface of the mouth. When you see a cat wrinkle its muzzle, lower its chin and let its tongue hang out, it is opening a channel to the Jacobson's organ.

Cats can land on their feet because they have a flexible spine. They can twist around better than most other mammals.

Most deaf cats do not meow.

Multi-colored male cats are very rare. For every 3,000 tortoiseshell or calico cats born, only one will be male.

Cats can see in the dark six times better than humans. But if there's enough light, humans can see objects 200 feet away clearly, but cats can see clearly for only about 20 ft. Humans see more color, too. Cats apparently see the world as shades of blue and gray.[48]

A third of American cat owners think their cat can read their mind.

Why do cats never have smelly armpits? Because they sweat only through their paws.

Why do a cat's back paws smell like Fritos? Maybe it has something to do with sweat. The more poignant question: Why do Fritos smell like a cat's back paws?

Cats respond to women more than men because women have higher-pitched voices.

A group of cats is called a *clowder.* The word came about in the 19th century, probably a dialect variation of the word *clutter.*

A male cat is a tom. A female cat is a queen or a molly.

The color of a cat's coat often indicates personality. And often it doesn't.

A cat's nose pattern is as unique to it as fingerprints are to a human. Look around the Internet and you can find companies that will help you make a silver model of a cat's nose. The process begins by pressing special molding material onto the nose to make a print. The company then fills it with silver to duplicate the nose.

Some of the foods that cats should not eat: chocolate, garlic, grapes, green tomatoes, onions, raisins, raw potatoes. Milk might make your cat fart. Aspirin and Tylenol might make your cat die.

From

Dr. Jamoke's Little Book of Hitherto Uncompiled Facts and Curiosities Regarding Bees

Busy as a bee? Which bee? How about busy as bee researchers at the University of Illinois who set up five hives, each with about 2,000 day-old bees. They fastened tiny transponders to a bunch of the bees so they could count, with scanners, how many were going out to forage. They found that 20 percent of a hive's bees accounted for 50 percent of the foraging activity. In other words, there were a lot of less-busy bees. When the scientists killed a number of bees who had been going out to forage, other bees were replacing them within a day. Whether the less-active bees were lazy, occupied with indoor activities such as housekeeping and child-rearing, or just held back for emergencies was not determined. In any event, not all bees are as busy as beavers.

* * *

Bees' lives are measured in days, not years. During the first three days of a bee's life, a worker bee is a chamber maid cleaning brood cells, but she will spend 20 percent of her day resting and 20 percent walking around. After age four, as her hypopharyngeal glands start secreting brood food, she becomes a nurse. By age 12, she knows how to sting and she goes to work in food storage, evaporating nectar to make it honey, packing pollen, building comb, and helping guard the hive entrance. At age 20, she's ready for dangerous work outside the hive, gathering pollen, nectar, water, and resin. By the time she's 28, she has worn her wings ragged and worked herself

* * *

When a bee consumes nectar from a flower, she swallows it into a "honey stomach." This organ is not part of the digestive system. It has no exit other than the entrance.

Back at the hive, she regurgitates the nectar repeatedly, taking turns with other worker bees to lap it up and heave it out. This ingestive-regurgitative process, which can take 20 minutes, uses digestive enzymes to hydrolyze the sucrose of the nectar to form a mixture of glucose and fructose. Yes, honey is bee barf...but natural!

* * *

The queen bee stays in her hive except to mate, which she may do 15 or 20 times during a single mating flight. She is not a queen in any sense of leadership, power, or privilege. She is more like a slave to those whom she has borne, fulfilling her sole function in life as fast as she can until she weakens, at which point her progeny gather round and kill her with suffocation and heat.

* * *

Male bees–the big, fat ones known as drones–have no known function other than sex. Even so, few of them will ever experience it, and those that do tend to have nothing but negative feelings about the brief relationship. Drones do not forage for food, care for the nest, raise the young, or defend the hive. Unlike females, they often leave the hive to take a nap outside. When winter comes, they assume they'll be welcome indoors, but there will be no mating until spring, so who needs them? Nobody. The females haul them outside and toss them over the edge, into the cold.

* * *

Drones mate with a queen during her mating flight. A fellow lucky enough to insert his endophallus into the queen and ejaculate therein will, upon retraction, have his endophallus and part of his abdomen ripped out. Sex is fatal to drones.

* * *

Whenever possible, bees carry waste, including their dead, away from the hive. If, however, a large intruder, such as a mouse, dies in the hive, removal is not an option. The bees will therefore encase the corpse in propolis, embalming it so that it does not rot, stink, or fester. If you were to bite into such a mummy at room temperature, you would find it gummy, and it would stick to your teeth. At cooler temperatures it would be crunchy on the outside, chewy on the inside.

* * *

Samson, of Biblical fame, was not only strong but clever, and honeybees came to play a part in an interesting event. Samson, it seems, had seen the woman of his dreams, but she was from among the uncircumcised Philistines who ruled over Israel. He took his parents to meet her. Along the way, he encountered a lion in a vineyard. He tore the lion apart with his bare hands, though apparently the altercation didn't create enough noise for his parents to hear. He never told them about it.

They met the girl, and, according to the King James version, "She pleased him well." He came back later and married her. On his way home, he looked for the carcass of the lion. He found it full of bees and honey! He dug right in, ate some, and took some home to his parents, though he never told them or his wife where he got it.

Later, he took his father to see his new wife. As was customary, he held a feast for his Philistine family. Thirty uncircumcised men were assigned to be his groomsmen. They befriended him. But not a lot. Sampson offered them a cruel riddle and told them that if they answered it in seven days, he would give all thirty of them a set of sheets and garments. But if they failed to answer it, they would have to give him thirty sheets and as many garments.

The offer was undoubtedly both intriguing and disturbing, but they agreed. And Samson said unto them, "Out of the eater came something to eat, and out of the strong came something sweet."

They couldn't figure it out. Desperate, they asked his wife to tease it out of him. His wife cried for a week and "lay sore upon him." She said, "You do but hate me, and love me not: you have put forth a riddle to the children of my people, and have not told it me."

Samson, nagged raw, finally told her, and she told them. And they told Samson the answer. And Samson said, "If you had not plowed with my heifer, you would not have solved my riddle."

The Bible does not mention how the wife felt about being called a heifer or exactly what Samson meant by "plowed," but it didn't matter because that marriage was effectively over. Samson, infused with the spirit of the Lord, went and killed 30 uncircumcised Philistines and took their garments.

And his wife? She was given to one of Samson's groomsmen. End of story? Certainly not. It got even more complicated. But that's the end of the part that involved bees.

* * *

Installing a Package of Bees

A bee package consists of three pounds of bees in a box with screen on two sides. You want to install those bees as soon as you get them. You can see the bees in there, eager to get out and get back to normal life. You can also see a can in there, hanging from the top. It's full of sugar water from which the bees have been sipping through little holes in the bottom. Beside the can hangs the queen cage, a little box the size of a clumsy carpenter's thumb.

(If you have received a queen only, without a package, to replace an old queen, the instructions are basically the same. Just make sure there is no queen in the hive or the new queen and the resident queen will end up fighting until one of the two is dead. If there's still an old queen in the hive, find her, thank her for her service, then behead her and leave her body outside the hive near the entrance so her loyal subjects get the message.)

The queen is in a cage because she is not the natural, original queen of the bees she is with. The bees in the package still see her as an intruder. If she weren't in a cage, they'd kill her. The complication of installing a package of bees is the process of not releasing the queen until she's accepted as one of the gang. Here's how:

1. Take the package to a hive that is all set up and ready to go, including a feeder with sugar water. A pollen patty would be good, too. This hive should be just a single brood chamber, or, better, a nuc (short

for "nucleus," a small hive with only five frames). A nuc's smaller size makes it easier for a small swarm to keep itself warm. Remove the top from the hive or nuc. Remove the inner cover. Remove a frame from the middle of the set of frames. Ideally, this frame will have comb on it. (Beg or buy a few frames with comb from another beekeeper. It will help a lot because the queen will immediately have somewhere to lay eggs.) In the upper part of the comb, in the corner that will be at the back of the hive, carve out a vertical space big enough for a queen cage, about an inch wide and three inches long. If the frame has no comb, see below.

2. Now it's time to get the queen cage out of the package. Pry up the flat piece of wood at the top of the package. See the can. See the silvery disk next to it. From that disk hangs the queen cage. If you pull it up, bees will start flowing up through the hole, each and every one of them in a bad mood. If you fail to prevent that, you'll be in a bad mood, too. So give the package a solid thump on the ground or the top of the hive. The bees will fall to the bottom of the box in a mass of confusion. This will give you a few seconds to pull up the queen cage and quickly set the flat piece of wood back over the hole before bees come flying out.

3. Look at that queen! Isn't she beautiful? She's long, slender and tan, like a girl from Ipanema with six legs, diaphanous wings, and a spermatheca ready to go. Look at her wiggle in there with her comfort maids. If the queen isn't wiggling, you've got yourself a dead queen and a real problem. Call a beekeeper or the jerk who sold you the bees. You need a queen, and quick.

4. There are two ends to the queen cage, each with a short tunnel capped with a tiny cork. You can't see the cork on one side because of the silvery disk that is nailed over it. Pull that disk off. Now you can see how one tunnel is packed with a white candy. The idea is, the queen and her attendants are going to start eating her way through that tunnel while the bees outside start eating their way in. By the time they meet,

the queen and the bees will have been in the hive long enough to become friends. The drones, of course, will be going absolutely nuts. So pull the cork out of the candy tunnel. Leave the other cork in place! It's an emergency exit. We'll get to that.

5. Nestle that queen cage into the place you carved in the comb. Best to put the candy tunnel facing up. This is so that if a bee dies inside the cage, her body doesn't block the tunnel. Set the cage so that the screened part faces the inside of the hive. This is so the bees can see and tend to their queen. Carefully set the frame back in place in the hive. Give the bees a pollen patty to help them produce comb. Put the inner cover on.

6. Now's the part where you might get stung. Once again, thump the package on the ground (not on the hive) so all the bees tumble down again. Now you've got a few seconds to pull that can out of its hole. This can be tricky. You'll need your hive tool or knife blade and some fingernails to pull it up far enough to get your ungloved fingers around it. Pull it up. Slap the wooden top over the hole. Did you get stung? Well, too bad. You're a beekeeper. What were you expecting? Utter the curse of your choice, pull the stinger out, and move on.

7. Now to let the bees go into the hive. Thump them down to the bottom of the package. Remove the wooden top and lay the box upside down on the inner cover so that the feeding–can hole is over the inner cover hole. Now the bees' only way out is into the hive, which is surely where they will go. It might take them an hour or two to make the move, but they'll like it in there. It smells good, there's some sugar water, it's nice and dark, and there's a queen who ain't bad lookin' even if she still smells a little funny. Why go anywhere else?

8. Go get something to sit on and a beer, unless you're a Mormon, many of whom are beekeepers, and for good reasons. They and other teetotalers might appreciate a lemonade at this wonderful moment.

Have a seat near the front of the hive. Drink your chosen beverage. You deserve it. You're a beekeeper, and you've just done the world a favor.

9. Before dark, put the hive cover back on. Leave that hive alone for three days. After that, puff a bit of smoke in the entrance and gently, furtively, pull off the top and inner cover. Check to see if the queen got out. If she didn't, pop the cork from the emergency exit and put the cage back. If she's out, you can assume she's doing her business. Remove the empty queen cage and close up the hive. Go read a book about beekeeping and see what you have to do next.

From

Journey to Chernobyl: Encounters in a Radioactive Zone

Chapter Four

Zones

Volodya had to go see his wife and son for the weekend. They live seventy kilometers from Kiev. I'm to stay in his apartment until he gets back, then move back to the Environmental Protection Society's hotel. His friend (who has the same name; I think of him as Volodya-II) takes responsibility for me. I'd say he speaks about twice as many words in English as Volodya-I. That puts him up around the range of about a couple dozen. Also his car is newer and closer to comfortable.

He picks me up at Volodya's house at 1:00 to meet Ljudmula [my translator] somewhere at 2:00. But, as it turns out, there was a delay in plans. We arrive at an unidentifiable stretch of sidewalk fifteen minutes early. So we sit in the car looking at the drizzle and snow until a big guy in a flattened fedora shows up with a limp flower. He hangs around on the sidewalk for a quarter of an hour, then finally comes over and asks, in crisp, perfect, forced English, if I'm the guy he's looking for. It turns out I am. Well, Lujdmula's going to be an hour late. Well, okay, now what? Well, now nothing. We wait. I sit with the door half opened while this poor guy leans vaguely down, afraid to pull away, afraid to get in. I warn him that his tan trench coat is up against the muddy car. He says that's not a problem. But after ten or fifteen minutes he says we should go to so-n-so's house and Ljudmula will meet us there. He will wait for her. He hands me the limp zinnia and says, "Please, give this to the hostess. Hostess, yes? Hostess."

So the Volodya-II takes me and the flower to a nearby address and up the rattletrap elevator to the tight clean apartment of a chemist named Alec who is on two committees that are measuring radioactivity all over Ukraine, figuring out which towns go in which zones. Zone 1, which is anywhere having more radiation than Zone 2, was supposedly evacuated in 1986. Zone 2 offers 3 curies of strontium, 25 of cesium and 0.1 of plutonium per square kilometer. Zone 3 has 0.15 curies of strontium, 5 of cesium and 0.1 of plutonium, with dosage exceeding 100 millirem per year. Zone 4 has 0.02 curies of strontium, 1 of cesium, and 0.01 of plutonium per square kilometer, with dosage not exceeding 100 millirem per year.

Whether these numbers are correctly translated I will never know. The exceptional power of Ljudmula's right brain has left her bereft on the other side - either that or the other way around. I mean she can't say, repeat, translate any number besides a simple integer. Decimals blow her away. We even get into powers of numbers. "Iodine-131 isotope" comes out as "131 isotopes of iodine." It's odd that she's this way. Her English is amazingly perfect in all other ways, though some of the atomic terms - ion, isotope, neutron and such - are new to her. She feels guilty about this and also about the fact that she gets emotionally involved in what she's hearing. She had no idea of the extent of the horror, the depth of the complications, the forces of evil at play in the radiation.

People are still being moved out of Zone 2, and those of Zone 3 have the right to be relocated. Those in Zone 4 have certain economic privileges. No agricultural production is allowed in Zones 2 and 3. Food is brought in to people still living there.

But of course things don't work out that way. People still live in all the zones, including the Prohibited Zone within 30 kilometers of the Chernobyl plant. In the absence of anything else to eat, crops are grown and consumed in all zones. Wood cook-fires send more radionuclides into the air. The Ukrainian government says that Kiev is not contaminated. Alec says that all of Kiev qualifies as Zone 4. Some parts of Kiev even qualify as Zone 3.

The trouble is, people living a Zone 4 area are entitled to certain benefits, including exemption from income taxation. If Kiev is in Zone 4, the government of Ukraine, already all but broke, will lose a major source of revenue.

Conclusion: Kiev is not in Zone 4. It's as clean as can be. It's just a matter of ignoring the numbers.

He explains how bathrooms pick up more radiation because radioactive water from the Dneiper per runs through the pipes, which pick it up and hold it. He shows me a little dosimeter. For 110 rubles I could buy one in any store, he says. Then I'll always know for sure. We turn it on. It says 0.13 miliroentgens. 0.10 would be normal. Outdoors, he says, it would be 0.14. This is called background radiation. It's always there.

Ljudmula and I go to a press conference back at the International Conference. No good news there. Genetic abnormalities are up 1.8 times. Cancer is way up, especially in children. But most of what I hear is the hogwash of people with political aspirations. When Elena arrives, we leave to go see a city deputy named Skripka.

Skripka's a former plant physiologist. He hasn't got any good news either. He's got all kinds of data and it looks organized, comprehensive, and accurate. I trust it because it's coming from a former plant physiologist who is wearing a suit and tie that are up to Western snuff. His data is on computer print-out.

Skripka's thesis is that there are more victims of Chernobyl than officially known. Some 30,000 liquidators and evacuees have registered as victims, but Skripka believes there are 20,000 more who haven't bothered. But even those numbers are low, he says. Everyone in Kiev - 2.6 million people - is a victim because radiation is much higher than officially acknowledged. His data falls in line with that of Alec the chemist. Though Skripka cannot verify it, some scientists he knows went to the Soviet Union's nuclear testing ground and took radiation readings at ground zero. The readings were lower than at any point in Kiev.

By Skripka's estimate, in the days following the accident, everyone in Kiev received from three to five rem from internal radiation. That's equivalent to the annual dose allowed nuclear workers in the United States (and fifty times the allowable dose for nuclear workes in the Department of Energy). This radiation was the alpha and beta particles emitted from radionuclides, the radiation that is relatively harmless as long as it's outside the body. Beta particles will barely penetrate human skin, and alpha particles will bounce off a piece of paper. They aren't a big problem unless they get inside your corporeal fortress. But if you inhale or eat them, the body may accept them as nutrients. Strontium-90, for example, looks a lot like calcium - same number of electrons in its outer shell - so bones readily latch onto it. The strontium makes itself at home and begins radiating the local marrow.

Similarly, iodine-131 is quite like regular iodine, so it tends to accumulate in the thyroid. (The purpose of iodine pills as a safeguard against radiation is to fill the thyroid so the radioactive iodine just passes out of the body as an unneeded nutrient.) Cesium is versatile enough to find many homes in the human organism. Once lodged in the body, these radionuclides keep emitting radiation, attacking the thyroid, the marrow, the blood that happens to pass by. It might give you thyroid cancer, leukemia, or any of various blood diseases. An invisible speck of plutonium in your lung is enough to give you lung cancer.

Kiev was also bombarded by gamma waves, which are more dangerous but shorter lived. They zap right through the human body, doing some damage on the way but not lingering to continue the attack. Today, scientists cannot determine how many rem of gamma waves people suffered six years ago.

Skripka gained access to some KGB files and found that the Soviet government knew a lot more than it let on. Children under the age of 1 had an average of .5 rem in their thyroids - five times the current annual dose allowed to hit non-nuclear workes in the United States. Pregnant women and their unborn were known to have equal radiation levels in their blood. Breast milk was contaminated.

Radiation wasn't the only poison blown out of the Chernobyl reactor. The atomic chaos of the meltdown created virtually every possible element and isotope, not to mention bizarre molecules. Some of the isotopes lived for mere nanoseconds; some will be around for millennia. The lead that helicopters dropped into the flaming crater evaporated and blew across the countryside. It finds its way into people via grass that cows eat. It is impossible to say how much of this lead is from gasoline, how much from Chernobyl, but whatever the source, it's all over the place.

A special well dug in the Prohibited Zone brings water up from 30 meters. Lately it's been showing radiation levels of ten to the negative ten curies per liter. If it were a byproduct in a nuclear laboratory, you'd have to take special measures to dispose of it. Dropping it into a well would not be appropriate. The Dneiper River, which runs through the center of Kiev, once had similar levels of strontium, but it has dropped to 10 to the negative 12 curies - acceptable though still above the ideal of zero.

So it's no wonder blood donor data shows that 80 percent of donors have abnormal levels of such things as white and red blood cells and immune proteins. It explains why 30 percent of children can't receive a vaccination because they come down with the disease the vaccination was supposed to prevent.

Skripka has data on increases in health problems. Among official adult victims, the death rate has increased 400 percent since 1987. Death by cancer is up 300 percent. Breast cancer is up 26 percent. General disease, up 500 percent. Problems in thyroids and other glands, up 400 percent. Respiratory disease, excluding cancer and tuberculosis, up 2,000 percent. Pneumonia, up 220 percent in adults, 260 percent in children. Allergy problems, up 41 percent in adults, 80 percent in children. Incidence of brain cancer, up 350 percent from 1988 to 1991. Genetic aberration, 10-13 times higher in contaminated areas.

This information flies in the face of the conclusion of the United Nations International Atomic Energy Agency (IAEA). The IAEA made a supposedly comprehensive and unbiased assessment of the aftereffects of Chernobyl to see if people who have not been evacuated are suffering consequences of radiation. (They did not examine liquidators or evacuees.) The IAEA conclusion: no problem. There is no illness, no cancer, no increase in birth defects. Even among people living in the most contaminated areas, the areas marked blood red on contamination maps, are suffering no more than they did under Stalin, Kruschev and Brezhnev.

Skripka says what the UN has done is certify the safety of nuclear war. If their report is true, he says, if 50 tons of nuclear fuel can be thrown into the atmposphere without harming anyone, why don't we dispose of nuclear waste the same way - just stack it on a pile of dynamite and blow it up?

Skripka announced a press conference where he planned to disseminate his information, which was probably the most complete and accurate available anywhere. Unfortunately, no one showed up. He suspects they were afraid to. They depend on the government for their paper and other supplies. The government of Kiev might like to have this information made public, but the government of Ukraine would not. He says he has many enemies on his committee. They don't like this information. They're bureaucrats, and it's information like this that makes heads roll.

He shows us a colorful map of topograhic-like lines that show where the cesium, plutonium and strontium lie in Kiev. Ljudmula and Elena check out the milliroentgens where they live. They're in Zone 4, which they see as somewhat of a relief. It could be worse.

* * *

Mr. Skripka remembers the days following the explosion at Chernobyl. He first heard about it in a minor item in the newspaper on Monday, April 28, two days after the explosion. It made no mention of radiation or evacuation. But rumors were bouncing around Kiev. On April 30, he checked instruments in his laboratory. They showed very high readings. Being a scientist, he knew what they meant. He called home and ordered his wife to bring their daughter inside, to close the doors, to change clothes and leave the dirty clothes outside, to take a shower, to tell the neighbors.

The neighbors didn't believe him. It was such a beautiful spring day. The sun was out, the breeze as nice as could be. The TV showed the May Day games and parades. Girls in marching bands were prancing around in short skirts, unaware of the deadly particles showering down on them. An international bicycle race charged off through the radioactive countyside, bikers huffing and puffing through the radioactive dust.

Skripka found an old Geiger counter in his closet, a relic of his days in civil defense. Somehow he got it working. It confirmed what he feared. Everything was hot, including his daughter's beautiful hair. He and his wife cut it all off with a pair of scissors. He kept calling people to warn them, but they told him he was crazy. As he watched the world continue as normal outside, he began to wonder if it was possible for one person to be sane and the all the rest not.

As rumors spread in the early days of May, TV programs actively denied problems. Peasants were interviewed. They said they felt as fine as ever. Scientists took readings near the power plant and found radiation levels below normal.

The news arrived in other countries first, though it tended to change fast. In some countries, it took a week to evolve from "There is no danger" to "Do not let children play outdoors." By the time the Soviet people had an idea what was happening, there were already riots in Rome and Athens. The news was especially slow coming into France, where the government was maintaining that the radiation had pretty much stopped at the border with Germany. Like green grass, it was much higher on the other side. The French Director of the Radiation Protection Agency went on record saying the highest elevations were 5-10 times normal, but by mid-May he was admitting he khad known they were 400 times normal.

On May 6, the panic began in Kiev. Desperate to leave the city, people mobbed the train stations - the worst place to be. Radioactive trains arrived pulling radioactive dust behind them. People with radioactivity in their hair and clothes were radiating each other. They would have been better off at home because the radiation levels were already decreasing.

On May 8, Hans Blix, Director General of the IAEA, held a press conference. He said that radiation levels at the perimeter of the 30-kilometer zone had been 10-15 millirem at the time of the accident but had declined to 0.15 millirem, a safe level. He did not mention that the level in Kiev, sixty miles away, was still at 0.4 millirem.

On May 12, Kiev City Hall announced that radiation had returned to normal. The definition of "normal," however, was being adjusted for the emergency situation. Instead of 0.5 rem per year, it would thenceforth be 10 rem per year. The new standard would let everyone relax because it would now take five years instead of two months to take on a dangerous dose.

From

Journey on the Estrada Real: Encounters in the Mountains of Brazil

Introduction

The Royal Road

In 1697 or so, the Crown of Portugal ordered a road built from the port of Praia dos Mineiros, where the Rio Inhomirim met the Atlantic, to Diamantina, where creeks were exposing diamonds to daylight. The Estrada Real, the Royal Road, was to surmount the Serra do Mar that stands steep, dark-green, and misty above Guanabara Bay, then probe north into the region known as Minas Gerais – General Mines. The Royal Road was to connect the cities producing gold and diamonds as nowhere else on earth. Tunnels dug into hillsides were turning up just about every type of gem known to man. São João del Rei, Tiradentes, Congonhas and Vila Rica were already thriving cities. Vila Rica was becoming the largest city in the Americas, and its name would some day change from Rich Village to Black Gold – Ouro Preto. Diamantina, in northern Minas, was rising from the muck of a diamond mine in a gully to become a Portuguese outpost worth the wealth it was sending south to Praia dos Mineiros – Beach of Miners – later to be called Rio de Janeiro. From there the wealth of Brazil sailed to Lisbon.

This winding dirt road connected some of the world's most miserable people to some of the world's wealthiest – the slaves in the mines of Minas Gerais to the Portuguese Crown, the ultimate beneficiaries of everything that could be stripped from the land of the ember-colored *brasa* wood – Brazil.

The Estrada Real was to restrict as much as facilitate transportation into the interior. The Crown did not want its colony to develop industrial capacity. It was to continue completely dependent on Portugal for food, metals, tools, nails, ammunition, equipment, and supplies. The Brazilian economy was to be based almost exclusively on the export of gems and gold. The Estrada Real, therefore, was to facilitate the inward delivery of manufactured goods to the interior while speeding the outward flow of mineral riches. The Estrada was also to remain the only route of transportation, making it possible for Portugal to control development and exploitation.

In a certain sense, the history of the Estrada Real is the history of Latin America. Unlike the settlers who came to North America from industrial nations, the colonizers of Latin America came from feudal lands. They came neither to build nor to stay. In Portuguese, the verb *explorar* means both explore and exploit. The language has no other word for either activity. As if by lingual necessity, the Portuguese did both at the same time, exploring a region so vast that even today it has not yet been fully mapped, exploiting the land and an ungodly number of native and imported people. Once the gold and jewels were gone, the people who remained were left with magnificent churches and abandoned mines but no infrastructure for any but an agrarian economy.

That situation hasn't changed much. At the beginning of the twenty-first century, the Estrada Real of the seventeenth century is still there. Most of the road is dirt, dust, or mud, though it becomes cobblestone as it passes through towns and villages. Many of the villages have a toehold on the twentieth century – undependable electricity, a single phone, two television channels, visiting doctors with medical degrees – but the lives of the people there haven't changed much since the seventeenth century. They still cook on open wood stoves, and they travel by horse, mule and foot. They treat their ills with roots and herbs, and they pray for rain. They live in houses built by their grandfathers and sing in churches built by slaves. They still have no infrastructure for any but an agrarian economy.

This is the cradle of Brazilian culture. It all started here, in the mountains of Minas Gerais. As urban Brazil struggles into modern times and the global economy, its slow, quiet past still lives along its first road. How has it survived? How long can it survive? Should it survive? What, if anything, can save it? The search for the answers – a walk down the road – turns up the seeds of an odd revolution. People who have yet to benefit from the global economy are already struggling against it. Some, poor as dirt, ignorant of the world, are satisfied with the happiness they've found in God. Others, more aware, appreciate the wealth of their ancient culture. And some, of course, want to trade their antiquated ways for the commerce and industry that brings the money that buys the stuff that promises to make life better.

This book is about the people, culture and history of the Estrada Real. The people are changing, some by resisting change, some by embracing it. The culture is in the balance. The history is there, as immutable as it is unfinished.

Chapter One

Mariana and Bento Rodrigues

I begin my journey on the Estrada Real in Mariana, Minas Gerais, for two reasons. One is that once upon a time I lived here, trying my hand at banana farming. I never knew that from my front porch I could see the oldest road in the Western Hemisphere rising over a hill to the east and north. The other reason is that there is no map of the entire Estrada Real, no guide book, no signs along the way. There is, however, a rough and often erroneous guide for the road from Mariana to Diamantina, its northernmost point. So, after fifteen years away from the place, I return, look up an old friend, Lázaro Francisco da Silva, tell him my plan, and spend the night at his house.

The plan I arrived with was to buy a no-frills horse and a basic two-wheel cart, called a *charrete*, and simply flog my way toward Diamantina. What a way to travel! Just sit there watching the scenery go slowly by. *Charretes* are fairly common in Brazil, but not, it turns out, in Mariana. We look around all day but find nothing. Lázaro has an alternative idea: a sedan. He happens to have one under construction – not a two-door car but a historically correct replica of a eighteenth century vehicle, a passenger booth on poles. It's the way royalty used to travel on the Estrada Real – carried by slaves, watching the scenery go slowly by. Instead of slaves, Lázaro suggests, we could hire a dozen beautiful women. It would pay off in publicity. Television coverage would be guaranteed. It was a tempting idea, certainly better than looking at the back-end of a horse for a couple of months.

But my budget did not afford the cost of a dozen beautiful pole-bearers, so I decided to just walk. My brother-in-law, a highly domesticated apartment dweller in the state capital, Belo Horizonte, calls my plan a *programa de índio*, an Indian plan, by which I think he means a plan that is not especially well thought out, more an idea than a plan. But what kind of planning can you do when you're going to a place that has no map? I load my knapsack, the same one I used on Boy Scout hikes thirty-five years ago, with toilet paper, a change of clothes, a sleeping bag, an umbrella, a bottle of water, a few other essentials, and a little duct tape just in case of disaster. Lázaro takes me into town to buy a straw hat. The spring sun is hotter than usual, he says, and the rains have yet to arrive.

But they arrive that very night, a ripper of a thunderstorm, an inauspicious introduction to a long hike. I awake when the neighborhood roosters start to crow, which must have been at about three o'clock in the morning. I roll around in bed in unquenchable anxiety, imagining the many ways in which I might be bushwhacked on the Estrada Real. Everyone, without exception, has warned me not to go walking alone in the outback. The crime rate in Belo Horizonte rose ninety-four percent in the past year, and the major daily newspaper, the *Estado de Minas*, always features a story of a purposeless murder. I think they have a special page reserved for reports of homicides and daring robberies. In general, across Brazil, the homicide rate is five times that of the United States. The rural areas are not subject to the same type of urban crime, but the Estrada Real does run through a region still relatively rich in gold. That's exactly why the road's there. The gold is in scant supply these days, but prospecting is still a last resort for men who can't find jobs. They muck around in the streams, panning for infinitesimal specks. Long-term investment in infrastructure is the last thing on their minds. To survive, they need gold, and if they don't find enough – and no one at any time in history has ever found enough – they are perfectly willing to steal gold from anyone else who has been lucky enough to find some. And of course the gold miner's code of ethics is silent on the issue of robbing tourists on a road far from town. Even a grubby, tattered backpack is worth more than the air in their pockets. Or so I have been warned by those who know.

I have a lot of faith in humanity, especially in Brazilian humanity, but I also know that all it takes is one bad apple – and Brazil has no shortage of those – to ruin a trip and leave a gringo dead in a ditch for buzzards to eat. Buzzards hold a strong presence in my pre-dawn fears, and they are also waiting at the place where the dirt road of the Estrada Real meets the paved road that goes out of Mariana toward the Timbopeba and Samarco hematite mines. If I were writing a work of fiction about a trip down this road, I would never dare have the protagonist begin his trip under the gaze of a dozen *urubu* buzzards perched on rocks and fence posts, enjoying the stench of something dead. They look like glum funeral directors who have been interrupted in the middle of a meal. They stare at Lázaro and me as we shake hands and slap each other on the back. He takes my picture, then drives away with a toot and a wave out the window. The *urubus* watch me as swing my pack to my back and trudge toward points north. I can say with authority that the gaze of a buzzard is palpable on the spine.

It takes me all of ten minutes to forget about being murdered. The tight weight of the pack is as welcome as a fatherly embrace. Birds chatter in the low, dry brush on the hills on both sides of the road. The only other sound is the crunch of my feet on the quartz gravel of the road. The road climbs through a series of switchbacks, then tips through a pass that looks over a wide view to the east. The downhill side of the road is dense with old eucalyptus and, farther down, the general *mata* of natural forest. Way down there, monkeys hoot up a mad orgy of excitement that suddenly quiets down, then rises into a another frenzy.

At the highest point I stop to take a few notes that might improve the SENAC guide book. It's already apparent that its author wasn't a very intelligent person and may well have been inebriated as he described the route. He refers to things that weren't there, such as the Fazenda Gualuxo and the bridge over the Rio Gualuxo do Norte. He is inconsistent in references to such landmarks as entrances to farms, sometimes noting them, sometimes not. He writes little paragraphs such as "Turn left. Go straight. Keep right," without reliable reference as to where these turns might be made. Often "turn right" seems to mean "don't turn left." In most cases, "Stay on the main road for the next ten miles" would suffice, and that's exactly what I do. Still, a little confirmation now and then would be comforting.

I soon give up trying to correct the guide book. I also give up trying to describe the scenery. I can generally describe the road as winding along the side of hills. The view to one side is usually a vista of ten or twenty miles over hills of varying shades of green that gradually blend into hazy purple. The other side of the road is the mountain I am walking around, usually a moderately steep incline with lots of rock, dried grass, low brush. Sometimes, though never for long, second-growth forest crowds in from both sides. By ten o'clock in the morning, cicadas crank up their whine. The road surface varies from red clay to white sand to brown gravel. On this first stretch of road, from Mariana to Camargos, half a dozen cars go by in four or five hours, raising dust in their wake. The passengers seem to be Mariana people on their way to picnics or the little farms, called *sítio* s, that Brazilians often keep just outside of town. I wave at them all, and they all wave back. A couple slow down and offer a ride by holding an up-pointed thumb out the window, but I wave them off with a wag of my forefinger.

Coming into Camargos, some ten or fifteen kilometers from Mariana (the guidebooks says 22, but I'm sure it's wrong) the road forks. I choose the one that doesn't go uphill. Camargos is just a hamlet of a few dozen houses, a town without sound. I soon come to a man who was fooling around with a bucket at a public spigot. A church, large but simple, stands atop a hill on the other side of the road. I ask the man where one could eat a meal in Camargos. He said there is nowhere. We talk a bit. His name is Fernando. He tells me Camargos was the first district of Mariana making it one of the oldest towns in the state. The church, Nossa Senhora da Conceição, is over three hundred years old. It's locked until the priest comes, which won't be that day. Still wary of thieves, I haul my pack up the long, steep stairs to the church, poke around, then come back down and continue on my way. I soon come to Fernando again, now with another man. He expresses his regret that the town has nowhere to eat, but he says he has some coffee, if I want some. Hungry and weak, needing the sugar, I accept and step into his house, which is flush up against the road. It's a simple and immaculate place many decades old. The floors are of a hardwood that no longer exists, at least not in the width of his floorboards. His living room walls have pictures of a saint, a cross, a prayer in a frame. Fernando explains that he gets his lunch from his *companheira*, and therefore he has no cooked food in the house. He pours me a generous dose of hot, sweet, strong coffee from a thermos and insists that I take at least three crackers from a package. We chat a bit about the wealth of the United States. And then off I go.

I soon come to a sign that says "Honey for Sale." Being a beekeeper, I want to go see. Honey for lunch is better than no lunch. I poke around a little lane that winds through the grass along a brook. A dump truck stands at the brook, its motor running, apparently there for the water. I ask a kid if he knows about the honey. He doesn't, but I see another sign that points over a pair of logs that cross the brook. I go across and head toward the only possible place with honey, a kind of shack next to a kind of corral under a kind of roof, a functional, slap-dash kind of place. I clap and call out, but no one appears until a few seconds after I turn around to leave. It's a tall, bearded man, dirty with work in the sun, his arms thick from the kind of work that might well include the cutting of trees, the pounding in of fence posts, lifting of calves.

"Do you have honey for sale?" I ask.

"I have.'

"You're the beekeeper?"

"I am."

"I'm a beekeeper, too."

That gets me a big smile and a strong, gentle handshake of apiary brotherhood. His name is Fernando. He says, "Come on!"

He opens a barbed wire gate, takes me back to his little shack, along the way asking, "You had lunch?"

As a matter of fact, I hadn't. I smell wood smoke. His shack doesn't quite qualify as a shack. I guess it's more like a hut, just some corrugated asbestos planks over a frame of poles, some plastic and sheet metal and cardboard around the sides. In one corner he has a jury-rigged, waist-high wood stove of sheet metal that once served for something else, a functional mess, a lot of stuff not out of place but hung and stacked wherever it goddam well belongs. His bee hat and veil are on top of a stack of stuff too vague to identify. His pots and pans are upside down on a plank of wood outside, black on the outside, shiny on the inside.

Lunch is a *mexido* of rice, beans, okra and herbs all mixed up in a pot, a delicious expediency typical of Minas Gerais. The first Portuguese *bandeirante* adventurers who came here carried shovels and muskets but no food or plows. They had come for gold. They had no time to plant. They learned about living off the land from the Indians, a people without alimentary taboos. They ate fruits they'd never heard of – *pitanga, araticum, bacupari, jatobá, guava, pequi, cagaita.* They ate fiddlehead ferns, wild squash, bamboo shoots, gooseberry leaves. They ate *tanajura* ants and *bicho-da-taquara* larva. They ate fish wrapped in leaves. They ate their corn raw, ground, boiled, baked, or roasted. They hunted alligator, monkey, quail, rabbit, dove, deer, armadillo, tapir, wild pigs, snakes, lizards. The ate manioc root baked, roasted, boiled, sweetened, ground, souped. From annatto seeds they made medicine, colored foods, decorated their bodies and defended themselves against bug bites. Of all these foods, only the *bicho-da-taquara* larva have fallen from the *mineiro* menu, though it was once a delicacy. They were mashed and boiled, their fat skimmed off for a tasty butter. As they were an ocean away from their women, the men suffered insomnia caused by "excesses of love." To get a good night's sleep, they ate dried larva with the intestines intact but without the head. The meal gave them wonderful dreams of brilliant forests where they ate delicious fruits.

Mineiro food, famous throughout Brazil, was born of hunger, first of the *bandeirante*s, then of the slaves. The slaves ate leftovers, the hooves and ears of the pig, the guts of the cow, the collards that grew in easy abundance, the corn mash that the horses didn't finish, and spices that came from the woods. Hunger necessitated invention, and the African women were culinary geniuses. The best foods on the contemporary Brazilian menu were concocted in miserable kitchens of slave quarters.

Fernando's mexido is manifest proof of the flexibility of *mineiro* food. He assures me that the pot is dirty on the outside but clean on the inside. I can help myself, have all I want. He rinses off a plate at a spigot fed by a tank up on the hill. It's good, hearty stuff, truly delicious. I've never tasted the herb that's in it, and the cook doesn't know what it's called.

Fernando lives in Mariana but comes out here on the weekends. He once wanted to build a house here, but his family doesn't like the place, so he comes here to be alone and is happy here, happy as a pig in mud, a man in his place. He used to work with a company messing in some way with environmental issues, but he lost the job, and now, it being hard to find another job, he spends his time on his little plot of land in Camargos, messing with a few cows, some bee hives, an organic garden. "*Sou homen do mato mesmo*," he said - a man really of the woods. He loves his grubby little place. I can't say it's dirty though I'm eating thirty feet from a corral with a cow in it. The big box of fine soil beside my foot, I'm told, is full of worms. But worms are not dirty, and I'll take cow-dirt over diesel fumes any day.

Suddenly I remember a beekeeper I used to know, an old guy named Ciro who sold his honey at the Saturday market in Mariana fifteen years ago. Ciro surprised me by speaking English when I complimented him on his honey. He was Brazilian but had worked for GM in Michigan for many years. Then he raised bees in a hamlet an hour outside of a town that was two hours from a state capital that no one outside of Brazil has heard of – Camargos, the place I have just walked through. Now Fernando tells me that Ciro died a few years ago. He praises Ciro very highly as an intelligent man who did things right. With deep nods over his plate of mexido, he emphasized how Ciro was good and smart.

Before he fetches some honey, Fernando rinses off a ladle and brings out a pot of milk still warm from his cows. It's good milk, creamy and earthy and warm. The only honey he has is a plastic container of one kilo, about four times the weight I want to carry. I costs five *reais* – two and a half dollars – which we agree is cheap. Any price for Brazilian honey is cheap because it's made by killer bees. Fernando and I have both had the painful pleasure of raiding their hives and extracting their honey. The price of killer bee honey is always too cheap.

Fernando tells me there's no hotel in the next town, Bento Rodrigues, but there's a little restaurant run by a guy named Juca. Juca is a fine fellow and will see to it that I don't have to sleep in the *mato*.

And off I go. Within a hundred yards I come to the most delightful little cascade, clean water pouring over rocks worn smooth. I change into trunks and wade into the main flow, which bounces horizontally through a sluice in the rock. I let the water pound down on my shoulders, which feels mighty good. Over to the side a lower flow sends a flood of bubbles swirling around under a pummel of water.

Along comes a young man with a very pretty young lady on his back. She strips to a tiny bikini and enjoys the water. He invites me to a place a few yards upstream, where they and some friends are cooking meat and drinking Cuba libres from an aluminum cup. With ice. They insist I sip a little. The coldness of it is very fine. They give me some chunks of chicken shaved from a spit. That is fine, too. The girls slide down a sluice in the rock, slowly, giggling, ignoring all orders and advice from the guys who are attending to the meat and the rum.

Then I take what I later find out was the long road to the village of Bento Rodriquez, a hot and winding road that curls high around a sierra. It's too high for tall trees, which means nice views but no shade. Much of the road surface is fine, white sand, which reflects the early afternoon sun up into my rapidly toasting face. What a glorious feeling it is to come around a bend and see Bento Rodrigues at the far end of a deep valley, still far away but within sight. With the Igreja São Bento at the center of town and fields all around, it's just as cute as can be, a place for Hobbits or fairy tale people. My feet hurt as I plod into town. At this late moment it occurs to me that I haven't walked this far in one day since adolescence some thirty-five years ago. Teetering with exhaustion and thirst, I pull up to the first bar and order a bottle of Skol beer. Then I sit down and drink it. It is cold and wet and good. I watch as rowdy a group plays pool at a little billiards table.

I inquire about Juca and am directed up the street to a bar that is just a small room that is filled to capacity by about ten guys playing a boisterous game of cards. At the crucial moments of laying cards on the table or transferring funds or resolving a dispute they're loud to the point of hurting my ears. They rather effectively pretend not to notice that a stranger has just walked in. At the little counter in back I introduce myself to Juca, make the connection with Fernando and in that instant obviously gain Juca's favor. When I ask him if he has beer, he gives me an answer that I've often heard and always thought would be a good line in a commercial for Antarctica beer: "We only have Brahma."

Brahma's the exact same thing as Antarctica, Skol, Kaiser, Bohemia and every Bud, Busch and Miller made in the U.S.A. – a light, hop-free, rice-based beer that is very, very good if too cold to taste on a day too hot to tolerate. Beer's a rich man's drink in the interior of Brazil. The guys playing cards are drinking *cachaça*, a drink so cheap that it rhymes with *de graça*, which means "free." It also with *desgraça* – misfortune with implications of disgrace. Rich guy that I am, and hot and thirsty, I opt for the Brahma and take a seat on a bench just outside the front door. I am sitting there, writing notes and resting my poor feet and wondering how to go about asking where a person can sleep around there, when along came an old, skinny black man with eyes that obviously can't see much and a knot of mutilated teeth at the front of his black and ragged gums. He asks if I am a "gringo" and offers his hand, which wavers about eight inches off course. He is not only half blind but three-quarters drunk. I shake it. In his garbled, gummy peon lingo, he asks if I'd buy him a *cachaça*. I cannot say no to a man who looks so poor and miserable. He should be entitled to every drop of *cachaça* he can hold. I tell him to tell Juca I'll pay for a dose. He goes in and tells Juca. Juca comes out to confirm. He has a game leg that isn't good for much except as a prop to keep him from falling over. To walk he has to swing it around with one hand. I tell him I'll pay for the drink if he wants to sell it to the guy; it's up to him. So he goes and gets a half a glass of it – a good four or five ounces - but he holds the glass out into the street so the guy has to physically leave if he wants to drink it. The guy downs it in one gulp, thanks me and, to my relief, leaves.

I then use Fernando's reference to ask Juca where a person can sleep in Bento Rodriguez, strongly implying that Fernando has passed this responsibility on to him. He indicates a Manoel Muniz, who lives down a grassy lane that runs beside the church. My weak and shaky legs stagger me on over there, arriving just as Manoel is coming through his gate with four plastic milk pails. A certain semi-mute I had seen in the first bar, who talks by huffing and squeaking and waving his arms around, is there with Manoel, apparently advising him of my imminent arrival. Manoel eyes me up and down as I explain myself and my mission and give Juca as my reference, strongly implying that I am here at Juca's request and recommendation. I recognize Manoel as a good man, the type with Christian love in his eyes, an older guy who still gets to do things with milk pails.

Manoel is a little concerned that he'll have to feed me. I say I'll eat at Juca's. He asks if I'm alone. Yes, I am. He asks how long I want to stay. I say I'd be out of there by dawn. I tell him I only need a little space on the floor. I just don't want to have to sleep in the *mato*. And in case he can't tell, I also need a shower, though I can certainly wait until he gets back from his milk business.

Well, he reckons he can put me up, so he takes me through the gate and around to the back of his house to where his wife is pushing coagulated milk into round cheese molds with her fingers, making the famous *queijo mineiro* - cheese Minas-style, a soft, salty cheese that can be anywhere from dripping wet to grainy dry. She is old and heavy and coughing and waving flies off her cheese. She shows no reaction to my presence. Manoel takes me to a bedroom, then leads me to the bathroom, a convoluted trail through the living room, kitchen and dining room. He shows me where all the light switches are, in case I have to get up at night. He explains that the hot water comes from a *serpentina*, a pipe that runs through the grill of the *fogão a lenha* wood stove, then up to a tank over the ceiling. The boiling water circulates itself up to the tank while drawing water down from the same tank. He doesn't need to explain that the supply of hot water, therefore, was limited but would be plenty hot. He also didn't need to tell me that the toilet might need an extra flush or two to really do its job. I can tell by looking at it.

It's a nice, clean, *casa mineira* with tile roof and blue trim around the doors and windows. The windows have no glass, just heavy shutters to swing shut at night. In this house, they swing into the room to open. In some houses, they swing out. The living room furniture is cheap and simple, just a leatherette couch, a chair, and a coffee table with a big Bible on it. The walls sport pictures of Nossa Senhora da Conceição and Santo Gabriel, a battery-operated clock in antique style, five starfish, a heavy-duty, oversized, only-for-show rosary, a picture of Jesus with arms held out to a nice lake, and the inevitable old photos of a husband and wife. I think just about every house in the interior of Minas Gerais has one of these pairs of photos in an oval frame. They are strange photos from deep in the past, often with formal clothes painted below the photo of the face. Someone told me that the photos are blown-up prints made from tiny contact prints. The rosiness in the cheeks is water color. Manoel tells me the photos are of him and his wife, taken fifty years ago, just after they were married. By the looks of the wife, she's been in a bad mood since day one.

Not just a bad mood, it turns out. Manoel tells me she's got mental problems.

It turns out I'm not the first foreigner to stay in this house. A guy from Germany, a backpacker who looked a little like me, was here not long ago, and a couple from Europe somewhere, and a whole busload of people from São Paulo who called beforehand and arranged to rent his whole house and *quintal*, where they slept and camped. They were friendly, peaceful people, members of a church. They had their pictures taken beside him beside his flowers, his chickens, his house and the little cow barn.

Manoel has a great *quintal*, a word for which there is no translation besides, inadequately, backyard. The *quintal* of a rural house in Minas Gerais is a lush area planted with food and flowers. In Manoel's case, it includes not only bananas, *jabuticaba*, lemons, limes, oranges, pitanga berries, mulberries, tangerines, and a lot of flowers but five dairy cows, three pigs, and twenty-one piglets that have been timed to reach table-size by Christmas. The *jabuticabas* are ripe, an event that takes place twice a year for about two weeks. These odd, black-purple berries grow right from the trunks of the many-stemmed tree, and a given tree produces far more than a family can consume. They can't be frozen or stored, though they can be made into a liqueur or jam. You have to eat them when they're ripe. They're a good fruit for eating outdoors because they involve a lot of spitting. You take each berry, which is a little larger than a marble, bite it hard enough to break the skin, then suck out the insides. You squeeze it to get the pit and pulp out, suck the pulp off the pit, then spit the pit out. There's probably a delicate way to do this, and I suppose it could be done indoors with a bowl on a table, but it's far more efficient and satisfying to project the pit into the great outdoors. As if the taste were not enough, the guilt of having a tree full of *jabuticaba* drives everyone to eat as many as possible. As with potato chips, it's hard to eat just one, or even just a pound, though as you binge toward a kilo, a certain limit is reached, usually all of a sudden. After two weeks of this, everyone's glad the season is over.

Manoel is seventy-six years old. He has a head of hair thick and black. One lens of his black-frame glasses is dirty and spotted with what seems to be white paint. He lives in a house with a roof that's a hundred years old, the house where his father was born. He's a fine fellow who loves his wife, his fruit trees, the chickens and ducks that peck around his sandaled feet in the *quintal* as he flicks corn scooped up in a blue plastic hard hat. He loves the piglets he will sell come Christmas. He loves Fernando of Camargos; he loved Ciro, the smart beekeeper who died, as I now learn, of a heart attack at the gate of his farm as he was about to leave for Mariana. Manoel loves his twenty-one grandchildren and the great-grandson who just turned one, at which point he had his little existence confirmed and glorified in a laminated card the size of a post card with the young lad bright-eyed and optimistic, looking for all the world like someone destined to become the mayor of a place with pavement.

We sit at Manoel's big dining room table, eating crackers and his wife's *requeijão*, a *queijo mineiro* that comes out soft and almost spreadable because at some point in its making it has been boiled. We also eat creamy *doce de leite* caramel that originated in his own cows. He gives me some manioc soup that had been warmed all day on his wood stove. We drink coffee which I believe he thinned down with water so there's be enough for both of us. His wife, suffering from a fever, keeps to her bedroom.

Ever-so-sore from my long hike, I sleep in exquisite soreness, window wide open, barely aware of the chilly fog that wafts in. It takes four hours of cock-a-doodle-doo, starting long before dawn, to get me up. For breakfast, Manoel makes me strong coffee – much stronger than that of the night before – with cheese and requeijão and store-bought cookies. It's good. He also boils me two eggs, serving them in a state barely beyond raw, which is the way I like them. One of the eggs had a greenish shell, the other a splotchy tan, both typical of the *ovos caipiras*, the eggs of truly free-range chickens who live off not chicken feed but whatever they can scratch up in the *quintal.* I contribute some of Fernando's honey, but it turns out Manoel has honey from a grandson who messes with bees. He has a vial of store-bought propolis, too, for medicinal purposes.

Before I leave, I ask if I can fill my two-liter plastic guaraná bottle. (Guaraná is a popular soft drink made either from the mildly stimulating seeds of that plant or from an artificial version of it. It's the only drink in Brazil that outsells Coca-Cola, though the Coca-Cola company has now come out with a guaraná drink of its own.) Of course Manoel is glad to provide me with water. In fact, he chills it for me by bringing from his freezer a block of ice in a war-torn aluminum pot. He draws water from his clay *filtro* tank and lets it cool over the ice before he pours it into my bottle. We fill the bottle in two batches, but that isn't enough. He uses a hammer and a lot of thumping to get the block of ice out of the pot. Then he cracks it into slivers that he slips into the mouth of the bottle. Presto! Cold water for my journey.

Then I ask him what I owed. Well, really, he says, nothing. If I write a book and bring more tourists to Bento Rodriguez, maybe some great-grandchild of his might someday open a little hotel in his house. It would be a great thing if that happened.

But I insist, and he finally says that any little thing would be fine. I slap him around the shoulders and tell him what other foreigners – the German, the Europeans, the church people in the bus – have told him: He knows how to work but he doesn't know how to charge. I give him ten *reais* – about five dollars – and he says it's too much and won't take it so I press it to the granite of his kitchen counter and tell him that's how much he gets.

And off I go with five pounds of cold water and the comfort of knowing I have to walk only nine kilometers to Santa Rita Durão. It's mostly uphill, however, and before I am a tenth of the way, I stop, dump my pack to the ground and drink as much of the extra weight as I can. A man comes up the road from behind me, a scythe and ax over his shoulder. I offer him water. He says he's hard put to swallow water. Just can't do it. I joke that *cachaça* is better, but he tells me he used to drink too much of it. A little dose (three or four ounces) in a glass wasn't enough. He needed a full glass, to the top. But then he decided to become a man again. He said that if you drink too much, you trade your friends for *cachaça*. So he stopped, and now he's going up the road to cut some firewood.

Chapter Nine

Morro do Pilar

Outside Itambé, about ten kilometers in the direction of Morro do Pillar, the serra turns rocky and sparse and eerie with huge, odd boulders that seem to have been thrust up as magma, frozen and cracked by ice, eroded for a millennium and left out to dry. The view to the west looks over a valley of hills washing up against the Serra Cabeça do Boi, with its stark, irregular humps, another range that starts at a cliff that must drop a quarter of a mile straight down to a narrow valley that separates it from Cabeça do Boi. From the looks of it, something ripped the ridge apart. The river that runs between them does not seem to have eroded its way through them. I'm at 3,100 feet, just below a layer of morning cloud that has risen from the earth and will burn off between nine o'clock and 9:20. The dawn light behind me slides a gilt patina across the bottom of the cloud. It's an unearthly sensation to be closer to the cloud than to the broad deep valley that spreads before me, rimmed at the far end by a ridge precisely as high as the one I'm on.

For most of two hours I hike uphill. The road changes from red clay to pink dust to sparkling quartz. Rock outcrops punched up through the sparse meadow loom over the road with Druidical mysteriousness. Under one of those outcrops, ten kilometers from Itambé, lives a well-known hermit named Domingos. To meet him, you have to know just where to stop – there's a little path heading uphill into brush and boulders – and there call out, as loud as you can, "Hooo, Seu Domingos!"

I find the spot and give a holler. Domingos answers with a hoot. I walk up the narrow path of granite sand to his home under a rock where he's got a living space of about thirty feet by ten. He's a stringy old guy wearing the remains of rags. His beard looks like it was trimmed with a dull knife in the dark. A ragged tuft of light whiskers sits above the center of his upper lip. On his head he wears the bottom of a plastic bag. He reaches out with his left hand to greet me. I reach out with my left. He touches it with one finger and pulls back. Then he squats on a rock behind his fence of jumbled bamboo and begins to talk in a voice jittery and slightly insane. But he's lucid and curious about where I come from. He is under the impression that the United States is part of Brazil. He's sure of it and knows for a fact that the two areas are connected by a bridge, or maybe that Mexico is part of Brazil and is connected to the United States by a bridge. He asks me if I came to Brazil by land. As a matter of fact I did, about thirty years ago, hitch-hiking from Fairfield,

Conn. to São Paulo, S.P. He asks me if I crossed a bridge on the way. As a matter of fact I did. Well, he says, there you go.

Domingos lives the most meager of lives. His brown shorts have a busted zipper and his shirt has only one button. The button is red. The shirt is a dirty rag. On his back he wears a shawl of plastic that used to be a shopping bag. He smells very bad. His knobby knees are scratched and scarred. As far as I can tell, he has no navel. He invites me into his broad narrow cave and in stuttering, maniacal chatter sets himself to looking for something clean for me to sit on. He finds some clean T-shirts that a woman gave him several months ago but which he's not yet gotten around to wearing. "I don't need much in the way of clothes," he says.

Most of Domingos' possessions are in two-liter soda bottles, tin cans and bamboo baskets that hang from his rock ceiling. They are tied with twisted strands of something sinuous that are pegged into cracks in the rock. The biggest thing he owns is a rusty milk can. He owns at least one small kettle, which also hangs from the rock overhead.

This is a man who can use some honey, and it so happens I've just lugged about 900 unneeded grams of the stuff up a long, hot hill. Would he like some? He's reluctant but not enough so to fully decline. His reluctance is in his having no food to offer me – a devastating deficiency in the Brazilian social context. Would I like some coffee? He could make some.

Noooooo...no thank you. I truly believe that you can judge a man's water by his house and garb. This man's water is hanging in age-old Coke and Fanta bottles, water probably from a clean source, a spring around there somewhere, but I'm sure the containers are veritable convention centers of germs and parasites. But that doesn't matter because he doesn't think he has any coffee anyway. He's mortified by his lack of anything to share. When might I be returning? In six months or year, I say. He says he'll have food for me then. So we pour, or try to pour, some honey into a plastic cup that had once held a retail serving of mineral water. But the honey's crystallized. It won't pour, so Domingos uses the broken blade of a pruning hook to shear the crud from a length of bamboo that then serves as a spoon. I say, "Don't let the ants get in there," but he knew that already.

Domingos talks and talks and talks, frenetically, sometimes stuttering with the urgency of getting a certain word out. He has a lot to say. He reviews his life for me, but his chatter is so quick and so scattered with peasant idioms that all I can really understand is that he's from São Paulo state and he's seventy-two years old. With pathological detail he recounts how he arrived in Minas Gerais, the time the train arrived, why it was late, where he went first, ad nauseam and beyond. I understand little of it, and I'm sure none of it matters. But a lot of what he isn't saying matters a lot – like why the hell does he live under a rock ten kilometers outside of a town which itself isn't much of a place to live?

A better question: Why didn't I ask him that?

I pretty much understand one thing: He may not be living under that rock much longer. The owner of that land died recently. Through convolutions of inheritance and deals, recounted now in excruciating and confusing detail, a woman has come to own the land. She has told him that he can stay for just two more years. Then he has to go find a rock somewhere else. Or so he thinks. I kind of doubt the reality of this danger. This land, too rocky for crops, to rough for cattle, too far from town for anything, is of no possible use except as a place to hide.

From

The Merry Burial Compendium

When in Palermo

Feel like a ghoulish tour? If so, the Capuchin Catacombs of Palermo is the place to go.

The catacombs have been there since the 16th century, when the Capuchin monastery cemetery ran out of room. To create more space, the friars began excavating caves behind the altar of the Church of Santa Maria della Pace. During the excavation, expired friars were stored in an underground charnel house. When the first catacomb was ready, the friars exhumed their fallen members and found, to their shock and awe, that 45 friars had barely decomposed. Their faces were still recognizable! It had to be a miracle, one of God's many mysterious ways.

The friars took it as a sign that they should not bury the corpses. Rather, the remains should be kept on display as relics of the miracle. They propped the bodies in niches along the catacomb walls.

The friars continued to store their dead in this way, embalming or mummifying them as best they could. They first dehydrated bodies by letting them dry out on ceramic racks for a good year. Then they washed the bodies with vinegar and dressed them in something appropriate for eternity. During epidemics, they bathed the bodies with arsenic, which did an even better job of preservation.

So lay people–especially rich lay people who could afford embalming–requested that they, too be mummified and put on display. A preserved body became a status symbol, the ultimate in dignity. In 1783, the catacombs were opened to anyone who requested interment there.

The place grew to house some 8,000 corpses and 1,252 mummies. The state of the remains varies from grotesque skeletons in formal clothes or priestly frocks to the beautifully preserved body of a two-year-old Sicilian girl named Rosalia Lombardo. Rosalia died of pneumonia in 1920. Despite the passage of nearly a century, she looks as if she's alive and merely sleeping.

Researchers found the hand-written notes of the embalmer (and taxidermist) who preserved the girl's remains. He had injected her with formalin, zinc salts, alcohol, salicylic acid, and glycerin.

Formalin is a mixture of formaldehyde and water that kills bacteria in the body. The alcohol dried the girl's body, allowing it to mummify. The glycerin kept her from drying out too much. The salicylic acid prevented the growth of fungus.

All of these chemicals are still used by embalmers, but it was the zinc salts–no longer in use–that did the trick. The zinc petrified the body, preserving it perfectly. It also made her as rigid as stone. If you leaned her against a tree, she'd stand there with no other support.

The catacombs are now open to tourists (not for interment, just for a tour). You can visit every day of the year. No, you can't take pictures, touch the dead, or eat anything. In fact, you probably shouldn't even think about eating anything. Turn your cell phone, keep your voice low, and, please, leave no trash behind.

Burial in the Air

No coffins are needed for a sky burial. In a sky burial, the corpse is expeditiously introduced into the lifecycle by allowing it to be consumed by birds, especially vultures. It has been practiced by Buddhists in East Asia, from Bhutan and Tibet to China and Mongolia for thousands of years, but a suspected sky burial site some 4,500 years old has also been identified at Stonehenge. Zoroastrians also practice sky burial.

In a sky burial, the corpse is left in the open, above ground, often high on a mountain. The practice is appropriate for places with a lack of firewood for cremation and ground that is too rocky for the digging of a grave. The body may be left on an elevated platform or high rock, or just left on the ground. Since many such burials are practiced in the same place, vultures are often waiting. They know what to do.

Transmigration of spirits is an essential belief in Buddhism. Buddhists believe that once the spirit has left the body, there is no need to preserve the body. In fact, giving the body to living beings is seen as an act of generosity by the deceased, a virtue of the religion. The process is believed to make it easier for the spirit to abandon the body and move on to the next life.

In Tibet, vultures are given all the time they need to consume all the flesh of the body. The body is then dismantled, the bones mashed with mallets, then ground up with barley, yak butter, or milk. The mixture is then fed to the crows and hawks who were waiting for the vultures to leave.

Some regions suffer a shortage of vultures. They can't consume all the bodies offered on a given day. This is bad news for a spirit trying to leave one body and find another. Ritual dances are performed to increase the appetite.

Other regions have too many vultures, and they're very eager to get their beaks into the deceased. Sometimes people involved in the funeral rites have to fend them off with sticks.

Apocryphal Anthropodermia

Did Nazis really make anthropodermic lampshades from the skin of murdered Jews? No. It was alleged that Ilse Koch, "The Bitch of Buchenwald," wife of the commandant of that concentration camp, had lampshades of skin, but at her post-war trial it was determined that the lampshades were made with the skin of goats. But that doesn't mean nobody ever made a lampshade of human skin.

The apocryphal report from Buchenwald inspired Edward Theodore Gein, an American murderer and bodysnatcher, to include a lampshade among many items he crafted from human parts, among them a wastebasket, seat covers, bowls, leggings, masks, and a corset.

And then there's anthropodermic bibliopegy–the use of human skin to bind books. Seventeen such books are known to exist, and several more are allegedly human though quite possibly of animals. Part of the binding of a copy of Dale Carnegie's *Lincoln the Unknown* is said to have been "taken from the skin of a Negro at a Baltimore Hospital and tanned by the Jewell Belting Company."

Dat Great Brick House

Was it folklore, disinformation, or reality? In the days of American slavery, blacks feared "Night Doctors" who sought cadavers–especially those of people who had neither voice nor right to life–for dissection and experimentation. These weren't necessarily corpses dug up from graves, which at the time was the only source of corpses used for experimental and training purposes. According to tales, if not verifiable reports, white doctors or their agents would abduct blacks, take them to some kind of medical facility, snuff them, and use their bodies for dissection. Blacks knew them as Night Riders, Night Witches, KKK Doctors, and Student Doctors. Historians say these were only vicious rumors generated by slave owners and, after Emancipation, white farm owners who wanted to discourage migration to the north. Men in white gowns would prowl around Afro-American communities, pretending to be looking for eligible victims. White people who wouldn't be missed–sailors in port, immigrants, indigents– could also find themselves on a slab in a classroom or operating amphitheater.

In the 1830s, the Transylvania University Medical Department in Lexington, KY, lost prestige for lack of corpses. Nearby Louisville Medical Institute, located where there were more blacks and transients, had no such problem.

The Medical College of Georgia in Augusta bought Grandison Harris for the purpose of janitorial work and the procurement of black corpses, which he did for 50 years, robbing graves and otherwise procuring specimens.

Whether doctors and students acquired black corpses by abducting living people is not known. But blacks and whites both ended up on dissecting tables, which is interesting in that blacks were considered something other than human while alive. Once dead, they were human enough.

The following poem, apparently written by a white imitating black dialect and making fun of black fears, was propagated in the late 19th or early 20th century:

THE DISSECTING HALL

Yuh see dat house? Dat great brick house?
Way yonder down de street?
Dey used to take dead folks een dar
Wrapped een a long white sheet.
An' sometimes we'en a nigger' d stop,
A-wondering who was dead,
Dem stujent men would take a club
An' bat 'im on de head.
An' drag dat poor dead nigger chile
Right een dat 'sectin hall
To vestigate 'is liver-lights-
His gizzardan' 'is gall.
Tek off dat nigger's han's an' feet-
His eyes, his head, an' all,
An' w'en dem stujent finish
Dey was nothin' left at all.

Stuff to Know about Cremation

First of all, it isn't spelled creamation any more than the process takes place at a creamery. It takes place in a cremator, which is an industrial furnace at a crematory, which is the business end of a crematorium. But it's where you end up if you get creamed by a car, asteroid, or ice cream truck, so the confusion is understandable.

Creamers are fake cream. A cremulator is a machine that pulverizes incinerated remains. Some cremulators are like blenders, others like grinders. Either way, it takes a good twenty minutes, and the results are the same: four to six pounds of remains, perhaps a little more for individuals who spent too much time chowing down at a creamery. These scant pounds represent just 3.5 percent of the human body. The other 96.5 percent is blowing in the wind.

It's considered politically incorrect to call the remains "cremains," which is seen as slangily disrespectful of the person they used to be. "The cremated remains of the late So-and-So" is preferred. "Ashes" in the same phrase would be also acceptable even if technically inappropriate. Anything resembling ash has been incinerated into smoke. What remains has the color and consistency of sand from a beach where nobody wants to go.

A word of caution: certain implants must be removed prior to cremation. It is the funeral director's job to see that this happens. A pacemaker can explode so powerfully that it could damage the cremator, even injure people standing nearby. Other little bombs in the body include spinal cord stimulators, bone nails, and implanted drug reservoirs. Breast implants are not a problem. Titanium hips, tooth fillings, and other metals must be separated after cremation lest they damage the cremulator.

Cremation offers a few advantages over burial. It's less expensive than embalming, vaults, caskets, a burial plot, and the interment process. Cremated remains are a lot easier to transport than whole bodies. And generally speaking, survivors can cast the ashes close to home or in an appropriate place.

Cremation is not as environmentally benign as some believe. Bodies are cremated individually, each requiring the burning of some 28 gallons of fuels during the 90- to 120-minute process. The combustion releases some 540 pounds of carbon dioxide into the atmosphere of an overheating planet. Embalmed bodies release chemical residues, and even the unembalmed release whatever toxins, such as heavy metals, the body accumulated during a lifetime in a polluted environment. Some but not all of these toxins are captured by abatement equipment. If a casket is incinerated along with the body, it, too, may release vaporized chemicals. The trees that died for the casket's wood will not be generating oxygen, and their combusted carbon contributes to global warming. In the case of mahogany and certain other fine woods, the trees may have been taken from a rainforest and shipped thousands of miles.

Natural burial is the most benign means of posthumous disposal. No fossil fuels are burned except in transporting the body to the grave site. (Some cemeteries offer a horse-drawn carriage for this trip.) The body is hastened into the ecosystem. Heavy metals and other corporeal contaminants remain in the ground, in many cases rendered harmless by decomposition and plant uptake. The body, its clothes, and the casket or shroud, all of biodegradable material, soon become a plant or animal. Who knows, maybe they will become grass, and then a cow might eat it and turn it into cream. And there you go: creamation. Maybe it should be a word after all.

Wake Up, America!

Buried alive? You've got a real problem and not much time to solve it. If you've been embalmed, of course, your problems are over. You are more than dead. Not even a worm would eat you. You're going to be more than dead for a long, long time.

But if you should find yourself in the situation of awakening in a coffin, first ask yourself how you know you're in a coffin and not just some dark, horizontal telephone booth. Do you remember dying? If so, odds are you aren't in a coffin. You're in bed and you're asleep and having a bad dream. Try waking up.

If waking up doesn't work, try going to sleep. That will minimize your consumption of oxygen. You'll live longer. And then die. Like everybody else. Just be glad you weren't embalmed.

But you may be too excited to fall asleep. Who could blame you? It's like your first day on a new job. You're confused. You're nervous. You want to do things right, but you haven't received proper training. They've thrown you into a new situation, and you've hit the ground running. Or in this case, lying down.

Relax. You've got enough oxygen for a couple of hours. You'll wake up in time. Because really, you're just dreaming all this.

With a little luck you'll dream you were buried with your cell phone. This is far more likely than being buried alive. Of course it's also likely your battery's dead. (That's why they buried it with you! Ha, ha–just a little coffin humor.) Of course if you were so fortunate as to have received a green burial–which may be why you weren't embalmed–they wouldn't bury you with a phone, not unless it's organic.

But maybe they forgot it was in your pocket, and the battery is no deader than you, and you aren't in a concrete vault six feet under, just four feet under and no vault, and in an organic cardboard casket in a cemetery not far from a cell tower. Try calling 9-1-1, see if they believe you. Then call the most dependable person you know who owns a shovel or, better yet, a backhoe. Tap your head gently on the bottom of the coffin, and then harder and harder as you listen to the detailed instructions on how to leave a message. Make sure you mention that you're leaving the message *after* the funeral.

Try texting. Text your entire list of contacts. And pray–pray that you aren't doing this in your sleep. Which you probably are. And they will never let you forget. And for the rest of your life, you're going to wish you were dead. And someday you will be–hopefully before you're buried.

From
Notions from a Time of Peril

The Doom of Wealth

Pope Francis chose the environment as the topic of a major encyclical for a good reason. In the environment – or call it nature – he sees something that knits together the principles and values that are most important to him and his global flock.

The smackdown of nature relates to the suffering of the poor, the worship of money, the wealth gap, the nature of capitalism, the value of families, a world mired in materialism, the discarding of inconvenient people, the threat to life in all its forms. Climate change affects the poor more than the rich. They tend to depend more on nature. Natural disasters hit them harder. They have fewer options when besieged by drought, storm, flood, pollution, or the social unrest that follows radical shifts in the basics of an economy.

Materialism – the pursuit of happiness through things – runs contrary to nature. Every product produced, without exception, requires the destruction of something in nature. Nature can reproduce some of those things, but others cannot grow back.

Under the principles of capitalism, a forest is worth nothing unless cut down. Capital-oriented accountancy has no way to value the oxygen lost, the extinction of species, the warming of distant seas, the far-removed effects on rainfall, the lives of people who depend on the slow, sustainable use of living forest.

The worship of money removes humanity and nature from the center of life. Nature and the dignity of humans are lost in the pursuit of cash. As nature suffers, humankind suffers, especially the poor. The poor become disposable, inconvenient consumers of dwindling resources.

Without much effort, the principle of disposable people extends to foreigners, people of other religions, the elderly, the unborn, the marginal, future generations, and whoever's economies are in conflict with capitalism's need to grow more, consume more, destroy more, discard more.

Pope Francis's encyclical embraces the importance – the miracle – of all life. Many lives and forms of life are threatened by the destruction of the natural environment. The extinction of life on our planet, already taking place, cannot possibly lead to any good. Nature is central to everything. As a moral leader, Pope Francis is obligated to defend nature in the defense of people everywhere. He sees the defense of nature and the prevention of climate change as a moral issue.

How ironic that the head of the Catholic Church is using reason and scientific evidence to counter institutionalized myths based on unprovable claims! How ingenious to base a morality on a global reality.

This encyclical should mark civilization's most significant turning point since the Industrial Revolution. With the industrial production of wealth, society began to turn away from God and the Church, increasingly believing that more physical wealth – more stuff – would bring about happiness.

But something has gone wrong. Physical wealth has not brought spiritual happiness, and the power of commercialism has perverted values to the point where the pursuit of happiness is confused with the pursuit of stuff. We pursue more and more stuff at the expense of nature and disposable people. It looks like progress, but as Pope Francis makes clear, we are moving in the wrong direction.

If we don't turn around, we are going to be very sorry.

Leave the Leaves Alone

It's that time of year when yellow leaves, or none, or few do hang upon the boughs where late the sweet birds sang. Now all but few are on the ground. My wife and I engage in an annual debate in many ways reminiscent of the Biden-Trump debacle.

At least we're smart enough not to do it on TV.

She wants those leaves disappeared. I want to savor their beauty until it's time to savor the beauty of snow.

The autumn leaves of New England are celebrated. Tourists come from afar to see the surrealism of it all. Media report the wave of color as it eases south. People grapple with the incomprehensibility of it all. They try to photograph the colors–a mountain of it or a single leaf with an impossible blend of orange and green–but such colors cannot be captured.

A sensitive few see beyond the sight of it. Fall comes with its own sweet, musty aroma. It comes with the sound of kids (me among them) scuffing through dry leaves just because they're there. It comes with the utter silence of a leaf departing a twig way up there, just letting go and dancing downward to land without a sound.

Around here, September's a month of blue skies over faint, warm hues of imminent change. October brings rain, pulling down the last of the stragglers and glistening the lollipop colors.

Later, frost edges the leaves with hairs of white. You can't see it from indoors, and it doesn't last long. You have to go outside early and look at it.

On the last day of this September, leaves on the lawn in question reflected the stress of drought. On one side, ruddy leaves of a maple covered the grass. On the other, it was the yellow leaves of a denuded black birch. Many trees around them were still as green as in July.

The deployment of the leaves was like orchestral music in that they told a story without meaning. The crimson leaves were dense around their mother maple but thinned as they stretched across the green and ochre grass. Across the way, the horde of yellow leaves reached reluctantly toward the maple. The grass lay like a valley between them.

I don't know what the scene meant, but it was too perfect to mess with. I let it lie. I watched it as it changed–the leaves browning, blowing around, settling down.

By spring, most will be gone, blown to wherever it is that dead leaves go. They'll be easier to rake in the spring, when it's good to get outside and do something.

There's really no need to mess with leaves now, no need to shriek them away with wind born of an internal combustion engine.

That's what an aesthetically challenged homeowner half a mile away was doing on the last day of September. Yes, I could hear it from half a mile away–his noise scaring *my* leaves on *my* lawn.

Why would anyone want to make so much noise just to blow the beauty from a lawn?

Remember the rake? So quiet, just a swishing whisper of steel tines. As you swished, you could hear birds and crickets. You could converse. You could think and not-think at the same time. It was exercise with a kind of open-air gym equipment, a kind of a back-scratcher for the yard.

One could dispense with the rake, too, by adopting a meadow instead of a lawn. A meadow is a garden that needs no gardener. Its beauty changes through the seasons, opening with dandelions and buttercups in the spring, then Queen Anne's lace and black-eyed Susans all summer, then asters and goldenrod, the harbingers of fall.

I don't know who decided that houses should be surrounded by monochromatic grass. I have a feeling the decision involved money. Keeping a lawn up to snuff requires the purchase of seed, fertilizer, pesticide, poisons, lime, trimmers, mowers, tractors, blowers, gasoline and oil. It requires a lot of noise. It takes a lot of time.

Give me a Monet meadow any day. Give me a Klimt bed of birch leaves. Give me quiet. Give me peace. Give me summer, autumn, winter, spring.

Paean to Pawnshops

I never pass up a pawnshop. They all contain mysteries and untold stories. No two are the same, though they all share a certain spirit.

In other words, pawnshops are like people—each unique and filled with their special collection of jewels, junk, oddities and backstories.

It would be too easy to say that pawnshops are the place where dreams go to die. Yes, some do—the guitars hanging by their necks behind the counter, each a dead dream of stardom. The beds of rings under glass, each with secret meaning reduced to memory. The fetish knives, so creatively lethal but unbloodied. Old tools—drills, sanders, nail guns, equipment for some reason no longer needed.

But as the National Pawnbrokers Association hastens to point out, pawnshops are oases of hope—desperate hope, yes, over-the-hump hope, yes, but that's when hope's worth the most. A pawnshop is a quick loan collateralized with something less necessary than a tank of gas, a bottle of medicine, a down payment on the rent, a bus ticket to somewhere better.

Pawnshops are the last safety net for 55 million people classified as—rather coldly, I think— the "underbanked." In fact, almost eight percent of Americans are utterly unbanked. No checking account, no savings, and all they can get out of a loan officer is a muffled guffaw. Mississippi ranks first in unbankedness; Connecticut ranks 21st.

I don't like to think of myself as "banked," but I guess that's one of many words for me. (Thank you, Chelsea-Groton, for your patience and understanding.) So a pawnshop, to me, is more of a cross between a museum and a yard sale. This is where I'm going to get an unparalleled peek at a side of the world that's pretty much inaccessible to the banked. I might also find that certain something special that can't be found at Walmart or a mall.

I'd always assumed that the word "pawn" derived from the defenseless and dispensable chess piece, itself related to "peon," the commoner, the laborer, a word going back to the Latin for foot soldier.

But no. It comes from an Old French word, possibly from an Old German word referring to a pledge or something given as security. It could also refer to booty or plunder. Or, I suppose, stolen goods.

Pawn's only synonym is "hock," derived from a Dutch word, "hok," referring to a jail or pen. Understandably, it became slang for debt. If you can't see the connection, go find an unbanked person and ask how deep debt feels.

And if you happen to be a burglar with stolen goods to fence, first of all, thank you for reading The Day. Second of all, don't be stupid. Don't take your pelf to a pawn shop. Every pawnshop can enter a serial number or description into a national database of stolen goods. The pawnshop will quickly discover whether you lifted that laptop in Reno. Also, you'll get your picture taken.

Philip Pavone, owner of AZ Pawn in Norwich, says he isn't interested in stolen goods even though business has been slow. Sales were brisk for a while as people snapped up anything that would make the quarantined life more sufferable–TVs, laptops, video games and such.

But lately there's been a drop-off of desperados coming in for emergency loans. Pavone lays the blame on the stimulus checks that families are receiving. For many, especially the underbanked with lots of kids, they've never had so much income. Their gas tanks are full. They've got their meds, their rent and no reason to leave town. No need to hock their dreams; they have enough to live on, at least for now.

Consider the Couch

I am the only person I know who's too lazy to sit on the couch and watch TV. I lack the requisite energy. By the time I figure out how to work the remote, I'm ready for a nap.

But that doesn't mean I don't respect the sofa. In these times of quarantined boredom, the living room couch is a lifeboat in a sea of contagion. It's a good reason to stay home.

Couch? Sofa? What's the difference?

Good question. Geography is a partial but inadequate explanation. "Couch" has been more traditional in North America, Australia, and Ireland. Yet in those countries' motherland, "sofa" predominates. In South America, it's pronounced "sofá."

A more complete answer lies in history and etymology–the source of the words. The Norman invasion of 1066 brought the word "couche" from France, where it derived from the verb "coucher," to lie down. This was furniture that the English had been sorely lacking.

The word in modern French, however, is "canapé." That word in English, of course, refers to a type of hors d'oeuvre. The derivation is understandable. A slab of fish on a tuft of bread bears an uncanny resemblance to a couch potato poised for an early season ballgame.

Sofa, on the other hand, comes from an Arabic word pronounced "suffa," referring to a bench or ledge. Yes, Arabic, the language that also gave us "ottoman," "alcohol" and "zero."

In Aramaic–language Jesus spoke–the word was "sippa," though it referred to something more like a mat. It is interesting to note that in the New Testament's only reference to Jesus sleeping, he was sacked out on what was arguably a rudimentary sofa. (Mark 4:35-41)

Given the historical roots of couch and sofa, one could say that a couch is for lying on, the sofa more for sitting on. So a couch would reside in the privacy of the living room, while a sofa would be found in the parlor for chats with guests.

And as long as we're on that topic, let me clarify: one lies, not lays, on a couch, unless one is a chicken, in which case, please, do it outside.

The word most common in anglophone Canada is "chesterfield," named after Philip Stanhope, 4th Earl of Chesterfield, who commissioned one for his sedentary preferences–leather, dimpled, and low-slung. Whether those preferences explain his two illegitimate sons is not known, but it should be noted that at one point he held the position of Lord of the Bedchamber.

(Yes, recent grads, that is an actual job. But openings are few, and appointment by Royal Warrant is much more a matter of who, not what, you know.)

Astute readers are by now wondering what the deal is with the "fainting couch." Contrary to common presumption, it has nothing to do with falling unconscious on a designated divan.

The fainting couch is identifiable by a high back at one end, sometimes wrapping around the side. It accommodated a person with a need to sit up while somewhat stretched out. During Victorian times, it was used to treat women suffering from "hysteria." The treatment involved a "manual pelvic massage" by a doctor or, depending on preference, midwife.

If you think Covid-19 is bad, be glad you weren't alive during the hysteria epidemic. It was so common that houses often had a fainting room for the fainting couch. The medical procedure often had to be applied weekly, sometimes for an hour or more. The fainting room ensured privacy while the specially designed couch facilitated proper posture.

So whether you have a couch, sofa, canapé, divan, futon, or daybed, show it some respect. Appreciate its loyalty. Thank it for being there. Give it a pat on the back. Do what Jesus did: take a nap.

Webs We Weave

Lying. We all do it, and it's done to us all.

We have a lot of words for it: Fibs. Shams. Whoppers. Yarns. Red herrings. Myths. Fairy tales. Propaganda. Trumped-up terminological inexactitude.

There are bald-based and bold-faced lies, white lies and blue lies. We bluff. We puff up and cover up. We deceive, defame, and disinform. We weasel and wax ironic. We fake, falsify, fabricate, prevaricate, confabulate, defraud and dissimulate. We speak with forked tongue in cheek. We con, twist, omit, and spin. We pile it on. We call it bull, B.S. and baloney and shovel it into crocks.

I know one such crock. It calls itself Country Crock. It isn't a crock. It's a plastic tub of congealed vegetable oil from the friendly farmers at Unilever. The fake crock bears a picture of a nonexistent barn on a fake and frilly placard faked with woodgrain. Above, it says, "Shedd's Spread," but Shedd does not exist. Below, a fake scroll says, "Country Fresh Taste."

I live in the county. Its fresh tastes are many: pine sap, pond water, sassafras, honey, mint, wild garlic, trout, raspberries, with aromas of rain, skunk, manure, and mown hay. But fresh congealed vegetable oil? Never.

Advertisers lie to buyers. Robots call us up to lie. Spin doctors blur lies into a foggy notion of maybe.

And that's not all.

We lie to ourselves. ("This isn't happening.")

We lie to simplify. ("Fine, whatever.")

We lie in politeness. ("How interesting!")

We lie in the name of love. ("Of course I love you!")

We lie to kids to give them hope. (Everything's going to be all right, and Santa Claus is coming to town!)

Men dress in pinstripe lies and lie about how much sex they've had. Women paste their lips with lies and lie about how little sex they've had.

Good fiction is a good lie, and it's even better if the lie tells the truth.

We live at the end of pipelines of lies. They're on TV. They're on the internet. They come in the mail and over the phone. They're dressed in the folderol of ads, packaging, junk mail, lawn signs, memes, sermons, soundbites, biases, platitudes, stereotypes. We usually know they're lies. And the liars know we know they're lying.

But without lies, what's left? Sometimes they're all that hold us together. No less than Napoleon said, "History is a set of lies agreed upon."

Candidates try to pull us together with cherry-picked half-truths in the guise of patriotism, accusation and hope. We know they're lies, so we vote for the liars whose lies we like, the lies that bespeak the way we wish life was. We hope the lies are gift-wrapped packages containing kernels of truth. And sometimes they are.

Lies come in so many packages and with so many intents and varying values that we have a taxonomy for them. To name a few...

The noble lie, told for the greater good but not without benefit to the liar.

The honest lie, really just a mistake without intent to deceive.

The white lie, harmless, told when the truth would hurt.

The blue lie, told by police to ensure conviction of the accused.

The big lie, so audacious that it seems beyond the scope of credibility.

The bluff, a tactic to gain advantage.

The defamatory lie, targeted on harming a reputation.

The half-truth lie, especially effective because it uses a fact to deceive.

The trade lie, a natural part of advertising, public relations, sales, politics, and other sad professions.

The jocular lie, the truth in an untrue jest, the tall tale, the deception of irony.

The fantasy lie, sometimes shared, sometimes kept to ourselves, in either case functional only if credible.

The lie of silence, the implied acceptance of a lie as truth.

We all live lies, like lies, need lies, and deal with lies. But lies are trouble. They require a commitment of memory and imagination. They are an indulgence that leads to suffering. Once revealed, they call all subsequent truth to question.

And they eventually fall apart. You can fool some of the people some of the time, and facts can be denied, but not for long. Tangled webs unweave. Truth necessarily prevails.

The only question is, does it prevail in time?

Certain Circles

I can't tell you whom I visited nor where he lives, not even his town. He's not sure if he's legal. He is sure, however, that he wants to stay out of the limelight. He's famous in certain circles, he says, circles in New York, circles that go around the world, circles of art and design. His name is known in Hong Kong. His stuff is worth money.

In his famous days, his money days, he lived on the 35th floor of an apartment on Central Park West. But that was no way to live, people all stacked up on top of each other in little boxes. It wasn't natural. Everything was artificial. Even the flowers in the lobby were artificial. He couldn't live like that.

So in 1981 he walked away from the city, the money, the certain circles, came back to where he grew up, near the high school that taught him art, Norwich Free Academy, Class of '48. He finagled a life-long lease on some land in the woods off a dirt road in a small town where people don't generally care if you've got a clutch of bantams roaming at will, a team of ducks, a muster of peacocks, or rather, now, just four peacocks, the ones too quick for coyotes.

Deer come to him, tempted by the piles of corn he leaves them every day. They know him. When he calls out "It's all right! It's all right!", they come in from the woods. They nuzzle him and eat corn from his hand. They are the most beautiful creatures, he says. So elegant and peaceful. How can hunters kill them? If the hunters want meat, he'll give them hamburger, though he himself does not eat meat. Why all the killing, he asks. Why all the killing? Too many deer? No, he says. Too many people.

He fought in the war in Korea. People tried to kill him. He landed at Inchon, a skin-and-bones kid, tromped over mountains with his M-1, slept in puddles and mud, got crawled on by big fat rats, lived off Red Cross jelly beans, won two medals for valor, another for thirty days straight under enemy fire, came home in one piece, did the New York thing, surrendered, and retreated to Windham County.

He's been building his house for 17 years. He uses second-hand materials, stuff he bums from builders, the remains of demolition. The house looks both ancient and unfinished. It hunkers under low scrub oak, as calm and confident as an English cottage, its steep roof graced with moss, its dormers in four sizes and designs, its old windows blurry with panes of old glass.

It's hard to tell where the woods stop and the yard starts. He likes a house and yard with everything in its place. His house and yard are cluttered with things not yet in their place. He has the things–statues, benches, bird feeders, gnomish odds and ends–and he has the places, but the things are still puzzle pieces waiting to come together. When he's done, 50 or 60 or a hundred years from now, his home will look like a picture on a jigsaw puzzle box.

So far he has no electricity, no running water. He's afraid it might not be legal to live this way. But it's the way he wants to live: out there with nature.

After so many years so close to nature, this is what he's noticed: There are no more birds.

His hand paints the scene with a fluttering sweep. A frenzy of birds used to assault his bird feeder all the time, a chattering free-for-all of titmice, chickadees, cardinals, gold finches, woodpeckers, blue jays and everybody else. His bird feeder is a magnificent homemade edifice with lathed pillars under a shingled roof with a copper weathervane, a Taj Mahal of wild bird eateries.

But now, no birds. Not one. We can't even hear any. He puts a hand to his ear to bring the silence into focus. We listen. We cannot hear a single bird, except...wait...yes, one, in the distance – a crow.

He doesn't like this ominous turn in the way of nature. He suspects the hand of Man. A slight quiver in his clear blue eyes reveals an unspeakable uneasiness with this encroachment of something sneakier than coyotes. He fled Central Park West, but it may have found him. It's out there, and it's not all right, it's not all right.

Here's what worries him more than anything else: That he might die up here in the woods and no one will know that his chickens need feeding, that they might be locked in their coop like so many apartment dwellers trapped on the 35th floor. He thinks some kind of high-tech phone might somehow resolve the problem, but phone lines don't pass anywhere nearby, and cell phone signals haven't found his secret place. Not that he really wants a phone. It just might come in handy that one time.

Dog Be with You

Mandatory dog accompaniment may be the best idea since unsliced bread and cross-country golf. Granted, that latter invention hasn't received the attention it deserves, but the dog idea is one whose time has come.

MDA is the legal requirement that all people be accompanied by a dog wherever they go. If two people walk down the street, they need two dogs. If a dozen slackers are hanging out at the Dutch Tavern, there are 13 dogs there–twelve for the customers, plus one to maintain order while her companion human tends bar.

Picture it: Dogs horsing around school playgrounds. Dogs sniffing people at City Hall. Dogs keeping people's feet warm at the Garde. Dogs getting seasick on the Block Island Ferry. It's going to be so much fun!

Consider the impact on crime. Nobody mugs somebody who's with a dog. Burglars don't sneak into homes that have dogs. Dogs can smell gunpowder and drugs. And who's going to rob a bank if it's going to involve a lot of barking?

Dogs are good for business, the foundation of an entire industry–dog food, dog accessories, dog training, dog walking, dog grooming, dog shows and, with so many dogs in town, dog accommodations.

In other words, dogs can be jobs, products, services, and money. Isn't that what everybody wants?

But it isn't just the economy. Dogs are pals. They're family. They're loved. A new puppy is of interest to the whole neighborhood. The death of a dog makes people cry. There's something about a dog that brings out the human in us, which is really something to think about.

And in a nation torn by cultural and political strife, I think we can all agree that we don't need to ask the dogs about MDA. They don't care! Unlike cats, gerbils and goldfish, they're always up for adventure, even if it's just a walk on a leash. And they're going to go nuts over restaurants!

Speaking of which, any restaurant worth its salt is going to expand its menu to include a little dog food. And if I know Americans–and I've known quite a few, some of them real doozies–they aren't going to be comfortable letting their best friends be served some kind of crap out of a can. Who's going to a restaurant that doesn't have a bone or two among the specials of the day?

And yes, you'll need to take your mandatory companion when you go to the rest room. Of course. But don't worry about his or her gender. As I said, they don't care! And if a human of questionable or objectionable gender walks in, it isn't going to be a problem. Who's going to get weird in a rest room full of dogs?

If you call an ambulance, you know what's going to happen. Two EMTs, a paramedic and three dogs will jump out the back. This will be not only thrilling to watch, but medically beneficial as well. Dog spit is bactericidal.

In ancient Greece, dogs were trained to lick wounds. In around 1320, St. Roch was cured of plague after his dog licked his festering buboes. In 1970, the medical journal "Lancet" published an article, "Dog Licks Man," that reported dog saliva healing a wound.

As they say in France, "Langue de chien, langue de médecin." (A dog's tongue is a doctor's tongue.)

(On the other hand, it depends on what was last in Dr. Dog's mouth. It probably wasn't Listerine. Dog licks have resulted in sepsis, necrosis, spinal infections, meningitis, and in rare cases, rabies. Other side effects may occur. Ask your doctor if dog spit is right for you.)

Let's face it: dogs deserve to be with us. They were our first domesticated animals. Over the course of 15,000 years, they've adapted to our behavior. They're adapted to the point where they couldn't live without us. (As opposed to cats, most of whom are just a few generations away from feral. They'd be fine on their own. They might like us, but they don't need us.)

All it takes to make MDA a reality in Connecticut is a single vote by the General Assembly. Write to your state reps and senators today and tell them what you think!

Just for Hics and Giggles

Once upon a time, there were a little girl named Gaby and a big boy named Barack. Gaby was in the eighth grade while Barack was being inaugurated president. It was an inconvenient time for either to get hiccups.

Unfortunately, it was Gaby who got them. She was watching the inauguration on TV at school. She hicked, and then she giggled, and the giggle made her hic. As she spiraled into constitutional disrespect, Mr. Marsico dispatched her to the principal's office. Hicking and giggling down the hall, she was a little scared but also relieved to get out of class. In such times, hiccups are good.

Gaby got off easy. Not only was she not given detention or charged with something akin to sedition, but her hiccups went away in a matter of minutes. Doctors never discovered the cause of her affliction. In fact, they didn't even try.

But the causes could have been any of many, including a hair touching the eardrum, a cyst on the neck, a tumor in the brain, a tumor somewhere else, devious elves, gastrointestinal reflux, laryngitis, encephalitis, meningitis, pneumonia, multiple sclerosis, stroke, traumatic brain injury, alcoholism, anesthesia, barbiturates, diabetes, electrolyte imbalance, kidney disease, chemotherapy, spicy food, carbonated beverage, steroids, opioids, malfunctioning pacemaker, or weighing a hog.

Actually, there's been only one confirmed case of someone coming down with hiccups while weighing a hog. This was in 1922, when it was delightfully normal for a man to be lifting up 350 pounds of unprocessed pork.

But something went wrong. The man, Charles Osborne, fell, pig in hand, banging his head on the way down and breaking a tiny blood vessel in his brain. He didn't feel a thing, but the hog was executed, hung on a hook, cut into pieces and eaten by scores of American consumers.

Osborne wasn't so lucky. As soon as he hit his head, he began to hiccup 40 times per minute. This went on for years. His wife divorced him, but he married a second, who didn't seem to mind. They had eight children.

Over the years, he managed to slow his hics to 20 per minute, but it was still hard to eat. He had to blend his food into a liquid to be able to swallow during brief opportunities.

It is estimated that Osborne hiccuped 438 million times in 68 years. Then one day he simply stopped. A year later, he died. He was 97.

Jennifer Mee, known to American consumers as the "Hiccup Girl," was about Gaby's age in 2007, when she came down with a case of synchronous diaphragmatic flutter so bad she hicked 50 times a minute for 35 days, long enough for her to appear on various TV shows and become a national celebrity.

Later that year, after the hiccups stopped, she ran away from home. Three years later she was arrested for involvement in a vicious robbery in which a victim was shot four times with a .38. Jennifer pleaded sort-of innocent. Her lawyer sort-of blamed Tourette's syndrome for the hiccups and the murder. A jury found her plenty guilty of the latter and sentenced her to life in prison without parole.

It wasn't her fault. She'd tried breathing into a paper bag, standing on her head, bending way over and drinking water, eating a big wad of peanut butter, and putting sugar under her tongue. Also, she didn't actually pull the trigger.

Other cures: Salt in yogurt. Cardamom tea. Chew ginger. Hold your breath. Hold a pencil in your teeth and drink a glass of ice water. Try again with warm water. Get scared. Sing loudly. Laugh loudly. Breathe carefully, thoughtfully.

Check your genetics. Hiccups go way back. Amphibians were the first hiccupers. It was a way to pull oxygen through their gills. In time, they grew lungs, kind of like the way gilled tadpoles turn into pulmonary frogs.

One thing led to another, and now all mammals hiccup. Dogs. Bears. Bats. Whales. A fetus hiccups in the womb, even without air to hic. It's an underwater myoclonic jerk of the diaphragm, a trial run at actual breathing. It could be said that one's first breath is a hiccup.

But back to Gaby: It would be fortunate indeed if we had a president inaugurated while he or she had the hiccups. Imagine it… "I do solemnly (hic) swear that I will faithfully (hic) execute…" And then he or she giggles, and then hics again. That's what we need. In such times, hiccups are good.

On Chocolate

Where were you on July 7? It was World Chocolate Day! If you weren't wolfing down a few pounds of the stuff, you were negligent. The chocolate cops are going to come after you.

But not to worry. Milk Chocolate Day is coming up on July 28. There's an International Chocolate Day on September 13, and if you miss that, there's White Chocolate Day on September 22, and National Chocolate Day on October 28 and yet another NCD on December 28, just a couple weeks after National Cover Anything in Chocolate Day, December 16, on which date all businesses and government offices will be closed so that people can stay home and do what needs to be done.

We have chocolate today thanks to the Mayans, who were enjoying xocolatl for 34 centuries before Christopher Columbus discovered it on his fourth voyage to India. (Lest history judge him wrong, let it be known that when he came across several local people paddling a canoe full of cocoa, he stole their precious crop.)

The Mayans consumed xocolatl as a hot beverage. The Aztecs imported it and drank it cold, or at least as cold as it gets in Mexico. They called the drink cacahuatl, literally "cacao water."

Both peoples associated cacahuatl with human sacrifice because the brew looked like blood. The Spanish thought it looked like something else, so for marketing purposes, they dumped the "caca-" and opted for a brand name more like xocolatl.

But don't let such facts ruin your Cover Anything in Chocolate Day.

(Etymological pause: caca dates back to the Proto-Indo-European ancestor of several modern languages. Derivatives of caca appear in Spanish, Greek, Russian, Hebrew, Gaelic, Finnish, Turkish, Icelandic, and Persian (but not Aztec), always referring to you-know-what. Our "poppiecock" comes from a Dutch word, pappe kak, meaning "diarrhea." Derivatives also pop up in cacophony (bad sound), coprophagy (bad job) and kakistocracy (bad government.)

As long as we're on words, let's clarify something you've always wondered: cocoa is the fruit of the cacao tree.

We know where caca, cocoa and cacao come from, but we have no idea where National Cover Anything in Chocolate Day comes from other than the obvious fact that she was an absolute genius.

While the plethora of chocolate-based holidays seem to have the year well covered, there are still opportunities for a place like New London as it struggles to make a name for itself.

There is no Chocolate Capital anywhere.

There is no Chocolate Hall of Fame.

There is no statue dedicated to Chocolate.

There is no statue made of Chocolate.

There is no statue that has been dipped in Chocolate.

There is no official celebration of Cover Anything in Chocolate Day.

So here's a question: How much of this confectionary vacuum could a city like, say, New London fill?

As New London struggles to draw the world's attention–and ideally some of its money, too–maybe chocolate is the key, the Punxsutawney Phil that puts the city on the media map.

So here's the plan: Every National Cover Anything in Chocolate Day, with all due pomp and ceremony, the city should dip its toppled statue of Christopher Columbus in a vat of bubbling dark chocolate. What better way to honor the first European to steal cocoa beans?

Such an event would certainly garner as much media attention as a groundhog. The world is nuts about chocolate. Global annual sales are $83 billion, half of it in Europe. The United States consumes only 18 percent of it. The British each eat an average of 24 pounds of it each year, about as much seafood as they eat. Americans, paragons of temperance, eat only half that much.

A few West African countries produce 60 percent of the world's cocoa, but the entire African continent consumes only 3.28 percent of the world's chocolate.

And that brings us to the dark side to chocolate. Though the world loves the stuff, cocoa farmers in Ivory Coast, which produces more than any other nation, earn less than a third of the U.N. poverty level of $2 a day. In that country and Ghana, 2.1 million children work in cocoa fields, and an estimated 12,000 of them in Ivory Coast are slaves subjected to harsh and abusive conditions.

Governments and chocolate companies have vowed to do something about the situation, but according to The Cocoa Barometer, "Not a single company or government is anywhere near reaching their commitments of a 70 percent reduction of child labour by 2020."

Maybe dipping a statue in boiling chocolate will give certain kakistocratic government and corporate authorities something to think about.

From
Lurking Doubt: Notes on Incarceration

Introduction

This book does not purport or pretend to be a thorough examination of the history or current state of imprisonment. It touches all too lightly, too briefly, on only a few of imprisonment's many serious problems. Its only purpose is to give the reader a sampling of the information that is available.

A lot of information is available. Innumerable studies identify innumerable problems with the current use of prisons as a form of punishment and personal improvement. Recidivism rates indicate clearly and undeniably that imprisonment fails to make society safer. As a deterrent, prisons are minimally, if indeterminately, effective. As a form of mandatory "correction," they fail miserably. They aggravate violence, destroy families, drain public funds, cause poverty, hurt children, and accomplish little more than temporarily isolating a criminal from society and giving a few people the satisfaction of revenge.

Some of those innumerable studies explore solutions. Some are just ideas, others actual programs proven to work. Shorter sentences, fewer sentences, more family visits, working with animals, religious conversion, art programs, college courses, meditation, shorter and less demanding paroles, more responsibility, restorative justice, less youth incarceration, even doing away with prisons altogether–there is so much that could be done, yet social, political, and economic pressures too often prevent change. The ever-popular "tough on crime" approach rarely recognizes the possibility that inducing a former criminal to go straight is more productive than making a criminal suffer. This book is one in a series of short books with brief narratives on a given subject.

The first books, however, were of a different nature. One looked at little known facts about bees. Another examined death and burial from unusual perspectives. Another took a light-hearted look at cats. They were all a bit frivolous, if a bit technical, meant to entertain as much as inform the reader. But the research into prisons, prisoners, and imprisonment quickly became too dark to treat so flippantly. Prisons are a real problem, a sad, painful, tragedy affecting, at the moment, over two million people in the United States, with millions more in the pipeline of racism, poverty, and erosion of generally accepted social values. The gravity of the problem and the existence of solutions led to a book that is distinct in the series.

In that each topic in this book is presented in just a few paragraphs, the author hopes that interested reader will refer to the documents cited in footnotes.

Many of these references are available on web sites, and they tend to have footnotes of their own, tempting the reader from casual reading into deeper research.

But neither reading nor research is enough. Something–a lot of things–need to be done. Solutions exist. They are known. What is not known is why the solutions are enacted only sporadically, if at all.

Meet & Greet

Welcome to your new home! It may not be as spacious as you like, but at least you'll have someone to talk to.

You may not be escorted to your cell. A guard will give you a cell number and point the way. If you can't find your cell, find someone who looks like you and ask where to go.

The first thing you have to do is meet your new roomie. This will be a big moment for both of you, and perhaps a bit awkward. The thing to do upon arrival is knock on the door. If there's someone inside, introduce yourself thus: "My name's Bob. They told me to bunk here."

If no one's there, go in, but don't touch anything. Don't lie on a bunk. Just wait. Stand up to introduce yourself.

Your cell mate may need some time to clean off the bunk that will be yours. It's a good time to break a little ice. Ask for advice. Where do I put my stuff? When do we eat? What's the rule on leaving and coming back? Don't ask any personal questions. Presume the best. Be nice–polite but not weak.

Keeping Women Busy

The programs and treatments at York Correctional Institution in Niantic, Conn., include 12-Step recovery programs, day job assignments, trauma recovery, alternatives to violence, anger management, artists in residence, book club, books for babies, Bible studies, Protestant and Catholic choir, Catholic retreats (Kairos, Emmaus, Legion of Mary, Life in the Spirit), literacy, English as a second language, public service projects, Habitat for Humanity, Warm the Baby/Warm the Elderly crocheting, Daybreak Protestant programs, puppy training, exercise classes, Good Works re-entry mentoring, greenhouse work (planting, garden design, etc.), grief and loss recovery, trauma healing for abused women, GED, how to be happy, certified nurse's aide, Islamic studies, Performance Project, childbirth support, library, life skills, Microsoft software, Miracle of Melody, Motivation and Self-Mastery, Overeaters Anonymous, parenting, pre-natal and post-partum education, Project Rap, Quinnipiac University, Weslyan University, and Trinity College for-credit courses, self-esteem, Seven Challenges, sex offender treatment, Sisters Standing Strong, Storybook Project, stress management, textile shop, certified cosmetology and barbering training, culinary arts, adult basic education, business education, computer education, hospitality operations technology, smoking cessation, women's wellness, creative writing, and yoga, and many others.

Don't Get Busted in Brazil

Brazil has one of the ugliest prison situations in the world. There may be places with worse prisons, but Brazil ranks fourth in number of prisons with close to 650,000 people behind bars, 42 percent of them just waiting for trial. The conditions are horrific. Prisoners are 30 times more likely to contract tuberculosis. Cells hold many times more than they were built for. A Minister of Justice called the nation's prisons "medieval dungeons." Brazil has the fourth largest prisonpopulation in the world.

The Curado prison complex in Recife, state of Pernambuco, holds some 7,000 prisoners in a facility built for 1,800. A reporter found 60 prisoners in a cell built for six. Cells are left unlocked because prisoners would suffocate if packed in at the same time. Guards cannot enter cell blocks, so keys are entrusted to powerful inmates. Conditions are so filthy that leprosy is a problem.

In 2016, during riots at two juvenile facilities in Pernambuco, 11 teens lost their lives and 11 others were injured. One of the dead had been attacked while in handcuffs in solitary confinement. A few days later, an uprising at the Caruau facility in São Paulo left seven teens dead, one of them decapitated.

Gangs control the prisons more than guards do, and their conflicts result in mass killings, beheadings, mutilated bodies, and sometimes mass escapes. An uprising and gang-versus-gang battle in a prison in Manaus resulted in 56 deaths and more than 130 escapes. President Michel Temer called it a "dreadful accident."

All Is Not Bad in Brazil

Brazil is finding success in a very innovative program called the Association for the Protection and Assistance to Convicts (APAC). At APAC prisons, prisoners are given respect and responsibility...and keys to their cells and even the main gate of the prison. Inmates wear their own clothes, prepare their own food, and, believe it or not, provide their own security. There are no guards or weapons. The inmates govern themselves.

And there's no violence. Inmates don't even want to escape. They are in the last years of their sentences, and their ultimate freedom depends on good behavior. Good behavior includes a strict routine of work and study. Some prisoners can leave the prison to do volunteer work for the community, reconstructing the social pact they broke by committing a crime.

The inmates are not called prisoners but *recuperados*, that is, people in recovery. Conditions are much better than in other prisons. The population is limited to avoid crowding. Consequently, recidivism is lower, and so is the cost of operating the prison.

Similar programs are operating in Costa Rica, Chile, and Ecuador.

APAC prisons work. They cost less and actually produce better citizens rather than better criminals. Why aren't there more? For one thing, the program depends on support by the Italian AVSI Foundation. For another, Brazilian politicians tend to put self-interest over concerns for country and people. For another, political will is always hard to sustain when the general population is boiling with anger over criminal violence. For another, communities resist the idea of hosting a prison where, under certain conditions, inmates are allowed to walk out the front gate.

Why aren't there APAC prisons in the United States? Same reasons.

Unfair Education?

Higher education in prisons is proven to work, and the success of the Bard Prison Initiative is no secret. Ex-prisoners become responsible, taxpaying citizens rather than go back to a life of crime. So why aren't all prisons offering college courses and degrees?

Money is certainly one reason. The inmates don't have much of it. Legislators, unable to see that college courses cost less than post-release crime and recidivism, see no reason to educate criminals. Even New York legislators turned down a proposal from Governor Cuomo to dedicate $1 million to finance college education behind bars. Colleges can't easily afford to dedicate professors and materials to a program, so they depend on donations.

But it isn't just the money. The issue has been swept up in a "get tough on crime" controversy, and many feel it isn't fair to educate prisoners when many taxpayers can't afford to go to college.

One of the New York legislators said the governor's proposal was "a slap in the face of honest taxpayers."

A Republican senator from Texas said it was unfair for felons to benefit from Pell grants when low-income students were denied them.

President Clinton signed a crime bill preventing prisoners from using federal funds for college courses, stating, "This bill puts government on the side of those who abide by the law, not those who break it, on the side of the victims, not their attackers."

A college professor whose daughter was murdered, said, "This does not make sense to me. What is the point?"

It's an old argument, that vengeance is sweeter than actually solving a problem

Easy In, Easy Out

Jack Sheppard (1702-1724) knew how to put the "escape" in "escapade." Before he finished his apprenticeship as a carpenter, he was tempted into a life of crime, not to mention an adventurous relationship with a prostitute much larger than his diminutive self.

At the age of six, little Jack was sold off to a workhouse to learn the trade of making cane-chairs. Over the next 14 years he worked his way up to an apprenticeship in carpentry. But by the age of 20 he'd had enough of the honest life of de facto indentured slavery. He started hanging out at a tavern populated by local thieves. There he fell in love with a prostitute. Her name was Elizabeth Lyon, though everyone knew her as Edgworth Bess. Jack began his criminal career with shoplifting and petty burglary. He had no legal problems until Elizabeth got arrested and thrown into prison. Jack broke in, freed her, and the two of them got away.

A while later, he and his brother committed a burglary. The brother got caught, and since it was his second arrest, he faced possible execution. The only way out was to rat out his brother Jack. When Jack got tempted into a game of skittles at a tavern, somebody fetched the local constable. Jack got arrested and locked in the upper floor of a building. He escaped through the ceiling and lowered himself to the ground with knotted bedclothes.

Within a month he got arrested for picking a pocket. When Bess came to visit him in the local slammer, she got locked up, too. They got transferred to a real prison. Within a day they filed through some window bars and again used bedclothes to lower themselves to the ground. This second escape ensured their working-class heroism.

Two months later a colleague in crime got Bess drunk in a tavern. She revealed where Jack could be found. He was arrested and sentenced to death for his thievery. Five days before his execution date, Bess distracted a guard long enough for Jack to remove an interior window bar and squeeze out. Disguised in women's clothing, he slipped out of the prison and got away.

Too cocky to leave town, he was arrested a few days later. He was put in handcuffs and leg irons in a "strong room," but he soon picked the lock of the handcuffs and, still in leg irons, made his way up a chimney, onto the roof, then through six barred doors to get into the chapel and from there onto the roof of a neighboring house, then down through the house (without awakening anyone) and into the street.

Within two weeks he was captured. This time he was chained to a 300-pound block in a cell under constant observation. He was soon relieved of a pocket knife he was planning to use to cut his gallows rope. An estimated 200,000 people accompanied his trip to the gallows. Due to his light weight, his hanging failed to break his neck, so he was left strangling for 15 minutes. The crowd, fearing he would be dissected–a common fate of the executed– closed in on his body, preventing an attempt by friends to whisk him off to a doctor.

Controlling Society Like a Prison

In the late 18th century, English philosopher Jeremy Bentham published an idea for a new kind of prison. It was new in both physical and psychological senses. He called it The Panopticon.

The name derives from a mythological Greek giant named Panoptes. Panoptes was so called because he could see (*-optes*) everything (*pan*). He had 100 eyes and thus was considered the perfect watchman. But one day Panoptes fell asleep and closed all his eyes. Along came the god of messages, Hermes, who bashed his head in.

Bentham's Panopticon prison was designed in a circle with cells around the outside and guards in the center. The guards, or even just one guard, could at any moment observe any prisoner. They could not, however, observe all the prisoners all the time. The prisoners would never know whether they were being observed. Louvered blinders would allow the guards to see the prisoners without the prisoners seeing the guards.

Bentham claimed that the Panopticon would not only save money but reform prisoners. It would save money by minimizing the need for guards. It would reform prisoners by inducing them to behave themselves all the time, not just when they saw a guard nearby. Theoretically, they would take that self-control with them when released.

No such prison has ever been built, though the theory has been applied in prisons and in public venues. People under the eyes of video surveillance cameras never know whether they are being watched. Cameras deployed in certain English cities actually have loudspeakers so distant observers can give information–or orders–to the public. The dystopian rulers in George Orwell's 1984 had cameras installed in all homes and other places. With draconian punishment for misbehavior, citizens would never take a chance that they were not under observation.

The theory of panopticism, therefore, has the potential to shift from control of prisons to control of society, rendering both not much different from each other.

Clink, Inc.

Governments often contract a private-sector company to run its corections programs. In some cases, a company owns the prison. In others, it administers a prison owned by a government. In either case, these corporations have a vested interested in a high prison population.

In 2016, the nation's largest imprisonment company, the Corrections Corporation of America (CCA), changed its name to CoreCivic. The change was an apparent attempt to shed the bad image it acquired when an inspector general found substandard living conditions, inadequate medical care, and higher rates of violence at 14 prisons run by the CCA and other companies. The company explained that it was transforming itself from corrections and detention to "a wider range of government solutions."

At the time of the name-change, the CCA was housing some 70,000 prisoners in more than 70 prisons or jails. It owned 50 of the facilities. In 2015, the company reaped a profit of more than $3,300 per prisoner. Part of its profit is made possible by "occupancy guarantees" that require the government to provide a certain number of prisoners. At one facility, the government is obliged to maintain an occupancy of 96 percent. Long sentences, mandatory sentences, stringent laws, and recidivism are means of guaranteeing a supply of prisoners.

The biggest investors in CCA in 2016 were the Vanguard Group, Blackrock, FMR, New South Capital management, Prudential Financial, and Bank of New York Mellon Corp. Meanwhile, Pershing Square Capital Management, Systematic Financial Management, General Electric, Columbia University, and many other investors divested themselves of all CCA stock and in many cases all private prison company stock.

Four Justifications for Imprisonment, None Good

Rehabilitation

Theory: The experience of incarceration will teach criminals a lesson. Upon release, they will be law-abiding citizens.

Reality: Incarceration alone does not improve the character or attitude of criminals.

Deterrence

Theory: Severe punishment, such as long prison sentences, will scare potential criminals away from criminal acts.

Reality: Studies show that high incarceration rates increase crime or have no measurable effect. Crime apparently increases because prisons tend to a) educate prisoners in the art of criminality, b) create antisocial attitudes, c) break up communities, d) break up families, e) prevent released prisoners from finding work.

Incapacitation

Theory: Criminals cannot commit crimes while they are prison.

Reality: Prisons are incubators of crime. Criminals continue criminal activity while in prison. Upon release, they are more likely to commit crimes.

Retribution

Theory: Prison is a form of vengeance. Victims and society are pleased to see perpetrators suffer what they deserve.

Reality: Vengeance–"pay-back"–does not create some kind of balance, nor does it negate the effects of the crime, nor does it deter criminals from criminal acts in the future. To the contrary, it leaves them angered and...seeking revenge! Future crimes are more likely and more severe. Ultimately, vengeance through incarceration causes communities to suffer.

From

Promised Land: A Nun's Struggle against Landlessness, Lawlessness, Slavery, Poverty, Corruption, and Environmental Devastation in Amazonia

Chapter One

Pistoleiros

I'm sitting in the back seat thinking, *nuns can't drive*. Or maybe it's just nuns with a lot on their minds. Or maybe it's just Sister Leonora, bearing on her sixty-four-year-old shoulders the weight of slavery, kleptocracy, landlessness, lawlessness, forest fires, hit squads, environmental devastation, and the ravages of capitalism. The year is 2010 and she's driving erratically down a ragged highway in the central Brazilian state of Mato Grosso, just south of a state called Amazonas. She speeds up, slacks off, squints into the dark beyond the headlights, then remembers the rearview mirror, then remembers the accelerator.

Half the problem, I think, is the woman sitting next to her, Elizete. She's telling a florid, multi-faceted tale of political shenanigans at town hall in Terra Nova do Norte. She works there, a sub-secretary of environmental issues, knee-deep in a political slurry of "detoured" money. She hates it. As she tells her tale of atrocities, her voice soars and sings with emotional involvement. I'd have trouble driving, too.

Then Leonora stops her with a finger tapping the rearview mirror. "They're following us," she says.

"Who?" Elizete asks.

"*Pistoleiros.*"

No matter how fast she goes, she says, they stay a few hundred meters behind, never closer, never farther. They've been with us since we filled the tank back in Alta Floresta, half an hour ago. She was pretty sure she recognized them back there, the car anyway. We're still an hour from the next town. Between here and there the houses are few, cars rare, the sky more than dark with the smoke of burning pastures and the scant patches of forest that remain in this part of Amazonia. It's a good place for a hit. There's no cell phone signal, but that matters little since there's no one to call. Certainly not the police. The guys in the car behind us are probably police, off duty for the moment. Leonora says, "If there's a police block up ahead, you two take care of yourselves. Don't worry about me."

Take care of ourselves? I have no idea how to do that if police are stopping us for the convenience of hit men. What are we supposed to do? Bribe? Bolt? Cower? Plead?

She hits the brakes hard at the edge of the bridge over the Rio Teles Pires. It's an especially rough hundred yards of narrow, cratered concrete. The car behind us is suddenly on our bumper, its lights filling our car and flooding Leonora's face. There's no backing up, no turning off, no dodging, nobody around. Leonora doesn't tell us then, only later, that she feared this was the moment she's been expecting for the last ten years, the moment she finds out for sure what God does with the dead.

On the other hand, maybe they're just following her, keeping tabs on where she goes and who she's with. They do that sometimes.

This nun, it turns out, can drive just fine. The *pistoleiros* stay on us as we rumble over the bridge, then fall back as Leonora picks up what little speed her little car can muster. She veers right onto the highway toward Terra Nova and swerves around a truck piled with furniture and peasants. Just up the road is the little eatery where we'd had lunch that day, run by a family that loves her. I offer the unneeded advice to duck off the highway there. The highway dips for a stretch, then rises, and there's the restaurant. While the car behind us is in the dip, its headlights out of sight, Leonora dives to the left, scoots behind a tree, snaps off the lights. Half a minute later, a car rises from the dip in the road and screams by. It's a dark blue VW Gol.

"That's them," she says.

Chapter Two

Renascer

A lot of people want Sister Leonora Brunetto dead. A lot more – maybe thousands – address her as Mãe. Mother. That's not a religious title. Avocationally, she's a Sister. But to fugitive slaves who have hidden in her house, to people who have been camping on the side of roads while waiting for land to which they're constitutionally entitled, to activists who have been guided by her confidence, to women Leonora has coached into their own small businesses, she is addressed as Mãe. As cruel, greedy and ignorant as certain people in Mato Grosso can be, they know what happens if you kill someone's mother.

I asked some men at an *acampamento* – an encampment – called Renascer on a dirt road near Terra Nova what would happen if someone killed Sister Leonora. It was dusk. We sat on crates and logs and busted chairs behind the patchwork hut of a nice, smart man nicknamed Nico. Under stars pinked with the smoke of distant fires, we passed around a *chimarrão*, the bulbous gourd of maté green tea more commonly pictured in the hands of Argentinian gauchos. Everybody sipped from the same steel straw. They rolled thin cigarettes of oily black rope tobacco in rectangles of notebook paper. Little boys growled around the ground, not waiting pushing pictures of trucks and honking at each other.

In his calm, deep, thoughtful voice, Nico said, "Nothing would happen. The Sister is our hope, and when she's gone, so is our hope. No one will do anything, just as they've never done anything before."

Someone else disagreed, saying that the murder of Leonora would spark people into action. The passivity of the *acampados* would turn violent.

I would have to agree with both of them. The history of the rural poor and landless is one of passive resignation. They suffer the abuse of rich squatters and mercenary polícia militar as if blessed with an infinite capacity to absorb punishment without resisting it. One reason, according to one of Leonora's leaders, is that it's the courageous who get murdered first.

One man at Renascer had been a slave. For 12 years he worked without pay, slept on the ground, was fed barely enough to say alive. Once he escaped, he did nothing to report the servitude. If he had, he may well have been killed. (In Mato Grosso in 2009, officials found 22 slavery situations and freed 308 slaves. In all of Brazil in that year, 4,283 slaves were freed. The number of existing slaves is estimated to be several times that number.)

Nico thinks it would be a good idea for me to interview someone from every household in the camp. He's impressed and grateful that someone from a foreign country has come to witness their most humble life, and he wants everyone in the camp to feel a bit of hope in the international attention. This is what they told me:

As for Nico, his real name is Adoni Medeiros. He's 51. His mother was from Italy, his father part Indian. His first name comes from the Bible, Joshua 10, wherein Adoni was a king of Jerusalem. If Nico has any such title, its Elder of Renascer. For the first part of his life, he worked with the land. Then he spent 15 years driving truck for a timber company and hauling trees out of the forest with a big tractor. Today he doesn't want anything to do with a tractor, except maybe a little one to pull a little plow on a little piece of land. His shack seems to be a little bigger than most in the acampamento. He has a nice enameled wood stove in a porched area behind the house. Fired up, it gushes smoke out the front, but most of it blows away, and whatever blows into the house soon wafts out the walls or seeps through the roof. It isn't the kind of house where smoke would be a problem.

Nico senses that Sister Leonora is getting tired, but he's sure she will not stop until they have their land. He's revolted by people who claim she takes money to prevent progress. "She came from God to be a *guerreira*," he says, a warrior, and without inflection of irony he adds, "If it weren't for that woman, we wouldn't be where we are today."

Antonio, 42, has been here for two and a half years. He says he is courageous but not a hero. Leonora is a hero. She does not give up. She could have her heart cut open, and she would not give up. She would still be where she had to be to talk with someone about what needed to be done. Antonio notes that at Renascer, there are no thieves. You can't say that about many places in Brazil.

Luiz V., 52, was one of the first to arrive at Renascer. Thugs were after him. When he arrived, nine years ago, there was no camp. To sleep, he lay on the ground and wrapped himself in plastic. Today, living alone in the camp, he's torn between staying in the camp, going in to town to care for his parents, who are in their 80s, and looking for work. He goes into town by bike, 87 km, 40 of them dirt. He leaves early in the morning, arrives mid-afternoon.

Luiz used to be afraid of the threats from the *pistoleiros*, thugs, ranchers, and police, but no more. He's in the struggle for all or nothing. And the tension has eased recently.

"Our life here is very hard," he says. "The shacks get rotten and there's no lumber to fix them. The roof leaks. But to give up would be worse than this. Even if I have to eat wood and stone, I will stay here until the end. I'll get my own land someday, *se Deus quiser*. It's up to Him. We have to wait until He's ready."

His father never had his own land, always worked for other people. He told his son that he never had the right to reap what he sowed, that when you work for others, you never have a future. Luiz's life has been the same so far. He's never had a regular job, just daily work at below minimum wage, no benefits. He has planted trees and then seen them cut down because their owner didn't want them there.

Would he have the strength to start a new farm at his age? He says his energy would double if he had his own land to work. That is his dream: To own his own land. It's a terrible thing, he says, to have a dream and not be able to reach it.

Germira, 67, was camped here until her husband died. Now she lives with her daughter on a lot that was awarded to her in an *asentamento* – a settlement onto land to which she was given title. She keeps a shack in the camp so that maybe someday she can leave a piece of land to her son, an itinerant worker who works for daily pay below minimum wage.

Ivani lives in a pre-*asentamento* just up the road from Renascer. She's been "under the tarp" for seven or eight years. Her house is on a slight hill, and since the floor is the ground, it slants with the hill. It's on land that INCRA – the Instituto Nacional de Colonização e Reforma Agária, the government agency responsible for land redistribution – has awarded her but without the deed and documents that make it really hers. A state judge says he can't give her the deed because it's Union land. But somehow the rancher gets to keep using this Union land. He doesn't respect the boundaries, put up a fence across the land designated to her, but there's nothing she can do about it. "INCRA put us here and abandoned us," she says.

Marlei and her husband, Saul, live a little farther up the road. They, too, have been allocated some land but have yet to receive title to it. INCRA is supposed to send them food and other assistance, but it never arrives. Marlei thinks this is part of a plan to wear them down, let them go broke and force them to move away. Saul says that slavery hasn't ended. It's only been modernized. He is very disappointed in the Partido Trabalhista, the Workers Party led by President Luiz Inácio da Silva, who is known to the world as Lula. The party has so much power, he says: the mayor, a state representative, a senator, the president...why does nothing happen?

Marlei says, "When Leonora sees us suffering, she suffers, too."

Evanete has been living at Renascer for five years. She has four small children. She likes it here, says the people are good and life is quiet. She will wait for her land for as long as it takes.

Nair has been at Renascer for five years after three years at another camp. She's been working the land since she was a child, and her dream is to own her own land. She might start up a chicken or pig business. Her husband picks up field work when he can. They have no children. She says, "God have mercy on us, and when He returns, may He find us on our own land, harvesting things."

Zélia, 63, is thin as can be, lively and talkative. She says she needs medical exams but can't afford them. She had tuberculosis and cancer.

She's been five years under the tarp. She is struggling to get land not for herself but for her children and grandchildren. She wishes she had a way to talk to all the poor people to tell them about the struggle.

The people camped at Renascer have been shot, beaten, robbed, arrested, and run out of town. In 2013, a plane sprayed something on the camp and crops planted around it. People got sick, and a planation of banana trees died almost instantly. Around that time someone shot bullets through a house that had children in it. Six people have been murdered. Just up the road, when they tried to occupy some land the federal government had promised them, one man got his spine broken. Several got whipped with fence wire. Skulls got pounded. Bulldozers flattened the camp. A young woman with a baby in her arms screamed at the police as they took her food away. They took everybody's food, the children's school books, everybody's documents, loaded everybody into a truck and dumped them in Terra Nova. It was only with the arrival of federal police that they were allowed to establish the camp where they live now.

But federal police don't just show up. They don't step into land issues without some kind of federal injunction. Federal injunctions don't just happen. Getting them issued takes a lot of brainwork and persistence. Things have to be done right. The process requires an attorney. Somebody needs to make sure the federal prosecutor receives the papers and that the prosecutor gets the papers to the judge. Somebody might need to remind the judge that he or she got the papers. A state judge might forget. A federal judge might not. Somebody needs to ride herd on all this, and Leonora's about the only one with the time, the sense, and an insistence backed by God. And that's why so many people would prefer to see her dead.

Mato Grosso is not a peaceful place. People kill each other over gold, land, labor, timber, and politics. In 2009, 21 serious threats of death, 13 attempted murders, four murders, and innumerable beatings were reported. Despite the assaults, the people in the camps remain passive, fearing that the least misdemeanor will eradicate the little progress they've made in courts. They also fear the polícia militar, against whom they have no defense.

Still, a few quietly – always quietly – suggest that violence might provide the oomph that gets INCRA to take action. Oddly enough, I never heard that from anyone in a camp, only from sympathetic people in town.

But the people in the camps deeply resent having to live in shacks on a narrow strip of land across the road from prima dona cattle in an endless Eden of grass.

"We have nothing, and they have everything," Nico tells me. They being the cattle, fat hump-backed brahmas within 50 feet of his hut. They have six thousand hectares; the camp has two. (A hectare is about 2.5 acres.) They have all the food they can eat; the camp lives on minimal nutrition sent occasionally by INCRA. They are protected by the police; the camp is assaulted by the police. They get medical care; people don't. They have electricity; the camp is in the dark.

And they are vulnerable. The six thousand cattle on that farm across the road are overseen by no more than half a dozen farmhands. A handful of peasants could do a lot of damage. They could make the ranch unviable. No one at this camp suggested such action, but it must have occurred to them. But there would be two problems: One would be the bulldozers, fires, broken backs, whippings, and gunfire. The other is a five-foot-two sister called Mother. She says *No.* And that may be one reason why no one has killed her.

Chapter Four

The Law Here Is Money

To keep the several hundred people at the acampamento Cinco Estrelas from giving up, she manages to get the Brazilian Commission on Human Rights to send a team to the camp. They shove off from the Hotel Avenida in Terra Nova shortly after dawn, one federal "Highway Police" at the wheel of each of four cars. I don't know what Brazil feeds its Highway Police, but these seem a lot bigger than the state polícia militar and everyone else in town. Dressed in camouflage fatigues and dark glasses, each carries a 9mm automatic, a bowie knife strapped to the thigh, enough ammunition to hold out for a while, handcuffs and other gadgets of the law. They wear thick, black bulletproof vests and crush hats snapped up on the sides. In one car they have at least one machine gun, just in case. They look grim, alert, suspicious, worried. They do the driving. Leonora rides in the back seat. I get to ride in front with agent Marco Antônio, who doesn't seem to like me. I have a feeling I'm a complication.

Cinco Estrelas is outside of Novo Mundo, a town 32 kilometers off Brazil Route 163. Some 180 families live in little homes of hardwood frames and veneer-thin slats of a soft wood. The roofs are plastic sheets with palm leaves tossed over them for a bit of shade and to keep the plastic from flapping. The floors are dirt, of course. The camp is clean, free of litter and garbage. They haul the water eight meters out of wells and dump it into plastic barrels with a spout at the bottom. Their outhouses have no roofs, but the walls are thick planks of rare tropical hardwood.

The land they've been promised is just across the road, the Fazenda Cinco Estrelas. The current squatter, Osmar Rodrigues-Cunha, bought it from Sebastião Neves, a.k.a. Chapeu Preto – Black Hat – a renowned pistoleiro who owns a few farms and administers a few others, hundreds of thousands of acres in all. His men have chased Sister Leonora for as long as three days. He has accused her of sending hit squads after him. He's been arrested for such things as slavery and illegal land deals, but he never spent more than token time behind bars.

The Human Rights team includes an attorney, a psychologist, a sociologist, a security technician, and a guy in charge. They are visiting Cinco Estrelas to learn the extent to which the people here have been forgotten by the law and the psychological impact of living under daily threats of death. They will conclude something and write a report. The Highway Police hang out in the shade of a hut while a couple dozen residents gather in a circle under a roofed area behind a little house. Sister Leonora explains why the visitors have come all the way from Brasilia.

In simple, graphic, ungrammatical terms, the residents report the stress they've been under. At first they take turns, but the testimonies soon break down into extrapolations of each other's stories.

Seven people have been murdered. One young man was granted permission to fish on private property, then shot for trespassing. Another got axed in the head and took six months to die. Another disappeared. Almost every day they receive death threats hollered out the window of a car or phoned into someone's cell phone. When they go into Novo Mundo, tough guys hound them. Their motorbikes get run off the road. Their children are threatened at the bus stop. When the men look for field work, no one will hire them. At night, motorcyclists shout threats from the road. Their tarps have bullet holes. With most of the men off looking for work, it wouldn't take many armed men to invade the camp and have their way with it.

On February 21, 2010, four months before the commission arrived, 22 military police and associated thugs ran everybody off the land, burned the camp, bulldozed everything. The people fled to Guarantã do Norte and stormed the INCRA office. They stayed for 35 days, demanding the land they'd been promised for so long. Finally, some federal support came along, and everyone got to go back and build another camp.

The people are angry because there's no reason for the delay in granting land titles. The federal government is sure it owns the land that Fazenda Cinco Estrelas illegally occupies. INCRA expresses every intention of deeding the land to the campers. Family plots have already been laid out. So why doesn't it happen?

"We want an answer," says one man, palms tilted to the sky.

Another offers an answer, "The law here is money. Who has the money determines the law."

An old man says "Seven years under the tarp is a long time."

A younger man says, "What do they want us to do? Go to a slum somewhere and live by robbing people? Do they want us to mine for gold? Do they want us to raise pirate cattle and not pay taxes on them?"

Another says, "We have no security here. They could come any night and kill us all."

Another has a joke: "We aren't landless. We have land. It's under our fingernails." During the meeting, somebody spots smoke rising from behind a hill a kilometer and a half away. It quickly turns blacker, seemingly angrier and closer. This has happened before. Someone sets a fire near the camp, hoping that either the camp burns or the people in it get blamed for the fire. Leonora notes that at least this time they have federal witnesses. Two guys start up a motorcycle to go investigate. Leonora tells them to be careful, not to risk too much.

In apologetic tones, the commission attorney admits that his group doesn't own the government and can't resolve the agrarian reform issues. "Our main concern here," he says, "is to keep you alive and continuing the struggle."

Leonora tells me later that the only purpose of the meeting was to show some federal presence and give people enough hope to hang on a little longer. The federal presence also makes her a little more secure. She's less likely to be gunned down if the bad guys think the repercussions might reach Brasília.

Chapter Five

Leonora Hunted

Leonora needs a well armed federal escort for good reason. In 2005, a few years after she had arrived in the area, she was helping a community organization establish a little factory to process Brazil nuts. It's a good product for the region because the nuts come from the stately castanheira tree, which can grow to a height of 35 to 40 meters. You can still see some of their charred skeletons in the pastures along BR-163, eerily majestic with their tall, straight trunks, unbranched on their lower half. It takes a long, long time to grow a castanheira from scratch, and the trees planted in plantations produce few nuts. The tree needs specialized bees to pollinate its deep blossoms, and these bees live only in the forest. As producers of nuts, they serve as economic justification for leaving the forest alive. All to0 often, however, a rancher-squatter will prefer the immediate value of the castanheira wood over the long-term value of annual harvests of nuts. Since his ranch will probably dry up and blow away in a few years, the financially smart decision is to take the wood.

But enough castanheiras remained in 2005 for a community to turn them into a business. Leonora was there to help them get organized. She didn't know that the mayor of the town had somehow turned the coordinator of the project against her. When he failed to appear at a certain meeting, Leonora asked his wife where he'd gone. The wife said he'd felt sick and gone to the hospital. That didn't make sense to Leonora. She already had a sixth sense of suspicion and recognized the situation as "black, ugly." The coordinator had actually gone to fetch the *pistoleiros* who were supposed to come eliminate her. When his wife invited Leonora to spend the night at their house, she resisted but eventually agreed. But once there, the wife insisted that she sleep with her window open. Leonora then knew something was up. After much insistence and counter-insistence, Leonora shut the window, and the wife went to bed. Leonora went to talk with the young man who was driving her around, told him to be alert, something was wrong.

She stayed awake all that night, pacing around her room to stay awake. Once the woman came back to peek in to see if she was sleeping, which Leonora pretended to be doing. At five o'clock she came out of her room and declined to have breakfast in the house. She told the woman that she had to go to a certain other community. But that was only a ruse to throw off whoever might be coming to get her. Still unsure what was happening – only later would she learn that the coordinator hadn't found the *pistoleiros* because they were off killing somebody else – she went back to the community center. She was giving a training session when the *pistoleiros* showed up outside. She recognized one of them from the assault on the Renascer acampamento.

She thought the best thing to do was to keep on with the training. The killers wouldn't do their business among of bunch of people. She called her driver and told him to be ready. They would have to get away somehow.

At about 11:30 she announced lunch and told everyone that they could rest afterward but if anyone wanted to accompany her to the other community, she'd be going there and returning that afternoon. Again, it was a ruse. During lunch, she stayed with the children, sacrosanct territory even for hired killers. She called Father Vitório. He said he'd send a car to meet her on the other side of the Rio Teles Pires, at the ferry landing. At a moment of opportunity, she slipped out one door and the driver slipped out the other. The driver took off in the car, hoping to draw the killer away. But they stayed, apparently figuring on killing her after she returned.

There was a truck nearby. Leonora pleaded with the driver to take her to the ferry at the river, but she made the mistake of telling him why. He refused to risk his life. Leonora said that if they took a few children, they'd be safe until she got out at the ferry. So he took her.

Then the ferry operator refused to take her across the river until a car arrived. He wasn't going to do it for just one person She begged him, offered any price, but he said they only had a wait a few minutes. He could see the dust from a car that was arriving.

It was the dust of the *pistoleiros*. Leonora asked if she could ride in the little tugboat that pushed the ferry across the river. The operator let her. She hid there while her hunters and their car rode the ferry.

Waiting on the other side was Ivaine, a church activist. As soon as the ferry landed, Leonora jumped ashore and disappeared into a group of people. It so happened that Ivaine's driver was a friend of the guy driving for the *pistoleiros*. He went over to talk with his friend, who then became afraid because he'd been recognized. He and the killer drove off toward Carlinda, some 60 km away. Ivaine took Leonora to the house of someone in his driver's family. They forgot to lock the car when they got out. Within minutes, the *pistoleiros* found the the car and stole the driver's documents from it. Ivaine sent someone to scout around for the killers and found them waiting at a fork in the road out of town. He and Leonora took a different road and drove to his house, where his wife, Bete, four months pregnant, had just received a phone call telling her that Ivaine was with Leonora and would not be coming home ever again.

They arrived safely and spent the night. The next morning there was a meeting at the house – some church people, a banker, and someone from the government – to finalize a credit agreement. The pistoleiro's car passed by outside. Ivaine's phone rang. It was them, telling the people to send Leonora out or they would come in and kill everybody. Ivaine suggested they come in to do their killing so a few of them could get killed, too.

They called Padre Vitório. He said he would swing by in his truck. They timed it so that he passed the house just as the *pistoleiros* were going around the block. Vitório took her to his house. She spent the night there, but by morning, the *pistoleiros* found her. Vitório managed to get ahold of an honest state representative. The rep got ahold of the polícia federal, and a few hours later they arrived in three cars. They took Leonora and the rep to Cuiabá, and from there Leonora went to Brasilia, where law and order are more respected, though it wasn't too long before Brazil's Minister of Justice asked her to leave town before something ugly happened.

During the days of this 2005 episode, Sister Dorothy Stang, an American from Dayton, Ohio, working in the state of Pará, to the northeast of Mato Grosso, was shot dead while walking down a road alone. She was 73. She'd been doing work much like Leonora's, defending the forest and promoting sustainable use of it. The man accused of ordering her murder, Vitalmiro Bastos de Moura, was convicted after his triggerman, Rayfran das Neves Sales, implicated him. But in a second trial – mandatory for sentences of over 20 years – Sales said he'd acted alone. After an international uproar, a panel of judges later overturned the exoneration, and a subsequent trial returned Moura to a 30-year sentence, though he was subsequently released pending an appeal. In 2013 the appeal failed, and the sentence was confirmed. Neves Sales was given a 27-year sentence, but he was released after serving less than a third of that. Another defendant, Regivaldo Galvão, was convicted in May of 2010 but was granted conditional release in 2012.

From

Quilombo dos Palmares: Brazil's Lost Nation of Fugitive Slaves

Introduction

Sometime in the late 16th century, forty "rebellious negroes" are said to have somehow escaped captivity at a sugar mill near Porto Calvo-Porto Calvo in the captaincy of Pernambuco in northeast Brazil. Sebastião da Rocha Pita, the Brazilian historian who reported this incident more than a hundred years later, gave no details of the escape, whether it was a violent uprising of slaves armed with no more than the tools of their trade – machetes, axes, hoes, scythes – or a silent slipping away into the dark of night. He did not report whether women and children joined the exodus, whether anyone took food or tools, whether they ran with shackles on their ankles. About all we can surmise is that they ran in bare feet and instinctively headed west, away from the coast – away from the civilization that had enslaved them – and into the dense *mata atlântica* forest.

The forest and terrain worked to the advantage of people who carried little and had no destination other than *away*. At the same time, nature hindered anyone carrying weapons, ammunition, armor, supplies, and chains. The people fleeing could go in any direction; the people chasing them had any number of directions to choose from, only one of which was correct. Even barefoot people in the remnants of shackles could outrun soldiers lugging the baggage of war and enslavement.

The fugitives, who could have been Africans or Indians, ran until they reached the hills of the interior – steep, long ridges that punched up out of generally level terrain. Like fugitives everywhere, they found security in the higher elevations. They settled in a place of palm trees, fertile soil, plentiful water, and an abundance of game. Over the years, more fugitives arrived, some quite likely from Bahia, the captaincy to the south. The population grew to hundreds and, by the turn of the century, thousands. Palmares became known to the Africans as a *quilombo,* from a word in the Mbundu language of Africa that meant *war camp*. Settlements grew into villages, and more villages took hold on more mountains. Sharing a common purpose, common problems, and a common enemy, the villages – called *mocambos*, a Mbundu word for *hideout* – formed relationships that would evolve toward a common government. The polity became known as Palmares for the region's many palms. Palmares became a refuge for more fugitives, and its men became bold enough to attack farms and sugar mills to steal what they needed and to liberate more slaves. By 1603, Palmares was a problem that the Portuguese colonizers knew they had to resolve. A society dependent on slavery could not survive alongside a society of former slaves.

Palmares thrived while the colony on the coast struggled against disease, corruption, and the inefficiencies of an autocratic, hierarchical government led by a distant king. While Pernambuco depended on slavery, the nation of fugitives proved that free people, even free black people, could sustain themselves without agricultural commodity production based on forced labor. Having formed a government and a religion that served its purposes, Palmares proved that the New World did not need the king of Portugal or the pope of Rome. Palmares also became a community of several races, not just blacks and Indians but whites who were fleeing society or the law. Palmares was a viable alternative to plantation slavery and Portuguese society. It was an attractive nuisance that lured slaves away from slavery and gave European plebeians reason to question the status quo. It was also an aggressive enemy that threatened public safety and the colonial economy. It had to be eliminated.

Over the next ninety years the Portuguese and, briefly, the Dutch, sent two dozen military excursions to Palmares with the objective of exterminating it. To say that these militias were "white" or European would not be accurate, though they were defending white European interests. Their ranks included black slaves and regiments of free blacks and free Indians. Judging by race alone, it would be hard to distinguish the defenders of the "black" nation from the defenders of the "white" outpost of Europe. The real battle was not only between an empire and rebels but between the wealthy and the poor, the enslavers and the free, the feudal past and an enlightened future that no one had even dreamed of yet. Almost all the Dutch and Portuguese excursions failed miserably until 1694, when a massive army, much of it mercenaries of mixed race, surrounded the Palmarian citadel of MacacoMacaco. After a month-long siege, they killed, captured, or dispersed its defenders, effectively eliminating Palmares as a nation, effectively erasing it from the face of the earth.

Today, not one bit of physical evidence remains from Palmares. The precise locations of all but one of its villages and cities are unknown. Historical information about Palmares depends entirely on documents produced by the invaders, and their version of reality is suspect. They recorded little about the society they were attempting to render extinct, and their reports were corrupted with ulterior motives. They had no concept of history, culture, or sociology, no interest in

Palmares except its elimination. They wanted it not just dead but forgotten.

But Brazil did not forget. The memories of the *Quilombo* dos Palmares evolved into Palmares and myths, and the myths fed into the political dialectic. Just as Palmares had offered an alternative to colonial society of the seventeenth century, it offered an alternative to socioeconomic problems of the 20th century. As a people on the losing end of civilization's perpetual struggles, the rebel nation was a useful symbol for later generations who opposed military rule, capitalism, class division, racism, and injustice. Thus myth became confused with fact, and, true or not, became an active and ongoing argument in the modern Brazilian culture.

Palmares was the largest and one of the most long-lived *quilombos* in Brazil but by no means the only one. There were thousands, and thousands remain in Brazil today, far-flung communities of people with complexions darker than average who still share communal land as their ancestors did. Many of these communities are under siege just as Palmares was. The invaders aren't militias but farmers, mining companies, developers, and others claiming land of undocumented ownership. The war that Palmares fought for nearly a century continues in myriad manifestations three centuries later.

This book recounts the struggle between Palmares and the European colonizers on the Brazilian coast. It depends extensively on the dubious documentation those colonizers left us. Those colonizers had little regard for the Palmarians as people or Palmares as a new and practical culture. The reports of militia commanders and government agents tend to focus on issues of battles, funding, and the threats Palmares represented. They report precious little about the Palmares way of life, its language and religion, its people and their point of view. The reports are also tainted with political efforts to wrest money and privilege from higher powers. This book reports what they *said* happened.

The book goes on to explore the struggle in modern times. That struggle has evolved with the times, yet it is remarkably similar. And, similarly, the truth is still hard to discern. Archaeologists, historians, and sociologists find it hard to detach fact from myth. Political activists struggle to use the symbol of Palmares to justify their positions. People who live in today's *quilombos* struggle for recognition and respect even as they struggle to hold on to land that has been passed down to them. A similar struggle, in fact, pervades Brazilian society, with its attempts to more equitably share revenues and land, provide justice for all, and, yes, still, end the modern equivalent to slavery. Palmares was real, and its myths have become their own reality. The story and the history of Palmares are over 400 years old, and they have yet to reach their end.

Chapter 1

A New World

Modern Brazilians are fond of noting, in a cynical sort of way, that Europeans discovered their country by either error or subterfuge. When a flotilla of thirteen ships left Lisbon on March 9, 1500, everyone expected them to head south along the coast of Africa, around the Cabo da Boa Esperança – the Cape of Good Hope – and then northeast to India. But for reasons unrecorded, the fleet swung wide to the west. Maybe a storm pushed them off course for a month. Maybe they already knew the currents of the Atlantic well enough to go west to grab currents circling to the south and east. Maybe they just swung too far west and stumbled onto a continent.

But Pedro Álvares Cabral, commander of the armada, was an accomplished navigator, and with him was Bartolomeu Dias, the first European to round the Cabo da Boa Esperança, though in all honesty he named it the Cabo das Tormentas, the Cape of Storms. (Dom João II, Dom João II, the king of Portugal, changed it to Boa Esperança in hopes of encouraging more trips to India.) Dias's brother, Diogo, an accomplished navigator, was also with the fleet. Cabral and the Dias brothers weren't the type to get lost. They knew about the 1497 voyage of Vasco da Gama, the first European to sail to India. On that trip, da Gama had swung south and west to grab the South Atlantic westerly current. Noticing seaweed in the water and birds in the air, he deduced land not much farther to the west.

Dom João II, Dom João II hastily assembled Cabral's armada not long after da Gama's return to Portugal in the second half of 1499. He was in a hurry to show some force at Calcutta. But the armada may have had another mission: to go look for the lands that had been given to Portugal in the Treaty of Tordesilhas. The treaty gave Portugal all lands anywhere up to 370 leagues (2,220 km, 1,375 miles) west of Cabo Verde, a small group of islands off the western bulge of Africa. (Spain was entitled to all lands west of that line.) But no one had ever seen most of the lands granted under Tordesilhas, or even knew for sure they were there, or even had the technical ability to find an imaginary longitudinal line drawn north to south across an ocean. On land they might, but even then they wouldn't be able to get to the line because it ran down the middle of an unexplored continent well defended by mosquitoes, snakes, swamps, thorns, jungles, diseases, and people, many of whom believed that the best way to honor enemies was to eat them. But before Portugal could find the Tordesilhas line, it had to find the land it ran through.

So we don't know whether Cabral was looking for something or just bumped into it while sailing west on his way to the East. If he was looking for something, apparently it was something other than what he found, a place he called an island, the Ilha da Vera Cruz, the Isle of the True Cross.

But of course he didn't discover it. Millions of people already lived there. (And, for the record, they were by no means all cannibals.) The tribes along the coast, largely of the Tupi-Guarani language group, included the Potiguar, Temembé, Tabajara, Caeté, Kairi, Tupinambá, Aimoré, Tememino, Goitaca, Tamoio, Carijó, and, in the area where Cabral came to land, the Tupiniquim, who had migrated to the area a millennium and a half earlier in search of a mythical place devoid of evil. Whether they had found that place of no evil or just stopped at the edge of the ocean, we do not know. They called the place where they lived Pindorama. But if Pindorama lacked evil, something at least a little suspicious arrived in thirteen ships on April 22, 1500. On the next day, men from the ships met men on the shore to exchange gifts and, no doubt, a raft of misunderstandings. Then the ships sailed on, poking along the coast until they came to a cozy little harbor they named Porto Seguro – Safe Harbor. All twelve ships (one had been lost at sea) tucked into the protective embrace of land and dropped anchor. Then the crew went ashore to get to know the Tupiniquim a little better. On April 26, the crew built an altar, raised a cross, and celebrated the mass that established their possession of Vera Cruz. This is the date on which Brazil considers itself born.

They danced with the natives, exchanged trinkets, and erected a cross that blessed the heathens with their first intimations of the goodness of Christianity. A writer described a girl as "dyed from top to toe with that red paint of theirs, and she was so well-made and rounded...that many women in our country would be ashamed at being somewhat less well-endowed." On May 2 they dispatched a ship back to Portugal to report the discovery of the new lands, and the others sailed off for India. They left behind a couple of JewsJews or criminals (the record is unclear which, or whether they were, by definition, one and the same), five deserting cabin boys, and a handful of volunteers who apparently knew a good thing when they saw it: terra firma, tropical sun, lots of fruit, friendly folks who slept in hammocks, lived off the fat of the land, and for some reason dressed a young woman in red paint. Why go anywhere else?

The name of Brazil came about in either of two ways. The least likely is that its discoverers thought they had found a place long rumored to have lain far to the west, an island known as Hy BrazilHy Brazil (or Ho Brazil or Ho Bresil or Ho Brasil or O'Brazil or O' Bresil or O'Brasil), supposedly discovered by a fifth-century Irish monk who was 105 years old when he sailed off in search of lands to Christianize (181 when he died), a land which had never been seen again, though once in a while sailors reported an oceanic oasis that evaporated as soon as they came near. According to Brazilian Historian Pedro Funari, PauloPaulo Funari, Hy BrazilHy Brazil means Island of Happiness or Promised Land – arguably a land without evil. Explorers were still looking for Hy BrazilHy Brazil in the early seventeenth century, well after Brazil had been found and Hy BrazilHy Brazil's hypothetical location still appeared on maps in the 18th century. A large island of the Azores archipelago has also been referred to as Hy Brasil. Yates, William Butler-William Butler Yeats wrote that he had talked with Irish fishermen who had seen the place and described it as an island without labor, care, or cynical laughter. The Portuguese may have thought they had discovered Hy BrazilHy Brazil, though that doesn't jibe very well with their naming the place Ilha de Vera Cruz.

The more widely accepted explanation is that the land was named after the natural resource of primary interest to the Portuguese, a tree they called pau-brasilpau-brasil or brazilwood. The question, then, is whether they named the place for the tree or the tree for the place. The pau brasil's red wood resembles embers – brasas. It also resembles a species of Asian tree – the Caesalpinia echinata – that had a vernacular name that sounded like brasil. In any event, the wood of this tree produced a lovely dye that had a special use. Europe had just begun an age of factory-made textiles. The sudden variety of clothes gave birth to the concept of fashion, and the mode of the day demanded the royal purplish-red that came from the brazilwood tree.

The crown of Portugal held a monopoly on brazilwood. The king owned each and every tree. His traders hired Indians – they called them gentio da terra, or gentiles of the land – to find and fell the trees, saw them up, and haul them to the coast. The traders paid in trinkets, textiles, knives, and tools. The gentiles could work independently, without supervision, instruction, or coercion. They could hustle or they could take their time. Those who delivered the wood took home a nice pair of pants or the head of an ax. Those who preferred to fish and hunt continued to walk around naked. It was a good system, the freest of free enterprise, forced on no one and blessed by a priest. Indians made pretty good lumberjacks and pack animals if left to their own time and devices.

For a while, Brazil didn't seem to have much else to offer. No gold, silver, or spices. Nonetheless, by 1532 Dom João III, Dom João III knew that he had not an island but a good part of a continent, and he wanted it tapped for whatever might be of value. Other European powers were ready to grab his land. The Treaty of Tordesilhas, Treaty ofTordesilhas was all but meaningless, and the French didn't respect it, probably because it neglected to mention France. Dom João knew that forts and trading posts alone would not protect his colony. He needed to settle it. He decided to impose a modified feudalism that had worked during medieval times and was still working on the islands of Madeira and the Azores. He would divide the land into twelve capitanias. They would extend from the Amazon River at the northern end to today's Santa Catarina state, down near today's Uruguay – some 735 leagues (4,410 km, 2,735 miles) of beach bordered by palm groves and *mata atlântica* forest. Each captaincy would be a slice between east-west lines that were ridiculously straight, reaching from the beach to the undeterminable line set by the Treaty of Tordesilhas. Dom João gave each captaincy to a nobleman. These grantees would serve as governors with almost absolute power over their captaincies' settlement and exploitation.

The Portuguese nobility, however, showed no interest in exchanging the comforts of Lisbon for the rigors of Brazil. Dom João therefore moved the necessary qualifications down a notch, granting the captaincies to twelve trustworthy men whose professions ranged from business to bureaucracy, shipping to soldiering. Of those twelve, four would never bother going to see what the king had given them. Three others went but either showed no interest or made no progress. Three others died not long after arriving. One other, accused of heresy, came home in chains to face inquisition.

One other, Pereira, Duarte Coelho Duarte Coelho Pereira, had the gumption to make it work. He was the bastard son of a peasant woman and a landed gentleman in northern Portugal. The boy's father took him on an expedition to Brazil in 1503 and apparently instilled in him a great degree of confidence. In 1506, at the age of 20, Duarte accompanied an expedition to India. By 1516, he was ambassador to Siam. In 1532 he was given command of a fleet tasked with scaring the French off the coast of Brazil. He was a natural choice for a captaincy in that new world. Dom João gave him Pernambuco, a choice cut of land, 60 leagues (360 km, 225 miles) of coastline on the southern side of the bulge that reaches out toward Africa. It would be a long time before anyone could probe the interior to the Tordesilhas line, so the precise depth of the captaincy made little difference. And since no one could walk a straight line through the land obstructed by jungle, mountains, and rivers, the borders had little meaning. The theoretical size of Pernambuco exceeded that of the mother country, but for practical purposes, a century of settlement would fail to move the frontier fifty miles from the coast.

Pereira had little interest in the brazilwood. The crown had a monopoly on it. There were plenty of coconuts around, but Portugal was already getting coconuts from Africa, just across the Strait of Gibraltar. The search for gold had turned up nothing but rumors and dirt. It was good dirt, though, well watered by rain and warmed under tropical sunlight. Together, these elements produced something just about as good as gold, gold a farmer could grow. Pernambuco was a perfect place to plant sugar cane.

Chapter 4

Early Palmares

Those fugitives of the last years of the 16th century necessarily survived at first as hunter-gatherers, living off the land, literally hand-to-mouth. In that they eventually settled in an area called Palmares–Palm Groves–we can presume that Palmarians ate a lot of coconuts and other palm fruits. Pernambuco offered a variety of species that produced coconuts, wax, açai, and the small, pulpy *coquinho* fruit. The pindoba coconut palm (*Attalea pindoba*) became a primary natural resource. Other palms in the area included the *ouricuri* (Syagrus coronata), catrolé (*Syagrus cearensis*), and the thorny, vine-like *titara* (*Desmoncus polyacanthos*). Palmarians drank coconut milk, ate coconut meat, and used scraped-out coconut shells as bowls and cups. They pounded the coconut milk into butter and fermented it into wine. They roofed their houses with palm leaves and weaved palm leaves into mats and baskets. They spun palm bark fibers into textiles and string. They ate the finger-sized bugs that lived under palm bark. They ate heart of palm, the tender white core of young trees. They cooked with palm oil and burned palm oil in lamps. They attached a small clay bowl to a bamboo straw to a coconut shell full of water to form a hookah through which they could smoke a certain hemp, fumo Angola, that gave them wonderful dreams and soothed their sadness when they missed Africa. No doubt they looked at the palms of Brazil and remembered the palms of the place they'd come from. After working in the merciless, unshaded expanses of cane fields, groves of palm, so much like those of Africa, must have felt like paradise.

Over the next few decades, more escapees arrived. Women had babies. Small settlements, called *mocambos*, sprouted here and there, often atop mountains with difficult access. Sometimes they joined with Indian villages, and sometimes Indians joined them. At first the *quilombolas*–the residents of *quilombos*–didn't identify with each other as a single political entity. But over the course of the first years of the seventeenth century, they recognized that they shared a common enemy, a common fear, and common needs. The use of the word *quilombo* in Brazil, adopted from the similar word in Mbundu, indicates that the war camps of Palmares probably adopted the Jaga tradition of integrating men from various cultures–various conquered territories–into a unified military brotherhood.

The word *quilombo* was apparently not generally used (at least by the Portuguese) during the time of Palmares, the full span of the seventeenth century. Existing documents refer to the villages of Palmares as *mocambos*. The first written reference to Palmares as a *quilombo* appears in a document of 1692, referring to mercenaries who were "making cruel war on the negroes, against whom there has already been some success from which it may be hoped that with the help of God the negroes will be dislodged from Serra da BarrigaBarriga Mountain and their fields incapacitated, without which they cannot sustain themselves or preserve that site and as a consequence all the other *mocambos* and *quilombos* in the Sertão." (In this book *quilombo* refers to all of Palmares since "*Quilombo* dos Palmares" is today a widely used expression and the aforementioned first use is in specific reference to Palmares. While *mocambo* can be synonymous with *quilombo,* here it refers to villages and towns of refugees from slavery.)

The *mocambos* that made up Palmares stretched across a band about 350 kilometers (200 miles) long and of varying width. This swath was some 80 kilometers (50 miles) or so inland from the coast of what is today Brazil's state of AlagoasAlagoas. Later in the seventeenth century the area of Palmares was thought to be "larger than the whole kingdom of Portugal." (This could be true only if one includes as part of Palmares the vast and unsettled area inland from there, the *sertão,* which the settlers on the coast could not reach because of the wilderness and *mocambo*s that stood between them and it.) The land rose gradually from the coast, forming a plain interrupted here and there by high, steep, ridges isolated from each other by forest, streams, and small rivers. Deeper inland, just beyond Palmares, the geography and ecosystem became the harsh, semi-arid *sertão* of thorn bushes, sparse vegetation, and gravelly soil. The southern end of Palmares and the captaincy of Pernambuco reached to the Rio São Francisco , a river reminiscent of the Mississippi in its length, width, tendency to flood, and, in the 19th century, paddle-wheel steamboat traffic. Some 2,830 km (1,760 miles) long, the river, later known as "Velho Chico" (Old Frank, "Chico" being a nickname for Francisco), begins southwest of Pernambuco in the gold-filled hills of Minas GeraisMinasMinas Gerais. It flows north east through Bahia before turning east and southeast to form part of the southern border of today's Pernambuco and then the border between AlagoasAlagoas and Sergipe. A few miles upstream from the Atlantic was (and still is) the city of PenedoPenedo.

In any given *mocambo*, people from various African cultures lived cooperatively. They worked out a language that may have started as gestures and pantomime and gradually built into a functional combination of African and Portuguese words, some Tupi-Guarani terms for local plants, animals, and places, and some words they made up as needed. Many of them shared the Bantu or Jaga language. *Mocambo*s distant from each other and in only occasional communication may have developed local dialects or accents. We have no evidence at all, however, of how these people communicated or whether they shared a form of writing. If they did use a written language, few knew how to do so.

Much of what little we know about life in Palmares comes from the report of a spy, a slave sent to Palmares by Manuel de Inojosa. An owner of land and slaves and a veteran of incursions against *quilombos* in Bahia and Pernambuco, Inojosa was ardent about eliminating the rebellious black republic. In or slightly before 1677 he offered freedom to one of his slaves if he went into Palmares, reconnoitered the way people lived there, and reported back. The slave did so, spending six months in Palmares before returning. Neither the reason for his return nor his subsequent fate are known. Inojosa sent a report to Lisbon. The report has been lost, but the document that accompanied it summarizes what the spy reported:

> Inojosa, Manel deManuel de Inojosa, for the sake of the conquest [of Palmares], sent a negro slave of his, with the promise of emancipation, to live among the negroes, pretending to flee captivity and thus enter into their trust and observe the way in which they live, work, marry, and govern because knowing the ways of the enemy facilitates success in war. For six months said slave was among the negroes as one of them, in every way gaining the confidence of not just residents but the highest leaders. Every negro who arrives at the *mocambo* fleeing his masters is soon heard by a counsel of justice that seeks to know his intentions because they are greatly suspicious and are not won over just because it is a negro who has presented himself. But as soon as they certify his good intentions, they give him a woman whom he possesses along with two three, four, or five other negroes. Since there are few women, they have adopted this practice to avoid contention. All the husbands of the same woman live in the same *mocambo* with her, all in peace and harmony, an imitation of a family but appropriate for barbarians without the light of understanding and shame that religion imposes. All of these husbands recognize themselves as obedient to the woman, who keeps order over everything in life as well as in labor. To each one of these so-called families the counsel of leaders gives a piece of land for cultivation, and this the woman and husbands do. They have these lands, but not as their own because they can't sell them, and they lose them under imprisonment if they fail to plant them as directed by the counsel of leaders. Among them, everything belongs to all, and nothing belongs to anyone, as the fruits of what they plant and harvest or what they make in their workshops they are obliged to deposit in the hands of the counsel, which divides to each according to what they need for their sustenance. They all arise to war when most needed, without the exception of women, who on these occasions seem more like wild animals than people of their gender. Complaints, be they of the pretend family or of the republic, are heard by the counsel of justice, without re-

> course. The leaders, all of them, are chosen by a meeting of the negroes who live in the *mucambo*, but the main leader is chosen by the leaders. The main leader resolves issues of war without consultation or contrary opinion of anyone whatsoever, and anyone who does not go into battle in conformance with his will he has put to death. In war, they use knives, spears, firearms, and gunpowder, of which they have copious amounts stolen in their attacks or bought from whites with whom they have an understanding. They are willing to die before they will abandon Palmares.

From the modern perspective, Palmarian society was in crucial ways similar to or centuries ahead of European society. Women were socially, economically and militarily empowered. Marriage and sexual morality were apparently established by necessity and efficiency rather than by religious edict. A parliamentary council was elected by popular vote, and the highest leader was elected by leaders in an electoral process. Property was communal, and, in an ante-echo of Karl Marxism-Marx, each citizen was expected to contribute in accordance with ability and to receive in accordance with need.

The communal aspect of land ownership was a tradition in Africa as well of the Native Americans who populated Palmares. In any event, ownership of land in Palmares would have been impossibly impractical. During an attack, people needed to abandon a village, which meant, of course, abandoning their land, not to mention most of their possessions, including stored foods. At the same time, new fugitives were always arriving and had no practical or or equitable way to take ownership of land. Survival and the common good held absolute priority over personal wealth.

In PalmaresAfrican culture inAfrica, these people had been farmers, herdsmen, hunters, artisans, potters, miners, artists, fishermen, blacksmiths, woodworkers, weavers, traders, housewives, soldiers, slaves, artists, and businessmen. They brought these skills to Palmares. They farmed, fished, and hunted. They made ceramics and textiles.

They mined hematite, smelted it into iron, forged it into steel, and hammered it into hoes, machetes, hatchets, and arrowheads. They traded with nearby farmers. They raised chickens and pigs but not cattle. In that they were human beings, it's quite likely they succumbed to the urge for artistic expression.

We don't know exactly what those early Palmarian settlers were doing to bother the Portuguese on the coast, but later records give us an indication. As soon as their ranks were strong enough, they started raiding mills and plantations to grab weapons, gunpowder, supplies, and tools. They also took gold and silver that they could use to buy arms, ammunition, and other manufactured goods from cooperative settlers. While there, they set fire to buildings and fields. Whether the destruction was revenge, an aggressive attempt to defeat or push back the Portuguese, or just a cover of chaos to hinder pursuit, we do not know. The logical guess: all three.

They also captured people – black men to join their ranks, and women of any color, presumably for reproduction and comfort as well as for household labor. Rape as revenge or act of cruelty was apparently rare. The many documented complaints about Palmares from landowners and local leaders never mention sexual violence. White women were often ransomed back to their families and returned unharmed.

Palmares needed to increase its population. Too few men had the courage to flee into the unknown dangers of the forest. Many were afraid of horrific punishment if caught. And of course many were simply unable to escape unless liberated. The Palmarian invaders had to effectively capture them from their captors and force them to flee–at least that's what the Portuguese reported was happening. In Palmares, these forced fugitives became slaves of their new captors. But it was slavery in the African tradition. They were not exploited for financial gain or abused to the point of death. They were more like helpers, doing the same work as everyone else. And they could win their freedom by raiding the coast and capturing someone else.

Even before Palmares became a unified political entity under a single ruler, it was a threat to the Portuguese society. The Jesuit Pero Rodriguez wrote a letter about the problem in 1597: "The primary enemies are the rebel negroes from Guinea [i.e. Africa], who are in some of the mountains from which they attack and give us trouble, and there could come a time when they become bold enough to destroy farms, as their relatives have done on São Tomé Island."

São Tomé, an island near the equator off the western coast of central Africa, had been successfully using black slaves to plant cane and produce sugar. Angolan survivors of a wrecked slave ship established a *mocambo* on a mountain, and soon fugitive slaves from the island were joining them. In 1574 they launched an attack against mills and plantations. Counter-attacks failed to eliminate the threat. Another attack in 1595 did even more damage. It failed to oust the white colonists, but the *mocambo* continued to be a problem for the next century.

In Brazil, the problem for mill and farm owners wasn't just the raids and abductions. It was the example. As a society and economy, Palmares was functioning effectively. Its people were working together and sustaining themselves. They still wanted and perhaps needed the European products they stole from the mills and farms they raided, but they did not need Portugal, its king, or its aristocracy. This was the beginning of a long-term trend in the Americas–a political and economic movement toward independence from a hierarchical and immobile tyranny. Like the revolution that would happen in North America 150 years later, it was founded on life, liberty, and the pursuit of happiness. Like the revolution that would happen shortly thereafter in France, it upheld (in practice if not in articulated statement) the principles of *liberté, égalité, fraternité*. Though it did not offer the social strata that would allow upward mobility through economic classes–it was a single class of workers and soldiers under a small elite of governors–it absorbed the tired, the poor, the tempest-tossed, the enslaved and huddled masses yearning to breathe free. The immigrants included not only fugitive blacks but poor people who were either fed up with oppression by the governor or a mill owner, or had been accused of a "crime." In the context of total tyranny and religious intolerance, a crime would include speaking out against the existing power structure, any conflict with the aristocracy, desertion, treason, destitution, witchcraft, prostitution, sodomy, loitering, and being Jewish. But the number of whites at Palmares was probably very small. The many incursions failed to capture or kill any whites, and documents offer very few references to whites in Palmares. It may well be that white settlers in Palmarian territory, with Palmarian permission, were considered part of Palmarian society even if not actively defending it. And of course in the panmixia of intermarriage, concubinage, and rape, the definition of white could become nebulous.

Palmares was demonstrating several fundamental alternatives to the Portuguese way of life. Blacks could survive in freedom, and they could live as equals with other races. A colony could survive without its homeland. An economy could sustain itself without gold, sugar, or ships. A society could function without aristocracy, Christianity, peons, racism, or the whip. And though a man couldn't own his own land, at least the land he harrowed and hoed didn't belong to anyone other than everyone.

In other words, Palmares counterposed Portuguese society in just about every way. To the Portuguese, the conflict went well beyond the issue of fugitive slaves. The struggle with Palmares was a class conflict: the poor against the wealthy. It was racial: black against white. It was cultural: two sets of irreconcilable values. It was social: two ways of organizing a community. It was economic: a collective economy versus a monocultural cash-crop under oligarchic domination. It was political: Portuguese subjects obedient to a king versus former Portuguese subjects doing perfectly well without the king.

Palmares proved liberty possible, slavery unnecessary. It represented hope. It had to be proven unviable. The best way to do that—the only way—would be to eradicate it.

Chapter 8

The Palmares Nation

Sometime in the first half of the seventeenth century, a man named Ganga-ZumbaGanga-Zumba became the leader of Palmares. Historians surmise that Ganga-Zumba had been a chieftain in Africa who naturally assumed leadership once he'd escaped captivity in Brazil. He may well have escaped enslavement with followers, or he may have been known as an African leader by people already at Palmares. It's also possible he was born there. If so, his old age in 1678 would indicate that he'd been in Palmares since it earliest days.

Three of Ganga-Zumba's children, named Toculo, Acaiene, and Zambi, were captured by the Portuguese in a raid in 1677. They and others bore Ganga-Zumba ten grandchildren.

Portuguese referred to the leader of Palmares as a *rei*, or king, and they believed the name Ganga-Zumba could be translated as *Grande Senhor* or Great Lord. It may have been the title of anyone in the position of supreme leader, or it may have been the individual's name. *Ganga* means *lord* in various languages throughout central Africa. The chief of a *ki-lombo* war camp was the *nganga a nzumbi*, a priest who dealt with the spirits of the dead. To the Portuguese, a Great Lord was a king. They had no other word for the top leader of a nation. "Prime minister" was a novel concept in Europe, referring only to the first of a king's several ministers.

Historians have debated the extent to which the central and local governments of Palmares may have been democratic or parliamentarian. The head of state of Palmares was autocratic enough that people who came to him had to kneel and clap their hands to show respect. The existence of a council of elders, however, implies that some kind of citizen or municipal representation held a certain power. According to the slave-spy whom Manuel Inojosa sent into Palmares, people elected elders to a council, and the council elected a general leader. This would imply that the leader would need some amount of political support to stay in office or make crucial decisions. The spy never used the word *rei* to describe the leader. The practice of village chiefs electing a principal chief was a tradition among the Imbangala of seventeenth century Angola, the same Central African area that had military training villages called *kilombos* by the Jaga. In that King Ganga-Zumba's mother, AqualtuneAqualtune, led the town that bore her name, it is evident that women participated in politics and perhaps could be elected to the top leadership position. The relationship also reinforces the possibility of hereditary selection not unlike that of Europe and some of Africa. The second-largest city of Palmares, Surupira, was ruled by the king's brother, Gana-ZonaGana ZonaGana-Zona. Though that could support the suggestion of rule by family lineage, history presents many cases of autocratic rulers appointing their brothers to control the military.

There is no indication that the leader was entitled to leadership through religious office, nor did he have magic or religious powers.

The secular election system was a solution to the practical situation of people of various religious beliefs and backgrounds and many different political traditions.

Whether Ganga-Zumba was as autocratic as a European monarch, we do not know. We have a few clues from a document written in 1678, titled *Description with Important News from the Interior of Pernambuco* (*Descrição com notícias importantes do interior de Pernambuco*) but the writer, whoever it was, gave no indication of how he came to know what he described. It doesn't seem possible that all these facts, if facts they are, were based on observation. They could have been the reports of prisoners or merely rumors.

> [In Palmares] are found all the structures of war, with higher and lower ranks, as much for the success in combat as for assistance to the king. All are obedient to one, who is called Ganga-Zumba, which means Great Lord, and all who were born in Palmares or have come from outside recognize him as King and Lord. He has a palace big enough for his family, is assisted by guards and officials, who usually have royal houses, and is treated with the respect of a King and all the honors of a Lord. Those who come into his presence kneel on the ground and clap their hands as a sign of recognition and acknowledgement of his excellence. They address him as Majesty and obey him with admiration. He lives in the Royal City, which they call MacacoMacaco, a name inspired by the death of a monkey in that area. This is the capital of the several cities and villages, and it is fortified with a wattle-and-daub wall with openings for defense, and on the outside there are iron spikes everywhere and pits so deep that they are dangerous even to the vigilant. The extensive city has more than fifteen hundred houses. Among them are ministries of justice for necessary actions, and all the semblances of any Republic can be found among them.
>
> Though these Barbarians have completely forgotten their subjection [to Portuguese rule], they have not lost all respect for the Church. In this city they have a Chapel where they retreat in times of trouble, and icons to

> which they appeal for their needs. Upon entering the Chapel, an icon of the Baby JESUS, quite perfect, can be seen, and there's another of Our Lady of the ConceptionOur Lady of the Conception, and another of São Brás. They always choose one of the more highly trained people, whom they venerate as a Parish Priest and call Ganga. This person baptizes them and performs marriages. The baptism, however, is not in the form determined by the Church, and the marriages are unique, not within the laws of nature. Their appetite is the only regulator of their marriages, each man having the women he wants. They teach each other some Christian orations, and they observe the documents of the faith that are within their capacity. The King who reigns in this city is accommodated with three women, a mulatta and two crioulas. From the first he had several children, from the others none. The style of dress is the same as ours, clothed more or less in accordance with what's possible.

And what was possible? Skirts of twined palm fibers. Tunics of wild animal skins. Precious lengths of manufactured cloth from Europe. Clothes stolen from farms. Sandals of twisted grass. Jewelry of polished wood, buffed nuts, fragments of shells, seeds of color, sections of bone.

As for the chapel, the icons of Jesus. Our Lady of Conception, and São Brás indicate that the Palmarians retained certain Catholic beliefs and rituals, but the deviations in sacraments tells us that they departed from others as necessary to satisfy their spiritual needs. São Brás–Saint Blaise–for example, was warned by God that he should hide in the mountains to avoid capture by Armenian officials. He is the saint of throats, the part of the body most often cut to execute a captive, and, like many rebels, he was decapitated. Conspicuously absent from the line-up of icons was Santo AntônioSanto Antônio, patron saint of Portugal and the one who is called upon to recover things that have been lost–fugitive slaves, for example. By the middle of the seventeenth century, Palmares included at least eleven *mocambo*s of notable size. MacacoMacaco, the de facto capital, perched on a steep ridge called Barriga. *Macaco* is Portuguese for *monkey*, but the word may have an African origin. Serra da Barriga*Barriga* meant *belly* to the Portuguese but may have come from a Kariri (Indian) word "Behig," meaning Reds, possibly a reference to people who had been inhabiting the mountain for centuries. Maybe the Portuguese thought the mountain looked like a belly; maybe they thought the Indians were calling it Belly.

Macaco was surrounded by double or, later, triple stockades and a wide scattering of pits studded with sharpened stakes. The city had some fifteen hundred houses and a population of perhaps eight thousand. Another village, Osenga lay twenty kilometers to the west between the Parabina and Jundia rivers. AmaroAmaro, fifty-four kilometers northeast of Serinhaem, had a thousand houses and five thousand inhabitants. Zambi (city)ZambiZambi was ninety-six kilometers (60 miles) northeast of Porto CalvoPorto Calvo. Thirty kilometers (18 miles) to the north of ZambiZambi were two *mocambos* named TabocasTabocas (which means Wild Canes). Acotirene was thirty kilometers north of ZambiZambi. Dambrabanga, possibly near today's town of ViçosaViçosa in the state of Alagoas, and the Dois Irmãos mountains, was eighty-four kilometers (52 miles) northeast of the TabocasTabocas and 50 kilometers (31 miles) southwest of Macaco. Andalaquituche was 150 kilometers (93 miles) northeast of today's AlagoasAlagoas. Alto Magano and Curiva were near GuaranhunsGuaranhuns, in today's state of Pernambuco. (These are the distances and directions given in "Guerras Feitas aos Palmares de Pernambuco no Tempo do Governo D. Pedro de Almeida, de 1675 a 1678." (See Carneiro, 202.) Unfortunately, there is no way to get them all into relative positions on a modern map. Dambrabanga cannot be northwest of today's Porto Calvo and the two Tabocas of Palmares yet south of Macaco. Macaco is the only site in a known location. It's near today's União dos Palmares, which is west-southwest of Porto Calvo. The only explanation is that the locations of Subupira and Dambrabanga are off by 180 degrees, both falling *south* of Macaco.)

SubupiraSubupira was the city that served as military headquarters. According to the "Relação" report, it was about 36 kilometers (22 miles) from Macaco, 48 kilometers (30 miles) north of Dambrabanga, and 270 kilometers (168 miles) from Porto Calvo. The city was fortified with stone and wood, according to a Portuguese document written during an incursion of 1678, "with eight hundred houses, a league and a half long across three very high mountains draining to the Rio Cachingi RiverCachingi (sic) and within which water is quite abundant, and this was the outpost where the blacks prepared for to combat our attacks. All of it was surrounded by deep pits, and where we attacked was spread with spikes."

It has been suggested that the names of some of the *mocambos* may come from African words. PalmaresAfrican culture inMacaco may have come the Luango *makoko*; TabocasTabocas may have come from an Mbundu word, *Taboka*; Andalaquituche may have come from a Kisama word, *Ndala* Kafuche; Osenga may have come from Kwango word, *Hosanga*; Subupira may have come from a Zande phrase, *sub-usupu hara vura*; Dambrabanga may have been formed from Benguella-Yombe words, *Ndombe* and *banga*. If the names of these places are indeed of African origin, it would indicate that the leaders of Palmares were from Africa, not *crioulos* born in Brazil. The scattered sources of the words, if they indeed they are sources, would attest to the multi-cultural population of Palmares as a whole, possibly with some concentration of African cultures at individual villages.

But those are only guesses based on the sounds of the words. They aren't necessarily even the real names of the places, the names the Palmarians used. They're only the words that the Portuguese reported that the places were called, and and the locations were only where the Portuguese estimated they could could be found. The distances could not be measured with any accuracy, especially to places the Portuguese may never have seen. The names of the places were only what they thought they heard from captives and others, people who spoke other languages and weren't inclined to tell the truth to their captors.

The descriptions of the locations don't lead us to any sites discernible today. The only exception is the mountain still called Serra da BarrigaBarriga that roughly fits the description of the site of the fort at Macaco. It stands above the Rio Mundaú , just outside of today's town of União dos Palmares in the state of AlagoasAlagoas. União dos Palmares, in fact, was known as Macacos until 1831, when the village was raised to the status of vila and given the name Vila Nova da ImperatrizVila Nova da Imperatriz. The Macaco (or Macacos) of Palmares may well have been a village on the Rio Mundaú, down near running water but under the protection of the massive fort on the mountain.

By mid-century, this archipelago of hamlets, villages, and towns had all the qualifications of a nation. At least some of them had local governments, at least some of those governments involving a chief and a council. These individual localities reported to and paid tribute to a central government. The entire population shared economic and military objectives. All of the *mocambo*s contributed conscripts to a common system of defense. The nation had laws and a system of criminal justice. Homicide, for example, was punishable by death. Adultery, theft and desertion were also capital crimes.

According to various reports, by 1677 Palmares was a cohesive, multi-cultural society within which social discrimination was, as far as we know, minimal. Blacks, Indians, and a few Europeans shared their community just as they shared their common needs and common enemy. They addressed each other as *malungo,* a term of solidarity not unlike the *comrade* used by later revolutionaries. The same term, from an Mbundu word meaning, "on the boat," was used between slaves who had arrived on the same ship. Its use united Africans of various cultures and Brazilian-born *crioulos* in a common cause.

Palmares had a small ruling class that couldn't have lived much above the living conditions of the general populace. At least some *mocambo*s had someone serving in the capacity of priest, but it's unlikely a religious order or hierarchy existed. Palmares had no leeway for divisive internal cultural, economic, or other social differences. The primary concern with survival–security and enough to eat–overrode such relatively petty concerns as racial or economic differences. They had to get along, speak a common language, and share common values just as they shared their food. The alternative was death or enslavement.

The population of this nation was growing. The Blaer, Captain JohnBlaer excursion of 1645 estimated the population of Palmares Grande and Palmares Pequenho to be around 11,000, though that probably didn't account for all the *mocambo*s in the Palmares territory. A report on excursions taking place between 1675 and 1678 estimated a population between 16,000 and 20,000. In a document dated 1675, Freire, Francisco de BritoFrancisco de Brito Freire, who had been governor 15 years earlier, wrote that he heard that the population of Palmares was 30,000. Granted, he had no way of counting the people in places his soldiers couldn't even find, but 20th century historian Paulo Freitas also surmised that the number could have been that high. Yale history professor Schwartz, Stuart B.Stuart B. Schwartz, on the other hand, estimates that the total captive slave population of Pernambuco during most of the seventeenth century averaged only 20,000, making it doubtful, to him, that the population of Palmares could have been that 20,000 or larger. Half the blacks in Pernambuco would have been living in Palmares. Other estimates of the number of slaves in Pernambuco in the middle of the seventeenth century are as high as 33,000 to 50,000. Archeologists Funari, PauloPaulo Funari and Orser, CharlesCharles Orser estimate the black Pernambuco population at about 60,000, Palmares at 20,000.

There are reasons to believe Palmares may have had such a substantial population. Slaves were fleeing to Palmares by the thousands, decreasing the number of slaves while increasing the number of Palmarians. At the same time, the black, white, and Indian women of Palmares, though relatively few, were having babies. If the men were sharing the women and the *quilombo* needed more people, the women probably had lots of babies, half of whom were female and by early adolescence bearing even more babies. By mid-century, some of the oldest women may have been pre-menopausal grandmothers of girls nearing puberty—three generations producing babies, quite likely as fast as they could. We have no information on infant mortality in Palmares, but if the women were strong, food supplies adequate, and the rural venue not prone to epidemics, babies born there may have been more likely to survive than babies born in Recife or even Europe. A few hundred women having ten or more babies would increase the population by a several thousand within a generation or two. If fertility was sufficient, the size of the population of Palmares over the course of several generations would have had little relationship to the size of the population of slaves in Pernambuco.

One clear fact, however, hints at a substantially lower population. More than twenty Portuguese and Dutch incursions never managed to find many people. People tended to flee as invasions neared, but it would be difficult if not impossible for so many thousands of people to disappear. Likewise, population centers of a thousand people or more could not be hidden. Another unanswered question is why a population of tens of thousands could not muster enough fighting men to overcome invading forces of only a few hundred.

Palmares was taking in blacks, Indians, and whites fleeing or taken from European society: deserting soldiers, political refugees, thieves on the lam, people in the wrong religion, kidnapped women, the homeless, the indentured, the poor, the emancipated who had no way of supporting themselves in Portuguese society. In the harsh and arbitrarily cruel Portuguese governmental/economic system, the weak inevitably lost any conflict. If any JewsJews or Protestants remained from the Dutch days, they were living contrary to both Church and crown. A broad demographic had good reason to flee to a place that was relatively equitable, prosperous, and free, a place of cooperation rather than cut-throat competition, a place where they could work a piece of land, albeit for a common rather than personal benefit. Between the fat of the land and farming dedicated to food crops rather than cash crops, the Palmarians lived and ate reasonably well. It is a testament to human dignity that a society without slavery was satisfying people's basic needs better than the society that had the supposed benefit of unpaid labor. Palmares demonstrated that the inefficiency of slave labor was caused not by the race of the workers but the use of force and violence to motivate them.

Brito Freire, Francisco de BritoFreire's *Nova Lusitânia* report (in which his name is spelled Freyre) noted that thanks to their industriousness and hard work, Palmarians enjoyed year-round abundance of food. Palmares controlled the best farmland, and Palmarians were trading with frontier settlers. Couto, Domingos Loreto deDomingos Loreto de Couto, a cleric, historian and literary critic who wrote about Palmares a century later, wrote that such commerce had to be carried out under "secret agreements" unknown to the government. Implicit in the agreements was the understanding that "homes and slaves would be safe" from destruction or capture by Palmarians.

Cattlemen from Bahia, wandering the stark outback inland from Palmares, living off milk and beef, clothed in leather to protect themselves from thorns and branches, "as brave and fearless as the *bandeirante*, as resigned and tenacious as the Jesuit...," paid tribute to Palmares. They exchanged gunpowder, salt, weapons, tools, meat, milk and tools for grazing rights in the *sertão*, the parched and thorny interior of northeast Brazil. They also provided information about troop movements and plans being made on the coast. These itinerant cowboys had no interest in the society on the coast. They didn't want the government taxing their products. They didn't want landowners claiming and fencing pasture land. They didn't want to be considered trespassers. They had no interest in owning slaves. Though by no means part of Palmares, they had every interest in the rebel nation remaining a force that preserved the freedom of the *sertão*.

It was through this secret and informal economy and trade that Palmares products–corn, tobacco, cane, sugar, potatoes, oils, baskets, and other artifacts –reached the coastal cities and to some extent sustained life there. By the same route, in barter, manufactured goods from Europe–arms, gunpowder, lead shot, tools, textiles–found their way to Palmares. Though Palmares and Pernambuco were at almost constant war, they found ways to support each other.

Chapter 17

Digging for Truth

In 1694, the same year that Palmares was overrun, paulista pioneers discovered gold in the mountains a couple hundred miles inland from Rio Rio de Janeirode Janeiro and north from São Paulo. They also found emeralds, aquamarines, topaz, and, in 1714, sdiamonds. The region would soon be known as Minas GeraisMinas Gerais–in English, General Mines. By 1697, the Estrada RealEstrada Real–the Royal Road–was under construction, a 750-mile road system connecting the ports of Rio de Janeiro and Parati to the gold mines of such cities as MarianaMariana, Ouro Preto, and Congonhas, and to the diamond mines farther north in Serro and Diamantina. Minas Gerais became the center of Brazil, the literal jewel of the Portuguese empire. Anyone with greed and gumption went there, and with them went their slaves. Pernambuco became a forgotten backland. The Brazilian sugar industry, unable to compete with Dutch and French plantations in the Caribbean, was all but dead. Had Zumbi held out another year or two, Palmares might have survived by default. With Pernambuco now of little importance to Lisbon, he might well have expanded his kingdom to the sea.

This is not to say that Pernambuco was of no interest to anyone. Domingos Jorge Velho, his officers, his soldiers, mill owners, land owners, the king, the governor, and the governor-general spent the next two decades arguing over who was entitled to the lands of Palmares. Not long after the last battle, Governor Caetano de Melo e Casto sent the king a letter in which he clearly stated, "I believe it will not be useful to the Royal Service of His Majesty that those people [i.e.

the *paulistas*] remain living in Palmares because the neighboring captaincies will experience greater losses to their cattle and farms than the blacks themselves had caused ... " In time, ownership would be determined by whoever had enough power to control a given piece of it. Men with the self-proclaimed title of *coronel*–colonel–used ragtag militias to pounce on land, snatching it from each other and from the many *quilombos* that survived or sprung up in the vast, arid central *sertão*.

But Zumbi was dead. His brave little nation was overrun, his people scattered, his head on a pole in Recife. If anything survived of Macaco-Macaco and the other *mocambos*, it was soon washed away in rain or digested, at least partially, into the earth. Today, nothing identifiably Palmarian remains, not one bullet, no scratch of writing, no trifle of art, no shard of pottery, not one bone, not one thing besides a few descriptions written by people who really didn't care.

The lack of remnants, however, does not mean people aren't looking for something. *Anything*. The implications of any discovery go beyond the academic domain of history and into Brazil's national identity and its contentious realm of politics.

Palmares was all but forgotten for over two centuries after Zumbi's death. During all those years it is mentioned only a handful of times in Brazilian historiographies and other documents. In 1726, Pita, Sebastião da RochaSebastião da Rocha Pita published his ten-volume *História da América Portuguesa,* which included twenty-six paragraphs about Palmares, some of it apparently based on reports from people who had lived during the time of Palmares. Pita's history included the glorious if unfounded notion that the two hundred people who had run over the cliff in the dark night of the invasion did so in a conscious act of preferring death over a return to slavery. Palmares didn't come into national awareness again until the early part of the 20th century. *Os Africanos no Brasil*, by Rodrigues, NinaRodrigues, NinaNina Rodrigues, was published in 1932. Though well researched and written in good detail, the book perpetuated the notion of Palmares as a regressive retribalization of Bantu culture that succumbed to the heroic efforts of the *paulista bandeirantes*. In 1933, Gilberto Freyre published *Casa Grande e Senzala: A Formação da Família sob o Regime de Economia Patriarchal* (*The Masters and The Slaves: A Study in the Development of Brazilian Civilization*), which exposed uncomfortable truths and myths about slavery and the role of blacks in the history of Brazil. In 1924, Taunay, Affonso de E.Affonso de E. Taunay started his eleven-volume history of the *bandeirantes*, *História Geral das Bandeiras paulistas*, which would take him twenty-seven years to write. It included the story of the conquering of Palmares. In the 1930s, Ramos, Artur Ramos wrote a ten-volume series titled "*O Negro na Civilização Brasileira,* praising Palmares as "the first great epic that the Negro wrote in the land of Brazil," eulogizing its economic organization as "perfect." In 1946, Carneiro, EdisonEdison Carneiro published *O Quilombo dos Palmares*, the first book dedicated to the history of Palmares. In 1959, Clóvis Moura published *Rebeliões nas Senzalas (Rebellions in the Slave Quarters)*, a Marxist interpretation of Palmares as historical class struggle.

None of these books became widely popular until the advent of a military coup in 1964 and subsequent rightist dictatorship. The coup was ostensibly a necessary measure to combat rumbles of nascent communism. Communist activity, however, wasn't much more than a minuscule band of ineffectual guerrillas, a small political party, some liberal tendencies by the president, and some inconvenient muscle-flexing by labor unions. Once in power, the military suppressed unions and oppressed anyone critical of the government.

Under this cloud of military repression, Zumbi and Palmares became symbols of resistance. Symbolically, the struggle between the

Portuguese (and their Indian and black allies) and Palmares (with its black, Indian, and Portuguese population) had not yet ended. To the politically repressed, Palmares symbolized resistance to tyrannical government. To Marxists, it symbolized resistance to capitalism. To the poor, it symbolized resistance to the rich. To the people of the miserably impoverished northeast, it symbolized resistance to the federal attention that was focused on the wealthy south. To blacks, it symbolized resistance to racism and white domination. To those espousing Liberation Theology, the Church's blessing of the annihilation of Palmares symbolized Catholicism ignoring the plight of the poor and the black. Seen in the right light from the right perspective, Palmares could symbolize any liberal cause. Unfortunately, the desire to adopt the symbol often meant interpreting history through a lens of something other than known fact.

No one knows the precise locations of any of the *mocambo*s of Palmares except for a mountain that is still called Serra da BarrigaBarriga in today's state of AlagoasAlagoas, a few hours inland by car, just outside the town of União dos Palmares, hulking above the muddy Rio Mundaú. As far as anybody knows, the *serra* has always been called Serra da Barriga, and it fits within the 17th century descriptions of the site: a long, broad ridge with steep slopes, a pond and a marshy area up top, and a nasty cliff. Until recently, União dos Palmares was called MacacoMacaco. In all likelihood, this is the place.

It certainly is celebrated as the place. In 1978, the Serra da Barriga was named a National Historic Site. Since about that time there has been a Zumbi memorial event on top of Barriga every November to mark his death. Every year until 1998, a bulldozer worked its way up from União dos Palmares, ironing out the dirt road, then leveling and pushing the vegetation off a site not far from the famous cliff. As it plowed back and forth, piling up rubble at the edge of the area, it clipped off innumerable prehistoric (that is, pre-Colombian or, in a term often applied to Brazil, pre-Cabral) Indian burial urns, the tops of which were just a foot or two below the surface.

Then a stage got assembled, and a few days later people congregated for celebrations, spiritual moments, speeches about freedom, and Afro-Brazilian music. Then everybody went home, often with a piece of prehistoric pottery in the pocket, leaving the mountain to the few dozen peasant families who have lived there since the 1960s.

It's a glorious and weepy place for such a ceremony but a nightmare for an archaeologist. Human activity and the search for evidence of earlier human activity do not combine well. No matter how intriguing a given artifact, if it is out of context–that is, separated from whatever lay near it the last time somebody actually used it–its message and meaning are almost entirely lost. It's the surroundings of an artifact that give it meaning and hint at its history. The chunks of ceramic burial urns piled up around the perimeter of the memorial site don't indicate much except that a bulldozer had been there and that for some reason people in the late 20th century had smoothed out the area once a year.

The first archeologists to take a look at Barriga were Charles E. Orser, Jr., of the Illinois State University, and Paulo A. Funari of the Universidade Estadual de Campinas in the state of São Paulo. In about two weeks in 1992, in the standard procedure of a preliminary survey, they dug a hasty trench, did a superficial assessment of the area, and identified a few stone artifacts and a lot of surface-level pottery, some of it prehistoric, some of it of European origin, some of it apparently made in Brazil but using technology that Brazilian Indians didn't have. They found a clay vessel under the soil. It appeared to be a typical Indian burial urn, but there were no bones in it. Since it was a bit chipped at the top, they theorized that it had been opened and closed many times. The archeologists suggested that it had been used as an underground storage vessel, which happens to be a tradition in Africa. Maybe, therefore, it was evidence that blacks had lived at Barriga. In an article about their findings, Funari and Orser wrote "The pottery used at Palmares thus attests both to the integration of the runaway polity into a much wider world of exchanges–from the Brazilian coast to Africa and to Europe–and to the polity's unique character. The material world of Palmares was not native, European, or African; it was specific, forged in their fight for freedom."

Funari went even further, describing Palmares as a place of racial harmony, home to Africans, Indians, JewsJews, Moors, heretics, sodomites, and witches. It was, in his words, a "Little Brazil," a utopian ideal that worked in the seventeenth century and therefore was not impossible in the imminent 21st.

The presumption of these archeologists, however, was a wishful extrapolation based on scanty information in documents. Nothing about the pottery, let alone its discombobulated context, indicated that escaped slaves were involved or that the artifacts had been produced in the seventeenth century. It didn't even indicate that Indians or anyone else had actually lived on the site. It may simply have been a burial site. Or pre-Colombian people may have lived there and abandoned the site before the runaway slaves arrived. Or the fugitive slaves may have joined the Indians in their village, as is known to have happened elsewhere. It's not at all unlikely that the residential village of MacacoMacaco was down at the Rio Mundaú, with only the fort up on the hill. As for the assortment of pottery, it's not unlikely that the Tupinambás had contact with the European culture (and its ceramics) in the hundred years that may have preceded the arrival of the first black refugees. Nothing in the pieces of pottery indicated African influence. Nothing indicated that anything had been "forged in a fight for freedom."

Broad interpretation based on a few artifacts is difficult if not impossible. There has been so little archaeology done in Brazil, and even less on the sites of *quilombos*, that there is no way to fit artifacts from Barriga into a bigger picture. They are as meaningless (and full of potential) as individual pieces of a jigsaw puzzle. One piece of a puzzle says almost nothing about the puzzle as a whole. Another dozen pieces don't tell much more. But from a thousand pieces one could not only guess what the big picture is but begin to put the pieces together and fill in the gaps of missing pieces. Take, for example, a smoking pipe found at Barriga. One edge of it is slightly raised. Archeologists wonder whether that slight difference in design might indicate African culture and therefore a Palmares. Or, they wonder, did the pipe have a certain purpose? Or was it particular to a certain clan or tribe? Or was it an artistic flair that was never repeated? Without more pipes from more sites, this particular pipe has no interpretable meaning. If archaeologists found similar artifacts at a site known to have been home only to former slaves who had been born in Africa, and at another site of slaves who had been born in Brazil, and at another of Indians who had never had contact with European culture or technology, and at another of former Africans who had lived together with Indians for a long time, a comparison of those artifacts with artifacts from Barriga would be very meaningful, very telling.

But Brazil is far, far from any such advanced stage of archaeological research. Rhode Island has many more archaeologists per archeology site than Brazil has, and indeed it was from Rhode Island–Brown UniversityBrown University, to be precise–that archaeology student Scott Joseph Allen, Scott JosephAllen came to Brazil in 1996 to begin research that would eventually add up to his dissertation for a Ph.D. Just barely beginning his post-graduate work, he came with what he soon recognized was an unscientific objective. He was looking for evidence of a black community where Indians and whites may also have lived. Like Funari and Orser, he was entranced with the idea of digging up the relics of a rebellious black republic, and he was predisposed to finding them.

But good archaeologists, like all good scientists, aren't supposed to be predisposed. They don't establish a conclusion and then go looking for evidence to back it up. Archeologists approach a site in search of whatever is there. They draw their conclusions from whatever they find, not from what's most exciting or politically relevant. They contribute their findings to the greater body of knowledge about ancient times. What they find might not tell them much about the place where they found it, but it might give clues about findings in other places.

Regardless of what Allen was originally looking for, what he found was the same tragic mix of prehistoric and modern rubble, the pieces of burial urns, and busted clay smoking pipes piled up with plastic water bottles, shopping bags, and cigarette butts. He also found a touchy political situation. Brazilians in general wanted very much to find something that would confirm the many stories about Palmares: the courage and high-minded principles of Zumbi; the existential leap over the cliff by two hundred people who would rather be dead than enslaved; the democratic essence of the Palmares republic; the communal, quasi-Marxist nature of Palmarian society; the harmonious intermingling of blacks, whites, and Indians in a community of mutual respect. Such interpretations bolstered the spirits and causes of the political left.

Allen soon cured himself of his predisposition. His dissertation ended up being not about what happened at Barriga or the culture that existed there or artifacts remaining today. The title was "'Zumbi Nunca Vai Morrer' ['Zumbi will Never Die']: History, the Practice of Archaeology, and Race Politics in Brazil." The first sentence is "I arrived in

Brazil in 1996 expecting to research and write a very different dissertation than the one that finally emerged."

What emerged was a discussion of the potentials of archaeology and the weaknesses of "official history." The official history of Palmares included not only myths but the reports and other documents written by the Portuguese of the times. Those reports hardly constitute solid scientific or historic information, having been written by people who couldn't write very well and, in the case of the *paulista bandeirantes*, barely knew Portuguese. The *bandeirantes* and the leaders of the many militias certainly weren't writing with the aim of describing a culture or establishing historical records. They did their writing in an era when journalism and sociology hadn't been invented and history was a concept recognized by only a few rare philosophers back in Europe. Their version of truth was clouded by prejudice, presumption, politics, avarice, rumor, and stupidity. Some of it was extracted by torture. Reports that reached the king weren't necessarily reports of what had happened; they were as likely reports of what the writer wished had happened or thought that the king would want to have happened.

Official history is typically written by the winners, that is, whoever dominates a given society. This is most often a government that uses propaganda and censorship to steer the official story, a story it would like to see become history. The same can apply to the awarding of grants and government permissions. They tend to go to researchers who can be counted on to present evidence that supports the official history.

In his dissertation, Allen quoted an academic article that warned that "erasure of local histories [is] one of the most cancerous products of international capitalism in both its colonial and its metropolitan manifestations. . . . Colonial and neocolonial powers manipulate the production of histories, encouraging certain forms of history while discouraging and even silencing others. The state exercises power over the production of local histories in various ways: *censorship*, the appointment of *official state historians*, the allocation of *resources for research and training* that serve to amplify knowledge about only the period in which the state is identified, the sponsorship of archaeological methods that ensure the *erasure of local histories* from the landscape, and *sanctions* against and outright suppression of those who attempt to challenge official histories." (Italics added by Allen.)

Official history can lead to myths, but myths are not necessarily undesirable. They serve a special purpose. Indeed, they are the story that steers history. Whether or not the stories sound true, the beliefs and values that guide them seem natural, unarguable, and inevitable. They are the basis of values and morality in the broader context of society. And of course if the myths seem to be based on or even part of history, their values seem all the more valid. The myths of Palmares, some based on original documents, others on wishful thinking, reaffirm such values as courage, independence, racial equality, human dignity, democracy, and communal economy.

Such values did not serve the purposes of a right-wing military government that ruled Brazil from 1964 to 1984, yet the history and myths of Palmares persisted and grew in popularity. Though the military dominated Brazil for two decades through the use of propaganda and censorship (and torture, arrests, and killings), it failed to establish a generally accepted history or to suppress the growing awareness of Palmares and the spreading of its myths. It didn't even try. The official history of Palmares was written not by the government but by left-leaning historians and academics. In fact the two main writers of histories of Palmares in the second half of the 20th century were leftists writing while in exile. Edison Carneiro, author of *O Quilombo dos Palmares*, fled Getúlio Vargas's rightist government of the 1930s and 1940s. He wrote his book while in Mexico and published his first edition there in Spanish in 1946. The first Brazilian edition was published in 1948 by Editora Brasiliense, which was owned by a Marxist historian. It was dedicated to the founder of the Brazilian Communist Party. Décio Freitas researched *Palmares: A Guerra dos Escravos* while in exile in Uruguay and Europe after the coup of 1964 and first published it in Spanish while in Montevideo.

In Brazil there is such a thing as a Palmarista*Palmarista*, someone who claims a political affiliation with Palmares. Trusting the accuracy of the original documents and then stretching them to the left, Palmarista historians depicted a glorious black republic that was not unlike the one they wished contemporary Brazil would become–a nation of racial harmony, cooperative spirit, equitable economy, and independence from foreign powers. Décio Freitas, for example, claimed, with scanty documentary evidence, that there was "civil and political equality among the Palmarians" and that all adults, presumably including women, shared political power. His book does not cite sources, and if sources support such statements, they are often unreliable and inadequate for such conclusions. Nonetheless, Freitas is a highly regarded historian, and his claims are generally, if only tentatively, accepted.

An interesting part of the generally accepted–or "official"–history is the claim, initiated by Freitas, that Zumbi knew Latin. Freitas based the claim–and the whole claim that Zumbi was captured as an infant and raised by a priest–on documents that have disappeared. They belonged to a Graziela de Cadaval, Contessa of Schonborn, whose family has been preserving a large number of books and documents, some going back to the seventeenth century. The documents relating to Zumbi were letters written by Fr. Antônio de Melo, the priest who raised him. They were written in 1696 and 1698, when the first duke of Cadaval was president of the Overseas CouncilOverseas Council.

These and many other documents of the time were passed down through many generations, their numbers dwindling as they descended. A fire destroyed some. Others disappeared when Napoleon invaded Portugal in1808, and the Portuguese nobility fled to Brazil, taking entire libraries with them to set up government in Rio Rio deJaneiro. An inheritance later divided the Cadaval documents, and some were sold off. Only half stayed with the Contessa. And then one day a researcher in a wheel chair visited the archives and absconded with Fr. de Melo's letters–or so Décio Freitas said. Freitas died in 2004, and as far as Scott Allen knows, no one else has seen the copy that Freitas said he had. But since Freitas is highly respected as a researcher who painstakingly sought out original documents, his undocumented claims are generally taken as tenuous truth.

The Zumbi-Priest-Latin story is part of the official history of Palmares. Though it is not based on solid evidence, it is accepted as true. True or not, it's a nice thing to believe in. It adds a beautiful human element to the story of Palmares. It glorifies the value of education. It enhances the image of a people that Brazilians like to imagine as embodying all that their country could be.

The myth based on the stampede of Palmarians over a cliff –that it was suicide, not panic in the dark–has been dropped from official history. Those who have studied Palmares know that there is no evidence that it was suicide, but great masses of people are content to believe it was. It was the historian Rocha Pita, a contemporary of Zumbi, who first declared that "Prince Zumby and his strongest warriors and loyal followers" had committed mass suicide. "Not wanting to die on our [i.e., Portuguese] swords, they climbed to the height of their eminence and willingly threw themselves off and with that style of death showed that they did not love life in slavery and did not want to lose it to our attack." Pita apparently made this claim without evidence, probably just generating a tragic and poetic image of existential heroism. Multiple documents confirm that Zumbi (or at least a man presumed to be Zumbi, or claimed to be Zumbi) was hunted down and killed almost two years after that final battle and the incident at the cliff. But the notion of a mass suicide, irresistibly romantic, has been repeated in many other books and articles right up to modern times.

Though archeology is not likely to prove that Zumbi knew or didn't know Latin, it can in other ways threaten official history. It opens the possibility of an alternative history, one that diverges from the image of Palmares as a black community with a culture of liberty, equality, and fraternity. Such a possibility is a threat to people of various liberal persuasions. So when Scott Allen arrived at Barriga, a rubble of artifacts wasn't the only mess he found. He also found a mess of politics. The military government was ten years past, and the left-leaning history of Palmares was alive and well, and few wanted to see it threatened. Academics and political activists were even less eager to see an American digging into the sacred heart of Palmares.

The Fundação Cultural Palmares is a governmental agency within the Brazilian Ministry of Culture. Endowed with legal authority over many issues relating to *quilombos* in Brazil, it would not allow Allen (or anyone else) to excavate at Palmares. This prohibition coincided with the first public awareness that the Serra da Barriga almost certainly included an Indian component, a reality, which, if proven, might wrest authority from the Fundação Cultural Palmares and transfer it to some other agency, such as the Fundação Nacional do Índio (FUNAI), which handles Indian issues. No one actually stated this, but to Scott Allen it smelled more like heritage politics than anthropology.

"The practice of archaeology is integrally linked to political agendas that are diverse, and archaeologists frequently feel the pressure of these agendas, which include the development of tourism, interethnic conflicts, and advancing of resources, etc.," he would later write in his dissertation. "...Generally researchers who challenge these official histories are prohibited from carrying out further studies by denying them resources or official permissions."

Allen had no intention of targeting a challenge on anything, but intentions are irrelevant in science. Any challenges would depend on whatever archaeology revealed at Barriga, and if nothing got dug, nothing would be revealed, and nothing would be challenged.

Stymied for the time being, Allen went surfing for a couple of months, then got down to researching whatever he could without actually digging a hole. At the same time, he probed the Brazilian bureaucracy, looking for a way to get something done at Barriga, where every year the situation worsened as the bulldozers went back and forth, erasing a few more inches of history to open up a space for the annual commemoration. Unfortunately, they were smoothing off an area known as "the plateau," the area most logical for habitation and therefore the most likely to yield artifacts.

The plateau was also the most logical place to build a monument to Palmares. Plans for a memorial park and museum had begun shortly before Allen arrived. On November 20, 1995, President Fernando Henrique Cardoso gave a speech in União dos Palmares, within sight of Barriga, to commemorate 300 years since Zumbi's death. With him were soccer icon Pelé, who was Brazil's Minister of Sports, and a black senator, Benedita da Silva. "I come here to say that Zumbi is ours," Cardoso said, "that he is of the people of Brazil, and he represents the best of our people in his the desire for freedom. [...] Zumbi has gone beyond his identity as an Afro-Brazilian."

In 1997, an act of the Brazilian congress named Zumbi dos Palmares a National Hero. The only other hero at that time was Joaquim José da Silva Xavier, more familiarly known as Tiradentes. An itinerant dentist and gold prospector in Minas GeraisMinasMinas Gerais. Tiradentes conspired to oust the Portuguese over a tax issue. The conspiracy accomplished nothing before its participants were betrayed and arrested. Tiradentes was hanged, beheaded, and quartered, his body parts left on display in Ouro Preto. His martyrdom, like that of Zumbi, is often likened to that of Christ. "Zumbi dos Palmares" was inscribed in the *Book of Steel* at a monument to Brazil's *Herois Nacionais* in Brasilia. In that same year, the president of the Universidade Federal de AlagoasAlagoas asked Scott Allen to join his faculty and to establish an archaeological presence at Barriga.

After much political wrangling, the Fundação Cultural Palmares came to understand that bulldozers were scraping away the heritage that the foundation was supposed to be preserving. They declared the entire mountain an archaeological site and put Dr. Allen in charge of it. The building of the memorial park and museum would proceed, but nothing was to scratch the surface of the earth without Dr. Allen saying it could scratch. His first project was to allow the construction of the memorial park on the plateau. This was a political, not archeological decision. Under better circumstances, he would never have allowed this until a thorough excavation had been completed. But the bulldozer had done its damage, and a few test holes confirmed that in all likelihood nothing remained. Bearing in mind that he had to balance scientific accuracy with the national passion for Palmares, he quickly gave his archeological nod to a boundary around much of the plateau. One side of the boundary was set at a point where they had found a clay smoking pipe. The pipe was interesting but not unusual. It could have been made by Indians well before Columbus set sail or by blacks during the time of Palmares, or sometime in between, or sometime well after. But still, it was something, and its undisturbed location indicated a good place to draw a line.

Architects came forward with plans for the memorial. Despite any evidence of how the buildings of Palmares had looked, architects wanted structures to be in some way authentic, and they wanted the structures in places that were either authentic or aesthetic or just practical. The governor of AlagoasAlagoas approved the final plan, not noting that the bathroom had been nudged over the boundary Allen had set. One end of the bathroom, in fact, was not far from where the pipe had been found. The governor had no right to approve the plan, but Allen wasn't tactless enough to try to get it unapproved. Sure enough, as workers began to dig the bathroom foundation, they found a burial urn. It had been clipped off by a bulldozer, but its bottom part was intact. Inside was a chunk of concrete. Either the inhabitants of Barriga knew the formula for cement or the context of the urn had been compromised. The former idea being virtually impossible, Allen concluded the latter. He already had plenty of pieces of out-of-context urn, but the presence of this one could indicate the presence of other artifacts nearby. He called a halt to construction of the bathroom until he and some students could excavate the area where the corner of the bathroom would go. Nothing would flush until Allen said it could flush.

Allen had heard suggestions that he dig first and most where he'd most likely find something integrally linked to the black community of Palmares–at the bottom of the cliff, for example, the one the 200 people fell over. Maybe there were still bones down there, or a ring or a button or something. But what would the findings tell him? At most (and this isn't very likely), that people really did fall over the cliff atcliff. But archaeology can never tell us *why*. Was it stampede, suicide, or murder? Did those people really prefer death over slavery? Or in panic did they take a wrong turn in the dark? Or did white men with guns and swords force them over the edge? The myth is more beautiful than the alternatives, Allen says. Why not just let it be? The same goes for the undocumented story that Zumbi knew Latin. These myths and questionable facts all put beautiful values–dignity, democracy, equality–on the pedestal of humanity's principles, and they make little difference in the study of how people lived in the past. Why not leave the myths alone, Allen says, and let archaeology sift through history's dustbin in search of simpler facts about human existence? If myths support the funding for archeology and the nobility of mankind, let them be.

The trench behind the bathroom turned up nothing. The Parque Memorial *Quilombo* dos Palmares now inhabits the plateau with reasonable representations of how people may have lived there before Domingos Jorge Velho arrived. The steep, palm-thatched domes of small houses look authentically African. Palm trees stand like flags. A platform at the edge of the plateau looks out over cane fields that stretch to the horizon.One can sit on a bench in the shade and think about it all while listening to recorded lectures about slavery, *capoeira*, and the African Orixá gods that are still worshipped in Brazil–Ogum (or Ogun), the warrior; Oxossi; the hunter; Omolú, the healer; Xangô, the judge. Though there is no physical or documentary evidence that Yorubá were worshipped at Palmares, a sign claims that beliefs in them sustained the beleaguered Palmarians.While one mulls the veracity of that sign, one can observe how nice and flat the bulldozer has made the land. A sign attests to the presence of Indians in the *quilombo*, though it refers to remains of buildings that are still visible on the site–a presence, if proven, that would certainly raise Scott Allen's eyebrows to a dangerous height. One can take a little walk to the Lago dos Negros, an algae-green pond that sustained Palmarians for a century. On one side there is a jumble of small boulders with deep scratches. People like to think that Palmarian warriors sharpened their weapons there. People also once liked to think that Zumbi had buried the treasurers of Palmares–gold and silver stolen from mills and farms–under the water of the pond. Wishful prospectors dug it all up, creating yet another archaeological nightmare, but found nothing.

Women still do laundry at the pond, squatting in the water in the shade of a broad, old *gameleira branca* (*ficus gamelleira*) with a dense canopy and roots that reach down from its lowest branches. Gameleiras are considered sacred, especially this one. It isn't old enough to have been around in 1694, but its mother may have been. The gameleira is an African tree now common in Brazil. How this one came to grow beside this pond is a matter of myth. The best or at least most beautiful guess is that an escaping slave wore an amulet with a gameleira seed from Africa. She planted it at the pond, and the tree has been there ever since. In fact, in a sense, it's mythically possible that it's the same tree because the gameleira starts its life as a parasite living off another tree. It typically sprouts in rotted leaves in the fork of another tree–perhaps its parent–and then sends roots to the ground. Little by little it overtakes the host tree and subsumes it–*becomes* it–as the ancestor fades into the soil.

That isn't just a myth. It's a metaphor. The gameleira that may have shaded Zumbi himself has disappeared, its molecules dissipated, but something has grown out of it. So, too, has Palmares disappeared, burned to the ground and wiped away by centuries of rain, rot, vegetation, and bulldozers. If anything remains, it hasn't been found. Maybe one of those eight cannonballs is still up there. Maybe under some undisturbed soil there's a smudge left by a Palmarian fence post. Maybe somebody scratched something unarguably African on a stone. But if we find anything, it probably won't tell us what most people would *really* like to know about Palmares.

It should be said that Palmares' and Zumbi's effect on Brazilian society is more through legend and myth than anything else. No technology or knowledge came out of it, no art, no music, no literature, nothing except certain values supported by myths. Whether the myths are based on truth or not, the effect of them, the *inspiration* of them, is all we've taken from Palmares.

In a sense, Palmares survives, or even prevails, in the way that the African cultures survive (and arguably prevail) in modern Brazilian culture. African musicAfrican music is the antecedent of *samba, bossa-nova, capoeira, axéaxé, maracatu, afoxé, batucada, batuque, lundu, choro,* and other kinds of music and dance popular today. African instruments–the *berimbau*, the *atabaque*, the *pandeiro*–are played in everything from *música popular* to opera. Foods once found only in the *senzala* (slave quarters) are now delicacies, one of which, the famous *feijoada* black bean stew, was made with the parts of the pig that slave owners considered undesirable. African-based religions–*candomblé* and *umbanda*–are still widely practiced, and every market has its kiosk selling soaps, incense, herbs, trinkets, candles, perfumes, and paraphernalia associated with mystical powers and a variety of gods, some of whom are disguised as Catholic saints.

And there are still places that consider themselves *quilombos*, and the politics surrounding them echo the struggle over Palmares.

From

Law of the Jungle: Environmental Anarchy and the Tenharim People of Amazonia

In the Beginning

A lot of people would like to know how Ivan Tenharim, chief of the Tenharim indigenous people in southwest Amazonia, died. He knew perfectly well how to handle a motorcycle, even in the mud of the Trans-Amazonian Highway. The things he'd bought in the rough-shod settlement known as 180 would not have thrown him off. The road was wide, the weather good, the traffic almost nil. But for some reason on a lonely stretch of the road, he lost control of his bike. His nephew found him unconscious, neck broken, head bashed in, gut swollen with internal bleeding, blood trickling from ears, nose and mouth. He survived a car ride 80 miles to the ferry across the Madeira River, then to the clinic in Humaitá, a regional town of some 45,000 people. From there he was taken to Porto Velho, the capital of the nearby state of Rondonia, where, on December 3, 2013, they pronounced him dead.

According to a Tenharim attorney, Ivan's family requested that, for cultural reasons, no autopsy be performed. If any was, it was not released. Police concluded that it was a fatal accident. But some people suspect something worse. The people of 180 are known as a brutish bunch. If their scrappy little settlement were on a map, the map would call the place Santo Antônio do Matupi, a district in the vast township of Manicoré, itself just barely on the map though it is larger than Connecticut, Rhode Island, and Massachusetts combined. The economy of 180 is based on clandestine sawmills, dirt-poor gold prospectors, and cattle ranchers squatting on federal land. Drugs and weapons come through from Bolivia on their way to urban Brazil. It's a Mecca of lawlessness for fugitives on the lam. Gunslingers are affordable. Murder can be contracted for under a hundred dollars, and many at 180 wouldn't mind seeing every last Tenharim dead or gone.

The story surrounding Ivan Tenharim's death is complex, and it relates to a complex life-and-death struggle going on across the interior of Brazil. Law is as tenuous as it was in the North American wild west frontier. Despite almost two centuries of progress elsewhere, indigenous people in the Brazilian Amazon face the very real likelihood of their physical and cultural extermination. The rainforest is being eradicated at an increasing rate. Rivers are being dammed into chains of lakes. Soil is giving way to sand. The regional economy, largely based on either the forest or the farms that have replaced it, is shaky if not, in time, doomed. Desertification threatens, and distant, drought-stricken cities to the south are wondering when Amazonia will send more rain. In a microcosmic sense, Ivan Tenharim was a focal point of all these problems, ground zero of a struggle in which many, many people will die–in riots and battle, on parched farms, on lonely stretches of road, in encampments of homeless families, in the myriad repercussions of cities suffering shortages of water.

* * *

It could be said that the struggle began in 1500, when thirteen ships out of Lisbon under the command of Pedro Cabral stumbled upon Brazil while trying to sail around Africa en route to India. A hundred and eighty years later, the first Catholic priests sailed eight hundred miles up the Amazon, then four hundred miles southwest up the mighty Madeira to the area of today's Humaitá. During the dry season, the river is a good half-mile wide there. During the rains of January and February, the width reaches several miles. Humaitá built up on the west side of the river where the land is high enough to avoid all but the worst floods.

* * *

The Tenharim arrived later, before they were given that name. Originally known as the Kagwahiva–the word apparently meant *us*–they lived well to the east of the Madeira, closer to the Tapajó, another major tributary of the Amazon. In the 18th century, as white society encroached, the Kagwahiva moved west to the area of the Marmelos and Maici rivers, tributaries of the Madeira. By the nineteenth century, the local Kagwahiva tribes were known as the Parintintim. By 1852, they were in conflict with whites. They formed three tribes–the Parintintim, the Jiahui, and the Tenharim. The three still speak Kagwahiva. The Tenharim settled in the general area where they live now, on or not far from the Marmelos.

The conflicts continued into the early twentieth century with the search for latex, the sap of the rubber trees. The trees, known as *seringueiras* in Portuguese, defied domestication, preferring to die rather than live on plantations. To thrive, they had to grow wild in the forest. Rubber-tappers had to hunt down the trees, slash them to collect the drippings, then dribble the sap over a spit above an open fire, gradually accumulating a ball of latex that was worth money–not to them, much, but to so-called rubber barons who became fabulously wealthy. The rubber-tappers themselves became fabulously short-lived. Following streams and trails into the forest, they suffered everything from snake bites to malaria. Alligators could be twice the length of a canoe, jaguars twice the weight of a man. And now and then an arrow of barbed bamboo flew out of the forest and killed somebody. And just as often a rubber-tapper shot an Indian because they wanted his women or just because he was there. But at least the rubber-tappers respected the forest, rarely clearing more than they needed to camp. They collected their sap and moved on, leaving a healthy tree behind.

In the 1950s, a trader came up the Marmelos River with a bunch of workers in a canoe. He dealt in forest products, not just latex but Brazil nuts and the sap of the *copaíba*tree, which was and still is used to make lacquers and varnish and is reputed to reduce tumors and infections. Some of his workers were Indians from other tribes, so he managed to befriend the Parintinim and marry the daughter of a chief. After she died, allegedly from a spell cast by a wife the adventurous trader had left behind, he married another of the chief's daughters. When the trader's son died, and he went back downstream. All he left behind was a deadly epidemic of influenza and a new name for the tribe: Tenharim or Tenharin, in either case a Portuguese spelling for a word the Indians had never written.

* * *

The bigger problem for the Tenharim, beginning in the 20th century, is the place where Ivan Tenharim died, the Trans-Amazonia Highway. In the early 1970s, Brazil's military government decided that the country had to start populating Amazonia–the vast river basin around the Amazon –before somebody else did. The rallying cry was *Integrar para não entregar*–integrate to not hand over –essentially *Use it or lose it*. It also wanted to give the impoverished, landless families of the drought-afflicted northeast Brazil a way to move west into the interior instead of south to cities already overburdened with slum-dwellers. "Land with no men for men with no land"was the official federal hype. The development project called for at least a few roads running through an area almost as large as the continental United States. The Trans-Amazonia was to reach west from the coastal state of Paraíba to the western edge of Amazonas state. Its official name was BR-230. From Paraíba the highway swung northwest toward the Amazon, then southwest to Humaitá, then northwest to the town of Benjamin Constant, where the headwaters of the Amazon –known in Brazil as the Solimõ–flow into Brazil from Peru. (The Solimões becomes the Amazon where the Rio Negro flows in at Manaus.)

Construction work was contracted to various companies. In the Tenharim area, it was a company called Paranapanema. Neither the government nor the company consulted with or warned the Tenharim or other indigenous communities that the road was coming through. No one asked where it might pass unobtrusively. In fact, despite the millions acres of Tenharim territory, the bulldozers pushed right past, and sometimes right through, most of the Tenharim villages. Cemeteries were plowed up and pushed aside, a traumatic sacrilege to a people who venerate ancestors and may take a year to complete funeral rites.

Tenharim men were enslaved, forced to work for nothing but food. They were given the most agonizing and dangerous labor, work that a bulldozer could not and white laborers would not perform–work in swamps, removing vegetation and moving mud. They often spent whole days waist-deep in swamp water, often dying of untreated snake and insect bites. Diseases that the Indians had never known –measles, hepatitis, yellow fever, influenza –decimated the population. Malaria spread. Women were kidnapped for days or weeks, then returned with sexually transmitted diseases. An oft-repeated phrase is still remembered by Indians and whites: "you want an Indian woman, you need to kill an Indian man." Children as young as eleven were put to work with domestic chores, such as cooking for workers. The Tenharim population withered from an estimated ten thousand to just two hundred.

The development that BR-230 brought seemed to the Tenharim more like destruction. It opened their land to a new kind of greed. Loggers took what they wanted. Ranchers burned off tracts to plant grass for pastures. Gold prospectors panned the streams and polluted them with mercury. Hunters and fisherman helped themselves to game and fish. The Paranaponema company probably used the federal funds to build another highway for itself. It happened to go from BR-230 to a deposit of cassiterite, the ore from which tin is extracted. There the company installed a mine, its profitability ensured by the new roads. Tenharim in a village nearby were told to move somewhere else, with no compensation offered. This side road became known as the *Rodovia do Estanho*, or Tin Highway. It, too, opened forest and stream to development and destruction. All these resources and activities were on federal land, but in the absence of law, invaders simply helped themselves to whatever they could carry away. The Tenharim could do nothing but avoid them. The Paranapanema mine is scheduled to be shut down soon, at which point its land will be converted to farmland. Paranapanema, however, is seeking government permission to open another cassiterite mine and build a small hydroelectric dam in the territory of the Waimiri-Atroari in Ipitinga, Amazonas. The mine would produce ore for about fifteen years and leave behind an open sore.

In 1985, after twenty years of torture, tyranny, theft, and the occasional massacre, the military government peacefully transferred power to the congress of Brazil, and in 1988, the nation ratified a new constitution. It recognized the special case of the nation's indigenous peoples and guaranteed them certain rights, including the right to their ancestral lands and the resources thereon. These lands were to be demarcated and registered within five years. Twenty-five years later, however, most tribes had yet to see their territory defined. The Tenharim were one of few peoples who did. Their reserve is on two plots, a total of nearly two and a half million acres, an area about twice the size of Rhode Island. One plot has no villages. On the other, all the villages are along the Trans-Amazonian between Humaitá and 180. Though proximity to the highway is an inconvenience and a danger, the Tenharim refuse to move. One reason is that the villages are near deposits of *terra preta*–"black earth," a fertile, anthropogenic soil made of charcoal, bone, manure, and other organic materials, a product of untold centuries of small-scale indigenous farming. But just as important as their manmade soil is the fact that they consider the land theirs. It always has been. If anything's going to move somewhere else, they say, it's the highway, not the villages that were there first.

The Tenharim land is mostly in the remote parts of the 12,769-square-mile township of Humaitá. The urbanized part of the town, perched above the Madeira River, has paved streets, electricity, and two traffic lights. The town has grown considerably in the last few years. The majority of the population is still on the low side of middle class. Of the 45,000 people, about a thousand are the Tenharim. In 2010, 2,136 families earned no more than minimum wage (at the time, R$510 per month, or about US$220), 616 families were earning less than half the minimum wage, and 2,599 were earning no more than twice the minimum wage. Until a few years ago, cars and even motorcycles were rare, and a bicycle was a sign of considerable disposable income. Today, motor vehicles are commonplace, and many of the bicycles are powered by battery. Thus the two traffic lights. A major wharf has been built on the Madeira, though it was so poorly planned that boats find it more convenient and secure to simply tie up to something on shore. A large number of stores, banks, restaurants, and hotels serve consumers. The economic improvement is attributed to Brazil's general economic growth, the Bolsa Familia program, which provides a stipend to poor families, and the opening of a branch of the Federal University of Amazonas, which has brought more educated and politically conscious people into town.

A common gripe throughout Brazil, and especially in Amazonia, is that land reserved for indigenous peoples seems to be "lot of land for a few Indians."In all, Brazil has just over five hundred indigenous lands, some 265 million acres, nothing less than twelve percent of Brazilian territory. In 2010, the total indigenous population was 896,000 with thirty-six percent living in urban areas. More than 517,000 lived on reservations of some kind; 379,000 did not. (In 2014, the total population of Brazil reached 200 million.) Indigenous peoples do indeed hold more land per capita, than other rural landowners, 135 hectares per Indian, 23.4 hectares per other rural landowner. That statistic does not include millions of hectares owned by the federal government but illegally claimed by *grileiros*, people who have laid claim to land by falsifying documents. In the case of the Tenharim, about two and a half million acres (about one million hectares) for about a thousand people can seem like a generous grant–roughly 2,500 acres per person. (If the original population of ten thousand were still there, it would be about 250 acres (100 hectares) per person. In other words, the per capita proportion seems high because white intervention reduced the population so much.) For one thing, the number of people living on the land is small because most of them have died due to white intervention.) But in Amazonia, farms of fifty thousand acres or more are not uncommon. The Maggi family, doing business as Grupo André Maggi, farms over half a million acres in the state of Mato Grosso. Cecílio do Rego Almeida claimed (without ever buying) almost fifteen million acres in the state of

Pará. In the state of Acre in 2001, Falb Saraiva de Farias had 31,784,547.5 acres registered in his name, an area larger than Portugal and Switzerland combined. In 2014, a plot of 2.28 million forested acres was for sale in the state of Amazonas. It is worth noting that a report issued by a special commission under the Ministry of the Environment estimated that twelve percent of the Brazilian territory, and *a full third* of the state of Amazonas, is occupied illegally.

An extremely large piece of land in private hands is known as a *latifúndio*. The phenomenon has existed throughout Latin America since the original Spanish and Portuguese land grants of early colonial days. *Latifundium* was considered a problem as far back as ancient Rome. In that *latifúdios* tend to concentrate power and wealth, they tend to be self-perpetuating. *Latifúndios* are associated with low productivity per hectare, low wages for agrarian workers, conditions analogous to slavery, low quality of life, little economic or capital development, little use of technology, lawlessness, corruption of government, and social instability.

Brazil's *Reforma Agrária* was supposed to reduce the presence and power of *latifúndios* redistributing land that was held by large landowners, unproductive land, and land illegally occupied. Unfortunately, redistribution has moved in the opposite direction despite twelve years of supposedly liberal presidents from the *Partido Trabalharista,*the Workers Party. During the four years of President Dilma Rousseff's first term— 2014–land held by large landowners expanded by six million hectares (15 million acres), an area three times larger than Brazil's smallest state, Sergipe. As of 2014, according to Brazil's *Sistema Nacional de Cadastramento Rural*, large landowners held a total of 244 million hectares (603 million acres). The 130,000 largest landowners –a number which does not include farmers claiming unregistered land, such as that third of all farmers in Amazonas –own

47.23 percent of rural land registered with INCRA. The 3.75 million smallest landowners own just 10.2 percent of registered land.

On a per capita basis on an Amazonian scale, therefore, the size of of the Tenharim territory is unexceptional, especially given its relative legitimacy, having been legally demarcated, not to mention occupied for centuries. But two issues make it exceptionally aggravating to many whites who live nearby, especially those in 180. One is the notion that the land was "given" to the Tenharim and other indigenous peoples. Anyone whose thinking has not been twisted into irrationality by self-interest can recognize the absurdity of that perspective. For another, the land was never "given" to the people who have been living there since, as one Tenharim chief put it, "the beginning." "Given to" would have to be equated with "taken away." But possession from before the time of money means that the Tenharim have never bought the land, which means that outside of their constitutional entitlement, they have no deed to it.

The other aggravating factor is the presence of natural resources. BR-230 gave loggers, farmers, and ranchers access to a long swath of Amazonia. Roads branched off the highway as loggers went after more trees. Seen from the air, the resulting pattern resembles fishbones of bare land. Between the proximity of the Madeira River, which can carry ocean-going freighters, and the Trans-Amazonia, the land around the Tenharim reserve was easy pickings. The forest around the reservation was soon cut down, sawed up, and shipped out. Ranchers burned off whatever was left and planted it with grass. The many saw mills at 180 became desperate for timber. They saw a fortune in the hands of a few people who were content with the slow yield of a living forest. So they went after it. They cut at the fringes, then bulldozed roads deeper into the Tenharim forest. They took what they wanted and left a wasteland behind. Trucks stacked with massive logs of hardwood rumbled past

Tenharim villages. The Tenharim reported it to federal authorities, but even though the crime was obvious, for many years the response was nil.

Under the same law that endows indigenous peoples with their ancestral land, the indigenous residents there are prohibited from harvesting their wood for commercial purposes. They are not allowed to clear land to plant marketable quantities of crops. They cannot mine their minerals. They are expected to live the lives of their indigenous ancestors, hunting and gathering, planting in small plots, exploiting the forest only in ways that don't kill it. Like any other Brazilians, they are legally prohibited from using violence to enforce the law, even in the absence of law enforcement. And if they tried to defend their land or its assets, however justifiably, they would fall under attack by the invaders and quite likely by the government as well. So the Tenharim, like Indians everywhere, are in a tough and untenable position. As roads, loggers, ranchers, miners, hunters, fishermen, and settlers encroach on their land, it becomes harder to find food and other forest products they need to survive. At the same time, they are prohibited from using their resources for revenues that they could use to buy food. Even complaining about it can get them in trouble, and that is exactly what happened shortly before Chief Ivan turned up dead.

Chapter II

Law of the Jungle

Law does not work very well in Brazil. Elected officials are notoriously corrupt and rarely punished. Courts are slow and inefficient. Law enforcement has a certain presence in urban areas, but it is often outmanned and outgunned by criminal gangs. In remote areas, which is to say in over half of the Brazilian territory, law enforcement is so sporadic as to be effectively nonexistent. Towns in Amazonia have police, but federal enforcement is at best called in only for emergencies. IBAMA, the federal environmental and wildlife management agency, is woefully unprepared for the task of monitoring the sprawling Brazilian outback. When IBAMA actually catches someone committing environmental crime, be it pollution, deforestation, the setting of forest fires, or the hunting of protected species, it can rarely muster the power needed to arrest people. If it does arrest people, the courts, often corruptible and easily influenced by elected officials, issue little or no punishment. Likewise, FUNAI, the federal Indian agency, is largely ineffective at actually protecting its charges. The local offices tend to be supportive, but when action requires federal enforcement or decisions in Brasilia, other interests trump concerns for people who have no money and few votes. Among FUNAI's responsibilities is the recognition and demarcation of indigenous lands, a function that has met paralytic political obstruction.

When loggers started invading Tenharim territory, the local FUNAI and IBAMA offices were unable to do much. They duly reported it to the powers above, the powers that could send in federal police, but nothing happened. One reason, certainly, was lack of funding or insufficient staff to oversee hundreds of indigenous lands throughout Brazil, most of them remote, each of them suffering similar problems. The lack of federal response could also be political pressure from a powerful caucus in Brasilia, the *ruralistas*. The *ruralistas* believe in supremacy of rural economic development, which is to say agribusiness, mining, and hydroelectric energy. They have no sympathy for indigenous people who are in the way. They see no use for a forest except to sell it and replace it with cattle or soy. They oppose the constitutional mandate that farms illegally occupying federal land should be divided up into family farms. They advocate giving federal land to whoever happens to claim it. They consider environmental concerns a farce that should be ignored in the pursuit of minerals and energy. They resist FUNAI'efforts to protect the indigenous.

The *ruralistas* have proposed an amendment or law opposing almost every one of the paragraphs in Articles 231 and 232 of Chapter VIII of the constitution of Brazil, the Chapter titled *Índios*. Article 231 recognizes indigenous social organization, customs, languages, beliefs, traditions, and rights. It also recognizes the land they have traditionally occupied, their rights to the resources thereon, including water as a source of potential energy, except by act of congress and then only with "consultation" of the affected peoples. It prohibits the removal of Indians from their land except in cases of catastrophe, epidemic, or threat to national sovereignty, and then only temporarily and only by act of congress. Article 232 recognizes indigenous persons, communities, and organizations as parties entitled to demand justice in defense of their rights and interests. Another article mandates demarcation of indigenous lands by 1993. Another allows the education of Indians in their traditional languages.

Two of the *ruralista* proposals to amend the constitution, known as PEC 215/2000 and PEC 38/99, would transfer responsibility for establishing indigenous lands from the executive branch, which oversees FUNAI, to the legislative branch, thus changing the demarcation process from an administrative function to a function subject to politics and legislation. Progress toward passage of the bill was stymied, at least temporarily, by an Indian invasion and occupation of the congressional hall in April of 2013. PEC 237/2013 proposes allowing agribusiness to negotiate with the federal government to receive permission to farm on Indian land. PLP 27/2012 would open Indian lands to mining, dams, pipelines, highways, railroads, airports, transmission lines, military training, and other uses that are determined to be in the national interest. PL 1610/96 would allow mining companies to exploit Indian land even if the Indians have expressly rejected the proposal. Portaria 303/12 requires more stringent conditions for the recognition of Indian land and would prevent the expansion of existing lands. Other proposals similar to these are in various stages in the two houses of congress.

The wording of PEC 215 narrowly–and perhaps only temporarily–escaped approval in late 2014. Congress was close to voting on the proposed text, but the session for the vote was postponed three times. The president of the house of representatives tried to schedule a last-minute session with little warning, but when word leaked out, sixty Pataxó invaded the building with bows, arrows, and clubs. They were stopped by police with tear gas, pepper spray, and riot gear. A police officer was hit in the foot with an arrow, and several Pataxó were arrested. The session was canceled, and PEC 215 was "archived." For a few weeks, indigenous people and their supporters hoped that "archived" meant "dead," but by February 2015, *ruralistas* were already resuscitating it. President Dilma Rousseff, after being narrowly reelected in October of 2014, appointed *ruralista* leader Kátia Abreu Minister of Agriculture. Known among environmentalists as "Miss Chainsaw," Abreu expressed support of PEC 215 as soon as she took office, saying "the Indians have come out of the forest and come down to the areas of production." An open letter from CIMI, signed by CIMI president Dom Erwin Kräutler, Bishop of the Xingu, decried the statement as so "out of place and disconnected from the reality of our country that it can only be the fruit of total ignorance and deep bad faith."

* * *

PEC 215 is hardly the first move to take land from indigenous peoples or prevent them from claiming land they are entitled to under the constitution. In 2013, President Rousseff decided, with dubious authority, to set aside the constitutional mandate that indigenous lands be demarcated and registered as protected areas by 1993. Under her predecessor, Luiz Inácio "Lula" da Silva, an average of ten indigenous lands were registered each year. Under his predecessor, Fernando Henrique Cardoso, eighteen per year were registered. In 2013, under Rousseff, only one was registered. These numbers are out of a total of 1,047 proposed or existing indigenous territories, only thirty-eight percent of which have been demarcated and registered. About thirty percent are in the process, and thirty-two percent have yet to begin the process. Of those in process, twenty-nine have no legal obstacles to finalization, yet they are not finalized. All they need are signatures by President Rousseff or Minister of Justice José Eduardo Cardozo. Five others are stopped on the desk of FUNAI president Maria Augusta Assirati.

Almost all of the registered lands are in Amazonas state. But according to the Brazilian 2010 census, 554,000 of the 896,000 Indians in Brazil live outside of Amazonas. For many of them, the lack of demarcation does not mean living on their own land while waiting for it to become officially theirs. It means camping in scrap-wood huts and tarp tents alongside highways beside land that is legally, or almost legally, theirs but is illegally occupied and used by non-indigenous farmers. The situation is similar to but crucially different from that of Brazil's many landless workers who camp beside land that belongs to the federal government but is illegally occupied by people who simply staked it out. That land is supposed to be divided among family farmers in accordance with the constitution's mandate for "reform." In the case of the Indians, the land was and always has been theirs, but they were forced off it by violence. Ultimately, they have a *historical* claim to it, while the landless have a *constitutional* claim.

The most ferocious struggle for indigenous rights has been in the state of Mato Grosso do Sul, far to the south of Amazonas, bordering Bolivia and Paraguay. The state is extensively planted with soy, corn, and sugar cane, and much of the land under FUNAI review has long been cultivated, not to mention bought and sold a few times. The threat to preserve the land is also a threat to the income of farmers who have been working the land for many years. The Terena and Guarani-Kaiowá peoples are camped along highways, where they suffer violence against which they have no defense. Some live on small reservations that allow barely one hectare (2.5 acres) per person, hardly enough to sustain a family that lives from the land. In 2013, just in Mato Grosso do Sul, indigenous people suffered thirty-three murders, sixteen attempted murders, fifty suicides, and ninety cases of infant mortality. In November, 2014, a group of Kaiowá–a young man and two young mothers with infants–were accosted by private "security" men on motorcycles. After a few minutes of terrorizing and threats, the men fired several bullets at the group, hitting the man and almost hitting the mothers. Similar incidents, often with more serious results, have happened all over Brazil.

The Conselho Indigenista Missionário (CIMI), organized by the Brazilian Conference of Bishops, is the only organization that accurately and honestly keeps track of crimes committed against indigenous peoples across Brazil. CIMI reports that murder of the Guarani is at one of the highest rates in the world. Brazil's rate itself is among the world's highest. In 2012 it was 25.8 per 100,000 people; the rate among the Guarani in that year was four times the national average, 34 out of 31,000 people. In Manaus, now a center of drug traffic coming out of Peru, Colombia, and Bolivia, the rate was 50.1 per 100,000 in 2012. (For comparison purposes, the rate in the United States is 4.7 per 100,000. In Canada, it's 1.6. In Mexico, it's 21.5. In UK it's 1.0.)

* * *

The bloodshed is by no means limited to Mato Grosso do Sul. In 2013, six Indians were killed in Roraima, four in Bahia, three in Tocantins, two in Pará, two in Paraná, and one each in Amazonas, Pernambuco, and Rio Grande do Sul. (The one in Amazonas was Ivan Tenharim.) There were also twenty-nine cases of attempted murder involving 328 victims in eleven states. In addition, nine Indians were killed by cars, seven of which did not stop to help. There were ten reported cases of death threats. Eight people were beaten, hit by rubber bullets, or injured by cars. Fifty-six people committed suicide, forty-one of them young men. Seventeen of the suicide victims were between the ages of thirteen and fifteen. Hanging has been the preferred method of exit. In Rio Branco, the capital of the state of Acre, the CIMI office was broken into, vandalized, and burglarized twice in 2014.

Three indigenous men were murdered in separate incidents in late April/early May, 2015. A Tupinambá known as Pinduca, an agent of the Indian Health agency, was ambushed when returning from a fishing trip with his family. He was shot dead. His wife was shot in the leg and back as she held her one-year-old son, but she survived. A teenage daughter escaped by fleeing into the woods. In Abaré, Bahia, a Gilmar Alves da Silva, a Tumbalalá, was run down on his motorcycle, then shot several times. The murder occurred on Tubalalá territory that had been declared a traditional indigenous area by FUNAI but was yet to be sanctioned as such. The murder was probably related to a regional conflict over a small dam that was being built which would disrupt indigenous farming. In Maranhão state, Eusébio Ka'apor, returning to his village on a motorcycle driven by another indigenous man, was shot in the back by men in a truck. The survivor identified the killers as timber cutters who were angry about Ka'apor actions to stop illegal cutting.

Nor is the bloodshed limited to indigenous people. According to Global Witness, an organization that investigates and campaigns to prevent natural resource-related conflict, corruption and associated abuses, in 2014 Brazil led the world in the number of land and environment activists murdered. Of the 29 deaths, four were indigenous people. (Worldwide, there were 116 killings in 17 countries–an average of over two per week. Forty percent of murdered activists were indigenous people. Honduras led in per capita killings.)

Many crimes and atrocities suffered by indigenous peoples are never reported, of course. They happen far from the law and the media, and the people are often isolated or misinformed to the point of not knowing that they live in a nation that exceeds the perimeter of their tribal territory. They do not know that at least in theory they are protected by a constitution and system of justice. But almost without exception they know that non-indigenous people are trouble. FUNAI has often let them down and rarely delivers on promises or obligations. CIMI is one of few organizations that they tend to trust.

CIMI doesn't promise much (or have much to promise), but it cares about and it advocates for indigenous peoples who are all but helpless in the face of "civilization." The Tenharim and Humaitá areas are within

CIMI's Rondônia region. The state of Rondônia is south of the state of Amazonas, bordering Bolivia. The Madeira River flows north out of Bolivia, through Porto Velho, the capital of Rondônia, and northward on to Humaitá and eventually to the Amazon. Sister Laura Vicuña Manso is coordinator of that region.

Sister Laura has the loving eyes, soft voice, and shy smile one would expect from a nun. But like activist sisters all over the world, she is also intelligent, well informed, politically astute, intensely focused on her mission, and unafraid to, say, take a canoe up Amazonian creeks for days at a time to reach indigenous communities within her fold. Her mission–CIMI's mission–is to promote human dignity, to strengthen the values, culture, and spirit of people who, if they are lucky, are barely noticed in the world. And when their luck runs out, as it is certainly doing very quickly, their land and resources fall under assault by outsiders. Much of CIMI's activities are focused on trying to persuade the government to obey the law.

CIMI's mission most explicitly does *not* include conversion to Christianity. In fact, Sister Laura thinks a lot of so-called Christians could learn a lot about Christian values from indigenous people who have spiritualities different from those of Christianity. They respect life in all its forms. They mourn the dead more intensely than most Catholics. They exercise their dominion over the earth with every intent of keeping it alive forever.

Laura has to work very slowly with these people. They rather wisely tend to distrust outsiders, but little by little she works her way into their favors. She learns something about their culture and a little of their languages. She eats their food and loves their children. She introduces them to such concepts as law, constitutionality, human rights, dignity, and the value of their culture in face of the bulldozer of the national and global cultures. She motivates them to defend themselves and their rights.

Outsider contact with these people, she says, almost always leads to dependence on outside technologies. Fifteen indigenous peoples in her region have yet to be contacted by non-indigenous people. These rare groups are known as "isolated peoples." Other peoples have only a tenuous grip on the modern conveniences. She knows of peoples that have managed to accumulate a few televisions, washing machines, and other high-tech devices, but they simply left all that behind and returned to their traditional lives. Others, such as the Tenharim, are more connected to outside cultures and technology, but they don't leave their traditional ways behind. With the help of their ancestors and CIMI's efforts, the Tenharim have learned the value of preserving their culture and the importance of actively defending their rights. But defending rights in Brazil can be very dangerous business. That, in fact, may have been among Chief Ivan Tenharim's last thoughts.

Chapter III

Catastrophe Under Construction

While Indians were being killed, beaten, robbed, threatened, run off their land, driven to suicide, and ignored by their government, the conversion of Amazonia to an economic engine picked up speed. After several years of a decreasing rate deforestation, in 2012 the rate shot up by twenty-nine percent. The rate was expected to increase in 2014. The rate in October 2014 was 467 percent higher than in October 2013. The increase could be attributed in part to a change in required forest reserves on private property that was pushed through by ruralistas.

As the forest is eliminated through logging and fires, it is generally replaced by cattle ranches and soy farms. The consequent widespread change in ecosystem in the north of Brazil is apparently impacting the climate in Amazonia and far to the south. The change was predicted in 2004, by Dr. Philip Fearnside, a scientist with the Instituto Nacional de Pesquisas de Amazônia (National Research Institute of Amazonia) and a member of the International Panel on Climate Change that shared a Nobel Prize with Al Gore. Fearnside predicted that deforestation would inevitably result in drought in the south and floods in the north. (He'd also been predicting global warming due to greenhouse gases since the early 1970s.) Ten years later, the Madeira River was eighty feet above normal at Humaitá, and the southeast of Brazil was suffering a drought that threatened the very viability of urban and agricultural life. Other scientists are now explaining that the drought is caused in part by a lack of moisture transpired to the atmosphere where the forest used to be. Huge volumes of moist air used to spill southward in "flying rivers" until it met cool air flowing up from Argentina. The collision produced the rains that fell on Brazil's largest cities–São Paulo, Rio de Janeiro, Belo Horizonte–and many others that make up the economic engine of Brazil.

The rainy season in that region is–or used to be–in the summer months between October and March. But in 2014, the rains were paltry. By the end of the year, São Paulo's main reservoir, Cantareira, was down to just 7.2 percent of capacity. January saw rainfall barely half the average for that month. By the end of the January, Cantareira was down to 5.1 percent of capacity. São Paulo and Rio de Janeiro were already arguing over the water of the Jaguari River, which Rio uses for energy and sewage dilution, while São Paulo, downstream from there, needs it to feed its Paraiba reservoir. Several cities were already rationing water. In Guarulhos, the location of São Paulo's main airport, some neighborhoods were receiving water only one day in three. In the first week of February, heavy rains exceeded average for the whole month. The downpours raised hopes, By April 22, the Cantareira reached 15.5 percent of capacity–slightly above the level on that date a year earlier–but rains were again below average for the month, and little more was expected until October.

Hydroelectric energy shortages also threatened. Reservoirs across the region were at one-fifth of capacity. In the deep south of Brazil, the five-mile-long Itaipu dam, once the biggest generator of energy in the world, cut production by eleven percent, losing its first-place position to China's Three Gorges dam.

Rainfall was down over most of Brazil. Thirty-six percent of the residences in the country suffered a lack of water at least once in January 2015.

Despite strong evidence that deforestation in Amazonia is causing the droughts, work continues on dams that not only flood existing forest but open new areas to the conversion of forest to farm. Nineteen new "dams"–hydroelectric installations of 30 megawatts or more–are planned for the next ten years in Amazonia. Hundreds of smaller dams are planned. The tributaries that flow into the Amazon east of the Madeira will become chains of reservoirs. If all the dams are actually built –in Brazil, plans are often no more than political pipe dreams –indigenous lands, which are invariably along rivers, will be almost entirely inundated. The reservoirs, deeper than the original rivers, will be able to handle barges, making agriculture in remote areas more cost effective. As a result, more forest will be removed, and Indian reservations and park preserves will come under financial and political pressure. More areas are being opened to transportation with the ongoing paving of BR-163, which reaches north from Rio Grande do Sul, Brazil's southernmost state, to Santaré, where the Tapajó meets the Amazon.

The dams are further evidence of poor planning and the flexibility of law in Brazil. Though federal law requires a rigorous approval process, it is often sidestepped, and the results of studies are often ignored. As a consequence, approved dam projects can be disastrous to local people, indigenous people, investors, and the environment. For example, 125 miles up the Madeira from Humaitá, two dams –Jirau and Santo Antô–are under construction and almost complete despite IBAMA's 221-page technical opinion opposing approval of the preliminary license, and 146-page opinion opposing approval of installation. The studies found that the Jirau dam is likely to cause flooding upstream in Bolivia. They also predict that the dams will cause year-round flooding of *várzea* floodplains, the ecology of which require seasonal flooding. Of the eight hundred species of fish that the studies found in the area, forty were new to science. The dams would prevent migration of certain species that are essential to the local economy. The slowing of waters was expected to cause mercury in the riverbed–a result of extensive gold-mining in the region–to methylate, becoming even more toxic than natural mercury. Despite these and several other problems, political appointees overruled the studies and approved the dams, creating a legal mess and bringing to question the validity of law and the wisdom of investment in Brazil.

Dams elsewhere have been condemned by studies but approved by legislators. The most controversial is the Belo Monte dam that is being built across the Xingu near the city of Altamira. FUNAI specified twenty-six "conditions" that would have to be met if the dam was to be approved. IBAMA specified forty. Few of the conditions were met before the license was approved and construction begun. The decision ignored the impact on nine indigenous peoples. The decision to proceed also ignored warnings that the dam would not produce enough electricity to pay for itself due to seasonal drops in river flow. During three to four months of the year, the turbines would be effectively turned off. In fact, the deforestation resulting from the dam and other projects may further decrease the amount of rainfall. The executive summary of a report issued by National Academy of Sciences of the United States in 2013 said:

When indirect effects were considered, deforestation of the Amazon region inhibited rainfall within the Xingu Basin, counterbalancing declines in [evapotranspiration] and decreasing discharge by 6%. Under business-as-usual projections of forest loss for 2050 (40%), simulated power generation declined to only 25% of maximum plant output and 60% of the industry's own projections. Like other energy sources, hydropower plants present large social and environmental costs. Their reliability as energy sources, however, must take into account their dependence on forests.

Monte Belo and other dams, in other words, may become victims of their own environmental consequences.

An analysis made in 2010 gave the Belo Monte dam an only 28 percent chance of profitability, based on a 2001 cost estimate of US$4 billion. The current estimate is closer to US$18 billion. In that work continues, it is feared that investors and the Brazilian government are secretly planning a series of dams upstream to ensure a constant, year-round flow of water through the Belo Monte turbines. The impact on rainfall, the environment, indigenous peoples, and other residents along the Xingu would be all the more devastating.

The Munduruku, an exceptionally politically activist tribe of 11,600, is threatened by Belo Monte and two dams dams on the Tapajós: the Jatobáand the São Luiz do Tapajós. The tribe has been exceptionally proactive in defending its land and rights. In 2014, a brigade of warriors forced several miners to leave tribal land and confiscated several dredges. In 2013, the tribe took three biologists hostage after they were found on tribal land, where they were researching the environmental impact of the Jatobádam for the Eletrobras company. In that same period, a 170 Munduruku invaded the Monte Belo project and set up camp to protest.

The two dams on the Tapajós–a long and beautiful tributary of the Amazon–threaten to swamp the 178,000-hectare (440,000-acre) Sawré-Muybu territory that has been claimed and populated by the Mundurku for many years. After twelve years of field studies, FUNAI completed a report confirming the area as historically inhabited by the Munduruku. The report justifies and mandates demarcation and preservation of the land. The Rousseff administration, however, has refused to release the report to the public. In November of 2014, a judge ordered the report to be released. Legally, if FUNAI has determined the land to belong to the Munduruku, it must be demarcated. If demarcated, it would preclude the possibility of inundation by a dam reservoir. No longer waiting for federal demarcation, the Munduruku have decided to demarcate it themselves.

Not far away, on the Rio Teles Pires, a tributary of the Tapajós, a planned dam, the São Manoel, threatens to swamp lands of the Munduruku, Apiaká, Kayabi, and peoples in "isolation." The Kayabi land, just a kilometer from the dam, would be worst hit. The legal contortions around approval of the dam illustrate the questionability of Brazilian law. Federal judges have blocked or suspended the license for the dam five times. On November 12, a judge halted the licensing process because the affected indigenous communities had not been properly consulted. Nonetheless, a week later IBAMA approved the license, invoking a federal privilege that was instituted during the 1964-1985 military dictatorship. In December, another judge suspended the license because over half of the preconditions, such as consultations with local populations, environmental impact statements, and monitoring programs had not been met. This fifth suspension was by no means the end of the issue.

* * *

Dams in Amazonia are part of Brazil's new "industry." This industry is based on the Clean Development Mechanism that allows developed nations to fund clean-energy projects in developing nations in return for credits that can be used to meet Kyoto Protocol targets. Dams in Amazonia would seem to be ideal clean-energy projects. Unfortunately, not to mention ironically, many of the planned and existing dams end up contributing to rather than replacing the production of greenhouse gases. Depending on the velocity of the flow of the river to and through the dam, some dams trap vegetation in a deep, stagnant layer of water where there is little dissolved oxygen. This includes grasses that grow in *várzeas* during low water and then are submerged when reservoirs fill. Under the anaerobic conditions in warm, tropical water, the carbon released in decomposition combines with hydrogen rather than with oxygen, producing methane (CH4) rather than carbon dioxide (CO2). A ton of methane has at least twenty times more, perhaps as much as thirty-four times more impact on global warming than a ton of carbon dioxide. An egregious example of environmental counter-productivity is the Balbina dam on the Uatumã river. The Balbina generates relatively little energy and relatively more methane, ultimately producing more greenhouse effect than a fossil fuel plant of equal productivity.

But the problem isn't the production of methane as much as the carbon credits that Brazil will be able to sell to other nations under the Kyoto Protocol. Power plants in other countries can buy the carbon credits and thus be allowed to burn more fossil fuels. So the dams end up producing methane while enabling the production of more greenhouse gases elsewhere.

The dams of Amazonia effectively export economic benefit while importing environmental, economic, and social liabilities. The electricity goes elsewhere. Humaitá and other towns along the Madeira, for example, though not far from the Jirau and Santo Antôo dams, have to burn oil brought in from the coast by barge, to generate their electricity. Likewise, the profits (if any) from the dams flow to distant corporations, none of them contributing much if anything to the economy in the regions of the dams. In fact many of those corporations are in other countries. Their investors are all over the world, all quite unaware of the source and true cost of their dividends. Those costs include not only the greenhouse gases and unjustifiable carbon credits but the damage of floods, the forced migrations, the disruption of local economies, the impact on fishing, and the swamped land, all of which all stay in the area of the dams, far from the energy and the dividends.

The Tenharim will be impacted by a dam planned for the Machado River, a tributary of the Madeira. With a margin of error of twenty percent, the reservoir of the Tabajara dam is expected to swamp areas within eight hundred meters of Tenharim land. It will inevitably impact the local ecosystem. At a meeting of several indigenous peoples in the area just a week before Ivan Tenharim was to die, the Tenharim and others declared war on the dam. Ivanildo Tenharim, who represents indigenous peoples at town hall in Humaitá, said that it would bring problems without benefits for his people. In late 2014, the impact of the dam was still being studied, but investors were ready to back the project, and construction was expected to start in 2015.

Mining is also expanding in Amazônia. Several bauxite, iron ore, and nickel mines are planned, a total investment estimated at US$24 billion. Much of the electricity from the new dams will be dedicated to smelting the bauxite. The mines will destroy forest, of course, but wider destruction will result from the roads and railroads to the mines as they open new areas to farming.

If anything can be uglier and more dangerous than dams and mines, more devastating than gold, it's oil. Brazil's national oil company, Petrobras, has been exploring Amazonia for many decades, and it continues to find new reserves. In 2012, the company discovered high-quality light oil in the Solimões basin in Amazonas. In 2014 it began exploring in western Amazonas in the Javari valley. Javari is home to several tribes that have had little or no contact with outsiders. Despite the constitutional requirement that indigenous people be consulted before any kind of development on their land, Petrobras moved fifteen barges of generators, piping, and mining equipment to land nearby. Brazil's national oil agency said that it had not authorized any exploration in the area.

The highways, dams, *ruralistas*, oil, mines, farms, fires, and general lawlessness pretty much doom the Amazonian rainforest. It's hard to imagine what kind of force would counteract the tremendous economic and political pressure that is already being put on land that is reserved for indigenous use, that is, land that's supposed to be preserved as forest. The grand economic scheme shows every indication of moving forward regardless of who or what might be in the way. If corporations want to build dams where they are legally prohibited, they will find a way to do it. If ranchers want to burn off thousands of acres of forest, no one will put the fire out. If loggers need Tenharim trees, they will come take them. And if a Tenharim chief happens to be alone on a motorcycle on an empty stretch of the Trans-Amazonia, there is nothing to prevent his elimination.

From

Bangs & Whimpers: The Ends of the Earth and Other Catastrophes

Global Warming

Will global warming be the end of the world or just a major reduction of Earth's population?

Good question. And no answer.

Scientists agree that the situation is going to get bleak. If the temperature rises by 2oC by the end of the 21st century, the situation will be merely "dangerous." A lot of people will die, especially in the less developed nations. A lot more people will have to adapt to droughts, storms, flooding, desertification, and higher sea levels. A lot of species are going to die.

Predicting climate change based on global warming is too complicated to draw accurate conclusions. How much greenhouse gas will be produced? How much will warming affect polar ice, the disappearance of which will affect the warming trend? How much, and when, will melting permafrost release methane from the tundra? How will warming affect ocean currents, and how will changes in currents affect climate? What will be the effects on civilization, and how will those effects affect climate change? Though predictions are not accurate, none of the predictions foresee improvement. The question is how serious the change will be. The answer comes down to probability.

Two university researchers assessed great amounts of existing climate and emissions data and calculated the probability of "catastrophic" climate change. Catastrophe will occur, they said, if the global temperature rises by 3oC. At 4o C, 74 percent of the world's population would be exposed to "deadly heat," and would need air conditioning to survive–a protective measure that would contribute to further warming by burning more fuel.

They calculated a 50-50 probability that temperatures will rise by 2.4o-2.6oC by 2050 and 4.1-5oC by 2100.

Five degrees is well within the scope of possibility, but there has been little research into what will happen under those conditions. The researchers therefore suggested a new category of disaster which they term only "unknown," that is, something beyond merely catastrophic. It's hard to know because the Earth hasn't been that hot since at least 20 million years ago. One possible consequence would be an end to life as we know it.

What are the odds of a 5oC rise in temperature? The researchers figured five percent by the end of the century. That's a one-in-20 chance. To put those odds in perspective, they posed a rhetorical question: Would you put your children or grandchildren on a plane that had a one-in-20 chance of crashing?

Because that's what we're doing.

Another Problem with Carbon Dioxide

Carbon dioxide (CO2) has received plenty of publicity as an agent causing global warming. Indeed, that is probably the most likely cause of the extinction of the human species. But rising levels of CO2 may cause yet another life-threatening problem: CO2 toxicity.

Human beings have always inhaled carbon dioxide. It's a natural part of our atmosphere, not to mention a waste product we exhale every couple of seconds during every living moment except, of course, the last. As a component of the air mixture we breathe, its concentration has been steadily increasing since 1820 and soaring since 1960. It used to be 300 parts per million. Now it's nearly 400.

Humans can tolerate something like 5,000 ppm for a day or so. But over a slightly longer term, just 600 ppm can lead to carbon dioxide toxicity. Among the symptoms of carbon dioxide toxicity are kidney failure, brain atrophy, cancer, neurological disorders and loss of brain function. This rarely occurs because people don't often go long periods without any fresh air at all.

What is not known, however, is the effect of constant, long-term, low doses–doses we can expect to be breathing within the lifetime of people alive today. Some models of atmospheric CO2 prediction forecast a level of 1,000 ppm within a hundred years.

There have been no studies on long-term low-dose exposure to carbon dioxide. No one knows what would happen if the entire human race were breathing 600 ppm during their entire lifetimes, all of them suffering some degree of mental impairment, starting at birth, or, indirectly, before birth. Just when people would need to be thinking clearly in a global emergency, they would be least able to do so. At the same time, they might be suffering a number of physiological ailments.

This would be happening all over the planet. Granted, some people–no doubt a tiny minority–would have access to an oxygen supply, but what about the vast majority who make civilization a viable operation? Could they be productive (and reproductive) elements of society if suffering constant dizziness, confusion, cognitive impairment, headaches, shortness of breath, and fatigue, dying young of kidney failure or cancer while, we must remember, the atmosphere is growing hotter, the sea rising, storms inflicting more damage, and climate changes causing droughts, floods, and forest fires, sending hordes of refugees to safer places?

Nobody knows.

The Monster from the Cold, Dark Swamp

For the 10,000 years prior to the Industrial Revolution, Earth's atmosphere had about 280 parts of carbon dioxide per million parts of atmosphere. Scientists figure that 350 ppm is considered the highest "safe" level for Earth's ecosystems to continue without adapting. Climatologists warned that if it ever reached 400 ppm, we would be passing a threshold indicating that we had moved way too far in the wrong direction. If it reaches 450 ppm, scientists warn, we stand only a 50-50 chance of keeping the global fever to 20C above pre-industrial levels. At that temperature, certain biological and geophysical processes would begin a lethal spiral of uncontrollable factors that cause planetary heating.

In February of 2018, the level reached 408.35, higher than it's been for 16 million years. By April 3, it was at 409.64. At the current rate of growth, it will reach 500 ppm within 50 years.

Unfortunately–*terrifyingly*–a lot more greenhouse gas is on the verge of surging into the air. It isn't the exhaust from cars and power plants. It's the methane trapped in the permafrost soil–that is, permanently frozen soil– of the Arctic. The permafrost contains more than twice as much carbon as is floating in the atmosphere today. If the permafrost thaws into a swamp, that carbon will be released as methane, a gas that is 84 times as powerful a greenhouse gas as carbon dioxide.

The permafrost is going to melt. Of this there is little doubt. It is part of a downward spiral known as positive feedback. Positive feedback means that a change in something causes more change in that something. In this case, it will be Earth's warming climate causing an increase in the cause of the warming.

The current effects of global warming are causing the melting of Arctic ice. The less ice, the less white. The less white, the less of the sun's light and heat are reflected back into space. The dark of the Arctic waters absorbs more heat, causing more ice to melt.

And on it goes until the permafrost, too, starts to melt, releasing methane, which causes temperatures to rise more, melting more ice and permafrost.

Meanwhile, the rising temperatures cause more evaporation, causing more cloud cover, which traps heat, worsening the other factors and itself. The higher heat causes forests to burn or die, quickly eliminating one of few effective means of removing CO2 from the atmosphere. Fewer trees means less shade, which means more solar heat absorbed, which means more ice melting, more permafrost thawing, more methane released. And as the dead trees fot, they release their carbon in the form of CO2.

Once this starts–and arguably, it already has–there is no going back. The absolute (and impossible) cessation of all fossil fuels combustion will not stop Earth from heating itself to the point of eradicating most forms of life.

Which is what happened 252 million years ago. Carbon dioxide and methane released from permafrost raised the planet's temperature by five degrees Celsius, killing 97 percent of all life on Earth. But that was then. This is now: We are adding carbon to the atmosphere at ten times the rate that occurred back then. And that rate is accelerating.

The trick–mankind's only hope–is to stop burning fossil fuels before Earth reaches the "tipping point" where the feedback starts.

Earthlings are apparently not willing to radically reverse the production of carbon dioxide. Some efforts are being made, but they are far from adequate. There is virtually no chance that the Earth will avoid the tipping point that sets off positive climate feedback. This is the way the world will end, and people alive today may well have the painful privilege of witnessing the beginning of the spiral to extinction.

Know Your Tipping Points

You can tip a bucket of water without spilling anything. You can always tip it back to level. You can tip it to the point where the bucket balances at an angle, and you can still tip it back. But if you tip it a bit more, the water takes over the tipping process. The tipping causes tipping. The bucket dumps. Good luck putting the water back into a tipped bucket.

In climate change, rising temperatures can push various geological and biological systems to a point where they tip into a self-generated destructive process. Destroying the vast Amazon forest, for example, is a linear destruction. If you cut 1,000 acres, 1,000 acres are gone. But if the forest around it survives, and the cut area can grow back. But when enough acreage is cut, the lack of trees reduces rainfall, which in turn reduces more forest, which causes less rain. That's the tipping point. After that, human-generated rises in temperature are not the driving force. The forest itself–its disappearance–drives the disappearance.

Earth has several climate-related tipping points. As temperatures rise, these earthly buckets tip. Scientific evidence indicates that tipping points can be triggered by a temperature rise of just two degrees Celsius above pre-industrial levels. Each tipping point will cause other systems to tip, a cascading effect that will almost certainly lead to the extinction of humankind.

A rise of 1-2 degrees Celsius could be enough to start the tip. For three years in a row (2014-2016), the planetary temperature was up by about one degree, reaching the highest since the last Ice Age. The moment of the tipping point will not be obvious, but that does not mean it didn't happen.

Here are some of the places that could tip, each causing other systems to tip.

Western Antarctic Ice Shelf (WAIS): As it melts, sea levels will rise by 25 feet or so. If it melts completely, the disappearance of its reflective white coat will reduce reflection of solar heat. Higher temperatures could melt the entire Antarctic ice sheet, raising sea levels by 180 feet. The WAIS over the sea has already begun to melt from warm water below.

Arctic Winter Sea Ice: As the planet nears the six degree temperature increase, Arctic sea ice will remain melted even in winter, causing a drastic decrease in reflected solar heat and ocean salinity.

Greenland Glaciers: These are already melting at a great rate. As their disappearance exposes darker land, melting will accelerate. As cold fresh water and icebergs enter the sea, levels will rise, currents will shift, and local climates will change.

Antarctic Bottom Water Formations: Antarctic bottom water is the densest water in the world. Its formation by cold water sinking along the coast of Antarctica is a major driver of the thermohaline circulation of the oceans. The melting of Antarctic glaciers slows that formation, thus weakening global seawater circulation and, in the long term, changing climate patterns all over the world.

El Niño-Southern Oscillation: The El Niño phenomenon is a temporary, recurring warming of global surface temperatures. La Niña is a temporary, recurring cooling. The former tends to happen more frequently, and over the last several decades, the El Niño temperatures have risen more. The increased frequency and extreme of warming may increase more frequent and extreme warming, affecting climate and weather all over the world.

East Antarctic Ice Sheet: It will start melting as temperatures reach the 3.8 Celsius level following rises caused by other tipping points. There will be no possibility of preventing submersion of all sea coast cities.

Thermohaline Circulation: This is global ocean water circulation as affected by water density. That density is affected by salinity and temperature. As air temperatures rise, more rainwater and glacial melt flow into the ocean, decreasing salinity. Warmer waters flowing toward the Arctic, e.g., the Gulf Stream, cause increased rain over Arctic ice, melting it. Circulation in the Atlantic seems to be slowing and could theoretically stop, causing severe and abrupt changes in weather and disruption of ecosystems in North America and Europe.

Arctic Summer Sea Ice: The melting is increasing each year. This does not affect sea levels, but it causes more absorption of solar heat in the area once there was ice.

Alpine Glaciers: Already melting at a great rate. Their gradual disappearance will accelerate the retreat.

Coral Reefs: A variety of human activities, from dredging to tourism, are killing coral at an increasing rate. Warming ocean water is a huge threat. As the seas absorb more CO2, they become more acidic, causing coral skeletons to weaken. An increasing El Niño phenomenon is raising water temperatures, to the detriment of coral. Rising temperatures also cause lethal coral bleaching. Rising sea levels reduce coral organism photosynthesis by reducing the sunlight that reaches them. Changing temperatures also change fish migration, with ecosystem impact on coral life forms. By the 2030s, 90 percent of coral reefs will be at risk.

Amazon Rainforest: It is still being destroyed, replaced with grassland and soy fields. The tipping point might be just under a four-degree rise in temperature. Less forest means less transpiration of water through leaves, causing drought in distant regions. Springs and streams will dry up. Soil will bake hard. The forest will not grow back.

Boreal Forest: Longer summers are killing the boreal forests, i.e., the taiga of northern latitudes. The forests are converting into grasslands and temperate forests, disrupting ecosystems and, consequently, climate.

Permafrost: The perpetually frozen ground of Siberia holds a huge amount of methane, a powerful greenhouse gas. As the permafrost melts at a temperature rise of about 1.5 degrees Celsius above current levels, the methane will be released (and more will be created), causing an increase in the rate of global warming.

Indian Monsoon Instability: Monsoon rains are created by the temperature differential between land and sea. Rapidly rising temperatures in the Indian Ocean caused a drop in inland rainfall, though possibly rising land temperatures may be having an opposite effect. As temperatures rise, variability in rainfall increases. At the same time, deforestation reduces evaporation and thus less rain.

Sahel: The area to the south of the Sahara is especially vulnerable to climate change. As the region nears the four degree increase, its ecosystem may collapse, causing further climate change. The Sahara will spread to the south. Nothing will grow in its sands.

Someday This Will Happen

One of the most probable threats that nature can throw at us is that of the "supervolcano." The massive eruptions have occurred a few times during the Earth's existence, at least once, some 250 million years ago, very nearly extinguishing all life on the planet. There were no humans (or even mammals) alive at the time, but next time, there may well be. Could they survive on a planet devoid of plants and animals? Not for long, not the centuries or millennia that a supervolcano can spew smoke, ash, and lava into the air and across the land.

The power of supervolcanoes is classified by the Volcanic Explosivity Index. The largest are classified as VEI 7 or 8. Some 60 VEI 8 supervolcanoes are known to have erupted since the Earth formed. Four VEI 7 eruptions have occurred in the past 2,000 years, nine others in the past 100,000 years.

Supervolcanoes will occur again. A big one is in process under Yellowstone National Park. It has exploded three times in the last 2.1 million years. The first was one of the five largest explosions ever to take place on the planet. So much material got blown into the air that the remaining depression, or caldera, was 60 miles across. Just 640,000 years ago, an explosion threw 240 cubic miles of rock, dust and ash into the sky.

It may happen again. Thick, sticky magma is building up not far below the surface. The ground above is already bulging, rising 10 inches over the last decade. From 2004-2008 it was rising three inches a year. Now the rate is slowing. No one can predict when or whether it will blow except to say it won't happen in the immediate future. It will be preceded by earthquakes.

If it erupts, its effects will be global and quite possibly very serious and long-lasting. With a little luck, however, rather than erupt in a massive explosion, it will gradually leak lava to the surface, possibly spreading a few hundred feet every day for several years, burying a vast region but not darkening the planet for years.

You can monitor volcanic activity in the United States at https://volcanoes.usgs.gov/vhp/updates.html. Keep your eye on Yellowstone.

Asteroids

An asteroid is one of few threats that really could effect the end of the world. A small one–less than 165 feet wide–would be a major inconvenience, resulting in the destruction of a city and a global collapse of agriculture, but some people–maybe even enough to constitute a civilization–would survive. A bigger one–say, more than 3,000 feet wide–would pound the whole planet with enough acid rain to destroy all crops, shroud the whole planet in sun-blocking debris, touch off tsunamis, earthquakes, and volcanoes, and consume a lot of oxygen in vast firestorms.

Smaller ones hit Earth every 100 years or so, the larger ones maybe once in 100,000. NASA knows of 900 large ones that cross Earth's orbit. The agency estimates there are 100 more out there somewhere. None are projected to collide with our pretty blue rock, but projections can't see very far into the future. On the brighter side, the larger they are, the sooner we'll see them coming.

On February 6 and 9 of 2018 two small asteroids passed less than one lunar distance from Earth. They had been spotted on February 4. The second, estimated to be 50 and 130 feet wide, was an astronomical close miss at just 39,000 miles away, less than a fifth of the distance to the moon. A NASA manager said that asteroids of that size rarely pass close to the planet, "maybe only one or twice a year."

February 4, 2018, was the same day that a rock a third of a mile wide and three quarters of a mile long passed within ten lunar orbits. NASA said it has known that particular chunk, known as 2002 AJ129, for a long time and has its orbit calculated for the next 100 years. We're safe from that one for a good while.

Comets

Comets have hit Earth before. It would seem the probability is infinitesimal, with the planet circling through a vast amount of space and the comet hurtling on a predestined course from the other side of the solar system. Of course gravity plays a little part, drawing the two heavenly bodies toward each other, but the gravity of the sun and the velocity of the comet are much more powerful factors than Earth's gravitational pull.

On the other hand, there's dumb luck. Over the course of eons, collisions are likely to occur. Earth has been lucky for – years. How long can that luck hold out?

Though they may be several miles in diameter, comets are hard to spot. Until they get within 400 million miles of the sun, they are black balls of ice against the black background of the universe. But as the ice approaches the sun, it releases gases, creating a bright tail that is visible from Earth. Once it's spotted, astrophysicists can calculate its projected path. We might have ten years to know that we're doomed. Or we might have no more than a few months.

Comets are less common than asteroids but more dangerous for two reasons. They can be much larger, perhaps 60 miles in diameter, and they are going much faster, a good 100,000 km per hour.

It is not known whether the object that created the Chicxulub crater on Mexico's Yucatán Peninsula 66 million years ago was a comet or asteroid. Whatever it was, it was probably a little under 10 miles in diameter. It pushed up a megatsunami that was only about a hundred yards tall because of the shallow waters of the Caribbean. Had it hit the ocean, the wave could have been almost three miles tall. The impact blasted material out of the atmosphere. When the material returned to Earth, flaming like meteors, it touched off fires all over the world. The impact also created global earthquakes and volcanoes. The particles in the air blocked the sun for a decade or more, cooling the planet and preventing photosynthesis. At the same time, the shock turned carbonate rock into carbon dioxide, leading to a greenhouse effect warming of the planet. It was a tough time to be alive. Three-quarters of the species on Earth, including all non-avian dinosaurs, were rendered extinct.

Would the human species survive such a cataclysmic event? Maybe a few if they survived the various initial shocks, had a ten-year food supply, a stock of seeds they could plant when the air cleared, and their human ingenuity allowed them to adapt to a radical climate change and the permanent disappearance of almost all life forms they had known before.

In 2014, there were 5,253 known comets, a number that continually increases as previously unknown comets arrive from out of the distant dark. Millions more are estimated to exist in the outer solar system. About one per year passes close enough to be seen by the naked eye, but for all of human history, they've been many millions of miles away.

Existential Dodgeball

Asteroids are rarely a problem for Earth, but when they are a problem, they are a huge problem–really the biggest problem imaginable. Can such a problem be avoided or mitigated? Is mankind capable of finding dark rocks in distant space and then move them? Asteroids are but specks in an infinite sky, but the ones big enough to end life on Earth would be terribly difficult, if not impossible, to move. No one has ever tried.

We can spot trouble coming a few months ahead of time. But to prepare a space mission to do something about it would take nothing less than four years–assuming these plans and rocket designs were already on paper, which they aren't. To give us a head start, a private organization, the B612 Foundation, started raising funds for a telescope that would be put into solar orbit to locate 90 percent of potential Near Earth Objects (NEOs). It was to be launched by 2016, but in 2015, NASA terminated its cooperative agreement with B612, and the project was abandoned.

Scientists cannot agree on the best strategy for avoiding asteroidal impact. One bunch recommends destruction of the NEO with either a bomb or a direct impact with something hard. Trouble is, destruction would be only partial, turning a large bullet into a large mass of buckshot. If any fragments are larger than 35 meters, they will not burn up in the atmosphere. They will have to be located and dealt with on a subsequent mission. Or missions. If there's time.

The other strategy is to deflect the asteroid or slow its orbit. This could be effected by a nuclear explosion if the asteroid isn't too large. To deflect the closest known NEO, an asteroid known as Apophis, which may be a pile of rubble or a semi-solid rock 30 meters wide, six 1.2 megaton nuclear bombs detonated in as many hours might do the trick. The rocket would need to be launched in the early 2020s to reach the target in time to prevent a slightly possible 2029 impact.

One proposal for destroying the asteroid is to hit it with at least two Hypervelocity Asteroid Intercept Vehicles (HAIVs). The first would create a crater that would allow the second to deeply penetrate the heavenly body. A Danish organization is trying to use crowd-funding to raise money to build a couple of HAIVs.

The National Nuclear Security Administration says it has some "canned subassemblies" of the nine-megaton B53 nuclear device, the largest explosive in the American arsenal. But assembly and deployment has been delayed due to concerns that it could be used as a weapon.

A more bizarre but theoretically viable plan: build a system of gigantic lenses in space to focus solar energy on the asteroid. The energy might vaporize the surface of the rock, which would thrust the thing in another direction or at least slow it down. A powerful laser beam might work, too.

Or: a gravity tractor–any large, heavy mass that could use its gravity to pull the asteroid off its trajectory over the course of many years. This would work on rubble as well as solid rock.

Or: tie a rocket–a really, really big rocket–to the thing and tow it somewhere.

Or (this is a good one): deploy a huge, hollow coil of wire in the asteroid's orbital path and charge it with electricity. When the asteroid, which usually contains a lot of iron, enters the electromagnetic field of the coil, it will shoot out the other side, and...*adios asteroid.*

Pre-Apocalyptic Collapse

If humanity knows of an imminent collision with a comet or large asteroid, society would probably begin to collapse immediately. The first people to know–probably NASA scientists and their friends, or maybe their colleagues in another country–would waste no time trying to prepare for the inevitable. They would inform their government, and the news would not remain secret for long. A government may make an announcement, confirming or denying the threat. Another government might do the opposite.

Society will quickly move from shock to desperate measures. With (let's say) weeks or months to live, no one is going to their jobs. Every company and government office will be effectively closed or dysfunctional. Trucks and deliveries will stop. Food supplies will quickly disappear from shelves. Infrastructure–power plants, dams, oil and gas lines, sewers, water systems, oil rigs, electrical systems–will hold up only as long as they can run on automatic and without maintenance. Cell phone service and the internet might work until power supplies fail. No news via television, radio, or internet, so everyone will make decisions based on local rumors.

Money and gold will lose all value. Orderly economic exchanges will give way to violent exchanges–chaotic looting perhaps followed by ad hoc gang-organized warfare. Police will not be available, and military order will break down as soon as the first officers abandon their posts. Hospitals and nursing homes will be vacated by staff with patients left to fend for themselves, many soon becoming cadavers. Fires will burn out of control. As buildings collapse, water mains and gas lines break, causing more collapse. Ships and barges will drift without crews, eventually wrecking and spilling their contents. People trying to evacuate by car will find themselves in permanent traffic jams.

Dead bodies will rot in the streets. The religious may flock to churches to apply the power of prayer. Drug addicts and alcoholics will become increasing desperate and violent. Families will try to dig shelters, but in a few weeks they will need to kill for food. Defense of the home against desperate hordes will be impossible. Nobody will have enough bullets, and everybody needs to sleep.

In other words, society would nearly extinguish itself before the comet or asteroid arrived. It might even do so based on nothing more than a rumor of a supposed collision. Since anarchy will not make anything easier, governments will probably try to keep the cosmic doom a secret. They will deny the rumors. A lot of people will refuse to believe the denials, seeing them as inevitable whether there's a collision coming or not. A rumor could prove more catastrophic than the actual comet, if any.

Solar Flares

Our Sun has been casting its life-giving rays in our direction since the first days of anything discernible as a planet. Every once in a while it burps up a solar flare–a flash of a few seconds that ejects electrons, ions, atoms, and electromagnetic waves into outer space. They travel in a somewhat tightly focused direction, possibly but not necessarily toward Earth.

Even relatively weak flares can create a radiation hazard to astronauts in space. They can disable satellites, mess up radio transmissions, knock out whole power grids, and light up the skies with auroras borealis and australis.

Solar flares happen several times a day when the Sun is in an especially "active" cycle, or once a week or so during calmer times. The biggest known flare–constituting a "geomagnetic storm"–was the "Carrington event" observed by Richard Carrington in 1859. It was strong enough to set telegraph offices on fire. One of equal size just missed the Earth in 2012. Had that eruption happened nine days earlier, the flare would have hit Earth and caused catastrophic damage to everything from toasters to national electrical systems. Recovery would have taken four to ten years, costing as much as $2 trillion in the United States.

Astronomers will know a flare is coming about 15 minutes before the first X-rays and UV radiation arrive. If there's time to announce the event on electronic media, the public will need to hear it in those first few minutes. After that, the flare will ionize the atmosphere, knocking out radio transmissions and GPS mechanisms. A few minutes later, the energetic particles arrive–an avalanche of electrons and protons that damage the electronics of satellites. A day or two later, billions of tons of magnetized plasma arrive. After that, you can forget about watching television, gathering information from the internet, or flushing your toilet. Your refrigerator won't work. Neither will your local, state, or federal government.

Another geomagnetic storm of Carrington power is almost inevitable. In fact, in 2014 a physicist calculated that there is a 12 percent chance it will happen by 2022–yes, a 12 percent chance that a large part of civilization will soon spend a few years in a modern Stone Age.

Superflares

Solar flares aren't the worst geomagnetic storms that can occur. Stars similar to our Sun have emitted superflares 10,000 times more powerful than the Carrington event. They don't happen often, and they don't happen on many stars, but they do happen.

A superflare from a distant star isn't a problem on Earth. But a superflare issued by our friend the Sun would cause several kinds of catastrophe to technology, the planet, and life forms. Satellites would be rendered inoperable. Damage to electrical systems would be severe enough to destroy switches and transformers. Electrical systems at nuclear power plants might be damaged too much to cool the reactor or spent fuel pools, leading to scores or hundreds of meltdowns. Ionization of the atmosphere would make radio communication impossible. The ozone layer would be decimated, in time causing cataracts and skin cancer. Plants would be damaged, many of them unable to grow for months or years. And you'd better hope you're not in a jet at the upper edge of the atmosphere when the radiation hits. You definitely don't want to be an orbiting astronaut.

Worse, superflares usually don't happen as single events. If a star does it once, it will probably do it a few more times.

There is no evidence that a large superflare has ever occurred in the solar system. It is only theoretically possible. Judging by superflare events on other stars, scientists figure a star such as ours might experience a relatively small superflare once in 800 years. There might be a stronger one in 5,000 years. A big one might happen once in 10,000 years.

If our Sun ever emits a superflare, odds are it will miss Earth. But odds are also that the Sun will take several more shots before it calms down.

Fiction

From

Passion in an Improper Place

Chapter One

Gumballs

This is the truth of what happened to Ysa, Kit and Soong Tan in Amazonia. The reporters didn't get the whole story, not by a long shot. The American consulate in Belém released only the official information, which is to say nothing. The officials probably knew more than they reported. They didn't mention the rain of porpoises or anybody getting sawed in half or the three crude coffins, small, medium and large. They alluded to a plane crash but not as a cause of death. Nothing about a war.

If it were anyone else but Ysa, it would sound like a make-believe adventure movie, the kind made for TV. But somehow she really got herself involved in such situations. A couple of years ago, for example, she found herself going to Burma and parachuting out of an airplane disguised as a nun. But, quite un-nun-like, she knocked off the biggest drug lord in the world, rescued the prettiest little girl you ever saw, and ended up the arms of Mr. Perfect. He moved right in. They didn't get married, but they're shacked up like married people except that when they had sex they made love, too.

The little Dutch-Burmese girl, the green-eyed Soong Tan, went right into the sixth grade. Ysa got a job identifying microbes in a pathology lab. Kit quit his job as a not-for-profit commando and opened up an ice cream stand off Virginia Route 169. Kit's Kones. Incredible place. A hundred and forty-four flavors. Blueberry-mango. Guava and cheese. Cinnamon-pumpkin. Bourbon. Bourbon and cloves. Cloves and cranberries. You'd weigh five hundred pounds before you tasted all his flavors. People came all the way from Washington, sometimes even whole busloads of people. He had congressmen in there. Senators. Ambassadors. Generals. People came to have an ice cream cone just to see who else was having an ice cream cone. He'd have a whole mess of famous people sitting around picnic tables, licking their cones and blotting ice cream off their shirts. Kit made so much in the summer he could afford to take the winter off.

Last winter he got a call from his foster-brother. Edgar. The last guy in the world named Edgar. Edgar lived in Brazil, right on the mouth of the Amazon in a city called Belém. Edgar had a Brazilian wife named Elizama. Kit hadn't heard from Edgar in years. Now all of a sudden Edgar just had to talk to him. He had big plans. He was going to get rich. He wouldn't tell Kit what it was. He wanted him to come down to Brazil and see it first-hand. Kit said, "This better not be some Amway deal," and Edgar said, "Amway's nothing compared to this."

Well, it was winter and Soong Tan had two weeks off for Easter and Ysa said she'd always wanted to see the Amazon. She packed safari shorts, half a dozen T-shirts, malaria pills, a blank diary book, a camera, binoculars for watching birds, a magnifying glass for weird insects, a little field microscope for tropical germs, a telescope in case there was an eclipse or something, a ten-pound first aid kit in case there was a war, enough other junk for Kit to consider taking a camel for their baggage. She called her friend, Susan, and said, "Can you watch my ferrets for a couple of weeks? I'm going up the Amazon."

Susan said, "The Amazon. Are you nuts?"

"I need to get away from civilization," she said. "Just for a while. I want to see how the planet used to be."

So the next thing you know, they're on their way. Varig Airlines down to Rio. Some rattletrap puddle-jumper up to Belém. Susan pictured it with vines and boa constrictors hanging off the wings. She could just see Soong Tan's round, Oriental face pressed up against the window, all wide-eyed and saying "Like, wow." But then a postcard from Ysa said it wasn't all that bad in Brazil. They were about halfway civilized, in the cities anyway. It was when you get out into the interior that you found your boa constrictors, anacondas, and pythons. Your alligators. Your piranha. Your malaria, yellow fever, elephantiasis, jungle rot and everything else the human body can catch.

So of course Ysa went there. She wasn't worried. She had Kit.

She's also had the kind of looks that let a girl get away with murder. Being of Dutch-Norwegian stock, she had green eyes and yellow hair. Being the kind of person with a little discipline at the refrigerator, she kept her feisty little butt in shape. She was the kind who, when she smiled, everybody just trusted her and liked her. Guys started clowning around. Women wanted to tell her their problems. Kids wanted to tell her stories about their little lives. Traffic cops let her go with a warning.

Yet she was nice. A regular person. She liked a cold beer on a hot day. She cut coupons. Sometimes her car didn't start. She got headaches.

Anyway, she and Kit and little Soong Tan made it to Belém without the plane crashing or anything. Edgar met them at the airport. They were two degrees south of the equator. The humidity was like something from dinosaur times but with garbage in the streets and a big outdoor fish market right downtown. Susan got a postcard that said it was like walking through clam chowder. Not that Ysa would ever break a sweat or anything. Not her. Not Kit. They looked like a deodorant commercial coming across the airport lobby, as fresh as a mouthful of Scope.

Edgar looked like Larry the Lounge Lizard in his flowery shirt unbuttoned halfway down his golden-brown chest and great gobs of 14-karat gold chain swinging around his neck. He was all over Kit with the handshakes and hugs and pats on the back. Ysa wrote in her diary that it felt like getting hugged by a reptile in a wet fur coat. He had yellow teeth and smelled like a half-empty cup of coffee that's been used as an ashtray. He had a kind of hatchet face with a nose that had steep sides and tall, deep nostrils which in certain light you could see up inside.

This was the first time Kit had seen him since Edgar left home and joined the Marines. Kit was just a foster kid in the house, three or four years younger than Edgar. The parents treated Kit like dirt. Edgar treated him like a gnat. So as soon as he could, Kit pulled an Edgar, except what he joined was the army. Edgar ended up being a cook at Parris Island. Kit ended up in Special Forces in Southeast Asia.

But first thing at the airport, Edgar bellows out, "Yo, bro!" and starts with the Brazilian-style back-slaps.

Kit backs off for a conventional hand-shake and just says, "Hello, Edgar. Long time no see."

"Boy, you can say that again, little brother. When was it?"

"A good twenty years ago. You were seventeen and full of pimples and had the grubbiest little mustache I ever saw."

"Haw! Time sure goes by, doesn't it? I could barely remember what you looked like. I had this memory of somebody about four feet tall who needed his nose wiped."

"Well," Kit says, "it's been wiped."

"Haw, haw, haw!" More back-slaps. Edgar loves his little brother. Suddenly they've been the best of bros since day one. Kit keeps giving Ysa looks of complete disgust. When he introduces her, Edgar not only moves in for a real tight hug but also, she's sure, feels around for her bra strap.

She pulls away and turns his attention to Soong Tan.

"What a little cutie-pie," he says, pinching one of her chubby little cheeks. "Jeepers, creepers, where'd you get them peepers, kid?"

The source of her pretty green peepers was a long story. Ysa didn't go into it. She just smiled wanly and said, "So do you have a car here or what?"

Edgar takes them home in his Fiat. He's got a big apartment in a building that looks to Ysa like a concrete block with windows. The apartment's got four bedrooms plus a bedroom for the live-in maid. Edgar never finished high school, but he's got a live-in maid. He snaps his fingers and the maid comes running. He says, "A little more ice for my drink, Maria," and she brings it. Even if the house were on fire, he wouldn't have to drag his heels off the coffee table. He could just snap his fingers and say, "Maria, would you put out that fire, please?"

Susan got a post card from Soong Tan, written on one of those first days in Brazil. All it said was, "Dear Aunt Susan: It is incredibly boring here. Hot, humid and nothing to do. TV sucks here. Why did they bring me to such a place? I don't get it. Yours truly, Soong Tan."

Ysa sent Susan a letter describing Elizama, Edgar's wife. It fit the stereotype of Brazilian women. Very tan. Very bright red lipstick so powerful it stains her big white teeth. Very curvaceous body, especially around the rump. A little heavy on the hips, maybe, but she moved them around like a professional. Great gobs of black hair. Nails to die for. Matching toenails. Lots of flashy rings on all her fingers. Jeans meant for women who get lots of exercise. She had big dark eyes that stretched waaaay open when something amazed her and that narrowed down to the size of snake eyes when she had something dark and personal to say.

Elizama had the apartment decorated all weird with Umbanda stuff. Umbanda is weird religion that got brought over from Africa by the slaves. Then it mixed with Catholicism to create bizarre gods and goddesses named after the saints but in charge of things like the sea, the sky, bad luck, lightning, and stuff. When believers worship, they burn candles and incense and go into trances and sacrifice chickens and practice voodoo. Edgar and Elizama didn't believe in it. They just had the stuff for decoration all over their walls and hanging from the ceiling and lurking on whatnot shelves. They had swordfish bills, porpoise eyes, dried monkey feet, rattles made from bones. And crucifixes. No air conditioning. Just ceiling fans. A little breeze came off the river, which is about ten miles wide there. Sometimes a rain storm would pass by and cool things off a bit. Ysa and Kit just sat around the apartment feeling like a couple of damp rags. It took all their energy just to snap their fingers for Maria to bring more ice.

Edgar treated them well. Big meals. Tours of the town. Juices you've never heard of. Fresh Brazilian coffee in tiny little cups. Elizama took Ysa out to have her fingernails done right and her body hair waxed so she could go to the beach in one of the itsty-bitsy *tangas* they wear in Brazil. Dental floss, they call it. Because it gets down into the crack.

While Ysa was getting herself tuned up to Brazilian standards, Edgar took Kit to a whore house. Not a bordello or anything. Just a whore house. Plain as can be. It reminded him of the lobby of a college dorm back in the days when college was cheap. He said he was afraid even to touch the walls. The lobby was just plastic chairs and drunk guys sitting around waiting to get laid. The closest thing to a frill was a humongous gumball machine over in the corner. It was the kind that's six feet tall with flashing lights and a million gumballs. When you buy one it rolls down a long winding chute inside a clear column under the globe of gumballs. Kit found that very weird. He never seen a gumball machine like that, and he never imagined he'd first see one in Brazil. And on top of that, he wondered, who would go into a whore house for a gumball? He figured it was probably for the girls. Whores are always chewing gum, right? He'd never thought of it before, but it kind of made sense. A whore house would have to have a supply of gum. But it was weird, this big thing standing there in the corner like some kind of a Martian with a huge head full of multicolored brainballs.

Edgar makes like he practically owns the place. "Take your pick," he says, calling out a parade of girls who didn't look old enough to vote. "Vanilla. Milk chocolate. Licorice. We've got 'em all here. Twelve dollars each. Buy two, get one free." He wasn't talking gumball flavors. Kit backed off. He didn't need to hire a girl. He had Ysa. She was gorgeous. Hair the color of white corn. The prettiest face in the world and legs that bring men to their knees. Her breasts look like something off a marble statue. Kit wasn't going to mess with some chick who probably had more diseases than a hospital.

So Edgar says, "OK then, be a chicken, see if I care. I've got a little business to attend to with my sweetheart here –" and he strokes this half-naked teenager who looks like she just got off the boat from Africa. "If you want, you can go across the street and have a beer, I'll be there pretty soon. The word's *cerveja.*"

And off went Edgar with his sweetheart. Kit had nothing against beer on a hot day, but before he went, he plopped a coin into the gumball machine, just to see how it worked. It took him a while to figure out which coin, but it turned out to be worth twenty-five cents, same as in America. He gives it whirl, and a yellow gumball drops down from the globe and starts down the chute, around and around and around. Something trips off a kind of a little siren, a pinwheel up on top spins around, whistling and shooting off sparks, and the yellow ball of gum pops out a little door down near his ankles and rolls across the floor.

Kit almost fell down laughing. It was the fanciest gumball machine in the world, and there it was, in a grubby little whore house on the outskirts of the Amazon jungle.

So he's across the street drinking Brahma beer and trying to fit all this on a postcard when Edgar comes out with a great big smile on his face. Kit thought that was odd. Men don't usually smile when they're done with a whore. They're always sad. But Edgar's got this big grin across the front of his head. He sits down at the table with Kit – it's a little metal table out on the sidewalk, under a canopy – and signals for the waiter to bring another bottle of beer. Kit says, "You look mighty pleased with yourself, Edgar. Something tells me you're out at least twenty-four bucks."

Edgar just ignores that and says, "So whadja think?"

"I hope that's not the business you brought me here to see."

Edgar smiles up a big mouthful of crooked yellow teeth. Kit feels like smacking him with a chair. But then Edgar says just one word: "Gumballs."

Kit's taken aback. He almost spills beer on himself. Gumballs.

"I heard you try it out," Edgar says in a sly tone, as if he were talking about one of the girls. "You couldn't resist, could you."

Kit thinks about it. He supposes he could have resisted just fine. He's sure he will next time. It was twenty-five cents down the drain. A little entertainment, maybe, but once you've done it, well, as he wrote to Susan, "It's time to move on."

Bear in mind: Kit's been around the block a few times. He's parachuted behind enemy lines. He's flown helicopters. He was in on Ysa's mission into Burma. He climbed Mt. Blanc in bare feet. He did survival training in the Congo. He was in the Olympic try-outs for marksmanship. So if a gumball machine manages to get a quarter out of him just once, well it must be a pretty good machine. But it's going to have to fly around the room backward to hold his interest for long.

Edgar isn't holding his interest any better than a fancy gumball machine. Kit's already getting bored with him and his constant pressure. He's always saying, Come on, have another drink, or You know what y'oughtta do, y'oughtta buy some land here, or Do you have any idea how many square meters of frog skins this country produces in a year? It's a lot of pressure when the temperature's a hundred and three and the humidity's almost as high and the city buses sound and smell like Russian tanks and everybody's got their TVs turned up all the way and there's nobody else to talk to but Edgar.

Edgar signals for the waiter to bring him a pack of Hollywoods. The waiters here have white jackets. Kit likes that a lot. It reminds him of the French colonies in Asia and Africa. So far it's the best thing about Brazil, besides the gumball machines. The waiter brings Edgar's cigarettes, waits until Edgar has one in his mouth, lights it for him. Kit likes that, too. Edgar hardly seems to notice. He squints through the smoke but doesn't say anything while some kind of impact's supposed to be sinking into Kit. All Kit's thinking is that he could make a fortune in this country if he started a brewery and made beer out of something other than swamp water and rice.

Finally Edgar leans in close and says something. Kit can't hear it because a bus is going by. He leans in a bit to hear it better. This time, just as Edgar says it, a kid on the sidewalk lets loose with two-fingered whistle and shouts something to somebody on the other side of the traffic. Kit just smiles as if he heard what Edgar said and leans back.

"You didn't hear me," Edgar says in a moment of relative lull. He looks hurt.

"Say what?"

"I say that was my gumball machine."

Well that raises Kit's eyebrows a bit. His half-brother owns the fanciest gumball machine in all of South America and he's got it installed in a roach motel. And by the look on his face, he's as proud as the father of twin boys.

Kit says, "That's quite an asset. Hell of a good location." He can already smell what's coming. He's glad it won't be tempting.

"That's just one," Edgar says. "I've already got ten of them deployed all over Belém."

"In whore houses?"

"Not all of them. One in a supermarket. One at the bus station. You probably saw the one at the airport..."

Kit tilts his head pensively. He searches his memory banks for the image of a six-foot gumball machine or even the distant whine of a siren. "'fraid I missed it," he says.

"Yeah, the idiots who run the place put it over near the police kiosk. It's safe, but who's going to go near cops just for chewing gum?"

Edgar waits. It takes Kit a while to realize he meant it as a real question. He wanted an answer. Who goes near cops just for chewing gum?

"Oh, um, well...I don't know. Other cops, I guess."

"Wrong! The answer is nobody. It's a wasted asset. If you want to make money off a recreational flavored multichewable snack dispenser, you need traffic. In the United States, it has to be kids. In Brazil, hell, everybody's a kid. These Wiz-Bang machines – that's who makes them, Wiz-Bang, Ltd. – are like carnival waiting for a quarter. I average two hundred and seventy dollars a month per unit. Ten units is twenty-seven hundred per month. In a country like this, that's money. But now look: a hundred machines, twenty-seven thousand. Per month. You know what that adds up to in a year?"

Kit doesn't even bother trying to figure that out in his head. Edgar sits back with his cigarette, waiting for Kit's jaw to hit the sidewalk. But

Kit's jaw remains locked. Finally, Edgar gives him the answer. "Three hundred and twenty-four thousand dollars. Per annum."

Kit whistles with disbelief and says, "That's sure a lotta gumballs." He knows what's coming.

Meanwhile, Ysa had two girls working on her nails at the same time. She was having them painted with rainbows on a background the color of watered-down Bordeaux.

Soong Tan was getting hers done the same way but quite against her will. She looked like she was getting her fingernails ripped out, not painted up. She came right out and expressed her opinion. "This is stupid," she said. "Even if they look like rainbows, it's unnatural. I bet it causes cancer."

"We'll just do it once," Ysa said. "For the experience. A little civilization to take with us into the jungle."

Elizama didn't hear any of this. She was under the hair drier. The few moments of solitude filled her head with things to say. As soon as she came out, she hit the ground running.

"Man in zis country, no good," she said. Her accent made her sound like a little girl. "I never marry wis Brazilian man. No way. Zey don't hispect you."

Ysa, half dizzy with fingernail polish, said, "Is Edgar a good husband?"

"Oh, yes. He's good. He comes home at night. He talks to me. He always tell me his plans. He's soooo eentelligent."

Ysa hadn't detected much in the way of eentelligence in Edgar. As a matter of fact, she thought he was pretty dumb. And to her he seemed the worst kind of dummy, the kind who thinks he's smart. Trouble was, he had irrefutable proof of his superior intelligence. He could beat just about anybody at just about any kind of board game or card game. He played Kit and Ysa in poker the same day they arrived and cleaned them of all their American coins. The next morning he whipped Kit's butt in chess. By afternoon Kit would play him in anything just because it gave him an excuse not to talk for a while. So Edgar beat him at Chinese checkers and then Crazy Eights and then backgammon. Kit knew his foster-brother was cheating just to see if he could do so undetected. He didn't care. At night they played a Brazilian card game something like gin rummy with a lot of extra rules. Pretty soon Ysa could tell Kit was just tossing in cards to get rid of them, handing Edgar vast combinations. Edgar beamed with joy as he clobbered everybody else by several thousand points. Smart dummy that he was, he couldn't see that no one else was even trying. Elizama didn't seem to notice much either. She never shut up.

Nor did she shut up at the beauty salon. Watching the work on Ysa's nails as if they might end up in a museum, she gave a detailed report on the errors and inadequacies of Maria, the maid. Maria had failed to clean behind a certain toilet where Edgar tended to leave a puddle. Maria bought wilted collard greens at the market. Maria always came back late after her day off. Maria neglected to fill the ice tray. Maria had fleas.

Ysa never knew what to say to Elizama. She tried to maintain a look of sincere concern, but when it came time to contribute to the conversation, she found her brain devoid of any possible offering. Once she managed to ask what Edgar did for a living. Elizama answered, "He has a booziness."

"A booziness?" She had no idea how one could earn a living at that. "What kind of booziness does he have?"

"Oh, I don't know. In Portuguese, we call it *negócios*."

Then Ysa understood. Negocios meant business. It sounded like the Spanish. That was how she was learning Portuguese. Every time a word sounded like the French or the Spanish, both of which she spoke, she learned it. This would come in handy later, out in the jungle, when things got serious.

Once they got their bodies all tuned up, Elizama took Ysa and Soong Tan to the beach. Ysa thought she was gazing out over the Atlantic until she swam and discovered it was fresh water. That vast expanse of sea was the Amazon itself.

The sun burned down from directly overhead. Ysa kept slathering on the Number 15 sun screen, but she still felt herself burning. When she asked Elizama to pass the sunscreen, Elizama reached over to squirt a blob into the palm of her hand. But rather than squirt, she gasped. Her index finger, with its incredibly long rainbow-streaked nail, darted to Ysa's palm and jabbed into a place just below the middle fingers. With eyes so wide her eyeballs almost fell out, she looked up at Ysa and said, "*Meu Deus*!"

At first she thought the pedicure girls must have done something to her hand, but then Elizama leaned in real-real close and poked the tip of her nail into a crack in Ysa's palm.

"Are you seek?" Elizama asked.

Except for the effects of the sun and some lingering dizziness from the morning of nail polish fumes, Ysa felt fine. She said, "No, I'm not sick...not that I know of."

"Is somebody in your family very hich?"

"Very hich?"

"Hich. Much of money. No?"

Ysa shook her head. No rich people in her family. No family, in fact. Her father was killed in Burma. Her mother died of cancer. No brothers, no sisters. She thought she had an uncle in Netherlands who worked in a bank, but she didn't even know his name. "Does it say I'm sick?" she asked, squinting into her palm.

"It says you die," Elizama whispered, looking up with wide-eyed wonderment. "But hich. You die, but vehy, vehy hich when you go."

Chapter Two

The Plan

But Ysa didn't believe that stuff. She was too rational. Susan had taken her to see a psychic once, back in Virginia, before Burma. Moi was her name. Moi told Ysa she was going to fall in love within a year. She told her she was going to have a child. She told her she was going to take a long trip to a warm place. And it all came true. She met Kit. She adopted Soong Tan. She went to Burma, and now Brazil. But Ysa still didn't believe it. She said that could have happened to anybody. Like everybody dressed up like a nun armed with a semi-automatic weapon and parachuted into jungles.

Elizama was a psychic, too. She read palms. She did Tarot. She saw the future. She looked at Ysa's palm and knew she was going to die and then become very rich. She saw a flock of parakeets and knew Kit was going to leave her for another woman and then become an angel. She looked at the last bit of coffee in a cup and knew Soong Tan was going to be alone for a long, long time, with danger lurking around her like jackals. Entrails in a butcher shop window showed her coffins headed for the sea.

That night, the same night Ysa got her nails done and Kit heard the Gumball Plan, they were in bed, maximizing their appreciation of human perspiration. As Ysa wrote to Susan, "When you're in Amazonia, you do as the Amazonians do. You sweat. You get into it. It's good for you. It cleans the pores. It cycles water through the body" They were in bed cycling a lot of water through their pores. Kit was fascinated with the dental floss lines of Ysa's new sunburn. Ysa didn't mind the attention at all, his fingers and lips walking the fine line between gringo winter-white and equatorial Brazilian tan. She was fanning the fire, licking the sweat off him, off just the right spots. He was doing the same. They licked sweat until the salt got the better of them. Then they drank vodka tonics. Then they licked more sweat from more places, which of course just got them sweating more.

Ysa paused from her lingual exploration of his thigh and said, "Do you think it's possible to tell the future?"

Kit said, "I think I'm going to love you forever. Care to take a bet whether it's true?" He pulled her up and licked a swath from her collarbone to her ear.

"No bet," she said in a close-up hush, kissing the dampness from his earlobe. "But that's not what I mean. I mean can the lines on your palm tell you how long you're going to live?"

Kit just chuckled. "I can see how maybe....just maybe something about your palms can hint at your health fifty years down the road. Maybe. But how could they possibly know that ten years down the road you're going to get run over by a bus?"

As soon as he said it, Ysa started thinking about bus accidents. She saw herself stepping into the street, looking left as from the right a bus came barreling along, the wrong way down a one-way street – illegal and unlikely, but that's how accidents happen. Especially in Brazil. She had no trouble imagining it. She could see little Soong Tan, her pinched, round oriental eyes in her own father's chubby Dutch face, eyes and face both gaping to take in the impossible scene of her big sister dead in the street, not believing it, suddenly gushing with tears as she rushes to her sister's crushed body. Suddenly she's alone again, on the street, defenseless, this time in a country foreign to the foreign country she moved to from Burma. In this irresistible nightmare that Ysa kept having – having in a dozen different forms – somebody eases Soong Tan from her fallen sister, leads her under a protective arm to a car, takes her away and throws her into the hell she thought she'd left in the slums and mountains of Burma.

She never ever mentioned these nightmare scenarios to Kit. Though scary, they were born of silly, baseless paranoia. She let each scenario play itself out, knowing that in the end Kit's strong hand would reach in to solve the problem.

That, especially, she never let him know.

She sucked the sweat from one of his longest fingers and said, "What about seers? Psychics? Can they know what's going to happen?"

"Edgar thinks he can. He sees glorious fortunes showering down upon him."

"Oh, really? And how's that going to happen?"

"Gumballs."

"Gumballs?"

"Tons and tons of gumballs. He's going to be the Amazonian King of Gumballs. I swear. That's his plan."

"Oh, he has a plan, does he?"

"Chewing gum far and wide. He's going to install these big fancy dispensers all over Amazonia. According to him, he's bringing civilization to the Stone Age. He says he wouldn't be surprised if someday they put up a statue of him."

"Yeah, right. And who's going to chew this gum? Monkeys? Jaguars? Toucans?" Ysa's mind treated her to an image of jungle animals blowing blue, red, yellow and green bubbles as they swung from trees and stalked the jungle floor.

"There's a lot of people living in the rain forest," Kit said. "You'd be surprised." He was quoting Edgar almost word-for-word. "There's Indians, gold miners, loggers, little villages, even some towns with ten to twenty thousand people."

"Oh, yeah? Name one. Besides Manaus."

Manaus she already knew. It was the only city of any size upstream from Belém. But she'd never heard of anywhere else. She tried to distract him by scratching the blonde fuzz at the top of his left thigh.

"OK," Kit said. "How about Itaituba."

"What kind of tuba?" She could tell he wasn't entirely focused on the city with the funny name. His scrotum was roiling with desire.

"Itaituba," he gasped as if it were suddenly irrelevant. "It's half...halfway up the Tapajós. Keep doing that."

"Hey, you really know your geography, don't you?" She was studying the geography of his groin, the mountains and valleys that were moving around like something in a slow earthquake. She was crazy about Kit. She couldn't keep her hands off him. She wouldn't let him talk geography for long. But he held out long enough to mention Jacaréacanga.

"Zhaca-what?" she said, wondering how he knew so much after three days in Brazil.

"Jacaréacanga. It's way upstream from Itaituba, which is already plenty upstream from the Amazon at a point which is way upstream from here."

Ysa pulled back from Kit's swelling desire. She smelled trouble. "What's that place got to do with us?"

"Well, it isn't us. It's mostly Edgar. He's got this plan to install gumball machines in all the places where there's nothing else. Jacaréacanga is just the jumping off place. That's as far as civilization goes. He's going to put one machine there and then branch out. Every Indian village is going to have one. Every gold mine. Every logging camp. Every little school and military outpost. Everybody gets a gumball machine."

"Wait a minute. Go back to the part about it's mostly Edgar."

Kit's strong broad hand cupped her shoulder blade and pulled her up to lie atop him. She loved to ride his chest as it swelled and sank, pressing to her breast and pulling back. In sleep, his heart beat six times between each exhalation, the slow k-thub...k-thub...k-thub of a healthy man at rest. He loved to stroke her silky yellow hair as she lay on he pillow of his chest. When he spoke, she could hear the words forming deep within him.

"Well," he said. "It is Edgar. But he's invited us to go with him."

Ysa raised her head to look him in the eye. "To that place?"

"Repeat after me: Jacaréacanga."

"Zhaca-reh-a-kanga. How do you spell it?"

He told her. She peeled her sweaty skin from his and grabbed Edgar's big green-and-yellow English-Portuguese dictionary from a shelf. With her elbows on Kit's chest, her breasts lightly against him, she searched the pages until she found half the word. Jacaré.

"Alligator," she reported.

"I like this place already. Look up the other half of the word. Canga."

Adjusting herself to keep her elbows from digging into her one and only, she flipped back through the dictionary, looking for the C's.

"Canga," she said. "Yoke."

"Yolk like egg yolk?"

"No, dummy, yoke for an oxen."

"Alligator Yoke. I love it. Let's let Edgar take us to Alligator Yoke."

That place sounded perfect – the frontier of civilization, the outskirts of the twentieth century. Exactly what she was looking for. Ysa dropped the dictionary and told Kit she loved him. He pressed his open mouth to her head, squeezed her hair in both hands, searched out her ear and breathed into it. Her sweat turned to ice in a wave that swept over her body, head to toes. He was strong and hard and ready. She arched against him and brought him inside, turning her belly to lava. He took her breast in his mouth, toyed with the nipple, sucked it to full height. She rose and descended, rose and descended, extracting his passion and filling herself with it. Then they fell back to the damp sheets and bathed in the caress of the overhead fan.

Yes, she would go to Alligator Yoke with Kit. She would go anywhere with him. But she worried about Soong Tan.

"Is it a place for an eleven-year-old?" she asked, quite out of the blue.

Kit knew what she meant. He said, "Hey, it isn't a war zone, you know? It's a town. People live there. Kids. I wouldn't want Soong to live in a place called Alligator Yoke, but hell, how bad can it be to visit?"

Ysa felt better. She trusted Kit. He could do anything. What could possibly go wrong?

Chapter Three

The Gumball Gods

The boat had rats. Elizama knew that before they arrived at the dock. She, Ysa, Kit and Soong Tan were still squashed up against each other in the back and front seats of a Volkswagen cab. The driver had the air conditioning on, but it did little good. It was a cab full of clam chowder.

Elizama hadn't actually seen these rats or even the boat they called home. She saw them in her head, a vision. "Kilo-rats," she called them.

Ysa almost threw up just thinking about a rat the size of a football.

But Edgar said, "Don't worry about it. They're down in the hold, with the bananas or whatever."

"No bananas," Elizama injected. "Bananas come down the hiver. We go up the hiver."

"What goes up the river?" Ysa asked, trying to eclipse the image of fat rats. "What products?"

"Oh, everysing ze peoples need. Oil for coo-king. Kerosene. Cigahettes. *Cachaça*. Everysing."

"And recreational multichewable coin-operated snack food dispensers," Kit added. "Can't leave without the recreational multichewable snack food dispensers."

"Is going to make much money," Elizama said, rubbing her palms together. When she smiled, her teeth looked big and white behind her bright red lips. Ysa thought she looked like the kind of woman who could make the most of a big pile of money. She looked like the shopping type, and from what Ysa had seen so far, she had little on her mind besides acquisition. Much of what she had acquired she was taking on her trip up the Amazon. It was in a footlocker in a taxi following behind them. Ysa could imagine the clothes therein – brilliant red Bermudas, filmy peasant blouses, T-shirts with things written in English, eighty-seven pairs of shoes, forty pounds of make-up.

Ysa wasn't that type. She didn't need florescent lipstick to make men notice her. It didn't matter what she wore. On this trip, she wore a simple shift held up by spaghetti shoulder straps. It let air circulate around her body. Kit seemed to like it. He touched her a lot. When he touched her shoulder, his finger went under a shoulder strap. When he reached for her knee, his pinky would go up under the hem. Ysa liked that. Meanwhile, he was always joking around with Elizama, trying to learn Portuguese, being a regular clown but not showing any kind of interest in her. Not that Ysa was worried. But she had her eye on him.

She had to. He was too close to perfect. Smart and loving and responsible and better looking than any normal person. Every girl in the world wants a man like that.

The taxi took them down to a dock on the river and pulled up at a boat that looked like it most certainly had rats. Kilo-rats. It seemed to lean up against the dock as if exhausted, arthritic, maybe a little drunk. A bunch of guys in nothing but little shorts were loading boxes and gunny sacks into the hold on the lower deck, which was only about a foot above the water. The men were dark, sweaty and muscular.

Ysa whispered, "They look like slaves."

"Zey are," Elizama said. "Zey work for food and cachaça and somesing like tree *reais* a day. Is nossing."

"But they look like they're having fun."

"Zey are. Zat's what ze *cachaça's* for. You give zem a little wiss lunch and zey sink zey are in heaven."

Cachaça had the same effect on Ysa, though she didn't drink it with lunch. It was made from distilled sugar cane juice and had a kick like a mule. But, as Kit said, what's wrong with getting kicked by a mule once in a while?

Kit wasn't worried about the dock workers. He was worried about the boat. It was made of wood and needed painting, which to him meant the wood had to be at least a little rotten, which might be OK in some places but not in a river famous for its piranha and electric eels. It had three decks: one down near the water for the cargo, a middle deck that was open on the sides, and an upper deck, really just a roof over the middle deck. Kit thought it looked like the kind of vessel you hear about sinking in thirty seconds flat in the middle of a school of piranha. But he didn't say anything. He just made plans for evacuation. As soon as he reached the end of the gangplank, he knew where the life preservers and fire extinguishers were.

Edgar wasn't worried about the boat. He was worried about his gumball machines. Only after a lot of asking around did he find out they'd already been put on board and stored down in the hold. Which made Edgar go berserk.

"*Não,*" he told some guy on the dock. "Não fucking way. Elizama ...explain to this guy..." Edgar spoke medium-advanced Portuguese, but when something really important needed saying, he called in Elizama. The really important thing in this case was that the gumball machines absolutely could not be down in the hold with the rats.

"Rats love bubble gum," he told Kit and Ysa while Elizama rattled off about ten thousand words that somehow added up to mean não fucking way. "We already learned that the hard way. Down at the bus station. They chewed right through the plastic and climbed up into the storage ball. They ate so much gum they died in there. Their guts busted open. Not that that gave me any satisfaction. I still had to replace half the stock."

"Half?" Kit blurted. "The gum was in there with dead rats and you didn't replace it?"

"Hey," Edgar said, leaning in close and shifting to a whisper. "These people don't care. Especially if they don't know. Did you know they still have elephantiasis in this town? Elephantiasis."

"They probably got it from the goddam gum."

Edgar liked that one. He guffawed through his big, toothy grin and smacked Kit on the back. "You kill me, bro," he said. "You really slay me."

Elizama reported. The guy on the dock could do nothing. It wasn't his job. It wasn't his boat. They'd have to go talk with the captain.

So they boarded the boat, the *21 de Março* – the 21st of March. Ysa said it reminded her of an old Mississippi steamboat, sort of, except smaller and with a pointed bow and no paddle wheel or smokestacks or steam, but it was made of wood and looked like it could burst into flames at any moment. They found the captain down in the hold, swinging in a hammock, smoking a cigarette, reeking of cachaça. He was wearing a tie-dye T-shirt over his rotund beer-belly, green plaid shorts over his spindly legs, black knee socks slung low around his ankles, and no shoes on his feet. He looked Elizama up and down as she explained the problem with the gumball machines and the rats and the importance of sanitation. When she finally finished her impassioned plea, the captain tilted his head toward Edgar and said, "You are married to him?" Ysa didn't understand until the man indicated his own wedding band.

Elizama confessed that she was indeed married to Edgar. That shifted the captain's sleazy gaze to Ysa. He looked her up and down but then saw Kit's hard, cold look and came back to Elizama. "OK," he said as if he already knew he'd regret letting these gringos onto the 21st of March. "Move your damned gumball machines. Put them up on the leisure deck. But don't ask my crew to do it."

So Edgar and Elizama returned to the dock to negotiate with the workers. Kit and Ysa stayed to string up their hammocks on the passenger deck. That's how you travel on these boats. In hammocks. That's your cabin. A hammock. You want to sit down somewhere, you sit in your hammock. You want to sleep, you sleep in your hammock. You want to change your clothes, you pull your hammock up around you and do it in there. You want to make love, well, you wait till the lights are out and then you do it quietly while you sway in the breeze.

Ysa summed it up rather well in a postcard to Susan. She wrote, "A Carnival Cruise it ain't."

At first she liked it. They set up their five hammocks like covered wagons in a circle, with all their baggage in the middle. They were all swinging in the breeze and thinking about lunch while Edgar hustled a crew of slave-types from the hold to the roof with twelve gumball machines, two men to each machine, twelve trips up and down. Edgar, nervous as an old maid watching gorillas handle her priceless china, had to supervise each twist and turn up the narrow ladders and through hatches barely wide enough. As each one came up onto the passenger deck, Edgar couldn't resist showing it off to the passengers. Each machine was a different model. One had the siren and pinwheel. One had little stairs going down instead of a spiral chute. One had stairs and a chute. One had a computer chip that said, "*Muito obrigado, amigo!*" – "Thanks a lot, friend!" Another one said, "Compra mais uma!" – Buy one more! All this in Edgar's voice, no less. The passengers marveled at the machines. Unfortunately ,nobody had money for gum. Most of them didn't have money for shoes.

Topside, Edgar had all the machines huddled together under a plastic tarp and bound with a rope so they wouldn't fall over. They looked like a bizarre Mardi Gras football team seeking shelter from the elements. When he finally joined his family at their hammocks, he went straight for a bottle of cachaça in his trunk. "I need this," he said, lying back to pour it straight into his mouth from several inches above. "I deserve this."

Elizama said, "*Tcht*," and turned her head to face away from him. "I hope you don't be drunk all zeh way to Itaituba."

"Not me," he said. "Maybe close to it, but not drunk."

Much to Ysa's surprise, Kit said, "Lemme try some of that." He took the bottle, leaned back in his hammock and poured a trickle right into his mouth the same way Edgar had done. He grimaced but said, "Cachaça and I could develop a relationship."

Ysa said, "You better not." She was surprised to hear herself saying it. Kit didn't drink a lot, and she never gave him any problem about it. As a matter of fact, she drank more than he did. But she had a woman's instinct about a man taking a little too much pleasure from a bottle, even for a second. It's a bad sign.

The boat finally got underway. It just kind of chugged along, hugging the coast. That's what Ysa called it. The coast. Because the river's so wide that sometimes you can't see the other side. For the first day it didn't matter that it wasn't a Carnival Cruise. They were just swinging in their hammocks and watching the jungle go by. Ysa had little binoculars so she could watch for animals. Elizama never stopped talking except when Edgar interrupted her.

Soong Tan was all over the boat, friends with passengers and crew alike. Ysa tried to get her to stay out of the hold, which she pictured as crawling with kilo-rats. But there was no stopping her. She was already speaking a funny little Portuguese crossed with English and Burmese. Kit kept quiet and took the occasional swig of cachaça.

But then Ysa discovered the bathroom. Three toilets for fifty passengers, most of whom weren't especially well potty-trained. Three showers, too. Ysa said the floors were so slimy she had to wear sandals or catch instant gangrene. The water was just river water. No hot. No cold. Just the temperature of the day.

Not that lukewarm was going to kill anybody on a hot tropical afternoon, but I think maybe Ysa was expecting just a little more comfort on her Amazon vacation. As for the leisure deck, the "leisure" part consisted of some benches you could sit on for as long as you could stand the sun. Benches and all the gumballs you could eat.

Edgar spent his time making enemies at the dining table that stretched across one end of the passenger deck. When it wasn't being used for a meal, men played dominoes there. Of course Edgar cleaned up. Not that the pennies of peasants amounted to much, but he took great satisfaction in scooping them in. They tried to win back their hard-earned pittances in poker, but again Edgar's game skills out-shined them all. He came back to the circle of hammocks patting a jingly little bulge in his pocket.

"They should have bought gum," he said with a big smile. " I gave them a chance. At least they'd have something to show for their money."

"Why don't you treat them to a round of gum, Edgar?" Ysa suggested. "Let everybody have a piece. Show off your machines. What the heck. It's their money."

Edgar tipped another squirt of cachaça into his maw, wiped himself off with his bare forearm, and tilted his head in consideration.

"Let's do it," Kit said, swinging around in his hammock. "Gumball kings, hell. Let's be gumball gods. Hey, gimme a snorta that stuff."

Edgar passed the bottle. Ysa gave him a look. He looked back, then took a quick hit. "Come on, Ed," he said, still looking at Ysa. "Let's go buy us some gumballs for the gang."

Good thing they went, too. Drunk or not – the jury's still out on that one – they didn't need a whole heck of a lot of brains to figure one thing out: their gumballs were melting in the hot tropical sun.

Not completely melting. They hadn't turned into tutti-frutti lava or anything. But they were all stuck together. Edgar loosened them by banging his fist on the plastic globe, but it was obvious they were going to have big gumball problems well before they got to Itaituba.

"We've got to get these things out of the sun," Edgar said.

"What an emergency!" Kit shouted to the broad equatorial sky.

"Trouble is, who's going to do it?"

"Never any slaves around when you need them."

"Maybe I can get some of those peasants to help me," Edgar said. "We're all friends."

Kit said nothing. He didn't expect much, and that's exactly what Edgar got. He lobbied all over the passenger deck, pulling on guys and saying, *"Vamos! Vamos!"* But they wanted nothing to do with him. Not after he'd taken their miserable excuses for life savings. He came back up to the leisure deck, wiped sweat from his eyes and said, "Looks like it's you and me, buddy."

"This is not a problem for a couple of gumball gods like us." Kit always liked a challenge, and he got bored much too easily. Moving twelve giant gumball machines down two decks looked a hell of a lot more interesting than hanging around in a hammock. He embraced one machine like a sumo wrestler, leaned back and lifted the thing an inch off the deck.

"How many gumball you got in these things, Ed?" he grunted.

"Two thousand, each one. It's the motor that weighs so much. That and the car battery."

Kit ended up dragging the thing across the deck to the ladder that led to the passenger deck. "You better get down there and support it from below," he said.

So Edgar went down first. Elizama came over to coach. "Be carefully," she said, her fists gripped tight.

Ysa said, "I think you'd be better off just letting them melt," but nobody was listening. Edgar shouted, "OK! Ease 'er down onto my shoulder." But that didn't work at all. The weight tilted him back. He lost his grip on the handrail and then on the stairs of the ladder, and then the gumball machine descended upon him, bouncing down the little stairs like a demon out of Disneyland. Edgar fell flat but rolled to the side just as the machine dived headlong to the deck. The plastic globe shattered like glass, and two thousand gumballs clattered across the 21st of March, dodging around the baggage, scurrying under the hammocks, rumbling past the dining table, diving over the side like lemmings blipping into the dirty brown water of the Amazon.

Chapter Four

Love in a Muted Womb

Things went downhill after that. Distressed at his busted recreational multichewable coin-operated snack food dispenser, Edgar slipped into morose depression. He lay in his hammock, hugging a pillow, staring at nothing. Kit, always the responsible one, used the power of the almighty dollar to persuade a couple of crew members to help him move the machines down to the hold. The machines, too, looked depressed, leaned up against each other in a dark area behind at least a thousand plastic cases of bottled beer.

"Rat bait," Kit told Ysa at the dining table.

"Do you think I care?" She reached across the table to help herself to a ladle of spicy fish stew. It was very heavy on the coriander and some herbs she had never tasted before. Twelve other passengers sat with them and Soong Tan. Three dozen others waited their turn. Those seated served themselves from three tureens. They were jolly folks, laughing and talking even though they hadn't met until the day before. Their dining behavior was both polite and crude. Before taking their first bite, they would make a symbolic gesture with their bowls to offer food to anyone who hadn't eaten. They spoke those magic words, *por favor* and *obrigado*. But they kept their elbows on the table and leaned in low to the bowls and slurped from their spoons and smacked their lips as they carefully plucked meat from the long, thin fish bones.

"Sweetness," Kit said, secretly touching her bare knee below the table. "Don't blame me."

"He's your brother. Soong Tan, chew with your mouth closed, please."

"He's only sort of my brother, and this gumball business is his business. We're just going along for the ride. Remember?"

"*Tcht.*"

She obviously wasn't enjoying the ride. Kit felt a little guilty but not real guilty. She was the one who wanted to see the Amazon. If she'd wanted to see it from the deck of a luxury liner, well, she should have said so.

Elizama wasn't having such a good ride, either. She didn't like seeing one of her gumball machines bite the dust before it had sold a single ball of gum. Nor could she suffer the destruction of a machine and loss of two thousand gumballs in silence. Standing over Edgar's hammock, she berated him in words visibly ferocious. Ysa, just a few feet away in her hammock, understood only a few of the words, including *estúpido* and *idiota*, which were repeated several times and punctuated with the longest, nastiest, sharpest index finger she had ever seen. Some of the other words could have been applied to the 21st of March bathroom just as well as they applied to Edgar. Everybody else on board understood everything, and Ysa understood their smirks well enough. The herd of gumballs that had escaped into the river would probably go down in Amazon history, becoming part of the lore of the river that would be passed down through many generations to come.

Soong Tan, running around in little yellow clip-clop sandals, mashed her big toe on something in the hold. When she first rose up through the hatch and came across the deck limping and bleeding –

but not crying – Ysa's first thought was that a rat had bitten her. But no, she'd whacked it up against an anchor or something.

That's when Ysa discovered that the hydrogen peroxide in her medical kit had spilled, probably because some irresponsible drunkard had been pawing through there in search of aspirin or something. If she needed disinfectant, she'd have to find it herself. God only knew what filthy, rusty, contaminated iron thing her foot had found down there in kilo-rat country. The obvious thing to do was go see the captain, which was going to call for some Portuguese. Elizama was asleep. Ysa thought it best to leave her that way. She could figure something out for herself.

So she and Soong Tan limped on up to the little cabin where the captain stood at his big, round wooden wheel. With his wide belly perched atop his short, stilt-like legs, he looked like an over-grown misshapen elf from out of the tropical woods. Ysa knocked gingerly on the side of the open door and said, "*Pardón, senhor capitão*...ummm" He took his eyes from the river for only two seconds. He spent the first second eating Ysa's face, the next second ravishing her body in a downward motion, the third second grasping the basic situation of the toe that she was pointing to. With a nod, he turned his attention right back to the river. After a slight alteration in course, he called out for someone named Rogério. Rogério popped in and took the wheel. The capitão took Ysa and Soong Tan to his cabin just behind the wheelhouse.

And closed the door behind them.

Oh, he had a first aid kit, all right. He gave it to Ysa and patted a spot on his little bed where she could sit to perform her little operation. She couldn't very well just walk out. Soong Tan was standing there breathing hard, her big toe, all bloody, sticking straight up in the air. So Ysa sat and had Song Tan sit next to her, turned sideways so her foot was in Ysa's lap. The captain sat down, too.

Real close. His thigh and hip against hers. His big belly all but in her lap. He made cooing noises and examined the toe very closely. His arm came around behind Ysa as if to hold her steady. Ysa just wanted to finish the job as quickly as possible and dash out of there. But just as she had one hand on Soong Tan's quivering foot and the other on a ball of cotton dripping wet with peroxide, the captain leaned over for a little nibble of her neck. She tried to shrug him off, but he stay in there, his tongue licking out to touch her skin like a hot garden slug. A nauseating stench of stale cachaça, sweat and cigarettes oozed out of him. His whiskery cheek scraped her neck like rough sandpaper.

Ysa wasn't one to put up with that stuff. If the capitão had known what she'd done to the drug lord of Burma, he wouldn't have been pushing himself on her. But he didn't know, and she was stuck with Soong Tan's throbbing foot in her lap and the hydrogen peroxide ready to go. It wasn't the right moment to dismantle the man. So, good nurse that she was, she pretended nothing was going on. She gently dabbed the disinfectant onto the toe while Soong Tan winced and sucked in air and the good capitão accepted the lack of resistance as evidence of desire. He went for her ear, first nuzzling it with his nose, then kissing it, then probing it with his tongue.

Normally, once a man's got his tongue in Ysa's ear, she's pretty much his. What happens after that is pretty much out of her control. In this case, however, she felt most disgust, but it was mixed with just a teentsie bit of desire.

Kit knew, too. So when he eased open the door just a bit, looking for his woman and little girl, he no doubt sized up the situation at first glance. Apparently the captain, his face buried under Ysa's sweet yellow hair, didn't even notice Kit's arrival. Ysa jabbed back with an elbow, but she had to do it lightly to keep from hurting Soong Tan. To Kit, it looked more like a nudge than a jab.

Kit said, "So, what's going on?"

That snapped the captain out of his desire. For a second, he looked scared. In Brazil, messing with another guy's wife is grounds for murder. But he quickly shifted that into a look of indignation. Kit read his face correctly. It said, What the hell are you doing in my cabin? Kit, not knowing Portuguese, came back at him with a look that said, What the hell are you doing with my woman and kid in your cabin? Ysa, smelling testosterone in the air, said, with typical cool, "Don't do anything till I'm done." And she continued to dab on the peroxide and examine Soong Tan's torn flesh. It didn't seem to need stitches.

Soong Tan shook her stinging foot and said, "Ooooooo, Ysaaaaa!"

"One second more. Then Kit can punch the nice captain in the nose."

The men continued to glare at one another. The captain said something Kit could not understand. Then Kit said something the captain could not understand. Ysa said, *"Momento...momento..."* and hurriedly wrapped a bandage around Soong Tan's toe.

"OK, gentlemen," she said, standing up. "Have at it." And she slipped out the room, Soong Tan in tow.

Kit could have pulverized the captain with his bare hands. He knows how to do that. And when Kit pulverizes somebody, they stay pulverized.

But Kit's not one to start a fight. Especially with the captain of the boat he's on. Kit's not dumb. Besides, he didn't really know what had been going on in the room before he showed up. Ysa hadn't exactly been fighting the guy off. So Kit did what he says is always best when you're faced with a fight. He turned around and walked away.

Ysa had expected more than that. She wanted some damage done. She really hated it when guys bother her, which tended to happen a lot . You don't get yellow hair like that from a box. You have to get it from

Norway and Holland. But what did it get her? Guys bothering her all the time.

For the rest of the day there wasn't a whole lot of talking around the gringo hammocks. Everybody was mad at everybody else. They all smelled like they needed showers. Only Soong Tan was happy. At Ysa's orders, she stayed within the circle of hammocks, keeping her foot clean by playing Crazy Eights with a couple of kids she'd met. She already knew enough Portuguese to explain the rules.

That night, as the passengers slept in their hammocks like fifty butterflies wrapped in colorful cocoons, Ysa awoke under the weight of a man. Without a word he slipped into the curved, muted womb of her hammock. She didn't even open her eyes. She knew who it was by his smell and the tongue that filled her ear like a warm animal burrowing into her head. She did not need to tell him to stroke her arms and then her belly and then up under her T-shirt to tease her nipples and gently rub her breasts in opposite directions. She did not need to tell him to put his mouth there. All she needed to do was keep quiet, to breathe without moaning, to try to keep the hammock from swinging too wildly as he kissed his way downward, across her ribs, across her tummy to the oasis of her navel. His tongue explored that fuzzy little cave as if it went so deep within her that he might find her soul in there. Indeed it felt as if he were extracting her soul through that little well of wet desire. Her fingers dug into his hair, moving his head in circles against her as she guided it places to where it felt really good. The hot, tropical air pulled sweat from every cell of her body and his, and her brain boiled over with steaming desire. Had she ever wanted him as much as now? She could not be blamed for what she did. Passion had taken control. It lifted her out of herself and left a throbbing body of flesh craving all the pleasure it could suck from any source it could find.

Lifting her hips, she let his hands slide her panties down, inch by inch, his lips in hot pursuit. He nibbled at her thighs, inside and out. He slobbered over her knees, returned to her thighs, kissing spots he'd missed on the way down. His hands searched for curves and nooks and spaces which they desperately needed to visit. She wanted those hands and his lips in all those places, too. She wanted them everywhere at once. No sooner had he gotten her toes into his mouth than she wanted his head between her breasts, his fingers between her legs, his tongue in her mouth, his lips sliding down the small of her back, all at the same time, an impossibility of contortion. She could not have him or any one man that way, so she took what she got. And she loved it. She loved his weight upon her, inside her hot, tight hug of arms and legs. His animalistic thrusting rocked the hammock in a shuddering contrapuntal sway. She didn't care if anyone noticed the unusual movement of their private cocoon. She didn't care if the whole boat rolled over. All she wanted in that hour of overheated passion she was holding tight within her total embrace. So the next morning they were in love again. At least for a while.

Chapter Five

The Prediction

Soong Tan wrote Susan a letter.. Susan thought it was pretty funny how kids can be doing something while grown-ups think they're doing something else altogether. But for some reason Soong Tan thought she could tell somethings to Susan but not to Ysa.

Dear Susan,

You're a grown-up. Maybe you can tell me. How come the bigger people get, the more they sit around doing nothing? I don't get it. We're going up the Amazon on a boat. It's so cool! And all Ysa and Kit and the others do is hang out in the hammocks.

I'm already friends with a bunch of kids. We went down in the cargo hold. They knew their way around. We went crawling and climbing all around the cargo. There's this one spot where's there's a hole a bout big enough to stick your foot into if you wanted to, which you'd be stupid to do because if you wait long enough, pretty soon a big, fat rat comes out. The kids had a sling-shot. We used it to shoot Brazil nuts at the rat. The nuts came from a big sack that we cut a hole in the bottom of. Pretty soon there were nuts all over the place, and we never hit the rat.

*The crew sleeps down there. One guy has a huge turtle in a gunny sack. I think he's smuggling it. When he showed me, he held one finger to his lips and whispered, "*Contrabanda.*" I'm pretty sure that means contraband. I couldn't think how to ask him why he was smuggling a turtle. I mean, I've heard of smuggling drugs, and I think I've heard of smuggling weapons, but smuggling turtles, that's a new one. I guess they smuggle different stuff here.*

We're traveling with this weird lady named Elizama. She keeps making predictions. Everything predicts something for her. She can read your palm, read your tea leaves, read the dried coffee in the bottom of a cup. When a flock of big pink birds flew overhead, she gasped like she was dying and said, "Soong Tan, you be sure to stay close to Ysa!"

Like, how far does she think I'm going to get? Where does she think I'm going to go? I said, "What do you mean?"

"I see danger. I see you all alone wiss great danger all around. Many friends and great danger." Then she grabs my head with both

hands and looks at me real close. She's got the grossest face, with bright red lips and blue stuff all around her eyes and her eyelashes plucked so she looks like a doll...an old doll with wrinkles a five o'clock shadow over her lip. She holds my head so close I can smell her lipstick and chewing gum. "You be carefully!" she says. "I do not know what weell hoppen, but you must be very, very carefully!"

Well, before too long I knew what she was talking about. I was down in the cargo hold playing hide-n-seek, which they call scondji-scondji *here, and I was just running for home when I stubbed my toe on a piece of pipe that was lying there for no reason. Yow! That really hurt! It bled and everything. But at least because of it I got to see the captain's cabin, and you know what? You're going to think this is weird, so I'm kind of glad it happened. Now it's over with. Elizama warned me, and then it happened, and now I can forget about it. Thank God. Because the stuff she predicts, sometimes it comes true.*

Yours truly,

Soong Tan

Chapter Six

The Bunnyhuggers

Edgar snapped out of it in Santarém, where the Tapajós flows north into the Amazon. There they had to change boats, a pretty big deal when you've got a dozen gumball machines and the temperature's way over a hundred and you've got a medium-sized crowd watching because you're the most interesting thing to come up the river in two hundred years. According to Edgar, this was the arrival of civilization, He'd figured out he could buy a new storage globe to replace the one that had broken. It wasn't the end of the world.

They had to spend all day in Santarém waiting for a boat up the Tapajós. Crack entrepreneur that he was, Edgar saw it as opportunity. He deployed his machines across the dock like a row of Beefeaters. Performing a shameless "Step-right-up-and-get-yourself-a-gumball" routine, pointing out the machines' features with some kind of pointer, he all but dragged people up to the face of temptation. He passed out twenty-five centavo pieces to get a few kids to try it. As the pinwheels spun and the sparks shot out, the crowd went nuts. The full splendor of civilization had arrived. And all it cost was the equivalent of a U.S. quarter.

Later, in a not-too-sleazy open-front sidewalk bar just across the street, Edgar counted his take. He had piles of coins all over this table, silvery columns among the sweaty glasses of beer. Soong Tan kept to her own table, where she worked on a postcard to her sixth-grade class at Beauville Elementary School. It said, "This place reminds me of Burma," she wrote, "but at least I'm not alone."

Ysa was scribbling away at a letter that already almost filled a notebook. She just kept jotting down her thoughts and observations. She thought that maybe if something exciting happened she'd write a book about it. So far, however, it was just rambling notes, a conversation with a friend who wasn't there to hear it.

His chin down at table level so he could see the little towers of his fortune, Edgar said, "Twenty-eight reais and twenty-five centavos in two hours." He nudged the columns around to make the money look like as much as possible. "Not bad."

Elizama took up her beer glass and rotated it to find a spot she had not yet stained with a curve of blood-red lipstick. The glass looked like it suffered from multiple lacerations. "What you can to buy wiff twenty-eight reais?" she asked in a cynical voice. She seemed to be thinking in terms of Mercedes Benzes.

"Fourteen bottles of Brahma beer," Edgar replied. He tapped one of the coins on the empty bottle. A waiter came to life and rushed over with another bottle.

"That's just two hours in one location," Edgar explained. "Now imagine twenty-four hours a day in twelve locations. You sure you don't want in on this, Kit?"

Ysa could tell that Kit was already tired of hearing about it. "I'll have to talk with my attorney," he said, gazing out over the river. It glimmered in the early-afternoon sun. Several buzzards soared in lazy circles, riding the heat while waiting for something dead to float by. "What happens if some kid chokes on a gumball way out in the jungle. Can I be held liable?"

"They don't have liability in this country," Edgar said, missing Kit's cynicism. "Responsibility is a foreign concept. Here comes more logs."

He pointed upstream at four barges stacked high with enormous trunks.

"I thought they stopped cutting down the rain forest," Ysa said.

"Ha! No way. They might talk about it, but as long as there's money in it, they'll keep cutting it down. It's entirely possible those logs came off a federal forest reserve. But they're worth so much that the loggers can afford to buy off the *polícia militar.*"

This disgusted Ysa. She was a confirmed bunny-hugger. Save the salamanders. No nukes. Adopt a dolphin. All that stuff.

"Don't they ever worry about oxygen?" she asked.

"Not till oxygen's worth money," Edgar said. Something about the gleam in his eye, a laser trained on a small fortune in logs, told her that he didn't give a damn one way or the other.

Kit said, "Where's the gold? I thought there was gold in the Amazon." He was happy they were off the topic of gumballs. He had his shirt pulled up a bit so his belly could cool off. He had his shoes off, too, his feet up on one of the shaky steel chairs.

"We'll be up in gold territory," Edgar said. "I wouldn't recommend drinking any river water unless you know what's upstream. It's all poisoned by mercury."

"They have mercury mines?"

"No, dummy. They use it to mine gold. When they've got a little gold dust mixed in with sand and dirt, they stir in a little mercury. It combines with the gold. Then they pour it off and heat it up. The mercury evaporates and leaves the gold behind."

"That doesn't sound too healthy," Ysa said. "Mercury's highly toxic. I wouldn't want to breathe it in."

"Health isn't their concern. Gold's their concern. And don't you see how all this relates to gumballs?"

Kit smiled wryly. "I had a feeling it would."

Edgar continued. "When you come right down to it, what good's gold? It's worthless. You can't eat it, can't live in it, can't brush your teeth with it."

"So?"

"So suppose the nearest supermarket's three days away by canoe. Your boss is paying you big money to muck around in the mud, not to mention poison yourself with mercury. The only thing you've got to spend your money on is cachaça and bubble gum. You're bored and you've got a hangover. So what do you do?"

Kit thought a second and said, "Any girls around?"

Ysa gave him a playful shove with her elbow. Edgar said, "Sure. Plenty of girls. And they've got every disease under the sun. And there stands a magnificent, disease-free gumball machine."

Kit was tired of this. Very, very tired. The heat hung over him like a heavy wool blanket. "I'd buy gum," he said. "I'd buy the goddam gum. OK?"

"My point exactly."

Kit surrendered in silence. Nobody said anything. They just sat, oppressed with the humidity, looking through the heat waves rippling off the street, vaguely seeing the gumball machines lined up on the dock, the little blue and white boat that they would soon board, the tan river beyond that, and the vast blue sky bleached pale from the sun. Ysa wanted nothing more than to climb into her hammock and doze off her beer-soaked doldrums as a light water-breeze drifted across the deck. She was tired of the Amazon. In fact, she hadn't even seen jungle yet. No monkeys. No anacondas. No jaguars or toucans or peccaries. Just an endless parade of medium-sized trees along the bank, second-growth forest replacing a jungle long ago cut down or burned. The upper Tapajós was supposed to be primal forest, but by this point, she really didn't care. She was hot, tired, sweaty, dirty, and her bowels felt like trouble brewing. At this point she was pushing on for Soong Tan's education and Kit McCracken's entertainment. She herself had had enough.

Due to lack of absolutely anything else to do, and to kind of pay rent at the table, and at Edgar's relentless insistence, they went ahead and had another beer. Soong Tan had another soda, some Brazilian stuff called *guaraná*. Everybody was just starting to think about the possibility of finally raising their overcooked carcasses and hauling them across the street to the boat when a couple of hippy-types came along.

Not hippies, exactly, but youngish, early twenties, she in a long flowery dress of translucent fabric, he in stylishly torn and faded jeans, both of them with backpacks, both pulling cardboard boxes on little luggage carts, both wearing sandals, both looking just as hot and sweaty as the other. Her ditch-water brown hair hung in a ponytail almost to her waist. His did, too, though it was blonde and prettier than hers. They'd come upon the bar by apparent accident, suddenly looking up and in, then saw Edgar's morose band of gumball hucksters. Their reaction was that of all gringos when they meet some of their species in a way-off place. They noticed and tried to pretend they didn't. But they couldn't. There was no denying it. They were all from the same place. The first words from the girl's mouth were crisply British: "Oh!" she chirped. "Gringos...right?"

The first thing Kit noticed about her was her light blue eyes. They sparkled. As he would later tell Ysa, they had absolutely no effect on him what-so-ever. It was just something he happened to notice.

To which Ysa would say, "Yeah, right."

The first thing Ysa noticed, of course, was that the girl had a large bead of sweat dangling from a single curly whisker on the end of her chin. And the guy, she said, looked like he hadn't shaved in about two days. Blonde beard.

She just happened to notice.

So there they were, everybody just happening to notice everybody else, and the girl's question was hanging in the air like wet laundry. Gringos, right?

Kit finally said, in clipped British, "Right...gringos."

"Whew," the girl said, and she stripped off her pack. It almost threw her off balance. The guy remained standing, his thumbs under the straps of his pack as if he expected to move on in the next thirty seconds. Ysa looked mildly miffed. Kit swung around a chair from a neighboring table.

"Have a seat," he said. "You look bushed."

Ysa said, "We were just leaving."

"Ve are lookink for a boat," the guy said. He had a German accent. "You haff heard off it?"

"Heard of it," Edgar blurted. "We've practically bought it. That's her right across the street. The one with the gumball machines on the...roof! Goddammit, I told them..."

"You're kidding," the girl says. She was one of those chicks who's just sooooo gushy about everything? "You're kidding," she gushed. "Are you going to...to...what's that place, Goose?"

"Jacaréacanga." With his German accent he made it sound like Transylvania or something. Ysa's skin crept. Two degrees south of the equator and she gets goose flesh. Maybe it was because he was wearing a little necklace of what looked like snake fangs. Behind her, Soong Tan slurped the last of her *guaraná* and said, "I'm still waiting for somebody to spell that place for me."

"Yeah, that place," the chick says.

"We sure are," Edgar said, taking control by reaching out his hand. "Edgar Entwhistle," he said. The girl shook it. Her name was Gaia. The guy was Gustav. He took off his pack before shaking everybody's hand.

"So," said Kit. "What's going on in Jacaréacanga?"

Gaia did all the talking. Ysa knew right then and there that Goose had to be the brains of the outfit. Gaia was the energy. She spoke at the speed of sound, her train of thought a discombobulated torrent on no particular track. In a nutshell, she was out to save the world. Step one: toss a thousand tiny purple porpoises out of an airplane over a logging camp a hundred miles south of Jacaréacanga. She extracted a porpoise from her cardboard box. It was wrapped up in a tiny green parachute.

Ysa said, "I don't get it."

'It's a statement," Gaia said, raising her chin in a gesture of defiance. "Clear-cutting the jungle doesn't just hurt the local ecosystem. It reaches into the sea and around the world."

"But aren't they plastic?" Edgar asked. "Suppose one floated downstream and a porpoise choked on it?"

"Don't mind him,." Kit injected. "Have some beer." He handed her his glass.

"They aren't plastic. They're pressed bicarbonate of soda and soy solids, with grape juice added for coloring. It dissolves in water." She handed Edgar the little porpoise, freeing her hand for Kit's beer. "You could actually eat it."

So Edgar bit off the tail. It was kind of gummy and stuck to the front of his teeth. "Weird," he said.

"It iss psychology," Goose said in a serious growl. "If ve convince vun logger zat he does wrong, ve sink he vill convince uzzers."

Edgar, using his fingernail to peel purple bicarbonate of soda and soy solids off his teeth, said, "Good luck's all I got to say to that." His lips buzzed as he struggled to spit out a fleck of porpoise.

"Ve shoot get tickets for ze boat," Goose said to Gaia.

Too exhausted to move, she waved faintly in the direction of the dock. "You do it," she said. "I'll watch the stuff."

Goose obeyed, scuffing across the street to the dock and the boat. Kit signaled the waiter for another beer.

Elizama looked oddly suspicious as she reached across the table toward Gaia. "Please," she said. "Let me to see your hand."

Gaia extended it to the center of the table. Elizama turned it over, perused the palm, traced a few lines. "I'm going to live a long time," Gaia said. "I already know that." She was squinting into the sun, watching her Goose negotiate with someone at the boat.

"Zat's not what it says here," Elizama cooed sweetly. "It says somesing very strange. It says you will get lost and you will divide in two pieces. I sink zat means you will die, but I don't know."

"Let me see that hand." Gaia snatched it back to herself and held it up close to her face. She picked at it, then spit on it and rubbed a clean spot. "You know what it is?" she concluded. "I'm a Gemini. That's all."

Elizama looked dubious. "Maybe is," she said. "Maybe is not."

Ysa became conscious of her own heartbeat. It was an odd sort of fear. She thought it might be sunstroke or something. She didn't tell anybody, though, and she forgot about it when Elizama suddenly said, "I feel a storm coming on."

The sky was blue for as far as anybody could see, but Kit took advantage of the break in subject. He dragged his feet off the chair, slapped both knees and said, "Then we'd better get our gumballs in gear." He stood up and held his hand out over the sidewalk as if it might catch a drop of rain from the clear, blue sky. "You mean like a thunderstorm?" he asked.

Elizama tilted her head to the left. "Yes," she said heavily, "and no. Yes, like a sunderstorm, but no...not a sunderstorm. Somesing worse."

From

Frankenstein on the Cusp of Something

Chapter One

Frankenstein Doesn't Play Ball

Frankenstein sat near you in the fifth grade. You've forgotten him. If he played on your kickball team, he stood so far out in the right field weeds that you couldn't see him. No one in the history of the game ever booted one out that far. He was safe there. He could think his thoughts.

He wasn't safe in the lunch line. You stepped on his foot and didn't notice. You jabbed him with a back swing of your elbows, the punch line of a joke he didn't hear. You left him with no place to sit except with the girls. He remembers that. He remembers you.

He remembers high school worst of all. Same deal but no girls. He still played obscure positions in obligatory ball games. He never sank a basket, never made it to first base, never knew what to do when the center hiked the ball. It didn't seem to matter what he did. Usually he just stood there. Once, in gym, during a basketball scrimmage, the ball came into his hands. Somebody loomed over him, huffing and puffing, preventing any throw or movement. He looked up into the hairy maw of the kid's armpit and said, "You want it that bad? Take it." And he handed the boy the ball. Remember that? The boy looked back as you dribbled away, ran as if he had water in his shoes, tried an easy lay-up but flubbed it.

Somebody might remember the time Frankenstein threw up in the hall between classes. Somebody might remember the time in the cafeteria when he slipped in somebody else's tapioca, fell beneath his own ravioli, green beans, creamed corn, juice. Somebody might remember the empty seat in the SAT exam. Frankenstein forgot to go. At the moment the proctor said, "You may now begin," Frankenstein was lying on his back under a thicket of laurel, wondering if there was a God.

While waiting for the next SAT exam to come around, he held a few jobs. He hosed the dog dew out kennel cages until somebody told him what he smelled like. He dried cars at a car wash until the skin came off his hands. He was the janitor of a big Catholic church until he applied full-strength Mr. Clean to the grime of an ancient crucifix. The paint wiped right off. He actually had Christ's blood on his hands while a priest blessed him out. He just stood there feeling stupid and guilty. Stuff like that happens to Frankenstein.

Nails bend under Frankenstein's hammer. Toilet paper has never ripped straight for him. Computers crash. Silent crowds give him hiccups. Dirt seeks him out, attaches itself where he can't see it but others can. His father left him before he graduated from kindergarten.

He went to college, barely crawled out. Somehow they let him graduate without a major. Then his diploma didn't have his name on it. Somebody in Registration had thought his name a joke. They get a lot of forms filled out for Mickey Mouse, Al Einstein, Chuck Wagon, Moe Rhon. Nobody's really named Frankenstein, so they left it blank. Before he took the diploma and photo ID to Registration, he lost both. Last he saw of them, they were on his mother's Oldsmobile. Not in. On. Regis-

tration, personified by a pasty-faced gum-chewing lady with bright red hair and a New York accent, wouldn't give him a new one. It's kind of like a blank check, she said. Anybody can write their name in there. And it's kind of not like a blank check because you can't cancel it. Somebody out there had a nice new diploma. Frankenstein didn't.

Love? It's not in the cards for Frankenstein. His nose, mashed to a mailbox at an early age, sits off to the left at the top, off to the right at the bottom. One ear definitely sticks out a little too far. It looks like it could flap. His teeth buck out a bit, and there's a dark gap between the incisors. His mustache looked pretty wispy for the its first two years. He grew a beard to hide the lack of meat in his chin, but somehow it got longer without getting thicker. Maybe his eyes are a quarter-inch too close together. He's worn glasses since the fourth grade, which only magnifies the weirdness of his eyes. His pupils are too dark to read. He seems to be hiding behind them. His mother described his hair as the color of a mule looking the other way. She's from West Virginia. She knows these things.

And he's short. Modeled after the common concrete block, he's squarish, open-faced and seemingly just knee-high. He's the kind of person you could practically trip over. But he's quick. He stays out of the way. He knows you won't see him. With your head up there in the rarefied air of conceit and self-concern, you don't notice much of what goes on below your haughty sight line. He's essentially invisible, and he knows it. He sees you coming and keeps to the side. You go by without noticing. Waitresses do the same. Right to his face they say, "Oh, I didn't see you."

Funny how he has the opposite effect when he hitchhikes. Drivers see him on the side of the road, standing behind his dirty white duffel bag. He doesn't hold out a thumb. He just shows them the palms of his hands. Cars pull right over, at least on good days. He tosses his bag onto the back seat, hops in front and off they go. Sometimes it's a drunk, sometimes a homosexual, sometimes a Jesus freak, a lonely person, a sleepy driver, an angel who can't help but help. Once it was a guy AWOL from the army and just as sad as could be. Once it was some yoga maniacs on their way to a festival. Once it was nine or ten Mexicans in an old Lincoln. Once it was a guy who had a rifle across his lap. One guy had no legs. A lady with a big yellow airplane propeller on the back seat, one end sticking out the window, had no voice. She had to honk through a little hole in her throat, but that didn't stop her. She yakked and yakked and yakked, even laughed, even sort of started to cry. Frankenstein went right along, taking cues when to laugh, look surprised or give a moan of sympathy--empathy even; he found himself beginning to imitate her huffy little honk. But he never knew if she was talking about her yellow propeller, her throat problem, the price of sow bellies, the weather or what. When it came time to leave the car, he kissed her hand. Her honk became a coo. As he pulled his duffel bag from the bag seat, he ran his fingers along the propeller, the only time he'd ever touched one. For the rest of his life he would squint at any low-flying aircraft to see if the propeller is yellow.

It's the Mexicans who drop him off across the street from a bowling alley. Big red letters across one wall say "Bowling." A flag over the door says "Bowling," too, its letters laden with blue icicles. This is in Arizona. The building is a refrigerator in a vast spill of lava. Frankenstein goes in. High-pitched thunder and bleating pop music fill the place. He hasn't bowled since the eighth grade, when he quickly learned that it was not his sport. It's safe to try again. He's not going to see how well he can bowl. He's going to see how long he can milk one game.

Can he bowl in sandals? A woman doesn't think so. She's just the cleaning lady sweeping up behind the counter, but she takes a look at his feet. They're filthy in their tire-rubber sandals. She hands him a pair

of purple bowling shoes with a zippy little yellow lightning bolt across the instep. "You got socks?" she asks.

"Sure do." They're a thousand miles away, in Delaware, at his mother's house, neatly folded in a drawer, just in case.

"Good. You gotta wear socks."

No he doesn't. He sets up camp at Lane 21, stuffs his naked, swollen feet into the shoes. They don't like it in there. It's hot and stuffy. But he knows that if he bowls in his Guatemalan Goodyears, he'll leave tread marks on the hardwood floor. He remembers a bank teller on the outskirts of Chicago. He left tread marks on the linoleum of her bathroom. Until that point, things had been going well.

He relaxes before choosing a ball. He thinks about it before giving it a roll. When he finally develops a satisfying strategy, he prances on up to the line and lets 'er go. The ball walks a tightrope down the middle of the lane, plows straight into the center pin. Everybody topples each other over like clowns.

Frankenstein fills with a scary satisfaction. He really doesn't want to get the knack of this. He doesn't want to be a bowler. He stalls around for a long while, then tries a shot with his right hand rather than his usual left. The ball sweeps wide, veers in, attacks from the side. The pins fall with a clatter of urgency.

He aims for the gutter but the ball won't go in. He sticks a wad of gum to it. No problem. It just rolls a little funny, a Caribbean two-step, tickwhump/ tickwhump/ tickwhump, all the way. They shouldn't all fall down on a shot like that, but they do as the ball pivots on its sticky little pink spot. He rolls it regular one time, tippy-toeing forward, sliding on his lead foot right up to the line. Even that works. A gathered crowd gasps with amazement, cheers at each strike. One ball to go and it's a perfect game.

The hush presses on him. Knowing he will fail, he refuses to do it right off. No time limit in bowling, right? Time segments. It stops and goes. It stops while Frankenstein goes to the bathroom. With his ball. He goes alone, assumes the solitary stall, a dented, black-enameled room neither clean nor dirty. His belt remains buckled, his zipper zipped. The global weight in his lap almost sparkles--pretends to sparkle--with golden flecks on a field of dusty black. He caresses it for the glory it has given him. It is so round and heavy, a model of the world, of heads, of atoms, the planets and distant suns, blow-fish, helium balloons, cantaloupes, milk-laden breasts, globs burped up in lava lamps, bubbles, cannon ammo, the dots of I's, monkey-fist knots--so much depends on the form of bowling balls. No wonder the pins fall! How could they resist? Who are they to stand when the holy sphere rolls in? Frankenstein uses spit to clean a spot on the ball, then curls his torso forward to set his lips to the cool plastic surface. So much depends.

The bathroom door swings open, swings shut. Feet appear below the stall door. Tutti-frutti bowling shoes, slightly duck-towed. Their owner says, "You all right in there?"

It's a woman--a big one by the sound of her.

Frankenstein says, "No problem."

"You got a ball in there?" The shoes don't move.

Frankenstein pleads guilty.

Big pause. Then, "I'm sorry sir. No balls in the men's room."

Frankenstein refrains from the obvious comment. He holds in his lap the model of the world, the universe and all that's equidistant from a point. And testicles. An eleven-twelfth's perfect game awaits his final roll. He cools his forehead on the ball, a slow rock from left temple to right. He says nothing. It's her decision. The ball, so to speak, is in her court.

"Sir?...Sir, I'm afraid I must insist."

It's still in her court. She can't get rid of it unless he talks. He feels his bowels and bladder swell. They know what toilet stalls are for, so, here, atop the round-holed seat, they assume what they've been brought here to do. Like hounds in a cage at the edge of the field, they're ready to cut loose. Frankenstein would love to drop his drawers and accommodate them. He'd like to a lot, but he has a bowling ball in his lap and danger at the door. If he puts the ball down--between his feet is the only space--she might see it and snatch it away. Then he'll have to go out and confront her. On full bowels and bladder, maybe even with his pants down. He doesn't want to confront her. He wants to take a dump, a leak, and be done with it. He wants to go back to Lane 21 and finish his game.

"Really, sir," she says, not unkindly. "Either give me the ball or I call the cops."

Nice try, thinks he. What's the crime? Taking a bowling ball into a men's room? Wouldn't that make a dandy court case. Almost worth getting arrested for. He'd insist on a full jury. He'd call in the TV cameras. He'd represent himself, present charts, diagrams, photographs, the single piece of solid evidence, the gold-flecked ball, plucked from obscurity and raised to legal fame, right up there with O.J.'s gloves and Liz Borden's ax. When the woman again says, "I'm going to call the cops," Frankenstein thinks, good. But when she says, "I really mean it," he knows she won't.

He takes the easy way out. He surrenders. He just rolls the ball under the door and says, "Save it for me, would you? Lane 21." He's glad he doesn't have to see her gloat.

Back at Lane 21, he finds, to utter horror, that his ball is nowhere in sight and that a bowling league team has set up camp. Four flabby people have re-set the pins, done away with Frankenstein's score sheet, rolled a few balls down his lane, busted his karma like...like....

They've lit cigarettes, shed shoes and jackets, draped their socks over the back of the long, fiberglass bench, dangled a large, stainless steel crucifix from the overhead projector. The bowlers' names glow on the overhead screen: Marilynn, Bob, Bill, Debbie. These people are plain vanilla to the core, but they've moved in and taken over. According to a red-on-blue nylon jacket, they are the Cindy's Country Skillet Sharks. They have seized his territory. If bowling alleys had historians and if these invading hordes had left any evidence of him, Frankenstein would be history.

What's he going to do--take on four flabby people? Not only do they fancy themselves sharks, but they have a whole bowling league behind them. Frankenstein's alone, a wimp out of Delaware. The hierarchy of authority here begins with the woman in the tutti-frutti bowling shoes. Above her, he supposes, are the police. Above the police are their grandfathers, the Supreme Court. Above them is God, if any. Given the incident in the bathroom, the embarrassment of police action, and the big, steel cross, Frankenstein has no hope. He has lost his lane, his ball and his last shot at a perfect game. Grounds for murder? He figures it depends whether the judge bowls. He treats himself to the image of a black-clad man billowing up to the lane line like a thundercloud, delivering his shiny black ball like a finely honed legal brief.

So Frankenstein can start a ruckus or just pay up and move on. Paying won't be easy. The lady at the counter is his friend in the tutti-frutti shoes. Now he knows more than her feet and ankles. She has the shoulders and broad back of a heavy-duty bowler. Her hips and thighs show signs of diet grazed at the bowling alley snack bar, fat rendered suet by lackadaisical exercise. Her face shows a certain ingrained sadness, perhaps a touch of shame for reasons he cannot guess. He feels a little sorry for her. Her face, he is sure, has never, at least since childhood, been gazed on as an object of beauty, an object of desire. If a man ever told her she was beautiful, he lied. For reasons that cannot be called reason, men avoid the pointed nose, the concave face, the down-turned lip line, the fatted underchin, the overbite of a suppressed IQ.

Frankenstein walks away from his lane, approaches the flier-and-warning-strewn glass counter. Socks required. No practice frames. Balls waxed: $1.00. Bowl a perfect game? Get one free! He leans into the counter, grips its cold chrome edge, looks up at the lady and says, "Nice eyes."

Taken aback, she shows surprise, then a second thought, the possibility that she might indeed have nice eyes. Frankenstein says, "I like brown," but that pushes it too far. She has indeed been told she's beautiful, it seems. Someone said that, ejaculated, and left. Now she looks at Frankenstein as if it had been him.

"Lane 21?" she says in cold business terms. He knows she really means to say, "You the guy with the ball in the bathroom?" From behind the counter she lifts his sandals and score sheet. "One game," she says. "One shoes. Plus tax. Five fifty-eight." She scans the lanes behind him, her clay-brown eyes unavailable for argument.

"I didn't get to finish," Frankenstein says. "The Sharks took my lane. I would've bowled a perfect game and you'd owe me a free one. Know what I mean?"

She glances at the score sheet, checks a machine that counts the frames of all the lanes. "Says twenty-three frames here. What do I look, stupid?"

Eighty-two percent pissed is what she looks. He's sure she's been pursuing the perfect game since she was waist-high to a bowling ball. He walks in out of nowhere and does it--boom, boom, boom--almost. No wonder she wanted his ball so bad. She probably thinks there's something about it. He searches her heavy, concave face for signs of stupidity. It's in there somewhere, he can tell. He wonders how it is possible to see ignorance in the topography of a face. He almost feels like asking, but he knows he'd be barking up the wrong tree. He just wants his sandals back. "Damned near a perfect game," he says. "Look."

She does, giving the score sheet but a flicker of attention. "Yeah, right," she says. "You come in off the street, take twelve practice shots, which you're not supposed to do under penalty of law, then bowl eleven strikes, then take your ball into the bathroom. A house ball. And house shoes. Sure. I'll let you get away with five fifty-eight if you cough it up now and, " she drops to a whisper,"never show your miserable ass in this bowling alley again."

Maybe she is ugly. To the core. Ugliness on the hoof. Ugliness defined, the very quintessence of the stuff. Right before his eyes and miserable ass. In a way, it's an honor. Why hurry through the experience? Better to linger in her shadow, savor the moment, milk it for all it's worth. He searches for her eyes, but they dodge him. They are beautiful, as all eyes are, and they accent her less palatable parts. They float like little brown lifeboats in sea of bloodshot moonlight. He wants to save those lifeboats. He knows what it's like behind them. "I'm sorry about the ball," he says. "I didn't want anybody to take it."

"Still gotta pay five fifty-eight." She keeps her eyes high in their sockets, pretending to check scores on the bank of screens above the lanes.

What's he supposed to do? Stand there and keep refusing to pay? Abandon his sandals, walk away, out the door in bowling shoes, forcing her to do something painful? Cough up the five-fifty-eight and call it a day? Tough choices all of them, each pitting his ego against hers. He wishes he knew the magic formula that would enlighten her eyes and let her love him just because for a moment he had loved a bowling ball that for eleven frames had done exactly what bowling balls are supposed to do. She runs a bowling alley! She wears bowling shoes to work! She probably knows the names of the ten best bowlers in America and their averages. Can she feel nothing above disdain for the house ball that made good? She says, "Five fifty-eight or I call the cops."

Frankenstein forks it over. Six bucks, keep the change. He pulls off his bowling shoes, tied, and holds them to her low and not quite far enough. Just as her fingers touch them, he retracts them an invisible bit, pulling her an invisible bit closer. He leans in and slides her a whisper audible only because it's on a frequency not reached by the rolling thunder and gentle explosions of bowling games. He says, "Want to know the secret?"

He senses her breath stop short. Their eyes meet. They are just as brown as can be, shot with black radii and glazed with melted glacier ice. The shoes between them conduct a certain juice, a voltage sufficient to make his face buzz hot. "Just roll the ball," he says in a sincere and caressing tone. "Just let it go."

She jerks back as if he he's just nipped her with a hickey. His sandals fly from her hand as if bursting with roaches. "Get the fuck out of here," she says, eyes burning. "Just get the fuck out."

With great relief and no regrets, young Frankenstein steps out of the stale cold air and into the warm humus of a summer's afternoon. The glass door closes on the explosions of devastated pins and the relentless bleating of pop-tune earwash. Frankenstein will never bowl again, of that he is sure, not if he has to do it in a bowling alley. He wonders how far he'd get if he invented cross-country bowling. Would people bowl in the woods if their balls drifted across pine needles and silently toppled logs into a bed of moss? Would they know they were having fun if they weren't pounded with pop tunes and parting with cash? Would the lady with the brown eyes and tutti-frutti shoes find happiness in a place that didn't need its rules posted? So many questions for just one bowling alley, but Frankenstein must move on.

Chapter Two

Frankenstein's Trip

In West Virginia, Frankenstein rode four feet from death. To save on gas, the driver of a rusty, yellow car of no discernible make slipstreamed an eighteen-wheeler almost all night long. He tucked his little car into the relative vacuum behind the truck and let it pull him through Appalachia. They rode so close to the bumper that Frankenstein could see individual flecks of grit where the one working headlight shined hard and close. The vast, towering back of the truck filled the little windshield. It seemed to move in slow motion, a surreal, neon monolith cut off from the night that sped by around it. Someone had fingered "Wash Me" in the grit. More grit had almost filled in the letters. Frankenstein just stared at the short, time-worn message. He wished he could lower the windshield, lean out and write, "Frankenstein was here." The truck was certainly close enough, and Frankenstein certainly had the time. But he feared he wouldn't need to write that message. If the truck driver just touched the brakes, Frankenstein's face would have left a graphic impression on its back door, his face and that of the tightwad at the wheel. All night long he kept nodding off, even in sleep assuming he'd meet his maker with a dirty face and nothing but nubs where his teeth used to be. Each time his head tilted forward, he snapped awake and for a terrifying second forgot that he and the truck were headed in the same direction. This continued until the shaky glow of false dawn, when the car ran out of gas. Frankenstein stayed in the passenger seat for a polite interval, then walked away.

In Georgia, on a straight state highway through fields of soy, a black Firebird thundered by. Flames graced its hood and front fenders. As it whumped by, an eight-foot orange rat snake leaped up out of the pavement, its spine crushed. In its horrific throes, it flitted as lightly as a butterfly and came right at Frankenstein. Aghast, he abandoned his duffel bag and scrambled away like an upside-down crab. The snake's agonized contortions wrenched it into a flapping, knee-high, uppercase W, a back-biting C, an impossible Q, an inverted z, a frantic S, a withering j, a spitting i in Palmer script, and finally an apostrophe draped across Frankenstein's bag. If it spelled something, Frankenstein didn't catch it. He was backing up fast, sucking in air through a constricted throat, screaming inwardly as if it were his own spine, his own ineffable anguish. The mashed nerves didn't let the snake die. Its tail twitched and its rust-colored head, as blunt as a bullet, convulsed to the side as if it might lick its wound with its little, red forked tongue. The white, ribbed roof of its mouth was as horrid as the underbelly of a cockroach. When it finally stopped twitching, pale goo oozed from its mouth. Frankenstein threw up.

For a long, long time he sat twenty feet away, spitting and wiping salt water from his eyes. His duffel bag had snake goo on it. If the bag hadn't contained everything he owned, he would have abandoned it. He could have lived without his dirty underwear, but he had a letter to his sister in there, over twenty pages on paper place mats from diners, segments of paper trash from the side of the road, napkins, even a regular postcard featuring the biggest truck stop in all of Oklahoma. He kept meaning to buy a notebook and transcribe it all to a coherent whole, but notebooks never crossed his path. Now it all lay under a dead snake from the Peach Tree State. It took almost an hour to become a reasonably normal situation. Then he crept forward, yanked his bag from under the snake, and wiped the worst of the goo off on a tuft of grass.

In Missouri Frankenstein kept thinking about home. He imagined his bed with clean sheets smelling of a thunderstorm. He conjured up an impossible trove of chocolate chip cookies. A mockingbird tootles its repertoire as he snoozes in a hammock in the dense shade of a sugar maple in his back yard. His mother brings him great books and calls him dear and has nothing to complain about. At night he watches hilarious TV shows, and a girlfriend he doesn't quite recognize comes over to stick her tongue in his ear and whisper things in a Swedish accent. Mid-state he crossed the highway and started hitching back the way he'd come.

But before long, he thought of the damp, gray sheets of his unmade bed and his mother's high-pitched opinion of his unmade bed, the dearth of edibles in the kitchen, the brutal noise of the neighbors' lawn mowers, his mother reminding him of certain facts, a girl with cold fingers and a tendency to whine. He crossed the highway again and wondered what it must be like in Utah.

The Swedish girl stayed with him for a long time. In Michigan, early winter, a fat guy asked about her. Was she cute? Did she have long legs? What did she wear in the summer? Was she blonde everywhere? What, exactly, was she like in bed? Frankenstein made up all kinds of stuff. He made up stuff about her sister, too. And her girl cousins who came to visit from the old country. He took the man on America's most erotic canoe ride, across a lake, down a river and over a waterfall. Everyone was killed but him. The man mashed down on the brakes, sending the car swerving and screeching across the road. "Get the fuck outta here," the man said, angry in his disappointment.

Frankenstein got the fuck out. He stood there as the car sped away, his duffel bag in the back seat. This was on the Upper Peninsula. They hadn't passed a town in hours. He didn't remember seeing another vehicle all day. He started walking in the same direction he'd been going in the car. He thought about the Swedish girl all the way. He wished he had a Swedish girl to travel with, a real one. If they got stuck walking across the Upper Peninsula, every couple of miles they could go into the woods and make love on a bed of pine needles. It wouldn't be so bad. But he didn't have a Swedish girl. All he had was sore feet and sense of worsening chill. Still, he couldn't complain. After walking for most of the day, he found his duffel bag on the side of the road. Things tended to balance out like that. Not that he'd trade a Swedish girl for a duffel bag with a snake goo stain, but it certainly could have worked out worse. Frankenstein doesn't complain.

In Texas Frankenstein found a perfect place to sleep--a sloppy pile of hay under a broad, lone tree at the corner of a pasture. It wasn't dark yet, but he wasn't going to pass up sleeping quarters this good. He thought it would be a nice place to do his plastic bag trick.

He does this sometimes, lies down in a comfortable, private place and puts his head in a plastic bag. Alone in there, he thinks about home a long time ago. On the wings of a deepening buzz, he can take himself back to the sunny age of five, a time when once his father knocked over a glass of milk at the dinner table. Like fanged slime, the milk lurched from its cave, stretching at his mother, slithering into her lap faster than she could back away. She screamed and leaped up, sputtering fire and crackling with little black lightning bolts. Daddy, silent, fuming, rose from the table, stomped quietly to the back door, slammed it so hard the house boomed.

His mother's anger, as wild as wasps, attacked not only daddy but little Frankenstein, his big sister, and all the other vile, useless subspecies of the world. Growling bad words from the top of her throat, she lashed at the milk with a dish towel, wrung its neck at the sink, came back for more, rubbed the table beyond all visible milk, rinsed the towel again, wrung it, rinsed it, wrung it, folded it into a tight little wad, dropped it into the trash can under the sink, then removed the white trash bag, twisted its neck, tied it shut, carried it outside like a dead thing, dropped it into a bigger trash bag and tied it shut. Then she went upstairs and took a long, long bath.

Daddy didn't come back, not even after dark. Frankenstein snuggled with his sister that night, both of them listening to the dirge of crickets, waiting for the back door to open again and trying not to wrinkle the bedspread. Somehow, next morning, he knew to go look in the shed.

That's what he thinks about most when he does his plastic bag trick. It's an old habit now, but he still thinks about how it must have felt to lie there in a dusky shed, stifling among tools and old paint cans. He thinks about the last sound his father heard, the same rhythmic crinkling of thin plastic, so soothing at first, so slow, then faster as he gasps at the humid warmth of his own exhalation. As he breathes more deeply, the moist plastic compresses against his cheeks and forehead, then expands away. He does this until he gets dizzy and desperate for breath. Then he removes the bag, sucks in delicious air and pants himself to sleep.

When he did this on the bed of hay in Texas, he emerged from the bag to find a black and white cow standing there looking at him, mulling its cud and breathing through its huge, wet nose in the heavy way of someone slightly short of oxygen.

Up in Canada, somewhere in Saskatchewan, he got hit with a bag of garbage – not some little litter sack but a thirty-gallon Glad formerly owned by someone who smoked Craven A's, had a baby, and ate lots of fried chicken. The bag had launched from the back of a pick-up truck and scored a bull's-eye. He saw it coming for about two seconds. It hovered beside the little truck, an impossible asteroid with Frankenstein written all over it. It exploded when it hit him, sent him reeling westward and then down to the sandy asphalt. This was in sunflower country, middle of the summer. Frankenstein had just been thinking what a wonderful place it was, an infinite sea with waves of sunny faces. If he had known how to paint, he would have set up an easel right there. But Frankenstein couldn't paint the broad side of a barn. Suddenly, that didn't matter. He was covered with household trash. Later, upon reflection, he thought he might have learned something from the experience.

Also up in Canada, coming into Vancouver, he got picked up by a drunk percussionist in a giant Oldsmobile. What a jolly fellow! How he loved his rye. Drank it from a leather-covered flask. He was driving all the way from Moose Jaw just to play the cymbals in a Rossini overture. It didn't pay much, he said, but it was easy and nothing in the universe was more satisfying. He described it in poetic detail, the swelling excitement, the build-up of tension, the climactic q'wizscj of the cymbals. Tchaikovsky's Romeo and Juliet, for example. Had Frankenstein ever heard it? Not that he could recall, not the cymbals, anyway.

"Not the cymbals," the man gasped with utter incredulity. "Not the cymbals." He gripped his flask between his legs and fished around in the glove compartment until he found the right cassette. "Listen," he said. With broad, drunken sways of his arm, he led an invisible orchestra toward orgasm. As the big moment approached, his eyes teared over and his jaw thrust toward the horizon. As the cymbals clashed in what even Frankenstein recognized as a sword fight, the man punched the air.

"Those cymbals," he said when it was all over. "See what I mean?"

Frankenstein saw it. He knew Rossini and could imagine cymbals in this man's hands as they burst with all the glory of the Italian renaissance. He asked if the man could sneak him into the concert hall, back stage, to watch it close-up. The man said he could do better than that. He'd let Frankenstein play them. Right there in the concert. Q'wizscj

Frankenstein knew better than to say, "Yeah, right." He'd been around. He'd seen plenty of stuff weirder than himself playing cymbals in an orchestra. But he also had a certain sixth sense for situations where he was likely to screw up. This was one of them. Out of respect for the music, he warned the man. With a wet, flabby-lipped embouchure, the man discounted the danger. He'd be right there. Frankenstein would feel the rhythm. When the man pointed at him, Frankenstein was to hit the cymbals three times in a row. They listened to the overture on a cassette. The man marked the rhythm with bouncy fingers, indicated the big moment coming up. Frankenstein could feel it. Yes, q'wizscj , q'wizscj , q'wizscj. It would be easy.

They walked into the concert hall as if they owned the place. The man was pretty well soused, but he found the rack of white shirts and black pants and had Frankenstein suit up. They practiced a couple of times. The man warned him not to hit the cymbals dead-on because they'd stick together, locked in suction. Frankenstein worked up a big sweat as he loitered just off-stage, two steps away from the percussion section. The cymbals stood on a special rack. The drunk percussionist did just fine with a series of gongs, raps and clicks. He was almost dancing to the rhythm. Frankenstein could hear the cymbals part coming up.

The man nodded for him to come forward. The conductor did not notice as Frankenstein took up the cymbals, but the entire audience had their eyes on him, the only guy in the orchestra with a beard half a yard long.

The big moment arrived. The man punched the air at the moment the conductor whipped the percussion section with his baton. Frankenstein slammed the cymbals with all his might. Q'wizscj. They didn't stick together. Rather, they inverted. The man didn't notice. He punched the air. Frankenstein had no time to think. He slammed them again. Klank. He then had everyone's complete attention. The orchestra played on but with a clear shift in intensity. It wasn't the Italian renaissance anymore. It was deepest, darkest Africa. The conductor stood there like a scarecrow, his mouth open, his baton frozen. It took two seconds for the next downbeat to come around. The conductor whipped his baton weakly, experimentally, as if only half hoping to repeat an experience. Klank.

And with that, job done, Frankenstein placed the cymbals on their special rack. He turned and walked off stage. As the orchestra played on, he hung up his white shirt and black pants, pulled on his bibbed overalls, and walked right out of the place. He would always wonder what became of the drunk percussionist. He probably never played in a concert again. He probably crept back to Moose Jaw, where until this day he sits sipping rye and not listening to Rossini.

Coming down the coast of California through a corridor of redwoods, Frankenstein got into the car of a woman who cried and cried and cried. It took him a few minutes to realize this. Though her eyes were brimming when he got in, she was smiling. Frankenstein took it for a warm and loving look. He hoped it wasn't that because she looked about fifty-eight years old. He had a way of attracting post-menopausal women. When he was a little boy, they used to come over to his family's table at restaurants. One lady buttered his corn-on-the-cob for him, right there in public. Another smeared spit on his cowlick. They'd been chasing him ever since.

So when this one smiled at him with those bleary eyes, he kept his own eyes pointed elsewhere. She didn't say anything for a long time. When she sniffled and mopped up under her left eye, he noticed. He suspected a trap but asked her if she was all right. She gave him the damnedest nod. It tried to say yes but at the same time shook no. Her golden earrings, fancy things that looked like wind chimes, clinked as they bobbled around. She sniffled again, hard, and dabbed at her eyes with the cuff of her blouse. Frankenstein offered to drive. She shook her head, choked a bit, kept both hands on the wheel. Increasingly upset, Frankenstein begged her to say something. He tried guessing if the problem was love, sickness, death, age, money. She just shook her head. She moaned through her gritted teeth and sniffled as hard as a bath tub draining the last of its water. She looked like she might bite her lower lip off. Spasms heaved her belly and chest. How could she drive? Frankenstein took a worried glance out the windshield. A logging truck stacked with redwoods came at them but rumbled by with only a warning. When he suggested stopping, for coffee or something, she just huffed uncontrollably through her nose.

So then Frankenstein started to cry. He knew exactly what the woman was crying about, but he couldn't put a word to it any better than she. They were crying simply because it was sad – the same "it" as the "it" that rains, the "it" that's hard to say, the "it" that doesn't matter, the little pronoun that means everything except itself. Frankenstein and the woman just cried and cried and cried.

In eastern Tennessee, Frankenstein dallied over a local paper in a little downtown diner. He read about the most horrific thing he had ever heard of. Somebody was in a one-car accident, got all busted up but not killed. He was stuck in his car, hanging out the open door, held in by his seat belt. Along came another motorist. This was up in the mountains somewhere, on a back road. The other motorist came over and just squatted beside the dying man for a while, watching, not saying anything. After a little while, without a word, he took out a pocket knife and slowly slid it into the driver's eye. Then he squatted there for a while and watched. Then he punctured the other eye. Then he patted the driver on the cheek and left. The image of the bad Samaritan haunted Frankenstein for weeks. He could picture the man's face, not cold exactly but serious and a little sad and a little excited, kind of like the face of an impotent man watching pornography. He always wondered if the man picked up hitch-hikers. He supposed so, and he knew the face to look for. He was sure of it.

Frankenstein slept the breadth of Indiana. In the back seat of a Chevy station wagon, his head in the harsh embrace of his canvas luggage, he swam, stumbled and struggled through three hundred miles of turbulent dream. He lost his voice in a riot of children. He fell into a bottomless hole. Something hot got stuck in his left nostril. He failed at more responsibilities than he could keep track of, something to do with his old job at the dog kennel, something else demanding intense thought at a computer screen from which damp, rancid breath puffed like smoke from a locomotive. A truck ran over him. A nasty-looking woman picked him out in a police line-up and accused him of not caring. He slid down a telephone pole. An asphalter laid pavement over his sandaled feet, pinning him to the sunny side of a dune. Bugs crawled on him. A medium-sized rat with a shiny black nose squeaked at him, but in a nice way that made a certain sense. A cop gave him a ticket for standing there. Somebody put him on hold so long that his skin grafted to the phone. Somebody else beat him up for the pleasure of it. He got gangrene. He woke up in the Land of Lincoln when a big, burly guy with a beard shook his shoulder and asked him if he wanted to get out or go to Chicago. He still doesn't know what a Hoosier is.

At a truck stop in Iowa (he thinks it was), he drank eighteen cups of coffee. A sky-blue waitress named Tina kept track. Frankenstein barely kept control of his mind. He had a booth to himself during a god-awful sleet-rain-hail-snow storm. Not entirely sure tornadoes couldn't happen in the winter, he kept asking for more coffee and place mats. On the back of the place mats he wrote letters to his sister. As the caffeine and sleeplessness snaked into his brain, his writing electrified into frantic, illegible scribbles. He kept wishing he could cry or something. He kept saying he was sorry: sorry he had smoked pot before being an usher at her wedding, sorry for the time he lit the leaves on fire under her tree fort, sorry he was such an inadequate uncle, sorry he had told her, fifteen years earlier, that Santa Claus had stabbed the Tooth Fairy, suicidally sorry he had shoveled his bit of dirt onto his father's coffin before he was supposed to, sorry he had left home without saying good-bye to his mother. He told her which parts of the waitress he desired most, then told her he was sorry he had told his sister such a thing. He told her he wished he could crawl into a dark little hole and just stay there.

He listed eight reasons to die (because why not, because it made a certain sense, because he wanted to see what would happen, because he was so sorry for what had happened so far, because he'd forgotten if he was on the westbound or eastbound side of the interstate and didn't see how it mattered but knew that it did, because absolutely everything went wrong for him, because he didn't know how to have fun and didn't think he'd ever figure it out) and two to live (because he wanted to see what would happen and because he was sure that dying would end up being a mistake). He told her about the lady who kept crying, the snake who got run over, a prissy, middle-aged man who drove with a Raggedy Ann in his lap, a guy who had been eating a Bible for the last three weeks and proved it by chewing on a page of Leviticus for half an hour but then choked on it so bad that Frankenstein had to slam him on the back until he coughed up a gummy wad which he looked at with disgust but said he'd save for later. When a drip of coffee plopped onto a blank space in his letter, Frankenstein doodled it into a face that looked shocked and windblown. He drew a bubble over it and wrote, "I'm sorry! I'm sorry!" and let the rest of the letter flow around it.

Chapter Three

His Name is Mud

A lady with half a brain dumps Frankenstein at the center of a rat's nest of interstates and ramps off ramps. A viscose rain, atomized by traffic, wraps around him like wet cobwebs. Overpasses soar above him. Underpasses pass below. These death ribbons have no walkways. Safety, a distant clearing of soggy twilight, hunkers beyond a forest of concrete columns that support an upper-story interstate. He stands at a bifurcation. Neither road is less traveled than the other. One curls around toward where he just came from. The other peels off toward infinity. Gross death roars all around. He's standing right in front of a giant yellow barrel that's supposed to absorb the vehicles of the sleepy, the stupid, the stoned, the indecisive. An amber light marks his location with a languorous flash. He cowers like a mouse among diesel cats, a fly among a mad flock of swatters, a tiny matador beset by Brobdingnagian bulls. He considers the easy way out: dashing to the guardrail, vaulting over the edge, tumbling into a murkish underworld of homeless Dumpsters, crumpled fencing, petrified car parts, fast-food excrement, flames of graffiti, chilled brimstone and wet litter.

But why risk a sure thing? Better to just start walking, see if he gets hit. With a little luck he'll get a ride in a cushy ambulance, a few days in a nice, clean, warm, dry hospital bed. Nurses will attend to his every need. He won't even get up to pee. He'll just watch TV all day. TV's a little better than hanging out at the big yellow barrel, waiting for a three-ton spear. It tips the balance. He goes for it. Sliding along a left-side guardrail, duffel on his shoulder, leaning away from the swish of traffic, he slouches toward somewhere else. By the time he gets there, his teeth are chattering with cold despondency. This other place is at the frontier of civilization. It's a body shop half buried in the carcasses of automobiles. The window beside the office door is protected by steel mesh and patched with cardboard and duct tape. The only light comes from behind an oily garage window, a dull glow and the sparky throb of a welding torch. The pavement between the curb and the door is slippery with rain and old oil. Frankenstein lifts his cold, naked toes away from the edge of his Goodyear sandals. The balls of his feet squeak against the wet rubber.

He touches the doorknob. In a heartbeat, a ghastly rampage of used lubricants creeps across his fingers, embeds itself beneath his nails, thrusts under his cuff, shoots up his arm, coats his armpits, swirls around his neck and dribbles across his torso to congeal at his crotch. A stalactite forms at the back of his scrotum. He thinks he feels the same stuff clogging the gaps between his toes, too. It is filth that will not leave him soon. It bonds with his coat of perspiration, a three-day build-up he had been hoping to scrape off in the comfort of a hot shower. Now impermeable to water, it has a half-life of at least a week.

He enters. The welding torch crackles just out of sight in the garage. Frankenstein says, "Hello?"

He peers in. A low dim light crouches behind something huge. With a little explosion of lightning, the torch crackles again. For a flicker of an instant, he sees an unearthly giant, a robotic thing, a mechanical cactoid as broad as a tree, a Godzilla of crankshafts, mufflers, axles, tie-rods, radiators, hubcaps, gears and junk he goes on to imagine in the dark. Less sure of himself, he says, "Hello?"

A man with a voice like a welding torch says, "Ain't that door locked?" He's behind the thing he's welding. Frankenstein can't see him.

"It was open," he says. He's never felt this cold, at least not cold this way. "I just wanted to use the phone. If you've got one."

"Be my fucking guest."

Before Frankenstein can decide if that's a yes or a no, the torch crackles and the lightning flickers. Blue orbs swim between him and the thing in the garage. He turns away. The orbs float around to a cast iron telephone, a junkyard dog of a pay unit on the wall. By the touch he can tell it's filthier than the doorknob, a phone that has never known a loving touch, that has tasted spittle tainted with the residue of Bazooka gum, Eldorado cigars, cold Chinese food, coffee sludge, yesterday's plaque, a phone that has transmitted every vulgarity known to men, a phone at one with the world around it.

He's heard better dial tones, too, but when he cranks the dial around for zero and the number of his sister outside of Bethesda, he gets the robot that talks him through the collect call routine. When it asks him to state his name, he hopes it's her, not her husband, who listens on the other end. If it's him--a computer peripheral sales rep with an almost erotic love of professional ball players--he'll say, "Yeah, what is it?" Frankenstein will tell him what it is, and he'll say that she's not home. Frankenstein's brother-in-law doesn't like collect phone calls, and he likes Frankenstein even less. They have opposing philosophies, and there's nothing either of them can do about it.

But it's her. She says, "Fred!"

It's not his name. It's an old joke. Nobody calls him that but her. In a dirty-old-man tone of voice, quivering through his filth, stretching his vowels, he croons, "Soooosie Creamcheese."

"Where are you?" she asks.

He looks around. He doesn't quite know how to answer. He'd never say to her something as simple as "greater Seattle." If he did, she'd say, "Yes, but where are you?" She's quite a sister for a guy like Frankenstein. He says, "I'm in a dark hole."

"Wow!" she says. "How is it down there?"

With those few words she resurrects him. Now he's glad he's in a dark hole. He remembers that this is where he wants to be. He says, "It's real clammy."

"Dandy?"

"Clammy!" he shouts. The little holes in the mouthpiece of the phone are clotted with somebody else's coagulated breath.

"I hate clammy!" She hollers it as if to someone at the bottom of a well. Her voice clatters out the earphone in metallic shards.

Frankenstein doesn't want to shout. He doesn't want the man in the other room to hear. Not that it matters. He just wouldn't want the guy to come stomping out with his welding torch and growling, "What're you calling clammy?"

He pictures his sister all in denim, shirt untucked, sleeves rolled halfway up her forearms, her hair in a pony tail tied with a rubber band looped around something she found at the beach. Bare feet. Traces of dried bread dough in the grooves of her knuckles, a smudge of oil paint on her cheek, a Band-aid around her little toe, Little Tom anchoring one foot to the floor. This is how she survives Big Tom. She keeps busy. She pretends he doesn't exist or maybe that he's someone else. She never said this. Frankenstein just knows. She's in a bit of a dark hole herself, but she makes the best of it. Frankenstein admires her spirit. She's always gung-ho. He can picture her in this grubby little auto body shop. Within ten minutes she'd have daisies growing out of the ashtray. She'd paint a sunny, Van Goghesque hayfield on the wall. She'd have ferns in the corner and vines across the window. She'd cook muffins on the coffee maker. She'd paint the steel desk yellow and put her feet up on it while she taught herself to play the accordion. Everyone around her would laugh a lot and keep their language clean. Under similar circumstances, Frankenstein might likely write a poem about the discomfiture of rigor mortis.

"I hate clammy, too," he says to his sister, "but sometimes it's all you've got."

"Sounds like you could use a nice, hot bath."

Somehow she always knows these things. He wishes she'd guess why he called. She's pretty close already. He doesn't want to come right out and ask. In due time he'll drop a hint and, if necessary, segue into a request. He says, "What's your mother up to this week?"

"You won't believe it," she gushes with half a laugh. "She has tilted her lance at the town dump. She says the place is a mess and she wants it cleaned up."

Frankenstein wrinkles his forehead. Clean up the dump. It sounds like the kind of oxymoronic impossibility she'd ask him to do. But he has trouble imagining his mother anywhere near the town dump. He didn't think she even knew such a place existed. He can, however, imagine her raging through town hall, berating, blaming, accusing, threatening, stabbing the long, red nail of her forefinger into state statutes, federal mandates, the mayor's gut, the sanitation department's gut and the guts of all others who look like they could use a little improvement.

"She got an editorial in the paper," his sister says. "She wants everybody to put their trash in white bags, and she wants all the bags laid out in even rows in an even layer so they can be sprayed with deodorant and disinfectant by a crop duster before they're buried."

"A crop duster!" It sounds like something he'd think up. He can see the lady with the yellow propeller swooping over the dump in her biplane, smiling down over the edge of her cockpit and cooing through the hole in her throat. "I wonder if she'll ever be happy," he says, meaning his mother.

"Not till she's got every speck of dirt in the world sealed up in white trash bags."

"That wouldn't leave much of a planet, would it? Where would she stand?" He pictures himself curled up and weightless in one of ten billion white trash bags orbiting the sun in a tidy row. His father's about ten bags ahead of him.

His sister giggles. She always does. "Antarctica!" she says in a tone of gleeful hope. "All alone in the clean-driven snow, queen of all she sees and happy at last."

"If she were there, I'd be happy, too." He lets two heartbeats pass, then says, as casually as he can, "Has she mentioned me?"

Two more heartbeats pass as his sister shifts gears. "Sometimes," she says.

He tilts his forehead to the concrete wall and says, "Like what?"

"Like. . . I wonder where he is."

He says nothing. He just waits. She adds, "Like. . . when's he going to come home or get a job or something?"

Yeah, he knows that. He says, "Tell her it's not time yet."

"I'm not going to tell her anything. You tell her. Call her."

"I will." But he knows he won't. It isn't time yet. Besides, he hates talking on the phone. He remembers that now. So he doesn't wait for her to ask. He says, "I'm in greater Seattle."

"Ah, Seattle," she sighs. "Land of. . . what?"

"Milk and honey, Nothing here but milk and honey."

"Hey. . . you know who lives in Seattle?"

He sure does. He says, "Who?"

"Angelica Pascapelli! Remember her?"

Frankenstein says, "Hmmmm. Rings a distant bell."

"My next door neighbor in the dorm, at State. Remember? Senior year?"

"Ohhhhh, yeah. Angelica. She used to wear dresses, right? Little matching outfits? Even to class?"

"That's her. Last I heard, she was living in Seattle. She became a flight attendant."

"I'll be damned."

Truth is, he's been thinking about Angelica since southern Idaho, and to that thought he has added a nice, warm bath. Now he remembers her last name. Things are fitting together. And then his beloved sister says, "You should call her!"

Beloved and omniscient. She knows why he called. He can tell. But he plays right along. He says, "Have you got her number?"

She says she thinks she can find it. Her phone clunks down. From Seattle he can hear her feet thump lightly across the room. They are indeed bare. A dog barks. He didn't know she had a dog. It's a mutt. He'd bet money on it. Unless it's Big Tom's dog. If Big Tom went nuts and bought a dog, it would be the kind that's worth money. By the sound of the bark, Frankenstein guesses its something between a beagle and a poodle, with a high IQ and very twitchy tail. A good dog for a kid like Little Tom. A pain in the ass for Big Tom. When Frankenstein's sister pads back to the phone and blows her bangs up with a phew, he says, "Did you get a new cat or something?"

She says, "Oh, that's Uncle Sam. You'd like her. Put her out and she wants to come in. Let her in and she wants to go out. You two would get along well. And boy could she use a bath."

"I know how that feels. You don't suppose Angelica's got a bathtub?

"If I know Angelica, she's got two. You ready to write this down?"

Of course he's not ready. Frankenstein hasn't been ready for anything since birth. He wasn't even ready for that. He was still working on a double back gainer with a twist. He assumed that's what life was all about. But then he saw the light at the end of the tunnel. He got curious. It was his first big mistake. He went for a peek, and boom--he's a person. He hasn't done a gainer since, let alone a back gainer. Twists? Forget it. He's lucky if he can keep both feet on the ground.

Wait," he says to his sister. He's got a dusty old Bic in his duffel somewhere, but it could take days to find. He's not about to ask the welder for a writing instrument. The little concrete block office doesn't look like a place to find such a thing. The gunmetal desk no doubt seized up decades ago. There's nothing on top of it except an ashtray dating back to the Mesozoic era. The trash can looks unfit for trash. Frankenstein's going to have to use his memory. He winces at the thought. He has no capacity for arbitrary data. Seven unrelated digits don't stand a chance in his brain. Just in case Angelica has one of those magical numbers like 345-6789, he goes ahead and asks. In a voice bogged with incipient depression, he squeaks, "What is it?"

"Area code two. . . "

"Fuck the area code."

"Okay, okay. 843-9271. Got it? 8-4-3-9-2-7-1."

He wouldn't talk like that to anybody but his sister. She understands. She knows he's standing there in semi-dark with the top of his forehead against a wall of concrete blocks painted with enamel and tobacco tar. She's just handed him the world's toughest phone number. It makes no sense whatsoever. She knows what he means when he says, with quivery desperation, "Does that spell anything?"

She hums for a while and mumbles combinations of letters. Then she says, "Well, there's no letters on the one, so forget it."

"How could they be so stupid?"

They being the phone company that didn't put letters on the one. But he knows who the stupid one is. If Angelica Pascapelli didn't have big brown eyes and a bathtub, he'd give up right there. She has a one in her phone number. He might as well go back up to the big yellow barrel at the fork in the road and wait for the first Buick with bad tie-rods. "Never mind," he says. "Give it to me one more time. Then I'm going to hang up and dial it quick. Okay?"

"I gotcha. Here it comes. I'm going to sing it. Ready? Eight-four-three-nine-two-seven-one." She makes it sound like Twinkle, Twinkle, Little Star. "Got it?"

He sings it. She says, "Yes." He sings it again. He feels a little pilot light of happiness blip into the darkness of his chest. He sings it again. His merriment means thanks and good-bye. He slams the receiver into the hook.

Eight-four-three-nine-two-seven-one.

He paws at his pocket for a coin.

Eight-four-three-nine-two-seven-one.

There's something in there!

Eight-four-three-nine-two-seven-one. How I wonder what you are.

He scoops them out, squints down close.

Eight-four-three-nine-two-seven-one.

It's a puddle of pennies. Not a bit of silver among them. He flings them across the room and slams his forehead to the wall. He's been lugging those damned things around for days.

Now he can't sing the number. He couldn't sing Twinkle, Twinkle Little Star if his life depended on it. Which it practically does. His belly undulates with the start of a good cry. All he wanted was a bath. . .

But God's good graces touch the telephone, and it belches Frankenstein's quarter. With a sense of Biblical significance, he extracts it from the little slot. He kisses it as if it were Angelica Pascapelli herself.

Eight-four-three-nine-two-seven-one. Like a diamond in the sky.

Whispering the numbers, he spins the black steel dial. The eight takes too long to mosey back around. It messes up the rhythm of the song, but he keeps cranking. He gets it right, he's sure of it. The ring sounds distant but cautiously optimistic. It rings again. It rings again. She's on a jet to Tokyo, he's sure of it. She's serving TV dinners in the stratosphere. Her answering machine is going to eat his last quarter, and he won't even have a message to leave. It rings again, and she answers. It's Angelica, yes, and yes, she remembers him.

* * *

Things move along well after that. She figures out more or less where he is. He walks to a certain intersection, waits on the corner for no more than a minute before a white Cadillac pulls up. It's far from new but remarkably clean and polished. The electric window glides down. A chubby-faced woman he would hardly recognize says, "Frankenstein?"

He's surprised most by her eyebrows. They're as thin and precisely defined as arcs drawn by a fine-point pen. She was working on them when he called, he can tell. She has a towel wrapped around the top of her head, a floppy mound stuffed loosely with hair. Sitting in the passenger seat, his cold fingers gripping each other in his lap, he wonders if she still has great gobs of black curls. She looks different than she used to, back when she lived next door to his sister in the dorm. Her former voluptuousness has rounded out to jolly curves. When he last saw her, he was a senior, he a freshman. Now she looks like a grown up and he feels like a kid.

The Cadillac moves through the washy-gray streets of Seattle like a fluffy cloud. She has the heater on full-blast, but it seems to produce only steam. It fogs the windshield. The wipers squeak as they rub away the misty rain. The bare areas remind him of the angels he and his sister used to make in the snow by waving their arms and legs. Then he notices key ring dangling at the ignition. It′s an angel, pure white and as big as a saucer. Angels, he guesses, are her personal motif.

She smells of soap. He's sure he smells of stale sweat. She cranks the defroster to full-blast, but when her fingers touch the window controls, it's his window that opens a crack. She says, "Do you mind?"

He's almost sure it's an oblique reference to the odor he's brought in from Idaho. All he can say is, "A little fresh air should help." It's an oblique confession of stench, an implied apology.

He likes Angelica's face. It reminds him of a pumpkin, but cute. The crowns of her cheeks are a little pink, not with heat or blush but well fed health. She'll be fat someday, he thinks. At her current stage of development, she's at voluptuous-plus but teetering on pudgy. She won't be fat, he decides, just buxom.

She asks about his sister. He tells her what little he knows. Angelica says she's quite a character. Frankenstein whistles softly. "I don't know what she's doing in Bethesda," he says. "I think she lives in an apartment."

"What's wrong with that? I live in an apartment."

"Oh, I didn't mean it that way,. I meant, like, she ought to be on a farm or something. Out in the country."

"Yes," Angelica says drearily. "With chickens or something."

He doesn't like the way she said that. Just by the sound of it, he knows that Angelica has never come, nor will she ever come, within a hundred yards of barnyard fowl. He's not too surprised to hear her ask, "Do you know anything about computers?"

Frankenstein tilts his head. "Computers," he says thoughtfully. "I know a little, but not much."

She says nothing in return. He's glad. He hates computer conversations. Back when he used to use one, he always felt a moment of quiet joy when he turned it off. He really enjoyed seeing the screen die, hearing the hard drive croak and the little fan sigh its last. He wished all his problems could be turned off with a little button.

Eager to change the subject, he says, "Do you still play harp?"

She turns her head to look at him. She looks longer than a Cadillac driver should. Then she turns back and says, "Yes. . . I do. Not as much as I should. But every once in a while."

"It's a beautiful thing, a harp."

"Sometimes I miss it. I'll be halfway into an all-night flight and all the passengers will be sleeping and I'll imagine sitting back near the galley, playing harp for everybody."

"That's beautiful," Frankenstein says, almost whispering. For the first time he ties together her name and her chosen instrument. He's now fully in love with Angelica Pascapelli–except those eyebrows still scare him. Why does she pluck them to such perfection when she could be playing her harp? Maybe it's in her contract. Would an airline claim that bushy eyebrows are a safety hazard? Frankenstein doesn't doubt it. Sex appeal would have nothing to do with it, of course. Eyebrow growth would have to be tightly controlled to prevent occlusion of the eyes during an emergency. Worse, unrestrained thickets of brow hair could burst into flames at the very moment when flight attendants have to remain calm and clear-headed.

Frankenstein doesn't share these thoughts. They go without saying. It's possible she likes to pluck her eyebrows. Some girls do.

And some guys have fantasies about having their back scratched by a harpist. Frankenstein's one of them. He thinks about it, then fully imagines it, all but feels it as his back breaks out in rampant itch. The itches march across him like a ragamuffin army through a salt marsh.

Angelica's apartment building looks like a motel, a two-story horseshoe with a swimming pool in its lap. She leads him up a short, wide flight of outdoor stairs, down a concrete walkway overlooking the pool, around a corner to 14-B. Neither of them speaks along the way. He lugs his duffel bag. She fiddles with her keys, finds the right one and isolates it with a jingly flourish. She opens the door and says, "Well, this is it."

It's an apartment with deep, cream-colored wall-to-wall carpeting, matching couch, love seat and chair, a coffee table with two neat stacks of magazines set at a jaunty angle. The back of the couch marks the border of the dining area, and a counter marks off the kitchen. The other rooms are down a short, dim hall.

Angelica removes her jacket. She's wearing a loose denim shirt unbuttoned to a hint of cleavage. Frankenstein notices this right off. It's a good sign. He lowers his duffel bag to the floor. Just to say something, he goes, "Whew."

Angelica looks back from the coat closet. "No, no," she says, signaling for him to pick it up. "Not there." The wag of her finger makes him feel like a bad boy.

He raises his grungy duffel bag from the cream-colored carpet and follows her down the dim hallway. She's not bad looking from the back. Her hips sway below her waist like a pendulum. She opens the other door at the end of the hall and stands back. There they are: the computer and the harp. Angelica says, "This is where I store junk."

She means his duffel bag. Granted, white though it might once have been, it doesn't exactly match her decor. Still, she could have phrased it better. But it's her apartment, not his, and she seems to have included her computer and harp in the category of junk. So his duffel's in with respectable company. He can't complain.

The computer looks like something dragged out of the sea. She hasn't been using it lately. A tangled glob of wires splays atop a tight crowd of stacked peripherals. Nothing's hooked up. It's waiting for somebody to come along to do it. Frankenstein inhales.

The harp looks even less used. It stands deeper in the room, beyond the computer, behind some file boxes, back among some milk crates and stuff in shopping bags. A dry-cleaned flight attendant's uniform in a plastic bag hangs from the pinnacle of the harp. It looks a little like a skeleton dancing with a ghost. He briefly considers asking her if he can take the plastic bag when he goes. Hoping to prevent mention of the computer, he says, "I thought harps had to stay in some kind of humidor or something." That is absolutely everything he knows about harps.

"Good harps, yes."

"What did it do," Frankenstein chuckles, "bite somebody?"

She smiles with only half her mouth. "I got it at a pawn shop. Cheap. Sounds like shit."

For an instant, Frankenstein wishes she wouldn't talk like that in front of it. "It doesn't want to sound like that," he says.

"Yes it does."

There's no discussing it. If Angelica says the harp wants to sound like shit, that's the way it wants to sound. It's her harp and her apartment. She says, "I suppose you want to take a shower."

"As a matter of fact. . . "

She points to the bathroom. "Right in there. I suppose you've got laundry."

Laundry would be putting it nicely. Filthy rags is more like it. Biohazardous waste. But not junk. It's all he's got. He says, "Well, yes, if I could borrow the use of a washing machine."

"You wash you, I'll wash the clothes." With a single finger to his shoulder she pokes him into the bathroom and closes the door behind him.

Nice can, thinks Frankenstein, maybe a little too nice. Everything's pink--pink sink and toilet, pink bath mat, seat cover and towels, pinkish wallpaper, pink tiles in the shower stall, pink angel around the light switch, pink silk flowers beside a bowl of pinkish potpourri replete with colossally pink odorizer. Pink, pink, pink, pink, pink. This crapper needs something like Frankenstein, something firmly unpink. His image in the mirror is so gross it's almost good, something salty after an overdose of sweet. He strips. He sits. He moves his bowels. It's a good one. He turns on the shower. The water looks so clean and steamy. Then there's a knock at the door. The door knob turns. Frankenstein thinks, This is it.

But it isn't it. It's only her voice and her hand with its bright red fingernails. She says, "Dirty clothes?" Her fingers snap. Frankenstein rolls them up, hands them over. The hands withdraws. The door closes. Oh, well..

It's a good shower. Even though the water temperature jumps around a bit as the washing machine commandeers the flow, Frankenstein appreciates the luxury as much as the wealthiest emperor might appreciate a trove of gold. He could live in a cave and eat charred rats off the end of a stick as long as he could take a hot shower at the end of the day. Modern technology hasn't developed much else of real import. Hot showers and the polio vaccine, that's about it.

While he's in there letting the wet warmth caress his skull, there's another knock at the door. It opens. He wipes a peephole in the fog on the ripply shower door. She enters. He barely makes out the creamy blur of her flesh as it twirls in. The door closes. He is immediately aroused. He wishes it didn't come on so fast so he could at least pretend not to have been thinking about it. The way things stand now, there's no pretending. It's as plain as the nose on this face. He lathers like crazy and sucks in his gut.

But she just stands there by the door, a smeary phantasm the color of moonlight. Frankenstein peeks again. She doesn't move. Something's wrong. He waits a while. Then he slides the shower door open a bit. It isn't her. It's a robe, hung by the scruff of its neck on a hook on the door.

Oh, well. What did he expect? She wouldn't be interested in someone like him. Maybe if he'd showed up with a couple pounds of roses and a bottle of good wine he might have inspired her. But all he brought was a sack of rancid clothing.

With a clunk of the plumbing, his shower goes cold. Frankenstein hops out, dries off, folds the towel as neatly as he can, hangs it back up nice and perfect-like. He puts on the robe, cinches the belt, looks down at his knobby, white knees. He doesn't recall wearing a robe before. He feels silly--vaguely Roman, slightly gay, very naked underneath. If she didn't mean for him to put it on, he's in big trouble. But what else can he do? She has his clothes.

He steps into an aroma of frying onions and garlic. Angelica's in the kitchen, stirring up some food. She's smooth and slow with her motions, swirling the stuff she's cooking, rapping the wooden spoon on the cast iron pan, peeking into the steam under the lid of big pot, jerking open the refrigerator, snatching something out, spinning off a lid, tilting something into the pan, peering into the jar, dumping the rest in. If he were on TV, he'd come right up behind her, slip his arms around her waist and kiss her neck. She'd lean back and say, "Mm-mmm." But something tells him to keep his distance. Feeling quite the soap opera stud, he says, "Smells good!"

"Pasta. I hope you like it." She doesn't sound optimistic.

"I love it. I really hadn't meant to impose. . . "

"No problem." She rinses her hands at the sink, wipes them on a dish towel. "Your laundry will be dry soon. It sure needed washing."

Frankenstein says, "I've been out there a long time." He likes the way it sounds, as if he's been up in the hills, fighting with the Resistance.

"And what are you doing?"

Standing there in a robe is what he's doing. That is absolutely all he can think to say, but he holds his tongue. She isn't looking for a wisecrack, and he doesn't want to author one. He considers saying that he's been fighting with the Resistance, then seeing if he can make it sound like he means something, something heavy. Resisting capitalism. Resisting American materialism. Resisting the System. But he isn't resisting anything. In fact, he's pretty much following the path of least resistance. Wandering around would sum it up well enough, but he says, "Just traveling."

"Traveling where?"

If she needs to ask, she'll never understand the answer. Trying not to sound too-too mysterious or stupid, he says, "To wherever I end up." He hangs humility across his face and shows her the palms of his hands.

"That's where we're all going," she says. "Do you think you could take a look at my computer?"

That's all she's been thinking about since he called from the body shop. That's why she did his laundry and is making pasta. She thinks he can fix a computer.

With weak hesitance, he says, "I don't know. . . "

"Guys know. It's a tool. Come on."

She takes him by the hand. He likes that. This is the first female to touch him in weeks. She drags him down the hall, past the bedroom, into the junk room. There's the computer, looking as morose as a teen at the opera. The ghost and skeleton dance behind it. Frankenstein swells with the best idea in the world. In the most seductive tone he can muster, he sings, "I'll fix the computer if you'll play the harp."

He's lying, of course. He can't fix a computer. But he can sure look like he's trying. And who knows. . . maybe he'll get it all connected and it'll start right up. Sometimes they do that. Like kids with sniffles, they get better. Whether he succeeds or not, he'll get to hear some harp. Live and close-up. It'll be like sitting in heaven while working on the tool from hell.

It takes Angelica a long time to finally say, "I really don't play very well. And this harp. . . " She shakes her head with something like disgust.

"How bad can a harp sound? You don't have to actually play. Just practice. I promise not to laugh."

She looks at the harp as if not trusting it. Frankenstein resorts to a whine. "Please," he says, "Please?"

Angelica backs up three inches and says, "I can't play harp."

"And I can't fix a computer." He's not lying. She is. He says, "Let's do it anyway." By "it" he means go to the clean sheets of her bed and make love, but he doesn't expect her to guess this, let alone do it. He'll be satisfied to hear her play the harp.

Finally she says, "I'll tune it." Like that's all he's going to get. No more.

"Good," he says. "A harp should be tuned now and then. You tune the harp. I'll tune the computer. This is going to be fun." He steps around the computer, slips a foot between two boxes of books, plucks the dry-cleaned uniform from the harp and hands to it Angelica. Without a word, she whisks it away to a closet. Frankenstein feels gargantuan as he leans here and there to pick up boxes and stack them away from the harp. Moving fast, he collects the stuff from a fold-up table, piles it on top of other stuff. He stacks the computer stuff into a precarious, teetering tower and lifts it all to the table. Now the harp stands in a little clearing. It already looks happier, even stately, a castle in a moat. By the time Angelica returns, he's set a milk crate upside-down beside the harp. With a flourish of his hands he says, "And now, Angelica Pascapelli on the harp."

Angelica Pascapelli says, "Wrong side." Gently, precisely, she kicks the milk crate around to where it should be. "Got that computer hooked up yet?"

The last person to mess with this computer must have really hated it. It took someone a lot of time to form such a convoluted ball of wires. They aren't just bunched together. They're tied in an ugly, senseless macramé of wires knotted around wires and plugs unnaturally inserted into odd sockets. Angelica is opening a little steel toolbox when Frankenstein asks, "Did you do this?"

"That was my ex husband."

He likes the way the emphasis fell on ex, but still, he's a bit shocked, maybe even just a teeny-weeny bit jealous. Some jerk who hates computers and can't appreciate a harpist has already been there and gone. On top of that, Angelica has already done the marriage thing. Frankenstein hasn't even learned to balance a checkbook. Again he feels way out of his league. She's a grown-up; he's a kid. He says, "Didn't like computers much, did he?"

"He didn't like me very much. He loved computers. It's all he did all day. He used to send me e-mail."

"He didn't live here?"

"Oh, he lived here. Right here in this room. He hardly ever came out except to go to work. He sent me e-mail so I'd have to use the computer."

"Not love notes, I take it?"

"Ha! That man couldn't write a love note any more than he could. . . could, I don't know, play the harp or something. He could download a love note off the Internet, assuming of course he ever thought of it, which he wouldn't."

Angelica places a winding key at shortest string of the harp and gives it a pluck. It sounds good to Frankenstein. He could listen to that note again and again. As long as she didn't pluck any other notes, that first one sounded fine. Without meaning to be funny, he says, "That sounded good."

Angelica's pinkie and thumb reach across an octave to pluck two strings. They aren't quite right. Now he can tell. He's standing with his back to the table, half sitting on it, grappling with the ball of wires. This is modern life, right here in this room and in his hands. He's in a white robe and quite naked underneath. A chubby little cherub--named for angels, no less--plays harp for him. Wires, however, demand his full attention. He wishes he could hurl them out a window and get on with life.

They are not easy to untie. Since they have big plugs and sockets on their ends, they don't slip through knots easily. The knots have to be loosened at various points along a given wire until finally an end can fit through. They're all the same color, so Frankenstein's fingertips have to feel their way along each wire like plumbers working in the dark. The minute precision of it makes his hands shake. He breathes hard and feels a little faint. He clings to the off-key harp notes as if they floated and he might not. "What did he do this for?" he asks.

Angelica plucks a string repeatedly as she tweaks the key that tightens it. The notes rise by the faintest nuances. She squints at thin air as if she can see the sounds. Only after she gets the string just right does she speak. "He took the computer, to which I said good, take it, go. But then I got made secretary of the Friends of the Goddamn Library so I have to type up minutes and get e-mail and maintain the web page and stuff. So when our court date came up, I said I wanted the computer. The judge said I could have it, so Frank brought it back. Like this. See, the judge didn't say I could have it not tied in a knot, so that's what he did. He was that kind of guy."

Frankenstein doesn't say anything. He's got his fingers worked deeply into the ball of wires. He's trying to picture what it looks like in there, what kind of sub-knot he's working on. Somewhere in there is a knot which, untied, will release all the rest. The ball will come apart into beautiful individual strands. Then he will be able to breathe normally.

Plim-plim-plim, ploom-ploom-ploom, boing-boing-boing--little by little, Angelica brings together the tones of her harp. It doesn't sound like shit. It sounds like droplets of condensed heaven coming down. She starts playing chords, then riffs of chords. Frankenstein gives his loose knot of wires a spastic shake. He's falling behind. She's practically tuned a harp and is moving fast toward Bach. All he's got to show is a three-foot monitor cable with a ball of dead snakes at one end.

Little by little she turns her tuning chords into long strokes of music. When she gets it wrong, she goes tcht and reaches for it again. Not that it sounds wrong to Frankenstein. If he could play the harp as wrong as that, he'd buy one and carry it wherever he went. He'd play it here and there, wherever he got the urge. He'd be a musical Johnny Appleseed. They'd call him Frankenharp. Future generations of kindergartners would sing songs about him. They'd draw crayon illustrations of him strumming a lyre in front of fast-food joints, in bus depots, near funerals, here and there on the interstates, calming the world one spot at a time. He'd become a myth, a legend, a folk hero. Kids wouldn't believe in him. They'd assume he was just more grown-up propaganda. They'd hear about him and think, "So what?"

But he can't play harp and could never learn. His fingers could not do what Angelica's fingers are doing, and she's just getting warmed up. He watches them while fingering the ball of wires. She isn't just stroking her harp. She's embracing and caressing it. Her fingers crook and stretch to find the right strings, set upon them as lightly as birds, grip them with just the smallest bit of finger-flesh, and pull them just so. Each gentle burst of sound becomes a glorious moment in the universe.

It's a glorious moment in the universe when Frankenstein's wires suddenly loosen and separate. In the time it takes to breathe once, he lifts them apart. They look good lying on the table, limp and roughly parallel. Harp strings they aren't, but he's just a little proud. She gave him chaos; he gives her order. Not that she notices. She's playing harp. Computer wires are as far from her mind as Mars. Frankenstein says not a word. He just sets about the business of figuring out which wire goes where. He kneels at the table, turns the computer around, tries to match up the wires with their outlets and peripherals. With the harp to his back and his nose to the ass-end of an electronic device, he feels like he's reading pornography under a pew in church.

The more she plays, the more futile his efforts feel. So what if he gets it all plugged in and working? Angelica Pascapelli should not be futzing with a web page. She should not be receiving e-mail. She and all other harpists should be banned from the Internet. Incoming correspondence should be censured of all but letters on parchment in the cursive handwriting of a fountain pen. Their radios should not receive the trash of hoi poloi. They should not be called upon to befriend the goddamn library or to rescue wet mutts from the rain, let alone do their laundry. They should live in cultural humidors and just let their eyebrows be.

Her music is too beautiful now. Her practice chords have evolved into Greensleeves. Frankenstein hasn't the faintest idea what greensleeves are, but their music tends to make him cry. He pictures lambs frolicking in a meadow of buttercups and rye. They frolic so well that they soon lose their way, and everyone wonders what happened to them. He vaguely recalls a hymn to the same tune. It's not about lambs but Jesus. What child is this, hmmm, hmmm, hmmm, something, something, something. Frolicking in a meadow of buttercups and rye, for all he knows. The image, the music, it's all too beautiful. A wetness swamps his eyes. He can't focus on the little dark sockets in the computer, can't even bring himself to stick in a wire. Something tells him that if he does, he'll short out the harp. Its strings will spit sparks and flames. Sweet Angelica will fall away, her fingers charred and smoking from the knuckles out. The invisible vastness of the Internet will not laugh. For all its omniscience, it won't even notice.

Frankenstein's not going to be the one to do it. He won't plug it in. In fact, neither will anyone else. He gets a great idea. His plan unfolds as if by divine inspiration. He never would have thought of this himself. The modem cable has a little transformer on the end, to reduce the power of the incoming electricity. He takes the modem power cord and loops it through the hinge of the leg of the table. Holding the table up with his shoulder, watching Angelica to see if she notices, he folds in the leg just far enough to snap the wire right near the little transformer. With his fingernail he slices between the two wires of the cord, then uses his teeth to pull off an inch of insulation from each. He plugs in the computer and turns it on. He plugs the modem into the back, then sticks the naked wires into the outlet in the wall. A hundred and twenty volts shoot into a unit built for six. He gets a little puff of smoke from the modem and suspects the same has happened within the computer. It's going to be a long time before Angelica Pascapelli goes online.

Angelica sniffs. The last of her harp notes fade. She says, "What's that?"

"Something's wrong here," Frankenstein taps the computer, clicks the mouse, looks as worried as he can. It isn't hard. He's got a lopped-off transformer on the floor and a lopped-off wire stuck in an outlet. Even the most dedicated harpist would recognize a problem.

"Damn Frank. I bet he screwed it up on purpose. I bet he gave it a virus."

"That's what I think it is," Frankenstein says knowingly. "You've got a virus in there. A bad one."

"Can you fix it?"

She's come closer now. She's right behind him, slightly to the side, with one hand on his robed shoulder. He's still on his knees. He clicks the end of his tongue and shakes his head as if he has a sore neck. "For a virus like this," he says, "you need a real expert. A specialist."

"I should throw the damned thing out the window and just play harp for the rest of my life."

"Yes."

"Unfortunately, Mr. Frankenstein, life's not like that." Having spoken her final word, she turns and marches back to the kitchen. Frankenstein hurries after her. She's moving very fast, her spine straight, her head back, her little hands in little fists. He almost runs to keep up. His robe flaps. Fresh air wafts in from below.

"Life should be like that," he says, wanting to grab her by the shoulders and impress her with some sense of the goodness of what he's talking about. "It could be like that."

"It could if you're willing to live out of a duffel bag and beg to have your laundry done. Then you can throw anything you want out the window."

He's about to say that he never begged, but that's not the point. The point is the part about throwing stuff out the window. She's not talking about computers. She's waxed philosophical. Normally he'd like that. But she's talking about him, something he's thrown out his personal window. He's not sure he wants to know what. Whatever it was, the lack of it left him standing filthy in the rain at a fork in the interstate with a bag full of clothes too rancid to wear. That's what she means. So the question isn't about what, if anything, he threw out his personal window but whether it was worth it. It would have been worth it if it had left him playing the harp. But it didn't. It just left him clammy.

How's he going to explain all that? He can't. All he can do is sit and eat fettuccine served with tomato sauce and guilt. He's sorry he let her wash his clothes, but he doesn't say so. He's not sorry he destroyed her computer. He doesn't say that, either. But he remembers he left the little transformer and the sliced wire on the floor in the junk room. He excuses himself for a moment, goes to the room, picks up the evidence, weighs it in his palm. If she finds this stuff, he's dead. All he can think to do with it is throw it out the window. What could be more appropriate? Only trouble is, the window squeaks when he opens it. He lets the peripheral amputations fall into an evergreen bush. The window squeaks as he closes it.

When he returns to the table, Angelica says, "What was that?" Her voice is cold, her jaw clenched. A tad of tomato sauce sticks to her tight lips.

Frankenstein packs fettuccine into his mouth before he says, "Nothing." He knows the lie won't work, but he has to say something.

Angelica resumes chewing. She gets up, clears her throat, walks to her bedroom and closes the door. Soon he can hear her in there talking on the phone. Figuring he has nothing to lose, he hangs around the door, listening. He can't make out much, but he does hear her say, "What I am I supposed to do with him?" He hears her hang up and then dial again. Then her voice murmurs in hushed conspiracy.

Afraid she'll suddenly open the door, he goes into the junk room and turns on the computer. It seems to be working, all but the modem. He goes to the harp, sits on the milk crate and very, very cautiously gives one string a little tug. A clear and perfect note hums forth. He tries another string. Again, the note is perfect and beautiful. Hoping to get an octave, he counts out eight strings, positions his fingers on them as Angelica had, and gives them a little tug. It's a sour combination. This is life, he thinks, right here in a harp.

Angelica opens her door, comes into the junk room. She looks quite relieved. Frankenstein says, "It works. I think I fixed it. See?"

She doesn't look at the computer. She just looks at him. She's smiling, but he'd guess it's against her will. She says, "I have some good news for you, Frankenstein. How'd you like to take a nice little trip on an airplane?"

From
Neighborhood News

Existentialist Injures Child

Justin Bulgarino, 8, received an injurious psychological trauma when an out-of-town existentialist hit him with the meaninglessness of life. The child was reported to be devastated, perhaps permanently.

The incident happened at the Baltic playground, on High St., when the stranger saw Justin leap gleefully from a swing and dash around the perimeter of the playground, screaming like a pterodactyl on fire.

"Your joy is meaningless," the stranger said, pointing hard at Bulgarino, his eyes glaring. "Your fun is utterly futile and without basis. You are nothing. Your mother's nothing. You come from nothing, and to nothing you are bound."

Resident state trooper Chris Johnson detained the man for questioning but was unable to link him to a specific crime.

"The suspect confessed to being an existentialist, but that's still legal in Connecticut," Johnson said. "All we could do was release him to his own responsibility and tell him to define himself, preferably in another town."

Consumadora Bulgarino, the boy's mother, said he has not been the same child since the incident. He has stopped watching television, loses video games on purpose, and lies awake in bed most of the night.

"The other day at dinner, he was just poking at his food," Ms.Bulgarino said. "And then he looks at me with his eyes all wet and he goes, 'Why broccoli?' and I go, like, 'Because it's *good* for you,' and he just looks at me like I'm an idiot, and then he just looks at his broccoli like it just fell there from outer space."

State poet laureate Leo Connellan, a Hanover resident, was called into offer the comfort of literary light on the incident and its disturbing implications.

"That was a rotten thing with which to hit a kid/ We ought to get him back, quo pro quid," Connellan said. "It was a tale told by Sartre or Camus/ full of sound and fury, signifying poo."

Trooper Johnson said he was considering visiting Sayles School to talk with the lower grades about the dangers of broaching the imponderable.

"Let's dare to keep kids off post-modern thought," Johnson said. "It starts at home, but it's up to each and every one of us in the community to keep a lid on the old *cogito*."

Robert Meya, president of the Hanover Philosophical Society, agreed that existentialism could be disturbing to the uninitiated. He suggested that Sayles School incorporate the philosophy into its curriculum, starting in kindergarten.

"Think of the benefits of having children realize, from a young age, that they are what they do," Meya said. "Being precedes essence. Or maybe it's the other way around, depending on which way you look at it. What's important is that it doesn't really matter."

Conquistadores Discover Sprague!

It's hard to say who was more surprised – the discoverers or the discovered – when 36 conquistadores rode into town last Thursday. As the town scrambled to find someone who spoke Spanish, the armored horsemen planted a flag on the bank of the Shetucket and declared the entire region a territory of Spain.

Dennis Delaney, town historian, noted that "this could be a serious problem" and cited an 16th-century incident in what is now Mexico, where a few dozen conquistadores toppled the Aztec empire, beheaded its emperor and massacred most of its people.

First selectman Stephen Papineau urged calm as he dialed 9-1-1 only to learn that the resident state trooper is on vacation until the end of the month.

"Just when you need him," Papineau said. "It's always like that."

Having no alternatives for the defense of Sprague, Papineau rallied the Baltic Fire Department, who arrived wearing yellow slickers and carrying battle axes but were clearly uneasy about confronting the mounted warriors, who wore cast-irron armor and carried swords, 12-foot picaderos and the head of Montezuma, former emperor of the Aztecs.

"On the front of the fire department there is a sign that bears our motto: *Nothing we can't handle*," said Daniel Nagle, fire chief, as he signaled for the town's two firetrucks to form a circle. "I think it's time we had that changed."

Glenn Cheney, former Sayles Spanish teacher and shameless polyglot, arrived on the scene to defuse the crisis. As the *Sprague Today* television crew recorded the historic mment, Cheney addressed the conquistadores from about 13 feet away.

"*¿Como está usted?*" Cheney asked.

The Sprague invaders responded by putting their picaderos to Cheney's chest and growling, "*¿Dónde está El Dorado?*"

Cheney recognized the name of the place they were looking for – *El Dorado*, the City of Gold.

"*No aquí,*" he said. "*Aquí es El Spragoo*, City of Affordable Housing. You want to take 395 south. Pick up 95 south. Keep going, keep going, keep going, keep going. Take *Exito 2*."

Apparently the invaders then realized that they had not yet reached the mythical city of infinite wealth. They were last seen headed south on Route 97 and were reported to have stopped at Occum Market, where, in a tragic misundertanding, they beheaded the owner after he handed them a bag of Doritos.

ED Commission Rolls Out Fat Rat

"An illustrative example of something..."

Sprague Economic Development Commission has unveiled the foundation of a major plan to stimulate the local economy.

It's a 32-pound rat.

"Work on the economic stimulus plan is ongoing," stated EDC chairman Ken Genron. "We aren't exactly sure how Ed is going to fit in, but we are certain we have the beginning of something here. We've made the hard decision. Now we just have to work out the details. A mouse that has attained such impressive size speaks well for the prosperity and advancement of our town. It's a symbol of growth, a potential tourist attraction, a model for our children and our children's children, and as far as I'm concerned, a work of art that harks back on our industrial heritage while harking ahead to a future of SmartGrowth and low taxes."

Ed is the rat. Genron said that he has been able to reach his current weight by specially formulated diet that began with milk and peanut butter, then dog food and an intravenous cocktail of transfats, high fructose corn syrup and Baltic tap water. Ed now survives on Wild Turkey and live cats.

Asked how a rat the size of a beagle would lower taxes, Genron said that the ED Commission and almost everyone else in town was in favor of lower taxes, a simple concept that seemed to evade the understanding of the Board of Finance, and that the full plan would be presented to the townspeople as soon as it had been developed and approved by the commission. Until then, he requested approval to proceed with the plan.

Several potential businesses had expressed interest in "employing" Ed for a variety of productive and promotional purposes.

"The International House of Gruel is definitely interested in bringing the town mouse into their business profile," Genron said. "And that's just one example of the many ways that other tax-paying enterprises can partner with the town to stimulate progress and bring folks a little tax relief."

Genron said that Ed would be used to help Sprague establish a thematic identity along the lines of frogs in Willimantic, roses in Norwich, and whales in New London. The EDC plans to take Ed to Sayles School as "an illustrative example of something" on which they can base lessons about economic development.

Swear Words Legalized

In a historical and unprecedented move, the Sprague Board of Selectmen has approved the legalization of all swear words, including [expletive], [expletive], [expletive], [expletive], and that old navy favorite, [expletive].

"[Expletive]," said selectman Kenneth Caisse as he emerged from town hall after Thursday's board meeting. "I've always wanted to say that. [Expletive] but it feels good."

The legalization of the long-prohibited words permits everyone over the age of 21 to use the so-called "four-letter" words at will, even in public and in the presence of children and pets.

The town ordinance also gives minors the option to use formerly borderline semi-swears such as those used to denote bowel gas and mucus in both solid and liquid form. The news is expected to touch off civil disturbance at Sayles School, where an underground network of middle-grade linguists has been passing down the words from generation to generation in an oral tradition that stretches back to the days of the Pilgrims.

Many in Sprague were surprised by how fast the ordinance was passed.

"We really had our collective [expletive] in gear for this one," said first selectman Stephen Papineau. "We've had an unbelievable amount of [expletive] in this town for so [expletive] long, but we never had the words with which to handle it properly. Now we can cut the [expletive] and say what needs to be said."

While many in Sprague rushed to utter the vulgarities they had never dared pronounce, Robert Meya, president of the Hanover Philosophical Society, said the lingual liberalization had merely shifted the problem to a new sub-set of verbal quandaries.

"Now that it is socially and legally acceptable to articulate these verbal expressions of and disdain, how do we curse?" Meya asked. "When you get a flat tire during a sleet storm and then find out your spare's flat, too, what are you supposed to say?"

In an empirical demonstration of the complexity of the issue, Meya put his thumb on the end of his nose and smacked it with a hammer.

"Now what is the appropriate oral response?" he gasped. "Ow?"

Glenn Cheney, editor of *Neighborhood News*, said he regretted not being able to use the words in the publication. Due to a Y2K glitch, his computer automatically corrects "misspellings," in this case replacing them with words such as *ship, trap* and *Shetucket.*

Teens Find Road to Rack and Ruin

Four teens have reported finding the mythical Road to Ruin. The well worn, litter-strewn trail began at the old "swimming hole" on the Little River and apparently led in the direction of New York and New Jersey.

"We're pretty sure this is the big one," said Stanley "Smoothie" Spidoonski, president of the Sprague Institute of Cool Ones. "We've been looking for it for a long time."

Spidoonski described the trail as wide, obviously well traveled, and littered with the bottles and cans of beer and alcoholic beverage. Marijuana and poppy plants grew wild along its edges. Unmentionables of an allegedly sexual nature were hanging from branches and lying on the ground. Vending machines offered snack foods and video games. Temptation was heard rustling in the brush.

A SICO exploratory team ventured down the road and returned with amazing tales of bliss and excitement. The road is easy to follow, they said, until it forks on the outskirts of New York City, where one road to leads to Rack, N.J., and the other goes over the Triboro Bridge.

"Watch out for the toll," Spidoonski said. "It's a little stiff. That's where we turned back."

Brunhilda Onus, town mother, warned residents not to approach the trail.

"Just because it's there doesn't mean you have to go down it," Onus said. "You're a lot better off staying right here and keeping your nose to the grindstone, where it belongs."

Tootsie-roll Taints Town Election

Registrar launches new word

Sprague election results were thrown into turmoil last month as an alleged Tootsie-Roll was found stuck to a key voting booth lever. Election officials suspect the involvement of a child.

The Tootsie-Roll, chewed and gooey, was found stuck to the lever of Democratic presidential candidate Albert Gore.

"I would describe it as gross," said Kathleen Boushee, registrar of voters. "It wasn't something you'd want to touch. And of course nobody was going to vote for the Green Party candidate besides you-know-who because Green is just too weird, Tootsie-Roll or no Tootsie-roll. And nobody in their right mind would vote for George Bush, so he only got

48 votes. That's more than anybody else got, but still, it doesn't seem like enough."

State police were notified. A milk crate found in the voting booth indicated that a short person may have been involved, perhaps a child.

"We're looking for someone between three and four feet tall with lots of cavities," said Chris Johnson, resident state trooper. "So far we have detained 372 suspects. We're also looking for a Republican with an off-beat sense of humor but so far we have found no one matching the description except for you-know-who and a couple of his friends, and quite frankly we suspect they are actually in the Bull Moose party. Also, they aren't the type to eat Tootsie-Rolls. If it was chewing tobacco, I might say maybe, but Tootsie-rolls just aren't their M.O."

Glenn Cheney, chairman of the town Green Party committee, said that many voters may have assumed that they were supposed to stand on the milk crate, as he himself did. The raised position made it difficult to reach the Green Party ticket, which was placed below the tickets of the two totally corrupt parties of the corporatocracy, where it was inaccessible to the sciatically disabled.

Boushee, who is also host of *Sprague Today*, a public access television program, interviewed herself regarding the electoral brouhaha.

"I think it's time we held our horses," Boushee said. "There's a lot of constitutional stuff involved here. Like can a child go into a voting booth with a parent or other adult? If so, can the child pull the levers? If so, does that give Republicans an advantage? Does the child have the right to take a milk crate into the booth? Does anyone, child or adult, have the right to stick a Tootsie-Roll to a candidate's lever? What happens if it is determined that a Tootsie-Roll, or for that matter a lolli-pop or a wad of gum, has affected the outturn of an election? This is obviously a case for the Supreme Court. They're the only ones who'll know what to do. Is that a word, outturn?"

Sayles Opening Doors to Grown-ups

Adults get a chance to "do it all over again."

In response to popular demand, Sayles School is now accepting grown-up enrollment for all classes, from kindergarten through eighth grade, starting in the fall.

"After hearing so many people say, 'I wish I could do it all over again...but knowing what I know now,' we decided to let Sprague taxpayers have their wish," said Michael Bychowsky, school board chairman. "Town residents of all ages can enter any grade they qualify for. We're putting the *public* in *public schools*, and for the first time in American history, taxpayers can really get what they pay for."

Screening will take place in early August. For entry into kindergarten, which Sayles principal Harrington "Mojo" Heifer-Tittlbaum expects to be especially popular due to the half-day sessions and the free graham crackers and milk, incoming students will need to demonstrate mature social skills. For other grades, students will have to take a written exam in various subject areas.

Heifer-Tittlbaum warns that upper-grade students will need to prove that they can add fractions of unequal denominators, remember key dates in European history, pass the state physical education test, and say at least *it* in Spanish.

"Let me give you a hint," Tittlbaum said. "*1492* is *not* one of the answers on the history test. Neither is *1776*, and neither is *0*. Ha, ha, ha, ha, ha, good luck."

Tittlbaum also said that *taco* does not mean *it* in Spanish, and that the state physical exam includes the ability to do 20 squat-thrusts on a full stomach.

B.Y.O.B.

Kindergartners taller than five feet are advised to bring their own blankies. To accommodate returning students, the school's lawn tractor will be fitted with a winch for lifting those who are unable to get up off the floor after naptime.

Local residents are very excited about the new program.

"I am definitely going to do it," said Thomas McAvoy, a town selectman. "I'm going to start at kindergarten and do it right. I'm going to follow instructions. I'm going to apply myself to my penmanship. I'm going to play clarinet in the orchestra and I'm going to stick with it. Instead of going into banking, I'm going to start my own salsa band because life is too short for banking. Also, I'm going to start dating as soon as I get into the first grade."

Fr. Emile Tito, St. Mary's parish priest, has shorter-term plans.

"I'm going straight into the third grade," he said. "Just one semester. My goals are to: a) at least once, tip over backwards in my chair on purpose, b) at least once, ask to go to the bathroom even if I don't have to, and c) ask a certain young lady if I can hold hands with her on the bus. Then I'm going back to being a priest. We were in love but too young to know it."

Bychowsky said that the board is still trying to resolve a possible conflict of interest involving third-grade teacher Edna Guertin, who plans to enroll as a third-grade student in her own class.

"I don't think that's half as schizoid as some people seem to think," Guertin said. "I'm going to be a model student, and I'm going to have myself sit at the head of the class. I'm going to write thank you notes to my teacher. I'm going to get straight A's, and I'm going to know how to spell diarrhea in the spelling bee. And if Fr. Tito tries to hold my hand on the bus, I'm kicking his ass out the exit door so fast his head'll spin." §

Loitering Penguin Baffles Local Authorities

Papineau: *Why does it just keep standing there?*

Local authorities admit they are clueless as to why an emperor penguin has been standing on the corner of Main and West Main streets in downtown Baltic. The curious bird, known locally as "the penguin," has been there, motionless, for almost a month.

"We have no idea where this penguin came from or why it's here or even whether a penguin needs to have a reason to be anywhere in the first place," said Stephen J. Papineau, first selectman. "We have notified the proper authorities. It's up to them to decide what to do about it."

Until the town receives an official response from the Connecticut Department of Inexplicable Phenomena, state police have been monitoring the penguin's movements, which so far have been nil.

Corrie Protubero III, a total braniac at St. Joseph's Elementary School and the closest thing Sprague has to an ornithologist, says the penguin probably came from Antarctica and that it may be hatching an egg.

Too bad for Daddy

"It's the male of the emperor species that hatches eggs which have been laid by the females," Protubero said. "He holds the egg between his feet and keeps it warm under his butt while the mother spends the next two months sliding around on her belly on an iceberg. If she happens to lay the egg on the corner of Main and West Main, then that's where Daddy has to stand. If it happens to be in the middle of the summer, well that's just too bad for Daddy."

Protubero has suggested that someone lift the groin feathers of the penguin to see if it is a male or female. As no volunteers have come forward, the task has been turned over to Sprague animal control warden Timothy Hawks, who has expressed reluctance to stick his nose where, in his opinion, it does not belong.

"Nooooo, sir," Hawks said. "There's nothing in my job description that requires me to peek under the groin feathers of a penguin. My job is to make sure it doesn't bite anybody, doesn't have rabies, and doesn't lie there dead in such a way as to threaten the public health. So far, the penguin is obeying the rules."

State resident trooper Chris Johnson says he has perused local ordinances, Connecticut state statutes, and the Constitution of the United States and found nothing prohibiting penguin loitering.

"It's a public sidewalk, penguins don't require a license, and my personal rule of thumb is not to arrest anyone in a feathered tuxedo because the one and only time I ever did so, it turned out to be a very big mistake," Johnson said. "Furthermore, one thing they never taught us at the Police Academy was how to handcuff a penguin, and I know that if I try, I will come off looking like an absolute idiot. It'll be worse than the time I busted Liberace."

Papineau says the motionless bird is an eerie sight that has begun to bother residents.

"Why does it just keep standing there?" he said, his voice cracking with emotional stress. "Why doesn't it run out in the road and get hit by a car? I'm giving it two months, and if it's still there, I'm going to go out there and hit it with a broom." §

Sprague Scientist Questions Earth's Location

For years scientists have believed that Earth is part of the Milky Way galaxy. Recent research at Sayles Elementary School, however, indicates that astrophysicists from out of town may be off by several trillion light years.

"Any dope can show you that we're not part of the Milky Way," said Seth Pellegrino, a Sayles astronomer who has been researching the issue. "We're standing on the Earth, right? It's, like, *right here*. And if you look up at night, there's the Milky Way, way, way up there. Obviously *we* are not part of *it*."

Researchers at the Harvard Observatory scrambled to explain their oversight. Harvard has always supported the notion that the earth and its solar system are part of the distant galaxy.

"It's rather difficult to explain in terms understandable to the layman," said Dr. Pearson P. Peabody, Professor of Astrology at Harvard. "To use a simple illustrative analogy, imagine looking at something through a telescope. It looks much closer than it really is. That's pretty much what happened, except the problem was compounded by us using a really, really big telescope."

Pellegrino said his discovery will be explained in a project demonstration booth at the upcoming Sayles School Science Fair. Using a simple picture of the universe and a 12-inch ruler he will demonstrate how the earth isn't part of any galaxy.

"It's just here," he says, "all alone in the dark."

Local Band Seeks Serious Players

The Baltic Apocalypse Band is looking for a few serious instrumentalists to help provide background music for the end of the world.

"We're primarily looking for qualified kettle drum players," said Stuart Woronecki, 30, band leader and, coincidentally, father of the commanding officer of NATO forces, Annie Woronecki, 4. "We could also use a choir, a harpist, and somebody who can play a big-ass pipe organ."

Woronecki himself will play bugle when the so-called "Judgment Day" comes.

Being a specialty group, the Baltic Apocalypse Band will have no need for trombones, banjos, or accordions.

"Piccolo players need not apply," Woronecki said. "We're thinking that there might be a place for the lowly kazoo not only for a much-needed sense of irony but also as a nod of recognition to the common man as the fifth angel falls from heaven with the key to the bottomless pit."

Woronecki explained that while the band members cannot expect to be paid in filthy lucre, they will have the satisfaction of knowing that as the plague of locusts with the power of scorpions torments mankind, fire-breathing horses with the heads of lions issue from the pit of Hell and brimstone spreads across the face of the earth, the band members will be be the last to go.

The band hopes to release a CD of the Judgment Day soundtrack, though Woronecki projects limited sales as few survivors are expected.

"Basically, we have to appeal to the innocent market," Woronecki said. "That's a pretty small niche, but we figure that if we call the CD

Told You So, everybody will buy a copy. We also plan to offer advance sales, so order now and receive a free VegeMatic. And that's not all! You'll also receive a free set of Gonzo throwing knives. Major credit cads accepted. Real operators are standing by."

Plain Hill Lab Busted for Controlled Substances

Acting on an anonymous tip, animal control wardens moved in on a Plain Hill Rd. residence last week and took a yellow Labrador retriever into custody on suspected drug charges and operating with an expired license.

The dog, Honeynuts Junior, 2, was reported to have been acting suspiciously.

"We began covert observations after receiving an anonymous phone call which we believe may have originated inside the house where the alleged perpetrator was known to reside," said Sprague animal control warden Timothy Hawks. "From an unmarked van parked across the street, we observed Junior engaging in various activities that had all the earmarks of drug use, among them chewing on a stick and flipping it into the air with unwarranted joy, sticking its nose under oak leaves and snorting an unidentified substance, and urinating in public."

Hawks said that Junior was also observed wagging its tail while panting and staring at nothing. On several occasions it barked nonsensically and without appropriate cause. When a cat of indeterminate breed walked across the yard, Junior wagged its tail from the neck on back.

Hawks said that Junior's drug dependency may have resulted from a lack of self-esteem brought on by castration at an early age. A companion animal's typical psychological response to being "fixed," Hawks explained, is to develop a strong imagination that engages in fantasies of hallucinogenic realism. Often these fantasies become fetishistic obsessions with rubber bones, tree branches, their own genitalia and even house guests who make the mistake of offering the animal a gesture of courteous affection.

"It was very sad to see how drugs had degraded this poor animal," Hawks said. "It was badly in need of a shave. It had mud on its paws and saliva on its chin and the breath of an Islamic terrorist. We pulled a parasitic, blood-sucking tick off its neck about the size of a teeny-weeny ping-pong ball."

The arresting wardens found a supply of heartworm pills and ear mite cream in the house as well as assorted drug paraphernalia, including matches, rolling papers, a Grateful Dead poster, plastic bags containing an unidentified white powder, a sawed-off shotgun, four hand grenades and an awesome hookah made out of a human skull and three vacuum cleaner hoses.

From

Life in Caves

Chapter One

psychosomatic: (adj) [< Gk. psyche, breath, spirit, soul + somatikos, symptoms] 1. Designating or of a physical disorder of the body originating in or aggravated by the psychic or emotional processes of the individual 2. an individual exhibiting a psychosomatic disorder

I remember the first time I saw the kid. I noticed him because he sat at Puker's table, which nobody but a new kid would do. He ate with his elbows down on his knees, his chin just above the table while his two hands fed a stiff, grey-brown grilled cheese into his face. Puker, tapping his lime Jello with a spoon, paid no attention him. I thought maybe I should warn the kid about Puker, but I really didn't want to get involved. A new kid's always a risk. You never know what kind of jerk he might be. I did a favor once for a kid from Connecticut - I showed him how to open his locker by whacking the lock with the spine of a history book - and for the next three months he stuck to me like wet toilet paper. Then I caught him and another kid in the gym locker room using my jock as a slingshot. When I told them to knock it off, some how it ended up with them laughing at me and my jock dangling from the branch of a maple in back of the gym.

Besides, this kid, the kid sitting with Puker, looked like he might have deep psychological problems. One sign: navy blue pants that looked like satin or something and had creases down the front and back of each leg. Another: his shoes, shiny black leather jobs with thick shoe laces and a rounded bumper of sole sticking out around the bottom. His shirt looked like the ones square dancers wear, plaid with fake turquoise buttons and fancy pointed flaps over the pockets. Something about the kid said, "Nebraska, born and raised" - nothing you'd want following you down the halls during the prime of your life. It's a reflection on your own lack of cool. I myself lacked enough cool already, and I knew it.

That was one of the two reasons I sat with Puker in the cafeteria. He didn't seem to mind it if I sat with him, and he was one of few kids I could ask for a pencil or something if I needed it. But he was the kind of kid nobody hung around with, especially at lunch, when he tended to need the little airplane puke sacks his father brought him from business trips. We sat at a four-seater ina corner where the janitor never swept. I often wondered what other kids thought when they saw me sitting there with Puker. They probably thought it was the most natural combination in the world. Either that or they didn't notice me at all.

I was chewing my fish sticks into a gummy wad when the kid from Nebraska did something so quick and so perfect I wasn't sure I really saw it. At first I thought he just brought a fist to his mouth to cover a cough. It even sounded like he coughed into it. But he had something in his hand, something as shiny as stainless steel and as long as a straw. An instant after the cough, I heard a sharp crack at the cafeteria clock, and in the next instant, Señora Wypychowski flinched. She was carrying a tray toward the table in back where the teachers sit when something seemed to hit her near the ear. She set her tray down and pawed at her hair until she found something. She held it between her thumb and forefinger. Somehow I knew it was a bean.

A kid coughs and a Spanish teacher pulls a frijole from her ear. Magic? Coincidence? I didn't believe it. By the time I looked back and forth between the kid and the target a couple of times, the kid had the grilled cheese up against his teeth again. But his eyes, still aimed at Señora Wypychowski, glimmered with secret amusement.

Something told me this kid and I shared common interests. Trying not to attract attention, I took up my tray, sauntered over to his table and slid in, smooth and low. Puker looked up from his Jello.

"You feeling all right, Puker?" I asked, ready to leap away. "You look great, you really do."

Puker had a weak stomach made worse by a patty of rancid butter a couple of years before, back in the sixth grade. But the nurse said the problem was psychosomatic, which I knew from my WordForce workbook, meant all up in his head. He vomited - by which she meant puked - because he thought he was going to vomit. After that, all he had to do was see a patty of butter. One kid found out we could set him off just by waving a softened patty near his nose. But that's the kind of joke that gets old fast. We saved it for emergencies.

He looked okay when I slid into the seat across from him, but not real okay. "Puker," I said. "Eat your Jello. It's good for the stomach. Very, very soooooooothing. I just had some. It's great. They did it right this time. No surprises inside."

Puker said nothing - he hardly ever said anything, except to burp - but lifted a wiggly green cube to his thin, pale lips and slurped it in. Then he took a slow breath and didn't puke.

I leaned close to the new kid and said, "What just happened over there?" With my chin I gestured toward Señora Wypychowski. She held the little brown bullet between her thumb and forefinger in front of Mr. Mundt, assistant principal in charge of pupil mutilation. But they'd never figure out where it came from. Out of the hundred-odd kids in the cafeteria, they'd never suspect the one who looked so scientifically interested in a petrified grilled cheese, the kid with bumper shoes. With the tip of his pinky the kid picked thoughtfully at the congealed cheese and said, "It was just a practice shot."

"That was practice?"

"Ricochets are tough, especially on a snap-shot like that. You never know where they're going to land. I was aiming for her spaghetti."

The kid spoke with a sort of western drawl, kind of slow, as if he talked off the back of his tongue. I said, "Where are you from?"

"Iowa."

"I was close. I figured Nebraska."

"You call that close? Nebraskans are weird. Completely different from Iowans."

"How come you moved to New Jersey?"

"It's a long story. Suffice it to say I'm Japanese."

Well that was the first corn-haired, freckle-faced Japanese I ever saw who was taller than me, and nobody every called me short. And his name, it turned out, was Rusty - surely another first for the Japanese empire. Middle name, just what you'd expect on a kid out of Iowa: Earl. And also Entwhistle. The two middle names together sounded more like something you'd get with a kid from California. But then came the weird part, the Japanese part. Matsunaga. Russell Earl Entwhistle Matsunaga.

I said, "Matsunaga?"

He looked me hard in the eye and said, "Want to make something of it?" By the way he held his grilled cheese I knew he could fit it up my nostrils if I so much as cracked a grin. Entwhistle Matsunaga's a hard name not to crack up over, but I prefer to eat sandwiches the old fashioned way. So I made my forehead wrinkle with deep concern and said, "My name's Mario. Mario McSweeney. I'm Irish. And Italian."

Then neither of us knew what to say, so I introduced Puker and gave a little of his background, the stuff he's famous for. Rusty put down his sandwich and leaned back in his chair. When his eyes shifted focus to look over the cafeteria crowd, I got the same idea he had. I wanted to see him shoot another bean.

"I got a lima bean --a cooked lima bean - into a teacher's spaghetti once," he said. "It was great. When she bit down on it, she must have figured it was a cockroach because she spit it out real fast, along with a mouthful of spaghetti and this incredible sauce they used to put on it. The meat was ground up dogs and cats. This kid I knew said he saw one of the cooks carry a dead schnauzer into the kitchen, and this wasn't a kid who told a lot of lies. I mean, it might have been a poodle mix or something, but for sure it was a dog from the side of the road somewhere. You could see the little bits of hair in the sauce. Sometimes you'd get a bone chip between your teeth."

"You shouldn't talk that way in front of Puker," I said. "And how do you shoot lima beans out a bean shooter? They're flat."

Keeping his eyes on the teacher's table, Rusty casually bent over and slipped two fingers into his sock. When he sat up, he kept his hand under the table but showed me what he had. Just like you'd expect a lima bean shooter to look, it was a flat tube, kind of oval shaped at the end. Not shiny like the other shooter, though. This one was just gray and crude-looking.

"A lima bean shooter," I said with total amazement. "Where'd you get that? "

"Made it in shop class. Back in Iowa."

"Too bad we haven't got any lima beans." Mrs. Wypychowski was talking so fast and hard at Mr. Mundt that I could see her teeth and tongue and half-chewed spaghetti from clear across the cafeteria. It wasn't a pretty sight, but it did make a tempting target.

Rusty said, "Lima beans? No sweat." From his shirt pocket pulled half a dozen beans, some brown, some black, some lima, even a few tiny lentils. "Limas are tough. They swoop around. Half the time they go the whole wrong way."

He lowered his chin to table level, slipped a lima bean into the six-inch tube, checked around for witnesses, and brought the tube to his mouth. With a quick, hushed toof, the bean took off. About halfway across, it sliced to the right like an F-16 showing off. It landed among some sixth graders who were giggling so hard they didn't notice. By the time I looked back at Rusty, he was coming back from his sock, hands empty.

I liked this kid. Very cool, very smooth. And he didn't have to talk about it, didn't have to make a big show out of being the best shot east of the Mississippi. Maybe west of the Mississippi, too, depending on whether every kid in Iowa could do what Rusty did so well.

Besides, I had this thing against Señora Wypychowski, who had some other thing against me. She hated me even more than she hated most of the rest of the English-speaking world. And not just the suckers who got stuck in her Spanish class. She refused to speak English with anybody. She'd talk to other teachers in Spanish. She talked to her dog in Spanish. When she passed me in the hall, she'd say, "Buenos dias, Mario. Como estás?" and smile with a wicked grin just daring me to come back with, "Oh, not bad, yourself?" She had fingernails, blood-red, grown long for kids who spoke English to her, and she had the kind of personality that could remove a kid's face with one swipe of her claws.

Maybe that's what they put in spaghetti sauce in New Jersey. Kids' faces.

Not that she needed to go that far. She had us trained well enough. She had a way of making a kid feel like he'd had his face clawed off. Like if your dog ate your homework, she'd make you stand up and sing Silent Night. In Spanish. It was amazing how fast our dogs learned to stick to their kibble. We had to memorize dialogues, too - not for punishment but just for her majesty's pleasure. Thirty-odd lines of dull-witted discussion between teen-age Mexicans. Not that I have anything against Mexicans, but why do I have to know how to say, "Who's the toreador?" in Spanish? If Mexican kids never had to learn to say, "Who's pitching?" in English, it wouldn't bother me a bit.

I had that toreador line to say - that or "I love meatballs!" depending on who started the dialogue - right after lunch on the day Rusty Entwhistle Matsunaga winged Señora Wypychowski with a turtle bean. There I sat in a puddle of sweat - it was late April and already hot - right behind the only person in the world who loved her Spanish teacher: Fluorine Dalwani.

Fluorine knew her stuff, be it Silent Night in Spanish or the chemical formula for photosynthesis or the geometric proof that a triangle has three sides. She was in the honors track because she was born too smart. I landed in the same fast-track because our school has a computer with a sense of humor. It put me in with the smart kids so it could watch me score low. Ha, ha, ha. Maybe it's just so the others would look better.

Fluorine ranked last among the five-point-two billion people on earth who I wanted to recite dialogue with. It was plenty hard enough without having to face an overfed female nerd in saddle shoes and a granny dress. That's what she always wore. Always. For as long as I had known her, which was since about kindergarten, she'd worn saddle shoes and granny dresses. She probably slept in them. I can't imagine where her mother found shoes like that. They didn't get handed down from older sisters because she didn't have any. Nor could they come from friends; she didn't have any of those, either. The thrift shop over in Newton wouldn't have them. You'd have to go to an antique store, or maybe there was a special shop for weird people.

The señora always paired off her estudantes for our moment in the sun. Depending on how many kids were absent between me and the left end of the back row, where she started picking the lucky pairs, I might have to face Fluorine at the front of the class. Or, in complete contrast, I might get to stand up there with the most beautiful girl in the world, Emily Fetschrift. I don't know what it was about that girl, but I loved her deeply. Also secretly. No one could possible suspect because we had never exchange a word except in Spanish, which, of course, didn't count. Emily didn't have the kind of prettiness your normal person would call pretty. Basically she was a skinny chick with hair the color of dirt. But I liked the way one front tooth kind of leaned out around the one next to it, and the way her jaw was kind of wide in back but pointed a bit at the chin. And she had dimples - five, to be exact: one in each cheek, one in her chin, and two others you could see only when she wore a certain pair of white jeans. No other girl in the world had dimples like that and such a sassy tooth.

Fluorine and Emily both had eyes, but they did different things to me up there in front of the class. I'd be standing there, sweat running a trickle from armpits to waist, and my dialogue mate would flash glances at me. If it was Fluorine, the flashes were of disdain, impatience, and disgust. If it was Emily, the flashes hit me with quick sparks of sympathy. She wouldn't quite smile, but I'd see a flicker of dimples, a peek of her tooth, and I'd know she knew how I felt. I knew she knew because she, too, had damp stains under her arms.

With the cruel smile of a sadist who knew of my love of Emily, the mighty Mrs. Wypy said, "Señorita Flora Doreen, Señor Mario, por favor..." and gestured toward the front of the room and a map of Mexico pulled down for the occasion. Fluorine planted her saddle shoes in a spot that seemed perfect to her and gave me a grin I'd just love to drop into the cafeteria trash can. In the voice of a cheerful Mexican teenager who really cared, she rattled off the first line, a tongue-twister I happened to know meant "Good afternoon, Pedro. ¿Would you like to go to the bullfight with me? I have some excellent tickets in the shady section."

New Jersey state law required me to say "Yes. ¿Who's the toreador?" but no law in the world could make me look like I wanted to go or to give a flying hoot who got to stab the bull. For all I cared it could have been the president of the United States in star-spangled glow-in-the-dark, red, white and chartreuse tights. In fact if I had known how to say that in Spanish, I would have. Not that our beloved señora gave extra points for creativity. No way. She wanted the R's to rattle like machine guns, the U's to sound like a pigeon's coo, the E's to come from where the top of the throat meets the back of the tongue, a kind of flat squeak, like Mickey Mouse in need of Pepto Bismol.

Worst of all, she wanted us to look like we cared. She wanted to hear those upside-down exclamation points and italics. If she heard murder in your throat, she'd make you say it again, and then again, louder. And in a day or two, for some minor infraction, you'd find yourself singing Silent Night before an audience of smirks.

But I'm the kind of guy who'd rather sing Silent Night in public than go to a bullfight with the likes of Fluorine. It was one of those lousy situations one could easily solve with plastic explosives, or even a beanshooter. I imagined an impossibly beautiful lima bean shot ricocheting out the door, swooping down the hall, around the corner and through the little glass plate of the fire alarm. The room clears, the fire trucks come. Before it's all over, it's time for gym.

I had no beanshooter, though, let alone the marksmanship to pull off a shot like that. Fluorine stood waiting for her answer, and Señora Wypychowski stood drumming the fingers of one hand on the knuckles of the other. I could stall no more. Being too honest for my own good, being the type who cannot resist going for the laugh, knowing I wouldn't make it to the thirty-fourth line anyway, and especially not wanting to get to "I just love meatballs!", I just answered Fluorine with the truth. I said, "No way, José."

The room guffawed, and poor miffed Fluorine let out with a bitter "Tcht!" that could have cracked concrete.

What did I get for my moment of truth and joy? An F for my recital and a two-hour detention for being an inconsiderate wise-guy.

That's inflation for you. I remember the days when you could be an inconsiderate wise-guy for only one hour of detention. Two hours was too much. It meant waiting for the high school bus that took the baseball and track teams home after practice. I wouldn't get home until after dark, about the time my father left for work and my mother disappeared into her bedroom for the night. Not that either of them bothered me much. I worried more about a certain snapping turtle I had chained to a tree at the side of a swamp in the woods. I also wanted to shoot some serious beans.

What exquisite happiness, then, to walk into Mr. Mundt's windowless chamber of boredom and see something besides cement block walls and half a dozen desk-chairs. What infinite joy to find a fellow cell mate in there, a freckled, yellow-haired, inconsiderate wise-guy with half a smile on his face and a general look of deep, deep thought. Nothing about him at all seemed in the least way Japanese.

"Rusty," I said. "It's good to see you here."

Chapter Two

sterile: (adj) [< L. sterilis < IE ster- barren] 1. incapable of producing others of its kind, barren 2. producing little or nothing, unfruitful [sterile soil, a sterile policy] 3. lacking in interest or vitality; not stimulating or effective [a sterile style] 4. free from living organisms

Rusty Earl Entwhistle Matsunaga had been sentenced to two hours of detention for a most exquisite crime: launching a wad of pink bubble gum so that it landed exactly on the corner of the desk where Mr. Mandia, crack health sciences teacher, tended to sit. Now Mr. Mandia had pink bubble gum in the center of his pinstriped pants, and Rusty had a running start on his Record. We could hear Mr. Mandia in Mr. Mundt's office arguing that the school should pay the dry cleaning bill. Mr. Mundt said school policy prohibited such expenses but that it was a valid tax deduction. Mr. Mandia said he didn't want a tax deduction, he wanted the gum removed from his pants. Mr. Mundt suggested squeezing it out of Mr. Matsunaga. That's when Mr. Mandia said, "I tried that. The idiot doesn't speak English."

When Rusty heard that he jumped up so hard he almost knocked his desk over. I grabbed his sleeve to keep him from busting down the door. Straining toward the invisible voices beyond the wall, he yelled, "That's my father you're talking about!"

"Easy boy," I said in a hard whisper. "Sticks and stones, right? They say that in Iowa, too, don't they?"

"We don't call people idiots," he said, "not for being foreign. What's wrong with being Japanese?"

I got him to sit back down, but he kept his eyes aimed through the wall into Mr. Mundt's office. "I'll get him," he said. "Gum's nothing."

"Looks to me like it did the trick. Listen to him!"

We crept to the wall and pressed our ears against the cement blocks. Mr. Mandia described the incident in detail. "Every kid in that room was laughing at me. It was the most humiliating experience of my life. It looked like I was pulling long pink tapeworms out of my butt. I felt like a clown at a two-bit circus. And it was slimy, like it had something on it."

I held my palm out. Rusty slapped it. "You're already even," I said. "He could call my father an idiot all he wanted if I got to watch him pull long, pink tapeworms out of his butt."

"We'll see."

"I got a question for you. How do you shoot gum out a beanshooter? Doesn't it get stuck?"

"You have to shape it like a little football and coat it with bacon grease. Then it slides right out. But for some weird reason, it sticks where it lands."

I shook my head with amazement. This kid knew his technology. I had a million questions for him. Where did he learn the bacon grease trick? From his grandfather! Was his grandfather Japanese? No, he was an Oakie, which does not mean from Okinawa but from Oklahoma, which is a whole different place from Iowa. Did everybody in Oklahoma coat their gum with bacon grease? Only when they had to. Where does one carry one's bacon grease? In one's socks. How did Rusty get a name like Matsunaga? He answered one syllable at a time, each as pointed as a dagger: "Be. Cause. My. Father's. Jap. Anese."

It sounded like on the one hand he didn't want to talk about it but on the other wanted the fact known. Or facts. Rusty had a story behind him, a good one. I couldn't resist. "Pray tell," I said, trying to sound funny, "wherever did you find a Japanese father?"

"He found me."

"What, were you floating down the Mississippi in a basket?"

Rusty, fiddling with a gum wrapper and not looking at me, tilted his head to one side. "Sort of," he said. "That's kind of what it felt like."

I waited a second before I said, kind of quiet, "What do you mean? You mean it was a raft or something?"

"I mean it was like being lost in a corn field, which is like drifting down a river in a basket. Ever been lost in a corn field?"

"Not really."

"It's about the scariest thing that can happen if you're five years old and the corn's twice as tall as you and you don't know which way to go and all you know is that there's a thresher out there and sooner or later it's going to bear down on you and you're going to get shucked, threshed, and blown out a pipe into a wagonload of corn. All you can see around you is stalks and leaves and the dirt under your feet and it's kind of dark. Home's one way and any other way is deeper into the field but you don't know which way's which. You can shout all you want, nobody's going to hear you, nobody's going to find you. So you start to run and run with all the corn leaves cutting at you but no matter how fast you run you're still in the field and everything looks the same. You can lie down and cry and cry and cry but nothing's going to happen and all the corn's just going to stand there."

For some reason I could imagine that pretty well. I could see how it was like floating down a big river in a little basket. Sort of.

Rusty was still looking down at something only he could see. I had a feeling he was going to start crying so I said, "And then along came a Japanese guy?"

"That was when I was little. Every kid gets lost in a corn field at least once. It teaches you something."

"Like what?"

"I don't know...kind of like there's no place like home."

I still didn't see what lost in a corn field had to do with a Japanese father. Rusty, looking like he had a sudden case of the sweats, pulled up out of his chair and flung himself back against one wall. "What do they have to lock us in a place like this for?" he said. "There ought to be a law against this."

I was feeling the same way, very closed-in, especially after imagining myself like Hansel lost in a forest of corn. I thought about my little lean-to out in the woods, how it was barely big enough to sit up in but somehow felt free and open. Tight, but open. Maybe it was because I could go there or leave there any time I wanted. Maybe it was because rain came in through the roof and wind swept in through the open sides. For a second I thought I might tell Rusty about the place. But in a second I decided no.

Then Rusty said, "This is what it's like in Japan," and held his arms away from his body, his palms pressed back against the wall. "Everything small, tight. You'd see a family of six living in an apartment this size."

"You've been there?"

"I saw a picture in National Geographic. A mother and father and three little nerds ate and lived and slept in one room. The kitchen was the size of a phone booth. Their dinner table was only six inches high. Can you imagine sharing your bedroom with your parents?"

The door opened and Mr. Mundt stuck his head in. "Russell," he said. "Could you step out here a moment?"

For a single hard second, Rusty didn't move from the wall. He looked kind of crucified there. But then he stepped to the door, opened it as wide as it would go, and walked into the late afternoon sun that filled the assistant principal's office. Mr. Mundt gave me a look of disgust before reaching way in to pull the door shut.

Alone in the concrete and linoleum cell, I thought about sharing a room with my parents. Actually it didn't sound too bad. They barely shared a bedroom with each other. They barely shared the same house. Dad worked all night and slept all day, seven days a week. Mom kept me outside until he woke up, around dinner time, which of course was his breakfast time. If you call meatloaf breakfast. So they barely saw each other and I barely saw both of them together. Sleeping in the same room with both, well, that didn't sound too bad, as long as they didn't fight, which of course they would,though of course maybe they wouldn't, being in the same bed and all.

For a while I wondered about being in the same bed with a girl, wondered how you could possibly get any sleep at all. I guess if the girl looked like my mother, or the guy like my father, you'd get plenty of sleep. Or you'd do like they did - use the bed in shifts.

Then I wondered again about sleeping in the same room with both of them. I imagined living in Japan, with the whole family of brothers and sisters and mother and father sitting around a table on the floor eating rice with chopsticks and then unrolling our straw-mat beds and going to sleep close enough to hear each other breathe. Having nothing else to think about, I threw in a little dog, imagined him curling up on my feet and snoring.

But then I wondered if Japanese had pet dogs. More likely they'd keep some kind of fancy bird with feathers that hung down to the floor. For all I knew, they ate dogs.

Rusty never came back into the detention room, not that day anyway. I later found out they took him home, presented him and Mr. Mandia's pants to his mother. She, poor thing, equipped with the courage and IQ of a squirrel, took ten minutes to figure out why they were pointing back and forth between a ten dollar bill and a sticky pink lump on a pair of pants. She thought they were offering her ten dollars to do Mr. Mandia's laundry. Rusty let her suffer for a while, then went to his bedroom and got a couple of tons of wrapped coins he'd saved up from left-over lunch money.

Rusty said she never figured out what it was all about. Blubbering out of control, she phoned Papa-san - they put san on the end of people's name, kind of like "mister" but nicer - and explained it all in a stream of Japanese that sounded, in Rusty's words, like a toilet flushing backwards. When the old man came home, he sent Mama-san to the bedroom and sat Rusty on the couch. Then he paced around while he flipped through a Japanese-English dictionary in search of a phrase to fit the occasion. Finally he put the book on the coffee table, held out both hands and said, "Hrdusty-san, why?"

Stuck with no possible answer, Rusty would only fall back on that old favorite: "I didn't do it."

To his utter amazement, Papa-san bought it. "Ah, no?" he said, pressing his palms together. "Oh, sodly, Dlusty, vedly sodly!" (That's how Rusty said he said it.) And Papa-san hurried off to tell his wife, who burst from the bedroom to give her son a tearful hug of apology. After a brief discussion, they pulled a neat wad of dollars from her purse, examined several of them, and forked over a pair of fives.

"It was too easy," Rusty told me later. "I didn't like it at all. Like taking candy from two babes in the woods. I felt sorry for them. I can't imagine what they must be paying for rent."

Of course I didn't know any of this on my way home. I had my own problems, namely the Activities Bus that carried all kids from the middle school and from Central High, in Newton, who stayed late. That meant it was full of all-American jocks whose main joy in life was to hold eighth graders upside down by their ankles and shake the change out of their pockets. Sitting near the front didn't help because Bob-the-bus-driver, a former jock who actually managed to hold down a job, had the same sick sense of humor.

I escaped by dashing off the bus about five miles before my stop, which normally is the last one because it's way outside of town, the only place they'd let us put a trailer home. But where I got off the bus this time wasn't too far from home as the crow flies. Or as the kid runs through the woods. The first mile or so cut through an arm of Piddle Nature Preserve, which was nice. The trees in these woods - oak, beech, black birch, maple - had been growing since the Civil War, when a guy named Piddle left his fields and went off to free the slaves. He never came back. The government got to keep his land - 1,843 acres - and in time his fields became a forest, which is basically all mine because nobody else goes there.

I know this from a library booklet called "Historical Pottsville." It's a pretty thin piece of literature. Not much history has happened around in here. In 1778, George Washington's army snuck through, but they didn't fight any battles. (Myth has it they only stopped long enough to take a leak and pick up a few cases of poison ivy.) Marion Francis, Swamp Fox, may have hid gun powder somewhere up on Potts Ridge. (Myth says it's still up there.) Isaac Piddle left here but didn't come back. (The myth: he bought a steamboat and called it the Piddle

Paddler.) Henry Phillips, inventor of the Phillips screwdriver, may have been born here. (Or maybe it was milk of magnesia.)

Anyway, the Piddle Preserve woods had huge trees growing in it, stone walls running all over the place, and enough poison ivy to hide the entire Viet Cong army and all their friends. It rose up into the trees in thick hairy ropes and covered the ground like a shiny green mat. People stayed out of the place, except for a few trails. I knew my way around, though, and could get just about anywhere. Down below the ridge, behind a no-man's land of poison ivy and pricker-bushes, was a little swamp. On the side of it was my little hut, and down in the swamp was Hercules, my killer turtle - a snapper, anyway. I suppose he could kill you if you sat there and let him chew on you long enough. Mostly he lived on bits of hamburger I snuck out of the cafeteria, bacon from home, and bugs I caught here and there.

The poison ivy had already leafed out that spring, but during the winter I had cut a well hidden passage way around the end of the ridge and under the thorns to my hut. There I found Herc's chain drooping down through the water. All I had for him was some dead flies I'd caught during gym - nothing worth waking a turtle up for. So I left them in a pile on a rock near the edge of the water and sat back to smoke a Marlboro Light and do a little reading. My library consisted mostly of illustrated human physiology publications. That's what I heard a kid in the locker room call his. To anyone else they were just filthy magazines. Mine were especially filthy, having been stored for a couple of years in a tattered plastic bag in a hole under a rock. I was pretty tired of them. The ladies, while practically flesh and blood when I first slid my eyes over them, had aged with exposure to the elements. Wrinkled and water-stained, they had become mere paper, mere memories of what they had been. And none of them came close to the tight, petite, innocent beauty of Emily Fetschrift. I often tried to imagine her in the place of the girls in the magazines, but it didn't work. Emily wouldn't show those parts of her body, at least not the way those girls did. It was hard to believe she even had those parts or would know what to do with them if she did.

I forced down about half my smoke before flicking it into the swamp. Then I got up and did a little housekeeping. I hauled in a good length of dead tree for firewood and brought over some stones from one of Piddle's walls. I had this plan for building a stone foundation and laying logs across it and gradually building up a regular cabin. My lean-to was okay, but only in good weather. So far I had about twelve stones and a page from a Sears catalog that showed various chain saws I might mail away for if a couple hundred dollars fell out of the sky. I had certain technical questions about exactly how to assemble the whole thing, but I figured I'd know the answer when I had the logs.

I figured if I fixed the place up good enough, I could move right in. I could have a dog - a lot of dogs - and eat what I wanted for dinner and just hang out all day doing nothing. How to pay for it all? Easy. Frog legs. Right at my doorstep I had all the frogs you could eat. If I caught a dozen good-sized frogs a day, I'd have enough to keep myself in Spam and popcorn and of course dog food for my little family.

Little? Not so. I had plans to liberate the population of the Pottsville dog pound and bring them all here. Depending on how things went I thought I might go on to free dogs all over the state, a regular Bolivar of New Jersey. I could have ten thousand dogs living on Piddle's Preserve, all citizens of the Republic of Piddle. As long as nobody knew, we'd be safe from invasion.

Dumb idea? Maybe. But that's one of the nice things about being thirteen and having a hut in the woods. There you can think whatever you want. Nobody can stop you, nobody can laugh or call you dumb.

But you have to be out by dark. I crawled out through my perimeter of raspberry thorns and draping poison ivy vines and headed for home. Mother let me in as soon as I knocked but, as usual, didn't say a word. She had a sponge in one hand and ammonia in the other, which meant she was working on her spot.

Mother's spot was a spot only she could see. She'd been working on it, trying to scrub it out of existence, for as long a I could remember. It kept moving. One day she'd be on her knees on the kitchen floor trying to scrub it out of the linoleum. Then she'd find it on the refrigerator. Next thing you know, she's found it behind the toilet. If I happened to walk by, she'd grab me and point me at it and say, "Look at that!" Then she'd glare at me like it was my fault. It was only some time after the eighth grade that I figured out she wasn't telling me to look at the wet patch she'd made with her sponge. She wanted me to see a spot that wasn't there. In fact, there were no spots anywhere in the house. No crumb on the counter, not a whisker on a sink, not a sock on a floor. At least not for long. the house was sterile except for the few moments that some bit of Pop's dirtiness lingered out of place.

That particular day, the day I met Rusty, Mother's spot seemed to appear on the back of my neck. Or a version of it, anyway. Just as I walked by her, she grabbed my collar and said, "Wait a minute, you little roach." She dropped her sponge and with her fingernails got ahold of a pimple on my neck. She squeezed it so hard it actually bled. Pain alarms went off in my head. She released me the way you release a used tissue and said, "If you washed yourself now and then that wouldn't happen."

Pop, just out of bed, was still stinking up the bathroom when she plunked three chicken pot pies on the table, and not for the first time that week. Or maybe it was turkey pot pies the last time. It didn't matter; they all tasted the same to me. I broke the crust with my spoon and let the steam swirl out for a while. Times like this a kid could use a good dog under the table. Or even a snapping turtle. But I dumped on enough salt to kill the taste and slurped it up like a good boy. By the time Pop came out in his green Dickies, she'd already rinsed out her little pie pan and crammed it into the garbage. She said nothing to him, and he said to me, as he always did, "Hey, buddy, how's it going?" and I said the usual "Okay," and he said, "That's good."

So much for conversation. Mother went to her bedroom (it was hers during the night), spraying lilac room deodorizer ahead of her as she went. The door closed behind her, shutting out me and the rest of the dirt of the world until morning. Pop slurped up his dinner like a good boy. I checked every channel on the TV–all four of them–twice and turned it off. Pop used his finger to wipe up the bottom of his pie dish clean before cramming it into the garbage. Then he put on his Mets cap and Mets jacket, and tucked his Mets lunch box under one arm. Snapping the thermostat down to three degrees below zero, he said "Hey buddy, have a nice day, hear?" and left for a night with a metal lathe.

I sat in front of the dead TV for a while and finally turned it back on. I don't remember what I watched. It was one of those shows about a family that argued all the time but with jokes. Every time somebody said something nasty, it was funny, though of course none of them laughed. I couldn't watch the whole thing. I preferred to read pages forty-nine through fifty-one of my history book, a heart warming tale of how the Visigoths, Ostrogoths and plain old Goths did to the Roman Empire what the Vandals in New York City would do if all their parents happened to go away on the same weekend.

But history, even good stuff like that, puts me to sleep. Even though I faced a quiz in the morning, I couldn't hammer into my head the difference between a Visigoth and an Ostrogoth. I fell asleep on the couch - I love to take a quick nap before I go to bed - and didn't wake up until the light in Mother's room was out and the house was dark and cold.

Chapter Three

sashimi (n)a Japanese dish of bite-sized pieces of raw fish eaten with soy sauce and horseradish paste

The next day, back at the cafeteria, back at the table with Puker, Rusty told me how Mr. Mandia had come to his home. Hearing the story of his parents' odd reaction, their amazing faith in their only son, I had to ask Rusty how he came to have Japanese parents. The answer was simple and predictable.

"I was adopted," he said.

"Just like that? Wham-bam and you're Japanese?"

"I am not Japanese."

"Well, sort of, you are, aren't you? I mean, you did say that, didn't you?"

"I was kidding. I'm Iowan."

Even Puker was paying attention to this. For the first time in several years, he didn't look like he had his belly on his mind. He seemed to keep forgetting his spinach-noodle surprise halfway between his plate and his mouth. He'd dip his head toward the dripping spoon but then back off when Rusty dropped another bit of data, such as, "I think they bought me." Who could possibly stick spinach-noodle surprise into his mouth after hearing a line like that?

I said, "They bought you?"

"Well," he admitted. "I'm not sure. But how else can you explain it?"

"Explain what?"

"How people have to wait years and years to adopt a kid, but I'm an orphan for three weeks and presto, somebody's got me."

That didn't quite make sense to me, but before I could straighten it out, Rusty went on.

"My mother died of cancer, about five years ago. *Brain* cancer. I was just a little kid then. I barely knew what was going on until it was too late. They never really told me she was going to die until my aunt came and said, 'Your mother's gone to heaven.' I can't imagine a dumber way to put it. Why didn't she say, 'Rusty, you're never going to see your mother again'? What did she think, that I was just going to shrug my shoulders and say, "Heaven? That's nice. She deserves it. She was a good mother.'? The next thing I know they've got me all dressed up in my Sunday suit and a red bow tie and we're down at the cemetery cranking her coffin into a grave."

"Cranking?"

"Yeah. It sits on a couple of straps and they turn a crank and the straps lower it down into the ground. Then everybody tosses in some dirt and we all go home for snacks. It's great." His mouth curled with irony.

I couldn't help but say, "Snacks?" Rusty had a weird way of cracking a joke but looking nasty, even mad, at the same time. I couldn't tell if he was serious. Did they really serve snacks? Did he stuff his face?

"Yeah, snacks," he said. "What, you never knew anybody who died?"

Actually, I didn't, except for a grandmother who died in Florida. I think I met her only once. I was about seven when it happened. There wasn't a funeral or anything. No snacks.

So Rusty's mother died of cancer. I'm not proud to admit it, but at the time, at the age of thirteen, dying of cancer meant nothing to me. I just sort of assumed people died like they did on TV - a few last words, a deep breath, suddenly the head leans to one side, and that's the end of that. Time for a commercial. I was as touched by the death of a lady in Iowa as I was by the Ostrogoths sacking Rome. I'd probably be more touched if my turtle had a hangnail. I mention this to show how smart I was in the eighth grade.

Still, it made an awful good story. Puker kept turning his head every time Rusty trotted out a new fact. He had spinach-noodle surprise all over his chin.

"And your father," I said. "Did he die of cancer, too?" The words sounded perfectly stupid as they left my mouth. Rusty, I could tell, agreed. I think he answered just so Puker would get the next spoon of food into his mouth.

"He died in an accident," Rusty said. "Got run over by his own tractor. Nobody saw it happen, but they think it kicked into gear just as he was getting out."

I didn't know what to say. Rusty was trying to look unconcerned, like maybe he was really thinking about where to shoot a lima bean. But I could see the sadness behind his face. He wasn't going to cry, though. Somehow I knew that nothing would make Rusty cry. His crying department had already grown up.

Puker mopped up his spinach-noodle surprise and was poking through his tapioca by the time I got up enough guts to ask Rusty what happened next.

He told me how he got passed to a great aunt who smelled so bad of lilacs he could hardly breathe. Then a regular aunt and uncle got him, but the uncle's army reserve unit got called up and the aunt had to do jury duty so their six kids - Rusty's cousins - got passed around the remaining family. A social worker with a mustache said that was no way for a boy to live and besides, she had a couple of wonderful parents for him if he wanted to move to New Jersey. He said he didn't want to move to New Jersey or to anywhere else but she said oh yes he did, he'd be glad, and he had no choice anyway. So the day after Christmas they packed his bags, took him to the airport, and handed him over to a stewardess who looked like Marilyn Monroe. She hung a chain around his neck. On the chain hung a yellow tag. As the plane revved up and lumbered down the runway, Rusty read the tag. It said, in a combination of type and handwriting, "Hi! My name's Russell Earl Entwhistle. I'm going to Newark to meet my father, Yoshiyama Matsunaga, who lives at 49 Wagon Wheel Lane, Pottsville, NJ. If I need help, please contact Westward Ho! Airlines or your local police department."

Rusty turned his head to look out the cafeteria window. "Then the plane took off," he said. "At first we were so low you could see cars on the roads and the tractors in the fields. I saw my school for about three seconds before we flew into some fog and it all got misty. Then we went into some clouds and everything was white. All I could think was, 'There goes the whole world.'

"When we landed in Newark, the stewardess took me through this place that was like a tunnel and then into the lobby. The place was huge. But somehow we knew right away Mr. and Mrs. Matsunaga were the Japanese man and lady all dressed up in navy blue. You could tell they were waiting for a kid from Iowa to come along and call them Mom and Dad."

"And did you?"

"No way."

"But didn't you kind of have to?"

Before he could answer, the bell rang. While it rang - all of two seconds - nobody in the cafeteria moved. Just like always. Then, just like always, everybody made one single move to grab their trays and stand up and surround the garbage cans like a bunch of cattle to a salt lick. Thirty seconds later, we were in the hall, automatically sorting ourselves out into the rooms where we belonged. This always amazed me. It reminded me of a science movie I saw once where a whole bunch of mice found their way through a maze to different nooks and crannies where there was food waiting for them. But they learned this by getting electric shocks when they screwed up, and kernels of corn when they didn't. And all the scientists said, Wow, aren't they clever? Somehow that applied to two hundred middle school students. Eight times a day they automatically rushed to their nooks and crannies - their study halls and science classes and whatever - without getting a candy bar for doing it right or a boot in the butt for screwing up, unless you count detention.

In the hall, before we split up, I had to ask Rusty one more question. "Did you?" I asked.

"Did I what?"

"Call them Mom and Dad. Just like that?"

"No way."

For some reason that made me feel good. Relieved. But then Rusty said something that really surprised me. He said, "It was worse."

"Why? What happened?"

He looked up and down the hall twice before he could say it, and then it came out as a whisper. He said, "I bowed."

My jaw must have dropped halfway to the floor because an instant later his knuckles were lifting it shut - gently, but, still, definitely knuckles nonetheless. "You bowed?" I said.

"Shhh! It isn't that simple." He pulled me in close so no one could hear. The hall was just about empty. "They bowed first. Then I bowed. Even the stewardess bowed. It was like we couldn't help it, like somebody had jerked our strings and down we went."

"And then what happened?"

"I realized what I was doing and stood up straight, real fast. So fast it made my nose bleed."

Then the bell rang. If I didn't get to my social studies nook within five seconds, a scientist was going to educate me with a cattle prod. But I had to ask again, "Then what happened?"

Rusty looked nervously up and down the hall and said, "Let's get out of here."

"What do you mean out?"

"I mean where do you hide in this school? Where do you cut class?"

I'd never cut a class before. Some kids did, but I had no idea where they went. I'd never even thought about it. Now classroom doors were closing fast. The hall was empty except for us. I felt like a cockroach caught in the middle of a kitchen counter when somebody snaps on the light. My urge, of course, was to head for the woods. I grabbed Rusty's arm and said, "Come on."

With a gesture of his hand he slowed me down to a calm walk. Unnoticed, we strolled past the administration office, through the big front doors, down the steps, along the windowless gym wall and around the corner to the vast open space of the ball field. A hundred yards way, behind the backstop, stood the thicket of trees and brush I was aiming for.

I doubt anyone saw us make the crossing. If they had, we'd still be in detention. They would have chained us to the wall and donated the key to the Houdini museum. For generations to come they would have paraded sixth-graders past us as an example of what happens if you attempt the unthinkable. As we walked quickly, stiff-legged across the lawn I was so scared I was shaking. The wind blowing across the grass still had a bit of the chill of winter, but it seemed to have a whiff of spring mixed in.

The area behind the bushes showed signs of high school kids: beer cans, a semi-gutted car seat, cigarette butts, charred sticks, a shoe, a beech tree all scared up with the initials of nature-lovers. Feeling myself in the midst of filth, I squatted with my back against the beech; Rusty sat on rock.

"So?" I said.

"So I bowed."

"Right. And then what?

"Then I got a bloody nose. Right there in the lobby of the airport. And this lady - my mother, right? - starts squawking like her only son's bleeding to death. Dear old dad whips a snotrag out of his navy blue suit and lets her try to cram it up my nose. It ws all crispy so I pushed it away and tried to keep breathing in. Then the stewardess, who I'd let be my mother any day, pinched a nice fresh Kleenex over my nose and said to the poor lady, 'Would like me to call the infirmary?'

"Well of course for all this lady knows, the stewardess is saying, 'He's got thirty seconds to live. What shall I do with him?' so she has to wait for her husband to translate. There's tears coming out of her eyes. They have a big discussion about it, and by the time they're done, the bleeding stopped."

What a way to arrive in New Jersey. It must have seemed like the gates of hell itself. The kid's three minutes into his new family and he's already caused the biggest stir since Pearl Harbor. I myself, at that point, would have headed for the runway and thrown myself into the nearest propeller.

But Rusty was cool. When the stewardess produced a paper for Mr. Matsunaga to sign, Rusty showed him where to do it. The stewardess snapped out a yellow carbon of the form, whatever it was, and everybody shook hands. They all bowed, too - everybody but Rusty. Then the Matsunaga family got into a blue Buick and drove home.

On the way, Mrs. Matsunaga sat sideways in the front seat so she could watch her boy. She kept asking things in Japanese and making Mr.Matsunaga translate. "What you like?" he asked. Rusty said, "Corn-on-the-cob." "You like lice?" he asked. Rusty, having once gotten lice from another kid's baseball cap and not yet knowing that lice meant rice, said, "No. I hate lice." Mrs. Matsunaga's face collapsed like a tire losing air. She made the mister ask again, "What you like?" Rusty tried "Spaghetti," but that wasn't what Mr. Matsunaga wanted. "No," said Mr. Matsunaga. "Before, you say...what you say you like?" Rusty got it then and said, in his best Iowa slur, "Cornacob." His parents still didn't get it, so five minutes later they're in a Grand Union, Rusty leading the way to the fresh produce department.

They found corn, all right, but, as Rusty told me, "It was dead. Corn-on-the-corpse. All wrapped up in styrofoam and plastic wrap, like a body bag. We might give corn like that to the chickens, but we'd sure apologize for it."

But they bought it. All of it. Fourteen pounds of posthumous corn-on-the-cob. They they went back to the meat department and had a long discussion about a fish. By his mother's upturned nose, Rusty knew the fish had died of mercury poison long before it hit the bed of ice next door to the pork chops.

At home, Mrs. Matsunaga hurried the corn into the freezer - "Just what it needed," Rusty said - and introduced Rusty to his bedroom. Apparently it had just about everything a kid could ask for: a TV connected to a computer beside a rack of electronic games next to a complete stereo system. On the walls, one baseball poster, one football poster, one basketball poster, a poster of Bozo the Clown, and a poster of "a skinny Japanese chick in short-shorts playing electronic drums."

"What's wrong with that?" I asked, standing up to look across the lawn toward school. If somebody came out after us, I wanted a good head start into the woods. Rusty looking unconcerned, opened a penknife and whittled at a piece of vine.

"Nothing wrong with it at all," he said. "But there was one other thing, right there on my bed, lying across it at an angle like it was put there to have its picture taken."

"Not a teddy bear!"

"Worse."

The only thing I could think of worse than a teddy bear was navy blue pants and black bumper shoes. Rusty saw me looking at them and said, "Even worse."

I couldn't think of anything worse than that until Rusty said, "A violin."

A violin. Yes, indeed, that meant trouble. It meant double trouble when Mrs. Matsunaga took the suitcase from Rusty's hand and led him directly to the instrument of torture she had laid there with such care. She picked it up, placed Rusty's hand on it, and guided it to his shoulder.

"They both applauded." His knife sliced hard through the vine as he said it, lopping off a six-inch length. "I was just standing there holding the stupid thing while they clapped and smiled and bowed. It was like they were proud I could hold a fiddle on my shoulder. I didn't know what to do. I wanted to smash it against the wall and run out and keep running all the way to Iowa. But they looked so happy. So I just stood there."

Mrs. Matsunaga, it turned out, had been a music teacher in Japan. Stuck in the United States, she had no one to teach because she couldn't speak English. So she vented her frustration on poor Rusty. One-on-one, hour after hour, again and again: Twinkle,Twinkle Little Star. This was two days into the month-long Christmas break, so he couldn't go to school, didn't know anybody, didn't have anywhere to go.

"She wouldn't quit," he said. "She kept saying, 'Goooood! Goooood!' every time I did something. She kept adjusting my fingers for me, tucking my elbow down, straightening my back, lifting my chin. Once she got me in just the right position, she'd say, 'O.K. You go!' and I'd do it again. But every time it sounded like a barn door on rusty hinges."

I looked at my watch. We had seven minutes before the next class. Rusty went on whittling the section of vine like he had all day. He shaved at the stringy bark, gradually exposing the dull white wood beneath. I wanted to head back to school before we got into too much trouble. "So that's it," I said."That's how you got Japanese parents. We'd better get back."

"That's not the whole story," Rusty said, looking up from his knife. "It's even worse than that."

"Worse than playing the violin all day? What did they do?"

"You mean besides the raw fish?"

"Raw fish? You can't eat row fish. It'd kill you."

"It's a big thing in Japan. I forget what you call it. They cut it up and wrap it around a hunk of cold rice so it's about the size of a Tootsie-Roll, then dip it soy sauce and...down the hatch."

"A hunk of cold rice? I think I'd throw up."

"But that's not the worst part. The worst is that they're moving back to Japan in September."

"How come?"

"The old man's here just for a while, to help his company set up an office. Or something like that. I couldn't really understand. But he showed me the date on the calendar. September 1. He pointed to it with his skinny little finger and said, "Setembah fust, we go. Jah-pahn!" and gave me a great big smile."

Japan. Land of Many Contrasts. That's about all I remembered from our geography book. I remembered some pictures of a girl in a fancy robe and a very white face, a snow-capped volcano, and one of those houses with funny gutters. And I remembered what Rusty had told me about a whole family living in one room. I pictured myself with a sister like the girl with the white face living in a house with funny gutters and a dead volcano out back and everybody sleeping in the same room. All in all, it didn't sound too awful bad, depending on what the sister was like. Probably not much fun, but better than a turtle on a chain. I pictured the whole family rolling out their bed mats on the floor, and everybody saying good night to each other, and then hearing everybody breathing and sighing in their sleep.

"That wouldn't be too bad," I said to Rusty. "Except for the raw fish."

Rusty snapped his knife shut and smoothed the piece of vine with his fingers. "There's just one problem," he said.

"What's that?"

"I'm not going."

He didn′t look at me as he spoke those words, and he said them with a smooth lightness that implied absolute seriousness. He wasn′t going to Japan. Period, end of discussion. He seemed more concerned with this length of vine. He twirled it between his palms, rubbing off the last of its fuzzy bark, and held it out to admire how straight it was. Then he put one end to his mouth, closed his lips around it and blew. I could hear the air come out, thin and hard. With a little smile he looked at me through one eye and said, ″Did you know these things are hollow?"

Chapter Four

An Idea

abscond: *(vi)* [<L. *ab(s)-,* from, away + *concete,*to hide] 1. To go away hastily and secretly; run away and hide, esp. to escape the law

So Rusty really had a problem. We did detention again, bukt this time I got dragged out for a talking-to. Mr. Mundy, sitting behind his gray metal desk, said he noticed me in trouble twice in connection with this new kid, Matsunaga. He hoped I I wasn't falling in with a bad crowd, wasn't going to besmirch–that was his word not mine–myj record because it was going to stick with me for the rest of my life. He held a folder in his hands that seemed to contain my record thus far. I didn't think it looked especially thick for a kid already more than halfway to college.

Behind me I could hear the occasional TICK-tick of a turtle bean ricocheting against two walls in the detention room. Rusty had one of those bendable straws with an accordion elbow. He was trying to perfect a shot that landed behind him. He knew he'd never gain any accuracy, but it would do for a diversion shot that seemed to come from nowhere.

Mr. Mundt went on about how shaky my future looked, how it was all up to me, how I should try to make my parents proud, how everything I did was a reflection on my mother.

My mother. All I could say for her, really, was that she didn't make me eat raw fish or play the violin. Not that I would say such a thing–no more than I would tell Mr. Mundt about Rusty's problem, about him not going to Japan.

Finally Mr. Mundt said, "Now why don't you go back in there and have a seat and think about what you've done. And take my advice. Stay away from that Matsunaga. He's trouble."

If you ask me, assistant principals are trouble. What a waste of taxpayer money. Sure Rusty was trouble. He didn't give a hoot for the rules and didn't mind getting punished. And after our second detention together, neither did I. Instead of seeing it as punishment, I saw it as something to do. It sure beat hanging around the yard waiting for Pop to wake up. Besides, Rusty really knew how to kill time He used it to perfect his been shooting. He showed me how to make a long, high lob that practically never missed the waste basket at the far side of the room. When he let me use this incredible three-piece shooter. When he screwed it together, it was almost a yard long. He kept it in pieces strapped to his calf. He showed me how to brace it by putting my elbow on the desk and using the bone of my forearm as a post. The shooter rested between the two knuckles of my fist. Bone, he explained, was steadier than muscle. I was getting pretty good at a short, two-well ricochet into the basket by the time the minute hand creeped up to five o'cock.

We hardly talked on the bus. One reason is that Fluorine Dalwani sat in the seat ahead of us. She'd gone to cheerleader practice, which was a joke because the high school football team got to vote on which girls would get to cheer for them. Fluorine wouldn't stand a chance. Too dumpy and weird. You'd think she'd be too embarrassed to go out n public in a little yellow and red skirt that showed her fat butt when she jumped up in the air. But Fluorine wasn't the type to get embarrassed. She was the type to; get up and do whatever she wanted, no matter what people thought. So they thought she was weird. She was so weird that even the high school athletes in the back of the bus didn't bother her. She must have scared them off of me, too, because they kept to themselves, whooping it up in the back seats growling dirty words, throwing hammer locks around one another, having a grand time which, thank God, didn't involve me.

Since Fluorine didn't seem to be paying attention to us, I whispered to Rusty, "So what are you going to do?"

He knew what I meant. All he said was, "Split."

Split! Just the sound of it filled me with a feeling of busting out, of escaping from everything–homework, washing dishes, the drudgery of school. But how could a kid of thirteen pull off something like that? How far could he get before they caught up with him and ragged him back? How long could he live without money? I'd thought of splitting before, but something I knew it was a good idea that wouldn't work–not unless you had a place to go and a big wad of money and nobody looking for you Rusty, as far as I knew, didn't have any of that.

So I asked him, in a whisper Fluorine couldn't hear over the rattle and bump of the bus, "Where would you go?"

He answered so easily, so readily, that I knew he'd done a lot of thinking already. "West," he said without looking at me.

West! What a perfect direction It broiught to mind a wagon train, Indians, cattle drives, land so big you could just stake out what you wanted and call it yours. Not that I belived the west was still like that. But every kid's got west in his blood. It points you west the way magnetism points a compass north. Every once in a while I put a little thought into heading west, but I knew they had state cops out there the way they used to have Indians. A kid wouldn't stand a chance. I said to Rusty, "But they'd catch you. Wouldn't they?"

"Yep. That's why I'm still here. I haven't figured out just how to do it. But I will. And then I split."

Suddenly Fluorine turned around, eyed Rusty from head to waist, glanced at me with a flash of disgust, then looked back at Rusty. Are you that new kid from Kansas?" she asked.

"Iowa."

"Pleased to meet you, she said. "I'm Flora." Her plump white hand snaked over the back of her seat.

Rusty, unsure of himself, gave the hand a little shake and said, "Rusty."

Pleased to meet you. Those words pretty much sum up the essence of Fluorine. She knew just what to say and wasn't afraid to say it. And she thought her name was Flora, which, as she was quick to mention, means Flowers. But any parents who name their daughter Flora Doreen do so only because they know the hospital won't let them name her what they know everybody's going to call her. Fluorine's name was Fluorine and had been since kindergarten. I know because that when I thought it up and spread it around.

Looking at Rusty, she said, "You should have seen your friend in Spanish class yesterday. Absolutely brilliant. *Muy humoroso.* He has a great future ahead of him. In Paraguay."

I've always tried not to talk to people like that. Anyone who thought Spanish class was for real obviously didn't see the world for what it was. If Fluorine wanted to insult me to all my friends, it didn't bother me. And Rusty was cool. He just said, "I'll ask him about it."

"Before or after you split?"

It's funny how girls can deliver a punch to your jaw with just a few select words. Fluorine's chosen few left Rusty and me stunned inm the repercussion of what she'd overheard. Anything Fluorine knew, thme world would know. If the world knew, then Rusty had to go to Japan to live out his years. And I, as accomplice, would spend the rest of my life in detention. They'd build a special room with my name on the door. I wouldn't see sunset until I was forty years old.

Neither Rusty nor I had an answer for her, so we were glad to see the bus pull up to her stop. She said, "Toodle-oo" to Rusty and left without looking back.

"That's Fluorine," I said.

"She looks like a real brain."

"She is. But *dumb.*"

We got a good giggle out of that. Then the buys came to wagon Wheel Trail, which was a long cluster of raised ranch houses with neat lawns. Rusty said, "See you tomorrow, buddy."

Buddy. It never occurred to me before that moment, but I don't think anyone had ever called me *buddy* before, except Pop, who didn't really mean it. No other kids lived without three miles of our house, and Mother wasn't one to haul me to cub scout meetings or baseball practice. I knew kids at school, but when the final bell rang, they all went home. Rusty did, too, of course, and as the bus pulled away from his stop, I watched him trudge up Wagon Wheel. He was going toward a home that wasn't his, a bedroom lorded over by the image of Bozo.

But at least his Mama-san and Pappa-san opened the door to let him in. As zi sat alone on the bud riding to the outskirts of the school district, I thought how life tends to balance out. Rusty had parents who doted over him but weren't really even in his family, and I had parents who barely talked to me but didn't make me play violin.

If there's one good thing about double detention, it means less time hanging around the yard watching for Pope to wake up. It was twilight when the bus pulled up at our trailer. Yellow light glowed in the living room, and white fluorescent glared from the kitchen. But Pop's bedroom and the bathroom were still dark. So I set my books on the back steps and at on them to keep my butt off the cold concrete. The air was cold, too, but not as cold as it had been all winter. It was probably warm enough now to camp out without shivering all night. In fact, I thought, maybe I'd do thta the very next day, which was Saturday. I'd pack up some smoked sausage for dinner, some bacon and eggs for breakfast, and some potato chips and Twinkies for the time in between.

I still had it in my head that maybe I should tell Rusty about my lean-to in the woods, take him up there, let him make himself at home. But I knew I could do that only once. After that, it wouldn't be a secret. He could show up anytime, even hang out there when I wasn't aroud. That wouldn't necessarily be bad, but who knows how things might turn out? I'd never never had a friend for more than a couple of months. Would Rusty be any different? And suppose he found other friends and started bringing them there? Then what would I do? Where would I go? It's a big move to tell somebody about your secret place, especially when it's as perfect as mine.

What I was thinking, though, was that it might be the place Rusty could split to. He couldn't live there or anything. It leaked and the wind blew right through it. But as camouflage, it worked, and nobody would ever, ever find their ways through the walls of thorns and poison ivy that suffocated that whole neck of the woods. The far end of the woods met up against a swamp, and the swamp lay at the foot of a steep ridge of boulders. A kid could hide out there for days. I knew because I had.

All this time, I could hear the television from the house–not loud enough to understand the words, but I recognized the burst of canned laughter and the shifts into the excitement of commercials. In the middle of it all, an odd sound in the house pulled my ears to attention. It could have been a grunt of strain, or maybe a gasp of breath. I held my breath until I heard it again, almost the same butnot quite. It definitely was not the television. People on television didn't make noises like that. It was too real.

I peeked through the door window. Nothing going on in the kitchen. Everything was a clean and orderly as ever.

But when I looked through the living room window, I saw my mother sitting at the dinner table. Her head rested on the bck of one hand, her hair blocking my view of her face. She shuddered, and then I heard the sound again. She was crying. I couldn't see the tears, but i could almost feel them dripping onto her hand and trickling down her wrist. Her head rocked and then turned so her cheek rested in her hand. She was facing me, and for a second I thought she'd seen me. But she couldn't see through the window into the dark. Her face, twisted in agonyj,m was raw red. She used a paper napkin to wipe a dribble of snot from her nose. Then she got up and went into the bathroom.

It's quite a thing to see your mother cry. I'd sure never seen it before. It scared me. I wondered what in the world would make a grown-up break down like that. It wasn't a soap opera sniffle or th ekind of tears you get from onions. I couldn't think of anything I'd done wrong, and Pop was still asleep. Had she stubbed her toe or something? No, that couldn't be it.

What's a kid supposed to do in a situation like this? Run in and say, "What happened?" and give her a big hug? Maybe with Rusty's mother you could do that, butnot with mine. Tell Pop? Somehow i didn't think she'd want that, either. Sit outside and wait to see what happened? I guessed so. SSitting back down on my books, facing the dark of the yard, I put my elbows on my knees and my head on my fists.

As it turned out, nothing happened. Nothing special, anyway. Pop got up and went to the bathroom, and Mother let me in. As usual, she didn't say anything. I heard the occasional sniffle from the kitchen as she put the finishing touches on a meatloaf and a jar of apple sauce. She sniffled through dinner and kept her eyes on her plate. Then she went to bed. Pop left for work, I roamed around and around the channel dial. Why did it have 13 numbers if there were only four stations? And why four if theres nothing on any of them? I turned the dumb thing off and, with dread, opened my Spanish book to the next dialogue, in which Fluorine will say, in a Spanish all a'twitter with interest:

"Where were you this weekend, Pedro? We looked everywhere for you."

And I will confess to have taken a trip to northern Spain.

"Northern Spain? How exciting? What did you see there?"

To make a long story short, a cave.

"The cave at Altamira? The one with the many interesting paintings on the wall drawn by primitive people of ancient times?"

Bingo.

"Tell me! What did they look like?"

Basically, dead buffaloes."

"How exciting! What more?"

A hand print. A smudge on the wall where a primitive person of ancient times wiped his greasy paw after a succulent dinner of buffalo haunch.

"How fascinating! Were you impressed?"

Not in the least...except...except I got an idea. Nodding off, slowly closing my likds on Dialogue 14, I remembered something. A cave. I'd never been there, but I'd read about it in the "Historical Pottsville" booklet they had at the library. In fact, the booklet had a crude, hand-drawn map of Pottsville, including Piddle's Ridge. The map had a big star on it, and somewhere under the ridge was a cae once inhabited by a historical figure known as The Itinerant Tinker. Hundreds of eyars ago he had wanted all over New Jersey, fixing people's shoes and pots and clocks and such. That was before the days of cheap motels, so he slept in barns and under bridges and in caves he somehow knew about. One of them was somewhere on Piddle's Ridge. Now it was vacant, grown over with poison ivy, up for grabs, just waiting for the Iowan refugee to move in and call home.

Chapter Five

Two Finds

hermitage: (n) [ME., OFr.: see -AGE] 1. The place where a hermit lives. 2. A place where a person can live away from other people; secluded retreat.

As soon as I had the idea i my head, nothing could stop me from finding the Itinerant Tinker's cave.Looking back, I can't imagine why I'd never thought of it before. Of course it wasn't in a very convenient place, but who ever heard of a cave across the street from a pizzeria. I was only thirteen but knew that life was not that kind to anyone. If you wanted a cave, you needed to take a long hike. In the case of a cave on Piddle's Ridge, it meant a long hike through a jungle of poison ivy.

So I prepared myself. I swiped one of y father's heavy-duty university work shirts from the laundry basket and got a pair of my mother's plastic dish-washing gloves from under the sink. Besides and baloney, eggs, bacon, marshmallows and potato chips, I packed a tube of stuff that claimed to stop rashes and itching. I got a scarf to wrap across my face and found a flashlight that worked. I even packed plastic work goggles to cover my eyes.

And off I went.

I didn't have much to go on. The map from the library wasn't of much help. A big black star indicated that the cave was a point of interest, but a footnote confessed that Piddle's Preserve was "undeveloped" and had no trails. The location of the star wasn't of much help, either. It was big enough to straddle several acres of the ridge. Obviously the map-maker, some little old Revolutionary War veteran at the HistoricalSociety, had just made a safe bet that the cave was up there somewhere.

Piddle Preserve did have trails, but not official ones. I guess deer blazed them, and then the occasional hiker followed them. I knew some of these narrow trails, knew they tended to follow a wandering route toward nowhere. And none went up the tumbled gray boulders of the ridge. As I understood it, the ridge had been in Canada until a glacier smuggled it on down to western New Jersey nd dumped it Pottsville. that's probably why Piddle gave up farming here and headed south, well out of reach of the next Ice Age. Our soil was rocky, and Piddle's Ridge was a forbidding mountain of busted, lichen-covered generic rock. Granite, I suppose.

Logic told me that if I stayed on the trails, I'd never find the cave, if indeed it existed. If it was near the trail, everyone would know where it was. There'd be signed pointing the way. The big, black star on the map would have been a tiny dot, and the footnote would list hours of operation. When you got there, you'd find it surrounded by velvet ropes strung up between shiny steel posts. There'd be a guy in a brown uniform standing there to tell you what not to do.

I rode my bike as far as my hut. From there I followed a trail around the swamp to the bottom of the ridge. Then I looked for the hardest place to forge into the venomous undergrowth. I must have looked like some zombie space alien with my eyes peeking through goggles between the blue bandana across the lower part of my face, and the ski cap pulled down over my forehead. Everything looked weird to me, too. My eyes sweated and fogged up the inside of the goggles. The shiny leaves of the poison ivy blurred as i eased past them or gingerly hacked through the hairy vines.

It was very creepy to walk in the midst of the worst of all possible deaths, itching so bad I clawed the flesh off my bones. As the glistening leaves brushed my socks and [ants and reached toward me from above, I imagined them the fingers of radioactive monsters whose touch left their victims writhing with terminal itch. All I needed to complete the scene was a heroine, a beautiful girl–Emily Fetschrift, say–to wrap herself around me as I led us through the deadly undergrowth and her clothes fell slowly away. We'd make it to the cave but be stuck there until late autumn, living off roots, berries, and venison. I'd treat Emily's poison ivy wounds by blowing softly on the little blisters, sending her into quivering agonies of bliss.

I didn't follow a map, path, or compass as I wound through the woods. I just went where it looked like no one else would go. I walked along the top of old stone walls, crept the length of fallen trees, hopped from boulder to boulder. I followed a scanty brook upstream. When it harrowed enough for ivy to arc over it, I waded through a tunnel of deadly green.

I felt myself quite the pioneer. How long had it been since a human being had last explored this territory? What would happen if I died in there. They'd never find me. Maybe they can shoot a rocket into space, but they will never ever send a posse into a sea of poison ivy. Assuming they'd even *bother* to look for me, they'd rein in their bloodhounds at the first thick growth and say "Naw, he wouldn't have gone in there. He wasn't *that* dumb."

All of which, of course, made Piddle's Ridge and the Tinker's cave a perfect little hermitage for a Japanese-Iowan to lay low in.

The ivy thinned out and disappeared as I came down to the boulders and shelf at the northern base of the ridge. Above me, scrubby oak and laurel grew where it could. I considered leaving my backpack behind but was afraid I'd never find it again. For that matter, Iwasn't too sure I could find myw ay back home or to my lean-to except by heading east until I came to the state highway That would put me ten miles form anywhere a person might want to be.

I didn't have to climb far before I knew that only an idiot or an itinerant tinker would set out to find a cave on this ridge. I had to climb one rock at a time, figuring out how to get around or over each one or whether to back up and go another way. And the cave, depending on how bit its opening, could be behind or under any one of them. In fact, I stumbled onto a lot of little caves in tje jumble of boulders. Not a stalactite kind of cave, just overhangs where I could could crouch in the event of rain. For all I knew, that's all a tinker would need to call home.

So how was I supposed to know whether I'd found the right place or passed it or should keep on looking? And how long would it be until I reach up over a rock and grabbed a copperhead? How long until I lost my grip on a rock and fell to my death? Or would I die wedged into a hole that looked like it might be a cave Several such holes tempted me in a little too deep, then gripped me at the hips and shoulders. I managed to wiggle back out only by breathing shallow and fighting off panic.

I knew I was the wrong kid for the job when I finally hoisted by weary butt to the top of the ridge. From there I could see far to the west–miles and miles of pine barrens where no one but mosquitos lived. To the east I had a real swell view of Piddle's Preserve. And in the sky, the sun looked like pretty soon it was going to do the same thing it had done the day before: set. Within a few hours I'd have to find a place to sleep. Going back the way I'd come wasn't going to lead me to anything new, so to the west, or really northwest, I descended. The lower I went, the more the land looked like a different world. The rocks had the greenish tint of moss and lichen, and the trees were stubbier than their cousins on the southeastern side. The leaves on the ground were gray with a dampness that looked permanent. Logs had weird growths of orange and red fungus growing out of them like some kind of parasite from Uranus. The sun didn't hit that side of the ridge until late afternoon, when the rays came in low and sideways. It looked like a nice place to find a cave.

I probably would have walked right by the place if the sun hadn't set low enough to darken the woods below while casting a warm yellow-red light across the upper third. There, up high, it seemed a spotlight was pointing it out. It looked like a picture I once saw in a book about primitive people. A huge flat rock extended out from a massive pile of boulders the size of cars. It looked like the visor of a baseball cap sticking out over a very ugly face. Underneath, several boulders formed a flat surface, and it looked like maybe the opening went back into the ridge. It didn't matter to me if this was the Tinker's old haunt or not. Night was coming, and I was going to sleep in that cave.

It took me a good half an hour to climb up that far and find a way up into the expanse under the flat rock. Rusty sure wasn't going to have to worry about attack by an army of fat guys, which ruled out Frank Kjelstrom, the Pottsville cop. And Rusty's new father didn't sound like the type to scale a cliff. If anybody came to drag Rusty out of this cave, it would have to nothing less than a squad of Marine commandos.

I wasn't the first person to hole up there. Charred sticks littered the ground, and a stain of smoke blackened the innermost corner. But that stuff could have been a hundred years old. I didn't see a single beer can or cigarette butt. Maybe I was the first person since the Indians or the Tinker himself to sit there and watch the sun set. Chewing on a hunk of cold kielbasa, I felt like quite the Neanderthal, a Paleolithic kid feasting on the intestine of a wooly mammoth. As the sky turned red, orange, and purple, with long, straight clouds shooting across at weird angles, I wondered the same thing the Indians and the cavemen did: who but a god could make the sky do tricks like that?

By the time the sky was easing from purple-blue to real black, I figured out one problem Rusty would face: firewood. The side of the ridge around the cave wan't quite a cliff, but you couldn't call it a hillside, either. To move around, you had to look before you leapt. But it didn't take me long to gather what little wood lay near the cave. If Rusty wanted a fire at night, he'd need to do some heavy-duty hauling from down below.

It was good to have a fire. A cave can be a weird place to sleep. You never know what kind of bears or snakes or wolves are going to wander in. A million tons of rock hover above, just waiting for that slight breeze to nudge it off the pebble that's been holding it up since the last Ice Age. Wolves in New Jersey? You never thing it's a problem until you're down to your last few sticks of firewood and your cave starts getting dark. Then you can smell wolf breath and hear the slither of mutant boa constrictors that have escaped from someone's aquarium. Alligators on the side of mountain? Stranger things have happened. Blood-sucking bats? Sasquatch? Coon Ladies? If you site in a cave at night and the only TV you've got is shadows flickering on the a wall of slimy rock, you know for sure that nature can do with you as it pleases, that myths aren't purely the product of imagination. You wonder about the headlines in the sleazy newspapers at the supermarket check-out line and imagine a photograph of your sneakers on the floor of a cave, your ankle bones sticking up out of them, licked clean. Under the picture, a headline reads, "LOCH NESS MONSTER EATS EIGHTH-GRADER!" In the cold dark loneliness, you review your religious convictions and consider the possibility of a few extra gods, like maybe the one for fire, the only thing standing between you and the jowls of death. You wonder if maybe Japan isn't so bad after all.

From

Acts of Ineffable Love: Stories

Billy Club Meets Dog Muffins in the Empty Lot of Life

It's easy to imagine a kid with a name like Butch: stocky, short-haired, a paunch you wouldn't expect on a seventh-grader. You can picture a kid like Butch with a club, the kind you hit people with. Not a caveman club, and not something meant to play croquet with or just some piece of a branch. No, it's a professional club, the kind a cop carries, a black nightstick with grooves where you hold it and a leather thong through a hole at one end.

Where does a seventh-grader get such a thing? He might swipe it from a cop if the cop's his father, and his father keeps it in the trunk of the family Dodge, a spare for emergencies. Butch finds it, and before long he's got it tucked up his pant leg and he's limping stiff-legged into Chester A. Arthur Middle School.

A club up the pants of a kid like Butch means trouble. He might be searching for any old trouble or he might have specific trouble in mind. The trouble might involve a kid named Pierce.

Imagine a kid named Pierce: scrawny, nervous, cold to the touch. Smart? Not really. Most kids would say wimp or nit wit before they said smart.

Butch limps down the hall. Smiling, one corner of his mouth a little higher than the other, the eye on that side squinted a little closer to shut, Butch pulls up to his locker. It's right next to Pierce's, which is right next to yours. You're down near the floor, rummaging through wrinkled old homework papers in search of the one you did but forgot to hand in. Pierce, all red in the face, is trying to open his locker. His combination lock needs to come within a split hair of the right three positions or it won't open. He's been dealing with this since the first day of sixth grade. The weather seems to affect it. Sometimes on hot days it never opens and Pierce gets all steamed up with fear of detention.

So when Butch pulls up and leans on his locker, he doesn't have to say anything. He just blows softly in Pierce's face. You know his breath smells of cigarettes because you've smelled him talking before. It smells like an old ash tray. He says, "Darn lock, right Pierce? Just can't get it."

From down near the floor you can hear Pierce trying to swallow and breathe at the same time. Without a word he spins his locker dial three times clockwise, cranks out his combination again. Butch moves in close and hawks up something from his throat. But he doesn't spit. He just blows softly on Pierce's red, hot face.

"I got this terrible pain in my leg," he says. Balancing on one foot, he bends one leg up to put his ankle across his other knee. "Well mercy me," he says. "Would you look at this?" His fingers reach into his sock to reveal the end of the nightstick. "Well would you just look at this."

Pierce and you look, and so do a few other kids. None of you has ever seen a nightstick up close, let alone coming out from a kid's pant leg. Butch pulls it out slowly, feigning surprise. "Would you just look at this thing," he says. "Whatever shall I do with it?" He looks at it as if admiring a fine piece of craftsmanship, then looks at Pierce, then at the nightstick, then at Pierce. Pierce tugs desperately at his locker door as if he needs to get in.

Your homework paper appears from within a damp wad of gym shirt. You remember, at a glance, why you didn't hand it in. It's an unfinished story titled "Dog Muffins," about an Olympic event involving the residue of a kennel. You weren't sure the teacher would accept such a thing even though you managed to avoid countless potential vulgarities and include a host of classic and original symbols. You were sorry you wrote it. But not too sorry. You couldn't bring yourself to throw it away so you did the next best thing. You shoved it under a gym shirt you'd been meaning to take home since Thanksgiving. Now, as if the topic weren't enough, the paper smells of old sweat and feels as soft and pliable as a T-shirt that's spent half the winter stewing in its own juices. But just as you pull it out and wonder whether to chuck it or hand it in, Butch says, "Whatever shall I do with it?", and something clicks.

It isn't the click of an empty revolver or a twig snapped in the dark. It's more like the click of a combination lock opening, a click that means nothing in itself, only that you may proceed, you may enter, you may move on to the next step.

The next step is to take your story to your creative writing teacher and explain why it's late: because it isn't finished yet. You tell her it's been stewing in its own juices and now you know what to do with it. Now you know how it's going to turn out. All you need is a little time.

Pierce is in your creative writing class. He's got a dog story, too. He reads it out loud from his desk, his voice thin, dry, famished, choking. It's a normal dog story, about a puppy, so cute and faithful and smart, but then one day day Daddy backs his truck over it and the puppy goes to heaven, "a big back yard in the sky."

You know you could write a story like that, get it done with, hand it in. But you've got a pile of dog muffins on your mind, and Butch has got a billy club. That click of Pierce's combination lock opened a door behind which the dog muffins and the club make sense together. You know they're in there, hiding under a gym shirt or something, but you can't quite see them. On the bus home, you don't notice anything around you, you just keep thinking, "Dog muffins, billy club. Dog muffins, billy club. Where's the connection?"

Your mother's still after you to do something with that pile of frozen dog muffins in the front yard, so, in hopes of inspiration, you draw up to it with a wheelbarrow and the only tool around, a post-hole digger. The dogs go wild with delight. Leaping, prancing, pawing, they bay and howl and bark for attention. You have to keep pushing them away or they'll wipe their snow- and mud-fouled paws all over your legs and shirt. You say, "Get away" and "Beat it" and jab at them with the post hole digger, but they take it as a game. Your sister's lab mix, whimpering, wagging from the neck back, beseeches you to take the filthy wet tennis ball from his mouth and throw it, just once, just once. With a thumb and forefinger you extract it from his teeth and flip it as far as you can. The lab and five brown puppies and a beagle who belongs to a man who went to Paris all dash after it. A St. Bernard-Newfoundland mix, the author of some breathtaking muffins the size of butternut squash, stands there like he needs a job.

No reason to remove the big pile if you don't get all the little ones first. They're scattered across the yard like stars, randomly yet clumped in identifiable galaxies. Mrs. Plevka's poodle leaves them in semi-circles. The Wilsons' malamute does it up a stump. Somebody's bichon frise seems to prefer the dark privacy of a hemlock.

Using the post hole digger like giant tweezers, you pluck up the muffins one at a time, then fling them toward the pile. It takes quite a bit of coordination but you get the hang of it. An Olympic event of this nature would be much better than the one with the ice chopper that you wrote about in your story. You get a little more serious about it. The rules come to include hurling the digger at a distant muffin, an event demanding the strength of the javelin thrower and the accuracy of an archer. Time becomes a factor. Hurl, dash, pluck, swing, release, until somebody says, "Why are you doing that?"

It's Pierce. His nose is bleeding. He's got his head tilted back as if trying to keep a puddle of blood in the gutter over his upper lip.

"What happened?" you ask, hoping the dog muffins and the billy club have just stepped out of the dark.

But Pierce says, "Nothing. This always happens. It just starts bleeding."

"Want a hanky?"

"Yeah, if you god one."

So you scrape the muddy snow off your shoes and fetch a swatch of scented toilet paper from the bathroom. You sit on the back steps with Pierce while he looks up at the sky, pinching his nose shut. Blood seeps across the lavender fleurs-de-lis printed on the paper. Something clicks again. Dog muffins, billy club, bloody fluers-de-lis – whatever shall you do with them? You ask, "Did you see that club Butch's got?"

Pierce says nothing, but you can tell from his upcast eyes that he can see Butch's club stretching across several clouds, as big as something God would own. After long thought, he says, "He's such a jerk. I hope he gets caught."

"Probably won't. His type never does."

"What did you think about my story?"

"Sad."

"She was a good dog. But why did she have to sleep in the driveway?"

All you can do is shake your head. You and Pierce have grappled with big questions before. They always start out interesting, but Pierce goes after the simple answers. Butch's type never gets caught for the same reason Leopoldina slept in the driveway and a poodle moves its bowels in a semi-circle. Because that's the way God wants it, and God works in mysterious ways. Pierce doesn't want to hear about the possibility of life's incidents being so many scattered dog muffins, each in its place but without plan or pattern. To you, life looks like a nice, neat semi-circle until you come to a stump or go poking around in the bushes. You think life's a combination lock that won't open, but then something clicks and the meaningless makes sense. But you can't explain that to a kid like Pierce.

While Pierce tends to his nose, you show him how the Olympic dog muffin event works. Pretty soon he wants to try it. He's a good shot with the post hole digger but lacks the swing-release coordination of a true champion. So you get him an ice chopper from the garage and let him pat the pile into a knee-high volcano. It works well. The semi-frozen muffins cling to each other, flattening when whacked, then freezing into place. As it gets higher, almost waist-level, Pierce pats it into a three-sided pyramid. It's quite a thing.

But it won't last three thousand years. In fact, you've got to get rid of it before your mother gets home. Using the digger and the chopper, you shovel most of the pyramid into a wheelbarrow, then walk it down the street to a sand lot strewn with chunks of concrete, wisps of plastic, and hulking stands of dead sumac. You say to Pierce, "Maybe this stuff'll help something grow."

"How?" he asks.

"It's fertilizer, dummy. Plants love it. Someday this lot's going to look like Eden."

So you dump the wheelbarrow and kick the stuff around until you hear an odd sound behind a clump of sumac at the far end of the lot. It sounds like a soft, muffled rifle shot. You sneak around, and there's Butch holding his nightstick down with both hands like a golfer. A cigarette extends down from his lips at about the same angle. Between his feet sits a chess board, the kind with built-in drawers. On the board stands a white figure about half a foot high. Butch lifts the club back over his shoulder, then swings down, catching the head of the figure with the tip of the club, decapitating it in one neat, tiny burst of plaster. The invisible smithereens clatter through the sumac. Butch grins so hard he all but drools. He opens a drawer under the chess board, removes another figure and sets it up.

Pierce, visibly aghast at the waste, asks, "What are you doing that for?"

Butch looks back over his shoulder, squints through the curl of cigarette smoke. "Because I like it," he says, his voice dry and tough. "It turns me on." He swings back again, wiggles his chunky hips a bit, squints into the distance and wastes a bishop.

Pierce rushes to the chessboard like a kindergartner to a Christmas tree. On his knees, eyes gleaming, he squeals, "Where'd you get this?" He pulls open one drawer. It's full of black pieces. He takes one out and holds it in both hands like an archaeological treasure. It looks heavy in his scrawny hands, and indeed it looks archaeological. It's a conquistador with helmet, shield, lance. Frantic with curiosity, Pierce pulls them out as fast as he can, giving each a quick look before reaching for another. The pawns look woebegone, the horses noble, the rooks Castilian. Their headless opponents, heathen Indians, lie in a jumble beside the board. The queen wears a necklace of spikes, holds a snake across her breast. The king wears a suit of feathers, holds a scepter with a skull on top. The rooks are Aztec pyramids, the pawns short, half-naked and forlorn.

Pierce, oblivious to the nightstick Butch is massaging in both hands, looks from piece to piece to piece. "What is this thing?" he asks. "Who are these guys?"

Butch again assumes his golfer's stance, but this time puts the club to the side of Pierce's head. "It's a chess set," he says with slow, dramatic coolness. "Not something for idiots. Hold your head right there, would you?"

But Pierce just brushes the club away. " Chess," he says. " I've heard of that. You play it, right?"

"Not idiots," says Butch. "Stop moving your head. There's something I want to do with it."

And that's when you make your move, a veritable chess move in its subtlety, the move that turns the game around and puts you in charge. You know how it's going to end. Butch has set himself up. When you ask him if he knows how to play, he can only say yes. When you hold out two pieces, one with head, one without, he can't help but choose one. You squat on opposite sides of the board, and Pierce kneels at the fifty yard line. Butch puts his club aside as you each set up your pieces. Pierce looks back and forth as if at a tennis game until his nose starts to bleed.

You say to Pierce, "Watch. Pawns can only move straight ahead. Two spaces the first time, one after that." You advance a pawn to king four. Butch quickly responds with the same move. He knows what he's doing. It'll be easy to let him win. By then Pierce will know the rules, and Butch will beat him, too, at least the first few times.

As the pieces step into position, they click like combination locks, but deeper in tone, resonating in the hollow drawers below. Their positions must look random and meaningless to Pierce, but to you they bristle with purpose and intrigue. So does everything else: Butch, Pierce, the club, the chess set, the excrement of man's best friend, all come together in the sand lot/chess board/blank page of life. The bully has stopped his senseless slaughter to join in a friendly battle of brains. A nit wit wimp witnesses something so deep it makes his nose bleed. A weapon lies forgotten in a field of fluers-de-lis made fertile by a writer who knew all along that the symbols and characters and conflicts were all there and would eventually come together to make sense. As soon as you get your pen and notebook, this story is going to come easy, as will every other story you ever write. All you have to do, you know now, is pay attention. When Butch says, "Sure is hard to tell these pieces apart without the heads," you don't say anything, don't need to say anything. You just clamp your molars together and think, *beautiful... beautiful.*

What Happens When a Dodge Gets Old

What happens when a Dodge gets old, when it loses what it had in '65? Tailgate won't drop, rear window moans and shrieks, kids - grandchildren - won't climb in through the back. The dog barks at it. It's an embarrassment in the driveway, but nobody wants it in the garage. It leaks in odd places, stains the floor, might even die and then there it would sit; you can't even get an old Dodge towed anymore.

Then one day it flunks its emissions test. A high school drop out, greasy, dumb, declares the brakes shot, ball joints shot, bearings shot, transmission damn near shot, the whole thing not worth fixing. He says he wouldn't touch it.

Now what's a Dodge to do? Not much choice but tank up and head west. It dodders in a slurry of commuters but then hits the interstate and breaks free. The revs build up to five grand, no sweat. It could go on like this forever. Three hundred and sixty cubic inches get cramped in the suburbs. They don't put tail fins on cars to make them go slow. All this Dodge needs is a little action in the back, some kids horsing around, trying to get skittles to stand up, arguing over the rules of Monopoly, sticking noses into the cooler for a whiff of bologna and tuna fish, waiting for the next place with a clean bathroom. It needs a retriever with its head out the window, ears blown back, nose feasting on the breeze. It needs a woman riding shotgun while she knits, Daddy at the wheel, fingers to chin, trying to think of one good reason not to ditch TV repair and start a dude ranch. Maybe it needs to pull over fast because the dog threw up or so a kid can hunker behind an open wing to pee on a guardrail. This Dodge has headed west before, but never like this, never empty.

For years the buttons on the radio haven't worked, though time and potholes keep nudging the frequency. It might play pop for a month, then nothing but static, and then suddenly it's all news through half the winter. The clunk-clunk, clunk-clunk of the concrete slabs on the interstate jiggles the needle to bring in Ukrainian music from Buffalo. Accordions, lutes, wails of a broken heart floating in a blizzard of static, music good enough for now and better than nothing by far.

The same could be said for the girl on the side of the road, a chick in faded jeans, a chamois jacket with fringes, dangling earrings, hair as fancy as a peacock in heat. She's just standing there, no thumb out, no baggage besides a tiny pocketbook, but it's enough to bring an old Dodge to a swaying, drawn-out halt. Taking her sweet time sauntering up from behind, she touches a tail fin, takes a while to open the door. She doesn't get right in but looks around as if into a cave that might have drawings on the wall. Her eyelashes, thinned to about five per lid, blink a few times. Seems she's never seen such a wide speedometer, such acreage on a dashboard, such a hump down the middle of the floor.

Peering way in over the stuff piled in back, she asks, "How far ya' going?" but something in her tone says, How far do you think you'll get?

The answer doesn't matter. She gets in, holds her pocketbook in her lap a while, then leaves it on her left. She looks out the windshield and chews her gum as if trying to mold it into a precise shape. Her name? Donna. Where's she going? West. How far? Vegas. What's the story? Her Datsun died. She left it on the side of the road, back in Jersey. What does she do?

"I'm a hairdresser," she says. "For the dead."

The dead?

"You know, cadavers. When people die, I do 'em up for the funeral. Perm. Bleach. Trim. Whatever. Doesn't bother me. I get seventy-five bucks and it takes me about an hour. And that was in Jersey. In Vegas they get two hundred bucks. A lot of people die there. They hit the jackpot and croak and there's nothing to do with their money but blow it on a big funeral."

Pets? None. High school diploma? Yes. Marital status? The day before yesterday, her boyfriend threw up on her. The next day she heard about Las Vegas and three hours had her Datsun fired up and headed west.

Family? Her mother's a hairdresser, for the living, and her little brother has some kind of a problem. He cries a lot for no reason. If he whines too much, her father smacks him. As soon as she gets some money together, she's sending for him. Then they're going to L.A., where she's got another brother. He left home the day after high school graduation. Now he follows migrant workers with a lunch truck. As soon as she gets out there, they're all going to move in together like a family, not married of course but together and being nice to each other.

"Like happily ever after," she says. "I'm going for it."

Has she ever seen a Dodge like this old Dart? No, not a station wagon, but her father has a '78 Caddy. He needs it because he's got a big belly. Has she ever seen an odometer turn over a hundred thousand? Yes. For the second time? No. Well she will in Tennessee, maybe Arkansas. It reads 99,258.6. She leans way over to see and gives her gum an extra loud crack before sitting up. Still looking over at it, she says, "You think you'll make it?"

She has reason to worry. Every few seconds, the motor skips a beat. For that instant, it's dead. But it catches, hums along for three seconds, then blinks again. Consistently. It gets neither better nor worse. They stop at a Sunoco for a look under the hood. She takes her little pocketbook to the ladies room while the Dodge knocks down a can of STP, chugs a quart of 10W-40 and tanks up on hi-test for a change. Back on the highway it seems smoother, but still there's that blink of unconsciousness.

Donna's never been in Kentucky before, but the Dodge has, twice. Once on the way to the Grand Canyon, the Missus went into labor in Frankfurt. She delivered a baby boy almost two months early. But since it was just as easy to head west as back east, they set up a little nest of blankets in the back and off they went, stopping at every rest area for a change of diapers. Did Donna know a baby's poop smells sweet as long as he's breast-feeding? No, she didn't.

The motor doesn't sound good. The rhythmic blinking has broken down into an irregular stutter. The radio skips channels more often: country-western, a preacher, two guys having a chummy talk about fishing. Laughing, Donna pushes the selector buttons. It's always two guys talking about fishing. But then one button pushes all the through and rattles down inside the dashboard. The needle slides way over to the left and it's one guy speaking in Spanish. Donna laughs and says,

"That's weird." She doesn't seem to know it's a bad sign in an old Dodge.

Just north of Knoxville, a cold mountain rain lashes at the windshield. The wipers, arthritic, unsteady, can't keep up. Neither can the heaters. Cool air streams in through the dashboard. Part way down a long hill, a baby raccoon lopes out from the median strip. The Dodge swerves and squeals. The little raccoon skitters across the right lane but stops, turns, tries to go back, stops again, turns around, cowers. The Dodge goes over it, thumpity-thumpity-thump. Donna, hands over her face, screams, "Stop! Stop!"

The Dodge coasts onto the shoulder. Donna sobs, "Go back. I want to go back." The raccoon's almost half a mile behind them, too far to back up, but Donna keeps saying, "Please. Go back."

There's nothing in the rearview mirror, so the Dodge swings a wide U-turn and heads back up the hill. They go all the way to the top without seeing a dead raccoon, then come back down, two wheels on the shoulder, very slow past the place. And then she sees it in the grass, stumbling as if dizzy. "It's alive!" she shouts. "It's alive!" She bursts out of the Dodge and into the rain, steps over the guardrail, kneels low beside the coon and nests it in her arms. Still trying to walk, climbing over her arms, it doesn't seem to know it's off the ground. Donna has to keep reaching so it doesn't fall. "Poor thing," she says. "I wonder where its mother is."

It's just a baby, a quivering bundle of wet fur. Donna strokes it and coos and says things like, "There, there. It's all right now."

But the engine won't start. It cranks and cranks, again and again. The only choice, the only hope, is to jump-start it -- no easy trick with an automatic transmission. If it catches by the bottom of the hill, they're still headed west. If not, it's the end of an old Dodge. After three tractor-trailers charge by, the emergency brake pops off and the

Dodge starts to roll. At first the gravel on the shoulder seems to hold the wheels back. The steering's stiff as rigor mortis. They're halfway down before the Dodge can lumber up onto the pavement and pick up real speed. Fifty yards before the bottom of the hill, the transmission slams into Drive. Donna crosses her fingers and squeezes her eyes shut. The Dodge slows, moans, shudders, falls silent, then kicks to life, backfires once, twice, falls silent, hesitates, coughs, and suddenly accelerates with the sound of a rocket. The windshield wipers come on and the radio plays Beethoven's Ninth.

Bit by bit, over the next twenty or thirty miles, the little raccoon settles down and seems to sleep, though it shudders now and then as if remembering. Donna's finger runs from its nose to its forehead times, smoothing the whiskers on each cheek. A thumb and finger massage behind its ears and dig into the fur around its neck. Her hand, wrapped around its body, slides down to the tail, where it shifts to scratch with her long, pink fingernails. The raccoon, nestled in the groove between her legs, chin resting on one thigh, doesn't move.

Donna says, "He's making a sweaty spot on my leg." When she tries to slide it to a different position, it jerks awake and starts squeezing out shrill moans, one with each breath. "Poor thing," she says. "Why doesn't it open its eyes?"

Maybe she should make a soft place for it in the back, unroll one of the blankets. Maybe it wants to eat. There's food in the cooler, maybe some melted ice.

The raccoon keeps moaning with the rhythm of a wet baby or a rusty machine. Leaning over the back of the seat, Donna fluffs the khaki blanket into a nest and sets the raccoon in it. Still it won't quiet down. It keeps moaning and trying to walk somewhere, never opening its eyes.

"It needs me," says Donna. "Is it all right to go back there?"

Of course it's all right. What does she think, a station wagon has snakes? Of course she can go back there. She'd be doing an old Dodge a favor.

She looks suspicious, like she knows the difference between the front seat and the back seat of a car. But then she wiggles over and starts arranging things, making walls of suitcases and folded blankets. A quick whiff of bologna and tuna fish drifts around, and then she and the little raccoon are both curled up in a sleeping bag, fast asleep.

Henney's Tubes

This kid I knew always wanted to go into TV repair. His father used to bring him busted TVs from his repair shop and show the kid how to fool around with the tubes. Before Henney got to kindergarten he knew how to take them out and snap them back in. He knew one tube from another. He'd bring them in for show and tell and talk about them. He could come into your house and tell you the problem with your TV set, why it flipped or buzzed or went dark.

So we all figured, "Henney's going to be a TV repairman." We knew that in the fourth grade when the rest of us still had our eyes on the astronaut training programs, major league baseball and the green berets. I don't know about the other kids, but I kind of envied Henney. He didn't have to sweat out the choice. A kid like me had it hard. I didn't really know what my father did for a living. He worked for the light company but had nothing to do with electricity. Whenever I asked, he'd brush off the question with a noise like a goat and say, "I just shuffle papers."

So I looked into other fields: archaeology, scuba diving, test pilot, DJ, submarine captain, animal trainer. A kid didn't have to watch TV long before seeing some other acceptable way to earn a living. Of course if the TV went on the blink, it never occurred to me to go into TV repair. I'd just read a book about race car drivers or something and wait until Henney came over to play.

Along comes the sixth grade. Time to look seriously at a career. We had to give oral reports on what we'd like to be. Torn between airline pilot and spelunker, knowing I'd change my mind before my age doubled to twenty-two, I choose the career that I could spell. I reported on the exciting and exotic world of airline pilotage. I based my report on information from books published before my birth. One had a picture of a pilot leaning out the cockpit window of a DC-3. Salary range: nine to twelve thousand, depending on experience.

Henney gets up there and talks for twenty minutes, no sweat, no three-by-five cards, right off the top of his head. Stuff you'd never think to even ask about TV repair. How to set up a shop in your basement. How much to bill. How to set up accounts with suppliers. Everything. Of course he got it all from his father. Never had to go to the library. His old man handed it to him on a silver platter.

It would have worked out right if the world followed rules. Henney would have had his own shop, built it into an empire of franchises, invented a miracle tube, then gone to work at NASA to build special little TVs for space capsules or something. I would have become a sharp shooter or a forest ranger or whatever, and all the girls would have divvied themselves into nursing, teaching, ballet or motherhood.

But the world doesn't follow rules. Sometime during the ninth grade, Henney's father ran off to Nevada with the mother of a kid named

Jack. Henney, fourteen years old, moved right into his father's shop. He knew just what to do. It almost seemed like his father had planned it that way, except of course he hadn't. Fourteen years old and Henney's a TV repairman.

Me, one thing led to another and I found myself under cars most of the time, swearing at rusted bolts and walking around greasy. After graduation, my girlfriend entered state trooper academy. I had a job at Tom's Texaco when Henney took off for South America. His mother had a new husband and Henney didn't feel like going to college. Without telling anybody, he started hitchhiking. Somebody saw him on Route 135 on the westbound side with his thumb out. Six or ten months later, a kid I knew who ended up down at the Post Office said a post card came through from Ecuador. A picture of the equator. On the back it said, "Dear Mom, I stood right here, one foot on each side. No big deal. There's no line or anything and it doesn't feel any different. I love you. Henney."

You can take words like that and see how maybe they mean everything that's in *Moby Dick* and the Bible combined. Or maybe he just didn't know what to write. Whatever the case, it kept me wondering. I wondered how it must feel to know exactly what your father does for a living, to be able to hold his living in your hand, even stick it in your pocket and take it to school to show other kids. The world must look as clean and simple as a quarter-inch nut and bolt just out of the box. But then how does it feel when a father like that slips away and leaves you behind? I imagine it being the way a TV looks when a tube blows and the screen suddenly looks and sounds like a blizzard.

As far as I know, Henney's still down there. I picture him married to some señorita, living in a bamboo hut and fixing Bolivian TVs on a banana crate in the back room. I picture Bolivian TVs as big cast iron things with the rounded lines of a DC-3 and dark translucent tubes that take a while to warm up. Henney might not even know about integrated circuits. For all I know he's never even seen a color TV. He's probably best off right where he is. What I wonder, what I'd really like to find out, is whether he knows that.

Science and the Art of Frogs

If you can't have kids, why not a frog farm in Brazil? If you're not tied down, why not go for it? It seemed like a good idea - not the frogs, necessarily, but the going for it. Rosilda would get to live nearer her mother, who was suffering arthritis and some vague deterioration of the spleen. Sam would get to ditch high school Spanish.

"You will learn *Portugûes* in one flash," Rosilda said, throwing the blankets off them and reaching for the light. Sam sat up. It was decided. They were moving to Brazil.

"How much does a place cost there?" he asked.

"Ten thousand," she said. "We can find a nice place for ten thousand. Plant flowers all around. Will be beautiful."

"Ten thousand," said Sam. "The whole thing? Just like that? Paid for?"

"Is cheap there," she said, "if you have dollars."

He didn't mention the frog farm right then. He still had it in the back of his mind, something he'd read about in Mother Earth News. Rabbits were in the back of his mind, too. Tropical fish, escargot, bees, silkworms - the back of his mind was an ark of esoteric livestock. For some reason, though, the frogs stood out. He didn't hear Rosilda going on about the house they'd build and the flowers they'd plant around it. He was remembering the details of the frog farm, thinking how he'd send back letters and pictures for the faculty bulletin board.

They scrimped and fretted and packed and planned. They bought stuff you couldn't get in Brazil: a laptop, certain seeds, maple syrup, everything written on the care and slaughter of frogs. On the last day of June, having collected their measly pensions and vacation pay, having cashed in their IRAs and held an everything-must-go tag sale, they flew to Florida for a day with Sam's folks, then on to Rio, and from Rio inland to the mountains of Minas Gerais. Her brother Victor met them at the airport with his old black Volkswagen.

"Be careful with him," Rosilda whispered while Victor tied the suitcases to the roof. "He's a little crazy."

But Victor talked of grand things. Sam understood enough of his Portuguese to catch words like capitalism and cosmos, names like Darwin, Nietzsche, Heidegger. It all related to frog-farming, which Victor had been investigating. He said something twice, emphatically, waving one finger in the air while trying to drive and look Sam in the eye. Sam asked Rosilda for a translation.

In English she said, "God's gift to earth," then switched to Portuguese to gasp, "Victor, watch the road."

Victor went on in high school English."You can eat the legs," he said, wiggling his fingers at his mouth.

"I know," Sam said.

"Eight dollars one kilo. The skin - " he pinched the hairless flesh of his forearm " - leather. Thirty-two dollars one kilo. *Dollars*."

"Wow," said Sam, impressed. He formulated an experimental sentence in Portuguese and launched it: "How many skins per kilo?"

"More or less twenty," said Victor. He took his hands from the wheel to hold up ten fingers.

"Only?" Sam said in Spanish. "Big frogs!"

Victor gestured again, indicating a monster almost the size of a Volkswagen windshield. Rosilda translated distractedly: "New breed. Only in Brazil. Twenty kilos."

"That's forty-four pounds!" Sam said.

"Forty-four," Victor said, nodding and smiling. "Only in Brazil. This is the promised land of next millennium. Frogs are the cattle of the future and Brazil is the land of frogs."

"Truck!" Rosilda said. "Cuidado!"

Victor glanced ahead, swung back to his side of the road and went on talking . "We will be the kings of frogs. It will be biologically impossible for anyone to catch up to us."

"We?" Sam asked.

"You and me."

"Biologically?"

"Genetic selection. Theoretically, you can make one frog as big as one sheep. Scientific fact."

King of frogs. Sam liked that. He could see himself, shepherd's crook in hand, looking over a swampy pasture of eight-hundred-pound frogs. He had to laugh.

"I'm serious," Victor said. He knocked on his wrist. "The bones. The best nutrient for plants. The viscera - " he patted his stomach - "guess who eats frog viscera."

"Don't know," said Sam.

"Guess."

"Japanese?"

"Ha! I liked that. No. Other frogs! Frogs eat frogs. You use the good parts to make money, the rest goes back into the system. One hundred percent recovery. No loss."

"A perfect system," Sam said.

Victor said, "You got it."

* * *

They found a place in a town called Cachimbo, an hour from the city. It wasn't the dream house Rosilda had foreseen, but it had plenty of room for planting flowers. And water: a stream tumbling off a mountain of rock. A canal fed a shallow pond about fifty feet wide. Victor declared the place perfect and they bought it.

Sam went along because he figured forty acres had to be good for something, and he'd never owned a water fall before. Rosilda approved but without enthusiasm. The house, a poorly built white-washed mud-brick structure with bent walls and concrete floor, had a porch overlooking the pond a good hundred yards away. The windows had heavy shutters but no glass. It was a house that could be knocked down and rebuilt later. The important thing was the land and the water.

Besides, their plans had changed. Rosilda would stay in the city at her mother's place, to take care of her. Sam would stay on the farm to do whatever he could to make money. Now they needed it. The place cost eighteen thousand, not ten, which just about wiped them out. But it was a perfect place for frogs.

Victor got hold of some baby carp and released them in the pond. "A delicacy," he said. "They taste like chicken. Six dollars a kilo. And what do you think they eat?"

"Don't know."

"Guess."

By this time, Sam was getting tired of guessing esoteric frog facts. Knee-deep in pond mud, he was making a Sisyphean effort to dig a post hole under six inches of water. He had just jammed the digger into his foot. Victor, giving instructions and advice from the bank of the pond, waited five seconds for Sam's answer, then came out with it.

"Frog dung," he said triumphantly.

Sam said he didn't understand. The frog part he got, but the other word was new. Victor gave the vernacular and illustrated with a quick sound effect. Sam got it but didn't believe it.

"Carp don't eat that," he said.

"They eat the algae. Frog dung has more nitrogen than any other dung, except that of worms. Put nitrogen in water, you get algae. Put carp in algae, you get fat carp. Only one problem..."

"What's that?"

"Carp eat tadpoles, too."

Sam already knew that carp ate tadpoles. That's why he was digging fence posts in the pond. They had to put up a fence between the frog section and the carp section. He wished he could say, "Good fences make good neighbors," in Portuguese, but then Victor came up with something even better: "Peaceful co-existence."

"This is a model of the world," he said. "The class struggle. Six dollars a kilo against forty dollars a kilo. And we are the imperialists, exploiting them all."

"Frog kings," said Sam, and Victor laughed like an idiot. Sam threw the post hole digger at him, overhand like a spear, and said, "Dig."

* * *

Rosilda got a job managing a store that sold fancy imported home furnishings. Sam made a little money giving English lessons to a dentist, a rich kid, and some engineers from a nearby graphite mine. When he wasn't in town, he stayed on the farm, preparing the pond for the frogs, building tadpole hatching tanks, insect larva tanks, frog retention walls. Once or twice a week Victor came to help or at least watch. On weekends Rosilda took the bus to Cachimbo but spent her time keeping her husband from looking neglected. She cleaned up the mud he tracked in during the week, re-washed the plates he had only rinsed, scrubbed the bed sheets in a galvanized tub. Feeling appropriately guilty, Sam told her she really didn't have to do all that. Rosilda agreed. She wanted to relax on weekends. Since a maid that far from the city would cost practically nothing, she asked around and found a girl to come clean the place every day and cook Sam a decent lunch. "You'll like her," she told Sam. "She has teeth like a frog and skin the color of mud." He knew what teeth like a frog meant. It meant Rosilda didn't like frogs and the girl had not been chosen for her beauty.

Not that they had money for such a luxury. Inflation was twenty percent a month. Rosilda suggested it might be better for them both to live in the city and visit the farm on weekends. Sam said they could get by on the farm if they had a good garden and made a little cash off the frogs and eventually some rabbits. He had plans.

"We can lead a poor but good life," he said as they sat eating dinner at the shaky card table in the living room. "We'll have enough. Most people in this country would give anything to have what we have. Most people in the States, too."

"Victor's crazy with that frog idea," she said. "I never heard about nobody make money off frogs. Coffee, cattle, sure. But no frogs. Somebody I know tried raise rabbits. Everybody died."

"The key is to think small," Sam said. "A couple of rabbits, a couple of goats. Half a dozen chickens, max. That' s how you start. Then you just make things grow."

"I don't know. I never heard about nobody try to be poor."

At dawn the Monday after, Sam stepped out the back door and found a young girl with buck teeth sitting on an overturned bucket. She was wearing a T-shirt and a beige, unhemmed skirt that barely came to her knees. Her skin was light brown but tinged with a bit of rosiness from the sun. Off-white spots bigger than freckles dotted her face and forehead, a genetic aberration Sam figured went back to a Portuguese slave owner.

He had no idea what to do with a maid. He motioned her inside, gestured at the mess and said, from the doorway, "Good luck." Her bank of teeth broke from her lips in a smile, but she quickly hid it with one hand.

He went down to the pond to work but kept coming back for glasses of water. Each time, she was in a different room, down on all four, rump up, leaning into the brush, schik-schik-schik-schik-schik, five scrubs to each patch of floor. He didn't know what to say to her so he stayed outside except once in a while came in for more water and a quick check. A maid. Schik-schik-schik-schik-schik. Another picture for the faculty bulletin board.

He was nailing up the knee-high anti-carp fence when Victor drove up the long driveway in his Volkswagen and stopped near the pond. He had the front trunk tied down over a heavy old apple crate. Sam came out of the water to look. Cowering in the bottom of the crate in a mat of wet leaves were a bullfrog the size of a shoe box and three females the size of shoes.

"Mancha rosas," Victor said. "See the rosy spots on the back? That's how you know. The bull's a prize winner. Had his picture in the paper. Look." And he snapped open a clipping with a photo of what the caption claimed was the largest tadpole in history: fifteen centimeters long - almost six inches - at the age when a tadpole's back legs first sprout. It looked like an amphibious Edsel.

"Let's go show the maid," he said.

"Maid?" said Victor. "We have a maid?"

"We?" said Sam.

"The frogs are ours."

"Okay. Yes, we have a maid."

"What color?"

After a moment's consideration, Sam said, "Cinnamon."

Victor guffawed. "I didn't ask what flavor!"

"What difference does it make?"

"Blacks cook better but they're slow. Mulattas are smarter but they give you more problems. Scientific fact."

Sam didn't address statements like that. Victor, nutsy indeed, was full of them. Scientific proof of pyramid power, rational proof of the existence of God. He was better left undisputed.

They lugged the crate up to the house, set it on the kitchen floor and called the maid. She looked in cautiously, suspiciously, then suddenly screamed and leaped back. Victor lifted the massive bull by the armpits and, making monstrous snorts, advanced at her. The girl screamed once, then again, harder, and fled to the bathroom, slamming the door behind her. Victor seemed to think that was pretty good.

They finished nailing up the fence across the pond, splashed around to herd the last of the carp through a gate to the other side, then opened the canal to feed in more water and released the frogs.

"Now it's only a matter of time and nature," Victor said as they sat on the bank, drying their legs in the sun, admiring the marvel of four frogs in a pond. "Next month we'll have a quarter of a million tadpoles. By January we'll have a hundred thousand frogs."

Victor left before noon. Sam went up to the house to coax his maid from the bathroom and formulate some kind of apology. She was already out, though, poking around the rusty kitchen cabinets. Before he could say anything, she asked what he wanted for lunch.

Not one to give orders, he gestured vaguely at the cabinets and said, "Anything."

"There's rice and beans and one egg," she said. "That's all."

He thought for a second and said, "Let's go into town. You can buy what we need."

So he fired up his Fiat and off they went. She sat quietly, one hand gripping the side of the seat, the other gripping the knob on the glove compartment. Watching her out the side of his eye, he thought she looked like a kid on a roller coaster. "First time in a car?" he asked.

"Oh, no," she said. "Many other times. But I like it."

He finally asked her name. It was Tânia. She was seventeen. She lived on the other side of the hill with her parents and nine brothers and sisters. Her father, it turned out, was Furão, an alcoholic chicken thief. Neighbors had warned Sam about him. They said to shoot him on sight. Sam didn't say so to Tânia. Something in her voice, though, revealed she wasn't proud to admit her father's name.

In the dark, dusty little supermarket, Sam felt both patronly and husbandly as he followed her down the aisles. Not knowing how to deal with Brazilian foods – he'd been living off rice, canned beans, sausage, eggs and Rosilda's weekend leftovers – he kept saying "Good," and "Okay" as Tânia lifted things from the shelves for his approval. She didn't buy much there, but then led him down a couple of streets to a cobblestone plaza of booths piled with vegetables and fruit. Again she showed him each item and he said good, okay, to each. He had trouble understanding the amounts of money she said to pay, so he handed her his wad of bills and let her do it. He carried the basket. It was a lot like being married.

* * *

One day during tadpole season Tânia showed up with a meaty bruise on her cheekbone and three little kids around her legs. When Sam asked what happened, she just said, "Nothing," then asked if her sisters could stay with her. "To help," she said.

They didn't look like they'd be much help. The youngest was about two, the oldest about six. But Sam couldn't resist. He scooped up the two-year-old and called for the other two to follow. He took them down to the pond and had them crouch down at the edge of the water to see the swarms of jittering black tadpoles. "Baby frogs," he said. "Pretty soon, big frogs." But they gave no response. Maybe it was his accent or his broken sentences, or maybe they were just dumb. They looked when he pointed at the ghostly shadows of carp under the water, but they didn't seem capable of saying whether they saw or not. Did they want to fish? He might as well have asked three fire plugs if they wanted to dance.

At lunchtime, Sam found his plate of rice, beans, collards and, today, breaded beefsteak awaiting him on the card table, as usual. Normally he ate alone, but today, when he saw Tânia seating her sisters on buckets and crates on the back porch, each with a plate in lap, he insisted they sit with him. Tânia insisted they couldn't, but Sam insisted and insisted, and finally they did. He brought in a long wooden bench off the front porch and got pillows for the kids to sit on. Tânia jabbered at them in clipped, harsh, peasant dialect. Sam couldn't understand the words, but knew by her tone she was telling them to behave.

Everyone ate in silence. Tânia never looked away from her plate. Sam got a good look at her bruise. It had worsened since morning. She'd probably been hit that same day. He asked her again what happened, but she seemed not to hear. "Tell me," he said, reaching out to touch her wrist. "Tânia."

Her arm jerked a couple of inches away. Without looking up, she shook her head just a bit. Sam looked at the little girls. The middle-sized was staring at him with big, brown eyes and clunking her feet against the bench. Sam smiled and said, "What's your name?" Her legs stopped swinging, but she didn't answer.

"Tell him," Tânia snapped. The little girl squeaked, "Rosamaria." Sam asked how old she was, but Tânia stood up and started scraping the girls' unfinished food into one plate. Sam was still chewing beef as she herded the girls into the kitchen and closed the door behind them.

Later that day, toward evening, he was surprised to find them still hanging around. Tânia was cooking his dinner, something she didn't normally do before leaving. When he saw her issuing dollops of rice and beans onto four plates, he knew she wasn't going home. Letting them eat on the porch, he sat alone at the card table, chewing slowly, thinking. When he delivered his plate to the sink, he put a hand on her shoulder and said, "If you want, you four can sleep in the other bedroom." Keeping her hands in the dishwater, she whispered perfunctory thanks.

During the night, one of the little girls started crying, and then the others joined her. Tânia tried to hush them by scolding, but it didn't work. Sam, quite awake in the next room, felt sorry for them all. He had no idea what to do about their situation and wondered whether to get involved. He didn't mind if they stayed for a while - the farm needed some kids on it - but he knew Rosilda wouldn't approve. She didn't even like frogs.

Two of the little girls stopped crying, but one moaned on. Soon Tânia came tapping at his door. Did the senhor have anything for an earache? He didn't think so, but he got up and pulled on his pants and went to have a look in his shaving kit. He found a single Tylenol tablet of indeterminate age.

"She can't," she said. "She won't swallow pills."

Sam said, "I know a way." In the kitchen, while Tânia looked around his shoulder, he crushed the tablet between two spoons, then dribbled honey on the powder. She followed as he led the way back to the room, spoon held high, one hand below to catch drips. Sitting at the edge of their bed, he groped for the little girl and told Tânia to turn on the light. Feeling quite the bwana, he looked into the kid's ear, up and down, left and right, then opened his mouth to make her open hers. She took in the honey. When a little dribbled out, he pushed it back in with a finger. He stroked her head, laid her down, covered her up, and told Tânia she'd be okay.

Sam now went to the city on weekends so Rosilda wouldn't come to the farm. He hoped the problem would resolve itself before she decided to visit again. When she asked him what was new, he said, "Nothing," even though he could have mentioned the growth of the tadpoles, the first of the frogs, and, most recently, the failure of a hundred thousand frogs to materialize. Sam doubted they had a hundred in all.

Not much new on Rosilda's end, either. Her mother's spleen was neither better nor worse. No one was buying imported home furnishings. The rent on the apartment was going up fifty percent next month but her mother's pension was frozen. Sam and Rosilda would have to make up the difference, which was only fair since Rosilda was, in fact, living there. Food and medicine and doctor fees were going up, too. Sam and Rosilda would have to chip in.

Which didn't leave much to invest in frogs. Sam was upside down under her kitchen sink when Rosilda assumed a seat on a chair from the dining room. She really didn't see how they could afford the luxury of a place in the country. He didn't say anything. Above him, the sink was full of week-old water Rosilda had been saving for his return. It smelled of sewage as it dribbled out of the pipe he had managed to loosen but not remove. When he grappled with the pipe, the water dribbled down his arm and off his elbow.

"We aren't rich, you know," she said. "Country homes are for rich people. You can't live with one salary in this country. We two have to work. Where are we going to work out in the country? I suppose you want more money for your frogs this week, right? You know how much that I pay for bread yesterday? Hmm?"

In a certain sense alone, his head and shoulders in the semi-darkness of the cabinet under the sink, Sam was just looking at the pipe now. He knew it hated him and wanted to make him suffer. He didn't doubt he deserved it. But it was better facing sewage in the dark than coming out of the cabinet to guess the price of bread.

She said, "Guess," and then, "Go ahead. I'm waiting." And then, after a good pause, in a dramatically lower voice, "You have one family to support, you know."

A burst of air rushed from his nose, something between a laugh and a snicker. He tried to smooth it over into a cough, but she caught it. "What?" she asked. "Why you laugh?" He gave a couple more coughs and didn't answer. She sat for a while, then got up and left.

Early Sunday morning, claiming to have adolescent tadpole problems – the first she'd heard of tadpoles at all – he packed his little haversack and headed back to the farm.

Tânia was hoeing in the garden when he arrived. The kids were playing with a distressed frog and a brown and white puppy that was prancing and yapping at it. They'd discovered a certain spot on the frog they could touch to make it jump. When they poked it with a stick it leaped three or four feet, arms and legs splayed out as it hurdled through the air. With each leap the kids collapsed with hilarity. Sam didn't like it, though. "Hey," he said. "Take that frog back to the pond."

But Tânia, looking over the bamboo garden fence, said, "No."

Sam looked at her. "Why not?" he asked, rather surprised she had spoken up against him.

"They saw a cobra down there."

The word made Sam gasp. He wasn't sure if "cobra" meant an actual cobra or just any old snake. Either way, it was bad news for frogs. He left his pack on the porch, caught the frog, got his machete from behind the woodpile and walked gingerly, vigilantly, down to the pond. The puppy came but the Tânia held the kids back.

The frogs didn't have much to say about a snake, but they did look concerned about the situation. They seemed to hunker a little lower in the water, and nobody was playing on shore. Dozens of yellow eyes and green brows poked up through the velvety pond scum, all looking at him. He could hear them thinking, What are you going to do now, Sam?

He thought the first thing he would do was sit on a convenient boulder and smoke a couple of cigarettes. Where were the hundred-thousand brothers and sisters of these terrified survivors? Digesting slowly inside cobras? Victor hadn't said anything about cobras. He'd given Sam pamphlets about diseases of the frog, history of the frog, stages of frog metamorphosis, but nothing about cobras. Maybe he assumed forty-pound frogs had nothing to worry about as long as they stayed off the highway.

Sam was peeling an orange and smoking his third cigarette when the puppy started barking and jumping around in the grass. Sam stood to see a low, dark, sinuous shadow slide from behind a bush. Even standing on the boulder, machete in hand, he couldn't tell how long it was. More than ten feet. It was black, with yellow spots on the back. Wondering if the spitting and flying and death-in-thirty-seconds cobras he'd heard about as a child were real, he whistled and called up toward the house. Tânia came out. He motioned for her to come. She walked about halfway before figuring out why he was standing on the rock. Only with a lot of gesturing and pointing and insisting did he convince her to come all the way down.

"Over there," he said, pulling her up onto the rock. "There's part of it under that bush."

"God in Heaven," she said. "It's going to kill us."

"Is it poisonous?" he asked.

"I don't know. I think so. It's going to kill us."

"No," said Bwana Sam. "It's looking for a frog."

Breathing hard, they watched as the snake wound silently around stones and tufts of grass, closer and closer to the pond, oblivious to the puppy's shrill yap. It looked endlessly long and thicker than a snake should be. By the time Sam discerned the tail, the head had disappeared. Only the front four or five feet of it groped over the frog retention wall and pulled into a tangled coil at the edge of the pond. The head rose. Tânia, torn between looking and cowering, whimpered at Sam's arm. The snake's head rose a bit higher, pulled back, dipped, froze, waited, waited, then jabbed into the edge of the water. When it pulled back, it had the hips and legs of a frog wiggling from its mouth. Tânia gasped so loud it was almost a scream. The snake pulled back, adjusted the frog a bit, then coiled all around to force it further in. It took a long time. Sam watched, open-mouthed, and Tânia sobbed so hard she retched.

Then they ran back to the house. Tânia called the children in and closed all the doors and shutters. Sam told her not to worry, the snake certainly wasn't going to come looking for them. But when he got in the car to go into town to call Victor, she looked dubious.

Sam described the snake over the phone. Victor said it sounded like a jararacuçu. "Be careful," he said."They're mean. And where there's one, there's more."

"If they've eaten a hundred thousand frogs, there's a lot more. What are we supposed to do now?"

"First thing, put dolomitic lime all around the pond. Snakes won't cross lime. Scientific fact.'

"That's all?" Sam said, wondering why lime hadn't ended the world's snake problems centuries ago.

"I"m going to get a gun," Victor said. "We'll kill them. I'll be there tomorrow morning."

Sam bought forty kilos of lime to hold the fort until Victor arrived with the artillery. Tânia and the kids watched from the porch as he sprinkled a wide white band around the pond, then sprinkled it again. He could imagine a snake licking it with its little forked tongue, then turning away. Maybe lime did the trick. Until sunset they all kept watch from the porch, the kids taking turns in Sam's lap while he held his binoculars to their eyes. They saw no snakes.

The next morning, though, when Sam and Tânia and kids and the puppy trooped down to the pond, they found what could only be the track of a snake across the dew-damp field of white. When Victor arrived, they showed him. He nodded heavily and said, "They're desperate."

He had a gun, a long-barreled .22 pistol loaded with tiny capsules of buckshot. When he shot it into the pond, the pellets ripped up two square feet of water. "With this," he said, "you can't miss. But you have to be close."

Sam shooed the kids away and then took five shots at varying distances across the carp side of the pond. The pistol had hardly any kick and the pellet groupings seemed tight enough at up to twenty yards. He re-loaded and tried to hand it to Tania, but she wouldn't take it. Victor protested. "Never give a woman a gun," he said in sudden English. "Especially a maid."

"I can't sit here waiting for snakes all day and all night," Sam said. "She'll have to stand guard sometimes. Tania, take it. For the frogs."

"You're going to be sorry."

She wouldn't take it. Sam said, "Sit here, like this," and sat on the ground, his back against the tall rock. "Knees up like this. Elbows on your knees, the gun out like this. Two hands. Point it at the snake and squeeze the trigger slowly. Keep looking..." And he let off a shot. "Easy," he said.

He coaxed her to the right position. Once she had her skirt adjusted to her satisfaction, he set the gun in her hands. She gave a nervous little laugh, like a kid doing something for the first time. Sam said, "That's the snake over there, that banana leaf. Go ahead. And don't close your eyes."

She had to turn her head away as she pulled the trigger, but she made the shot and even hit the leaf a little. Sam said, "Do it again," but she wouldn't.

* * *

Victor and Sam were swinging in hammocks and drinking beer under two mango trees - Tânia was down at the pond, standing guard - when Victor proposed yet another anti-cobra idea. Geese, he said, attacked snakes. In fact their reputation was strong enough that they didn't have to attack snakes. Snakes knew the smell of a goose and stayed away. But there was one problem: geese ate frogs.

"Then to hell with the frogs," Sam said. "Let's raise geese."

"Escargot. If you want to make money, you want to look into snails."

"But don't geese eat..." And that's when they heard the crack of the pistol and the rhythmic wails, lungful after lungful, of a maid face to face with reptilian death. Well before they reached the pond, they saw the violent throes of a long, black snake thrashing above the grass, writhing in agony, flailing and twisting and lurching back on itself, showing the ivory white of its belly and the inside of its mouth. Tânia was gripping her face in her fingers and screaming, screaming, screaming. Sam took the gun from between her feet and emptied it at the snake, shot by shot knocking it down until they heard it only twitching in the grass. While Victor poked at it with a long stick, Sam put his arms around Tânia's shoulders and said, "It's okay, it's okay." Gradually her screams became sobs and then a low, damp whimper. When Sam tried to lift her to carry her to the house, she stopped him, then got up and went alone, still holding her face in one hand.

For the first time since Sam had met him, Victor had nothing to say, no comments or revelation of fact. He kept to himself, walking slowly around the pond, arms crossed over his chest, looking down, thinking. An hour later, he handed Sam a box of ammunition, said, "Be careful, hear?", then got in his car and drove off.

For several days, Tânia stayed within five paces of the house and kept the kids within her sight. When the kids asked Sam to bring them a frog to play with, he brought three and made a big to-do about organizing them into a jumping contest. Of course they wouldn't stay put on the starting line, so Sam kept hopping after them, rolling over in somersaults, even catching one in mid-air. The kids giggled and squealed and fetched frogs and held them to the ground at the starting line. Tânia came to watch. When the kids realized one frog could jump remarkably further than the others, they wanted to get more from the pond to see who was the grand champion. But when Sam said, "Okay, let's go!", Tânia, suddenly serious, said, "No."

She agreed to go, though, and walked down with Sam, each of them carrying a cardboard box for the catch. They were poking through the pond scum with sticks when Sam saw something whitish whisk by under the water. It was a carp.

He decided to drain the pond and solve the problem immediately. While Tânia sat watching from the boulder, Sam pulled the sheet of plywood away from the drain screen at the low end of the pond. As the water descended across the upper end, it uncovered a host of frogs Sam hadn't known he had - certainly not a hundred thousand, but plenty just the same. Uniformly the size of children's tennis shoes, they might have had a little elbow room if they'd spread out evenly. But, uncomfortably exposed to daylight and air, they leaped in silent desperation, colliding, falling all over each other, forming amorphous piles that melted, dispersed, and reformed.

It was a lot of frogs. Tânia, still up on the rock, gushed with a confluence of giggle and scream. Trying to look and not look, to back away and look closer, she wrapped her arms around her torso and hips as if trying to hide nakedness from a crowd.

The screen fence had risen above the mud at a point near the middle of the pond. Sam kicked off his sandals and rolled his shorts up as high as they would go. Careful to keep off the frogs, he stepped gingerly into the mud. His foot sank way in, and when he moved his other leg forward, he sank in halfway to his knee. By the time he reached the middle of the pond, the mud was up to his thighs.

The screening had come loose from a nail several inches below the mud. He thought he'd be able to hook the hole in the screen around the nail, but he couldn't pull it down far enough. He needed more weight. He looked toward his maid and said, "Tânia, come here."

She inhaled audibly and shook her head at the impossibility of doing such a thing, at the surprise of being asked. But Sam said, "Yes. Please. Hurry. Come on. Yes."

And she did it. She touched the mud with her big toe, as if testing the temperature, then stepped in a little, then again, up to her ankles. With each step she sank a bit deeper and gave a little hoot and raised her skirt to keep it above the mud. Deeper and deeper, higher and higher, until she knew she should stop. By then, though, it was too late. She was sinking. Trying to turn, she lost her balance and swayed into even deeper mud. She didn't have anything on under that skirt, so when a mound of frogs lurched under her and she lurched at Sam, he brought her in close and tight and then kissed her. For a second it was like kissing a post with teeth, but then she let him, and then she kissed back. Frogs swept around, leaping and flopping against them like children sensing a secret and wanting in.

* * *

After that, they slept together every night. Sam felt a lot like a teenager in love. He even saw the potential for poetry. She was a cinnamon swirl, sweet and buttery, their bed a toaster oven. The kids didn't seem to attach any significance to the change. And really, it was all quite the same except that they got to keep a box of frogs in their room. Tania was still the maid, Sam still the benevolent patron. They still didn't talk much, but Sam touched her whenever she was near, and sometimes their eyes met. At night, she slept curled up inside his arms and legs. On weekends, he slept with his wife.

How did Victor find out? Maybe the kids told him. Maybe by some instinctive perception he knew enough to ask them where their sister slept. Whatever it was, Sam knew because he could feel Victor watching him. When Sam looked back, Victor looked away. And he wasn't talking. Sam had never heard him so quiet. It was an odd reaction. This kind of thing was normal in Brazil. Standard. Victor didn't say anything until finally, down at the pond, when they were alone, he said, "You're sleeping with her?"

With a shy little smile of confession, Sam said, "More or less."

"How can you do that? She's a peon."

"She's very nice, actually. I like her."

"But she's black."

"Mulatta."

"Same thing. More trouble. And how old is she? Seventeen?"

"Eighteen, pretty soon."

"When?"

"When the rains come," said Sam.

"The rains?"

"That's what she said. I don't think she knows about months."

"And Rosilda?"

"Have you decided yet what we're going to do with all these frogs?"

That shut him up. He looked at the pond as if trying to see how it had something to do with his sister. But he didn't say anything, and pretty soon, without a word, he steamed off to the house, got in his Volkswagen and drove away.

Now what? Was Victor going to honor the rule men had, or would he act to preserve the virtue of his sister? Sam figured he'd find out Saturday, that he probably had three days to decide between an illiterate cinnamon swirl and good old Rosilda. But it was only two days before Victor's car came up the driveway, his sister in the seat beside him.

Still wearing her calf-length business suit, Rosilda came through the door looking hard for evidence. Tania was in the kitchen: *schik-schik- schik-schik*.. Sam slipped out, closing the door behind him. Victor, not looking at him, tried to maneuver around, but Sam grabbed him by the front of his shirt, knotting it up under his chin with both fists to pin him against the wall. Victor laughed and convulsed as if being tickled. Sam, an inch from his face, growled in plain English, stressing each word, "*You. Fucking. Idiot.*"

"I didn't tell her," Victor said, but Sam didn't let go. "I just told her you had kids living here. That's all."

Sam dropped him to go into the house. Rosilda, just coming out of the kids' room, stuck her head in Sam's room, gave it a quick look – right, left, down, up – then marched to the kitchen. "You," she said to Tânia, cutting off the schik-schik-schiks. "I want those kids far from here. This isn't an orphanage. And get those frogs out of the bathroom."

Sam looked around her. Tânia, squatting beside a galvanized bucket of suds, brush in hand, teeth out, scared, meek, whispered, "Sim, senhora."

Rosilda said, "What?" and Tânia had to say it again a little louder.

"Okay," Rosilda said. Then she turned to Sam and said, "I want to talk with you."

They went outside on the porch. Rosilda still had her purse over her shoulder. She said, in Portuguese, "We're selling the farm." Sam said nothing. He heard Victor barking at Tânia inside the house. "My salary doesn't give even for rent," said Rosilda. "This place eats money and produces nothing. I talked with a real estate agent. He's bringing people here Sunday."

"What about the frogs?" Sam said in English. "They're doing very well. That's what we came here to do."

"Victor says they're big enough to kill and snakes are eating all. You never told me about snakes."

"There's lots of things I never told you."

"Like what?" Sam didn't answer. "Like what?" she asked again. "Hmm?"

"Nothing," he said. "If you want to kill the frogs, we need a freezer."

"We brought some ice chests. I found one restaurant will buy all frog legs we deliver. I'm going back with the car today. You and Victor are going to kill the frogs. Sunday I will come back with the agent and pick the legs. Okay?"

Okay? What was he supposed to say to that? He didn't say anything. Inside the house, Victor was barking at Tânia. Sam leaned on the porch railing, looking down on his frog farm until Rosilda went through the house to the car. Victor drove her down to the pond, where they pulled three red and white ice chests from the back seat. Then Rosilda drove away alone.

Tânia was in the kids' room, door closed. He almost knocked but then didn't. He went down to the pond, where Victor, pants rolled up, using a long-handled shovel for balance, was just stepping into the mud. The herd of frogs, which covered the basin of the pond, parted before him as he uprooted each ankle and swung it forward, heavy with mud. Panicking, the frogs piled into two rolling waves that percolated with the few who managed to wriggle free and leap away.

"Where are you going?" Sam asked as lightly as possible.

Victor turned from the shoulders, looked Sam up and down, then turned back to face the frogs. Up to his knees, he could go no farther without getting mud on his pants. So he steadied himself and lifted the shovel back over one shoulder. When a frog leaped into the clearing before him, he crouched a bit and swung the shovel over his head and down like a sledge hammer, whacking the frog so hard it disappeared in the mud.

Sam heard a chorus of gasps way up at the house. He turned to see Tânia on the porch, the kids around her legs, her fingers to her teeth. He wanted to say something to her, though he had no idea what and she was too far away for anything less than a shout.

Using the shovel for support, Victor leaned forward to pluck the dead and broken frog from the mud. Holding it by one leg with the tips of his fingers, he swung it back and then forward, releasing it so it arced to the bank and flopped into the grass near the ice chests. Sam looked back toward the house. Tânia and the kids were gone.

Victor pointed to one ice chest. On top of it lay a kitchen knife. Sam picked it up and tested the blade with his thumb. Very sharp. Victor, shifting the shovel to his other hand, put a finger to his groin, then traced a line to his chin. Sam was still looking at the dead frog at his feet and the knife in his hand when he heard the sharp crack of the pistol at the house. Victor flinched, and a few spent pellets of buckshot blooped into the carp side of the pond. The pistol cracked again. Victor yelped and slapped a hand to the back of his neck. When he took it away, a tiny bead of blood appeared. Stuck in the mud, he could only hunch against the next shot. *Crack*. He flinched again and twisted to glare at Sam and growl, "See?"

See what, Sam wondered. See why you shouldn't give a girl a gun? Why you shouldn't sleep with a peon? How *mulattas* make more trouble? That scientific fact prevails in the end?

Victor staggered to the edge of the pond and collapsed dramatically. Sam looked over his wounds. The spent snake shot had broken the skin in a few places but hadn't really penetrated. All he needed was a few dabs of peroxide.

But technically, legally, he'd been shot. If he got his hands on Tânia he'd hurt her bad. If Rosilda found out, she'd have her thrown in jail. She wouldn't stand a chance in a trial. With no clear idea what to tell Tânia, he left Victor on the ground and walked slowly up to the house. The kids' bedroom door was closed. No sounds came from within. Sam sat down at the card table and tried to think of something. He waited a long time before knocking on the door, then opening it. They weren't in there. Most of their stuff was gone, too. Sam dashed to the back door. He didn't have to look long before he saw them walking single file up the path over the ridge, Tânia in front, a large bundle on her head.

The warm and soft places inside him wanted to call them back. But he had no idea what to tell them if they came. Should she run away, leave the state before Rosilda had the police after her? Would she be safe back in the hills, wherever it was her father lived?

Running away wouldn't work, he knew, and yes, the police could find her if they tried. The only solution was in Rosilda. She could be dissuaded. She'd be ready to abandon the whole thing – farm, frogs, charges of assault – if he let her. That's what she wanted.

As Tânia and the kids faded into the brush near the top of the ridge, he let the thought grow. Dumping the farm was a very logical solution. It solved all the problems, from snakes to spleen to rising rent. He could teach English in the city and not have to worry about things. It wouldn't be news for the faculty bulletin board, but it would sure be easier.

Hot, barbed pangs swelled up around his heart when the bundle on Tânia's head disappeared over the ridge. That was the end of her. He could turn his back and go down to the pond and patch up his brother-in-law with a little peroxide. Then they could get on with it and by Sunday be gone.

From

Poems Askance

The Cure

If the cure's in a cave,
and a cave is a space in the earth,
and the earth is in space on a loop
where its up could be down,
its down could be tipped,
and the curse is a tear
on the tip of a stone like a teat
from a roof underground
in a space like a womb
where a shout tumbles down
into petrified hush,
a lump of a sound underground
in the dark of a day
with a curse without cure,
for the cure's in the drip on the teat
where the bats flap around
in a screech of a song
in a space filled with dark they can't see.

The curse has no name,
and the cure has no name,
but the dark has a name,
but the name is a lump underground
on a loop through a space
where its down is the up,
and the teat's in the womb
where the curse is just spit
on the lip of a bat in a swirl,
in a swoon without name,
like love in the dark of a room where you
– yes, you –
just you and that nook you call soul,
that womb in your heart,
that space cut in half where it hurts,
just you and it inside each other,
tumble stuffed with loneliness and want.

The cure to the curse and the curse of the cure
caress like worms in a bunch underground,
in a swirl in a place with no space
in the dirt in the dark,
dank as a stone in a cave,
love after love without aim,
without up, without warm, just a squirm
in a swoon all alone.

Life in Caves

The cure's in the hush of your room
in the woods with the womb of your soul
on the sweep of your lip, yes,
you are the cure,
the breast and the warmth
in the swoon of the sun
where the clouds are a roof,
and the worms and the bats
are at bay in the earth,
and the tear on your lip
is as sweet as the song of the sky.

Teeth of Lions

You can stomp them, poison them,
yank them up and strangle them,
run over them with a mower
sct on low, lop off their little heads,

but some night you'll need to sleep,
and when you awake to a foggy dew,
you'll see those sunny faces in the mist,
faint wands of wispy seeds,
brave wafting paratroopers of propagation,
bearing the banners of egalitarian beauty,
ineluctable, irrepressible, innate and simple
eternally reborn of its own accord.

How It Ends

One of these springs the daffodils
won't melt the snow, the dead snow
will drool into iridescent mud, the fox
won't come around to snatch my hens, no gnats,
no mouse-ear maple buds, no peepers in the dark, the breeze
putrid of whatever they use to embalm Spaghetti-O's,
and you, my dear my warmth my heaven, I fear
will freeze over of the same malaise, pummeled
by the ads and preservatives, flogged
by the glitz, sucked in by the petroleum slick, all
I love in you turned to a plastic daffodil,
cold to the touch, dustier by the day, doomed
to wander like styrofoam in the desert of the dead.

This is Your Last Warning

"Don't be stupid," she said, "don't do stupid,
don't go near stupid; stupid," she said,
"is out there looking for you."

And along came stupid,
found me on the corner
all dressed up, ready to go.
It picked me up and off we went,
stupidity and me, a oneness
on our stupid way.

We slopped wine, lost keys,
whacked our thumbs with hammers,
took wrong turns, tried to save seals,
stop war, start a business, stick it to the man,
took stupid stabs at the impossible,
failed at the facile, too,
destroyed a miscellany of stuff,
trusted and failed to trust.
We fell in love all wrong.

Pigs in pokes, we bought a few,
Gift horses in the mouth we gawked,
counted our chickens before putting
the eggs in an iffy basket

in a canoe with no paddle
up a creek with a can of worms
in search of a golden haystack
that might have a needle or something,
anything, anything interesting,
even if just plain idiotic.

We left tracks, let history repeat,
went our merry ways,
the wrong ways and back,
ways to nowhere, didn't care,
it was just a journey to
stupidity somewhere else.

Oh, we had a great time, sure,
for a while, but stupid
comes with its own deadline,
its own punchline, its strings attached,
its payback hangover, its karmic judgment day,
the doom of stupid – out there,
somewhere, waiting for us one and all.

Ode Alone on a Stump

Dump. Jump. Hump. Clump.
Some mighty nice words
can rhyme with Stump.
So gimme some bourbon
(hic) and a handful of snow
and something to stir with,
maybe this stick – hey, whaddya
know – it's hemlock! How aptly
Socratic, for bourbon and sap's
like dope to an addict:
It's pleasant and kills
and eliminates pain, and for some
reason's better on a log in the rain.
It's certainly better than a Brooklyn Bridge jump,
to drink and think all alone on a stump.

But wait! Hold off! Admonish me not!
I won't do it, it was only a thought.
It all rhymed so sort-of, so easy and quick,
I won't do it, I swear, at least not with a stick.

Cave Lucem

Fancy splinters down at foot level –
Microscopic timbers, deadfall in dusky sloughs.
They lie mong the boulders of the night's dishevel,
Daggers, stingers, punji ambuscades for toes
Curled back as if in flinch against the coming unseen stub.
Paleo-slimey things, cousins to the eel,
lurk midst hexapods of mustard/mayo mixed, a bug or grub,
God knows it's no place for an atheist to kneel,
dally, tarry, hesitate or stop when just another stride
Might reach the switch and drive the demons back and bore
A tunnel past necrophagous things with scales that abide
In fossiliferous lairs of darkness left from yore.
    This we must remember in the luxe of modern caves:
    Mankind lives in light just as long as dark behaves.

Last Leaves

Fall's last leaves,
dry, light, hunched, danced
on winter's first ice,
slick as a mirror,
blued with the sky,
gray in its own right,
backed by water dark
with oak tannin.

They danced with desperation,
skittering hither, looping yon,
waltzing away and back,
whirling up like ballerinas,
swooping light as larks,
as resilient as children,
as if to stop would make them
nothing more than dead leaves.

The wind played with them
as they with the wind,
lofted with each chilly bluster,
sails of nothing more than themselves,
avoiding the shore where other leaves,
less lucky, lay damp and dead,
hunkering into humus,
waiting for winter, praying for spring.

Everything Screwy

A kid I knew, now grown
(but crazy still, like kids)
wrote that brief, sly book
of dubious topic titled
Ventriloquism for Dummies.

When I phoned for an autograph, he said
I could sign it myself, put his name
in rounded script with donut
dots on the i's, a swirly tail
on the end of Screwy, and underline it
with a crosshatched scroll.

I thought that cute and did it, practiced, even,
going for the John Hancock of someone
wild with irony, an Evel Knievel
in a station wagon who mowed his lawn
in bare feet and kept a rooster
just to crow at.

Screwy soon got busted for internet fraud,
hacked into a federal agency, issued himself
a Purple Heart or a pilot's license or something,
did community service at a school for the deaf,
coached acting there and himself
learned sign language.

He married one of the teachers,
a homely thing with sagging cheeks and peach fuzz
in her oblong dimples, an amateur puppeteer
who could read his lips but never knew
he was always saying something else.

Translations

From

The Size Switch, by Monteiro Lobato

Chapter I

Clarion Sunset

"Today's sunset is a trumpet," Emília said, hands on hips, her little feet on the gate post where that afternoon, after a walk in the woods, Dona Benta's folks had stopped. They never missed a chance to appreciate nature's spectacles. During a strong rain, Littlenose had her nose glued to the window, watching it come down. If the wind blew, Padrinho ran to the porch with binoculars to watch the dance of dry leaves. He said, "I want to see if there's a Saci inside." And the Viscount gave scientific explanations for everything.

The sunset that day really was beautiful. It was a trumpet sunset. Why? Because Emília made it up that on certain days the Sun "played a trumpet to call together all the red and golds of the world for a spur-of-the-moment party. Standing before a trumpet sunset, no one felt like talking because anything they said would sound silly.

But Dona Benta couldn't contain herself.

"What a wonderful phenomenon a sunset is," she said.

Emília gave the Viscount a wink on account of that "phenomenon" and decided to start some trouble.

"Why is it called a "sun set, Dona Benta?" she asked with her famous air of angelic innocence. "What does the Sun actually set? Some kind of egg?"

Dona Benta sensed it was a trap question, one of those that force a certain answer and set the stage for Emília's famous "Well then..."

"The Sun doesn't actually set anything down, silly girl," she said. "The Sun sets itself down."

"Well then the Sun is its own egg. That's funny!"

Dona Benta had the patience to explain.

"'Sun set' is a manner of speaking. You know perfectly well that the Sun doesn't eve*No table of contents entries found*

r really set. It's the Earth and the other planets that move around the Sun. But our impression is that the Sun moves around the Earth–and therefore it rises in the morning and sets in the evening."

"I'm tired of knowing that," Emília declared. "My issue is with that 'set.' 'To set' always meant to put something in a certain place. A hen sets an egg in her nest. The Viscount sets his top hat on his head. Pedrinho sets his finger in his nose."

"Liar!" Pedrinho shouted, quickly pulling his finger from his nose.

"But the Sun," Emília continued, doesn't set a top hat on its head, nor does it have the terrible habit of pulling gold from its nose."

"As I just explained, it's a manner of speaking," Dona Benta said again.

"I see that all the things that grown-ups say are manners of speaking," the little pest continued. "That is, they are little lies. And then they go around telling children not to lie! Oh! Oh! Oh! Certain poets, for example. What are they doing if not lying? Last night you read that poem by Castro Alves that ended with 'Andrada! Pull this flag from the wind

"'Columbus! Shut the door to your seas!'

"It's all a lie. How can this poet tell Andrada, who's already dead, to pull a flag out of the wind when there's no flag in the wind, and even if there were, a flag isn't a tooth that gets pulled. Flags come down the flagpole on a rope. And how does this poem, this plain soldier, dare to give orders to Columbus, an admiral? And how does he order Columbus to shut the 'door' on 'his' seas if the sea doesn't have a door and Columbus never had seas? The one who's got seas is the Earth."

Dona Benta sighed. "Manners of speaking, Emília. Without these manners of speaking, which we call 'poetic images,' Castro Alves wouldn't be able to write poetry."

"But is it or isn't it a lie?"

Dona Benta was just opening her mouth to answer when a man on a horse appeared on the curve of the road. It was the mailman who brought the mail every other day. Everyone took their eyes from the sunset to set them on the mailman.

The man reached them and bid everyone a good afternoon. He dismounted with an air of eternal awkwardness and opened his grimy canvas bag to take out Bona Benta's newspapers.

"There is also a letter for Mr. Viscount Corncob," he said, handing over the package.

Emília threw herself onto the letter like a cat on a sardine head and yanked it from Dona Benta's hands the same way that the poet wanted Andrada to yank the flag from the winds.

"It must be a response to an inquiry I made about the vitamins in pirlimpimpim powder," the Viscount explained modestly as Emília got ready to rip open the envelop and Pedrinho sighed through his lips.

"Don't open it, Emília!" Littlenose screamed.

"Grandma said that the the privacy of correspondence is inviolable. A letter is a sacred thing. Only the addressee can open it."

Emília made a pout, stuck the letter under the Viscount's nose and said, "Eat and drink your privacy."

Meanwhile, Pedrinho unfolded the newspaper and read the enormous headlines and subtitles about the war.

"Another bombardment of London, Grandma. Hundreds of airplanes flew over the city. A monster of bombs. Whole blocks destroyed. Innumerable fires. Deaths all over."

Dona Benta's face grew dark. Whenever the thought of war gripped her, she grew so sad that Littlenose ran to sit in her lap and cheer her up. "Don't be like that, Grandma. It was in London, a long way from here."

"No such thing, my dear. Humanity is all one body. Every country is part of this body, every finger and fingernail, every hand, every arm or leg makes up part of our body. A bomb that falls on a house in London and kills a grandmother like me over there, and injures a little granddaughter like you or leaves a Pedrinho over there crippled, it hurts me as much as if it fell here. It's such a monstrous perversion, this bombing of innocents, I'm afraid I just can't stand the horror of this war much longer. I just want to die. Ever since this huge disgrace started, I can't do anything but think about the suffering of so many millions of innocents. My heart aches for all the grandmothers and mothers so far away who cry over the slaughter of their children and grandchildren."

Dona Benta's sadness continued into dusk at Yellow Woodpecker Farm, where it was otherwise happy and joyful. And it was precisely this sadness that led Emília to plan and carry out the most tremendous adventure that there ever was in the whole world.

Emília swore to herself that she would put an end to the war, and she fulfilled her vow–but she just barely didn't put an end to the whole human race.

That night, in her corn husk bed, she couldn't sleep.

Anyone going into her head would read a thought like this: "This war is taking too long, and if I don't do something, those infamous bombardments will go on, going from city to city until they end up here. Someone turned on the war switch. Somebody else has to switch it off. But where is the war switch? Nobody knows. But if I take a pinch of that super-powder that the Viscount is making, I'll be able to fly to the end of the world and find the Switch House. Because there must be a Switch House, with switches that control everything in the world, like the electrical switches in the hallway that control all the lights of a house."

The Viscount was in fact studying a mysterious super-powder capable of wonders even greater than the old pirlimpimpim powder. That's why he spent his nights awake and even got scientific letters from foreign countries.

But that night Emília heard some snoring. "Could that be the Viscount?" she said...and she went to see. Yes, it was the Viscount, who, after nights and nights awake, was sleeping the sleep of that lazy little pig Rabicó.

"If he's fast asleep to the point of snoring," Emília thought, "it must be because he has solved the super-powder problem. The snore of a wise man means a clear head, an invention invented."

With that in mind, Emília went tip-toeing to the Viscount's little laboratory. She messed around with everything until she found in a little matchbox a substance that looked like ashes. She sniffed it. The smell reminded her of pirlimpimpim powder.

"This must be it," she said, and she courageously took up a pinch.

Chapter II

The Size Switch

Fiiiuuuunnn!!!

When Emília opened her eyes and slowly returned from her dizziness, she found herself in a foggy place, kind of like the air before dawn. She couldn't make out trees or mountains or anything else. There was just a large and mysterious house far in the distance.

"This must be the End of the World, and that house can only be the Switch House. The Viscount's powder is perfect!"

Still a little dizzy, she got up and went to the house. Exactly right! Big lettering on the front said simply, "SWITCH HOUSE."

Emília spent a while with her nose in the air and her eyes on those lit-up letters. She saw an open door. Filling herself with courage, she went in. There was nothing inside, no thing, no machines. Just that same fog that came in from outside. But she made out a set of switches on the wall, like electric switches, all of them switched up.

"They must be the switches that regulate and calibrate everything in the world," Emília thought. "So one of them is the switch that turns wars on and off. But which?"

Emília held her chin. She thought as hard as she could. There was nothing different about any of the switches. All exactly alike. No letters or numbers. How to know which was the switch for war?

"The only solution," she thought, "is to apply the experimental method that the Viscount uses in his laboratory. I have to move the switches, one by one, until I hit the one for war."

The switches were in a row eight hands from the floor, therefore out of the reach of a little creature only two hands high. How to reach the switches?

Emília looked all around. She saw no ladder or chair or crate she could climb onto. There wasn't even a stick. The solution would be to go back to the super-powder. "If I sniff half of the smallest of the little grains I brought in this box, I'll rise up there and grab hold of one of the switches."

And that's what she did. She picked out the smallest grain of powder, broke it in half, and inhaled that little piece. It worked. Just a sniff of that bit of super-powder was enough to raise her up to the switches, allowing her to hang off one of them. She didn't even need to use her strength. Her weight was enough for the switch to go down almost to the end.

But what happened was the most unforeseeable thing in the world. Everything changed before her eyes, and an enormous cloth, like the tent of a pony circus, toppled down onto her. Emília felt herself surrounded by cloth. The floor was cloth; above her, only cloth; all around her, cloth, cloth, cloth. And with the weight of so much cloth, she could hardly stay on her feet. She ended up lying down like something squashed. But she had to get out of there or at least try to get out. She was already feeling herself without air. She started crawling under the cloth in a blind attempt to get free. There were so many folds, so many that at every moment she had to go around and around to move ahead. She went on crawling, getting around the folds that were getting her all mixed up. Sometimes she even managed to get up, when a larger fold gave her space. Emília remembered the Labyrinth of Crete, where the Minotaur lived. It was dark in there, nothing more than the dark of the middle of the night. Emília had the impression she was spending a century crawling around the labyrinth until at last she made out some light in the distance. "That must be the hem or the end of the dang cloth," she thought as she dragged herself in that direction. It was, in fact, the hem. Emília, almost out of breath, bathed in sweat, got out of the labyrinth and fell exhausted to the floor with an Ooof!

She lay on her back for a while, her arms out, not thinking anything. First rest, then move on. She looked up at the switches on the wall. She didn't see any switches at all. "What's this? Did the switches evaporate?"

Looking harder, she confirmed that they had not evaporated. The switches were there but much, much higher up. The wall had grown tremendously. It seemed to go on forever. Everything had gotten phenomenally larger. And on the floor she saw something new that hadn't been there before. It was a pedestal carpeted in yellow paper.

Emília found herself lying exactly atop this pedestal. Then, looking at her little rag doll body, she saw that she was naked.

"What's this?" she said to herself. "Me, naked as a worm up on top of a yellow pedestal full of black scratches beside a mountain of cloth...and the switches way up there...and everything enormous...Am I dreaming?"

She set herself to thinking as hard as she could. She examined the carpet on the pedestal.

She realized that the scratches were letters. She had to stand up to read them one by one. The first was an M, the second an A, the third a T. When she got to the last, she saw that they formed the word MATCHES. And then she made out another word...KITCHEN. She put it all together and it said, KITCHEN MATCHES.

"Is that possible?" Emília exclaimed to herself. "Am I on top of the biggest box of wooden matches in the world? But if so, then each match stick may be practically a beam of pine."

Since the box was open, she looked inside. She didn't see any beams at all; rather, she saw some kind of rough sand of exactly the color of the Viscount's super-powder.

At that moment, a beam of light illuminated her brain.

"Ha! I know what it is. This is the matchbox that I brought here and is still the size it always was. It's me that shrank. I became teeny-weeny. And since I'm teeny-weeny, everything looks hugely big to me. The same thing that happened to Alice in Wonderland has happened to me. First she was so large that she practically can't fit in a house. Then she was the size of a mosquito. I've become teeny-weeny. Why?"

And she set herself to thinking even harder than before.

"It could only be for one reason: because I pulled the switch down. So that switch is what regulates my size. But does it regulate only my size, or does it regulate the size of all living creatures? Does it regulate the size of all living creatures, or only that of human creatures? My God, so many problems!"

She thought and thought.

"If all creatures have become teeny-weeny like me, the whole world must be totally confused and everybody's heads are spinning as much as mine. But war has ended! Oh yes, it's over! If men are all as teeny-weeny as me, they can no longer kill each other or wield those terrible steel weapons. The most they can do is poke each other with needles or thorns. At least that's something..."

She thought and thought and thought.

"Yes, I moved the Size Switch and all living creatures became small because it would be absurd to have a switch just for me. If there was a switch for each and every person, in this room there would have to be almost seven billion switches because the population of the world is almost seven billion. Therefore the same switch works for all people.

Therefore all of humanity is "shrunk"–and prevented from making war. Oh yes, I have done away with war. Hurray! Hurray!"

She thought and thought and thought.

"The proof that this switch only regulates the size of living creatures is here in this matchbox. If this matchbox had also shrunk, it would be proportionate to my body and not huge the way it is."

The situation was so new that her old ideas just didn't work anymore.

Emília understood a point that Dona Benta had explained, that our ideas are daughters of our experience. Now the change in the size of humanity had made ideas as useless as a wooden nickel. The idea of a matchbox, for example, was the idea of some little thing that people carried around in their pockets. But with creatures shrunk to the point where a matchbox was the size of the pedestal of a statue, the "idea-of-the-matchbox" wasn't worth anything. The "idea-of-a-lion" was the idea of a terrible and very dangerous animal, an eater of people. And the "idea-of-a-baby-chick" was that idea of a harmless little animal. Now it was the opposite. The chick is the dangerous one.

Emília felt a chill in her heart. She began to lose confidence that she had done something tremendous, the most tremendous thing that had ever happened in the world.

She thought and thought and thought. Then she decided to figure out what size she was.

"I can calculate my size by comparing the letters in the word MATCHES. These letters were about a tenth of an inch back when I was 16 inches tall. Now, if I was 16 inches, I was 160 times bigger than a tenth of an inch. And now: What is my size in relation to the letters?"

To make the measurement, Emília lay down on the M and saw that the M was one third of her height. So she had shrunk to about an inch.

"Amazing," she exclaimed. "I've shrunk to just a third of an inch. I used to be 16 inches tall. I'm one-forty-eighth my size. That means Pedrinho, who was four-foot-six, must have shrunk to a little more than one inch. And Colonel Teodorico, who boasted of being five-foot-eight must be a little less than an inch and a half–the size of a grasshopper."

Emília thought and thought.

"Now what do I do? I have several options to choose from. One is to just leave everything the way it is. Another is to go up to the switch again and leave everything the way it was. That seems better to me because if I go back to the farm at this size, I probably won't make it across the yard. The baby chick who's always there will eat me as if I were an ant."

She looked up.The switch that was pulled down seemed to be way, way up there...48 times higher than before. But that made no difference to someone who still had plenty of super-powder. So, wiggling her hand into the matchbox, Emília grabbed a grain and sniffed it up. The powder threw her all the way up to the switch. But her strength, diminished 48 times, wasn't good for anything.

She didn't even have a way to hold on to the switch, which seemed like a giant doorknob as wide in diameter as her whole body–the same as a giant tree trunk for men in the olden times.

Yes, in the olden times, because, if all men were now as reduced in size as her, anyone who wanted to refer to the men of the day before would have to say 'the men of olden times."

Emília sat on top of that enormous tree trunk, not knowing how to go back down.

"Now what?"

She thought and thought and thought.

"I'm going to throw myself down," she decided. "My weight must be like the weight of an ant, so if I throw myself down, I ought to land as light as a mote of dust, not to mention that there's a mountain of cloth down there."

And so that's what she did. She threw herself into the air and landed on the mountain of cloth.

And that's how she discovered something: the cloth of the mountain was a farm of enormous branches of red roses, just like the roses on the dress of hers that had disappeared. And then she understood everything. The enormous mountain of cloth was none other than her own dress dropped to the floor. When she pulled the switch down and instantly shrank, she found herself in the middle of the dress which, without her body to hold it up, collapsed, giving its minuscule owner the impression that a circus tent had fallen around her.

"Amazing!" Emília exclaimed. "That huge cloth that formed a labyrinth all around me was my own dress. I was lucky the box of super-powder was in my hand and not in my pocket. If it had been in my pocket, how would I ever be able to take it out from inside that enormous mountain? What a job!"

Emília thought for a few more seconds. She was going to have to abandon all that precious powder here, even though it was all they'd had at the farm. Because how could she take this pedestal-box back? If she were dressed, the few pinches of the powder would fit in her pockets. But the way she was, naked as a worm, all she could take back was whatever she could hold–just one grain in each hand.

But better that than nothing, and Emília picked up a grain of powder in each hand.

Then she sniffed up a third little grain and...*fiiiuuuunnn!* Off she went with the wind, back to Dona Benta's farm.

Chapter III

Because of the Chick-without-a-Tail

Trips with the super-powder were instantaneous. A blink of the eyes. Emília closed her eyes there on the pedestal and opened them at the gate of the farm.

Saints alive, what a colossal gate! Too hundred times her height. Far in the distance she saw an enormous animal grazing: the cow Mocha. And farther on, a colossal sleeping mountain. And the house? Oh, the house, at the end of the vast yard, was, for her, as Sugarloaf Mountain was for the men of olden times. The roof seemed to bump the clouds.

How was she to cross the hundred yards of the yard on foot? A hundred yards in the olden days meant nothing to the "big" Emília. But now, it would take 33,353 steps, since her step has diminished to 3 millimeters.

She was thinking about that when a horrendous monster rose up from the yard: the baby-chick-without-a-tail.

"Incredible!" she muttered. "That chick was no more than a simple chick like all the other chicks in the world, the ones you call with a 'chickee-chickee-chick!'" Emília calculated that the chick must been twenty times her size, that is, the size of an ostrich seventy yards tall for a man like Colonel Teodorico.

"Can a monster of that size see me" she said, not feeling like crossing the yard.

But the baby-chick-without-a-tail was very good at seeing. It had the eyes of a microscope.

As soon as Emília set out, step by step, the chick saw her and came toward her with its beak open, ready to eat her. Emília barely had time to resort to the super-powder she'd brought with her. She quickly put the two little grains to her nose and sucked them in.

Fiiiuuuunnn!

She awoke far away, up in an enormous tree, caught on a branch. The leaves were as blue as the sky and shaped like rounded hills.

"Leaves? No. This was never a leaf. This is a flower. And those hills are bunches of flowers. But what kind of tree makes blue flowers like these?"

Emília then remembered about hydrangeas, and with a little effort she saw that she had actually fallen into an enormous hydrangea blossom. It was hard to keep herself there because human creatures, endowed with only two feet, need flat surfaces to keep their balance, and on that blossom, there were only one or two petals in a horizontal position.

Emília tried to get down.

"For people-creatures, there's really nothing like flat land," she thought. So before getting down, she looked around.

"What I thought was a forest is actually a garden. An immense garden, the largest garden in the world, with roses the height of trees, and that flowering jasmine plant is the size of an Amazonian Victoria-Regis lily pad, and around the edge there's grass that's most like the banana plantation in Cubatão. My God, how big everything got!"

And up ahead? Emília focused her eyes. A greenness reached way up, and way up there spread itself across horizontal beams.

But Emília was quickly learning how to "interpret" the immense things she was seeing.

"Yes, I get it," she thought. "That greenness is a vine on a veranda, and what looks like beams are the wires holding it up. Veranda? Well then that huge white thing that seems to reach up to the clouds is the front of a mansion."

She focused again. Great big rectangles way up there: the windows! The flat roof was so far up there she could barely see it.

"Yes, it's a mansion, much bigger than Dona Benta's house. It's going to be hard for me to get used to the new size of things. For ants, of course, this big size of stuff is natural, because that's the way it always was for them. Red ants can't even comprehend what a house is. They must see houses like parts of the world, of things that have always been, like hills, boulders, rivers, and trees. That's why they're not afraid to walk around a house, going up and down the walls, even making their little ant hills in the cracks of sidewalks. When they come out and see a person, for sure they don't understand that it's a person. They think it's only a moving immensity, like rivers or the ocean. For ants, the world must be divided into moving immensities and unmoving immensities. A house or a hill is an unmoving immensity. Moving immensities come out of houses–people, dogs, cats. And out in the fields are immensities with horns, which we call cows and cattle. But even though I'm now the size of an ant, I have the same intelligence as before–and I know it. I know that these immensities I'm seeing are no more than mere fleas beside even bigger things, like mountains. And mountains are no more than mere fleas next to something bigger, such as the Earth. And the Earth is a flea next to the Sun. And the Sun is the sneeze of a flea next to the Infinite. My God, how I know things!"

Emília set herself to philosophizing, thinking about the strange animals around her, some with wings, others without wings, some black, some green, others squishy–but all with legs.

"So many legs in this world that so long ago I called "the world of bugs" and now has turned into my world! So I've also turned into a bug. I see my fellow bugs in all sizes, some smaller than me, some bigger. Like that inchworm I see coming this way, for example. For me its a monster, since it's five times longer than my height–the same as an anaconda 25 feet long for a man of olden times. But at the same time it's the same little caterpillar I used to hold in the palm of my hand."

From

The Reform of Nature, by Monteiro Lobato

The Reformer of Nature

Américo Blink-Blink had the habit of finding flaws in everything. To him, the world was wrong and Nature was just foolishness.

"Foolishness, Américo?"

"Well yeah! Right here in this orchard you have proof of it. Over there, that big jabuticabeira tree holding out little berries, and way over there I see a colossal squash stuck to the stalk of a plant creeping along the ground. Wouldn't the exact opposite be more logical? If I were to reorganize things, I'd swap those fruits. I'd put the little jabuticabas on the squash plant and the big squash on the jabuticabeira tree. Am I not right?"

Américo went on talking, proving that everything was wrong and only he was capable of intelligently sorting out the world.

"But the best thing to do," he concluded, "is to not think about any of that and just take a nap under these trees, right?"

And Américo Blink-Blink, blink-blinking to no end, stretched out face-up in the shade of the jabuticabeira.

He slept. He slept and dreamed. He dreamed about a new world entirely remade by his own hands. It was so beautiful!

But then, right at the best part of the dream–*plaf!*–a jabuticaba fell from a branch right onto his nose.

Américo leaped awake. He blinked and blinked. He thought about the situation and finally recognized that the world wasn't as poorly made as he'd said. And off he went toward home, thinking, "What a bummer! Because if I remade the world, the first victim would be me. I, Américo Blink-Blink, killed by a squash that I myself had put in the place of a jabuticaba. Let's just forget about reforms. Let everything stay just as it is, which is fine."

And Blink-Blink went on blinking his way through life. From then on, he lost obsession with correcting Nature.

When they heard Dona Benta tell that story, everyone agreed with the moral...except Emília.

"I always thought Nature was wrong," she said. "And after hearing the tale of Américo Blink-Blink, I thought it was even more wrong. Because isn't it wrong to make someone blink-blink? Why so much blinking? Everything excessive is wrong. And the more I "study Nature," the more I see mistakes. Why does Aunt Nastácia have such big lips? Why does a cow have two horns on the front and none in the back? Enemies attack from the back more often than the front. And everything's like that. Very, very wrong. If I were to remake the world, I'd leave everything a delight, and I'd start by reforming that story and that Américo Blink-Blink."

The discussion took off that day. Everybody was against the reform, but the feisty little girl wouldn't give up. She hollered that everything was wrong and that they had to reform nature.

"When, Marquesa?" Littlenose asked ironically.

"The first time I'm left here alone."

Frog Shows Up

Just such an occasion was approaching. Once she knew Dona Benta had received an invitation from the leaders of Europe to go straighten out that poor continent, Emília jumped for joy. With the idea of reforming Nature in her head, she declared that she wasn't going.

"What do you mean not go, Emília," Dona Benta said. "Do you think I can leave you here alone?"

Emília hid the real reasons she wanted to stay. She said that she just wanted to avoid scandalizing the Peace Conference.

"Yes," she said. "If I went, it wouldn't be just to sleep in a hotel! I'd also want to take part in the Conference. And you wouldn't believe some of the facts I'd like to tell those dictators. And inevitably it would turn into a brouhaha. It would turn into a scandal. That's what I'd like to avoid."

Dona Benta thought for a while and went to the kitchen to consult Aunt Nastácia.

She found her housekeeper scouring a pot to make guava jelly.

"Nastácia," she said. "Emília's making trouble. She wants to stay. She says that if she goes to the Conference, the dictators will break out in a brouhaha and there will be an international scandal. And that's what I'm afraid of. I hate scandals."

"Yes, ma'am, it'll be a brouhaha, all right. After that story with the Size Switch, Emília just got too full of herself. She doesn't put up with anything. She'd make a scandal, all right. She could even ruin our work over there. Pedrinho said that over there in Europe it's worse than a junk yard when you look for something and can't find it. Everything's turned upside down and all around, he says. Total chaos, just a big mess. Our job is huge, ma'am, and with Emília messing things up, we won't be able to get anything done right. In my opinion, she can stay here."

"But stay here alone, Nastácia?"

"She can stay with the donkey Counselor and the rhinoceros Quindim. What more do you want? They've got common sense to spare. I'll talk with the Counselor and explain everything."

Dona Benta thought and thought and finally convinced herself that Aunt Nastácia was right. Under the control of the Counselor and defended by Quindim, what could go wrong?

And Emília stayed.

But Littlenose, the one who knew Emília the most, didn't believe that pretext of not going so as to not start a scandal.

"That's just what she says, Grandma! Emília actually likes scandals. I know why she wants to stay alone–so she can hang out like a bum and do something even crazier than that Size Switch thing. If I were you, I would not leave her alone."

But Dona Benta was democracy in the flesh. She would never abuse her authority to oppress anyone. Everyone was free on the little farm, and that is exactly why they were bathed in happiness. Emília didn't want to go? Well then, go she would not. How to force her to go? Who had the right? And what good would it do to force her to go against her will, all stubborn like a mule? So Emília was allowed to stay home.

That was right on the morning that the invitation arrived. A month later, the commission arrived to take Dona Benta. The commission arrived on the last ship in the world. All the others were resting at the bottom of the sea, victims of submarines and aerial torpedoes. Dona Benta packed the bags and put on her yellow grosgrain dress from the time of Dom Pedro II. She had Aunt Nastácia put on a new skirt with little green baby chicks on it, and off they went to board the ship.

Pedrinho and Littlenose accompanied their illustrious grandmother as good grandchildren. The Viscount, with a thick briefcase of science under his arm, went along as Scientific Consultant.

Emília, the Counselor, and Quindim were there for the send-off at the gate, and they listened to Aunt Nastácia's last instructions on the chickens, the piglets, and the nest of baby chicks that were just being born.

"Don't go helping the chicks get out of the shell or they'll die," she said. "Chicks know how to take care of themselves. And don't forget to water the collard seedlings in the garden."

Hearing these sensible instructions, the men of the commission looked at each other like someone saying, "With people of such lovely, practical spirit, so careful with everything, the Conference is going to be a veritable triumph for humanity." (And they weren't wrong.)

As soon as she found herself alone, Emília ran to the typewriter and typed up a letter to a girl in Rio de Janeiro with whom she'd been corresponding and planning "things" for some time.

Dear Frog:

I am alone–alone-alone-alone-alone! Everyone's gone to Europe to straighten out the countries more smashed up than old tin cans and now I need you to come spend a little time here. You are like me, the type who don't agree. We can carry out our plan to reform Nature. Américo Blink-Blink was a blissful fool. He reformed Nature looking no farther than his own nose, and it's too bad the squash in his dream didn't really squash his head. It would be one less fool in the world. We will do better reforms. First we'll remake things here on the farm. If it works out well, the whole world will adopt our reforms. Your mother isn't going to want you to come. She's an "adult," and adults are Américo Blink-Blinks.

Take a sniff of half a pinch of the powder in this little paper bag—only half; otherwise, instead of stopping here, you'll end up I don't know where. They left this morning and I'm already feeling very lonely."

(After Emília learned that "solitary" was a synonym of "alone," she started using the word "alone" instead of "solitary." "It isn't grammatical," she said, "but it's shorter."

Frog, who was called that because she was a skinny eleven-year-old girl, was very much like Emília, the type who doesn't agree with anything. As soon as she read the letter, she jumped up and down ten times and tried to divide the powder in the little bag in two "bisolutely" equal parts. Emília always went around using the word "absolutely" spoken that way. Before reforming Nature, Emília had already reformed language several times.

"What are you doing there," Frog's mother asked when she saw the girl dividing the mysterious powder.

"I'm "bi-ing" something that takes and brings so that I can be taken away and brought back," she said in the language of the Oracle of Delphi. (In Emília's language, "bi" meant "dividing in two.")

The mother was sure she didn't understand anything, but since she was used to her daughter's enigmatic answers, she just gave a sigh and went on to take care of something else.

Froggy sniffed the powder according to the instructions in the letter. Her eyes immediately shut, and in her ears she heard the famous *fiunn!*. An instant later, she felt herself drop to the ground. She opened her eyes. A yard! It could only be the yard at the little farm.

But she didn't see anybody. The house was closed. In the air, just two sounds: a snorting, which must have been Quindim the rhinoceros rooting around, and the sound of chewing that could only be the pig Rabicó.

Still sitting and still a bit dizzy, the girl shouted, "Emília! Emilita! Emiloca!"

The Nest-Bird

The answer from the orchard was "Here!" Running toward the voice, the girl found Emília so absorbed in a little bird that she didn't even look over. She was pressing down on the back of a tico-tico, a Brazilian bunting. All little birds have convex backs, that is, rounding upward. Emília was making a bird with a concave back, with the rounding going down into the shoulders. Frog looked on without understanding it at all, until Emília explained.

"I'm making a new kind of nest, a 'nest-bird,'" she said, "a nest in a bird. Idiot Nature made things screwy, without thinking. Little birds, for example. Nature taught them to make nests in trees. Could anything be more dangerous? The eggs and the babies are left out in the rain, open to snakes and ants and gusts of wind. Last year there was such a bad wind that it knocked down this tico-tico's nest, right over there in the pitanga tree. And there were three little eggs, so cute, all spotted. And once again I was convinced of the torture in things. I started to reform Nature because of that little bird."

Frog didn't understand that reforming nature was something like that, so she asked, "What's the denting of the tico-tico's back supposed to be for?"

"Well it's a nest," Emília answered. "I make its nest right here in the shoulders, and there we are! Wherever it goes, its eggs and kids go along–and there's no danger of snakes or wind or rain."

"Well, there's still rain," little Frog said. "In the nests in trees, the female is always on top of the eggs. But here..."

Emília stuck out her lips with an air of superiority.

"I've already foreseen that hypothesis," she said. "I'm going to make its little tail more movable so it can turn around and cover the eggs when necessary, like a little roof."

Satisfied, Frog paid close attention to the preparation of the world's first nest-bird.

"Ready!" Emília finally exclaimed. "Now all we need are the eggs. Run back to the house and bring me the female tico-tico that is in the birdcage."

Frog went and returned with the little bird. Emília took it very carefully and squeezed it so that three spotted eggs came out. She very carefully set them in the nest of feathers she had made on the back of the male tico-tico–and she let them go with a *prrrr!*

Emília was radiant.

"Off they go!" she exclaimed. "No more disturbances, no more fears of snakes, ants, or wind. And no more unfairness with females doing all the laying and brooding. Men are always abusing women. Dona Benta says that in the olden days, and even today among Indians, grown men get the cushy life, whistling in their hammocks, keeping themselves busy with no more than hunting and war while the poor women do all the work and spend their lives washing and cooking and sweeping and putting up with the kids. And if they don't walk just right, they get spanked on the bottom. Males have always abused females, but now things are going to change. That tico-tico, for example, has to take care of the eggs. The female still has the job of laying them, but the male has to take care of them.

"But then the eggs won't hatch," little Frog said. "To hatch them, the females have to sit on them for a certain number of days. Hens spend twenty-one days brooding."

"I've already foreseen this hypothesis," Emília said, "and the reforming is ready. In my bird-nest system, it's the sun, not the female, who does the hatching, just as with alligator, turtle, lizard, and snake eggs."

"And when there's no sun? Sometimes days go by without the sun coming out."

"In such a case the eggs will have to be patient and wait for the sun to appear. Why hurry?"

Frog had nothing else to say. She was right. It was only then that Emília remembered to greet her and ask how everyone was doing at home. She also checked Frog's fingernails to see if they were dirty. And made her turn around and jump three times. It was the first time the two of them had met.

"I like the looks of you," Emília said after the examination. "I was afraid you weren't going to go along with my idea. Often people imagine a person one way and they turn out to be another way. I really liked your last letter about reforming cities and people. I adore you, Frog, because you disagree."

"Oh, I really disagree!" Frog exclaimed. "I always disagree. In ourselves, people, for example, so many things are wrong! Why two eyes in the front and none in the back? And if I were reforming people, I'd put one eye on the forehead and the other at the nape of the neck. That way I'd double people's safety."

"Well I'd increase the number of eyes," Emília said. "Why only two? Jut as we have ten fingers, we could have ten eyes. I'd put four on the head–to the north, south, east, and west. I'd put two on the big toes to keep from stubbing them. The other day, Pedrinho stubbed his toe on a brick and almost lost a toenail. With an eye on each big toe, there's no danger of stubbing them, or stepping on thorns or splinters. And I'd put one on each little finger. The little finger's a regular bum on the hands. It doesn't do anything. It spends its whole time watching the others do their work. Now, if the 'short man' had a little eye at the tip, it could help out. Sometimes you want to see something in between your teeth or see if there's wax in your ear and you can't see. With an eye on the little finger, it would be so easy!"

"And that little finger eye," Frog added, "could be like a microscope, able to see tiny things invisible to regular eyes. But there would be one inconvenience, Emília. Hands work with everything. They work a lot, and those little finger eyes would always be getting dirt in them or getting scratched."

"Nothing could be easier to prevent that," Emília recalled. "Just wear thimbles. They would be covered when they have nothing to do. But for now, we can't reform people because there's nobody here. All the humans on the farm have gone to Europe."

"And Rabicó?"

"He's inhuman and so four-legged. I've thought a lot about reforming Rabicó. We could turn him into a biped and..."

"And do away with that insane desire to eat everything he finds," Frog continued. "This is what I'd do: On his snout I'd put some kind of mousetrap, always set. When he went to get into candy or whatever else, like Littlenose's wedding crown, the trap would trip and grab him by the snout. And I'd also give him the legs of a turtle so he can't run away when Pedrinho chased him with his slingshot."

Emília looked at Frog with a suspicious eye. The ideas seemed absurd. The mousetrap would keep Rabicó from eating not just macaroons and cookies but everything else, too. He'd die of hunger.

"'Bsurd, Frog!" she said. "The mousetrap would end up killing Rabicó and Dona Benta would get mad."

"You don't understand, Emília. The mousetrap would work only when he wanted to eat cookies. For squash, corn, manioc and the rest, it wouldn't work."

"But how is the mousetrap going to know when it's a cookie?"

"By the smell. I'll put a good nose on the mousetrap."

Emília looked sideways at Frog. The girl seemed kind of crazy.... Nevertheless, she decided to reform Rabicó. Frog changed the subject.

"In the letter you sent me, Emília, I found the word 'bsolutely,' and now you're saying 'Bsurd' instead of 'absurd.' Are you reforming words, too?"

"Not yet, but I've thought about it. For now I'm limiting myself to cutting a letter or two when they bother me. The 'a' in certain words makes me open my mouth too much. My jaw could fall off, like Nha Veva's daughter's. Try saying 'absurd' without opening your mouth."

Frog tried and couldn't do it, but she said "bsurd" with her mouth almost shut.

"Well there you go!"Emília said. "Everything wrong, even the 'a' in certain words. The world's a big mess. Why, for example, put a little tail on Rabicó? The tail has a purpose on Mocha the cow. It's to scare off flies. It's a scarer-offer. But on Rabicó? What good's that hairless little tail?"

"To decorate that end," Frog recalled.

"What end?"

"Rabicó's end. All ends have a little tail. It's the final touch. Mommy says that it's ugly to eat and leave your plate clean, or to drink a glass of liqueur and not leave a sip in the bottom. Those are little tails. They're the final touches of a good education."

Emília was trusting Froggy less and less. She seemed like Alice in Alice in Wonderland. She just came up with ridiculousnesses. She said, "Decorations are useless. I don't want to hear about any decorations on my reformings. Everything has to have a scientific purpose. That idea in your letter about reforming Quindim seems crazy to me. Girl, I think you want to play with nature. I want to correct nature. I want to make it better. Know what I mean? This isn't a game. It's serious business. That's the difference between us. In your last letter you talked about replacing Quindim's leather with velvet. That's dumb."

"But what does Quindim need with such a tough hide, here at Yellow Woodpecker, where there aren't any African thorns?"

"I agree. He could use a finer leather, like suede. But velvet, that's just too much. Sometimes I think you're sabotaging my idea of reforming nature..."

Remaking Mocha

For a long time the two went on talking about how to reform, and, since they were sitting under a jabuticaba tree, they ate the delicious little fruits as they talked. At a certain moment, Emília said, "This jabuticaba tree, for example. Don't you think it's a shame that such a big tree produces such little fruits? Meanwhile, over in the garden, we have a squash plant that produces enormous squashes, and it's a plant that's barely a plant–just a soft stalk that squashes when you step on it. I'm going to change it. I'm going to put jabuticaba fruits on the squash plant and the squashes on the jabuticaba tree."

"But that's what Américo Blink-Blink did," Frog said, "and the dream opened his eyes."

"That's because the idiot slept under the jabuticaba tree. Know why? So the story would work out right.The storyteller was a big scaredy-cat. He wanted to tell a story that made it scary to change, so he made up that fable about Américo sleeping under the jabuticaba tree. I've already re reformed that fable."

"How?"

"By having Américo not sleep under any tree at all, and La Fontaine had no way to end the fable. I left just one part of it. An unfinished fable like that famous symphony. And with no moral."

"A fable with no moral is an immoral fable," Frog said. "It's a Rabicó tale, a tale without a tail. It's good for nothing."

"His nose is good for nothing," Emília responded, and she went about doing the reformation.

The squash became very uneasy and discouraged to find itself hanging from the branches of the enormous tree, and the little jabuticaba berries were mad about being on the ground, held down by squishy stalks and leaning against the dirt. What they liked was being disguised. On the other hand, they were covered with dust. Still, they looked sick, sighing how they missed the old branches.

Frog watched the changes and went on giving her opinions.

"The oranges," she said, "I'd make them grow with a little knife inside. How many times have you had an orange in hand and nothing to peel it with?"

"It would be a lot better to make oranges blossom already peeled," Emília said. "Why do they need a skin? It's only good for getting your hands dirty with juice."

And that's what was done. All the oranges in the grove had to be naked. They were ashamed of themselves with their insides showing, and only on the lowest branches. The ground filled up with so many peels that Rabicó came over and sniffed around.

Little Froggy, who hadn't known the famous Marquis Rabicó, was delighted at the sight of him.

"Emília, he's so chubby and shiny! Is he still a marquis?"

"What to do?"Emília bawled. "A title's like a nickname: once it grabs someone, it never lets go. Not far from here there's an old Black guy, 70 years old, who has the nickname Tadinho, as in 'poor little guy.' Know why? Because when he was born, everybody called him Poor Little Guy. And so he was stuck with Tadinho his whole life, a Black guy of his size."

"But you, Emília, you seem like you no longer remember that you're a marquesa."

"Sometimes I remember, but with no pleasure whatsoever. What pleasure is there in being the marquesa of a marquis like him? You know what my dream is..."

"Yes–to be the woman of a great pirate, to command a ship. Why not get married to Captain Hook?"

"What a great idea!" Emília exclaimed. "No pirate can discourage people more than he. First, he doesn't have one arm, and now he doesn't have a ship, either. The Hyena of the Sea turned into the Hummingbird of the Waves, as you well know. And today he's just something for little Pedrinho. I wanted to marry one of those great pirates from the time of gold in Peru, the ones that attack Spanish galleons out at sea, with knives between their teeth. There's one, named Morgan, who would be good enough for me. I also thought about an underwater pirate, but I gave up. Being under water takes my breath away."

Rabicó only smelled the orange peels. He only liked peels with fruit inside.

"And Mocha the cow?" Frog asked. "Are you going to reform her, too?"

"Of course–and right now. Come on, let's go."

And off the two went to Mocha's pasture, where she was patiently chewing some corn cobs. They stood before her, hands on hips, discussing the reform.

"I would change the milk tank," Froggy said. "Put a faucet on her udder to avoid what happens now: to take out the milk, the farmer has to pull on her udder with his filthy hands. With the faucet system, his hands wouldn't touch the udder."

Emília let loose a delicious laugh.

"That's nuts! It's so easy to see that you're just a girl from Rio de Janeiro. Because don't you know that udders are for giving milk to baby calves? How's a baby calf going to suck milk from a spigot?"

"We'll teach the calves to open the spigots."

"No,"Emília declared. "Too complicated. For Mocha I want some useful reforms just for her and not for people who exploit her. I'm going to put a tail on Mocha right in the middle of her back because the way the tail is now, it can reach only half her body. How's the poor cow supposed to wave off flies that land on her neck if her waver only reaches to her ribs? It's all wrong..."

And she planted Mocha's tail in the middle of her back, right where she'd be able to wave off flies from her whole body–north, south, east and west. And she moved the teats on the udder over to the sides, half on the left, half on the right.

"That way we can milk her on one side while the baby calf sucks milk on the other. Reforming isn't a game. It needs science."

"Great!" said Frog. "And we can put the spigots on the teats on the right side, for the milkers. The ones on the left can be as they are, for the calves to use."

Emília approved the idea. Then they moved on to think about the horns.

"Every respectable cow has horns," Emília said, "except this poor cow Mocha. I'm going to give her some long horns, but without sharp points."

Frog remembered that fencers use foils with a pad on the tip. They could give Mocha two pointed horns but with padded tips. Emília immediately perfected the idea.

"Instead of a pad, Frog, we can stick a soft rubber ball on the tips–a removable ball, that is, one that can be taken off at night."

"What for?"

"So she can defend herself against any nocturnal attack. Horns are her only defense, the poor thing."

"But what kind of nocturnal dangers are there around here?"

"Jaguars, my dear. Uncle Barnabé says that in a former life, Mocha was eaten by a jaguar. So during the day, Mocha can use the rubber balls because jaguars attack only at night."

And Mocha was armed with two splendid horns elegantly twisted like corkscrews, with two soft balls on the point–removable balls.

The hide of the cow also underwent reform. It became as sleek and iridescent as plush silk.

They were busy reforming Mocha when a beautiful blue butterfly flew overhead.

From

The Best Chronicles of Rubem Alves

Walking in the Morning

FOr the past two weeks I've been starting my days by committing theft. I don't know how to avoid this sin, and, to tell the truth, I don't want to avoid it. The guilt is from a mulberry tree. Disobeying the commandment of the wall that fences it in, it thrusts its branches over the sidewalk. Not satisfied, it loads them with fat, black, appetizing, tempting mulberries [in Portuguese, amoras] within reach of my hand. It seems that the fruits are, by vocation, invitations to theft: changing the order of a single letter is enough. I think that the case of the mulberry tree proves this linguistic thesis: Everything depends on a name. Because amora is a word which, if repeated several times, amoramoramoramora turns into amor–love. And isn't that what love is?–a desire to eat, a desire to be eaten. The wall, much like a commandment, says it is prohibited. But love is not contained. Cross-dressed as a mulberry, it jumps the fence. Thus it was in Paradise...

The few strollers passing by at that hour of the morning were perhaps surprised to see a man with white hair picking prohibited mulberries. But if they pay attention, they will see that the person who's there isn't a man of nearly seventy years. It's a boy. And since it was the son of God himself who said to enter the Kingdom of Heaven you need to return to childhood, I pick and eat mulberries with redoubled conviction. And just so no doubts remain about the theological inspiration of my deed, as I chew and the purple juice stains my fingers and mouth, I repeat the sacred words: "Eat and drink, this is my blood..." Ah! The divine mulberry, sacramental gift of grace! My day begins this way, stealing the magic fruit that works the miracle of everyone who dreams of returning to childhood.

Body and soul reinvigorated by this divine manna fallen from the skies, I continue along my morning walk. I walk no more than fifty steps and I'm under a long alameda of pines. On them there's no fruit for me to steal since they don't produce anything that can be eaten. Pines aren't for the mouth. They are gifts for the eyes. It's still early. The sun, just risen, illuminates their green needles, which shine like crystals. I am reminded of Le Corbusier, who said, "The essential joys are sun, space, and green." But the pines know more than the architect, and the joys of light feed the joys of smell. I breathe deeply and smell the aroma of resin.

If they ask me what I think, I answer with a line from the Tao: "The sound of water says what I think." I think the mulberries, I think the pine, I think the light of the sun, I think the smell of resin.

It's the season of *sibipiruna* tree blossoms. Green and yellow, they grow on both sides of the street where I walk, transforming it into a long, shady tunnel. During the night, their flowers fell, covering the sidewalk, turning it into a golden carpet. I step off the sidewalk and walk on the asphalt so to not tread on them. I am reminded of the mysterious voice that spoke to Moses from inside the burning bush: "Put off thy shoes from off thy feet, for the place whereon thou standest is holy ground."

To contemplate this spectacle, you have to get up early because soon the housewives and their brooms will take care of restoring the concrete to its cold cleanliness. This hurts me, and with the pain comes a thought. I ask myself about the perverse education that makes people become blind to the generous beauty of trees, treating their blossoms as if they were dirt. But the *sibipirunas*, indifferent to the blindness of humans and broom, will repeat the miracle during the night. Tomorrow the sidewalks will again be covered in gold.

I walk a bit more and come to the grove called the Bosque dos Alemães. It awaits me with another delight, the delight of the ears. An infinitude of birdsong mixes with the sound of leaves blown by the breeze. I am not alone. Many other people dedicated to the exercise of morning walks and runs keep me company. They are there in fear of dying before their time. It's necessary to exercise the heart. But it seems that's all they're exercising. But no matter how hard I try, I can't manage to see in their faces signs that they are also exercising the delight of their eyes, noses, and ears. They run and walk with eyes fixed on the ground, serious and focused, compelled by medical necessities. And for that reason they do not know how to see and hear, can't handle a stirring love affair unrolling before them. I'd been sensing romance for a while when I heard sighs came from on high. Up there, far from indiscreet eyes, a giant eucalyptus and a cork tree embrace. Their intertwined branches manifest the passion of lovers. I think they're making love because as the wind makes their bark rub against each other, they moan with pleasure...and pain.

I walk all morning. For medical reasons, it's true. But, even if they didn't exist, I'd walk the same way, with the light and joyful thoughts that nature makes me think. Nature is a good psychoanalyst, charging nothing for the dreams of love she makes us dream.

Popcorn

Cooking fascinates me. Once in a while I even dare to try it. But the fact is, I am more competent with words than with pots and pans. For that reason I've written more about cooking than actually cooking. I dedicate myself to something that could be called "literary culinary." I've written about a great variety of entities in the world of the kitchen: onions, ora-pro-nobis, chopped beef with tomato, rice and beans, cod, soufflés, soups, barbecue. I even reached the point of dedicating half of a philo-poetical book to a meditation on the film Babette's Feast, which is a celebration of food as a ritual of sorcery. Aware of my limitations and competences, I have never written as a chef. I wrote as a philosopher, poet, psychoanalyst, and theologian–because the culinary stimulates all those functions of thought.

Foods, for me, are dream entities. They stimulate my capacity to dream. At the same time, I never imagined that the day would come when popcorn would make me dream. But that's precisely what happened. Popcorn–dried corn, tough, rounded grains–always seemed to me a simple little joke, a delicious game, without metaphysical or psychoanalytical dimension. But a few days ago I was talking with a patient who mentioned popcorn. And something unexpected happened in my mind. My ideas began to pop like popcorn. Then I saw a metaphoric relationship between popcorn and the act of thinking. A good thought is born like an unexpected, unforeseen burst of popcorn. So popcorn revealed itself to me like an extraordinary poetic object. Poetic because as I thought about popcorn my thoughts started popping and jumping around like the kernels in the pot.

I remembered the religious meaning of popcorn. Popcorn has a religious meaning? For Christians, the sacraments are bread and wine, which symbolize the body and blood of Christ, a mixture of life and joy (because life, life alone, without joy, is not life...). Bread and wine should be taken together. Life and joy should exist together. So I am reminded of the lesson I learned with Mother Stella, the powerful Bahian candomblé wise-woman: that popcorn is a sacred candomblé food.

Popcorn is a withered, underdeveloped corn. If I were an ignorant farmer, and if some of these runty spigots appeared among my full-blown corn, I'd get mad and get rid of them. From the perspective of size, popcorn can't compete with normal corn. I don't know how this happened, but the fact is that someone had the idea of shucking the spigots and putting the kernels in a pan over a fire, expecting the kernels to get soft so they could be eaten. After the experiment with water failed, they tried with oil. What happened next, no one would ever have imagined. All of a sudden the kernels began to burst, jumping in the pan with an enormous noise. But the extraordinary thing was what happened to them: tough, tooth-breaking kernels turned into soft, white flowers that even children could eat. Thus the bursting of the kernels went from a simple culinary operation to a party, a game, foolishness that everyone, especially children, laughed at. It's very funny to see corn popping!

And what does this have to do with candomblé? It's that the transformation of hard corn into soft popcorn is a symbol of the great transformation that all people should go through so they can be what they ought to be. The popcorn kernel isn't all it ought to be. It ought to be that which happens after the pop. The kernel is us: hard tooth-breakers inappropriate for consumption. By the power of fire we can, all of a sudden, transform ourselves into something else. We can return to being children!

But the transformation takes place only under the force of fire. Kernels that don't pass through fire go on being kernels forever. That's what happens to people. The great transformations happen when we pass through fire. Whoever doesn't pass through fire remains the same their whole lives. They are people of a sameness and an astonishing hardness. It's just that they don't realize it. They think their way of being is the best way to be. But all of a sudden there's fire. Fire is when life thrusts us into a situation we never imagined. Pain. It could be fire from outside: to lose love, lose a child, get sick, lose a job, become poor. It could be fire from inside. Panic, fear, anxiety, depression–sufferings whose causes we do not know. There is always recourse in medicine. To put out the fire. Without fire, the suffering diminishes, and with it the possibility of transformation.

I imagine that the poor popcorn, closed up in a pot, thinking, as it gets hotter inside, that its time has come, that it's going to die. From inside its hard shell, closed up inside itself, it can't imagine any other end. It can't imagine the transformation that is being prepared. It doesn't imagine what it is capable of. Then, without warning, under the force of fire, the great transformation happens: Pop! And it looks like something else, something completely different, something it had never dreamed. It's the ugly, crawling caterpillar coming out of its cocoon as a flying butterfly.

In Christian symbology, the miracle of popcorn is represented by the death and resurrection of Christ. The resurrection is the popping of a kernel. You have to stop being one way to be another. "Die and transform yourself!" Goethe wrote.

In the state of Minas Gerais, everybody knows what *piruá* is. Talking about *piruás* with some people from the state of São Paulo, I discovered that they don't know what *piruás* are. Some even think I was kidding, that *piruá* is a nonexistent word. I found myself forced to check the *Aurélio* dictionary to confirm my knowledge of the language. A *piruá* is a popcorn kernel that has refused to pop. My friend William, an extraordinary research professor at Unicamp–the federal university at Campinas, São Paulo–who is a specialist in the area of corn, unveiled the wonder of popcorn popping. He certainly has a scientific explanation for *piruás*. But in the world of poetry, scientific explanations don't count. For example, in Minas Gerais, "*piruás*" is the name that they give to women who never marry. *Old maids*. My cousin, over forty, laments, "I've become a *piruá*!" but I think the metaphorical power of *piruás* is much greater. Old maids are those who refuse to change no matter how much they are scorched by fire. They think that there can be nothing more wonderful than the way they are. They ignore what Jesus said: "Whoever preserves their life loses it."

Their presumption and their fear are the hard shell of the kernel that doesn't pop. Their fate is sad. They will remain hard their entire lives. They won't give happiness to anyone. When the joyous popping is done, in the bottom of the pot remain the old kernels who were never good for anything. Their destiny is the trash.

As for the kernels that pop, they are adults who go back to being children and who know that life is a big game...

Mental Health

I was invited to give a lecture about mental health. The people who invited me supposed that I, as a psychoanalyst, ought to be a specialist in the subject. And I thought so, too. So much so that I accepted. But as soon as I stopped and thought about it, I regretted my decision. I saw that I didn't know anything. Let me explain.

I began my thoughts by making a list of people who, in my point of view, have had a rich and exciting mental life, people whose books and projects are food for my soul. Nietzsche, Fernando Pessoa, Van Gogh, Wittgenstein, Cecília Meireles, Vladimir Mayakovski. And then I was shocked. Nietzsche went crazy. Fernando Pessoa was given to drink. Van Gogh killed himself. Wittgenstein was happy to know he would die soon; he no longer tolerated living with such angst. Cecília Meirles suffered chronic light depression. Mayakovski committed suicide. All of them were profound, lucid people who will continue to be bread for the living long after we have been completely forgotten.

But did they have mental health? Mental health– that condition in which ideas behave themselves, always balanced, foreseeable, without surprises, obedient to the commands of duty, everything in its place like soldiers in rank order, never allowing the body to miss work or do something unexpected. It isn't necessary to take a trip around the world in a sailboat. It's enough to do what Shirley Valentine did. (If you haven't seen the film yet, do.) Or have a prohibited love affair, or, more dangerous than all of this, the courage to think what's never been thought. Thinking is a dangerous thing...

No, mental health they did not have. They were too lucid for that. They knew that the world is controlled by crazy old people in neckties. Being owners of power, the crazy go on to become the prototypes of mental health. Of course none of the names I cited would survive the tests that psychologists would have subjected them to if they were to look for employment in a company. On the other hand, I've never heard of a politician who had stress or depression. They always go parading around the streets of town, passing out smiles and certainties.

I feel like my thoughts are the thoughts of a crazy person, so let me hurry on to some obligatory clarifications.

We are very much like computers. The function of the computer, as everybody knows, requires the interaction of two parts. One of them is called hardware, literally the hard equipment, and the other is called software. The hardware consists of all the solid things that the appliance is made of. The software is made up of "spiritual" entities–symbols that form the programs and are recorded on discs. We, too, have hardware and software. The hardware are the nerves of the brain, the neurons–everything that makes up the nervous system. The software is made up of a series of applications that are recorded in our memory. Just as in computers, what remains in the memory are symbols, gossamer-light entities that could be said to be "spiritual," the most important application being language. A computer can go crazy through a flaw in its hardware or its software. So can we. When our hardware goes crazy, we call in the psychiatrists and neurologists, who come in with their chemical potions and scalpels to fix what went bad. When the problem is in our software, however, potions and scalpels don't work. You can't fix an application with a screwdriver. Since software is made of symbols, only symbols can get into it. To deal with software, you have to make use of symbols. For that reason, whoever deals with disturbances in human software never sees anything good in physical resources. Their tools are words, and they may be poets, humorists, clowns, writers, gurus, friends, or even psychoanalysts. It happens, though, that this computer that is the human body has a peculiarity that differentiates it from others. Its hardware, the body, is sensitive to things that the software produces. And isn't that what happens to us? We hear a song and we cry. We read Drummond's erotic poems and the body gets excited. Imagine a sound system. Imagine that the record player and accessories, the hardware, had the capacity to hear the music that it played and to be emotionally moved. And imagine that the beauty is so great that the hardware doesn't behave and breaks down with emotion! Well that's what happened with those people I cited at the beginning. The music that came out of their software was so beautiful that their hardware couldn't stand it. Given these theoretical presuppositions, we are now in a position to offer a recipe that will guarantee, for those who accept the risk, mental health until the end of their days. Opt for modest software. Avoid beautiful and emotionally moving things. Beauty is dangerous to hardware. Be careful with music. Brahms and Mahler are especially contraindicated. Rock can be taken at will. As for readings, avoid those that make you think. There is a vast literature specializing in impeding thought. If there are books by Dr. Lair Ribeiro, why risk reading Saramago? Newspapers have the same effect. They should be read daily. Since they publish the same things every day with different names and faces, it is guaranteed that our software will always think the same things. And on Sundays, don't forget Silvio Santos and Gugu Liberato. Following this recipe, you will have a banal but tranquil life. But since you have cultivated insensibility, you will not sense how banal it is. And instead of reaching the end that the people I mention reached, you will retire to realize your dreams. Unfortunately, however, when you arrive at that moment, you will have forgotten what they were.

On Politics and Gardening

Of all the vocations, politics is the most noble. Vocation: from the latin vocare, "calling." Vocation is an inner call of love. Not love for a man or woman but for a thing-to-be-done. This thing-to-be-done marks the place where the called want to make love with the world. There, in the place of their thing-to-be-done, they want to penetrate, ejaculate, fecundate. Psychology of the lover: to do without wishing to gain. To do even if their thing-to-be-done puts them in danger. Many lovers have died because of ephemeral moments of pleasure with a prohibited love.

Political vocation is a passion for a garden. Let me explain. "Politics" comes from *polis*, city. A city was, for the Greeks, a safe place, orderly and tame, where men could dedicate themselves to the pursuit of happiness. Political vocation, then, is at the service of citizens' happiness, the happiness of people in the city.

To the contrary of the Greeks, for the Hebrews this living space was not represented by the city. God did not create a city, he created a garden. Their God was not an urbanist; he was a gardener, an inventor of paradises. Perhaps it was by the fact that they'd been nomads in the desert. Those who live in a desert dream of oases. So the garden, for the Hebrews, was that which the *polis* was for the Greeks. If we asked a Hebrew prophet "What is politics?" he would respond, "The art of gardening applied to public things."

Vocational politicians are in love with a big garden that's for everyone. Their love is so great that they give up the little garden that they could till for themselves. What good is a little garden if all around you is a desert? The whole desert needs to be turned into a garden.

I love my vocation, which is to write. But I know that the beauty of literature is weak. A little poem by Emily Dickenson:

To make a prairie, it takes a clover and a bee,
One clover, and a bee.
And reverie.
The reverie alone will do,
If bees are few.

It would be good if it were true. But the fact is, fantasies aren't enough to plant gardens. To turn into gardens, fantasies need bees: hands, tools, power. But power is what the poet does not have. But the politicians do. Politicians by vocation are poets with power. They have the power to dig, plant, care for, pull up, prune, make walls. Politicians make laws and take measures for them to be obeyed. The nobility of the political vocation is in that it has the power to transform the dream of a garden into a real garden where life takes place.

It is such a pleasing vocation that Plato suggested that politicians do not need to possess anything as private property. It doesn't make sense to have a private garden when you're the gardener of the big garden. For that reason it would be undignified for the gardener to have a privileged space better or different than the space occupied by everyone else. Laws for the politician are laws for everyone. I know, and have known, many vocational politicians. Their lives were and continue to be a reason for hope.

Vocation is different from profession. In a vocation, the person finds happiness in the act itself. In a profession, pleasure is found not in the act but in the gain derived. The professional who is only professional does his *thing-to-be-done* not for the love of it but for the love of something outside of it: the salary, the gain, the profit, the advantage. People motivated by vocation are lovers. Professionals, to the contrary, don't love their lovers; they use them for their own advantage. They are gigolos.

All vocations can be turned into professions. Prophets are followed by mercenaries. Gardeners by vocation give their lives to everyone else's garden. Gardeners by profession use everyone else's garden to build their own garden even though, for this to happen, the desert and the suffering around them must increase.

Thus it is with politics. There are many professional politicians. So therefore I utter my second thesis: Of all the professions, professional politics is the most vile. This explains people's total disenchantment with politics. No one believes what politicians say.

Guimarães Rosa, asked by Günter Lorenz whether he considered himself political, responded:

I could never be a politician with all the charlatanism of reality... Politicians are always talking about reason, logic, reality, and things like that and at the same time practicing the most irrational acts imaginable. Unlike "legitimate" politicians, I believe in mankind and I wish us a future. The politician thinks only in minutes. I am a writer, and I think in eternities. I think about the resurrection of man.

Anyone who think in minutes doesn't have the patience to plant trees. A tree takes many years to grow. It is much more profitable to cut them down.

Our future depends on a struggle between politicians by vocation and politicians by profession. The sad thing is that many who feel the calling of politics do not have the courage to attend to it in fear of the shame of having to get along with gigolos. I'm one—but now it's too late.

I speak to you, the young, to seduce you into becoming gardeners. Maybe there's a dormant politician inside you (like in the story of *Sleeping Beauty*). Hearing the vocation is hard because it is disturbed by the noise of the expected choices: teaching, medicine, engineering, computing, law, science. All of them are legitimate if they are vocations. But they are all funneling: They all put you into a little corner of the garden that's far from the place where the fate of the garden is decided. Wouldn't it be a lot more fascinating to take part in the fate of the garden?

We recently celebrated 500 years since the discovery of Brazil. The discoverers, when they arrived, didn't find a garden. They found a jungle. A jungle isn't a garden. Jungles are cruel and insensitive, indifferent to suffering and death. A jungle is a part of nature still not touched by the hand of man. That jungle could have been transformed into a garden. It hasn't been. The politicians that attended to it were not lovers. They were woodchoppers. Gigolos. And that's how the jungle, which could have been turned into a garden for the happiness of all, was transformed into deserts flecked with luxurious private gardens where a few found life and pleasure.

There are discoveries of origins. More beautiful are discoveries of destinies.

So maybe, if the politicians of vocation take possession of the garden, we can begin to write a new history that does not repeat the past but a history that celebrates the future. But this can only happen if the woodchoppers are thrown out and replaced by gardeners. So instead of deserts and private gardens we would have a big garden for everyone,. It would be the work people who loved to plant trees in whose shade they would never sit and who would feed themselves with food that birds brought from the future (Nietzsche). We would have the happiness of seeing men, women and children living and playing in a garden...

From
Tender Returns, by Rubem Alves

Love Letters

I should believe it or doubt it. If I believe, I doubt. I doubt because I believe. Because it was he himself who said–or better, his other person, Fernando Pessoa–that he was a pretender. "All love letters are ridiculous. They wouldn't be love letters if they weren't ridiculous..."

In my office I have a reproduction of one of the most delightful paintings that I know of. *Woman in Blue Reading a Letter*, by Johannes Vermeer (1632-1675). A woman, standing, reads a letter. Her face is lit by the light of a window. Her eyes read what is written on that piece of paper that her hands hold, her mouth slightly open, almost in a smile. She's so absorbed that she doesn't even notice the chair at her side. She reads on foot. I think I'm capable of reconstructing the moments that preceded the one that the painter froze. Knocks at the door interrupt the household routine. She opens the door, and there's the mailman with a letter in his hand. By simply reading her name on the envelope, she knows who sent it. She takes the letter, and with that gesture she touches a distant hand. That's why love letters are written. Not to give news, not to tell anything, not to repeat things already known, but so that hands far apart touch each other by touching the same sheet of paper. Barthes cites these words of Goethe:

> Why do I see myself once gain compelled to write? It isn't necessary, my dear, to ask such an obvious questions because, in truth, I have nothing to tell you. However, your hands will receive this paper...

I return to Álvaro de Campos. Could this be the cause of the ridiculousness of love letters–the mismatch between what they say and that which they really want to do? Because the explicit purpose of a letter is to give news, and that's why they are made up of words. But what they really mean to accomplish is always above and beyond the written word. They want to accomplish that which separation prevents–a hug. Anyone who wants to try to understand a love letter through an analysis of the writing will always be off the mark because what it contains is that which isn't there, that which is absent. With any love letter, what matters isn't what's found written in it, only talk of desire, of the pain of absence, the longing to meet again.

That letter made everything stop. The woman closed the door and walked through the house without seeing anything, just looking for one thing, light, a place where the words would be illuminated. What difference does a chair make to her? She forgot that she's pregnant. Her eyes go over the words that came from the same hands that had hugged her. Her body is suspended in that magic moment of impossible affection that that little piece of paper opened in the time of her daily life.

A love letter is a paper that connects two lonelinesses. The woman is alone. If there are other people in the house, she's left them behind. It could very well be that the things written in the letter are no secret, that they can be told to everyone. But for it to be a love letter, it has to be read in solitude. As if the lover were saying, "I write so that you can be alone..." It is this act of solitary reading that establishes complicity.

Because it was in loneliness that the letter was born. The love letter is an object the lover creates so the abandonment is tolerable.

I look at the sky. I see Alpha Centauri. The astronomers tell me that the star I see now is that star that was two years ago. Because that's the time that the light took to get to my eyes. What I see is that which no longer exists. And it would be useless for me to ask myself, "How is it now? Does it still exist?" I can get answers to these questions only two years from now, when its light reaches me. Its light is always late. I always see that which has already been... In this way letters are like stars. The letter that the woman has in her hands, which defines her moment of solitude, belongs to a moment that no longer exists. It says nothing about the present of the distant lover. Thus her pain. The lover who writes extends his arms to a moment that does not yet exist. The lover who reads extends her arms to a moment that no longer exists. The love letter is an embrace of space...

"It's good the phone exists," retort modern lovers who no longer have to live love in the space of absences. Mistake. A telephone call isn't a spoken letter because it lacks the essential. The silence of solitude, the calm of the pen poised over the table, waiting for and choosing thoughts and words. The telephone does away with solitude. In a telephone call we never say that which we would say in a letter. For example: "I was walking down the street when all of a sudden I saw a blossoming pink *ipê* tree that made me remember that time when...." Or "Re-reading Neruda's poems I found this one which I imagine you would like to read...."

The difference between a letter and a telephone is simple. The telephone is an imposition. The conversation has to happen right then. It lacks the essential element of the word that is said without expecting a response. And once it's over, the two lovers are left with empty hands.

But the woman has in her hands a letter. The letter is an object. If she had not been able to take it into her solitude, she would have been able to put it away in her pocket in the delicious expectancy of an opportune moment. A telephone call can't wait. The letter is patient. It stores its words. And after being read, it can be re-read. Or simply caressed. A letter against the face–could anything be as loving? A letter is more than a message. Even before being read, even inside its closed envelope, it has the quality of a sacrament: a palpable presence of invisible happiness...

These thoughts came to me after reading the letters of a young scientist, Albert Einstein, to his girlfriend, Mileva Maric. It was they that led me to the poem by Álvaro de Campos. They were ridiculous. All love letters are ridiculous. I think the editors thought the same. And as an excuse for their indiscreet act of making public something ridiculous that was a secret between two lovers, they wrote a long and erudite introduction that transformed the ludicrous love letters into documents of the history of science. They were worth something because, mixed in with the ridiculousness the lovers fed each other the editors found trails that give historians keys for the understanding of "the sources of the emotional and intellectual development of the correspondents." Not knowing what to do with (ridiculous) love, they put the letters into the archeology of science.

It was then that Vermeer's painting had me see the scene that letters hide. And the woman with a letter in her hand and a child in her womb? She might very well be Mileva, pregnant with an illegitimate daughter that was given up for adoption and about whom nothing is known. The child was given up. But the letters were kept. And for what reasons might a person have to keep ridiculous letters? Her absorbed face and half-open lips give us an answer. For those who love, ridiculous love letters are always sublime. I return to Álvaro de Campos's poem and therein find what was needed to finish the scene: “but in the end, the only ridiculous things are creatures who have never written love letters.”

Bullshit and Politics

One look was enough to know he was up to something... His face was that of a mature man, but his shifty smile said that inside resided a brat who had just committed some kind of art...art in both senses: the artifice of a brat and the creation of an artist. Because that’s what he was. In the end, there isn’t a whole lot of difference between the two.

The brat as much as the artist does what reality does not allow. I remained quiet, waiting to hear what he had to say.

“I have been contracted to decorate a space. I walked around, looking up, waiting for inspiration to come to me from on high. But one who looks up doesn’t see where he’s going. As a result, I stepped in a cow pie. I got mad. My boot sunk into that malodorous green pasta. But my anger soon passed as my eyes discovered delicate details in that work that an unpleasant contraction at the end of a ruminant’s alimentary canal had produced without needing any special inspiration.

“I looked around and found similar works already dried in the sun, which allowed for a more detailed inspection–to the point of actual manipulation with no great danger. And thus I was crouched in scatological contemplation of the aesthetics of cow shit when inspiration came to me... In a fraction of a second I saw the work of art I was going to produce.

"I collected a pile of the most beautiful bovine turds, carefully took them to my atelier (there was always the danger of such fragile things to break). I spray-painted them gold and tied them together with clear nylon string. I turned them into mobiles that floated in space...

"People came along and stopped, looked and were enchanted. 'Such lightness,' they said in admiration. Then they asked me about the technique I used in fabricating those golden metallic discs. But of course I didn't say anything. I kept my secret..."

And he fell down laughing. And so did I.

A laugh is a sudden ejaculation of joy. And it happens when the unexpected appears before us and trips us up. Every good joke-teller knows this. The punchline has to be an ending that no one was expecting. It's the unexpected wit that makes the body explode in laughter.

A laugh reveals one of the secrets of the soul. The soul doesn't like to march. In a march, everything is equal, predictable, done in a military parade. The soul is a ballerina that likes most to dance. And that's why, in its original state (and this is the lesson that psychoanalysis teaches us), the soul is a playful child. It's a sorceress who delights in the most unheard-of and prohibited transformations. It's a poet who writes, and the world is never the same. It's a clown who laughs because the world is so much like a circus...

And that's what my friend was at that moment: a boy, an artist, a dancer, a clown, a sorcerer who puts a bull flop on his hat and, abracadabra, the hat turns into floating gold. This was the secret that the alchemists wanted to discover. But, poor things, they were looking in the wrong place, in complicated laboratories without knowing that anyone can make this magic happen.

It's been a while since that happened, but all of a sudden I recalled (nice word, that one, wanting to say "call again" that which has been kept in the heart...). Because it was children who made me go back to the heart, children and adolescents, kids going somewhere, singing and following the song. I never imagined that I would ever see this again, black clothes, the color of mourning, gloomy and harsh, feces, excrement, who could it be who made them dress this way: But their faces spoke otherwise, faces painted, joy, hope, jokes, laughs...

Sometimes very strong magic is needed to awaken Sleeping Beauty! Sometimes you need a lot of shit to make the unconscious soul awaken from its sleep and say, "This is not what I am! I am Beauty! I am a golden floating mobile! I am a flower!"

In no way similar to political parties with their flags, their erected fingers, their rasping throats, their mottos and commands, the outpourings of youth were pure explosions of life, laughs, ejaculations of joy before the unexpected, the unexpected being that Beauty still exists despite the malodorous excrement leaving the end of the insatiable alimentary canal of the powerful.

Neruda said once that poets (those bad politicians) began the happiness revolution. So I think that this is what the young are proclaiming: that in the middle of shit (pardon this word, but no other does justice to the reality!) it is possible for a flower to sprout. Because, as everyone knows, cow shit, after composting for a while, is good manure. We can make a garden with the excrement of the powerful....

On Princes and Frogs

Many, many years ago, before asphalt, when the Fernão Dias Highway was either a sea of dust or a sea of mud, trips were adventures. I lived in a rural area of Minas Gerais, and the way to come to Campinas to see my girlfriend was to arrange a ride in some truck. One of those times the driver, delicately, to begin a conversation that promised to be very long, asked me, "What do you do?" I could have answered simply, 'I'm a professor." This he would understand perfectly well since he had gone to schools, knew a lot about professors, and would have gone on to tell about his accomplishments in arithmetic and his difficulties with his native tongue. But I, foolish and inexperienced, and to give myself an air of importance, answered, "I am a professor of philosophy..." The driver's face lit up in a wide smile. "At last," he said. "For so many years I've been wanting to know what philosophy is and until today I haven't found anyone who can explain it to me. But today I have the fortune of having a professor of philosophy as a travel mate. Today I will have the explanation. When you come right down to it, what is philosophy?

I have no memory whatsoever of what I told him in my useless explanation. But his smile comes back to me whenever I reveal to someone that I am a psychoanalyst. Because inevitably the same question comes up: "What is a psychoanalyst?" The wisest ones, who have already heard of or read about the subject, dispense with introductions and go on to examine the issues. "And what line do you follow?" It makes me want to say I prefer curved lines to straight lines–which would not be faithful to the spirit of psychoanalysis, where the curve is always the shortest distance between two points. but I know they would not understand because what they want to know is whether I am a Freudian, Kleinian, Bionian, Jungian, Lacanian, etc. It so happens that's not my way. Preferring curved lines to straight lines, I follow the counsel of Guimarães Rosa: I only give answers to questions that no one ever asked. So, half in an oriental style, half in an evangelical style, I tell a story:

"Once upon a time there was a prince with a wonderful voice who sang to all the creatures that would listen to him. His song was so beautiful that he even seduced the witch who lived in the black forest and with whom he, too, fell in love. But, different from the other listeners, who felt happy just to listen, she decided to sing, too. What a lovely duet we will make, she thought. And she set herself to singing. As it happens, however, witches never manage to sing very well. As soon as she opened her mouth, the most bizarre sounds came forth. They soared like the toads and frogs. The booing was everywhere. The witch filled with crazed envy and cast on him the most terrible of spells: If I cannot sing as you sing, then I will have you sing as I sing! And the prince was turned into a toad. Ashamed of his new form, he fled and hid in the bottom of a swamp, where he lived with the toads and frogs. In every way he looked like the batrachians. Except for one thing. He continued to sing as beautifully as ever. But now the ones who didn't like the singing of the new toad were the toads and frogs who only knew how to croak. The new song soared around their ears like something from another world, which disturbed the harmony of their monotone marsh. They sternly warned him, whoever lives with frogs and toads must croak like frogs and toads. The toad-prince stopped singing and had no other choice: he had to learn to croak as all the others did. And he repeated it so much that he ended up forgetting songs of the past. No, no...he didn't forget... Because when he slept, he remembered and heard the old, prohibited music singing inside him. But when he awoke, he forgot. But not everything. He had an undefinable longing.

Longing for he didn't know what. Longing that told him that he was far, far away from home..."

That is a summary of psychoanalysis, as I understand it. It's a story that is mixed with love, beauty, and spells of forgetting. Do you feel fooled? You were expecting famous names, complicated concepts–and instead I told a fairy tale. Words to put children to sleep, they said. But I reply: It's to make adults wake up.... Psychoanalysis is a struggle to break the spell of the bad word that puts us to sleep and makes us forget the beautiful melody. It's an attentive listen to a song that can be heard only in the intervals of silence in the croaking of frogs, and that comes to us like fleeting little disconnected fragments. It's a battle to make us retake the destiny written in the depths of the sea of the soul.

I've read the classics. But it was from the words of anonymous tellers of stories of enchantment and of the enchantment of the word of poets in which dead words become living things. Fernando Pessoa tells these secrets of body and soul better than I. Read these lines. But read slowly. Read them again. He is speaking of our mystery. It is our mystery that he invokes:

Cease your song!
Cease, for, while I listened,
I have heard another voice
coming as if in interstices
of the soft charm
as if your song came to us.
I heard you and heard it
at the same time and different
to sing together.
And the song that wasn't,
if now remembering it, makes me cry.

And he asks:

Was it your enchantment voice which,
unwilling, at this vague moment
awakened some alien being that spoke to us?

Could that be it? Some other being lives inside us? In the interstices of croaking, a song? What other being is that?

What angel, as you raise your voice,
without your knowing,
comes down over this earth where the soul wanders,
and with his wings fans the embers of an unknown hearth?
Living inside us an other who does not forget our truth...

Some think that psychoanalysis and poetry are the stuff of the insane. There's even a saying: *Everyone has a grain of the poet and the insane.* The toads and the frogs, hearing the songs of the poet prince, must have said: *He's a poet! He's crazy!* And tried to cure him, educating him on reality. For them, to be normal is to croak as everybody else croaks. But the soul, in the middle of the noisy monotone of life, continues to heave a voice in the intervals. It continues to cry when it hears a melody that wasn't there. It continues to hear the talk of an alien that lives within us and visits us in our dreams.

He continues to be burned by the embers of longing for a forgotten hearthstone from which we are exiled.

It is quite possible that toads and frogs live more tranquilly. For them, all the issues have been resolved.

But there is a happiness that resides only in beauty. And this we find only in the song that soars, forgotten and repressed in the bottom of the soul.

Love's Reasons

Mystics and those in love agree that love has no reason. Medieval mystic Ângelus Silésius said that it's like a rose: "The rose has no why. It blooms because it blooms."

Carlos Drummond repeated the same thing in his poem "The Non-reasons of Love." It's possible that it had been inspired by these same verses without his ever having read them since the causes of love are blowing in the wind. "I love you because I love you..."–non-reasons... "You don't need to be a lover or ever know how to be one."

My love does not depend on what you do for me. It doesn't grow from what you give me. If it were that way, it would flow with the power of your acts. It would have reason and explanation. If some day I no longer have your gestures of love, it would die like a flower plucked from the earth.

"Love is a state of grace and is not paid with love." There is nothing more false than the popular Brazilian saying that "love is paid with love." Love isn't transacted with the logic of commercial exchange. I don't owe you anything. You don't owe me anything. Just as the rose blooms because it blooms, I love you because I love you.

"Love is given gratis. It is sown in the wind, in the waterfall, in the eclipse. Love escapes the dictionaries and various regulations... Love is not exchanged... Because love is love-nothing, happy and strong in itself."

Drummond had to have been in love to write those lines. Only people in love believe that love is that way, so without reasons. But I, perhaps for not being in love (which is a shame...), I suspect that my heart has regulations and dictionaries, and Pascal would support me because it was he who said that "the heart has reasons that reason itself does not know." It's not that the heart lacks reasons but that its reasons are written in an unknown language. Drummond himself was aware of these reasons written in a strange language and asked himself: "How can I decipher pictograms of ten thousand years ago if I don't know how to decipher my own interior? The essential truth is the unknown that resides in me and each morning punches me."

Could that be love–a punch from the unknown?

To the person in love, the deciphering of this language is prohibited because if he understands it, the love will go away. Like in the story of Bluebeard: if the prohibited door is open, happiness is lost. That was how paradise was lost: when love–that fragile soap bubble– not content with its unconscious happiness, lets itself get bitten by the desire to know. Love doesn't know its happiness can exist only in ignorance of its reasons. Kierkegaard commented on the absurdity of asking lovers for explanations for their love. To that question they have only one answer: silence. But if asked to talk about their love without explaining it, they will talk for days without stopping...

But, as I've said, I am not in love. I look on love with suspicious eyes. I want to decipher its unknown language. Contrary to Drummond, I seek the hundred reasons for love...

I go to St. Augustine in search of wisdom. I re-read his Confessions, the text of an old man meditating over love without being in love. Possibly there one can find the most penetrating analysis of the reasons for love that has ever been written. And he confronts me with a question that no one who's in love would ever ask. "What is it that I love when I love my God?" Imagine if a person in love asked that question about his or her lover: "What is it that I love when I love you?" It might be the end of a love story. Because this question reveals a secret that no lover could ever stand: that to love the beloved, the lover is loving something that is not beloved. In the words of Hermann

Hesse, "What we love is always a symbol." He concludes the impossibility of focusing your love on anything on earth.

Variations on the impossible question: I love you, yes, but it isn't actually you I love. I love some other mysterious thing that I don't know but which I seem to see flowing on your face. I love you because in your body some other thing is revealed. Your body is a lake where reflections swim like fugitive fish... Like Narcissus , I stand before it... "In the depth of your aqueous light my eyes swim in search..." (Cecília Meireles). That's why I love you, because of the enchanted fish...

But they are slippery, the fish. They flee. They get away. They hide. They make fun of me. They slip between my fingers. I embrace you to embrace that which flees me. When I have you, I'm happy in the illusion of having it. You are the place where I meet that other thing which, by pure grace, without reasons, came down over you as the Wind descended over the Blessed Virgin. But, by being grace, without reasons, in the same way that it came down, it can go away again. If that happens, I will give up loving you. And my search will begin anew...

That is the pain that no one in love can tolerate. Passion refuses to know that the face of the beloved (present) only suggests the dark objective of desire (absent). "Love begins as a metaphor," says Milan Kundera. "Or better: love begins at the moment in which a woman inscribes herself with a word in our poetic memory."

Now we have the key to understanding love's reasons: love is born, lives, and dies by the delicate power of the poetic image that lovers think they see in the face of the beloved...

From

On Time and Eternity, by Rubem Alves

Soufflé Time

Our subject today is cooking. I have chosen the gastronomic topic soufflé.

Soufflés can be made with practically anything. There are soufflés of asparagus, cheese, chayote, shrimp, banana, chocolate, salmon, strawberry, ham, carrot, and so on. This variety of soufflés owes itself to the fact that that which characterizes a soufflé isn't the thing it's made of but the ethereal, pneumatic substance that goes into all of them.

I found it strange, then, that that substance, the soul of the soufflé, never gets mentioned in cookbooks that I look through. I went to the famous *New York Times Cookbook* to see if it said something about the soul of soufflés. I read the recipe for "cheese soufflé." The necessary ingredients are listed: butter, flour, milk, salt, Worcestershire sauce, Jamaica peppers, shredded cheese, eggs. Only. But the soul of the soufflé, which which it cannot be made, isn't mentioned. Dona Benta's book is no better. See the recipe for "cod soufflé: cod, potatoes, milk, eggs, parmesan cheese, butter, seedless raisons, and olives. Again, total silence on the soul of the soufflé.

The word soufflé, for those who don't know, come from the French. Soufflé comes from the word *souffler*, "to blow." The soul of the soufflé is the air. The pneumatic and spiritual qualities, in that "souffler"–wind and spirit–are etymologically the same thing. If it weren't for the snobbish craze of finding the French word more elegant, if the soufflé had been invented in Minas Gerais, for sure the word for it would be *assoprado,* or "blown." Chayote blown, shrimp blown, asparagus blown, etc. Which should not be shocking in that, according to what it says in cookbook *Fogão de Lenha* [wood-fired cook stove], which records some 300 years of cooking in Minas Gerais, there was some kind of sweet called "Little Blown Girls, what was made of beaten egg whites, three ponds of sugar, an ounce of bitters, a little carmine. If there are Little Blown Girls, there must also be "Blowns" of the housewife, too.

If you aren't convinced, remember that the essential element of in the making of a soufflé are the whites of the eggs, beaten until stiff. But what is the purpose of these egg whites? It's obvious and simple: the whites are nets for catching air. The circular-rotational whipping motion of the fork beating the whites is the same as the motion of a fisherman throwing his net to catch fish. But here, what you want to catch is the air, which egg whites do well that they go from the consistency of goo to that of foam: thousands of little transparent bubbles, each one of them with a tiny bit of air stuck inside.

From this pneumatic and spiritual quality of the soufflé comes it essential characteristic: the soufflé is fffffluffffy. You can't say ffffffluffffy without blowing air through your lips. Webster's dictionary defines soufflé as a *fluffy* baked dish.

This pneumatic characteristic of the soufflé, which is its glory, is, unfortunately, also its weakness. Because everything that is full of air, such as balls and balloons, turns mushy and empty at the most minute puncture. It's what happens to the poor soufflé. It has to be eaten as soon as it comes out of the oven because its erection is precarious. If it cools down or gets hit by a puff of cold air, it suffers a seizure: first, a slight tremor, then vertical and horizontal movements–6.5 on the

Richter scale–there's a cry for help, and the golden-brown blush on the surface suddenly sinks to the bottom of the form.

I remember when this happened once in my house. I was a boy. We had guests for dinner. Astolfina, our cook, prepared a wonderful soufflé. But it got hit by a waft of cold air and turned mushy. Astolfina was desperate. She decided it would be worth heroic measures. She went into the back yard and cut a hollow papaya twig and carefully threaded it into the soufflé, the same way one inserts the pin of an air pump into a ball. And she blew softly. The soufflé seemed to resuscitate, filling up again, becoming as beautiful as it had been. But as soon as she extracted the twig, the soufflé fell back down. There is no way to fix a sunken soufflé.

As a patient of mine once said, thinking about the fate of women, "It's like a soufflé. Doctors say that menopause is climacteric. I say its soufflé time. Until then, the flesh behaved itself with relative elegance. The power of air gave it lightness and held it up. But all of a sudden, the forces of the Earth become stronger, and everything that floated in the air begins to weigh down. And it falls. I don't need to name the parts that fall nor describe their flaccid and mushy condition."

I had to bow before that powerful metaphor. But I thought to myself, "What about men? Is there a soufflé time for them, too?"

Soufflé time is the time for generalized panic, like Astolfina's, everyone trying to use a papaya twig to raise up what has fallen. Diets, seaweed creams, turtle soap, hair dye, skin cleansing, gyms, plastic surgery, girdles, acupuncture, prosthetics...

All futile. There is no way to refill a sunken soufflé. The little straw always fails. All you can do is laugh when it falls. And it's good to know that the fallen soufflé, even though it isn't as beautiful as the other, if served with spices and humor and laughter, it is quite delicious.

On Male Sexuality (II)

The ferocious North American feminists say that the idea of a father God, masculine, is an invention of men, with the purpose of making women submissive to the phallus. For that reason they are trying to change the sex of God. For them, God isn't a god; she's a goddess.

I'll sign that petition. I think they have total reason. The divine powers that decide the fates of men must be feminine. If the divine powers were masculine, they would not allow the evils that are done to men. All one has to do is assess the asymmetry between men and women to see that humble situation of the men.

Men, fooled by the fantasy that they have something that women lack, don't take into account their own fragility. And, in an incomprehensible blindness to anatomic and physiological facts, they say that they "eat" women. Pure error. To eat is an act in which something is put into the mouth, the mouth being an empty orifice that extracts from the referred-to object, through rhythmic movements, its substance and juices. Now, the anatomy is clear: it's the woman who is the empty orifice that receives the male object, which in the end appears mushy and drained. Woman is mouth: man is fruit. In the end, the only thing left is the peel of the orange. At the end of every sexual act, the man loses his penis. The woman, on the other hand, eats and grows fat. Psychoanalysis customarily says that women suffer from a "castration complex" because something is missing. Totally wrong. The ones who suffer this pain are the men. They are the ones who lose the penis at the end of the sexual act. With what they don't have, women can have as many of what the men have as they want. In the words of Norman O.

Brown, what happens with the penis is a crowning followed by decapitation.

The second asymmetry is another punishment from the goddesses. On a par with anatomo-functional asymmetry, the goddess imposes on man a punishment of honesty. He can't hide it or pretend. He can't, by rational decision, give his penis an order. The penis has its own ideas. It doesn't obey, it just does what it pleases.

It's different for women. She doesn't run the risk of humiliation. By means of a rational decision, she can have a relationship with the person she loves. She can pretend, and the other will never know. Maybe the greatest pleasure in a sexual relationship is the pleasure of being the object of someone else's pleasure. "Someone desires me. I can satisfy that desire." Babette, marvelous cook, took no pleasure in eating the food that she prepared. She only tasted it. Her pleasure was in giving pleasure. This is as valid for eating at the table as for eating in bed. And the woman is like Babette. She can give pleasure whenever she wishes. That can't happen with a man.

The venerable St. Augustine stated, in his *De Civitate Dei*, that this was the primary punishment that divinities inflicted on man: they separated the penis from reason so that at inappropriate moments the former would set itself to doing things it shouldn't, and at appropriate moments to not do what it should. That's why the gods, feeling sorry for man, covered them with clothes: to hide their shame. And is there anything more shameful than a penis numb to the desire of a woman? Zorba said that that was the only sin for which man would go to Hell. St. Augustine concluded that the ideal would be for the male organ to function the same way the finger functions, moving without ever disobeying, as ordered by reason. To which every man ever born or to be born says, "Amen!"

Then comes the fantasy of "her being just too much sand for my little truck." Of course there's always the recourse of making two trips. But the asymmetry continues. In culinary terms, my food is too little for her hunger." In technical terms: "I, as an object of desire, am too small for her desire." And women are the first to speak out on the enormous size of their desire. Adélia Prado said, "For my desire, the sea is but a drop." Ah! So then men need to be gods to satisfy this oceanic desire!

So men start to fear women's desire. "Better a woman with no desire. For if she has no desire, I won't go through the humiliation of not being able to satisfy it." For that reason men of generations past want virgin brides, not for reasons of religious purity, but to prevent the possibility of comparison. Men can't stand imagining that the desire of their beloved, which he can't satisfy, could be satisfied by someone else. Hence the terror of a woman's infidelity. No, don't be fooled. The wound isn't from being without her; the pain isn't the loss of her. The greater pain, intolerable, is narcissism. For "to be unfaithful to me and abandon me, she is proclaiming to the four winds my incapacity to satisfy her desire: she reveals the secret of my incompetence." What will be intolerable to the man isn't the absence of his woman but the looks of his peers–men. Sexual identity is also defined "homosexually" through its confirmation by others of the same sex. "My masculinity should be recognized not only by the woman but also by my peers." Saunas are still sanctuaries of recognition. But if the woman doesn't have desire, the man will be protected from this horrible metaphysical danger. Virginity, the excision of the clitoris practiced by some African tribes, sexual indifference, and, at its most extreme, crimes of passion, are means of possessing a woman through the destruction of her desire. "A woman without desire is always mine."

The brute appearance, the muscles sculpted by weightlifting, the tales of sexual prowess, the visual productions in accordance with male standards–all of these are tricks of a fearful being before the fascinating mystery of women. "So weak, so fragile–and still, it is before her that I will be exposed. It will be she who expose whether I am the food that can end her hunger." Those who do not feel anxiety are those who don't understand, like dogs: they still haven't heard the news. Soon her flesh will surprise them with the message. And from then on, they will be permanently lost.

Now tell me: do the goddesses need to do such evil to men?

The Revolutionaries are Coming

Some psychologists said to be specialists in adolescence advise, as a remedy for the disturbances characteristic of that phase, a lot of dialog, a lot of love, a lot of understanding. Parents should create conditions that let their kids talk with them about their problems, and that they should make an effort to understand them. Through love and dialog, they guarantee, parents and teens continue to be friends, and the family will go back to being as happy as they had always been when the teens were tots.

I disagree. In the first place, nothing convinces me that adolescents are after their parents' love. After love, yes. But their parents? Doubtful. In the second place, there is nothing teens want less than to be understood by old people. In arguments between husband and wife, there is a moment when one of the two says, as a final argument, "I understand you very well..." –an affirmation always made with a certain pause and a sneering smile. It's a way of saying, "Stop lying. I have you figured out inside my head. I can see through you. I've already done a CAT scan of your soul...Anything you say will be futile.

I understand you. I have already solved your mystery." To understand is to dominate.

And do you really believe that adolescents want to be understood by their parents, those big cast iron balls the kids have to drag around, chained to their ankles, parents the teens still have to depend on so disgracefully for money and car, who watch over them like the eye of God and who ask for explanations of where they've been and what they've done, beings who can be escaped only at the price of lies and trickery? What prey wishes to be understood by a hunter? If the hunter understands the prey, it will know where to set the trap.

The hunter needs to understand the prey without depending on the good will of the prey to have a discussion. And the understanding begins when one realizes that the teen is still mentally a child; the only difference is the size of the body. And that's what makes all the difference.

Understanding children is easy. All you have to do is read the tantalizing comic strips about Calvin, which appear every day in Section C of the *Correio Poular*, that prestigious newspaper. (All newspapers need to be referred to as "prestigious" the same way that the pope is his holiness, the president his excellency, and the dean his magnificence.)

A child's head is dominated by fantasy, by wonder: Calvin is an astronaut, his mother is a tractor, a bicycle has its own ideas and acts on them, he's an incredible modern sculptor who makes amazing sculptures of snow. For absolutely logical reasons, 6+5=6, and the stupid teacher marked it wrong on the test. In the head of a child, everything is possible.

"Buy it, daddy? Buy it!"

"But I don't have any money," the father responds, lying.

But the child counter-attacks. "Pay with a check."

In the old days, fairies used magic wands. Now they use checkbooks.

Children think adults are omnipotent. When I am in a full elevator and I see a small child on the floor, splayed out in the middle of the adults, I imagine what the kid's seeing when she looks up–enormous towers. I think it was from similar situations that fantasies of giants were born, giants who eat children. For children, adults are giants of uncommon strength who can do anything.

If Calvin had power, if he were big and had a checkbook, the world would be totally different–all toys and adventure. Unfortunately, his mother and father, the dominant class, owners of the means of production, have reduced him to the miserable conditions of a slave and thus oblige him to eat what he doesn't want to eat, do stupid, meaningless homework–can there be any greater alienation?–and go to bed when there are still so many entertaining things to do. Adults are guilty of his unhappiness. But the day will come when the shout of revolution arises: "Children of the whole world! Unite!" Children will take over. The dominant adults will not be shot, as they well deserve, because children know how to forgive. It will be a classless society, the return to Paradise. When this moment arrives, Calvin will be an extraordinary revolutionary leader.

And then, out of the blue, the moment will come, gloriously announced by the hair cropping up in places previously smooth. Ah! The hair! Finally...How much envy and how much fantasy were teased up in the heads of boys and girls as they thought about those symbols of the condition of adulthood.

The psychological importance of that hair has not yet been sufficiently analyzed. My clinical research on the subject led me to a curious discovery: the hair is responsible for a syndrome characteristic of adolescence, yet to be described in scientific compendiums. I have baptized it with the term "the Samson Syndrome."

As you know from biblical mythology, Samson was a hero of uncommon strength. He, alone, defeated an entire army, an army armed with swords and lances, he himself armed with no more than the jawbone of an ass. Next to Samson, Rambo was anemic. Well Samson's strength was in his hair. All Dalila had to do was give the hero a haircut for his strength to wither like a punctured balloon.

The Samson Syndrome is mental disturbance that causes adolescents to identify the growth of their hair with the growth of their strength. And this illusion is confirmed in their heads by the development and growth of organs adjacent to the hair, newly sprouted, which start working at a touch of the "start button," even under the most adverse conditions, such as early winter mornings. Which contrast with the paternal Studebakers that, under similar conditions, demand a new battery and only work after several attempts, their functioning interrupted by coughs, breathlessness, sudden shutting down, to the embarrassment of all.

Yes, the children are no longer children. Besides the growth of the hair, there is the growth of the body. Now the children looking up in the elevator have become enormous adolescents who look down. They are bigger than their parents. Not only bigger but better. The latest model. The model of the parents is already obsolete. "The elderly..." Already out of production. Old Studebakers, rambling along, dented, smoke spilling from the tailpipe. To go out with them is an embarrassment.

The glorious moment: the taking of power. The revolution. Adolescence has arrived. To understand adolescents, you need to understand the sociology and psychology of revolutionaries.

The oppressed class does not go around with the dominant class. It doesn't go to the same places. It doesn't speak the same language. It doesn't want to converse. The worker does not converse with the boss. Workers demand their rights. If they don't get them, they go on strike. Teens don't want to chat with mom and dad. They no longer visit the family farm. They don't spend New Year's Eve at home. They don't listen to the same music. If it's prohibited, it has to be transgressed. With the teen, a new order is begun. The teen is a militant. Adolescence is a anarchic revolutionary party. If the political situation were anything else, your kid's place would be at demonstrations, possibly as a guerrilla. But today, the way things are, the teen can't pass up a party.

From

Concerto for Body and Soul, by Rubem Alves

On Simplicity and Wisdom

They asked me to write on simplicity and wisdom. I accepted the invitation happily, knowing that, for that request to be made, I would have to be old.

Youth and adults know little about the meaning of simplicity. The youth are birds that fly by morning. Their flights are arrows in all directions. Their eyes are fascinated by ten thousand things. They want them all, but none of them give the young rest. Youth is always ready to fly again. Their world is the world of multiplicity. They love it because in their minds, multiplicity is a space of freedom. With adults, the opposite happens. For them, multiplicity is a spell that imprisons, a trap they fall into. They hate multiplicity, but they don't know how to free themselves. If, for the young, multiplicity is called freedom, for adults, multiplicity has the name of duty. Adults are captured birds in cages of duty. Every morning, ten thousand things await them with their orders (for this, there are agendas where the ten thousand things write their orders!). If they are not obeyed, there will be penalties.

At dusk, when night draws near, the flight of birds is different. In no way does it look like their flight in the morning. Have you ever watched the flight of pigeons at the end of day? They all fly in one direction. They go back home, back to their nests. Birds at dusk are simple. Simplicity is this: when the heart seeks just one thing.

Jesus told parables about simplicity. He spoke about a man who possessed many jewels, though none of them made him happy. But one day he found a jewel, dazzling and unique, and fell in love with it. So he then made a deal that brought him happiness. He sold the many and bought the one.

In multiplicity we lose. We ignore our desire. We act in fascination with the seduction of ten thousand things. It happens that, as the second poem of the Tao Te Ching says, "The ten thousand things appear and disappear without stopping." The path to multiplicity is a path without rest. Each point of arrival is a point of departure. Every meeting is a good-bye. It's a path where there is no house or nest. The last of the temptations that the Devil tried with the Son of God was the temptation of multiplicity: "The Devil took him to a high mountain, showed him the kingdoms of the world and its glory, and said unto him: "All this I give you if you fall down and worship me." But what multiplicity does is shatter the heart. The heart that pursues the "many" is a fragmented heart, a heart without rest. The word of Jesus: "What is it worth to gain the whole world and ruin life?" (Matthew 16:26)

The path of science and of learning is the path of multiplicity. A sacred writer warns: "Of making books there is no end, and much study is wearisome to the flesh." (Ecclesiastes 12:12). There is no end to the things that can be known and understood. The world of knowledge is a world of sums without end. It is a path without rest for the soul. There is no knowledge before which the heart can say: "I have finally arrived home." Knowledge isn't home. In the best hypothesis, it is bricks with which to build a house. But the bricks themselves, know nothing about a house. The bricks belong to multiplicity. The house belongs to simplicity: a single thing.

Says the *Tao Te Ching*: "In the search for knowledge, something is added each day. In the search for wisdom, each day something is subtracted."

Says T.S. Eliot: "Where is the wisdom we lose in knowledge?"

Says Manoel de Barros: "Whoever accumulates a lot of information loses the wandering of guessing. The wise one is the one who guesses."

Wisdom is the art of savoring. On wisdom, Nietzsche said: "The Greek word is linked, etymologically, to *sapio*, I savor; *sapiens*, the savorer; *sisyphus*, the man of the most perfect taste." Wisdom is, therefore, the art of savoring, distinguishing, discerning. The man of knowledge, in the face of multiplicity, "plunges into every thing that it is possible to learn, in the blind eagerness of wanting to know at any price." But the wise one is in search of "things worthy of being known."

Imagine a buffet. On the table, an enormous multiplicity, an infinitude of dishes. The man of learning, fascinated with the dishes, throws himself at them. He wants to eat it all. The wise one, on the other hand, stops and asks his body: "In all this multiplicity, which is the dish that will give you the most pleasure and joy?" And then, after meditating on it, he chooses one...

Wisdom is the art of recognizing and savoring joy. We are born into joy. Bachelard says that the entire universe is destined to happiness.

Vinicius de Morães wrote a beautiful poem with the title *Remain*...Already old, having walked the world of multiplicity, he looked back and saw what remained–what was worthwhile. "What remains is this heart, burning like a candle in a cathedral in ruins..." "What remains is the capacity for tenderness..." "What's left is this old respect for the night..." "What's left is this desire to cry before beauty..." And so goes Vinicius, counting the experiences that gave him joy. They were what was left.

The things that remain survive in a place in the soul called longing. Longing is the pocket where the soul keeps that which it tasted and approved. The approved were the experiences that gave joy. What was worthwhile is destined to eternity. Longing is the face of eternity reflected in the river of time. This is why we need gods, so that the river of time is circular: "Cast your bread upon the waters, for after many days thou shalt find it..." We pray that that which was lost in the past be returned to us in the future. I think God doesn't mind if we call it the Eternal Return–for that is all we ask of him, that the longed-for be returned.

I wander through the caverns of my memory. There are many wonderful things: scenes, places, some heavenly, others strange and curious, trips, events that mark the time of my life, meetings with notable people. But these memories, despite their size, don't do anything for me. I feel no desire to cry. I feel no desire to return.

So I consult my pocket of longing. There I find pieces of my body, pieces of joy. I look carefully, and nothing I find shined out in the world of multiplicity. They are little things that weren't even noticed by other people: scenes, paintings: a young son launching a kite on the beach; a night of insomnia and fear in a dark room, and in the middle of the darkness the voice of a son saying, "Daddy, I really like you"; a daughter playing with a puppy now dead (I cried a lot over her, Flora); a boy riding a horse before sunrise in a field perfumed with ripe hay; an old man smoking a pipe, contemplating the rain that fell on plants, saying, "See how grateful they are!" Friends. Memories of poems, of stories, of songs.

Guimarães Rosa said "happiness only in rare moments of distraction..." Correct. It comes when it isn't expected, in places unimagined. Jesus said: "It's like the wind: it blows where it wants, you don't know where it comes from or where it goes..." Wisdom is the art of tasting and joy, when it comes. But this art is mastered only by those who have the grace of simplicity. Because joy lives only in simple things.

From Addition to Subtraction

At the end of the year, for reasons unrelated to my will, my body goes through a metamorphosis. I become different. I feel like its software is changing.

Software refers to the program, the logic a computer works with. During the year, my body is driven by a software that only knows the logic of "addition." I add up all the time. I add on things. I don't throw anything away. I make annotations. I don't forget. Memory is also a way of adding up.

There are two reasons that lead me to add up. The first is love. I save because I love. That's the case of letters that arrive. They are letters from people who wish me well. They tell me good things that make me happy. Love can remain without response. The right thing to do would be to answer the letters at the exact moment I read them and become happy. But life has urgencies greater than those of love. The letters go without answer. So my solution is to add them up in piles, to be answered in the future. But what was true on one day is true for them all. The piles go on growing. The year comes to an end. The pile is enormous. The letters remain unanswered.

The second reason is utility. It's possible that the object in my hands, of dubious utility, may have some use in the future. So, availing myself of the benefit of the doubt, I save it. At the end of the year, my drawers are a mess that I don't understand, messes stupid with an unbelievable quantity of varied objects that, out of shame, I am not going to list.

But now, as year comes to an end...

(End? Evidently referring to man's illusion that the means of marking time represents the beating of the heart of the universe–thus the festivities, the champaign, the feasting. We really believe that a certain time is agonizing: an evil old man whose death is toasted with parties. Now another time arrives, newly born, blank pages without memory, accounts zeroed out, and everything will change. It is only this childish belief that explains the enormous brouhaha made because of a change of calendars–because that's all that happens. An old calendar into the trash, a new calendar on the wall. The stars, time keepers, ignore it all and continue to watch over us with the same indifferent eyes and silences as always, to the horror of Pascal...)

...but, as I was saying, now, as the year ends, my software changes. The program that "added up" is uninstalled, and in its place, the "subtraction" program begins to run. The "add up" program is a nasty conjuration: the more it accumulates, the heavier it gets. We lose lightness. Walking around becomes difficult. There's too much fat and muscle. The body sinks from too much weight. It's the devil who adds up. The "subtraction" program is the opposite. It breaks the add-up spell. We lose weight, become light, shed scales. Scabs peel off. The body loses bulk and grows wings. "Adding up" makes us grow old. "Subtraction" returns us to childhood. The devil adds up: he has an implacable accounting that does not forget. God subtracts. He has no accounting. Every forgiving is a forgetting.

The piles of letters: until a few days ago, possessed by the logic of adding up, I looked at them and became anguished. They were telling me there was a duty to fulfill. Love letters must be answered. The pile of letters was telling me that I was not fulfilling my duty. But, all of a sudden, the logic of adding up went away, and the logic of subtraction took its place. Álvaro de Campos agrees.

Ah! The freshness of not fulfilling a duty! What a refuge, to not be worthy of trust! I breathe better now...

I am free, contrary to clothed and organized society. I am naked, and I dive into the water of my imagination...

So I give myself to the grace of "subtraction." With the eyes of someone saying good-bye, I looked at the letters that the sense of duty was obliging me to answer. I am going to deliver them to forgetting. I am going to subtract them from the place they occupy. They will no longer remain there, in front of me like a liability. I tenderly take them in my hands. I will say good-bye to each of them. I re-read passages, and I smile, happy once again. I ask forgiveness from the friends who wrote to me. The letters will remain without written response, though the response of my heart has very much been given in the joy they created in me. This does not mean a lack of love. It's that I am not the Lord of Time. I need more time than I have. Not even love can deal with it. It is from this impotence of love in the face of time that art is born.

Tempus fugit–this Latin phrase is engraved on a wooden plaque on the door of my office. *Time flies.* I saw the phrase, the first time, on one of those antique clocks that toll every quarter hour, monotonously repeating: *tempus fugit...tempus fugit.* A Biblical psalm says: "Teach us to number our days that we may gain a heart of wisdom." Wisdom begins when we learn to tell time. Those who tell time know that time does not add up, it only subtracts. And that's why the letters will have to go without response. My friends will understand. They will forgive. If they don't forgive, it's because they weren't my friends. I am going to start the year off very light, without letters to answer. In the place where they are now will be the delicious emptiness on the varnished surface of wood, a space that isn't telling me something.

I look at the rest of the house. The logic of subtraction has its work cut out for it. I rummage through drawers, shelves, boxes, closets, in search of things that have accumulated during the year. Before each thing I ask two questions. First: Do I love it? If the answer is positive, the decision is made. Things that are loved must remain. If the answer is negative, I ask a second question: Is it useful? If the answer is negative again, the sentence is rendered: It will have to vacate the space. My house, for the new time, must be full of emptiness.

Álvaro de Campos, euphoric with the freedom of not fulfilling duties, ends by saying, "I am naked, and I dive into the water of my imagination."

Water is the great power of subtraction. Wherever it passes, it cleans. So I imagined a ritual for the celebration, not of the dubious passing of the year but of the body's joyous return to childhood–the dive into the waters. The waters have the power of subtracting, from the body and the soul, the heavy things that the passage of time built up in them. The waters carry us to forgetting. They wash the aged body, and the body returns to being a child.

A dive into the waters: sea water, rain water, river water, lake water, the water of a waterfall, a shower, a bathtub, a swimming pool, a squirt, any water–or, if for some reason these dives are not possible, a *dive into the water of the imagination.*

It isn't by chance that the religious symbol for metamorphosis is a sinking into water. Rising from the water, the old person who went down is dead, and in the person's place a child arises with a new name. I am going to think of a new name for myself.

The Stepmother's Eyes

If I were intimate with the Creator, I would tell him that there's something to be done to alleviate the suffering of children. Just change their parents' eyes. In the place of their eyes, put the eyes of the grandparents. The eyes of grandparents see grandchildren in a way that's different from that of parents.

I know this from experience. When I was a young father, I looked in a hurry. My eyes ran agitatedly over ten thousand things that swirled around us. They hadn't yet learned how to distinguish the essential. To see what is essential in a child, one must have a vagabond look, a look that strolls unhurried over the child who is playing. A child playing is a happiness that passes very quickly. The eyes of parents are administrative eyes. They try to administer infancy, thinking that this can guarantee the future. (Fools, they don't even know if there will be a future...) The eyes of grandparents are wise eyes, wise in the precise sense of the etymology of the word *sapient*. *Sapio* in Latin means "I savor." Children are objects of savoring.

I really feel sorry for children. They are victims of their parents' disturbances. How much wrong is done to them, from sadistic beatings and torture that often end in death, to the normal, daily wrongdoings done with the razor of a look or the punches of the voice. And they, poor little things, children, are weak. There's nothing they can do. The only thing they can do is shrink back in fear. Infantile reason can't do anything against the adult arguments of force. Dostoyevsky tells about one of these victims of parental malfeasance–alone on a cold night, closed in a dark room, as punishment for some transgression she'd done. And she beats on the door with her little hands, crying... And the author comments that nothing, absolutely nothing in the whole universe, can justify or pardon such cruelty.

I really like children's stories, the old ones, the classics, with all their horror. The Disney films ruin them. The horror is taken out. The classics are transformed into cute little stories. Robbed of the horror, they become innocuous diversion. They lose their power of revelation and recovery. The old stories weren't written for enjoyment. They were written to horrify. Often it's in horror that revelations and transformations happen.

In the Old Testament there is a wonderful incident. King David seduced and impregnated Bathsheba, wife of Uriah, one of his generals who was off at war. Not knowing what to do, David imagined that the death of Uriah would get him out of that intolerable situation. He gave orders to his captains to abandon the cuckolded husband during combat so he would be killed by the enemy. That they did. Crime consummated, the prophet Nathan came before the king and told him of a situation, asking the king for a decision.

"A rich man had thousands of sheep that he loved very much. His neighbor was a poor man who had just one sheep, which he loved very much. So the rich man, wishing to eat some mutton, stole the single sheep from his neighbor, killed it and ate it." The king, infuriated with the story, rendered his sentence: "Let that man be killed." The prophet looked the king in the eye and said, "You are that man."

That's how the trap-stories go. You think they're talking about someone else in a distant land many years ago, and all of a sudden you realize that that story is our story. We talk about the story of Snow White, the story of Cinderella, and we think they are false stories that never happened–once upon a time in a land far away–we don't realize that they are happening in our own house.

Reading these stories, I imagine the situations that would have brought them about. I know they were born from wounds. Stories are the bleeding that runs from wounds.

From what wound does the Cinderella story run? The suffering of a child.

Who made it up? I think it was an old nanny who looked at the girl with the eyes of a grandmother. She was the one who made the girl sleep in the maid's bed while the ball took place in the salons on the other side of the closed door. She told this story to make the girl sleep.

The story tells of a stepmother. Women who do what that one did could only be stepmothers. But was it really a stepmother? Storytellers know that real names cannot be spoken–as in dreams. The nanny was afraid to say the real name. It is dangerous to denounce the boss. I don't think it was a stepmother. I think it was the mother herself.

Disney made a sweet interpretation of the story. The stepmother was real, evil, and ugly. Her two daughters were horrible and spiteful. The three could not stand the beauty of the husband's daughter. Gnawed with jealousy and taking advantage of the father's absence, they tried to get her out of the way. They shut her off in the kitchen.

But there's another hypothesis to consider. Mother and three sisters. Of the three sisters, two were pretty and smart. The third was disheveled and ugly–possibly with a deformed foot. If she had had a normal foot, there's no way to explain the fact that only one shoe fit on her foot. Some other girl in the kingdom must have worn the same size. It is even possible that she had Down Syndrome. The girl was a cause of shame, a cause of embarrassing scenes.

When the mother looked at her two pretty daughters, her eyes smiled. And the girls knew it. But when she looked at the other daughter, her eyes filled with shame. And the girl felt it.

She was the mother of the first two. Because a mother can be seen by her look.

The third was aborted by the mother's look. Now, at a time when so much is discussed about abortion, religious people don't notice that among animals, motherhood is a matter of uterus. It's not like that among humans. Human beings are created in the eyes of mothers. The eyes have the power to communicate beauty or ugliness, to transmit life or death.

It is certain that the mother of the first two daughters was the stepmother of the third. The girl caused her shame. How to explain to others (Oh, the eyes of others, the traps of our body!) that the girl was her daughter, that she had come from within her? She could not stand not being able to show that daughter to the eyes of other mothers in the game of comparisons and envy into which mothers and fathers throw their children.

That was the girl who was put in a place "far from eyes," in there with the ashes and cinders. What was her name? It is not known. We only know her nickname: *Cinderella,* she whose body was made of ashes. Or *Cinder Cat*, she who was with the cats in the cold, sleeping beside the warm cinders to stay warm. She didn't enjoy the happiness of human warmth in a mother's eyes. That kitchen where she lived was the eyes of her stepmother.

The Fire Is Coming...

The silk floss tree was gigantic. Actually, I don't know if it was really gigantic or if I was small. I know that it was very old. Its bark was dark and wrinkled. Where the trunk went into the earth, there was a big, dark, bottomless hole. In the afternoon, after dinner, the men of the neighborhood sat around on the roots of the tree to roll corn husk cigarettes and tell stories. Many were ghost stories. We kids listened in terror. Once we heard some prophesy about the end of the world. That the world would come to an end was a sure and inevitable thing. Because everything that has a beginning has an end. Everyone agreed that if the first time the world drowned in a flood of water, sparing only Noah and his animals, the second would be by fire. No one would be spared, for we can make no arks to float above fire. And we imagined the terrible scene, the fire falling from the sky like rain, the same way it happened at Sodom and Gomorrah and at Herculaneum and Pompeii.

A Sunday afternoon. The sky was absolute blue, thinned by an excess of sunlight. Suffocating heat coated the face with drops of sweat that ran down. Not a single cloud offered shade. No promise of rain to extinguish the bonfire in the middle of the sky. The car ran down the road through a sad scene. Trees were scarce, lost in the poor fields of wild and stubborn grass. If the heat were to continue, the trees and grass would die. No form of life resists heat for long. I remembered the silk floss tree and the prophesies of the end of the world back in my childhood. I realized that the images of our imagination were wrong. The world would not end with a rain of fire that would burn everything in a raging fire. The fire of the end of the world would be more cruel, like the fire of that afternoon, the fire of a low-heat oven roasting slowly.

In times past, the scene was something else. The countryside was green forests where brooks of cool water ran, full of ferns, bromeliads, orchids, animals and birds of every kind. Where there is forest, there is water. Where there is water, there's life. The forests were cut by businessmen, developers, lovers of profit who were short on vision. A tree standing up isn't worth anything to them. A tree on the ground is worth money. They cut the forests to plant coffee and raise cattle. Now the ground is good for neither pasture nor coffee. In a short time it has turned into desert. What was left was the forests in the mountains. The forests in the mountains were saved not out of love but because they were no good for cattle or coffee. What was left was the forests useless to progress and profit. It is in them that green life found refuge–precarious oases in the middle of a desert of development.

That was in the state of Rio de Janeiro. But wherever you go, you find the tracks of businessmen and developers. Fifty years ago, in the region of the city of Governador Valadares, in Minas Gerais, everything was green, alive with forests, springs, and creeks. Men saw the forests and did not love them. They saw them standing up, beautiful and useless, and they figured out their value lying down, dead and profitable. Today, all that's left is a sad countryside where eucalyptus are planted. As soon as they grow, they're cut down and turned into firewood. The fresh perfume of the forest was replaced by the smell of hot smoke.

The same happened with the pine forests of Paraná state, in the south of Brazil. In their place stretches an endless green carpet–the beautiful plantations of soy that get lost at the horizon. Around here are the plantation of sugar cane. Seen from a plane, they look like immense lawns. But they are deserts. In the fields of soy and sugar cane, there are neither trees nor springs nor animals nor birds.

Now the businessmen and developers turn to what is still left: the Amazonian forest. I visited a region of the Amazon forest that had been devastated by profit. It was like a beach. The only thing missing was the sea. Pure sand. Once the trees are cut, the water evaporates and the forest turns into a desert. It is possible that in some not-too-distant future where there was once the Amazon forest there will be only a continuation of the Sahara desert.

A president of the United States once wrote to Indian chief Seattle with a proposal to buy his land. The Indian chief's answer is one of the most beautiful and moving manifestations of love of nature ever produced. He knew what the fate of his land would be if civilization took ownership of them.

> *There is no calm place in the cities of the white man. No place to listen to the blooming of flowers in the spring or the beat of an insect's wings. And what is left of life if a man cannot hear the solitary cry of a bird or the croaking of frogs around a lake at night? The Indian prefers the smooth murmur of the wind wrinkling the face of the lake and the smell of the wind in rain or the perfume of pine.*

I am horrified by our powerlessness before the destructive power of companies that raze nature for the love of money. But I'm even more horrified to feel that other people are not horrified. They don't love nature. For them, it is natural to treat nature like a garbage dump. I remember the sadness I felt in Pocinhos do Rio Verde. Ahead of me was a pick-up truck of happy, middle-class youngsters who had just graduated from school. They were calmly tossing empty beer cans to the side of the road as if this were the most natural thing in the world. School had taught them many things, but not the essential. Once I took a hike in the Ecological Park and never went back. The sight of soda cans and plastic bottles along the trails just made me mad. They told me that once the entrance exams were over at the PUCC university, a company passed out boxes of soda to the kids as they left. That night the street was piled with trash. At the Unicamp state university at Campinas, São Paulo, there was a day denominated Open University. The day after was tragic. The campus was an absolute garbage dump, covered with plastic bags, cups, bottles, soda cans, paper, napkins and detritus of all kinds. My dear friend Herógenes, a professor and director of the garden, now deceased, told me that after that day all the young trees had to be replanted because the future university students had broken them for pure pleasure.

I believe that the preservation of nature is the most important challenge of the present time. It has to do with the preservation of life, the future of our earth, the future of our grandchildren. It's more important than all the doctrines preached in churches. Because, to believe the sacred scripts, our primordial vocation is that of gardeners. God gave us a mission to take care of Paradise. It's more important than all the science that can be taught in schools. Because all of science will be empty and useless if our work is turned into a desert.

I'd like to be able to go back to the silk floss tree in whose shade I first heard the forebodings of the end of the world–just to read a counterfeit sacred script, a prophesy of a new world being born:

The poor and needy seek water, but there is none, their tongues fail for thirst.

But rivers shall open in desolate heights,

and fountains in the midst of the valleys;

the wilderness shall be made a pool of water, and the dry land springs of water.

In the desert will grow the cedar and the acacia tree, the myrtle and the olive, the cypress and the pine, the elm and the box tree together...(Isaiah 41:17-19)

From

Ex Cathedra: Stories by Machado de Assis

Ex Cathedra

"Godfather, with all respect, you'll go blind that way."

"What?"

"With all respect you'll go blind. You read with desperation. No, sir, give me that book."

Caetaninha pulled the book from his hands. Her godfather got up, walked around, ducked into his study, where he did not lack books, shut himself in and continued reading. It was his vice. He read with excess, read morning, noon and night, at lunch, at dinner, before sleeping, after a bath; he read walking, read stopped, read at home and at the country house, read before reading and after reading, read the whole cast of books but especially law (in which he had graduated), mathematics, and philosophy. Lately he was also given to the natural sciences.

Worse than blind, he went lunatic. It was around the end of 1873, in Tijuca, when he began to show signs of cerebral disturbances. But since they were slight and few, only in March or April of 1874 did his goddaughter note the change. One day, during lunch, he interrupted his reading to ask her:

"What's my name?"

"What's your name?"she repeated, scared. "Your name is Fulgêncio.

"From now on, call me Fulgencius."

And, burying his face in the book, he went on with his reading. Caetaninha referred the case to the slave women of the house, who told her they'd noticed something wrong for some time, that he wasn't right. Imagine the girl's fear. But the fear passed quickly, leaving only pity behind, which only increased her affection. And besides, the mania was narrow and slight. It never went beyond the books. Fulgêncio lived for the written word, the press, the doctrinal, the abstract, the principles and formulas. In time he came not to superstition but to hallucination of theory. One of his maxims was that liberty never dies where there's still a sheet of paper on which to declare it. And one day, awakening with the idea of improving the condition of the Turks, he drew up a constitution which he sent as a gift to the English minister in Petrópolis. On another occasion he immersed himself in the study of books on the anatomy of the eye to verify whether they really can see, and he concluded yes.

Tell me where, under such conditions, the life of Caetaninha could be happy. She lacked nothing, it's true, because her godfather was rich. It was he himself who had raised her since she was seven, when he lost his wife. He taught her to read and write, French, a little history and geography, to say the least, and he had one of the slave women teach her embroidery, needlepoint, and sewing. All of this is true. But Caetaninha turned fourteen. Though at an early age toys and household slave women were enough to entertain her, she reached an age where toys fall out of fashion and slave women are less interesting, where no readings or writings make a paradise out of a lonely house in Tijuca. She went out on a few occasions, rarely and quickly; she didn't go to plays or dances, didn't visit or receive visitors. When she saw a cavalcade of men and wives pass by, she put her soul in the saddle and let herself go, leaving her body at the feet of her godfather as he continued to read.

One day at their country home she saw a young man mounted on a little beast stop at the gate, and she heard him ask if that was the house of Dr. Fulgêncio.

"Yes sir, it's here."

"May I speak with him?"

Caetaninha responded that she would see. She entered the house and went to the study, where she found her godfather mulling, with a most voluptuous and saintly expression, a chapter from Hegel. Young man? What young man? Caetaninha told him it was a young man in mourning clothes. Mourning? repeated the old doctor, suddenly closing the book; it must be him. I forgot to tell you (though there's time for everything) that, three months earlier, a brother of Fulgêncio, in the north, had died, leaving one natural son. Since the brother, before dying, had written to him to recommend the orphan he was to leave behind, Fulgêncio sent to have the orphan come to Rio de Janeiro. Hearing that there was a young man there in mourning clothes, he concluded that it was his nephew. And he didn't conclude badly. It was him.

It seems that up until this point there's nothing that doesn't fit into a fondly romantic story: We have an old lunatic, a lonely and sighing young woman, and we see a nephew show up unexpectedly. In order to not descend from the realm of poesy in which we find ourselves, let it be said that the mule on which Raimundo arrived was led by a black from whom he'd hired it. I'll also bypass the circumstances of the accommodations for the young man, limiting myself to saying that, living to read, like the uncle, having completely forgotten that I had sent for him, nothing in the house was prepared for him. But the house was big and well stocked. An hour later, the young man was settled into a beautiful room from which he could see the country home, the old cistern, the washtub, plenty of green foliage, and the vast blue sky.

I believe I still haven't said the age of the guest. He's fifteen and sprouting a shadow over his upper lip. He's almost a child. Later, if our Caetaninha is overcome, and the slave women go around spying and talking about "the nephew of the old *sinhô* who came from somewhere out of town," it's because life there didn't have much happening, not because he's a made man. This was also the impression of the master of the house, but here's the difference. The goddaughter wasn't aware that the job of that shadow is to become a mustache or, if she thought about that, did it so vaguely that it isn't worth putting here. It wasn't that way to Fulgêncio. He understood that he had there the dough of a husband, and he resolved to get them married. But he also saw that, unless he took them in hand and kneaded them, happenstance might lead things in a different fashion.

One idea begets another. The idea of marrying the two jibed with one of his recent opinions - that calamities or simple unpleasantness in matters of the heart happened because love was practiced empirically. It lacked a scientific base. A man and a woman, once they understood the physical and metaphysical reasons for this sentiment, would be able to receive and feed it more effectively than another man and woman who knew nothing of the phenomenon.

"My little ones are still green," he said to himself. "I have three or four years ahead of me, and I can start now to prepare them. Let's proceed with logic. First the foundation, then the walls, then the roof. . . . instead of starting with the roof. The day will come when learning to love is like learning to read . . . On that day . . . "

He was dizzy, dazzled, delirious. He went to the shelves, pulled down a few tomes, astronomy, geology, physiology, anatomy, jurisprudence, politics, linguistics, opened them, flipped through them, compared them, here and there extracted bits, until he formulated a teaching plan. It had twenty chapters in which entered general notions of the universe, a definition of life, proof of the existence of man and woman, the organization of societies, a definition and analysis of the passions, a definition and analysis of love, its causes, necessities, and effects. In truth, the subjects were tough. He understood how to tame them, turned them into ordinary, everyday sentences, lending them a purely familiar tone, like the astronomy of Fontenelle. And he said with emphasis that the core, not the skin, was the essence of the fruit.

All of this was ingenious, but here's the more ingenious thing. He didn't invite them to learn. One night, looking at the sky, he said that the stars were shining a lot - and what were the stars? By any chance did they know what the stars were?

"No, sir."

From here it was just a step to begin a description of the universe. Fulgêncio took the step with such agility and so naturally that he left them enchanted, and they asked for the whole journey.

"No," the old man said, "we are not going to exhaust the whole topic today. Nor can you even understand this except slowly. Tomorrow or later . . . "

Thus it was that he began, surreptitiously, to execute his plan. Every day the two students, amazed by the world of astronomy, asked him to go on, and even though in the end of this first part Caetaninha got a little confused, she still wanted to hear about the other things her godfather had promised.

I'm not saying anything about the familiarity between the two students since it's obvious. Between fourteen and fifteen years of age, the difference is so small that the bearers of the two ages didn't need to do much more than one offer a hand to the other. That was what happened.

After three weeks, they seem to have been raised together. That alone was enough to change Caetaninha's life. But Raimundo brought her more. Within ten minutes of watching her look longingly at the cavalcades of men and ladies who passed by on the street, Raimundo ended her longing, teaching her to ride despite the reluctance of the old man, who feared disaster. But he gave in and hired two horses. Caetaninha had a beautiful riding jacket made, and Raimundo went into the city to get her some gloves and a crop with the money from his uncle - as you know - who gave him boots and the rest of the masculine accoutrement. Soon thereafter it was a pleasure to see them both, gallant and intrepid, up and down the mountain.

At home they played freely, played checkers and cards, took care of birds and plants. Often they bickered, but, according to the slave women, they were make-believe fights, only for them to make up afterward, a passing peevishness. Sometimes Raimundo went into the city, sent by his uncle. Caetaninha waited for him at the gate, watching anxiously. When he arrived, they argued because she wanted to take the largest packages from him under the pretext that he was tired, and he wanted to give her smallest ones, alleging she was a weakling.

At the end of four months, life was completely different. It could even be said that only then did Caetaninha begin to wear roses in her hair. Beforehand she often showed up for lunch with her hair unbrushed. Now, not only was her hair brushed early, but even, as I said, she brought roses, one or two. Either she picked them herself the evening before and kept them in water, or he picked them that same morning to bring to her at her window. The window was high, but Raimundo, standing on tip-toe and raising his arm, managed to hand the roses to her. It was around that time that he picked up the habit of smoothing his filmy whiskers with his finger. Caetaninha took to smacking his fingers to get him out of that bad habit.

Meanwhile, the lessons continued regularly. By then they had a general idea of the universe, and a definition of life, which neither of them understood. Thus they came to the fifth month. On the sixth began the proof of the existence of man. Caetaninha couldn't suppress a laugh when her godfather, expounding on the topic, asked them if they knew that they existed and why, but she quickly got serious and answered no.

"Nor you?"

"Nor I, sir," the nephew agreed.

Fulgêncio usually began conceptually, with deeply Cartesian reasoning. The next lesson was at the country house. It had rained a lot the previous days, but the sun now flooded all with light, and the country place seemed like a beautiful widow who changes her mourning veil for that of a bride. Raimundo, as if he wanted to emulate the sun (the great tend to copy each other), sent out a vast and faraway look from his pupils. Caetaninha took it in, throbbing like the country home - a fusion, transfusion, diffusion, confusion and profusion of beings and things.

While the old man talked - straightforward, logical, stalwart, enjoying the formulas, his eyes fixed on nothing - the two students made thirty thousand efforts to listen, but thirty thousand events distracted them. At first it was a pair of butterflies who played in the air. Do me the favor of telling me what could be extraordinary about a couple of butterflies? I agree that they were yellow, but the circumstances aren't enough to explain the distraction. The fact that they flew one after the other, now to the right, now to the left, now down, now up, does not explain the detour, seeing that butterflies never fly in a straight line like simple soldiers.

"Understanding," the old man said, "understanding, as I just explained . . . "

Raimundo looked at Caetaninha and found her looking at him. They both seemed confused and shy. She was the first to lower her eyes to her lap. Then she raised them to look somewhere else, somewhere far off, the wall around the grounds, but as they went there, since Raimundo's were still there, she looked off as quickly as she could. Fortunately, the wall presented a spectacle that filled her with wonder. A couple of swallows (it was a day of couples) hopped around on the wall with the grace of people with wings. They peeped as they hopped, saying things to each other, whatever it was, maybe this - that it was quite nice that there was no philosophy on the walls of country homes. But when one of them flew - probably the lady - the other, naturally, the boy, did not let himself fall behind. He spread his wings and went the same way. Caetaninha lowered her eyes to the grass on the ground.

A few minutes later, when the lesson was over, she asked her godfather to go on. When he refused, she took his arm and asked him to take a walk around the grounds.

"It's rather sunny," the old man argued.

"Let's walk in the shade."

"It's rather hot."

Caetaninha suggested they continue on the veranda, but her godfather told her, mysteriously, that Rome wasn't built in a day, and ended up saying that only two days later would the lesson continue. Caetaninha withdrew to her room, stayed shut in there for three-quarters of an hour, sitting, then to the window, back and forth, looking for things she had in her hand, and reaching the paroxysm of seeing herself on horseback, the road ahead of her, Raimundo to her side. Suddenly she saw the boy on the wall outside, but she focused better and saw it was a couple of bugs humming in the air. And one said to the other:

"Thou art a flower of our race, the flower of the air, the flower of the flowers, the sun and the moon of my life."

To which the other responded:

"No one outdost thee in beauty or grace. Thy hum is the echo of divine speech, but leave me . . . leave me . . . "

"Why leavest thou, soul of the grove?"

"I have already told thee, king of the pure airs, leave me."

"Do not speak to me this way, charm and party of the woods. All above and around us is saying that you speak to me in another way. Dost thou know the song of the blue mysteries?"

"Let us hear it in the green leaves of the orange tree."

"Those of the mango tree are more beautiful."

"Thou art more beautiful than any others."

"And you, sun of my life?"

"Moon of my being, I am what thou wantest . . . "

In that way the two bugs spoke. She heard them ruminating. As soon as they disappeared, she went into the house, saw the time and left the bedroom. Raimundo was out. She went to await him at the gate, ten, twenty, thirty, forty, fifty minutes. When he got back, they spoke little. They came together and separated two or three times. The last time it was she who brought him to the veranda to show him an ornament she thought she had lost and had just found. It does them justice to believe that it was pure lie. Meanwhile, Fulgêncio moved the lesson up, gave it the next day, between lunch and dinner. Never had the word left him so lucidly and simply. And that's the way it should be. He talked about the existence of man, a deeply metaphysical chapter, in which it was necessary to consider everything from all sides.

"Do you understand?" he asked.

"Perfectly."

And the lesson went on to an end. At the end, the same thing happened as on the day before. Caetaninha, as if afraid of being alone, asked him to go on or to take a walk, and he refused both, patted her paternally on the cheek, and shut himself in his study.

"This week," the old doctor thought, giving the key a turn, "this week I go into the organization of societies. All next month and the next is for the definition and classification of the passions. In May, we will move on to love . . . by then it will be time . . .

As he said this and closed the door, something echoed from the veranda - a thunder of kisses, according to the caterpillars of the yard, but for caterpillars any little sound is worth thunder. As for the authors of the sound, nothing is known for sure. It seems that a wasp, seeing Caetaninha and Raimundo together on this occasion, concluded a consequence from the coincidence and understood that it was them. But an old grasshopper evinced the inanity of that conclusion, alleging that he had heard many kisses, a long time ago, in places where neither Raimundo nor Caetaninha had ever set foot. We agree that this other argument was worth nothing, but such is the prestige of good character that the grasshopper was applauded as having once defended truth and reason. And from that it can be that that's the way it really happened. But a thunder of kisses? We suppose two; we suppose three or four.

From

Trio in A-Minor: Stories by Machado de Assis

Fulano

Come with me, reader, to the opening of the will of my friend Fulano Beltrão. 1 Did you know him? He was a man close to sixty years of age. He died yesterday, the second of January, 1884, at eleven-thirty at night. You can't imagine the strength of spirit he showed throughout the illness. He fell on the evening of the Day of the Dead, and at first we supposed it was nothing, but the illness persisted, and after two months and a few days, death took him.

I confess to you that I am curious to hear the will. It necessarily contains some determinations honorable to him and of general interest. Before 1863 it wouldn't have been this way because until then he was self-absorbed, reserved, living on the road to the Botanical Garden, where he went by omnibus or mule. He had a wife and son living, an unmarried daughter of thirteen. It was in that year that he began to occupy himself with other things besides his family, revealing a universal and generous spirit. I can't affirm anything about the cause of this. I believe it was a friend's testimonial on the occasion of his fortieth birthday. Fulano Beltrão read in the Jornal do Comércio, on the fifth of March of 1864, an anonymous article in which beautiful and honorable things were said of him: - good father, good husband, dependable friend, dignified citizen, a soul uplifted and pure. To be given such fair praise was a big deal; but anonymously, it was most unusual.

"You will see," Fulano Beltrão said to his wife, "you'll see that this is by Xavier or Castro. We'll tear off his hood before long."

Castro and Xavier were two frequent visitors to the house, constant partners in games of *voltarete*[2] and old friends of my friend. They used to say friendly things, on the fifth of March, but it was at dinner, in the intimacy of the family, among the four walls. In the press, it was the first time he was blessed with praise. I could be wrong, but I think the gesture of fairness, the material testimony thanks to which good qualities and good acts don't die in the dark, was what motivated my friend to get out, to appear in public, to be seen, to give the human collectivity a little of virtues he was born with. He thought how thousands of people were reading the article at the same time he was reading it. He imagined that they commented on it, questioned it, confirmed it. He really heard it by a phenomenon of hallucination that science has yet to explain though it is not rare. He distinctly heard some of the voices of the public. He heard that they called him a good man, a distinguished gentleman, a friend of friends, a hard worker, honest, all the qualifications he had seen at work in others and which, in the life of the wild animal he was leading, he never presumed applied - typographically - to him.

"The press is a great invention," he said to his wife.

It was she, D. Maria Antônia, who tore off the hood. The article was by Xavier. Xavier said that only out of concern for her was he confessing authorship, and he added that the appearance wasn't complete because his idea was for the article to come out in all the newspapers, but he hadn't done it because he finished it at seven o'clock in the evening. There was no time to make copies. Fulano Beltrão made up for this failing, if it could be called a failing, having the article transcribed in the *Diário do Rio* and the *Correio Mercantil.*

But as this fact did not explain the change in our friend's life, another fact remains, to wit, it was from that year on, and properly from the month of March, that he began to appear in public more often. Until then he'd been a stubborn man who did not go to company assemblies, didn't vote in political elections, didn't go to theaters, nothing, absolutely nothing. Right in that month of March, on the twenty-second or twenty-third, he showed up at Santa Casa de Misericórdia hospital with a ticket from the grand lottery of Spain and received a letter of commendation from the director, thanking him in the name of the poor. He asked his wife and friends whether he should publish the letter or put it away, seeming concerned that to not publish it would be a disrespect. In the end, on the twenty-sixth, the letter was given to all the papers, one of which commented on the piety of the donor. Of the people who read this news, many of them naturally remembered Xavier's article and connected the two occurrences: "Fulano Beltrão is the same one who, etc.," the first building block of a man's reputation.

It's late. We have to go hear the will. I can't be telling you everything. I'll summarize that the unfairness of the word in the street set off in him an active and eloquent vengeance, so that the wretched, chiefly the dramatically wretched, the victims of a fire or flood, found in my friend the initial rescue that in such cases should be quick and public. There was no one like him for one of these efforts. It was the same with the freeing of slaves. Before the law of September 28, 1871, it was very common for slave children to show up at the Commerce square to beg businessmen for money for their freedom. Fulano

Beltrão made three-quarters of the contributions so successfully that in a few minutes the price of freedom was covered.

The fair treatment that was done him encouraged him. The fairness even brought him memories which, without the fairness, he possibly never would have noticed. I won't even mention the dance that he gave to celebrate the Battle of Riachuelo victory because it was a dance that had been planned before the arrival of the news of the battle, and he did no more than attribute to it a motive higher than simple family recreation, putting a picture of Admiral Barroso with a navy trophy and flags in the hall of honor, before the portrait of the Emperor, and at dinner raised some patriotic toasts, as reported in the newspapers of 1865.3

But here, for example, is a quite characteristic case of the influence that the fairness of others can have on our behavior. One day Fulano Beltrão came from the Treasury, where he had gone to discuss some tax payments. As he passed the Lampadosa church, he remembered that he'd been baptized there, and no man has a memory of that without reviewing the passage of a lifetime and things that happened, to lie again in the maternal lap, to laugh and play as he never again laughs nor plays. Fulano Beltrão did not escape this effect. He crossed the churchyard, entered the church - so simple, so modest, and for him so rich and beautiful. As he left, he made a resolution which he put to work within a few days: he sent the Lampadosa a gift, a superb silver candlestick with, besides the name of the donor, two dates: the date of the donation and of the baptism. All the newspapers ran the news, and they even received it twice because the church administration understood (and with good reason) that it would also do well to spread it to the four winds.

After three years, or less, my friend had entered the public cogitations. His name was remembered even when no recent event had suggested it, and not just remembered but adorned with adjectives. Now in some places his absence was noted. Now they sought him for other places. So D. Maria Antônia saw the biblical snake enter Eden, not to tempt her but to tempt Adam. Indeed her husband was going so many places, taking care of so many things, showing up so often at the door of Bernardo's on Rua do Ouvidor, that the old conviviality of his home slackened.[4] D. Maria Antônia told him so. He agreed that it was so, but he argued that it couldn't be any other way, and, in any case, though his habits had changed, his feelings hadn't. He had moral obligations with society. No one belonged to himself exclusively, so therefore there was a little dissipation of his care of things. The truth is that they had been living too secludedly. It was neither fair nor attractive. It just wasn't proper. Their daughter was getting to marriageable age, and the closed up house created the stifled air of a convent. A carriage, for example, why was it they didn't have a carriage? D. Maria Antônia felt a shiver of pleasure, but a short one. After a moment of reflection, she protested.

"No. A carriage for what? No, never mind a carriage."

"It's already bought," her husband lied.

But here we are at the probate's office. Nobody's here yet. Let's wait at the door. Are you in a hurry? It'll be twenty minutes at most. So it's true, he bought a beautiful victory. And for someone who, only in modesty, had traveled so many years on the back of a mule or squeezed into an omnibus, it wasn't easy, later, to get used to the new vehicle. To this I attribute the salient and inclined attitudes he went around with in the first weeks, the eyes he stretched to one side and the other in the way of people who are looking for someone or a house. In the end, he got used to it, went on to adopt more laid-back attitudes, albeit without a certain feeling of indifference or lack of concern which his wife and daughter felt, maybe because they were women. They, on the other hand, did not like to go out by carriage, but he insisted so much that they went out, be it to go everywhere or to go nowhere, that there was no other way but to obey him. And in the street, it was known that as soon as a tip of the clothing of the two women appeared in the distance, and on the seat a certain coachman, everybody said, "Here comes Fulano Beltrão's family." And that, maybe without him realizing it, made him more widely known.

In 1868 he got into politics. I know the year because it coincided with the fall of the liberals and the rise of the conservatives. It was in March or April of 1868 that he declared his assent to the situation, not slyly but loudly. This was perhaps the weakest point in my friend's life. He had no political ideas. When he made an effort, he put forth one of those temperaments that substitute for ideas and make people believe a man is thinking when he's just sweating. But he gave in to a moment of hallucination. He saw himself in the town council opining an aside, or leaning over the balustrade in conversation with the council president, who smiled at him in a serious intimacy of government. And that's when the gallery, in the exact meaning of the term, had to think about him. He did everything he could to get onto the council; halfway there, the situation collapsed. Recovering from the shock, he remembered to affirm to Itaboraí the opposite of what he'd said to Zacarias, or beforehand the same thing. But he lost the election and dropped politics. He went around much better adjusted, going into the issue of the Masons with the prelates. At first he kept quiet. On one hand, he was a Mason; on the other, he wanted to respect the religious sentiments of his wife. But the conflict took on such proportions that he couldn't hold his tongue. He went into the issue with ardor, the expansion, the publicity that he put into everything. He held meetings in which he spoke at length about the freedom of conscience and the right of the Mason to wear a robe. He signed protests, petitions, congratulations, blatantly opened his wallet and his heart.

His wife died in 1878. She asked to be buried without anything fancy, and that's the way he did it, because he really loved her and held her last desire like a decree from heaven. He had already lost his son, and his daughter, by then married, was in Europe. My friend shared his pain with the public, and though he buried his wife without pomp, he did not neglect to have a magnificent mausoleum sculpted in Italy, which the city admired on display on Rua do Ouvidor for nearly a month. His daughter came to attend the inauguration. I haven't seen them for some four years. Recently the illness arose and, after a little over two months, took him to a better place. Note that before the agony began, he had never lost his reason nor the strength of his soul. He spoke with visitors, got them to know each other, didn't forget to tell the ones arriving about the ones leaving. It was pointless because a friendly newspaper was publishing their names. On the morning of the day he died he still heard the newspapers read, and in one of them a relatively small item reported his illness, which in a certain way seemed to reanimate him. But by afternoon he weakened a bit. At night, he expired.

I can see you're annoyed. They're really taking a long time... Wait, I think that's them. It is. Let's go in. Here's our magistrate, who begins to read the will. Can you hear? This genealogical minutia isn't necessary; it's an excess of small print. But this telling of the whole family, from the great-great-great-grandfather, tests my friend's patient and precise spirit. He didn't forget anything. The funeral ceremony is long and complicated but beautiful. Now he's starting the list of inheritors. They're all religious people; a few industrialists. Watch the soul of my friend.

Thirty *contos*.

Thirty *contos* for what? To start a public subscription aimed at erecting a statue of Pedro Álvares Cabral?[5] "Cabral," it says there in the will, "must not be forgotten by Brazilians. He was the precursor of our empire." It recommends that the statue be of bronze with four medallions on the pedestal, to wit, the portrait of Bishop Coutinho, president of the Constitution, one of Gonzaga, head of the rebellion in Minas Gerais, and of two citizens of the current generation, "notable for their patriotism and liberalness," as chosen by the commission, which he himself appointed to take charge of the project.

What this accomplished, I do not know. We lack the perseverance of the founder of the fund. But if the commission follows through and this American sun ever sees the statue of Cabral put up, in our honor it should think about putting a portrait of my late friend on one of the medallions. Don't you think? Well, the magistrate's done. Let's go.

Cabriolet Anecdote

"Cabriolet is here, yes sir," said the black who had come to San José cathedral to call the vicar for the last rites of two dying people.

Today's generation hasn't seen the entrance and the exit of the cabriolet in Rio de Janeiro. Nor will it know of the time when the cab and the tilbury came into the ranks of our private and livery vehicles. The cab didn't last long. The tilbury, the first of the two, promises to go to the destruction of our city. When the city's done for and the excavators of ruins arrive, they'll find one stopped, with the horse and the coachman in bones, waiting for the usual customer. Rain or shine, the patience will be the same as today, the melancholy greater no matter how much the sun shines, because it will bring together the now and the specter of time. The archeologist will say exceptional things about the three skeletons. The cabriolet had no history. It left only the anecdote I'm going to tell you.

"Two!" the sexton exclaimed.

"Yes, sir, two, nhã Anunciada and nhõ Pedrinho. Poor nhô Pedrinho! And nhã Anunciada, poor thing," the black said, continuing to moan, walking back and forth, afflicted, out of himself.

For anyone who reads this with a soul confused with doubts, it's natural to ask if the black really felt that way or if he wanted to pique the curiosity of the curate and the sexton. I believe that everything can be agreed on in this world as in the other. I believe he really felt that way. I don't disbelieve that he anxiously desired to tell some terrible story. In any event, neither the curate nor the sexton asked him anything.

It wasn't that the sexton wasn't curious. Actually, he was a little more than that. He knew the parish by heart, knew the names of the worshippers, their lives, the lives of their husbands and their parents, the endowments and resources of each, and what they ate and what they drank and what they said, their clothes and their virtues, the dowries of the unmarried girls, the behavior of the married couples, the pining of the widows. He looked into everything. In the intervals, he helped with Mass and all the rest. He was called João das Mercês, a man in his forties with scant beard, graying, thin, a man of average height.

"Which Pedrinho and Anunciada are they?" he said to himself, walking with the curate.

Though the sexton was burning to know, the presence of the curate would preclude any question. The curate walked so piously and quietly, heading for the church door, which compelled the sexton to show the same silence and piety. Thus they walked. The cabriolet awaited them. The coachman removed his hat and some neighbors and passersby kneeled as the priest and sexton got in and the vehicle wound down Rua da Misericórdia. The black strode back along the same route.

Let donkeys and people walk the streets, clouds, if any, walk the skies, and thoughts, if any, walk through heads. The sexton's head had several, and they were confusing. They weren't about the Our Father, though he knew how to offer it, nor about the holy water and aspergillum he was carrying. Nor was it about the time – 8:15 p.m. – and anyway, the sky was clear and the moon was appearing. The cabriolet itself, which was new there, replacing in this case the chaise, that same vehicle wasn't occupying João das Mercês's whole brain, except for what he'd caught about nhô Pedrinho and nhã Anunciada.

"They must be new people," the sexton was thinking, "but hosted in some house, for sure, because there are no empty houses on the beach, and the house number is that of Commander Brito. Relatives, perhaps? What relatives if I've never heard of them...? Friends, I don't know; acquaintances, maybe, just acquaintances. But then would they send a cabriolet? This same black man is new to the house. He must be a slave of one of the dying, or of both."

João das Mercês went on cogitating, and not for long. The cabriolet stopped at the door of a big two-story house, precisely that of Commander Brito, José Martins de Brito. There were already some people down below with candles. The priest and sexton got out and climbed the stairs, accompanied by the Commander. At the landing his wife kissed the priest's ring. Grown-ups, children, slaves, a hushed hubbub, low light, and the two dying people waiting, each in a bedroom in the back of the house.

Everything went as it ordinarily does on such occasions. Nhô Pedrinho was absolved and given unction, and so was nhã Anunciada, and the curate excused himself from the house to go back to the church with the sexton. The latter did not say good-bye to the commander without asking to his ear whether the two were relatives of his. No, they weren't relatives, Brito answered; they were friends of a nephew who lived in Campinas, a terrible story... João das Mercês's wide-open eyes heard these two words, and they said, without speaking, that they would come back to hear the rest – maybe that same night. It was all quick because the priest was descending the stairs, and it was necessary to go with him.

The stylishness of the cabriolet was so short that this one probably never took another priest to people dying. What remained was the anecdote, which I'm about to finish, so skimpy it was, an anecdote about nothing. It doesn't matter. Whatever the size or importance, it was always a slice of life for the sexton, who helped the priest put away the holy bread, to take off his surplice, and do everything else before saying good-bye and leaving. He left, in the end, on foot, up the street, along the beach, until halting at the the commander's door.

Along the way he recalled the whole life of that man, before and after the command. He built his business, which was supplying ships, I believe, the family, the parties, the parochial, commercial, and electoral posts, and from here the rumors and anecdotes were no more than a step or two away. João das Mercês's big memory stored all things, maximum and minimum, with such detail that they seemed to be from yesterday and so complete that not even the subject of the memories was able to repeat them the same way. He knew them like the Our Father, that is, without even thinking about the words. He prayed just as he ate, chewing on the prayer, which left his jaws without being felt. If the rule was to pray three dozen Our Fathers in a row, João das Mercês would say them without counting. It was the same way with other people's lives. He loved to know them, to look into them, to memorize them, and they never left his memory.

Everyone in the parish wished him well because he neither got entangled nor spoke badly of others. He loved the art for art's sake. Often it wasn't even necessary to ask anything. José would tell him about Antônio's life, and Antônio about José's. What he would do was ratify or rectify one with the other, and the two with Sancho, Sancho with Martinho, or vice-versa, everyone with everyone. That's how he filled the empty hours, which were many. One time, at Mass, he remembered an anecdote of the evening before, and at first started asking God's pardon. But he stopped asking when he realized that he hadn't missed one word or gesture of the holy sacrifice, the two were so consubstantiated within him. The anecdote he had relived for an instant was like a swallow that flies over a vista. The vista remains the same, and the water, if there is any water, murmurs the same sound. This comparison, which was his, was worth more than he thought because the swallow, still flying, is part of the vista, and the anecdote became in him part of the person. It was one of his acts of living.

By the time he arrived at the commander's house, he had gone over the litany of the commander's life. He stepped in with his right foot so as to not step out badly. He had no thought of leaving early, no matter how afflicted the occasion became, and fortune helped him out. Brito was in the front room talking with his wife when they came to tell him that João das Mercês was asking about the state of the dying. The wife left the room, the sexton entered, asking pardon and saying it was for a short time; he was passing by and remembered to find out if the sick ones had gone to heaven, or if they were still of this world. He would listen with interest to everything said regarding the commander.

"They haven't died, nor do I even know if they will survive; she, at least, I think will die," Brito concluded.

"They look pretty bad."

"She, mainly. She's also the one suffering most from the fever. The fever hit them here in our house, just after they arrived from Campinas a few days ago."

"They were already here?" the sexton asked, astonished that he hadn't known.

"They were, for fifteen days, – or fourteen. They came with my nephew Carlos and caught the illness here..."

Brito interrupted what he was saying, or so it seemed to the sexton, who put on his face the full look of someone waiting for the rest. However, since the other was biting his lips and looking at the walls, he didn't see the expression of expectation, and both remained silent. Brito ended up walking up and down the room while João das Mercês said to himself that it must be something more than fever. The first thought that came to him was whether the doctors had erred in the illness or the remedy. He also thought that it could be some other hidden problem that was called fever to hide the truth. His eyes followed the commander as he walked back and forth all around the room, softening his footsteps so as not to bother the people inside anymore. From inside came whispered conversation, a call, a message, a door opening or closing. All of this would be nothing to anyone who was worried about something else, but our sexton now wanted nothing other than to know what he didn't know. At least the sick people's family, status, current state, some page of their life, anything that could be known no matter how far removed from the parish.

"Ah!" Brito exclaimed, stopping short.

He seemed to have an impatient urge to report an affair, – the "terrible story" he had mentioned to the sexton a little earlier. But he didn't dare ask for it, nor did the other dare to tell it, and the commander took to pacing again.

João das Mercês sat down. He saw perfectly well that the situation called for him to excuse himself with some good words of hope or comfort and to come back the next day. He preferred to sit and wait. He didn't see any signs of disapproval on the other man's face; to the contrary, he stopped in front of him and sighed with great weariness.

"Sad, yes, sad," João das Mercês agreed. "Good people, no?"

"They were going to get married."

"Get married? They were engaged to each other?"

Brito confirmed with a nod. The tone was disconsolate, but there was no sign of the terrible story, and the sexton waited for it. He noted to himself that it was the first time he had heard something about people absolutely unknown to him. Their faces, seen just a while ago, were the only sign of these people. Not even for that did he feel less curious. They were going to marry...It could be that this was the terrible story. In truth, hit by something bad on the eve of something good, the bad must have been terrible. Engaged and dying...

They came to bring a message to the owner of the house, who asked the sexton to be excused so quickly that there was no time to say good-bye and leave. He ran into the house, and there he remained for fifty minutes. Finally he arrived at the room in suffocating tears; then, soon, the commander turned.

"What did I tell you just a while ago? At least she's going to die. She died."

Brito said this without tears and almost without sadness. He'd known the dead woman a short time. The tears, he said, were for the nephew from Campinas and for a member of the dead woman's family, who lived in Mata-Porcos It took the sexton but an instant to go from that to imagining that the commander's nephew had liked the dying man's fiancée, but the idea didn't hold for long; it wasn't forceful, and later, if he himself had accompanied them... Maybe he'd have been the best man at the wedding. He wanted to know, as was natural, the name of the dead woman. The owner of the house – either for not wanting to give it, or because he now had another idea in his head – did not state the name of the bride or the groom. It could have been both of those causes.

"They were going to marry..."

"God will receive her into his holy care, and him, too, should he come to expire," the sexton said, full of sorrow.

And that word was enough to extract half the secret that seemed eager to leave the mouth of the supplier of ships. When João das Mercês saw the expression in his eyes, the movement with which he raised the window, and the request he made to swear – he swore by all his loved-one's souls that he would listen to it all and not talk about it. He wasn't a man to expose the confidentialities of others, much less those of people as noted and honored as the commander. At which the commander said he was satisfied and enthused, and he then confided the first half of the secret, which was that the two lovers, raised together, had come here to get married when they heard, from a relative in Mata-porcos, abominable news...

"And it was...?" João das Mercês hastened to say, sensing a certain hesitation in the commander.

"That they were brother and sister."

"Brother and sister how? Really siblings?"

"Really. Siblings on the part of the mother. It was the father who wasn't the same. The relative didn't tell them everything nor was clear about it but swore that's the way it was, and they were thunderstruck for a day or more . . ."

João das Mercês was no less shocked than they. He resolved not to leave until he knew the rest. He heard the clock strike ten, and he would hear all the other hours struck that night, would watch over the cadavers of one or both, as long as he could add this page to the other pages of the parish, even though it wasn't of the parish.

"Let's go, let's go, so it was the fever that took them...?"

Brito clenched his teeth to not say any more. But when people came to call him inside the house, he responded quickly, and half an hour later he was back with the news of the second passing. The weeping, this time weaker in that it was more expected, now no longer having anyone to hide it from, delivered the news to the sexton.

"There went the other, the brother, the groom... May God forgive them! Now you can know everything, my friend. Know that they wanted each other so much that a few days after learning of the natural and canonical obstacle to the union, they did some thinking and, satisfied that they were only step-siblings, not full siblings, they jumped into a cabriolet and fled from home. The alert soon went out, and we caught up with the cabriolet on the road to Cidade Nova, and they became so remorseful and ashamed with the capture that they took ill with fever and ended up dying."

What the sexton felt as he heard about this affair cannot be written. With difficulty he kept it to himself for a while. He learned the names of the people from the newspaper obituary, and he matched the circumstances he'd heard from the commander with others. In the end, without considering himself indiscreet, he spread the story, but hiding the names and telling it to a friend, who passed it on to another, and he to others, and everyone to everyone. He did more. He got it into his head that the cabriolet they fled in was the same as that of the latest sacraments. He went to the coach house, chatted with an employee, found out yes. Which led to this page being called, "cabriolet anecdote."

About Glenn Alan Cheney

Glenn Alan Cheney is a writer, translator, painter, and managing editor of New London Librarium. He is the author of more than 30 books on such topics as the Pilgrims, Abraham Lincoln, cats, the end of the world, nuclear proliferation, Mohandas Gandhi, Brazil's Estrada Real, the Quilombo dos Palmares, Chernobyl, nuns, incarceration, environmental issues, bees, and Swaziland. He has also written a few novels, hundreds of articles, scores of op-ed columns, and a book of poetry. Peggy Montgomery, to whom this book is dedicated, was his high school creative writing teacher.

New London Librarium

New London Librarium is a boutique press that specializes in books that merit publication but which are unlikely to reach sales levels expected by larger publishers. Many of NLL's titles explore culture, literature, history, and current issues relating to Brazil.

Other series focus on history, Catholic issues, fiction, and art. Among translations are works by Machado de Assis, Rubem Alves, Mário de Andrade, Paulo Leminski, Rubem Alves, and João do Rio.

For more information, see NLLibrarium.com.

www.ingramcontent.com/pod-product-compliance
Lightning Source LLC
Chambersburg PA
CBHW020302030826
48979CB00027B/2006/J

* 9 7 8 1 9 4 7 0 7 4 6 7 5 *